*Wish*daughter

To Mike
who travels & travels
& is just becoming
a father!

Ady

To Gabriele Rigó-Titze
In Love and Friendship

*Wish*daughter
Adrian Mourby

seren

Seren is the book imprint of
Poetry Wales Press Ltd
Nolton Street, Bridgend, CF31 3BN, Wales
www.seren-books.com

ISBN 1-85411-361-5

A CIP record for this title is available from
the British Library.

The publisher works with the financial assistance of the
Welsh Books Council.

Printed in Plantin by Bell & Bain Ltd, Glasgow.

The Lord is long-suffering, and of great mercy, forgiving iniquity and transgression, and by no means clearing the guilty, visiting the iniquity of the fathers upon the children unto the third and fourth generation.

Numbers 14:18

❖ THE FUTURE

"PLEASE DON'T ASK MY GENERATION TO FORGIVE," says the old man.

"Sure, there is a time for reconciliation." He stands up, his shoulders bent in a permanent arch of defiance. "But only after I am dead."

He takes his newspaper, the old man in open-necked shirt and jacket. He does not express his thanks for the coffee, neither does he offer to shake hands. And Bill knows better than to proffer. The old man does not touch others. His friends make allowances. His family makes allowance too. Presumably his wife learned to love him in her own way. Or his way. He is one of the *Nizolim*, this man, a Survivor, and allowance is always made for Survivors. How can we reproach those whom humanity sought to destroy? After all, we are humanity. It is us the old man holds responsible for his suffering and for the suffering of an entire race.

"They won't have long to wait!" he continues, in a tone that prods the world with sour reproach. And Bill feels himself beginning to lose the admiration he wishes to feel for his guest. This survivor, he reminds Bill too much of his father-in-law. His *ex*-father-in-law. Like others of his generation Lev Davidov considers himself a living rebuke to the naive and ignorant. To the world in fact. In him curdles the obscenity of genocide, the even greater obscenity of survival and the final obscenity of people like Bill Wheeler, his host, relatively young, relatively fit and born into a time – and parentage – where mankind does not seek to obliterate you.

"Measure yourself against me," say the old man's stooped spine and hollow cheeks. "Measure yourself against me and you will all be found wanting."

Bill can't help wishing the old bugger would go. Those who suffer deserve our compassion but Davidov would tax the patience of his Maker. It takes him an age to stand up and retrieve his copy of *Yediot Aharonot*. Not because he is frail but because he expects the world – and God – to wait. Bill now knows every fold in the old man's neck, every melanoma on his weather-beaten skin and each of the thousand creases round his eyes that have given this remarkable Survivor the semblance of a cruel old iguana.

"Yes, measure yourself against me," say the old man's lizard eyes. "No-one departs from my side without shame."

As Davidov prepares slowly to leave, Bill recalls how, even before their divorce, Tamsin's father had been unable to forgive, before their marriage even. Michael Walken could not forgive. Anyone. For anything. He too held the world responsible for a unique atrocity.

Why do I let myself in for this? Bill asked himself. Standing now out of politeness. He no longer attended Walken family parties in Swiss Cottage but he seemed to come to Israel every year and ask those who spoke for the Survivors' generation the same set of questions.

Because I'm paid to. That was the answer. Paid even though the answer invariably proves the same. "No, not now. Not in our lifetime." The Survivors speak and the country listens, for they built the country. Had they not sacrificed everything for Israel? Who would disrespect them now?

"I am an old man," says Lev Davidov, his newspaper rolled like a baton. "You shouldn't have long to wait!". Bill raises his hands as if to show there is no contention between them.

"I'm a journalist," he explains. "I really don't ask these questions to persuade you. This isn't my cause."

But the old man is giving no quarter. He smiles his lizard smile and nods his head once more as if to say, "I would not expect you to be capable of having a cause of your own. What have you and your sort done with your lives? You have lived. Nothing more. You have not *survived*."

There were times when Bill hated coming to Israel. The same old interviews with the same old Jews: liberals, musicians, politicians, rabbis and men like Davidov who seemed to hold the world in contempt. It was true that Bill's paper would ask for the views of the *Nizolim* to be reduced to little more than a paragraph but that did not mean that they belittled his suffering. Bill Wheeler was here to write about the future of music in Israel, not the martyrdom of Chaim Levi Davidov. Was there, since the Holocaust, only one subject deserving to be written about? True Theodor Adorno had said that after Auschwitz there could be no more poetry. But surely journalism?

Did Davidov really want life to stop out of respect for those who did not survive? Maybe. Or maybe it was out of contempt, contempt for those who never had a number tattooed on their wrist.

The old man was already gone, taking his grievance along Tel Aviv's Herbert Samuel Esplanade. Bill had known that he would not enjoy meeting Davidov again but his New York editor had wanted him to re-interview the same people he'd spoken to two years ago. Had they changed their opinions? Had they hell. Nothing would change in Israel. Politicians would still strike poses, the liberals would still defer to snakes like Davidov and the snakes would carry their venom to the grave. Bill knew it was folly to place himself in the firing line of such a man. He had done so because, in the end, he was paid to do so and because doing so took him round the world. His was a better job than most. The check-out girl in a hypermarket gets in the line of fire from time to time. At least when Bill Wheeler was mauled it was usually several time zones from home.

He regarded the beach from his roadside seat and then signalled to pay. The sun had already fallen low enough to cast an incandescent orange glow around the youthful bodies playing ball games between the marina and Aquarium. Bill could not help but derive animal pleasure from the energy and sheer physical grace of those who had come to the shore that evening. The New Israel. Far less European. Far less angry. Yet how far beneath the skin of those tanned, muscular men and women lurked that same black seam of suffering that disfigured people like Davidov and Bill's father-in-law? Maybe Michael Walken had been playful before the last Kindertransport left Bavaria and European history began its grim subdivisions. Male and female: different queues. Parents and children: different queues. Dysentery and Zyklon B. Dead and Dying. All filing silently into the final darkness.

Tamsin had not been like that. Tamsin had believed in the future when they met. But then they were each other's the future. Maybe the brightness in her eyes was the light shining from a life she could foresee, a future to which she clung. We move towards the light, Bill thought, because love renews us. Hadn't Davidov said that he had been engaged to be married when his family was denounced, arrested and gradually subdivided down to extinction in Poland? In whose eyes had Chaim Levi Davidov once seen light shining? Whose eyes did he carry in his heart until the SS finally divided Davidov from his humanity and left him scrabbling like an animal for survival in the last dark months before liberation? Bill knew such stories. Tamsin had known many more. All her family were Survivors or descended from Survivors. Old people who had caught a last glimpse of their children as they were led away to extinction. Middle-aged people who still remembered their parents' last words, telling them to have courage. Yet she had been able to put the past aside, at least when they met. How could a woman like Tamsin Walker dwell on the past when the unborn future cried out in her? The future that was Bill and their many children, each one shining in her eyes.

Bill had delighted in that idea. He was excited by Tamsin pregnant with their firstborn, until he came to think of the future as more boys for

Tamsin's father to circumcise. Bill had found himself dreading the idea of anyone claiming the right to mutilate his child. Tamsin had always told him that she'd want their children to grow up aware of their Jewish inheritance but Bill had never thought this through and Tamsin had been very relaxed about religious matters when they met. She hardly observed the Sabbath. Naively Bill thought a Jewish inheritance meant one or two services (which he tended to like) and the occasional meal with Tamsin's noisy extended family (which he liked less). He hadn't thought of mutilation. While she slept, noisy, huge and inaccessible, Bill lay awake trying to think of a way in which he could broach the subject. He never did.

But then Reah was born and Bill loved Reah. He was happy to see his daughter welcomed by that noisy argumentative gaggle of women who were Tamsin's nearest relatives, even though they saw no role for him. He felt happy that Reah was Jewish. It suited her. His children could be anything: Muslim, Taoist or tree-worshipper, as far as he was concerned. Just as long as no one snipped bits of skin off them. It was primitive, Bill admitted, both what was done in the name of the tribe and the extent to which he reacted against it, but in the event Bill and Tamsin Wheeler had no other children and Bill was glad now that he had never had to do battle with Mr Walken and Tamsin, and all her sisters, over the preservation of a foreskin. Particularly Old Man Walken. He was no easy man to argue with. Like Davidov, Michael Walken believed that life had taken everything from him except the moral high ground, and that he had no intention of surrendering, ever.

The bodies of Tel Aviv's younger generation kept Bill distracted until he had collected his change and was about to leave. He thought of wandering down to the shore, of circling those young sybarites. Their skin attracted him. He wondered if passing by them would recall his ex-wife's wonderful skin, and the future they had once looked forward to together.

Bill calculated a tip and supposed that now it was time to go. Part of him would have been content just to sit and rest. To sit and not even see what he was looking at. To take time out of time. For a moment he realised again how deeply tired he was. Then he rose. He had to act, to move on. And at that moment a voice intercepted him.

"Mr Wheeler?" It was an unwelcome voice. Doubly so given that Bill had just decided that closer proximity to a sea of young nubile bodies was the appropriate antidote for this past half hour with Davidov. "Mr Wheeler, the journalist?" When Bill followed the voice he saw a fat man in early middle-age and a white suit. He also saw a young woman with thick dark Levantine hair that reminded him of his daughter's.

"I have been called worse," said Bill, and he extended his hand.

"Do you have a moment to meet someone who wishes to meet you?" the woman asked, her eyes bright, her smile intoxicating.

Bill reflected ruefully that young women on their own never asked him that kind of question. "I'm due back at my hotel," he told the couple.

"This will only take a few minutes," said her companion. His accent suggested he could be German or American, it was difficult to tell. He had yellow hair plastered across his head. Not blond but an unhealthy nicotine-yellow, as if smoked that colour. Like haddock. He also leaned heavily on a stick. Now that Bill looked more closely, it seemed the young woman was actually supporting him.

They drove a little way to the old town of Jaffa which lies to the south of that long sequence of hotels that is Tel Aviv's shoreline. The young woman took the wheel, the nicotine man – who had not introduced himself – had squeezed in alongside her. Bill sat in the back and watched beach-life fly past. He knew something of the ways in which people kidnap journalists and this was not one of them. He had not been sandwiched between two minders. At any traffic light he could simply open the car door and step out.

Bill's hosts did not speak to him and he resisted the temptation to ask them where he was going or whom he was going to meet.

The journey to Jaffa took only a few minutes but turning through oncoming traffic into the old town took longer. Getting the fat man out of the car and on to the sidewalk took longer still. As he straightened up he seized a paper tissue from the woman's shoulder bag and mopped his face with it.

"In here!" He lifted a finger from his stick. This podgy, imperious gesture propelled them into a small mosque-like restaurant on Mifraz Schlomo that overlooked the bay. The fat man's tone had suddenly become one of irritation, as if he had grown tired of Bill's obtuseness about their destination but once inside he seemed to cheer up. He spoke to the waitresses with great warmth, like a benevolent regular or even, perhaps, the patron. He also expressed exaggerated delight at the table on the terrace to which he and Bill were shown. Bill had been so busy watching all this bogus bonhomie that he hadn't noticed the woman with the gorgeous hair disappear. Wasn't it just his luck to be left with the wheezing bastard?

"Sit down! Sit down!" cried Bill's host as he reached round to find somewhere to rest his stick. "Isn't this a glorious view?" he asked. Bill did not sit down but he did take in the view. The sea below them, the few stumps of rock which were all that remained of the island on which

Andromeda was chained before her rescue by Perseus. If you believed that kind of thing. Several militias over several generations and numerous occupations had used her prison as target practice. All that remained now were those blackened tooth-stumps.

"I thought I was meeting someone here."

"So you are," said the man. "Please. Do sit down."

"You?" Bill asked without surprise. The fat man gestured to the chair opposite him. "We could have talked where we met," Bill took a chair. "Why the cloak and dagger?"

"You won't regret it," said the fat man and he caught the arm of a passing waitress. "Can we have a bottle of that special Reserve, the Binyami. No? And two glasses please."

Bill sat back with his arms folded. Until this man was ready to speak there was clearly no point in objecting further. They both of them regarded Tel Aviv's hotel skyline for a moment, the pink glow of Opera Towers dwarfing everything else. Then the fat man turned his attention back to Bill. He smiled. "Martin Katz." He offered his hand. Bill noticed that in Katz's tongue the name Martin sounded much more German. Almost German, but not quite. Maybe Katz was American, of German or Austrian parentage.

"How do you do?" said Bill.

"And you are the famous arts journalist, Bill Wheeler."

"I'm not famous," said Bill.

"But you write for famous papers all round the world," Katz protested. This was not flattery. He clearly wanted to be sure he'd got the right man.

"When they want me," said Bill.

"People trust you."

"Those who employ me do," Bill replied.

"Well I have for you the story of the century," said Katz with another smile. His was not a good smile. Not conspiratorial, as between two fellows, but a greedy smile. A phoney smile. The smile of a wolf who can see rich pickings ahead but who pretends to this little piggy that his interest lies only in getting him better insurance against all occurrences of huffing and puffing in the neighbourhood. Bill didn't like the porcine role assigned to him.

"Ah, excellent!" cried Katz as the wine made its way over. "Now we can drink a toast to your great success."

"What success?" asked Bill as Katz filled the glasses.

"The story I am going to give you. Tell me, what are you in Israel for?"

Bill hesitated. He disliked the way Katz was playing this self-appointed role of master of ceremonies. And he particularly objected to fulfilling the function of Martin Katz's audience. Twenty minutes ago, Bill thought, I might have been wandering the beaches of Tel Aviv, drinking in the beautiful bodies, singing praises to the future. Instead I am regretting the present and drinking local plonk.

"I imagine you know why I'm here," said Bill. "That's why you chose to contact me."

"Too true," said Katz with a gulp. The man was already halfway through his first glass. "That is why I am here too. The Wagner Question. When is the music of one of the greatest composers of the 19th century going to be heard in Israel? I read you in *The New York Times* last year. Or maybe the year before. We are now in the 21st century and yet still Wagner is not forgiven for associations that his music had under the Nazis. The Philharmonic want to perform Wagner, New Israeli Opera wants to give its Ring – because every international company wants to give its Ring – but they dare not, nobody plays Wagner, not even the radio stations, because to do so will upset too many people alive in Israel today."

"It will happen one day," said Bill, and he stole a glimpse out to sea again. Yet as he did so Bill caught sight of Katz seeming to shake his head. The irritating gesture of a man who wishes you to understand that he understands better. Bill turned back and saw the fat man's relish in having regained Bill's attention with such a paltry device. Katz paused to top up their glasses.

"Drink!"

The two men regarded each other.

"To your story," said Katz, raising his glass.

"What story?" Bill asked.

"What would you say if I told you I had a piece of paper that would ensure Wagner is never heard in Israel. Maybe not anywhere in the world. Ever again!"

Bill found himself smiling. Now he knew this was all nonsense but he was amused by the hubris. Katz's belief that he had access to such an unlikely story made Bill warm to him. The fat man was no longer an egoist with yellowing hair. His egotism was childlike. He had made a naive miscalculation.

"No piece of paper could do that," he replied. Katz shrugged, playing his game. He wasn't going to argue with Bill. He was going to retreat into the superior oh-so-worldly silence of those who know better.

Bill drank some more of his wine. "What is it? A love letter from Wagner to Adolf Hitler?"

"Wagner died six years before Hitler was born," said Katz.

I know that, thought Bill. Or at least I could have known it if I'd looked it up. He put down his glass. "Quite," he bluffed. "Nothing can touch Wagner directly. It's all by association. His wife quite liked Hitler, his son's wife Winifred was mad about him, the Wagners at Bayreuth were the nearest thing Hitler had to a family. And the Reich used his music as the sound-track to world domination. It leaves a bad taste in the mouth for those who suffered under the Nazis. Of course it does. But as the years go by that association gets consigned further and further to the past. And in time Wagner will be performed in Israel. We all know it. Barenboim's tried already. Even the Survivors acknowledge it will happen one day."

Katz shook his wise head again. Bill really wished he wouldn't do that "It ain't *necessarily* so."

"Please," said Bill. "Can we stop these games? I've got a meeting at..." he looked at his watch. Actually it was for any time from now onwards although Phee had said she would almost definitely be late.

"What would you say if I showed you a letter that could blow the whole Wagner industry out of the water?" said Katz. "People, important people, wish to buy this letter, to suppress it. Now would that be a story, eh?" As the waitress passed he took her arm again and asked for a second bottle.

It was over an hour later that Bill checked outside and took a look up and down Mifraz Schlomo. The Mediterranean twilight was dimming now to a point where street lights would be needed. The air was moist, crickets were beginning their evening din. A lot more than two hours seemed to have passed since Bill Wheeler first met the dubious Mr Katz. Of Katz's hired car and hired driver there was, of course, no sign. Katz himself was drunk now and insisting they go on to a casino. Bill felt he had not had such a wasted evening for many years. He was half tempted to abandon Katz in the tiny restaurant but any such plans were at that very moment being denied him. As Bill turned back down the mosque's short flight of steps he met his host being gently ejected by two waiters, one of whom was suggesting that someone should pay the fat man's bill.

"Do you have any money?" Bill asked Katz, but the oaf was almost asleep on his feet. With bad grace Bill settled the cheque himself and asked one of the waiters to find him a taxi. "Where is your hotel?" he asked Katz as the waiters placed their burden against a lamp post for safe-keeping. "Where do you live?"

Katz mumbled something.

"He said the Renaissance," announced the waiter.

"Renaissance Hotel?" Bill asked. He wasn't convinced the waiter had heard properly. The young man was eager, as indeed Bill was, to get shot of Martin Katz. Now they were joined by the driver of a white taxi who appeared from nowhere, shook hands with the waiters and then began speaking to one of them in earnest.

"*Esrim*," said the young waiter, turning to Bill. "He wants twenty."

"To the Renaissance?" Bill asked.

"No, twenty is for him," said the waiter. "Renaissance is on the meter, maybe ten."

Bill understood. The driver wanted an up-front payment in case Katz failed to respect the backseat. He wasn't entirely surprised. "Have you got any money?" Bill asked Katz again.

The fat man took Bill's hand in his own. "We are going to make our *fortune*," he smiled. This prophecy was the sum total of Mr Katz's contribution to their evening out.

"OK," said Bill. "No money."

Bill put Katz in the back and sat up front with the driver. He was paying an extra twenty. No reason why he should be splattered by Katz as well.

As the street lights ticked by back to Tel Aviv Bill thought back over one of the least productive interviews of his life.

It turned out that Mr Katz, a man of no fixed abode and even less integrity, was claiming to have in his possession a letter that he would not show to anyone but which he insisted could do a lot of damage to the reputation of Richard Wagner. Katz wouldn't say who the letter was from. Or to. He wouldn't say how he came by it, when he came by it or even when it was written. If indeed it was written at all and not just a figment of Katz's addled imagination. In fact it transpired that all Katz wanted Bill to know was that the letter existed and that he, Martin Katz, had placed three copies of it in three safety-deposit boxes somewhere in Switzerland.

"Every week as long as I log on to my personal computer the location of those deposit boxes remains a secret but if for any reason I do not log on, if anything should happen to me, then an e-mail will be sent to you – and to two other famous journalists – telling where you can pick up your copies."

"Where is the original kept?" Bill asked.

Katz had gazed at the bottle in front of him. "Ah!" he chuckled. "That's the clever bit. I'm not going to have my room turned upside down! You see one of those copies *is* the original."

"Which one?" asked Bill, deciding that Katz was probably making most of this up as he went along. Katz thought again and then gave out an explosive laugh. "I don't know!" He looked at Bill as if he expected that he too would find this uproariously funny. "I don't know! The original could go to you, Bill Wheeler. It could go to..." He paused. "Any one of a number of famous internatural journalists. Who knows who it could be!"

"You realise this story – if it is a story at all – doesn't stand up unless we have the original letter so it can be verified."

"Oh stop being so *serious*," Katz grumbled and he tried to pour them each another drink but ended up soaking the table.

Bill knew that he was rarely the life and soul of any party but an evening with Martin Katz would kill off anyone's *joie de vivre*. It was all nonsense. And yet he failed to see any purpose to it. Why had Katz gone to such lengths to lead him towards a story that could not be told?

"You know I can't write anything about this until I get sight of the original," Bill reminded him.

"Well maybe I don't want you to get sighting the original," Katz suddenly snarled. "Maybe I don't want to end up dead in a hotel room just so you can see a stupid letter."

Bill was thrown. "Who said anything about ending up dead?" he asked, putting down his glass.

"You are my *insurance*," Katz was gazing at the bottle again. "They know that if anything happens to me, you get the letter."

So that was it. Maybe. This wasn't about a story at all. It was all about a fat man called Katz using Bill to warn off person or persons unknown, person or persons unreal, in all likelihood. Martin Katz, for whatever reason, wanted Bill to be in a position to publish this letter so that knowledge of Bill's involvement would deter anyone who meant Katz harm. He was spinning a yarn and Bill didn't believe a word of it. The only thing that puzzled him still was why Katz had gone to such lengths to try and convince him. And, presumably, these other journalists. What was in it for him? Looking at the obese sleeping bullfrog on the back seat Bill didn't believe he was going to get an answer to that – or any other question – tonight.

They pulled up outside the Renaissance, its apron a beacon of calm good sense in a world that had grown tawdry and foolish that evening. Getting Katz out of the cab wasn't easy. The driver left it to Bill and one of the doormen.

"I believe this gentleman is staying with you," Bill explained. Katz, half in and half out of the taxi, struggled into life at this point and began fishing noisily in his pockets. "No problem. I have a room key," he announced as a sheaf of hotel stationery cascaded out of his breast pocket and on to the floor of the cab. Bill picked up a sheet, saw that it was headed Hilton Continental and realised that they had just had a wasted journey.

It took a further twenty minutes and several more shekels on the meter before Katz was successfully delivered and out of Bill's life for good. Bill's last image of him was as a large white-suited figure slumped over a baggage trolley beneath the hotel awning, two doormen gazing balefully down, wondering what to do. He had not bothered asking about any contribution to their evening. This was just one of those nights you wrote off. Maybe it would make a good story to tell Phee, assuming she were still around.

Bill had met Phee in the long queue at passport control. She seemed to be some kind of management consultant over from London, here to lead a three day brain-storming session in Tel Aviv. It had taken a further half an hour for the two of them to clear the airport by which time Phee and Bill had established they were staying in the same hotel and Bill had invited her for a drink the following evening. He didn't hold high hopes for their date. He couldn't even remember Phee's surname for certain but she was attractive and intelligent and he met very few women these days. As the taxi finally pulled up in front of Bill's hotel he found himself wondering whether Phee would find the tale of his evening with Martin Katz funny or appalling.

The driver was leaning into the back of his cab checking to see whether Katz had indeed done the damage for which Bill had paid up-front. "OK?" Bill asked. "Thirty-two," said the man as he surfaced. "You owe me twelve."

"Oh come on," said Bill. "There's nothing wrong with the cab, is there?"

"Twenty and twelve for the journey," the man replied implacably.

"I'd like a receipt please," said Bill.

As he entered the hotel Bill glanced over to where, in the best of all possible worlds, an auburn management consultant with an unusual name – and a highly developed passion for journalists – would be waiting by Reception. She'd be smiling and, with luck, more glamorous than he'd remembered. Even better, her presence at the desk would save him the bother of having to recall her name accurately to the desk-clerk. But, before the glass doors had slid noisily shut behind him, Bill found he'd been rejoined by that annoying little taxi driver. "I really hope you're not after a tip," he thought darkly.

"You left these," said the man, handing over what seemed to be a wad of Hilton Continental stationery. Now that was impressive. He'd actually made a point of checking underneath the seats before setting off in search of another fare.

Well at least I will not be without a souvenir of Martin Katz, thought Bill as he thanked the man and took his place in the queue for Reception. Ahead he could see a note in his pigeon hole. From long years of travelling, Bill always harboured high hopes of the pigeon hole. Once upon a time he used to have rolled-up faxes from Tamsin waiting for him. There was another woman who used to fax him in foreign hotels, too. She, for all her faults, had been remarkable at tracking him down. He'd even had notes from her when he had no idea she knew his whereabouts. And once or twice when Bill had been away for a long time he'd had faxes from Reah too, which her mother had let her send. These days he didn't expect anyone from work to contact him on paper. The technology of text-messaging and e-mail had moved so rapidly that the fax had all but been superseded.

"You have a note for me," Bill pointed out as the clerk, a slight young man with pixie ears, became free. "Room one-eleven."

"One moment sir," clicked the pixie.

"And I need to call someone in another of the rooms," said Bill, but before he had finished speaking he noticed the piece of paper now delivered to his hands was signed "*Phee*".

Bill – Sorry we'll have to call off this evening. Heavy day and another tomorrow! 9pm. Gone to bed now. Hope you had a great evening.

Bill folded the piece of paper tightly and swore quietly. If he were honest with himself he hadn't had a chance in hell of ending up in bed with an Irish management consultant but he would liked to have had the chance to discover that in person. And to be honest he would have liked to have had some real conversation too. He took the stairs.

It was only when he got to the door of Room 111 and was fumbling for his key card that Bill realised he still had all those Hilton sheaves stuffed under his arm. He must have looked a curious sight in Reception, he thought. What kind of kleptomaniac steals freebies then trails them from one hotel to the next? Despite himself Bill laughed as he looked around for a bin to dispose of the stuff. There was only a tall brass cigarette sand-tray in the corridor, so in the end Bill took Katz's booty into 111 and binned the sheaf in the bathroom bucket as he passed.

He kicked the sofa glumly and decided to have a drink. The Divine Bastard worked to tight deadlines, Bill thought. Every day another day. Inevitably some of them were going to be substandard. He looked at the minibar, squatting under the TV, smug with its hidden array of overpriced luxuries. Living by himself had made Bill cautious about drinking on his own. He knew he'd already helped Katz through quite a lot of wine. But a whisky or two wouldn't do too much harm, he supposed. It might help settle the seething irritation within.

Bill paced the room and then pulled the curtains shut. He was still angry at the day for sending him Davidov and Katz. And at himself for coping badly with both. All he wanted to do now was switch off the anger, let it go. But this was like the arguments he used to have with Tamsin. It could take hours for the rage to seep away, hours until Bill was able to un-poison his heart. He used to go for long walks during that time, tire himself out if possible, burn up the bile. Then he'd come back and Reah would run out to greet him and everything would be OK again. Picking her up in his arms Bill could believe once more in the future and when you believe in the future the rest hardly matters. The great thing about the past, after all, is that it's passed.

But in the absence of his daughter – and because he felt unwilling to stir outside for a walk along the beach – Bill decided whisky and ice was probably the answer. He really wished he read more. This would be a good time to lose oneself in a book. But he'd travelled light. Too light. Bill broke the tab on his minibar and decided not to even check how much they'd hiked up the prices.

Bill had had a girlfriend some years back who meditated every morning and spoke of centring her being by listening to her own breath. That was what Bill always felt he got from whisky. Some benign demon in the alcohol reached his stomach and then spread. He felt it move like calming hands across his abdomen and suddenly all was still. It was as if the genie in the bottle had stemmed a tide of raw energy which he had been wasting in fragmented fury. 'Be still,' said the spirit. It did not speak like the voice that told Moses "Be still and know that I am God." It simply told him to stop. Better still it *enabled* him to stop. To be still. It possessed him.

Bill sat for a moment wondering whether there was any point in putting on the television. Then he remembered he *knew* there was no point in putting it on. The debate in his head was merely whether or not he was going to give in to the joyless temptation of wasting what remained of his evening in front of either CNN or some age-old BBC comedy repeat. He took another sip of whisky and then remembered something else. Something he hadn't even been aware of when it happened but that now he knew. When he threw the Katz detritus into his bathroom bin there was more than hotel stationery amongst that pile of papers. His hand had known that at the time. The package was far too bulky but Bill had been sufficiently chewed-up by rage to miss what his hand was telling him, to miss what his armpit had been telling him all the time he was struggling to open the door to Room 111.

It was curious but quite, quite clear in his mind now. All Bill had to do was walk back to the bathroom and retrieve whatever had landed in the bin with such an inappropriate thump. Obviously it wouldn't be Katz's stupid letter. It probably wouldn't even be the key to that safety deposit box. It might be Katz's wallet of course. Maybe Bill would find out who Martin Katz really was before returning it – minus half the cost of this evening's entertainment – to its owner. Bill liked to believe he had scruples even when rifling someone's pocket book.

And yet he found himself unwilling to get up, the spirit in the whisky reminded him that deep inside him dwelt a need to sit and rest forever. He'd been told that at the beach too. Time to take time out. But he had to act, he had to move on. Bill rose.

It was a small padded envelope of the size that might be used to send an audio cassette through the post. It had the look of something that may have been opened and resealed several times already and yet there was no writing on it. The only clue to its origin was the opaque adhesive tape that held it together. Bill knew this was not of a kind he recognised. Not English, not American in all probability. Bill took out a pocket knife that he kept on his belt and cut through the seal in the spirit of true journalistic enquiry. He expected a cassette to fall out when he shook the package but nothing did. Bill put in his fingers to see what plums might come tumbling down. Something gnawed at him that spoke of unresolved significance. He might do well not to probe any further with this. But it was, as ever, too late.

A small plastic bag was tucked inside. As Bill withdrew it he saw within the bag some folded paper. Even before he opened the bag Bill knew. Martin Katz was not lying about the letter. He may have lied about many things. Certainly he had lied about keeping the original in one of three safety deposit boxes. For *this* was the original. A letter on two folded sheets of paper. Whatever it said, whenever it was written, and by whom, this was the letter that was supposed to destroy one of the greatest composers Europe had ever known.

Ridiculous.

❖ THE PAST

HOW ON EARTH could you make anyone think less well of Wagner?

Bill was still pondering this as he stood in line for the security staff at Ben Gurion Airport. He had no liking for Richard Wagner. Who was it said "Wagner contaminated everything he touched?" *Nietzsche.* And he was a friend! Didn't Wagner himself say something about his sufferings as an artist giving him a superior right to steal, lie and run up huge debts all over Europe? Wasn't it Wagner who appropriated other people's houses and other people's wives as he felt he needed them? And didn't his music so overwhelm mad Ludwig that the young man let Wagner bankrupt the Wittelsbach dynasty with his grandiose plans?

The only way this letter could shock people today was if it showed Wagner taking in stray cats and baking strudel for the homeless.

"Good morning, we would like to ask you a few questions," said the beautiful young woman from airport security. Bill had been coming to Israel often enough now to know that this would be a long process. They would keep him standing at a table in the departures hall and ask him what he was doing in Tel Aviv. Everyone got something of this although Bill suspected that the guys in hats and plaits got less than him. The interrogators were always young. Bill wondered if this were part of their national service. They were frequently beautiful too. And invariably thorough. They would ask him for proof that he was a journalist, proof that he had had meetings with the people he claimed to have met, they would ask to see a copy of one of his articles and seize on all possible incongruities, such as why a British journalist should be paid to cover an Israeli story for an American newspaper.

"You'd have to ask the *New York Times* about that," Bill replied. He knew from past experience that the sooner this woman found something wholly implausible in his story the sooner he'd be on his way. Professional terrorists never sounded quite as suspicious as real people. Bill didn't resent her questions although he found it alarming how quickly one could be made to feel dubious, even to oneself.

"Is this your luggage?" continued the young woman. Bill was impressed and distracted by the fact that she managed to be beautiful despite the regulation white blouse and grey slacks. Refocusing, he agreed that, yes it was and that he had indeed packed it all himself.

"During your time in Israel has anyone given you anything and asked you to bring it back with you?"

"No," said Bill.

"Have you bought any gifts, souvenirs?"

"Just a present for my daughter," said Bill.

"May I see?"

It was a large fluffy camel crammed into his suitcase.

"How old is your daughter?"

"Thirteen."

"Isn't this a childish toy for a girl of thirteen?"

"It's the kind of thing she usually wants," Bill replied, immune to the impertinence. "She's been ill. I spoke to her on the phone. I said I'd bring her a camel."

"What is her name?"

"Rachel."

They always reacted with interest at that.

"But we call her Reah." Today Bill felt he wanted to be helpful. "My ex-wife is Jewish. She lives in Britain."

The woman was now flicking through Bill's passport.

"Your daughter is not registered on your papers."

"No longer necessary in Britain," said Bill. "She's had her own passport for years. She likes fluffy camels but she has her own passport." He immediately regretted the tone of irony. What was the point of antagonising these kids?

"You have changed your ticket," said the woman. She was now going through his flight documents. Bill found himself noticing the downy hair on her cheek.

"I had to stay on longer to get an interview. Somebody my editor was very keen to have me speak to," Bill explained. "He postponed our meeting."

"The editor?"

"No, the man."

"What is his the name?"

"Lev Davidov," said Bill.

"Do you have a letter from him confirming that your interview was postponed?"

"No, I don't," said Bill. As if Davidov would do such a thing!

"One moment," said the young woman. She was going to get a colleague. Bill knew this tactic of old. It sounded ominous but it usually meant that she could think of nothing more to say.

Bill watched her go and wondered if women like that ever went to hotel rooms like his. If the average male thinks about sex every five minutes what a very poor return we get on all that mental investment, he thought. Bill found himself wondering how Richard Wagner would have coped with all this officialdom. Ever in debt and frequently in trouble for posturing as a revolutionary, Wagner was always slipping across borders. In fact it took royal Ludwig to square things before the Leipzig *Übermensch* could return openly to Germany. Bill was sure that was part of the life story. Ludwig then fell out with Wagner after he discovered that Liszt's hook-nosed daughter, Cosima, was carrying out her amanuensis duties in a horizontal position. He'd refused to attend the first Ring Cycle at Bayreuth and only turned up at the third. He'd even laid claim to intellectual ownership of *The Ring* because of all the money he'd given Wagner over the years.

Bill felt an old familiar distaste rise in his gorge. It was a long time since he'd thought about Wagner, the man or the composer. Wagner was indeed a sickness. He had concluded that years ago. Wagner, Nietszche, Schopenhauer. All those mad Germans. And all the people who worshipped them. On the whole he steered clear of Wagner premieres. He had his reasons.

"Good morning, I would like to ask you a few questions," said an even more attractive young woman from Israeli security.

"Is this your luggage? Did you pack it yourself? During your time in Israel has anyone given you anything and asked you to bring it back with you? What is the purpose of your visit?"

"I am a journalist. I have been interviewing people about cultural issues in Israel today."

"Do you take notes or tape-recordings of your interviews?"

"Both."

"May I see your notes?"

Bill wasn't expecting that one but he knew which pocket in his shoulder bag to unzip.

The woman studied the pad in front of her with its mixture of shorthand, scribble and doodle.

"What is this?" she asked pointing to a cartoon he had drawn of a large, gentle and rather apologetic assistant he had met at New Israeli Opera. Seeing the caricature through another's eyes Bill suddenly realised how anti-Semitic it must look.

"Someone I spoke to," he replied.

"So do you also provide line drawings for the *New York Times*?" asked his interrogator.

"I was bored," Bill apologised. "I did it while I was waiting."

"And what about this?" asked the woman. Leafing through Bill's pad she had disinterred a slim padded envelope which contained some pages of an old-fashioned script. A Germanic script that men of Lev Davidov's generation would have recognised as *Fraktur*.

"It's... a letter I'm studying."

The woman eased the pages halfway out with her thumb.

"An old letter," she observed. Bill's heart leapt into his mouth. He had debated whether he was entitled to take the letter with him but in all his moral contention one thing that had never occurred to Bill was that possession of it might attract attention at Ben Gurion Airport. He fought down any desire to say more.

Just don't ask me where I got it, Bill thought to himself.

The last thing he wanted to admit now was that he had been given the letter while in Israel. Actually he hadn't been given it but that nicety was not what was worrying Bill at the moment. What mattered was that he had lied when asked about receiving something to carry through security. Lied without even thinking about it. Lied because, contrary to how he would claim he normally behaved, Bill had appropriated someone else's property.

"This letter," said the young woman. "Who is it from?"

"Richard Wagner," said Bill. "The composer."

The letter still rested under her thumb, halfway in the bag and halfway out.

"Who is it to?"

"I don't know. There is no envelope. I'm still working on that. I'm writing about Wagner's music. That's why I was in Israel, to ask when his music might be played here." He could feel his speech starting to speed up.

"These words..." said the woman who suddenly seemed much less attractive.

"German," said Bill.

"This plastic bag..." said the woman.

Bill felt the noose tightening. "I use it to protect the letter. It's quite old. The letter." Don't ask me where I got it, he thought to himself.

"It has been sealed using adhesive tape," said the woman.

"I'm sorry?"

"This brand of adhesive tape is sold in Israel."

"Yes..." said Bill, wondering what she was getting at. "Yes, I had to seal it up again. I'd taken it out..." Was she thinking the letter was Israeli property? Hell! Maybe it was. Maybe it was a national bloody artefact. Come on, Bill thought to himself. Work it out. All I did was bring the letter to

Israel, open it and use hotel sticky-tape to reseal it.

"I'm, er, trying to discover what it says. It's... research for an article."

The woman looked at Bill. He determined not to say anything and even gazed around the security hall with what was meant to be a nonchalant gesture. Israel invested so much time and manpower in these bloody interrogations. Would they ever stop a professional terrorist this way? he wondered. Had anyone ever been led off from this hall, bags chockfull of explosive? Un-bloody-likely. Only idiots like him got caught. And why? Because Israel wanted a reputation that no-one messed with El Al or with any airliner carrying the Chosen People out of Israel. It was part of Jewish victimhood, he thought bitterly. Make clear to all the world the threat that Israel perceived to its own existence. That was the propaganda value of . requiring people to check in three hours early and screwing about with them like this.

The woman was still looking at Bill's letter. Katz's letter. How could he have been so foolish? Bill tried speaking to himself. Mossad weren't after him. All he had done was save the letter from being thrown out with a pile of stolen hotel stationery which Katz had left in the back of a taxi.

That, and of course to lie to two pertly-breasted interrogators at Ben Gurion Airport. Bill wondered whether the women in front of him would look kindly on his distinction between 'being given something' and 'stealing'?

"What is the purpose of your visit?" the woman asked again.

"I am a journalist. I have been interviewing people about cultural issues in Wagner today. In Israel, today. About why Richard Wagner is not performed in Israel."

"And you carry with you a letter from Richard Wagner?"

"Yes," said Bill. She had put two and two together and ended up with a sum that worked in Bill's favour. This sounded better.

But what if Katz had woken up sober and telephoned the airport to tell the security services that a journalist called Bill Wheeler was making off with stolen property? It was a nightmarish thought. Bizarre but surely possible. Bill said nothing and tried not to see the cell door closing ahead of him. Bang. Strip lights. Strip search. Hours of interrogation, missed flights and pure bloody tedium as the state of Israel decides whether it wishes to be involved in this squabble between a fat man called Katz and a slightly dodgy journalist called Wheeler.

Bill looked at the letter in the woman's hand, a hand that might have done wonders in Room 111 last night. God, he hoped like hell that it wasn't Israeli property. Had Katz swiped it from some archive in Tel Aviv? Possibly. Please God don't let it be stolen, Bill thought.

"I'm sorry?" He suddenly realised the young woman was speaking to him.

"This letter from Richard Wagner, is it addressed to anyone in Israel?" she asked. "No," said Bill, surprised.

"Is Mr Wagner asking in this letter why his music is not performed in Israel?"

"No," said Bill, numb with incipient relief. "No, Mr Wagner is dead. This is an old letter. I just carry it to try and understand what it says."

"Do you read German?" the woman asked.

"No," said Bill. "Only a little," he added. "Not this kind."

"What kind of German is this?"

"*Hochdeutsch*," said Bill, fumbling. "The handwriting is old-fashioned German. It was used until the early twentieth century."

"You realise that anyone born in Germany before 1928 is required to fill out a special application to visit the state of Israel," said the young woman.

"Yes," said Bill. He had seen that notice in the arrivals hall but reference to it now confused him utterly.

"Have you shown this letter to anyone while you have been in Israel?"

"No," said Bill. "No I haven't." He could feel the pulse of blood in his brain. Just stay calm, he told himself.

"OK, thank you," said the young woman turning back to her colleague. They exchanged some words in Hebrew. Bill struggled with the hope that perhaps he was in the clear.

"May I have my letter back?" he asked. The woman looked at Bill in surprise, reinserted the letter and handed it over.

"Have a nice flight."

Bill didn't even look at the little plastic envelope until his flight was in the air. He sincerely wished he had not just gone through all that. This piece of paper could easily have deprived him of a few days' liberty. Bill breathed out. What a precious commodity freedom was.

"Can I get you something from the bar?" asked the steward.

"Yes please," said Bill. "A lot."

The clouds were particularly beautiful today. Bill drank his gin and tonic and imagined them as the tops of snowy mountains, a fantasy he'd enjoyed ever since he began to fly at the age of twenty. Bill's family hadn't travelled. His father hadn't drunk. Bill had come to air-flight and alcohol at about the same time. The two experiences were inseparable for him now.

The spirit within the gin and tonic reached Bill's stomach and spread its calm. He thought of Libby Ziegler. Now that was a strange thing to do, but the thought was not wholly unconnected with all that had just happened. Libby after all was the person who had introduced him to Wagner all those years ago. But Bill hadn't entertained thoughts of Libby for three or four years, possibly more.

Bill looked at the letter in his hands. He did not wish to remember her today. He took his notebook out of his shoulder bag, folded the letter tightly within it and zipped the whole thing up. He had had enough of Wagner for a while.

In any case the letter currently held no meaning. Bill had realised that almost as soon as he'd opened it in his hotel room last night. The script across the first page was florid but clear, the writer reserving his flourishes just for the beginning and end of words. Bill noticed the letter B at the front of one sentence spiralling outwards expansively and open at its base. The script was hurrying on to whatever minuscule vowel came next. He had also spotted the end of a word that looked like '*Niebelung*', the tail of the G looping back on itself and then tearing splendidly up the page. The writer gave the impression he was enjoying himself hugely, but what was he saying? The use of German was different from anything Bill had seen before.

Mein Werther Freund, Welch Schuft bin ich, so lange zu warten –

There was no way he was going to get any sense out of it working on his own like this, but of two things Bill was certain. At the bottom left hand corner of the second page a section was torn away and deliberately so, as if some kind of postscript or address panel had been removed. Secondly, the signature that finished this letter was clear. It read *Richard Wagner*. This was weird. It felt as shockingly banal as reading Hitler's signature. Each letter was surprisingly clear. The R was open and very like the capital B on page one. Its top whirled up high and then swept precipitately down into what might be an I. The C and H were looped together as were the final D of Richard and the W that began Wagner. It might be argued that the G of Wagner looked more like a P and the N was so open at the top that it read much more like a U but, given that the surname Wapuer was uncommon in nineteenth-century Germany, Bill felt that whoever had signed this letter had almost definitely gone by the name Richard Wagner.

Moreover he didn't find it difficult to imagine this as Wagner's handwriting. It was passionate, self-important yet slightly feminine. It matched with Bill's recollection that Wagner claimed to be both male and female because the artist must have the Eternal Feminine within him, or some such nonsense.

Yes, but what did it say? Bill wondered, as he heard the drinks trolley rattling towards him again. The greeting looked like '*Werther Freund*', presumably 'Worthy Friend'. Unless of course Wagner had a friend called Werther. And even if he did, such a mode of address seemed unlikely. So what was Wagner telling his werther friend that would shake the music-world to its foundations two centuries later?

Bill would obviously have to get help with this.

The steward came by to explain that they would be serving lunch soon. Did Bill want another drink? This was a question with more than one answer. One part of Bill, the part that had already bid the spirit welcome, cried out enthusiastically for more. But his mind heard that cry and feared it. It was not the quantity of alcohol, ultimately, that worried him. What really mattered was whether or not Bill needed it, whether he responded not from appetite but because his body was sensing the absence of intoxication. Once down that route we will always want more. Bill knew something of the body's needs. This wasn't like sex. This was a compulsion that would grow and grow until need was everything and everything was need and quantity really would be an issue. Demand would be fuelled until demand, and nothing else, became the purpose of existence.

Bill thought of some of the old hill farmers he knew as neighbours who clamped a bottle of whisky and two glasses to the kitchen table as soon as night fell. He thought of the Finns he had visited in Helsinki who came home from the opera and embraced the long winter nights with a toast to oblivion. Recognising the way his heart leapt at the idea of another drink, Bill felt sure that this was no time to say yes.

"Just a bottle of red with the meal," he replied and continued sipping his gin.

Libby, Bill thought, as he looked at the clouds in the last wave of pleasant intoxication. Libby Ziegler. And the image of a woman with wild flowing clothes and provocative ideas floated before him. Yes, Libby Ziegler was the last person to whom he should show this letter. Not because she didn't know how to read Wagner's letters – she could probably translate these two sheets and authenticate them on the spot – no, Libby was the last person anyone should consult about anything. Besides, Bill did not know where she was anymore, did not want to know and did not intend to find out.

Bill drained his gin and tonic. Damn Wagner. Damn him for reminding Bill of Libby Ziegler and her wonderful long hair. His hand strayed towards the bottle of red. It was a choice of two intoxications. For the moment she proved the more powerful. Yes, he was hooked again, hooked on the idea of Libby. As he looked at the clouds Bill felt that same sense of potent significance that he had felt when he opened Katz's envelope last night. That same knowledge that a route had suddenly opened up ahead of him, down which he could so easily travel but that he should not. Last night he had felt like a man standing on a high cliff, believing himself compelled to jump. All he had to do was step back. From Libby yes, not from the letter. The letter was safe territory.

He had taken it with him for all manner of reasons, each of which made it possible for Bill to justify such an action. He had given into instinct, yes, an instinct he had subsequently justified to himself with specious reasoning about keeping it safe. But ultimately the letter would do him no harm. Words were safe. Libby was another matter. Whatever happened, he was not going to contact her.

At Heathrow Bill used the time waiting for his luggage to ring London University. By the time his suitcase was taking its fluffy camel round the carousel for the fourth time he had tracked down three academics who were willing to look at fragments of a letter that this polite but determined journalist had come across. In Bill's experience academics were always surprisingly willing to help anyone connected to the media. They could have hardly imagined that they were furthering the cause of scholarship by doing so. Nor could they have expected much kudos thereby, although Bill did notice that mentioning the *New York Times* notched up the level of interest in what he was saying.

Clearing security, without anxiety this time, Bill persuaded a BA official to let him photocopy the two pages of Katz's letter, then he cut the copy into three sections. This way he'd not be asking for a full sheet of translation from each expert. Bill's consideration masked a darker motive. He wished to keep the letter's ultimate significance for himself. I'm becoming like Katz, he thought as he posted each of the envelopes.

Bill collected his Jeep from the Terminal 4 car park and began weaving laboriously out of Heathrow towards the M4. It was already late and he could see the sun ahead of him as he headed west. It glanced across the windscreen, graphically delineating just how splattered his car had become on the journey up. Bill switched on the windscreen washer and fell to thinking about what he had put in motion today.

Katz's letter was in his notebook. Bill hoped to keep hold of it long enough to be able to get a proper authentication, but first he would find out what it said. Each of his highly obliging German-experts had agreed to fax or e-mail him, probably tomorrow if they received the text in time. One, an old donnish character who gloried in the name of Rory Llewellyn Goetz, sounded far too keen to explain how difficult was the act of translating nineteenth-century *Hochdeutsch* into modern English and might well hold everything up. On the assumption that the meat of Wagner's letter probably did not lie in its opening salutation, Bill had therefore assigned Llewellyn the Loquacious his first third. The second section, consisting of the bottom of page one and top of page two, had gone to an ambitious young man who asked – in recompense – for a contact name at the *New York Times*. The third had gone to a reader in nineteenth-century German who had sounded far too busy to speak on the phone but who'd nevertheless said he'd do it once Bill had, in exasperation, asked whether there might be anyone else in his department who could help.

Bill was stumbling blindly towards one Wilhelm Richard Wagner (1813-1883). These men were going to be his eyes and ears over the next few days. They could lead him to the man, help him hear Wagner's voice. Bill felt a strange sensation of the past brushing against him. That letter came from another time. If Bill could get beyond its impenetrable German, the spirit of Wilhelm Richard would address him direct, bursting out into the world through all those whorls and loops like a calligraphic genie.

Bill imagined Wagner bustling about in that letter. Somewhere on the other side of this paper silence he imagined the Meister's high-voice, full of self-importance, throwing out commands, demanding silks for his boudoir and lavishing praise whenever it seemed necessary. Didn't Berlioz say "*Wagner is mad*"? And, if Bill was remembering correctly, Bizet accused him of being so insolent that criticism couldn't touch his heart, adding ruefully, "Assuming that he has a heart."

Wagner the Disease. The profligate egomaniac who made music sick, so sprach Nietzsche. And he should know a thing or two about mental illness. Wagner the Whirlwind. Bill felt a frisson of excitement. He had gone to Israel to discuss an age-old debate about laying the past to rest but he had returned with a living portion of it. Suddenly history no longer felt so inert, so ripe for internment. What might he discover?

Passing south of Swindon, Bill found his thoughts turning back to Katz and the letter. His intention had been to hang on to it only until he had discovered its contents. Then he would return it to Katz, wherever Katz might be. Until this moment it had not occurred to Bill how exactly he might locate his fat beneficiary. The easiest thing would have been to try him at the Hilton that morning. No matter. Katz would find him. Katz had been able to track him down in Tel Aviv. Katz would certainly find out how to reach him in Britain. Besides, Bill now realised he didn't just want to read this letter. Whatever it said, he wanted it authenticated, even if the words within were just an enquiry after the cost of Parisian silk.

As he drove westward the traffic eased. Fewer and fewer people had a reason to take the motorway this far from London. Bill called in a service station to refuel his Jeep. It was a big unnecessary car, he admitted. He and Tamsin had bought it when they moved from Chiswick into the Wye Valley. This was to be the family car for their new country existence; she would keep the town car but as things had fallen out Tamsin actually spent far more time in the Wye Valley than Bill. Nevertheless, when they divorced, she insisted on taking the small runabout saloon. It was not well suited to getting up the lane to her farmhouse, but Tamsin claimed to feel far more secure in something small. Bill found this perverse. He had a sentimental attachment to this beast however. It used far too much fuel, it had the aerodynamics of a Norman cathedral but it was a tough old bruiser of a vehicle. It gave the impression of being pretty certain it could cope and Bill believed it.

At the till Bill spotted a cassette labelled *"Wagner's Greatest Hits"* which tempted him. Even when the temptation had passed he couldn't help but be amused thinking of how Libby Ziegler would react to the idea of Wilhelm Richard's Greatest.

Libby was no snob but she did believe absolutely in Wagner's idea of replacing opera's arias, recits and choruses with open-ended expanses of music, "through composition" – the kind of seamless interminable slidings and crashings-about that ought to make it impossible to extract Ten Top Tunes For Today's Teutonic Lovers.

Unendliche Melodie Libby had called this kind of composition. Music without beginning or end. That was probably what Wagner called it too. Bill could remember the syllables of that word *Unendliche*. Libby had spelled them out to him one heady evening when they were locked into some discussion or other at London's ICA. He couldn't remember what was exciting her so then but he remembered Libby's American accent just discernible under her studied German, how sensual he found the reference to unendingness. And how he almost forgot the time that evening and was grateful Tamsin hadn't asked him where he'd been.

"Which pump?"

Bill realised he wasn't in this world at all. He was remembering a young woman who had taken over his every waking thought seven years ago. She'd probably been in his dreams too. That he and Libby had connected surprised them both, he reckoned. She was a rising young media star. He was a journalist in his early thirties moving belatedly from news to the arts. And married. With a child. Why did she feel the need to tell him everything? Why did he need to listen? It was all folly. Folly and disaster. And then she disappeared.

"I'll have this cassette as well," said Bill, reaching across to where the Greatest Hits were stacked.

"I've just put this through," replied the till girl reproachfully.

"I'll pay cash."

Back in the car Bill intended to put the cassette in straight away but it seemed inappropriate to listen to Wagner as he was manoeuvring across the garage forecourt. Inappropriate, too, as he headed down the slip road and moved from the inner to middle lane. Wagner did not write music for changing gear and looking in the rear-view mirror. Wagner wrote music for driving your car faster than it's ever been driven before, driving it as if no-one else is on the road, crashing through all barriers – artistic, moral and literal – and then exploding in a fireball of redemptive incandescence. Bill hadn't listened to Wagner for years but he knew it was the kind of music best not heard when driving. "Only mediocre performances can save me," Wagner had written while he was composing *Tristan*. "Good performances will drive the listener mad."

Bill was surprised he could remember so much about the Meister but he did not need to ask himself why. He knew these words not because he had studied Wagner in depth but because he had studied Libby Ziegler. Libby, who had thrown down the challenge of Wagner to him almost as soon as they met. He was a staff reporter in those days. She was... goodness knows what she was. She was young, deep and difficult. Hadn't she been living with some distant great-grandson of a famous German conductor and come to London when that broke up? Or maybe they'd been married. Bill wasn't certain. Libby said very little about her past life. As far as Bill could remember she'd started training in psychology but discovered Wagner and Schopenhauer at about the same time and given up science to work on Wagner manuscripts. That was how she'd come to meet the great-great-grandson. Bill couldn't remember his name. Was it one of the von Bülows, Furtwänglers or Karajans? Somehow she'd arrived in London with this series of lectures at the ICA. Her rise had surprised people, but then everything about Libby surprised people. She was gloriously out of step and it was the world around her that had its priorities wrong.

Funny, Bill would have claimed that by now he remembered very little about Libby; but he could remember in exact detail the occasion on which she told him that marriage reduced love to property and utility. Wagner's word, that "*Versorgungseinrichtung*". He remembered the relish with which she spoke it. Libby Ziegler was nobody's utility. She was Isolde, Brünhilde, Sieglinde. And what did those Wagnerian heroines have in common? Now Bill could hear Tamsin's voice. "They none of them feel guilt about adultery, Bill. All Wagner's women love someone other than the person they're married to. Well I'm sorry, that may be all right in opera but it isn't all right in the real world and that's where we're living in Bill! You. Me. Reah!"

And Reah had begun to cry.

He was coming up to the Severn Bridge. Bill decelerated for the toll booths. It was shocking how clearly he had heard Tamsin's voice just then, how he'd seen her in his mind's eye holding one of Libby's ten page faxes in her fist, tearing at it. Fighting her corner, a corner into which Bill had never intended to push her. Tamsin the mother, scrabbling to protect her marriage while he, the father, the man who had held the future in his eyes, was being dazzled by Libby Ziegler.

"It isn't fair!" Tamsin had cried. "She's a single woman. Or at least she behaves like a single woman. She spends hours writing to you, impressing you, flattering you, while I'm trying to bring up your daughter. I'm tired, Bill!"

"We're not having an affair," Bill told her and Tamsin had struck him with the rolled up fax and Reah had wept to see her parents fighting.

He paid the toll in a daze and didn't even remember asking for the receipt which was handed to him with his change.

Bill crossed the Severn Bridge but he did not play the cassette of Wagner's Greatest Hits. Though the long white suspension towers reminded him of the gods' entry into Valhalla, Bill did not play *Rhinegold*. Though he saw an Army helicopter circling overhead from its base on the River Wye he did not play *Ride of the Valkyries* either, even though the index card told him it was "as featured in *Apocalypse Now*, with Academy Award-winner Marlon Brando".

Bill flung the cassette away. It bounced across the passenger seat. He did not want to hear Wagner. He did not want even to read that man's bloody letter. Bill swung the Jeep up past Chepstow. After a while he stopped it in a small, dark-forested car park that overlooked the river. He thought of getting out and hurling both the cassette and letter down into the Wye, getting rid of that poisonous little man. But he did not.

Bill leant back in his seat. He recognised what had happened. It was so simple. He had become reintoxicated, both by the idea of Libby and by the idea of Richard Wagner. They were both creatures who could do that kind of thing to you. He had gone to the cliff edge again. Logically, if he wished to avoid whatever it was that Wagner represented in his life, all he had to do was step back. He did not need to destroy anything. Besides, Bill did not believe in destroying the written word. Or even a plastic cassette. He was only a journalist, a mere footsoldier in the literary crusade, but he did believe that there was something sacred about the word once written. Of course once we have read the written word then the onus is on us to behave morally, in response to it, but the word itself is above morality. And below it too.

He did not like all art, Bill thought as he flicked on the Jeep's headlights and restarted the engine. The valley lay in mist before him. And he certainly did not like Wagner, not at the moment anyway, but he would not destroy one note, not even a letter, particularly this letter. Censorship disturbed him. Who was he to destroy anything?

Except his marriage.

Winding up through the white shrouds of Wye Valley mist, Bill reflected on how this landscape had been their new beginning. After Libby, he and Tamsin sold up in London and bought Holt's Farm, two buildings separated by a small field. They lived in the cottage while the farmhouse was being done up. Once they moved into the farmhouse they would raise more children and be happy again, she said. But none of that happened. It was all in the past now. After a difficult year living in the farmhouse together Bill moved back into the cottage. Two years ago Tamsin had asked for a divorce. Reah was now thirteen. It was seven years since Tamsin had hit him with that rolled-up sheaf of fax paper and Reah had cried and Bill had realised how far things had gone wrong.

He drove up the track that led to Holt's Farm. Turning right before the broken gatepost that marked off his land from Tamsin's, Bill parked in front of a small dark cottage just below the crest of the hill. In the distance he could make out a warm glow of lights coming from over the ridge. There lay the farmhouse where Tamsin and Reah lived together now. He would see his daughter tomorrow. But not tonight. That was how wrong things had gone.

The future, once so bright, was forgotten, but my God the past was with them still.

❖ TRIUMPH OF THE LIVING

THERE WAS NOTHING to suggest how much he would lose that day.

Bill woke to find the sun burning off the mist below. Holt's Farm was well above the valley with its slopes of dark coniferous forest. There were many mornings like this when Bill would open the curtains of his office and find the valley full of cloud, as if a dank white sea had rolled up in the night, drowned the abbey at Tintern and claimed the Wye as its estuary.

Beep.

"Bill, I've sent you a fax," said the answer-machine. "And I believe Siobhan's e-mailed you. Sorry to bombard you but I don't think your mobile works when you're abroad."

"Yes it does," Bill told the machine. He was sipping coffee at the window of his tiny office. Bill often drank the first coffee of the day here. When he and Tamsin had bought Holt's Cottage this had been a store-room but it proved just big enough to take a desk, a chair and an ancient sofa which some long deceased dog had made very greasy before Bill Wheeler bought it for a song and shoved it under the makeshift book-shelves.

"So now. What was I going to speak to you about?" continued the voice of Louis Montgomery. Bill was perversely fond of these games. Louis knew exactly what he wanted to speak about. He had just waited until Bill was out of the country before ringing him. "Oh yes, this man in Vienna. Sounds appalling but I really think we should feature him and I'm sure you are the only person who can handle him. I have faith in you, William."

"You mean nobody else will do it," Bill told the machine.

He loved this view from his office although it had taken a few weekends hacking down brambles and saplings before Bill finally found the vista he'd always hoped was there.

Two hundred feet below lay the river. It was an effort to see far into the valley. It dropped away too suddenly. So in the mornings Bill often stood on the sofa to get a better view. And he'd open the window too. The sheer freshness of country air had been a revelation to Bill Wheeler. It alone justified the move from London. If anyone were to come upon him now, windows wide open, coffee cup in hand, standing on the furniture in his nightshirt with his head scraping the ceiling, they might have thought the owner of Holt's Cottage very odd. But no one came this way. Holt's was the end of the line in more ways than one.

"Anyway give me a bell when you get back. What's that?" Bill listened as Louis covered the mouthpiece and conferred with his assistant. "Oh it seems I'm going to be in Barcelona when you get back, so speak to Siobhan will you? She'll arrange tickets and hotels."

Bill laughed. Typical Louis. He stepped down and shut the window. The room was cold this morning. In fact his whole cottage was cold. It seemed to die when he went away. Now Bill stood by the desk with an old black jersey over his night-shirt. His feet could feel the cold striking up through cracked tiles. He'd covered them with a threadbare Indian carpet that might have been thick enough for Rajasthan, but not Welsh Wales.

Those tiles. This secondhand desk. That narrow sofa which afforded such a view. This was home. It would soon warm up. He would light a fire to supplement the storage heaters.

Beep. Louis again.

"Bill, I don't know if you got my fax but if you didn't the last message probably didn't make much sense. Look, how would you like to interview Paolo Bardini in Vienna on Friday? He knows your work, thinks well of you. I've been hoping to feature him for some time. Ring me as soon as you can."

Presumably Bardini was notoriously unreliable or difficult. That's why this call hadn't been delegated to Siobhan. As it happened, though, Bill knew neither Bardini nor his reputation. There were still a lot of gaps in Bill Wheeler's knowledge of the music-world. While Louis had gone from Oxford directly into publishing, Bill had come into the music-world indirectly. He'd started in the newsroom of a London paper, developed an interest in writing about the arts and only then discovered opera. When he'd left to go freelance he was struggling to catch up. And still was.

That had been eight years ago. Bill could still remember those days and the determination to make his the most useful telephone number in any editor's address book. He would go anywhere at any time night or day. It had been an exhausting and exhilarating crash course in the arts but Bill's training as a journalist had given him the edge over Louis' college chums. They often knew far more about the subject than the person they were interviewing but they couldn't turn a story around in four hours.

Beep. Bill had just picked Louis' fax off the floor when the next message broke into his life. "Bill, my name is Vita," said a woman from New York. "Call me the moment you get in. I'll be seeing your article through its various stages."

He hated the 'various stages' to which the *New York Times* submitted an article – and the person who'd written it. Between the studied vagueness of Louis and a hard-nosed American called Vita, Bill knew he'd take Louis any day. Except Louis wasn't there was he? Louis had skipped abroad on yet another a freebie, which meant that Bill would have to deal with Siobhan and Siobhan was far worse than either.

He would speak to her later in the day.

"Hi Dad, it's *me*," said a voice that he recognised: Reah, from yesterday, sounding as if she were making an effort to come over light and cheerful despite phenomenal woes. Bill knew that tone well. "Just wondered if you're back yet. Jethro is being a right pig," Reah continued referring to her kitten. "Mum thought you wouldn't be back till really late but I thought I could see your car. I really liked speaking to you when you rang, Dad," Reah continued with just a little sadness in her voice. "Anyway I'm over the tummy thing now. Ring me when you get in, OK? Bye!"

In Reah's world it was Easter holidays, Bill reminded himself. In her mother's family it was Passover. Either way she would be coming to stay while Tamsin went to London for a few days on her own. Suddenly Bill remembered how much he was looking forward to it. Parenthood to Tamsin was an ocean of concern permanently engulfing her, whereas for Bill it was a relatively tranquil sea he dipped in and out of. When he was away he might go a whole day and not think of Reah, but when he did it was with such rich pleasure – and virtually no anxiety. He particularly loved the idea of her coming to stay with him. They had their Wednesday evenings together and alternate weekends when they usually drove down to Chepstow to rent videos. In this way he'd introduced her to black-and-white greats like *Casablanca*, *The Maltese Falcon* and *Double Indemnity*. They were friends, Bill liked to think. In a way that he and his father never had been. Reah was his unexpected bonus in life. Someone to come home to.

The machine beeped yet again. An acknowledgement of the safe receipt of his American listings guide written for a Danish publication. The editor was so polite.

And another beep. On this occasion Bill heard no voice but some definite breathing. "Yes?" he demanded of the machine. The breathing continued. Frustrated. The breathing of someone who felt that Bill really ought to be there. Then a note of exasperation and the phone went down with some force. Someone wasn't happy.

That was the end of the messages. Bill dialled 1471 but a machine simply told him, "You were called yesterday at 22.31 hours. The caller withheld their number." It could have been any one of a number of

London editors whose offices used the PABX system. Or it could have been a mobile. Or someone abroad.

Bill turned back to Louis' fax. An accompanying article referred to Bardini as the genius who reduced everyone to tears, but not in the same way Puccini did. Paolo Bardini usually only worked with young singers. He wished to mould new talent, to gain access to the voice before it had been corrupted by outdated nineteenth-century projection techniques. Probably means that none of the old hands will put up with him, Bill thought to himself.

The cutting, which from its spelling of words like *center*, *maneuver* and *theater*, must have been from some American publication, went on to talk about a scandal in Berlin where one of Bardini's young cast had had a nervous breakdown and had to withdraw from a production of *Rigoletto*. The girl's agent attributed her collapse to Bardini's way of working with singers. He of course had insisted she was unhinged before they ever met.

A second, smaller cutting referred to the fact that Bardini was starting rehearsals in Vienna for *Elektra* shortly. Now that would be interesting. Bill could see the story Louis wanted. How was the man who drove singers to distraction going to approach an opera that deals with mental breakdown? Tacky. But intriguing.

Presumably Bardini was giving interviews, but was he really going to let Bill draw him into making such parallels? Bill could see why Louis didn't want to talk to him directly. He didn't want his tame reporter to have the option of saying "No".

A door banged shut. "Hi Dad!" said Reah from the living room. Bill went to greet his daughter and found her putting down a huge black overnight bag in front of the TV. "Well? What d'you think?" she asked, posing.

"Very nice," said Bill automatically. It was rare that he had a clear idea what he was supposed to be admiring. "You're early aren't you?"

"Mum's got to get off to London," Reah explained and she struck her pose again.

"Oh. Just a moment," said Bill. He'd wanted to see Tamsin and make sure she was OK. Bill knew she would have dropped Reah off rather than let her lug that great unnecessary bag across the field. She'd be outside still, engine running, checking her daughter had gone in safely. Bill opened his front door but already he could see Tamsin's motor disappearing down the lane and into the woods. It was unlike her not to talk, not to hand over bits of information and superfluous instructions. She must be late.

"How was your trip?" Reah asked as Bill came back with the post.

"Fine."

"What's the desert like?"

"I wasn't in the desert. I was in Tel Aviv. Tel Aviv's like Milton Keynes."

"You know you really shouldn't wander around like that, Daddy dear," said Reah, looking archly over her shoulder at him. This was obviously one of her frisky mornings. Sometimes Reah would come in and collapse on the settee in angry despair about her hair or thighs. Today was not a body-image day.

"Like what?" Bill asked. Before realising that Reah was referring to his fetching nightshirt and pullover combo.

"You really ought to have a smoking jacket. There's this shop in a place called Jermyn Street, right?, that does the most wonderful dressing gowns and things, Dad." Bill went on to automatic pilot as he checked through the post that he'd brought in last night. There were times when Reah needed all his concentration. There were times when she was just burbling for the fun of it.

Nothing but bills and press releases.

"Ooh!" shouted Reah suddenly. "My programme's on. OK if I watch it?" She was already scrabbling across the sofa towards the remote control. "I'll go on cans."

"Do you want anything to eat?" Bill asked.

"No thanks, Daddy-Boo," said Reah as she lost herself within the silence of Bill's heavy-duty headphones. Bill stole a glance at the screen. It was the usual boy-band nonsense. He'd make himself some more coffee and put the washing in. Then he ought to get dressed. Reah was just thirteen. Bill was unsure whether the sight of his legs mattered. Might she really suffer traumas in later life simply because he didn't have a smoking-jacket of the kind they sold in posh parts of London? Bringing up a teenage girl was difficult. Tamsin told him that frequently. As for bringing up a teenage girl who wanted to shop for smoking jackets in Jermyn Street, that sounded difficult *and* expensive. How on earth did a child of her age even know about Jermyn Street?

Reah was still sitting cross-legged and happily plugged into the TV when Bill took his coffee into the office. The ground floor of Holt's Cottage was entirely open-plan, apart from the office, which meant that Bill could watch his daughter from the kitchen sink as he reloaded the espresso machinetta. He marvelled yet again at the thick mass of black hair bobbing around on either side of those headphones. Reah's hair was extraordinary, it curled and waved as if Nature were simply having fun when it created Rachel Christabel Wheeler. She of course hated her hair but Bill could not get over what he took to be the magnificence of her Jewish inheritance. Tamsin's hair had always been straight. He could not see where those dense dark curls had sprung from. As for Tamsin's mother, she had always worn a wig as far as Bill could remember. And her father had always had very little. The old man had shared in Bill's delight once Reah's mop had begun to sprout in this spectacular way. It was vibrant proof that the forces of destruction could not succeed. She herself was the triumph of life. Bill had liked the quiet way old Mr Walken smiled upon his grand-daughter. That was how the past should be put to rest, he thought. Not by banning operas.

He was back in his office now. Soon he'd have to check his e-mails. Thoughts of Wagner stirred memories of that impenetrable letter. Bill put down his pile of press releases and took it out of his notebook. He thought of the letter as Wagner's but really it was the property of the person to whom Richard Wagner had addressed it. That is how it would be referred to in an article. The *von Bülow* letter. The *Laussot* letter. The *Wesendonck* letter. Funnily enough the only names Bill could remember from Wagner's private life were the husbands whose wives he had appropriated. "*Werther Freund*" it began. "*Welch Schuft bin ich.*" Something something have been I... Bill knew this was wasting time but nevertheless he reached for a pocket dictionary.

Welcher; welche, welches. Pronoun *what.*

What a *Schuft* have I been! There was no entry for *Schuft* in this dictionary, alas.

Schuhmacher, Schublade, *Schopenhauer.* Curious how bits of what Libby had told him kept coming back when he started thinking about Wagner. In middle age Richard Wagner had become a great convert to Schopenhauer but the two never met. It was something about Schopenhauer's belief in the pre-eminence of Will that so caught Wagner's imagination. Allegedly.

Bill got up and reached over to where a paperback dictionary of philosophy sat under a pile of telephone directories. A post-Kantian philosopher was Herr Schopenhauer. Bill skimmed down both columns to see if there was any reference to Richard Wagner. "*Art as the sole arena in which man may escape subjection to the will in free aesthetic contemplation*" he read. Fair enough. But how did this "escape" relate to Wagner? Wagner was nothing but Will, surely? He took money and wives off all those he met because his sufferings as an artist raised him above bourgeois constraints. His Will was wholly unconstrained. So what did he see in Schopenhauer's view that we need art in order to escape it? Maybe Wagner found the daily act of living the life of a monster arduous. He had called something that Schopenhauer wrote "My gift from Heaven" "My salvation". Bill could remember Libby reciting those words to him in German. She had lain much emphasis on Schopenhauer. How she had recited him. They had never kissed but Bill had spent months distracted by her lips.

With a start Bill realised that he had spent the last ten minutes at a total tangent, diverging yet again in the direction of Libby Ziegler. He wasn't even supposed to be piecing together the disjointed elements of Wagner's philosophy. What mattered at the moment was to whom this letter was written – and what it said. A combination of those two elements would be what had made Katz consider it dynamite. Well, the latter he might find out when he got some replies. As to the addressee, Bill wondered whether that piece of paper torn from the bottom left hand corner of page two might have contained the formal name of Wagner's *Werther Freund*. He'd seen that practice on nineteenth-century English letters.

Bill picked up the phone and dialled a number.

"Cardiff University."

"Could you put me through to your music department?" Bill asked.

After talking to a number of secretaries, all of whom sounded dismayed whenever he asked if anyone in the department might keep facsimiles of Wagner's correspondence, Bill found himself speaking to a librarian who remained calm long enough to impart the knowledge that there were two books on the stacks with plates illustrative of Wagner's letter-writing style.

He'd have to go down and compare handwriting. Bill felt absolutely certain in his own mind that this letter was written by Richard Wagner. He'd never doubted it but he needed to make that test. "I'm probably coming down to Cardiff today," he began. "Is it possible I can call in and look at those two books?"

He'd been so busy he hadn't seen Reah waiting in the doorway but suddenly there she was, arms outstretched and bouncing on to his lap. "Did you bring me a present?" she asked. Her weight was not insignificant.

"Of course," he said, awkwardly trying to reach under the desk.

"I love you, Daddy Boo"

"And I brought a necklace for your mother, as I was back a day late."

"She's been awful," said Reah.

"She had to look after you while you were sick. She was probably worried."

"No it wasn't that," said Reah, absentmindedly turning over the dictionary of philosophy, then fiddling with the phone. "She's been crying again. And she's always nagging me. Then she starts crying again. Or singing. That's worse. Dad, you *know* she can't sing."

Bill always found it disturbing when Reah talked to him about Tamsin. It was as if she could see someone who was invisible to him. Literally speaking, Reah did see Tamsin when he didn't. His ex-wife and daughter were together most weeks for most of the time but to hear Reah talk was to believe that Tamsin had become another person entirely, a character whose existence was entirely circumscribed by Reah's reportage.

These days Bill only knew Tamsin as the person with whom he discussed Reah, with whom he tackled money matters and practical issues, like trying to get the lane to Holt's Farm made up and the gatepost fixed. These days the Tamsin he met was always upbeat, even if she seemed a little tired at times. The Tamsin whom Reah described to him was much more volatile. Often in tears, sometimes angry, frequently undermining Reah's confidence for "absolutely no good reason" (Reah's words) and putting pressure on her to do "stupid Jewish things" (also Reah's words).

Bill was cautious about getting involved, particularly on that one. As far as he was concerned Reah was Jewish when she was with Tamsin and not so Jewish, if Jewish at all, when with him. Bill had no discernible religion and no wish to get involved when Reah grumbled to him about Shabbat or complained that everyone else had Christmas trees but not her mum. Yes, the Jewish thing was difficult but then everything was potentially difficult in their current situation. What was most frustrating was that if he and Tamsin were still married he'd have no hesitation about telling his wife to let up, not to get in a state if Reah wouldn't wear dresses when visiting her grandparents, skipped prayers over the candles on Friday night or openly ate bacon cheeseburgers. Tamsin herself had been a rebel once. What she needed now was to regain her sense of proportion. Not the kind of advice a woman takes well from her ex-husband.

So far Bill had kept his silence over whatever Reah told him. He noticed with some relief that the persecutions varied. As for religious issues, Bill knew that Reah remained close to her grandparents, so it wasn't really Judaism she was rejecting – it was her mother. Unfortunately for Tamsin, Reah's rebellious phase seemed to have coincided with Tamsin's rediscovery of her faith. Poor Reah: bad enough in these parts to come from a broken home but a broken Jewish home! *Not good.*

"How would you like to go to Cardiff?" he asked, his arms wrapped around hers.

"I'd rather go somewhere really interesting," she replied.

"Bad luck, we're going to Cardiff."

"So what did you get me?"

"You said you wanted a fluffy camel."

Reah shrieked with embarrassment.

"What's wrong with a fluffy camel?"

"I know it's babyish," she admitted, "but I'm allowed to be a bit of a baby when I'm ill, aren't I?"

"Absolutely."

"Is he very fluffy?"

"Any fluffier and he'd be a one-humped kitten."

Their's was a good relationship, Bill thought.

He made a few phone-calls to chase up editors, then faxed a note to Siobhan: "*Just back and received Louis' fax. No time to talk at present. Off to Cardiff. Do you want to ring me on the mobile this pm?*"

Two could play at Louis' game.

The journey down to Cardiff was one that Bill enjoyed. The M4 west was effortless and the distant hillsides were rich with trees and old stone farmhouses. This was the borderland between England and Wales with the architecture of one and the countryside of the other. As Tamsin had remarked when they first arrived, "Thank God it wasn't the other way around." Bill had tended to agree. He had moved to the Wye Valley without even realising that it was in another country. Nationhood was not something that interested Bill. He identified with the Native Americans who, when told they were American now the USA had bought Alaska, failed to be impressed. Russia and America were just words. Their valleys were no deeper now, their mountains no higher. "Nationhood," Bill once said to someone who listened too intently, "should be optional." It was just a concept and certainly not one worth dying for.

Too many bad things had been done in the name of nationality. He wondered why we persist in dignifying it. Fortunately the worst Welsh atrocity he'd witnessed in this part of the world was the imposition of bilingual road signs on places like Chepstow where no one spoke Welsh outside the classroom. It got a little more serious when someone sprayed 'CYMRAEG' over the sign to Holt's Farm, soon after Bill and Tamsin moved in. It was an action that had shocked Tamsin deeply. It reminded her of the people who'd daubed 'JUDEN' on her great grandparents' house in Munich. Ever since Reah's birth, Tamsin had reconnected with the Nightmare. She'd not gone out for days afterwards. Bill knew that she spooked easily.

He parked by the University, a series of unexpectedly imperial build-ings from the city's period of Edwardian affluence. Reah had wanted him to park in the city centre so she had easy access to the shops but Bill was impatient to seek out his quarry.

He didn't find it hard to locate the music building, as the calm librarian had described it accurately. Modern, brick, with a Henry Moore outside. "What's that?" said Reah, pointing to the statue.

"It's famous."

"What for?"

"Good question," he conceded. Bill would not have been able to explain a Henry Moore. How could one tell if Moore had ever done a bad one? He'd had that kind of debate with the woman who listened too intently. She'd had the answer, of course.

In the library Reah lost her nerve. She had tried asking if they kept anything on Dooley Wilson, who sang 'As Time Goes By', but when the librarian expressed surprise that a girl of her age knew of *Casablanca* she clammed up and hung lumpishly round Bill while he took some photocopies.

But even before he'd studied the plates, Bill knew. The handwriting was very, very similar. Yes, here were those sudden flourishes as letters tore up and down the page, here in the signature was an R, very open and very similar to Wagner's capital Bs. As before, certain letters hardly seemed formed at all. And why did an N in Wagner's hand so much resemble a U? Nevertheless it was clear that Bill's letter – Katz's letter, the letter now in his hand – was either written by Wagner or was a very good forgery intended to give the impression it was written by Wagner.

To compensate for her boredom in the library Bill took Reah to the docks. They sat on a terrace outside the Sports Cafe overlooking Cardiff Bay. It was just warm enough to eat outside. Reah would rather have stayed within and played with the video games but Bill wanted to talk. "I miss our conversations when I'm away," he told her.

"Mm," said Reah.

"You know what I always think when I'm setting off?"

"Where the hell's my passport?" said Reah. Bill laughed and took one of her chips. "OK, what do *you* want to talk about?" Reah shrugged but Bill didn't mind. There was an easy intimacy between them.

"School?" he suggested.

Reah shuddered. "Those bitches? No way."

"Jethro?"

"OK," she conceded.

"*So*, what about Jethro?"

"Well, he's very sweet and he's started walking across my homework when I'm doing it and sticking his tail up my nose."

"Does Tamsin still want to have him done?"

"Yes," said Reah, pretending gloom. "And it's not fair. I wanted to have some kitties."

"I don't suppose Jethro will be too pleased either."

"Mum says it doesn't matter while we're living in the country but if we move, then he might get into lots of fights with other cats."

"But we're not moving," said Bill.

No, not moving. Tamsin's car disappearing down the lane.

There must have been something in his tone that threw Reah. Looking back on that awful moment in the days that were to come, Bill realised that he had probably sounded more definite than Reah had expected. More surprised too. It was an awful shock, a shock that hit him with a sickening thud.

Reah's words made no sense but, like that moment when he had disinterred Katz's letter from the hotel bin in Tel Aviv, Bill knew immediately that something was spinning out from this moment. A line that went from the present into an unknown but significant future. It had been the same when he had first met Libby Ziegler all those years ago. He had wanted quick quotes from media personalities and someone in the office had said ring this woman, and within one minute of their conversation Bill had known something was going to come of this, something that in due course wrecked his marriage. Can we put the phone down at that point? Can we stop the conversation or throw away the letter? We can. In theory.

But we don't. Bill remembered the Norns. Wagner's stupid, stupid Norns at the beginning of *Götterdämmerung*. Three women sitting on the top of a mountain winding the fates of the world into ropes from which no one escapes. Not Siegfried, not Brünhilde nor the gods themselves. Is it all so predetermined? Is the most we can ever ask for the simple perspicacity to glimpse ourselves clearly as we are tangled, ever further, in those ropes? Any attempt to free ourselves is doomed. Like flies trapped in a web, the more we struggle the less chance we have.

"Does your mum say you're moving?" But at that moment he already knew she did. He also knew – and Reah did too – that this would lead to difficult times. Awful times.

"Mum said she was talking to you about it."

"About what?"

"Us all moving back to London."

Ridiculously Bill tried for a moment to remember such a conversation.

Of course there had been none. And this morning Tamsin hadn't waited to speak to him. She'd driven off, her car disappearing down the lane, into the trees, taking his daughter with him. Gone. Reah out of his life forever.

"When?" he asked, looking out across Cardiff Bay, looking out on a new world, a landscape blighted by shock. Normally he would not pump his daughter for information but this was different. Tamsin had driven off to avoid speaking to him. Down the lane. *Forever.*

"Mum said we'd all be going," said Reah, looking scared now. Bill didn't know why. What was she seeing in his face?

"When?"

"She said I'd be going to a nicer school in September."

"Where?"

"Near by where Grandpop and Gramma live."

"But what about her job?"

"She's given in her notice. She's getting a better one, she said."

Bill was silent.

"I thought you knew..." said Reah.

Bill could not believe the moment he was living through. What had Tamsin done? What was she doing? He reached for his mobile phone.

"Dad, Mum said she was speaking to you about it. She's probably just forgotten because you were away." Reah was clearly agitated now. "And because I was ill. She was probably going to tell you yesterday but you came back late."

The number was ringing, ringing.

"Hello?" Tamsin's voice. Anxious. Bill knew that her mobile displayed the caller's name. He could hear how she had hesitated before picking it up.

"Tamsin. Bill. What is this Reah tells me about you moving to London?" There was a pause. Silence, then the sound of a car in traffic. Then Tamsin's voice again.

"I can't talk about this at the moment, Bill, I'm driving. It'll have to wait till I get back."

"You know what we agreed, that we would stay nearby each other so Reah was brought up by us both."

"I can't talk about this at the moment," repeated Tamsin. "It'll have to wait until I get back." She hung up.

Bill tried Tamsin's number again, but she had switched off her phone. He sat in silence, cold with anger. They had had an agreement.

"You can come too, Dad," said Reah. The poor girl was earnestly searching his face for some traces of good humour, of humanity even.

"Mum says you're a freelance, you can work anywhere."

"Yeah," said Bill. "That's right." But what he also knew – and what Tamsin knew too – was that he had no money to move to London. All their joint capital was vested in the farmhouse which Bill had transferred into her name when they divorced. All Bill had was a mortgage on a two-bedroom cottage, and property prices in the capital were easily twice what they were around Chepstow; near where Tamsin's family lived, probably three or four times as much. He was stranded.

Bill was sure he could detect the long arm of Michael Walken in all this. Old Man Walken had never wanted his daughter and granddaughter to move to the Welsh borders. He wanted his family around him, and if that meant marooning Bill in Chepstow, then so much the better.

It was a moment Bill would long remember. The light extinguished and his daughter far from him.

Darkness.

❖ FALLING APART

IT WAS ANOTHER DAY, and the world was cruelly determined to be cheerful. Even the bell-ringers of St Mary's had decided to join in. God, thought Bill as he emerged into the sunlight of Upper Castle Street, Tamsin knew Reah meant the world to him and he meant the world to her. Didn't she realise how lost he would be if she took Reah away? Of course she knew. That was why she wasn't returning his calls.

The meeting with the solicitor had not gone well.

"I'm afraid we can't go back to court and vary the terms of the consent order," Bill was told. "You see you paid off the mortgage on the farmhouse and transferred it into Mrs Wheeler's sole name as a one-off sum in lieu of maintenance."

But Bill didn't want to vary terms. He wanted his daughter living nearby as she always had. Legal opinion however was adamant. The former Mrs Wheeler was a free woman. "She can live where she wants. There is nothing in the agreement that commits her to living in any particular place."

Bill wandered down towards Bridge Street and past his favourite second-hand bookshop. He had no appetite for browsing today. No appetite for the rather attractive young woman who worked there either. He was heading towards the castle, which was where he had said he'd meet Reah. All he wanted to do now was gather her to him and retreat back into the hills.

"The consent order says nothing about *levels* of contact," the solicitor had reminded Bill. "By exchange of letters you agreed that Rachel will have a home with your ex-wife and that she will stay with you – 'staying contact' we call it – as often as is reasonable."

How often is reasonable when Tamsin's living in London? Bill wondered. And why now after they'd been down here six years? To be honest he had no idea what he'd signed at the time of the divorce. Everything was so vague and painful then. All he could recall now was the sadness that it had come to this, when the Wye Valley was supposed to be their new beginning. They had slept together for one last time the night he signed the papers for Tamsin. No, now that he thought about it, that wasn't the last time, the night of the kitchen and the candlelight. There was another time too. But the night he signed he remembered how they had taken their pain to bed and found compassion. Yet afterwards, as he lay by Tamsin's side, Bill had felt that old painful need to escape her, sadly now stronger than ever.

The narrow terraces curving down Bridge Street ended abruptly at the Three Tuns Inn and then suddenly, round the corner, there was the castle on its rocky outcrop, one broken stump sitting on another, with Chepstow's bijou modern visitor centre and toy-town car-park down below.

It had not survived the neglect of generations well, this castle. Were it not a monument it would be an eyesore, Bill thought. He decided not to wait in the car but to sit on the lawned embankment next to the battered old Public Works Portakabin which seemed to have become a permanent part of the castle's outer defences.

Bill seated himself on slightly higher ground where he could see his car and gazed across the narrow Wye to England. He knew this spot well. He had seen it in summer and winter. Today however it was graced by a riot of pink blossom. Even the birds were singing. Why was everything so bloody perfect? he wondered. Nature can be an ironic bitch sometimes, sending doves to coo as your life falls apart.

No it wasn't falling apart, he thought. This was yet another final stage in the disaster that had been their marriage.

"I think really you have to wait and see what your ex-wife has to say," the Law had concluded. "How far she is willing to compromise."

And Bill had smiled. In all of this the one thing they knew for certain was that the former Mrs Wheeler didn't have it in mind to compromise. She had driven down the lane and into a future without him.

Bill stretched out on the embankment. "I must warn you though, Mrs Wheeler's solicitors will have told her that there is no way she can be compelled to stay in Chepstow. If she were planning to move Rachel abroad, now that might be a different matter..." Bill sat up. There was no way he would be able to settle today. He switched on his mobile again but decided there was very little point in ringing Tamsin. That had become obvious after his third attempt last night. She was screening him out. Short of going up to London, Bill was stuck. He couldn't make a move until he knew what his ex-wife intended.

Suddenly the mobile burst into life, vibrating in his hand as the caller display screen lit up. It trilled and buzzed with urgency. Bill stabbed the OK button without even looking at whom this might be.

"Is that Bill?" asked a voice, which for a moment he could not recognise. "Bill, it's Siobhan. You're not returning my calls."

The last thing Bill wanted at the moment was to listen to the relentless reproaches of Louis Montgomery's hatchet woman. Siobhan was probably quite a likeable person when you got to know her but Bill doubted either of them would live that long. Her Presbyterian Scots accent endowed every utterance with a dour gravitas that belied her twenty-something years. She was grim in her loyalty to Louis, something he exploited of course, placing Siobhan in the front line of all but his most intricate dealings.

"Bill, Louis gets back on Monday. If he finds we're no further forward with this Bardini interview it's really going to throw things out and he's got such a pressured week."

Bill wondered why, if Louis' week was so pressured, he had taken a freebie to Barcelona. Life was never difficult for Louis Montgomery except on the rare occasions when Siobhan took a holiday.

"Can't someone else go?" Bill asked. He really felt the need to concentrate on the Tamsin bombshell.

"We've asked Tom," said Siobhan. "He's reviewed Bardini several times but he's busy for the next two weeks."

Bill had guessed the short notice meant he hadn't been first choice for this particular jaunt. Why should he be? There had to be some journalists who'd heard of the infamous Bastardini.

"Isn't there anyone else?" Bill asked.

"No one else can bluff like you," Siobhan replied.

"I do not bluff," Bill snapped. He would take that from Louis because Louis always teased him and Bill knew he genuinely respected his ability to assimilate background detail quickly. Louis also seemed to genuinely like Bill's writing.

There was a silence which was probably the sound of Siobhan coping with the unfamiliar feeling of being wrong-footed.

"Get someone else," Bill grumbled and he switched off.

Damn – he should ring back. But before Bill could, she did.

"Sorry," said Bill. "Bad day."

"You cut me off," said Siobhan reproachfully.

"Yes, I'm sorry," Bill said again. "Lot of problems down here."

Siobhan took a breath.

"Life isn't easy for any of us," she told him and Bill could see those irritating little creases that formed around Siobhan's eyes whenever she was keeping Louis' boys in line.

The pair of them were lost in silent stalemate for a moment. Bill almost said, "My ex-wife is taking my daughter away" but he doubted that Siobhan would be touched by that or by anything that didn't relate to poor

Louis and his allegedly heavy workload.

"So do you think you could go at the end of the week?"

Bill really wanted an end to the depressing relentlessness of Siobhan. Could he go at the end of the week? Well he'd only got Reah for three nights. He doubted that Tamsin would delay her return from wherever she'd gone. It wasn't like her to let Reah down.

"I could go on Saturday," he conceded without enthusiasm.

"And when could Louis have copy?"

"Tuesday."

"Morning?"

"Yes, OK. Tuesday morning," Bill grumbled, adding, "11 am." But he doubted if Siobhan picked up on irony. Never before had Bill regretted making himself indispensable.

Siobhan started to give him the details of a hotel that would host him for as long as he needed.

"No," said Bill, for he could see Reah coming across the car park now. "No, I've got things to sort out here, Siobhan. I'll do the interview but will you fix the accommodation please?"

"Very well, Bill," said Siobhan. She only ever used his name pointedly.

Bill wandered down to meet Reah who looked at him sadly and then snuck into his shoulder. Unbearably lovely, he found her today. Bill tousled her hair.

"Dad!"

Bill had forgotten. They were in Chepstow. Her so-called friends from that rotten comprehensive lived in Chepstow. Bill was not supposed to show signs of affection.

"Good shop?" Bill asked but his mind was already elsewhere. Tamsin's car disappearing down the lane.

"They hadn't got the CD I wanted," Reah explained. "So I got one I didn't want." She looked up at him. That was supposed to be a joke. Their joke, Bill realised.

"Let's go back," he said. He didn't want to be out. He wanted to get back to Holt's Cottage. To sit inside and light a fire even. The instinct to hole up was ridiculously strong.

"What about a video?" Reah asked. They'd been going to choose something together.

"Sure," he said, making the effort. Whatever happened, Bill told himself, whatever happened he would always make the effort for her.

On the way back up to Holt's Cottage Bill tried to grapple with his anxieties. He knew that what worried him most was not knowing what

Tamsin had planned. This was what had had him driving down to the solicitors first thing, even before Lee had arrived with the post. That Tamsin would not speak to him about this projected London move alarmed Bill as much as news of the move itself.

Had she really been offered another job? No. Primary school teachers don't get headhunted, he thought. Even those with special needs qualifications. Perhaps she'd applied for a job in London and got it. But that would mean she'd been planning this for months. Why hadn't she told him?

He didn't know. He just didn't know. Once he had the measure of what he was dealing with Bill knew he'd cope. Somehow. One did. Meanwhile his mind was throwing up images of Reah wrested away from him, of never seeing her again. As they turned out of the sunlight and up into the dark wooded lane that led to Bill's cottage he found himself imagining parents divided from their children. The dark, unforgiving forest. Dogs barking. How the legacy of another century haunts us all, he thought, and how clever of the Nazis to tap into everybody's worst nightmares and give them substance. Bill knew he was being ridiculous. Tamsin was a sane and compassionate person.

"Dad, what are you doing with that?" Reah asked. Bill was standing in the doorway of his cottage, stepping back from the hook on which he kept a shotgun for scaring rabbits off the vegetable patch. Bill genuinely had no idea what the gun was doing in his hands. He had no recollection of parking the Jeep either.

"That's not for Mum is it?" Reah joked. She knew of course that there was a reason why Bill had been to the solicitor that morning, why he had sat silent all last evening with his arms around her as they watched TV.

Bill broke the gun to show her there were no cartridges inside.

"Just checking," he said with a smile.

"Post," said Reah, holding up some envelopes she'd brought in from his mailbox. "You forgot your post."

For a moment Bill wondered whether there might be a letter from Tamsin in the pile.

"Let's have some coffee," he said nonchalantly. He really mustn't alarm Reah any more.

"This one's from London," she said.

From London. Bill felt significance hanging in the air. Nevertheless he took his time and put down the machinetta carefully. That envelope either is or is not from Tamsin, he thought. How quickly a man crosses the room to open it does not change what's inside.

University of London, the envelope said. Bill exhaled and lightened up.

A long time ago in a world that made sense, he'd asked three men to look at a letter written in German.

"*Dear Mr Wheeler*," the letter read, "*I enclose the extract you sent me.*"

Bill checked the signature. This was Tony Something-Or-Other, Tony Scribble-Scribble, the young man who'd wanted a name at the *New York Times*. To him Bill had given the middle section of Katz's letter, the bottom of page one and the top of page two. Bill laid it to one side and finished preparing the machinetta. Then he wandered down to where Reah was loading her new CD into the hi-fi.

"I'll go on headphones, Dad."

"Great," said Bill, patting her hair distractedly as he went into his office, letter in hand. This was what he needed. Something that had to be done. Something that didn't hurt. Bill was already scanning Scribble-Scribble's typescript for words of a sensational nature. As it happened Dr Tony had ended up with the briefest section. There at the bottom of his translation however Bill immediately picked out the words *Siegmund*, *Sieglinde* and *Brünhilde*. Well, well. Dr Scribble-Scribble probably had a pretty good idea about the author of this letter by now!

Bill closed the door of his office and started to read what he'd been sent from top to bottom.

"Here however, my friend, things get worse," ran the first sentence. "*Wie auch immer, theurer Freund, hier verschlimmert sich die Lage.*" Tony had done a thorough job, providing not just a translation but also the German original running underneath. Rendered into reliable Times Roman even nineteenth-century Fraktur seemed penetrable.

> *I had hoped, as you know, to endure no more special relationships of the kind that scars me still.*

Tony had asterisked this section.

> **Wagner actually says "that eats up my soul." He uses quite a few archaisms, some of which I would imagine he's invented. Where possible I've found a modern idiom, hope this is what you want..*

So it hadn't taken Dr Scribbleman any time at all to deduce the author's identity. Bill's subterfuge suddenly felt naive.

> *I have courted the affection of nobody, as you know, and I leave people to think of me as they please but if a finger of unconditional love is held out to me from anywhere I seize the whole hand and draw that mortal towards me.*

What on earth was he talking about?

Ich bin so ein Kind.

I am such a child! I know no first or last midst those my heart belongs to. I've only one heart and whoever dwells there is sole tenant from top to bottom. You know dear friend of the one I spoke of whose love for me was of the purest, noblest kind.

This one however I love as my own child, as the All Father his daughter. Yet what hope is there for me? She cannot love me as I her. Siegmund in that dark land had the love of his sister and Siegfried his Brünhilde but I am allowed no such consolation and will allow myself none.

So Wagner is in love, thought Bill. But surely Wagner was always in love? Usually with women married to other men. That is why they cannot love him as he them. What fresh scandal is there in this?

The *All Father* was Wotan, Bill remembered. Wotan the builder of Valhalla, compromised by his own ambition. Wotan who by the end of *The Ring* is willing the destruction of his own kind in a gloom worthy of Schopenhauer. Bill checked the German typescript and then Tony's photocopy of the manuscript itself. Yes. *Der Allvater.* "*Wie der Allvater seine Tochter.*" As the Allfather his daughter.

Brünhilde.

So Wagner loves this new tenant of his as Wotan loved the Valkyrie, Brünhilde. Brünhilde who disobeys him and tries to save Wotan's son, Siegmund, because she knows that is what Wotan *really* wants.

Bill remembered reading about the Valkyries: they were Wotan's illegitimate daughters, with ridiculous names like Gerhilde, Grimgerde, Ortlinde and Flossysomething. Or was she a Rhinemaiden? He fished out a *Walküre* programme to check the list of characters. Anyway, their job was to carry out Wotan's will, that was it, wasn't it? But Brünhilde goes too far, doesn't she?

"*Obliged by Fricka*", Bill read, "*his vengeful wife, to kill Siegmund, his illegitimate son, Wotan tells Brünhilde that she must abandon their plan to save the hero in his forthcoming battle with Hunding.*"

Hunding, the husband of the woman with whom Siegmund – in true Wagnerian fashion – has just slept. But Brünhilde knows that the Allvater is really on the side of her half-brother and tries to save him. She fails. Wotan shatters Siegmund's sword and Hunding runs him through. As a punishment Wotan imprisons the Valkyrie on a rock surrounded by flame.

So that is the model for the love Wagner feels for this woman, this new sole tenant of his heart? Not exactly illuminating, Bill thought as he let the programme slip from his fingers. And what would Cosima make of this latest girl? Bill remembered Tamsin's words. "I'm sorry Bill, that may be all right in opera but it isn't all right in the real world!"

All Wagner's heroes love someone other than the person they're married to. Moreover the Meister didn't just put adultery on stage. He portrayed incest too. Siegmund really did notch up a few basic transgressions while the old man slept. No wonder Wotan got an earful from Fricka and found himself obliged to destroy his son. Oh the sacrifices we make for marriage, Bill thought.

Siegmund dead when he is only doing Wotan's will. Then Siegmund's son, Siegfried, the product of that incestuous union, has to die too. One steps outside the commonality of life at one's peril. The sins of the father extending to several generations, Bill thought. But Brünhilde was different. Brünhilde knows where Wotan's heart lies. She is wholly outside the commonality. She is his *Wunschmaid* with a divine simplicity that comes from living in the heart. Compromise means nothing to her.

So this is the model for the woman Wagner now loves. Someone who understands the *Allvater* and will go further than even he dares. Bill fished out the letter. When was it written? he wondered. At what stage in Richard Wagner's outrageous personal life did he discover this new Brünhilde? Maybe that piece of paper torn from page two held the date.

Bill gazed at the original. He felt frustrated, like an orangutan who's just been handed a mobile phone. He was so ignorant of its meaning, knowing only that it symbolised things far beyond his understanding. *Damn.* How Bill now regretted his caution in dividing up the letter.

The sun was making wonderful patterns on his window. Wind was stirring the branches. Bill wanted to get up, crane over his desk to see what colour his river was today, but he found himself unwilling even to rise. Sunlight might play outside but Bill was tired within, tired and deeply undermined. Once again he was overcome by that old, old sense of needing to sit and rest forever. The need to take time out. But more than ever he had to act. He had to move on. There were articles to write and e-mails to send. He had lost a morning at the solicitors. If this business with Tamsin came to a legal battle over Reah he would need money. Lots of it. He could not afford to stop working now.

Bill switched on his PC and, as the machine whirred and beeped into life, he got up to make some more coffee. Pausing in the doorway he looked at Reah. She sensed his shadow, glanced up, smiled then went back to the TV. She is lovely, thought Bill, and she has no idea. No idea. And that is how it should be. He had tried not to interrogate her about what was going on with Tamsin. It was important that Reah just thought this another silly quarrel between her parents, like all the silly quarrels they used to have in the aftermath of Libby Ziegler. "Mummy and Daddy are being silly," Tamsin had once said through her tears, and that had made sense to six-year-old Reah. It became the family fiction: Daddy stormed out and walked furiously for an hour or so because he was being silly; Mummy lay down on the bed and banged her fists into the pillow because she was being silly too. Mummy and Daddy were like naughty children, and little square, curly-haired Reah knew best.

But Reah had not been able to stop the ultimate silliness of Mummy and Daddy's divorce. Fortunately, for all concerned, by the time Tamsin said she wanted things finalised Reah was nine and life was a lot calmer. The die was cast. They no longer argued. The night they decided on the divorce arrangements there was sadness but not anger.

"I'll have the farmhouse outright," Tamsin said. "No mortgage. That way I won't have any worries."

"I don't want you to be worried," Bill had said, refilling her glass.

Had she set him up? Bill wondered as he gazed at the screen. No, he didn't believe that. Tamsin could get very angry, she had even proved that she could be downright nasty during that time in Chiswick when they were falling apart, but he could not see her planning a revenge that came to fruition years hence. If she hated him it was in the fire of the moment. It takes a particular kind of sick mind to create misery in cold blood. Ask Lev Davidov.

Once coffee was made Bill returned to the office. There was something about his training as a journalist. Give him a keyboard and a screen and a different part of Bill took charge. He would be here until hunger or the need for the lavatory intervened.

In fact it was an hour and a half later that the interruption came. Bill was just beginning to remember that he must feed Reah sometime when the phone rang and a certain American called Vita came on the line.

"Bill, I'm going to be seeing your article through its various stages." *Oh, great.* "How did you get on in Israel?"

"Fine," he said. "No one's budging much."

"Pardon me?" said Vita.

"No one's shifting their positions. But the politicians were interesting."

"When can I see something, Bill?"

"End of the week?" he suggested. That would mean banging something out before he went to Vienna. The problem with the *New York Times* was that it was dangerous to send in an early draft. The moment Vita got her hands on it fact-checkers would probably descend in their swarms with the result that he'd find himself locked into negotiating the minutiae of something that was never intended to be set in stone.

"End of the week would be fine, Bill." Women kept using his name today. Siobhan to reproach and Vita, presumably, to impress.

"I had an interesting conversation while I was out there..." Bill began. The old freelancer's instinct for an extra commission had not died in him yet.

"Oh yes?" said Vita with a deliberate and wholly polite show of interest which Bill wished could be taught to British editors.

"A man I ran into is hawking round a letter that he claims could wreck Wagner's reputation in Israel for good, possibly do substantial damage elsewhere too."

"Have you seen this letter, Bill?" asked Vita.

"Not yet."

"Is this really likely?" Vita asked. "I would have thought Richard Wagner's reputation was about as low as can be. What about *Mein Leben*? What about *Das Judentum in der Musik*?"

Bill was thrown for a moment.

"I'm sorry but *Judaism in Music* is the most meretricious publication," Vita ploughed on, inadvertently helping Bill climb back on board their conversation. She was quite a woman, this Vita. Not only had she read Wagner's great polemic about Europe's spiritual crisis – and the drastic cure he proposed – it sounded as though she'd done so in the original German. Bill on the other hand had relied on extracts supplied to him by a professor of Jewish Music whom he'd interviewed in London. OK, so a New York intellectual might have time to read one of the building blocks of nineteenth-century anti-Semitism, but Bill Wheeler had a living to earn.

"Let me look into it, Bill," said Vita, much to his surprise. "Speak Friday."

Bill was thrown. He was simply trying to elicit another commission from Vita, not proposing to hand the story over to her. Besides, it wasn't a story. Wagner had found his Brünhilde, someone who wanted to play Valkyrie games in the attic of his soul. There was nothing there to rock the music-world. The lady Vita was probably just being polite. After all, she hadn't even asked him for Katz's name.

In the afternoon he liked to take a walk for half an hour. Reah tagged along on this occasion although she put up her usual complaints about the countryside, the omnipresent mud and any form of exercise.

"When we moved here," said Bill. "You were so keen on living in the country."

"I didn't know it smelled," said Reah, gazing with distaste at the ground. She was teetering, as ever, on her platform heels. They made an odd combination, Bill in his wellies and waxed jacket, Reah dressed for shopping in Oxford Street. "Besides, when you first talked of moving here I thought you and Mum were going to stay together."

"We were," Bill replied. She made these little digs from time to time. Emotional aftershocks. His role was to absorb.

Most of the time, however, Reah seemed reasonably happy with the way things had turned out. These days she had the pretty-much-undivided attention of two parents with only a mere 100 yards' hobble on platforms between them.

"We didn't intend to get divorced when we came here. We all lived together in my cottage first, do you remember? Then we lived together in the farmhouse—"

"Then you went back to the cottage," Reah snorted. "On your own."

"We were arguing all the time," Bill reminded her.

"And then you got divorced," said Reah. "Nobody told me I'd end up in the smelly country with two divorced parents, a rotten school and fat thighs."

They walked on in silence for a moment. Bill put an arm round her shoulder. She shrugged it off, stopped walking for a moment and then reached towards him with her arms outstretched. Bill encircled her in his arms and looked down on the effulgence of Reah's amazing hair.

"I'm not leaving here unless you come too," said Reah into his chest.

They were standing in a clearing with conifers all round them. Bill liked this walk. Today however the trees summoned up new images. Oh God, Bill suddenly felt that he was holding Reah for the last time.

"I'm going to have to speak to Tamsin," he told her. "Find out what's going on."

"She keeps crying," said Reah. "It's like one moment she's talking to me and then her eyes go all sad and she can't speak and she runs out the room. She spends ages on the phone."

When they got back to the cottage the light on Bill's answer-machine was flashing and for a moment he thought this might be Tamsin but no, it was that same stupid silence he'd heard on his return from Israel. Someone there on the other end of the line, waiting a moment, breathing out in displeasure then cutting the connection.

Bill didn't think any more about his mystery breather until that evening in front of the fire. Reah was sitting drawing and Bill was trying to read a biography of Wagner that he'd picked up in Cardiff. They often sat in silence. It was one of the things he liked best about his time with Reah. Tamsin always talked. Her whole family talked, sisters, cousins, aunts. For them it was as if the world didn't exist unless it was being obliterated by their torrent of words. Maybe Reah was like that when she was with them, but here she was peaceful. Bill was sure there had always been peace between them. Their relationship worked at an almost biological level. It was as if her very scent told him 'This creature is of your kin. You need not be on your guard, nor need she be on hers. All is well.' He had loved Tamsin but theirs had not been an easy love. Maybe love of that kind was never easy. They were too different.

"Goodnight," said Reah with a kiss. Halfway up the steep modern staircase, that was already beginning to splinter since Bill's hasty DIY, she leaned over the banister, "Dad, I don't like it up there. You come and tuck me in?" And Bill stopped thinking about the heavy breathing on his answer-machine.

Later still, after Reah had talked nonsense and snuggled down, he closed the door on her small room under the eaves and went downstairs. He could almost feel the cottage exhale and slip into its night-time silence. Such a welcome silence, broken only by the occasional snap and settle of wood in the fireplace.

Was Tamsin cracking up? That was one possibility.

After a while Bill got up and wandered out of the cottage and across to where his car was parked. The night was shockingly bright with an enormous moon just visible over the treetops. Bill walked across the field to where he could see Holt's Farm bathed in white light. He rested against the broken gatepost that divided them. Bill knew he had to see where the threat was coming from. At this distance the farmhouse seemed all roofs and dormitory windows. Reah's room was dark tonight. Of course. When Bill first moved back out into the cottage he used to look across the field and find it so hard when the light was on in her room. His child but not his night with her. Many divorced fathers must feel that, he supposed, but not many lived this close. At first it had hurt like hell, but the heart can adapt to almost anything. It is our most volatile, yet most resilient organ. How easily it breaks and how raw the damaged pieces feel, so raw you think you'll never cope again. That was how he'd felt when he gave up Libby. Tamsin had taken them away on holiday, just the two of them. Reah had stayed with her grandparents. It was supposed to be a new beginning and yet he'd been grieving inside. Had she realised? She may have chosen not to notice, but for Bill the agony was both visible and insuperable. He had no idea how he got through those days. He had no idea how he would cope with the years that lay ahead. And yet his heart *had* adapted. It absorbed and neutralised the pain. It patched over the fissures and now it was bearable to think of Libby. She was just a person. Of course being angry with her had helped cauterise the wound. But that came later.

Sometimes, however, we ask too much of our hearts – and the hearts of others – Bill thought as he returned to the cottage. Tamsin was not going to take his daughter away from him. He stood in the doorway of his cottage and suddenly the black bile of anger ripped through him like a gunshot wound.

Bill realised he had his hand on the rifle again. He must have reached up. This is how I take it down, he thought. This is how I check the barrel. This is how I protect what is mine. The shotgun felt cold and that coldness strangely reassuring. He would never use it, Bill told himself. But he was glad it was there. Bill returned the gun to its hooks. Then he touched it once again for luck. Tamsin would be back the day after tomorrow.

Bill thought about having a glass of whisky before bed. He needed to find some sense of calm. The spirit could always give him that. He didn't drink alone, he reminded himself, but then he wasn't alone was he? Reah was upstairs.

Unimpressed by his own sophistry Bill went to get some ice from the fridge. One glass, he told himself.

The ice cubes cracked as Bill poured in a generous measure. Then he put the bottle back. Not on the coffee table, not on the sideboard but *inside*. Close the door on it. Make sure it's easier not to have a second glass. Easier to say no than yes to the beckoning spirit. He drank by the light of what little fire was left and waited for the alcohol to arrive in his stomach and disperse its calm around his system. It did not disappoint. He almost wished it would. If only he could feel this centred without inebriation.

It was in a state of chemical serenity that Bill went to bed. Tomorrow would be another such day as this, he thought. Tomorrow would be quiet and then Tamsin would return and we would see.

"Dad have you seen mum's Anne Frank book?" Reah asked. "I'm sure I left it here." Bill was just coming in from the mail box. He hadn't heard Lee's van as it drew up but when he looked outside the front door its little red tail was disappearing.

"I can't find that stupid book of the country either. Ooh two from

London!" She knew Bill was always awaiting cheques. "And look you've been offered a Gold Card *and* American Express!" Reah was clearly impressed.

"I don't need any help spending my money," Bill grumbled. "What I need is a bit more coming in."

"I bet your credit rating is enormous," said Reah taking the envelope from him.

But Bill didn't hear her. The first envelope was, by the looks of it, a translation from Goetz, but the second – there was something odd about the second. It was addressed to W.R. Wheeler, Esq and of unusual length. Thin too. Legal dimensions.

Bill sat down and opened it. With a shock he took in the name of a firm of London solicitors, the very same solicitors who had dealt with their divorce.

> *Dear Mr Wheeler,*
>
> *We write to inform you that we have received instructions to act for your ex-wife, Mrs Tamsin Wheeler, in the matter of the sale of Holt's Farm.*

Bill sat down in shock. He knew that he was in shock because he felt so extraordinarily calm. All he had to do was read to the end of the letter and then he'd know the depth of the pit. There was nothing difficult about that.

> *It is Mrs Wheeler's wish that you be kept informed of any relevant developments solely through us. She will however continue to discuss matters relating to the day-to-day welfare of your daughter Reah directly with you.*
>
> *With regard to your contact with your daughter our client wishes to resolve the matter on an amicable basis if possible, however, if you are not minded to do so, or agreement cannot be reached in early course, we are instructed to apply to the court for the appropriate order. Kindly do not correspond directly with our client on this matter.*
>
> *If you have any queries relating to the matter of contact or the sale of Holt's Farm please contact the writer.*

The writer was a person called Charles Aaronovich. He signed himself "*Yours Sincerely*", with a pleasant open signature, not a cocky and flamboyant Wagnerite flourish. Charlie Aaronovich probably was sincere. A sincere and pleasant person whose task it was to separate Reah Wheeler from her father. Bill crushed the letter in his fist. Tamsin's bloody father was behind this.

"What is it?" asked Reah. Bill didn't know what to say. There was no point in pretending that he hadn't just been hit, and hard. No point in lying either.

"Your mother's selling the farmhouse."

Reah nodded. This didn't surprise her much.

"You can sell this place," she told him and snuggled on to his lap. Silly Daddy had forgotten. In all that was going on he'd forgotten that he could move as well. It wasn't as if Reah's dad worked in Chepstow like other people's dads. Reah wasn't like other people and occasionally this had advantages. Bill could work anywhere, *ergo* he could live anywhere.

"There are some really nice flats by Grandpop's and Gramma's."

Bill nodded. Reah had it all planned in her kind optimistic head. Life wouldn't change, just the location. But what Reah didn't realise was that really nice flats in Swiss Cottage cost about four times what Holt's Cottage was worth. Why should she?

"Sure," he said. He felt he didn't want any more conversations on this subject at the moment. He didn't want Reah to witness his feelings. Whatever his feelings were. Bill couldn't exactly tell at the moment. They were elsewhere, happening to someone else.

"I'd better get on with some work," he said, standing up. Reah began to ask Bill if he minded her watching the TV but Bill had agreed long before he'd even heard what she was saying. He just had to get in his office and work.

He shut the door. Sat down. Then he took up Tamsin's letter again. *Dear Mr Wheeler...*

Tamsin had not stopped to speak. She drove down the lane, into the trees and went to see Mr Charles Sincerelyovich.

Bill stared up at the ceiling and exhaled. He felt he might remain in this position for the rest of his life. It would be easier than ever looking at the world again. Why was she doing this? Why was she relying on Charlie Aaronovich of Knapp, Letterman & Rose? Why would she not explain? He kept coming back to that question.

> *If you have any queries relating to the sale of Holt's Farm please contact the writer.*

Bill picked up the portable phone and dialled. A male receptionist fielded his call. No Mr Aaronovich wasn't in at the moment. No, it wasn't known when he would be in. Probably the next half hour or so. Did the caller wish to leave a message? Bill resisted the temptation.

"I'll ring back."

He sat and looked at the screen. How had she managed to put the farm on the market without his knowing? More than the shock of losing Reah was the shock of Tamsin doing all this behind his back. And it was a hundred and thirty miles to London. Three hours door-to-door in the car to where Tamsin's parents lived. How often was it going to be possible, let alone convenient, for him to see his daughter now?

Bill switched on his PC. He would try and order his thoughts on the screen. Work out the possibilities. By the time the computer had started up, Bill was still sitting in the same position, the cursor flicking impatiently at him. Maybe he should ring that solicitor in Chepstow. Find out what he should be asking Charles Aaronovich.

Reah meant so much to him. When he was in Britain Bill saw her face almost every day. She called over whenever she wanted to, and she wanted to a lot. She was the richness in life. His treasure. His purpose even. How could Tamsin take her away like this? That was the kind of question he wanted to ask at the moment. He didn't need a solicitor. He needed a friend. A *werther* friend. Like Wagner.

"Here, my friend," thought Bill. "Things get worse."

❖ THE SUN IN OUR EYES

HE WAS WIDE AWAKE. Of course. Bill sat by the small low window beneath the eaves of his bedroom and stared out. Trees moved silently in the darkness. It had been raining since midnight and the pattering on the skylight had made it impossible to get back to sleep. Bill had grown tired of staring up into the dark nothingness of a clouded sky. That was why he'd moved to the window. Nothing but trees. But what was he looking for?

An hour later he was sitting downstairs in front of a fire that had been prodded and goaded into new life. It crackled sulkily in the grate.

Half an hour later still a bottle of whisky sat at Bill's feet. Tamsin would be back tomorrow to collect Reah and then the whole picture would emerge.

Bill sighed as he remembered that he hadn't even looked at Goetz's translation. He'd done nothing that day except complete a first draft of the *New York Times* piece, talk to Reah and make plans, pointless repeated exercises in contingency for what he might do when all became clear.

Bill upended his glass then regarded the fire through the bottom of it. Tamsin wished to resolve this matter on an amicable basis. It was after all a friendly gesture to take from him the person he loved most in the world. This had not been a satisfying day. Bill wondered again about going to get Goetz's translation. It was in the office and he was in the living room with a bottle of J&B for company. Somehow that bottle didn't want to be left alone. No, dammit, he would go and get the translation. He was not going to become the kind of person who won't even get out of his chair because he has made his bed for the night with a bottle of booze. It was becoming too familiar, that bottle. It should never become his friend.

Two minutes later Bill was slumped back on the sofa. He removed Goetz's typescript from its envelope. Unlike Tony Scribbleman, Rory Llewellyn hadn't transcribed the German text. He'd just launched straight into translation. His covering letter was surprisingly brief too.

Dear Mr Wheeler,

I won't bore you with details of the author's irregular orthography, which should be viewed in the context of the relatively late date at which spelling was standardised in the German Empire. Wagner's sentence construction – for example "In diesen Momenten, wer weiss, was ich schreibe?" – is also quite unusual and he uses some curious idioms. These I have left in their original form and merely suggested modern equivalents.

Bill took another sip. He was amused how everyone seemed to spot straight off the identity of Richard Wagner. So much for his subterfuge.

If I can be of any further assistance do feel free to contact me.

Rory Llewellyn had signed himself simply "Goetz". Bill sighed as he began to read, but he was relieved to enter another world.

My worthy friend,
What a brute I am to wait so long before replying to your solici-
tous enquiry! I must excuse myself on the grounds that many things
have been happening here of a distressing nature, as you may imagine.

So a *Schuft* was a brute, Bill noted.

But what were these things of a distressing nature, these things that only got worse?

That S—— places these things in the world [is going around saying
these things] makes the suspicion sprout in me that he too might be a
Jew!
Dear Friend when I am in the midst of musical composition it is
possible for me only if I am in a constant ecstatic state and behaving
to all the world as a complete eccentric. In these moments who knows
what I write?

Bill was getting lost in all this indignation and self-justification. And who exactly was S? As for the Jewish reference, how curious that he hadn't spotted the word *Jude* himself.

When I consider the phrase our friend refers to I believe he may be
right that I did use that old song beneath the guiding motif.

Here Goetz had added "We know this phrase 'guiding motif' better in its German form '*leitmotiv*', a term that Wagner himself invented." Bill had never really thought that '*leitmotiv*' had a literal meaning. How strange that one can make a career out of words and yet overlook their etymology completely. His father used to talk about London's Blitz without realising the word simply meant 'lightning' to Germans. And it had been many years before Bill had twigged that a philosopher was literally a 'lover of knowledge' or that nirvana in Sanskrit is actually the verb to 'blow out' or 'extinguish'. On a windy day a barbecue might easily achieve nirvana without the remotest sense of spiritual awareness. Intrigued by Goetz's ramblings, and more than a little distracted by his own, Bill had to go back a little to regain the sense of Wagner's sentence.

> *When I consider the phrase our friend refers to I believe he may be right that I did use that old song beneath the... leitmotiv... that accompanies the hero Siegfried to his funeral pyre but this does not mean that I intended the march to signify Death To The Jews.*

Bill sat up. The headline writer within him had suddenly clocked on. What was this? Siegfried's Funeral March a coded reference to the destruction of Judaism? What were Wagner and his friend talking about?

> *I merely drew on ABCGH because it served my purpose.*

Now Bill was completely lost. He reread the last few sentences.

> *When I consider the phrase our friend refers to I believe he may be right that I did use that old song beneath the leitmotiv that accompanies the hero Siegfried to his funeral pyre but this does not mean that I intended the march to signify Death To The Jews. I merely drew on ABCGH because it served my purpose.*

ABCGH? What the hell was ABCGH? Puzzled, Bill read quickly through the rest of Goetz's translation:

> *The death of Judaism and of Jesuitry will be achieved by means greater than my music but if my music can play its part in this mechanism of wheels I would be delighted!*

Goetz had shoved in another set of brackets at this point:

> *(Of course 'in diesem Räderwerk' in English is a redundant idiom. I have retained it however in order to demonstrate Wagner's stylistic finesse. I'd also point out that Wagner's phrase for 'to come about' [zu Stande kommen] is curious. More regular orthography would require 'zustandekommen'.)*

"Yes, yes," thought Bill impatiently. And the writing paper was probably bought in Dresden from a shop on Tiefengriefenstrasse. Dammit, he wanted to know how this bizarre paragraph ended.

> *However if S jests with you again I would urge you not to take him to your knowledge [to ignore him]. Having answered his letter once I see no reason to do so again.*

Here, however, things get worse, said Bill to himself putting the two translations together. Worse than what? Worse than someone going around telling Wagner's worthy friend that Siegfried's Death March was a blueprint for the Final Solution. What were these things? And what on earth did it mean? Particularly ABCGH? What bizarre kind of code was that?

"Dad?" Reah was standing at the foot of the stairs. Bill looked up, surprised. "Dad, I've been calling for ages. I'm feeling funny again." She looked tousle-haired and so much his own child. Bill held out his arms. Reah came across to him, wrapped in an enormous baby-soft dressing gown. He felt her forehead, hoping to be able to say that everything was OK and not to worry but in fact Reah *was* hot. Even so Bill held her a moment longer for both their sakes before standing up.

"Right," he said. "You lie down here. I'll get you something to drink. Did the doctor give you any medicine?" He moved to the kitchen area. "Have you brought any medicine with you from Mum?"

"Dad," said Reah, holding out her arms from where she now sat abandoned on the settee. "*Cuddle.*"

An ill child is a sobering experience. Doubly sobering for those who've been drinking alcohol. Bill gave Reah hot Ribena to sip and a paracetamol-based syrup. He did not lift his eyes from the spoon until it was all gone. It was as if the magic would only work if he imbued it with all his concentration.

Reah sat back, smiled as if to comfort her father, and promptly fell asleep again. Bill made sure she wasn't too tangled up in cushions and blankets then took his seat opposite her next to the fireplace. At four o'clock in the morning he woke, checked Reah again and went upstairs to sleep. Her temperature was down a bit now.

Bill found he had come to bed clutching the two halves of that Wagner letter in his hand. He put them down on the chair beside his bed and made a mental note to try and check what exactly it was that Wagner was saying publicly about the Jews at the time this letter was written. What possible hold could this S—— person have over Herr Wagner? And who exactly was S——? Schumann, Strauss, John Philip Sousa for goodness sake? Not, in all likelihood, a fellow composer, although there were plenty to choose from: Salieri, Schubert, Simon and Garfunkel...

Bill knew tiredness was overcoming his thoughts. Who in the immediate circle had a name that began with S? Schopenhauer? But would Wagner have talked so slightingly of his spiritual saviour? No. God, Bill needed to rest.

As he slept, terrible dreams invaded him but each had faded by the time he struggled awake, leaving only the image of those trees outside and his father's face, devoid of animation, dead. Bill recalled his father's spirit-less features as he struggled through the tangle of sheets. The old man dying alone. What a terrible thing that was to happen to anyone. But was it better to die together in those shallow graves out in the forest? Reah's head flung backwards.

What was he thinking? This was the Wye Valley, after all. He had the Tourist Board brochures downstairs to prove it. Look, there they were, torn into confetti, floating down into his father's grave. Bill slept again, deeply this time even as the light around Holt's Cottage grew bright and the birds sang. Neither woke Bill Wheeler but the sound of a car drawing up outside had him instantly alert and pulling on his trousers.

Tamsin.

He rushed downstairs, checked on the sleeping Reah and did a theatrical double take when he noticed the bottle of whisky at her feet. Bill hid it in the sideboard and then headed for the front door just in time to see Lee waving goodbye from his red Post Office van.

No, not Tamsin.

Time anyway to tidy the place up. Bill made some coffee, binned most of that morning's post and wandered into the office. His view down to the Wye was spectacular this morning. From where he stood on the sofa Bill could see the engorged river snaking dark grey round blossom-strewn meander-loops below. Sometimes the Wye sparkled white. Sometimes it reflected the placid sky. Other times, after heavy rain, it would be red as clay but today it swirled dark, in ominous contrast to the bright colours of the valley that channelled it slowly towards England. Oh you gaudy blos-soms – yellow, white and pink – cascading down in riotous profusion. It was a view worth having lived for these many years, thought Bill. He could grow old here. A thought suddenly reminded him of something less happy. He might very well grow old here, old and alone like his father unless he and Tamsin could resolve something over Reah.

Bill noticed the answer-machine was flashing. He must have had a call last night and not noticed. This surprised him. Maybe it was while he was out in the moonlight looking at Tamsin's cottage, sizing up the foe.

He pressed play and heard silence. Silence but no breathing this time. As soon as Bill heard the receiver at the other end begin to go down he hit 1471 expecting to hear the electronic voice telling him in all smugness "You Were Called. Yesterday. At 23.16 hours." But in fact the grand elec-tronic dame from BT was more forthcoming this time. "Telephone number 0117..." It was a Bristol number. Someone not far away. Bill scrabbled for a pen but his memory of the six subsequent digits was scrambled 460-what? He put down the receiver, tried to clear his mind, was about to ring 1471 again when someone rang him.

"Yes?" said Bill, snatching it up in surprise.

"Bill, it's Tamsin," said a voice calling on a car phone.

"Did you ring me last night from Bristol?" Bill asked.

"No!" said Tamsin, now just as surprised as Bill.

He remembered they had more pressing things to talk about but before he could raise them Tamsin cut in.

"I'm about half an hour away. I thought I'd call and collect Reah as I drive past."

"Fine," said Bill.

"I don't want there to be any trouble in front of her," Tamsin added, trying to sound matter of fact.

"Neither do I," said Bill. There was a silence. Bill could feel her discomfort. It wasn't like Tamsin to be so unaccommodating. He resisted the temptation to say any of the things that had come into his mind during the last 24 hours. Tamsin had clearly psyched herself up for the possibility of a fight. Had someone been preparing her, he wondered. Who was feeding his ex-wife these crisis management techniques? Bill, however, was determined not to fight.

"Reah had a temperature last night," he announced.

"Is she all right now?"

"She's still asleep."

"I packed some medicine in her overnight bag."

"You should've told me," Bill pointed out.

Tamsin caught herself before she replied. Bill could hear the abrupt silence that followed her sudden intake of breath and the noisy surge of car engine that moved in to fill that silence. He could tell Tamsin was uneasy about the way she'd dropped off Reah on Tuesday.

"I don't want any arguments," Tamsin reiterated.

"I wasn't arguing," said Bill.

"See you in half an hour," said Tamsin.

Bill put the phone down. This was clearly going to be difficult. He had rather hoped it might not be; he'd even had some naive hope that he and Tamsin would see each other and remember who they really were, that she'd speak openly about all that was happening and he would be forgiving and in ten minutes this whole silly lawyer business would be redundant. Clearly it was not to be so.

Damn. With a sinking feeling Bill tried 1471 on that Bristol number again but of course the electronic lady was now responding to his conversation with Tamsin. "You were called. Today. At 10.05 hours. We do not have the number to connect you."

"Thank you Tamsin," Bill muttered under his breath.

Half an hour was an uncomfortable unit of time to fill, a ridiculously short interval, suitable only for soap operas and situation comedies. It was too brief to do something worthwhile, too long to sit and wait. He ought to try and get Reah up, possibly even fed. But as she showed no sign of stirring, Bill checked the ticket details he'd received in the post from Siobhan, packed Reah's bag and put it by the front door. He also did the washing-up from last night, had a shave, made some more coffee and checked the clock more often than was necessary.

At one point Bill ventured out, knowing full well that doing so was bound to make it less likely that Tamsin's car would pop up from the forested lane that led down to the valley floor. Life was like that. The sheer coincidence of Tamsin being visible at the exact moment when he went to look made it just about impossible she'd be there. So why was he looking? The same universal law of non-coincidence made it impossible for any scene with Tamsin to play the way he had already imagined it. Nevertheless he had to do something. Bill was beginning to feel a prisoner of expectation. He wanted to step out, swing his arms around, sing loudly. Anything that wasn't constrained by the imminent arrival of his ex-wife.

Everything outside was bright and glorious. Even the trees, even the verges with their tangled grass steaming in the unaccustomed sunlight, seemed beautiful on a day like today.

Bill knew this vista well. His failed attempt at a vegetable garden, the potholed track, the Forestry Commission's dark screen of trees that were his horizon to the left and the open field beyond the gatepost that led to Tamsin's farmhouse on his right. He knew the scene so well in fact that he could immediately tell there was something odd about it today. People. A person. In the woods. Bill could make out a figure – possibly two – about 100 yards away on the edge of the treeline. He wasn't sure but this person, these people, seemed to be looking at him. Then he, or she – or both of them – turned and the scene was empty. Nothing odd in that. Walkers did come through the forest. Some had even stopped and asked for a glass of water in the past but that departing figure, or figures – something was wrong. Bill stared at the line of trees. He must get his eyes tested. Now he had it. The thing that had arrested his attention was not the figure but the speed at which that figure, once observed, departed.

Then he heard it, the sound of Tamsin's car, and suddenly its roof became visible as she approached the brow of the hill leading up from

Chepstow. Bill thought about waiting for her to draw up alongside. It might seem unfriendly to suddenly disappear inside the cottage. On the other hand he ought to get an update on Reah.

Bill found his daughter still very much asleep but with a reasonable temperature. He straightened the blanket he'd put over her, gathered up some cushions and magazines and went outside to greet his ex-wife. Tamsin's car had stopped a little way up the road and she was walking quickly towards him.

She smiled. A reflex. Bill noticed over her shoulder that someone seemed to be sitting in the passenger seat.

"Hi!" he said.

"Hi," said Tamsin. Friendly but business-like.

How many times has she walked into my life? thought Bill. How many times has Tamsin arrived, as she arrives now? That deliberate walk. That tight skirt. Those eyes that always seem to see me so clearly. Hungry. Angry. Always immediate.

"Is Reah ready?"

"Still asleep I'm afraid."

Tamsin glanced up into Bill's face and in doing so the sunlight over his shoulder caused her to wince. She looked unhappy. Reah wasn't awake and Bill was shining the morning into her face.

"I did ring you half an hour ago," she pointed out.

"I thought of waking her but it seemed best not to," said Bill, his eyes flickering towards Tamsin's car.

His ex-wife was uncomfortable. She had clearly seen this scene proceeding in a particular way and now it wasn't.

"Who's in the car?" Bill asked.

"Jessica," murmured Tamsin, as if her sister's presence could not possibly be of any consequence to Bill. Jess, one of the middle sisters with Tamsin, the one with bangles all the way down her arms and a loud voice. Jess the Protector.

"Why don't you invite her in?" Bill asked.

"She's got David with her," said Tamsin. Bill vaguely remembered that Jessica had a son by that name.

"He can come too," said Bill. "We are all family." He tried not to let it sound ironic.

"Please Bill," said Tamsin, wincing again at the light that still blazed over his shoulder. "Don't make it difficult."

"I think I'm making it very easy for you indeed," said Bill. "The only thing I'm not doing is waking Reah up and bundling her out of doors the moment you arrive."

"This is exactly what I wanted to avoid," said Tamsin, exhaling in annoyance and looking away. Her breath was fresh in the morning light. Spring was still in its tentative stages. Tamsin seemed uncertain in this atmosphere. What to do? What to do?

"Oh why don't you bring Reah over when she's woken up," she suggested, looking uncomfortably at his front door.

"Don't you want to see her?" Bill asked. He was genuinely surprised. Tamsin breathed out again, an opaque cloud of irritation. In the middle distance Bill noticed the passenger door open. Jessica half rose out of the car. From this distance he would not have recognised Jess had Tamsin not identified her. This woman, this Jess, uncertain whether or not to get out of the car, seemed larger than Bill remembered his sister-in-law. She didn't seem to have Jessica's cascade of black hair either. It had been years ago of course.

"I'd better go," said Tamsin, aware of the door behind her.

"She is your daughter..." Bill began to say but at that moment Reah appeared in the doorway, tall, tousled and tangled.

"Hello, mum," she said blearily.

"*Bubbeleh*!" said Tamsin, her face brightening as she hugged Reah. "How are you, my baby?!" Bill noticed with some surprise that Reah was up to her mother's shoulder now.

"Ooh, is that Aunty Jess?" Reah asked looking down the lane.

"Yes. And David, they've come down to help me for a few days."

"Help you do what?" asked Reah, still slightly fuzzy.

"Oh, pack. You know."

"I wonder if we ought to move inside," Bill suggested.

"Hi Auntie Jess!" shouted Reah, waving a big arm.

"How about you get dressed?" said Tamsin to Reah. "And Dad and I'll finish our conversation."

"OK, but no arguing," said Reah turning to go. "OK?"

They both said OK but, once Reah had gone inside, felt unsure what to do with each other. After a moment Bill said, "I'd like to know what your plans are. I can hear them through your solicitor but that just costs both of us money."

"I think it's better that we deal formally on this," said Tamsin, not looking at him.

"Why?"

"To avoid any unpleasantness," she replied.

"Isn't this unpleasant?" Bill asked.

"No," said Tamsin. "This is sad. It's sad we're having to deal with each other in this way but it isn't unpleasant. At least you're not abusing me."

Bill was shocked.

"I've never abused you," he insisted.

"You can be very angry," Tamsin told him. Bill didn't feel this made sense.

"We've both been angry with each other in the past. It doesn't mean we can't deal reasonably with each other now."

"No, I'm sorry Bill," Tamsin had suddenly lifted her hands. It was as if she were pushing him away, drawing a boundary, insisting there was to be no more. "I can't talk to you about this, I'm sorry," she said. "When Reah's ready, send her over to the car will you?"

And with that she walked back to where Jessica now stood, waiting on the roadside. Bill watched as Tamsin almost lost her footing at one point. He noticed how the skirt tugged spasmodically round her thighs, like Reah's, and how the pockets of her short quilted jacket were taut and distended by Tamsin's fists. He also noticed the way Jessica glared up at him as she put an arm round Tamsin.

What was going on?

After Reah had bounced happily into the car, loaded her enormous bag inside, squeezed cousin David and then waved goodbye, Bill went back inside his cottage and wondered what had got Tamsin in such a state. It was without a doubt the most bizarre conversation he'd ever had. So much had been left unsaid, in fact, that it could hardly be called a conversation at all.

Bill felt the need to do something normal. Listen to the radio, put on another track from that CD he'd picked up from Tower Records in Chepstow. But no, jazz was last night's music, wasn't it? It would seem pretty incongruous to wash up along to 'Memphis Moaner Blues'. The wail of clarinet and throb of bass had their place but not now, not in the wake of Tamsin's neurotic departure and in the tactless sunshine of early spring.

He ought to pack for Vienna. Bill knew he may as well do it now. It is a curious thing about the human spirit that we all hate packing. Everyone delays it till the very last minute and yet it is such simple job. Did nomads feel the same? The time Bill had spent in the desert with some Bedou, they'd never seemed to care, but then their concept of home was wholly independent of place. Home was a Platonic ideal to be discovered wherever shelter, safety and comfort coincided. You stopped your camel when you found a wadi or rocky outcrop that came close to making it possible to reconstitute the ideal. That way home was never destroyed by moving on.

And what Bill had learned after years of having to take off suddenly for work was to start packing the moment the idea occurred. Nothing was gained, he knew, by giving in to our perverse temptation to stall.

As he threw things into the suitcase upstairs Bill wondered about his Wagner letter. Was it worth taking that along in case he got stranded somewhere? Maybe if he telephoned his third translator he could get something faxed over this afternoon so that he'd have the full text in English and German to play with. Bill picked up both translations from the bedside chair and stuffed them into his notebook alongside the original. He had a file downstairs marked 'Wagner' with the photocopies of handwriting he'd made at Cardiff University. No point in taking that along too but he sought out that biography he'd borrowed and chucked it on top of his case.

Feeling disproportionately better for having packed, Bill decided that he could do with going for a walk before getting down to polishing off that *New York Times* piece. He left a message on Grice's answer machine, slammed the door behind him and set off into the woods. Walking on your own was so different from walking with someone else, particularly if that person happened to be Reah. It felt more like exercise. You concentrated on pushing your body round the next corner or up the next hill, all the time asking of it just a bit more than it wanted to yield. Walking with others was social. This was physical.

He was out for about an hour. The going was muddy underfoot. For such an upland area the ground was surprisingly water-logged but Bill pushed on and was completely ready to write when he got back in. Those trees which had haunted him since yesterday no longer seemed like the same mute witnesses to mass murder. The forest was no longer unfriendly. It simply didn't notice him today. Bill went straight to his office, switched on the machine and poured himself a glass of water while the slow old beast loaded up. Then he was away.

An hour and a half later Bill e-mailed the text through to Vita, sat back in his chair and felt good about life. Then it was that he noticed his footprints on the stone floor. What a mess. He hadn't thought to wipe his feet. But worse, neither had someone else. Bill went back into the living room and saw what he'd missed when he first arrived home, full of the need to work. Another pair of boots had been in Holt's Cottage, possibly two pairs. It was difficult to tell now, given that Bill had been stomping round too. One pair however definitely was not his. Seized by anger and fear, Bill checked where he kept his money then ran upstairs. Someone had been in the cottage. If that person were still there now he would break heads. And even if no one remained Bill certainly wanted to know what had been taken.

He looked into Reah's room. They'd better not have been in there. Then he ran to his suitcase. Even before he got there he had a presentiment of what he would find. Nothing disturbed, but that borrowed copy of the Wagner biography was missing.

Bill swore, but swearing was not enough. He picked his suitcase off the bed and slammed it down on the floor. He wanted to make the loudest noise possible, ideally by kicking the head of whoever had broken in. Luggage had to suffice for the moment.

For the second time that day Bill asked himself what was going on. This time, though, he felt he knew.

Someone wanted the letter. They had been very delicate the way they had let him know it. His cottage hadn't been trashed but one significant item relevant to Wagner had been taken.

What about the third translation? Bill suddenly thought that might have come through while his burglars were at work. He raced downstairs and tried dialling 1471. The machine – fortunately – was still telling Bill that he had been Called Today by Tamsin.

"Bastards," said Bill. He could see in his mind that figure standing at the edge of the trees this morning. One person, maybe two, watching his cottage then ducking away. Had they been waiting for him to go out?

"Bastards!" he shouted. He blundered outside, ready to do battle. No one there of course so Bill marched purposefully round the corner to where the logs were kept. He had an axe but chopping wood would not be enough. Inside the woodshed Bill kept a few old cups, chipped and without handles, which held screws, bolts and nails. Seizing one he hurled it with all his might at the stone wall of the cottage. The sound of crunching disintegration and scattering nails created a surge of a relief. But it was still not enough. Bill ground his boot repeatedly into the shards until nothing was left.

Two cups of coffee later Bill wasn't exactly calm but he was feeling more capable of dealing with the minutiae of going away. The first thing he had to do – obviously – was to stop any post coming to the cottage while he wasn't around to collect it. A call to Lee's boss down in Chepstow would see to that. Then he'd better secure all the catches on the windows although Bill felt certain that whoever had broken in before was pretty adept and wouldn't be deterred by locks. It was a curious assumption to make. After all Bill often went out leaving the front door unlocked. He probably had on this occasion. Certainly he had no memory of turning a key in the door on his return. Whoever removed the Wagner biography might easily have been some opportunist passing through Holt's Farm.

No, he dismissed that notion. It was no coincidence the book on Wagner had gone. And anyone who'd come from Germany or Israel to put the frighteners on him like that would have to be a professional. He'd just made it easy for them by leaving the door unlocked. Nevertheless this time he'd make sure.

Angrily Bill backed up all his documents so that no one, be they from Mossad, CIA or Bayreuth's 1st Mounted Valkyrie Division, could damage his work. Then he stuffed the disks and his bank account pass-books into a small holdall that would zip into the suitcase he'd be carrying.

Bill was just making up a large sign that read THERE IS NOTHING WORTH STEALING HERE which he thought he'd leave on the living room floor when the phone rang. Convinced this would be someone in league with the burglars, Bill ran into the office and seized it up.

"Wheeler!" he snapped.

"Bill?" said a voice. The calm, well-read and procedural voice of a woman in New York who was not expecting to be challenged. "Bill, this is Vita."

"Oh," said Bill. "Hi. Sorry about that."

"Just to say, Bill, that we have received your piece *in extenso* and we will be getting back to you shortly. You say that you are out of the country this weekend."

"I'm in Vienna," said Bill.

"Ah, palatschinken or mohnstrudel?" asked Vita. Bill was just about to tell her the address of his hotel when he got the strudel reference. Vita was asking him what he was planning to eat in Viennese cafes. This was what passed for humour among the Manhattan erudite.

"Sachertorte," he replied.

"Ah Kärntner Strasse," said Vita who was waxing very lyrical, whatever time of day it was over there. "Well, Bill, one of my colleagues will revert to you on your return."

"I shall look forward to it," Bill lied.

"Oh and that story you told me of. The rogue Wagner letter. It seems it's quite well known. No one has ever seen the letter but two journalists of my acquaintance have been approached by someone who claims to have a letter that would seriously damage Richard Wagner's reputation."

"Do they know where the letter's come from?" Bill asked.

"If it exists," said Vita flatly. "I wouldn't concern yourself with it Bill."

"I'd be interested in knowing if there's any story about how this letter has suddenly popped up."

"Stolen," Vita declared flatly. She was clearly not impressed by Bill's dogged pursuit. "That is if there is such a letter. Which I very much doubt. Hoaxes of this kind are not uncommon, Bill. Someone wants a little publicity, wants to feel important, wants to be taken out and dined by gullible gumshoes. As I say, rumours of this letter have been circulating for a month or so now and no one has seen even a photocopy. My guess is that a kite is being flown."

"Odd thing to do," said Bill.

"The world is full of very odd people, Bill" said Vita. "Enjoy Vienna."

❖ A HELPING HAND

BILL was doodling in his notebook.

"*Question*" he wrote, "*Who is Wagner's worthy friend?*"

> *Question 2: Who is S—— who spreads these rumours?*
> *Question 3: How much does Louis actually owe me?*

He'd done a small sketch of Louis, dark skin and Eton collar, leaning in a dandified way up against some bass clefs. Further up the page Bill had already written "*ABC GH*" several times, drawing attention to the curious omission. Was there significance in that? Bill could see none. His mind turned to that phonecall with the sceptical Vita and her belief that the letter currently nestling in his notebook actually didn't exist.

"*What is in this for Katz?*" he wrote. And who had broken into his cottage looking for Mr K's letter?

It was this last question that intrigued him most. There was nothing in the two sections of Wagner's letter so far that might damage the man's reputation. Not even that outrageous reference to the destruction of Judaism, given that Wagner was already *persona non grata* in Tel Aviv. So why did Martin Katz want people in Britain and America to know he'd got it? Why did he want it back so badly, badly enough to hire person or persons unknown to break in and leave that coded message? Bill recognised that he was making a big assumption about the significance of that singular theft. But then who, other than people working for Katz, would come to his cottage and steal a biography of Richard Wagner? The Chepstow Music Society?

It didn't make sense and, simply because it didn't make sense, Bill assumed the most puzzling aspect of it all must hold the clue. ABC GH...

Bill looked round the cafe of Hotel Sacher. His reasoning was more than a tad intuitive, he had to admit. The obscure wasn't always significant. Look at serialism in music. Total cultural cul de sac. For every William Blake ahead of his time there were hundreds of conceptual artists who would never make sense, regardless of the decades rolling by, because they were no bloody good.

He gazed round the hotel again. Coming, as Bill did, from the Wye Valley's subtle greenery, via the plastic anonymity of two international airports, all this red, white and gold was a shock. The resplendent gold S for Sacher monogrammed on every chair, the doorman with his huge white handlebar moustache, the liveried staff who grouped together respectfully waiting to serve, even the newspapers presented for perusal on bamboo canes – it was like discovering a corner of the world which believed the Romanoffs still ruled Imperial Russia.

Bill had finally got his meeting with Bardini and this cafe was his reward. The Beast of Berlin had actually been very pleasant to interview. A large, quiet man in an expensive grey cardigan, Paolo Bardini had a certain graceful ugliness about him that was irresistible. After five minutes talking to this Swiss Svengali Bill would not have had him looking any sweeter. The apparent brutality of the man's features served only to bring out the compelling candour of his eyes.

"That girl, it was unfortunate," Bardini told him. "I asked too much of her but she was wrong not to tell the company manager that she was already under treatment. I always push my singers but I expect them to be healthy. This is not unreasonable I think?"

They had met at the Staatsoper just opposite and talked in depth about Bardini's conflict with contemporary conductors over the sound that singers should produce. For an opera producer Paolo Bardini seemed to have an almost fanatical dislike of the accepted sound of opera singing. Bill's dictaphone faithfully stored everything the man had to say about how the nineteenth and twentieth centuries destroyed the human voice. Bardini was clearly already in conflict with his new conductor and intimated to Bill that henceforth he might only produce new work. They spoke only intermittently of Richard Strauss' *Elektra* so Bill had to seize any chance that came his way to ram home Louis' question. "Do you see parallels?" he asked trying not to apologise too much for the asinine turn that their interview was taking.

"Between Elektra's madness and that unfortunate girl in Berlin?" asked Bardini. His eyes gazed blank and limpid at Bill as the smoke curled upwards from his cigarette. Bill felt pinioned by the man's directness. "Do you like music, Mr Wheeler?"

"Yes."

"And yet you have come all this way to ask me that question?" Bardini asked.

"Would you do me a favour and not answer it?" Bill replied, switching off his dictaphone. It had till that moment been such an interesting conversation.

"No I will answer it," said Bardini. "I will answer it if that is what your readers want to know. Elektra is suffering grief and anger that she may not express following the murder of her father. She is condemned by her mother and stepfather to live and eat with the dogs. The utter misery of her bereavement has made her implacable and inhuman in her desire for revenge. She is unable to forgive and this inability results in her own destruction. Failure to forgive poisons the human spirit and, by extension, humanity. The girl who played Gilda in Berlin had stopped taking her Valium and not told the company manager that she was on medication. Now, tell me, do you see a parallel?"

Bill decided he should go.

"You tell your editor," said Bardini. "You tell this man in England that there is no story for him there. If you don't believe me talk to her."

"No, that's OK," said Bill, but Bardini was already fishing and fumbling in the pockets of his cardigan.

"Here," he said, passing over an empty envelope. Bill noticed the sender's address in Mestre was written on the left-hand side of the back flap. Bardini held up the letter itself, which he had just extracted, between finger and thumb. "This I will keep but – you see – we are still in touch. Talk to her."

"It's not necessary."

Bardini insisted he take the envelope nevertheless.

The rest of the interview had been enjoyable and Paolo Bardini had been keen that Bill should come back to review his *Elektra*. Bill was flattered. He felt at home with the man, taken into his confidence even. On the way out of the Staatsoper Bill even raised the question of that other letter in his pocket.

"What is your interest?" Bardini asked.

"You know how the journalistic mind works," Bill told him. "If someone tells you this is dynamite, it's very tempting to light the fuse."

Bardini thought for a moment. "I have never worked at Bayreuth but I would say that Wagner is unassailable for those who admire him and unredeemable in the eyes of everyone else. Do I see what harm any letter could do to his reputation? No, I don't."

All of which had done nothing more than confirm that the mystery of Martin Katz was indeed abstruse. Bill tried to imagine what his own motive with this letter might be if he were Katz. But what if Katz were a total fool? The problem with our approach to solving mysteries, Bill thought, is that we always assume our opponent has some brilliant masterplan which it will take all our wit to divine. Maybe Katz was just a self-dramatising, inebriated, overweight oaf. That after all had been Bill's first impression of him, and first impressions should be respected. After all, they usually form the bases for our falling in love and setting up home together.

Bill savoured his coffee. It was bitter but worth making an effort towards. In truth he only really liked Italian coffees. The Viennese mochas were brutal, their espressos dull.

He noticed a tiny old lady at the table next to him, holding the in-house newspaper, *Die Sacherzeitung*, on its cane and reading so slowly she seemed to nod between words. Bill looked at the fur on her coat collar. It was always strange to come to the Continent and see dead animals draped around the necks of respectable dowagers. Reah would be outraged, he thought.

A mobile went off. Bill realised it was his. A few heads turned in his direction as he reached inside his leather shoulder bag. Suddenly that sign on the opposite wall, the one that read KEINE HANDYS, loomed very large. "Bill," said a voice. The ever-so-slightly aggrieved voice of a woman whose standard currency of communication was reproach. "Where are you?" Siobhan asked as if wherever he was he shouldn't be.

"Vienna," Bill replied.

"Have you spoken to Paolo Bardini yet?"

"Yes."

"Did you get any pictures?"

Bill was thrown. "Pictures of what?"

"I believe Louis asked you to see if there were any pictures of Bardini and the girl."

"No he didn't," said Bill. "And even if he did Bardini is hardly likely to have brought them to Vienna with him is he?"

There was a silence at the other end. Siobhan was obviously talking to Louis. Bill watched a man sitting below the Handys sign pour a mountain of sugar into his coffee with slow deliberation. It was as if he were trying to displace the liquid in his cup entirely. Bill waited in vain to see it over-flow but it just absorbed.

"Bill," said another voice. Louis this time. "Delighted it went well. It did, I assume?"

"I got his denial," said Bill. "He's says there's no parallel between Elektra and that girl. He was quite eloquent in fact."

"Excellent," said Louis. "Eloquent is good. All the more justification for running it. Let's have dinner. What time are you back?"

"Five this afternoon," Bill replied. "I need to head home really."

"Drinks then," said Louis. Do you know the Overseas?"

"You've taken me there before."

"Half past six," said Louis. Bill was about to object and point out that coming into London from Heathrow meant heading in the opposite direction from where he lived. This fact always escaped Louis but what the hell. He could always use the opportunity to hand in his expenses.

Waiting at the airport, Bill reflected glumly on how much foreign travel was really just a question of queuing in rooms, showing pieces of paper and shuffling on to queue in more rooms where one showed even more bits of paper and then shuffled on again. Room after room. *Check-in. Passport Control. Security. Departure lounge.* The only way to tell these places apart was the photographs on the wall. Were he leaving Ben Gurion Airport there would be a picture of the Dome of the Rock. At Marco Polo it would be the Leaning Tower of Pisa. In Vienna the Schönbrunn.

Eventually the plastic rooms led down to a tunnel where people in uniform welcomed you with smiles and nodded in the direction of your seat, down a narrow aisle where one shuffled and queued again and bags fell on your head. Human beings had not yet learned how to board an aircraft without creating instant log-jam, Bill thought.

Then, two hours later, we start the whole process again. We stand up, things drop on our heads and we make our shuffly way through another sequence of rooms: *Passport control. Baggage reclaim. Customs.* Only this time the photos on the wall show the Tower of London and Hampton Court. Finally this whole weary, dreary system of rooms disgorges us into Arrivals where we find ourselves conspicuous, gazed on by a sea of faces all looking for someone else as we take our trolley for a walk.

Oh God, I am growing discontent with my lot, he thought. There was a time when Bill had leapt at the chance of travelling abroad. Of course in those days, he'd had a marriage to travel away from.

What a provocation to sadness, Bill thought. He ordered a gin and tonic from the stewardess, forgetting, once again, that he'd given up drinking on aircraft.

Bill wanted to be at home. He had done his talking for the day. Living on his own he realised how much speaking to another human being demands of you, particularly when you are giving them the kind of attention Bardini required. All he wanted now was to get back to his cottage, light a fire and rest. How good it would be if Reah were there when he got back. Reah fitted into life in the cottage so completely that Bill was hardly aware of her presence most of the time. When she was not there however he missed her. It was perhaps a good thing that he wasn't going straight home tonight.

The Royal Overseas was shabbier than some of the London clubs that Bill had been taken to. Snuck into a dead end near St James' Palace, Overseas House bumbled along affably beneath a plaque which proclaimed its intention to promote friendship amongst people of all nations (whilst serving them over-priced booze). The bar was populated by colonial types, men and women who were far too old now to moderate the orotund manner in which they addressed each other. Bill could not help but catch the strains of 'Jonesy' and 'Hugo' speaking freely to each other with what he liked to think of as veranda-mentality, that very English belief that any stranger within earshot was probably only a servant. The main lobby, by contrast, was home to a greater mix, both socially and ethnically. As Louis was late, Bill decided it was better to sit here, which he did, watching a group of tall African women with extravagant headwraps laughing amongst themselves. Better than being stuck in the bar with Jonesy anyway.

"Bill, my dear fellow," said Louis extending his hand to clutch at Bill's arm. "Crisis upon crisis in the Evil Empire. Apologies. Drinks! Let's go to the bar."

To Bill, Louis was a mystery. His exquisite clothes and the anachronistic precision of his English accent would have made him a marked man in Chepstow and yet Siobhan had intimated there was heterosexual past, a former fiancée who had broken his heart and gone to work in India. Whatever effect she had on young Louis' emotions his dress-sense remained clipped and stylish and his jet-black mop was cut in a most expensive manner. He moved in a light but measured way. No gesture was ever out of place or unnecessary. The word for Louis was graceful, Bill supposed. Manly but graceful. Oh they'd definitely have had him up against a wall in Chepstow.

"And how is Reah?" Louis asked as they made their way up the wide flight of stairs that led back to the bar. Louis had a facility for remembering names, dates and relationships. It was the gossip's attention for detail. He also had an interest in the lives of others that bordered on the prurient. Bill said nothing about his problems with Tamsin. Some things were too serious for Louis.

"And what about Bardini?" said Louis as he signed for their drinks. "I take it you were charmed?"

"More than charmed," said Bill. "He's genuinely talented, I think, which makes him different from the rest of us."

"Ah," said Louis as if he thought this rather amusing.

"I'm not saying that morally he's not to be judged like other men," Bill continued. "But maybe it's just that he doesn't bother to cover his tracks quite so cautiously. I certainly felt there's another side to that story. It's just that Bardini isn't too concerned about telling it."

"Well, I'd like to hear it." Louis settled back in his chair.

"It's not as good as the one you sent me for," Bill warned him. Louis made a small wave of his hand as if to say he would be the judge of that. Bill was irritated but he kept going.

The bar was beginning to fill with a party of mature Oxford women who had come up to hear this evening's talk. As Bill recounted his meeting with Paolo Bardini he couldn't help but take in snatches of their conversation. The speaker tonight had been in Nepal and written a book about his time there. Had anyone who'd been to Nepal *not* written a book?

Louis was leaning back in his seat, a knowing smile on his face and an index finger under his chin. "I think you should go to Venice."

"Why?"

"Try and find this girl."

"Are you going to pay for me to fly over and play private eye?" Louis waved his hand again. Cuffs perfectly white, Bill noticed. Bill's shirts used to be good but he had never had cuffs like that. Nor cufflinks to put in them.

"Oh you can take in whatever's on at La Fenice at the same time," Louis was saying. "Review something."

"And who's paying for all this?" Bill asked.

"We are," said Louis simply. "*Arts International*. Don't we always?"

"Eventually yes," said Bill. "Since when have you got to be so generous with foreign travel?"

"Oh, it's nearly the end of the financial year," Louis replied. "I don't want those weasels clawing anything back."

There was a silence between them while Bill regarded Louis with suspicion. "Which weasels?"

"Indulge me," said Louis, concentrating on the single peanut he had just picked up. The man was up to something.

The two of them talked and drank. Bill always warmed to Louis eventually but he usually found the ensuing intimacy one-sided. He knew nothing of Louis' life. Louis by contrast knew too much of his. Bill deliberately kept things light on this occasion. He didn't mention Tamsin once.

"I don't know why you don't want to go to Venice," said Louis, returning to this evening's main theme.

"Yes you do," said Bill.

"My dear man, it's a big city. You're hardly likely to end up sharing the same gondola. Besides, she's probably not there any more."

Bill regretted having told Louis about Libby. He had never intended to but it turned out that Louis actually knew of her. Her name had come up in conversation between them on one occasion and Louis had immediately spotted Bill's morbid interest. After a little probing Bill had ended up admitting to Louis that Dr Ziegler was the woman who'd done so much damage to his marriage.

Louis had been intrigued. "I'd heard a rumour that she'd been married when she was in Germany. Briefly. Some scion of one of the big conducting dynasties. But I didn't know she'd had a paramour in London."

"She didn't," Bill told him forcibly. "*We* didn't."

He'd noticed ever since that from time to time Louis would play a game with him. It would turn out, surprise surprise, that there was a Venetian angle to whatever story they were discussing. Louis seemed to select these stories specially, just to be provocative.

"Do you know any German?" Bill asked, changing the subject.

"Good Lord no," Louis smiled. "Siobhan does all that. Why do you ask?"

"I wondered whether there was some significance in ABCGH. In Germany."

"The letters?" Louis asked pulling distractedly at his cuff. "Do you mean the letters ABCGH or the notes?"

"What notes?"

Louis was now adjusting his cufflink. It looked like very good gold, Bill thought. Not that he knew about such things. "The letter B in German represents the note B-flat while the letter H represents B-natural. Everyone knows that," said Louis."

"No they don't."

"Bill you never cease to amaze me. It's why Bach was able to sign compositions with his name. B-flat, A, C, B-natural."

"So ABCGH could be notation. If it's in German."

"Of course," said Louis.

"And everyone knows this?"

"Bill the gaps in your musical education are legendary."

But Bill wasn't interested in riposting. He wanted to dig out the Katz letter straight away. What were the words in Goetz's translation: "*I merely drew on ABCGH because it served my purpose*"?

"Would you excuse me a moment?" he asked. Louis looked on humorously as Bill took the translation out of his notebook and studied it.

When I consider the phrase our friend refers to I believe he may be right that I did use that old song beneath the leitmotiv that accompanies the hero Siegfried to his funeral pyre but this does not mean that I intended the march to signify Death To The Jews. I merely drew on ABCGH because it served my purpose.

So ABCGH was a tune. A tune that Wagner used in Siegfried, an old song that somehow signified Death To The Jews? Bill stared at the paper in front of him. A, B-flat, C, G B-natural. He must find a piano.

"Now?" laughed Louis.

"Yes."

"Well, I think there's one in the Queen Elizabeth room but it's probably locked."

The two men made their way out of the bar and up the steep interconnecting staircase that linked the various mansions out of which Overseas House had been created. The Queen Elizabeth Room was not in fact locked but, as Bill feared, there was a function in progress, with forty or fifty people already drinking and chatting therein. The piano however was open and just visible to the left of the gathering.

"Sorry Bill," said Louis but Bill wasn't going to be stopped that easily.

"I need to hear those notes," he insisted. "Come on, Louis, you can get me in there."

"That is someone's private party, Bill!" Louis was outraged by Bill's sudden transformation from journo to fanatic, yet enjoying his outrage too.

"Please Louis, you look respectable. Just get me in, get me to the piano and let's hear those notes."

"Why?" Louis challenged him.

"It's important." At the glass doors ahead a man in a dog collar and faded purple dinner-jacket was looking curiously at them as they approached. "Trust me."

"I'm not trusting you until you tell me what all this is about," said Louis in a stage whisper.

"Well what the hell kind of trust is that?!" Bill hissed back. The man was distinctly unhappy about them now. At any moment he was likely to decide Bill and Louis were up to no good. "I'll tell you afterwards," Bill insisted. "Look, my place has been broken into and those notes are some kind of clue."

"You're mad," said Louis. "Burglars do not break in looking for German sheet music."

"Louis, please." Bill realised he was squeezing Louis' arm.

"What has got into you?" Louis was delighted. "This isn't Bill Wheeler at all."

"Can I help you?" asked the cleric whose politeness was cutting in a manner unique to the English middle classes.

"Look I'm very sorry," Louis began smoothly, "But my colleague here is playing in this room tomorrow. Do you think we could possibly check whether the piano needs tuning?"

He sounded ridiculously plausible. Louis had retained that Head Boy quality which stands young men in good stead for the first decade of adulthood. The sharp suit and subdued necktie helped the illusion but it was something about that respectful but superior manner in which Louis Montgomery dealt with authority that made Bill think of them as two sixth-formers getting round the chaplain of some minor English public school.

"I'm afraid this is a private function," the cleric replied.

"Absolutely," said Louis as if he were agreeing with him. "And you don't finish for another half hour."

"Hour and a half," the man corrected.

"Absolutely, absolutely and by then it'll be far too late to arrange a tuner for tomorrow. They stop taking bookings after 7.45, as I'm sure you know. Look, it won't take a moment. We'll be discreet. Otherwise I'm going to have to book a tuner on spec and if I have to cancel, the call-out fee is monstrous."

The man in the dog collar looked Bill up and down, pondering the logic of Louis' appeal. Bill was not dressed for London club-land. He might well be a pianist though. He had the look of someone who had just jetted in, and the best of them could be scruffy in mufti. "Very well but please be quick."

Bill and Louis made their way to grand piano like a pair of schoolboys who were trying to play down the fact they'd just conned their way into the staff room and were fully appraised of where the booze and magazines were kept. "You are amazing," said Bill. "I will never believe a word you say again."

Louis sat down, tossed off a quick three octave scale and asked Bill to repeat the note sequence: "A, B-flat, C, G, B-natural." Louis picked them out with his left hand. First slowly then quickly, then a third time so Bill could record them on his dictaphone.

"Mean anything to you?"

"Siegfried's Funeral March?" asked Bill hopefully.

"Not a chance," said Louis. "Now come on. I have to try and retain my membership of this place."

As Bill drove home that night he tried to work out where he'd gone wrong. Playing the notes over and over again did no good. They didn't sound remotely like the Siegfried Funeral March, nor even for that matter like something that might have been played under the March. Wagner's harmonies were ambitious, Louis had reminded him. Despite all his din the master actually wrote so every instrument could be heard. But that sequence did not sound like anything that he might have put into an accompanying phrase. Besides, where is the scandal in a few notes hidden down in the trombones? The audience can only hear one tune at a time. That was Bill's view.

Louis didn't agree. "No, Wagner was a musical miniaturist," he pointed out to Bill as they left the club. "He writes chamber music on a vast scale but every note is supposed to register. That was Nietzsche's view, by the way."

"I thought Nietzsche said Wagner was a sickness," Bill replied.

"A man can have more than one thought in his lifetime," said Louis who was now standing beneath a lamp-post shooting those cuffs again. "Go to Venice. You know who knows more about Wagner's manuscripts than anyone else. Well anyone else who is also sane."

Louis was always cheerful, always in control. Bill was feeling grumpy with him. Libby Ziegler was not someone to be visited just to fuel the man's inexhaustible appetite for gossip. Why didn't Louis get a life of his own? "Scandal attaches to the melody, not the harmony," Bill had insisted "If it bloody attaches at all. I could be barking up the wrong tree entirely you know."

Louis knew all the Katz story now, except for how Bill had come by the letter. That Bill had managed to conceal. "It's a great story," Louis told him. "If that letter checks out just the fact that it exists and wasn't incinerated after Cosima's death, that alone means that it's important. Whatever it says. You have to get it authenticated." Bill had muttered something about trying carbon-dating. He was being very ungracious and he knew it. "I'll get Siobhan to ring you about tickets," said Louis, patting him on the elbow.

It was after 10.30 by the time Bill got back to Holt's Farm. He parked the car and went to look if the lights were on at Tamsin's. Just the one in the kitchen that she always left to deter burglars. Nothing in Reah's room. Bill suddenly felt very far away from his daughter. He didn't actually know where she was although he assumed it was London. North London. Far too distant and far too expensive.

He unlocked the door and saw his own handwritten note to burglars still resting on the floor. Bill had to smile at the extremity of his own behaviour and yet the fact that no one had removed the sign made him naively confident that the place hadn't been broken into again – as if Katz's minions would have scrawled 'Oh yes there was' when they forced the door a second time.

He knew there wouldn't be any post because he'd signed a form to keep it in Chepstow till tomorrow. Bill wouldn't normally bother about messages either, not until the morning, but he felt the need for contact in this cold empty cottage. Now that he looked at the folded blankets on the sofa, he felt the absence of Reah acutely.

Bill went into his office and sat down to dial. There was one fax. For a moment he hoped Grice had ignored his request not to send anything until after Vienna. But it wasn't Grice. It was Goetz offering his apologies and making some damnably pedantic point about the German word *neben*. Bill tore it off and sat down to dial a local number.

The voice at the other end was dark and rather smoky. A dull, late night voice.

"Hi it's Bill."

"Oh hi," said the woman's voice. Monotone.

"How're you keeping?"

"OK."

There was a silence between them with which Bill wasn't entirely comfortable. "I've been in Israel and Austria."

"Ah." There was a pause and then the voice at the other end of the phone added. "I've been here, but then you know I'm always here."

"I was wondering about coming over tomorrow," Bill said. Another pause.

"Sure," the woman said.

"Eight o'clock?"

"Sure."

Bill didn't feel much happier having made that call. He wondered about a glass of whisky and decided that it could be his reward for looking at Stupid Goetz and his Piece of Pointless Pedantry. At least he could make sure the damn thing was worth binning.

> *Dear Mr Wheeler,*
>   *I took the liberty of showing a colleague the extract you faxed me*
> *and he, having a better knowledge of music than I, pointed out an*

ambiguity regarding Wagner's phrase "ich tatsächlich jenes alte Lied neben dem Leitmotiv unterlegt habe, das den Helden Siegfried".

Yadda, yadda, thought Bill. But the word *Siegfried* revolved in his mind. No, he'd better not bin the thing just yet. Better file it.

Neben is an ambiguous word in German and while my suggestion of "beneath the Leitmotiv" for "neben dem Leitmotiv" is wholly acceptable...

Bill smiled. Goetz was clearly worried about something but he was making sure there was no question over his professional expertise. Bill pulled out his new clandestine file that went under the title 'Swalec.'

... it is also quite possible that 'neben' might be translated here as 'besides' or even 'before'. I'm sure you as a musicologist appreciate the difference between a tune that is heard beneath the Leitmotiv and one that is heard before it.

Bill sat up and the file slid out of his hand. Something was being said to him here of significance but he couldn't quite grasp it. He was too thrown by the coincidence. He had just driven back from London frustrated by the fact that the phrase Louis had played him could not possibly be a harmony to be heard under Siegfried's Funeral March and what was this here? Goetz telling him that ABCGH was more likely to have been heard before the March. *Before.* Not beneath...

What happened before the March? Bill didn't possess a recording of *Götterdämmerung*. Damn! He had thrown out all his Wagner after Libby. How in the depths of the Wye Valley do you hear an extract from *Twilight of the Gods* after 11 pm? Now Bill realised why people lived in cities and why one should always esteem insomniac Wagner-loving neighbours. He was seized with frustration. If he'd had Louis' home number he would have rung him straight away. But he didn't and nowhere was open this late. Nowhere in Britain anyway...

Bill dialled and got through to Vita's extension at the *New York Times*. Unfortunately she was on voicemail.

"Vita, it's Bill. It's urgent. If you get this message before you go, can you ring me at home? I absolutely need to listen to, say, the five minutes that precedes Siegfried's Funeral March in *Götterdämmerung*. If there's anyone over there with a copy that they can play to me down the phone please give me a ring."

Bill sat back in his chair. He may just have done a very foolish thing. After all there were more important matters to think about than some coded squabble that, even one hundred years ago, hadn't been taken seriously by the main protagonist.

But no. No, something in this matters. Bill was just damned if he knew what. A hunch like this was the essence of being a journalist, he felt. Of course, he reminded himself as he went upstairs, history only celebrates the journalists who follow their hunches to a successful conclusion. Who now remembers Peter Giffard who was convinced that Harold Wilson was poisoned by the KGB? Bill came across Giffo when he was just starting out in journalism. Giffard was a maverick who eventually got himself sacked for ignoring every other story but Wilsongate. Quite a few people were convinced that he'd be back. In fact, so the gossip ran, when Giffard proved his case he'd be reinstated as editor. But Giffo never did. The story didn't stand up. Giffo ended up drinking too much and editing the property pages of some local paper in Salisbury.

Bill decided he ought to lay off the whisky. Time for bed.

He woke to the sound of Lee beeping his horn. "Been anywhere nice?" said Lee, handing over a pile of press releases.

"No," said Bill as he signed for one Registered envelope. "Vienna."

"What's that like then?" Lee asked. He had such a cheery disposition and such natural curiosity some days that Bill couldn't help but like him.

"*Flat.*"

"Oh aye," said Lee. "You said Rotterdam was flat too."

"Amsterdam," said Bill.

"Right."

"Amsterdam *is* flat," Bill told him, handing back the signed book.

"What *is* it you do?" Lee asked, tucking the book back in his pocket.

"I go to opera houses and interview people."

"And they build all these opera houses in flat places do they?"

Bill could never quite tell if Lee was having him on. An image of Bayreuth at the top of its hill flashed into his mind. "Usually," he said.

"Why's that then?" Lee was grinning good-naturedly from ear to ear as if anything this crazy English recluse said was bound to amaze him.

"Don't know. Probably because it's easier for an audience to get to flat places and the only reason for building up on a hill is if you're trying to defend yourself."

"Like with a castle," said Lee. "Is that it?"

Yes, or if you're as mad as Richard Wagner, thought Bill.

"You're not going to be doing much of this are you?" Lee asked. "I mean this cloak-and-dagger-asking-for-your-post-to-be-stopped stuff. Only, if you are, Vaughan – that's the PHG – he says you got to come down and pick it up yourself."

"No," said Bill. "I don't think I'll be going undercover much more now."

It was good to have seen Lee. Bill knew nothing about him but he realised how much he looked forward to his ruddy face and shaven head. He imagined Lee worked out somewhere. Whether he chased the local girls or not Bill couldn't tell. He talked sometimes about 'The Match' which meant he supported rugby – and that his national orientation in this border valley was clearly towards Wales – but that was the sum of Bill's knowledge about his early morning friend. Funny, he reflected, he probably saw Lee more often than anyone else in the whole world apart from Reah. It was rare they even talked and yet Bill genuinely valued him.

Back inside Bill put the coffee on and opened his Registered letter. When he'd seen the London postmark his heart had pounded but no, this was not from Tamsin's awful solicitors. It was Dr Grice right on cue and taking Bill's message about his post being interfered with seriously.

> *Dear Bill Wheeler,*
>
> *Thank you for your message. I am taking the precaution of sending this letter registered although I think you will find its contents uncontroversial. Can I remind you that the University appreciates acknowledgement of all assistance given to publications?*
>
> *Yours sincerely,*
> *Edward Grice*

Well, thought Bill, you could have asked me if I'd had a nice trip. He sat down in his dressing gown intending to read the translation which Grice had typed on the second page of this letter. But he got up and decided to dress instead. Nothing in what Herr Wagner had to say was so urgent that Bill couldn't put on some warmer clothes first. After all it had all been done and dusted over a hundred years ago. It could wait for some decent coffee too.

He wandered into his office to check on the Wye. From the puddles on the rutted road outside there'd obviously been more rain while he was away. Would the river be chocolate brown yet? Bill wondered. Then he saw the light flashing on his answering machine. Someone must have rung last night while he was asleep. *Louis.* He was sure it was Louis pretending to complain about their evening in the Royal Overseas and nagging him about Venice. But in fact it was some very badly recorded music. Then a man singing some extremely high notes in praise of a woman called Brünhilde. "*Heilige Braut! wach' auf! Öffne dein Auge*".

Bill listened with amusement. It had to be Vita. He had either discovered a hitherto unsuspected streak of humour in his New York sphinx or the woman was dangerously humourless and had taken him wholly at his word. Bill smiled as he listened to the compressed signal but it was impossible to distinguish any tune beneath the *heldentenor* notes once a phoneline had got hold of them. Then in the background some laughter cut in. Vita probably had people round. They were no doubt in hysterics about the fact that the only way an alleged English opera critic could get to hear music these days was down a long distance telephone line. Silence, then a voice. "Mr Wheeler, my name is Speight MacNamara. I work for the *New York Times*. I hope we have been able to help you." There was another burst of laughter from the distance, cut short by the beep of Bill's answer-machine.

Bill felt rebuked but kindly so. He must get a grip on this obsession. But not before he'd sat down and read what was bothering the great Richard all those years ago.

> *As for my wife, she refused this morning to embrace me. She knows my heart as well as I do. You will understand therefore why this matter of S—— has not touched me but I thank you, my friend, for concerning yourself with it on my behalf.*

Bill noticed how Grice, unlike Goetz and Tony Scribbleman, seemed to be able to translate without resorting to footnotes and stylistic glosses. So the great Wilhelm Richard had wife trouble, so much trouble that he couldn't care about the rumours that S—— was spreading about letters ABCGH. *Cherchez die Frau*, thought Bill as he unfolded the page further to look at paragraph two.

> *Our dearest Lusch leaves to meet her father at the end of this month. This matter hits me at the deepest bottom of my soul...*

Bill laughed silently at the idea of Wagner's soul having a bottom, a series of bottoms in fact, of which this was currently the deepest. Obviously Grice had had to grapple with a few tortuous idioms.

> *... as you may imagine. I am tolerably well in other respects...*

Yes, yes. Bill put the translation down. He could see in what followed that Wagner was moving towards an elaborate farewell, talking about the "stage-festival-consecration-play" which he hoped to see finished this year. That would be *Parsifal* presumably. Bill sat up. Excellent, now he could date the letter! It had to be around the time that *Parsifal* was completed or, at most, a year before, assuming Wagner's prognosis hadn't proved wildly inaccurate. Bill was just about to fetch his Grove dictionary from the pile on the sofa when he noticed the last line before Wagner took his formal farewells:

Forgive me my despair!

That didn't fit. Why was Wagner despairing? His wife was giving him a hard time so he couldn't be bothered about the rumours S—— was spreading, Lusch the chambermaid was off to meet her dad, *Parsifal* was not yet finished, but for some reason something was hurting Wagner in the depths of his soul and he was ear-bashing his worthy friend with despair. What was going on between the lines of this letter?

Bill spent the morning writing up his interview with Paolo Bardini and went for his usual lunchtime walk. As he left the cottage he noticed that the gatepost that let into Tamsin's field had loosened even further. Tamsin had scraped it on a number of occasions when driving back late at night and had asked Bill whether he could arrange to have the thing dug out. Certainly, as there was no longer a gate separating her farm from the cottage, it seemed they might as well widen the gap properly. That was of course before Tamsin decided to sell Holt's Farm.

Now, looking towards the farm in all this bright spring sunshine, Bill couldn't quite believe that somebody else was going to occupy it. This had been Reah's home for most of her childhood. His disbelief was enforced by the lack of any FOR SALE sign. But then why should there be? Unlikely to get any passing trade so far from a main road. But the absence of a sign did make it all seem much less real just as, paradoxically, when they were preparing to leave Chiswick, the presence of a SOLD sign on Park Road had shocked both Bill and Tamsin with the incipient reality of that move.

Bill idly palmed the gatepost, rocking it to and fro. It would still take a good twenty minutes to dig it out he reckoned. And why should he do that now that Tamsin and Reah were leaving? He squinted against the sunlight over Tamsin's farmhouse and suddenly in his mind's eye he saw Reah running towards him. Not as she used to in the days when he would go for those long furious walks but as she was now. Her hair flying in the wind. Her eyes are bright, he thought. Her skin is wet with the rain. And mud. She falls towards me and clings.

It was a curious image. He had never seen Reah run towards him streaked with mud and tears like that. She was crying, running, arms outstretched, falling, clinging. Bill tried to think of his other images of Reah. Reah as a tiny child telling him and Tamsin not to fight, Reah singing "Oranges and Lennons" over and over again, Reah playing a shepherd in the nativity scene at school (despite Tamsin's reservations) but all he could see now was her falling forwards, head thrown back, the tall trees surging in the wind as his daughter dropped to the ground.

Bill shuddered. He was increasingly haunted by genocidal images but this with Reah was something different. And disturbing. Bill decided to change his walk today, not to pass the place where the bodies were buried. He would walk to where you could catch a glimpse of Tintern from the Devil's Pulpit, providing the foliage was being kept down. Hackneyed Wordsworthian images were far more welcome than the nightmare clichés of genocide.

When he returned there was a fresh message on the answer-machine from Siobhan, resentful as ever that his mobile appeared not to be working.

"I never take it with me," Bill told the machine.

"Anyway I do now have flight details for Venice, when you're ready to discuss them. Louis says can you get over there in the next seven days." There was a pause during which Bill was sure he could hear Siobhan's hand covering the mouthpiece. "He also says that he hopes the piano lessons are going well." Siobhan delivered this last in a slightly suspicious tone as if she suspected she was being used in some joke between the boys.

Bill sat down to review what he'd made so far of the Bardini interview. On the screen it read strangely. None of the man's charm came over. How was Bill going to convey that? He'd assumed that Bardini's arguments would speak for themselves but looking at them transcribed on to a PC, the man simply seemed dangerously opinionated, bizarre even. Sure, he had an unusually creative mind, but Bardini also had a way of asking if his ideas were unreasonable which, while wholly engaging when you were with him, read out of context like the hectoring of an ideologue. That flow of interrogatives beat down all opposition.

Bill sat back and glared sullenly at the screen for a while. It was all right as articles went but where it went Bill wasn't much interested in travelling. Nevertheless it was what Louis had asked for and if he got the piece in now he'd be able to prompt Louis to chase up his expenses yet again. Bill printed the piece off. Words still made more sense to him when they appeared on paper.

Miss Maguolo, she was like a child to me. But all my singers are chil-
dren to me. I need their trust and in return they learn from me to
grow. Is this so strange?

Well now you mention it, mate, thought Bill. OK, so Louis would be
pleased with this sketch of the Beast of Berlin but Bill wasn't. Words
mattered but the words before him revealed either a dangerous side to
Bardini or Bill's inability to handle them properly. Worrying either way.

At 7.45 Bill got into his Jeep with a bottle of red wine and drove down
to the valley floor. It was already dark and the canopy of trees that over-
hung sections of the A466 made it pitch black. He turned north towards
Tintern and after about a quarter of a mile swung the Jeep up a lane that
ran parallel with his own. The track soon deteriorated into a series of pot-
holes and Bill had to engage four wheel drive. Where he was headed was
another hilltop farm no more than two miles north of Holt's Cottage. On
a good day it ought to be possible to walk across the top of Bill's hillside,
through a tangled forest and a swamp, to the next upland stretch, but
travel in this area had always been along the valley floor. There were no
connecting roads up here. Anyone living above the Wye always went
down, drove north or south and then came up again when they drew level
with their destination.

Where Bill was heading was a large shambling farmhouse with
mullioned Tudor windows which had seen much better days. Vehicles
littered the yard in front of it, most of them hadn't moved in years – not
surprising given that their tyres had long ago been replaced by bricks.
Dogs barked as he got out of his Jeep. The house – which must once have
been splendid – was spattered, three feet high, with the mud of centuries.
Yellow lichen had claimed what lay above. Some window panes were
cracked, more were simply missing. Hardboard was nailed across the
larger gaps. It was a chill place. Coldness of a kind that has been accreting
for centuries hung in the air. It would take more than a few hot summers
and global warming to get this place habitable again.

But one person did live here. Marika who kept the dogs and worked the
farm in a far from enthusiastic fashion. Marika who gave the impression
that she did not like the countryside – or animals – very much at all but
who took her living from the land, with about as much enthusiasm as a
prisoner takes food from his jailer. This was all that she had. Didn't mean
she had to like it.

Marika was a few years older than Bill but a lifetime of cigarettes gave
her the appearance of more years still. Standing in the doorway she

regarded him at first with the same weary insolence with which she looked upon the whole useless bloody world, the world that had stranded her here. Marika Thomas was the daughter of a Czech woman who had many years ago fled the Eastern bloc, taking her daughter with her. By a crazy sequence of events she had ended up as housekeeper to a Welsh farmer living at Tredossor while her illegitimate daughter ran wild in the badly tended fields. The old farmer had developed a fondness for his house-keeper which manifested itself in a series of sexual encounters verging on the brutal. When she died the old man developed that same fondness for Marika but she fought him off. Nevertheless two years later when his will was read the farm was found to be left to a woman known as Miss Marika Thomas and here she had been ever since. It was her prison and the buggers (her cattle) were Marika's only company.

She dressed in a series of tatty pullovers and jerkins. It was the way you kept warm in Tredossor. This accumulation of garments gave Marika the appearance of bulk, but, as Bill noticed when he first came here, her legs were slender. Her body in fact was almost emaciated. She had gone from an eating disorder in her teens to the simultaneous discovery of alcohol and cigarettes. Whatever nature had intended for Marika Thomas' body she had always had her own wholly destructive ideas. It was as if she had a wish to be withered, Bill thought, but the first time he had slipped his hands inside her clothing he had found breasts of unexpected, even youthful, firmness hanging free. It was for these that he came back from time to time.

Marika's world-weary scowl lifted to something like a smile at the sight of Bill. "Hi."

She closed the door behind him. The square oak lobby with its staircase that could have been Jacobean if it made the effort was dirty and chronically unheated. Piles of tinned food bought in bulk were stacked at the foot of the stairs. Everywhere else there were dog baskets, dog blankets and discarded outdoor clothing. Boots torn and collapsed, coats crumpled, gloves forgotten. Marika used the house as if she didn't have a single cupboard or shelf where things might be put away. Everything had a place here and that was where it was dumped. Bill thought of Reah in Tredossor. How she would hate it.

"There's a fire upstairs," said Marika and she extended a hand to lead him up, past the broken cardboard boxes and buckets of peelings on their way out to be mulched.

Marika had no curtains in her bedroom so as a concession to Bill she usually lit a fire. This way the room became almost as warm as the air outside. The first time Bill had ever taken Marika up on her invitation for some whisky they had ended up having sex on the floor of her living room, a very uncomfortable experience for both of them. The room was uncarpeted and at one stage her dogs attempted to join in. Nowadays they used the bedroom and the fire lent a warmth to their coupling which was all but absent in emotional terms.

Bill sat down and opened the bottle with his penknife and poured it into glasses that were warming on the hearth. He took a sip from his and Marika did the same. She regarded him directly, but with no discernible show of feeling, then removed her torn quilted jerkin. The two of them didn't really have anything to speak about. At this moment Bill often felt something bordering on dislike for her but when he put down his glass and hiked up her pullover and teeshirt he always felt the same intoxicating surge of desire. Moving up from her waist and running his hands over the taut skin on her ribs Bill rediscovered once more the possibility of human intimacy. Her pale skin was always warmer than he expected but the moment his hands cupped her breasts Bill was lost in the grip of something black and dangerous. Their encounters never varied. Marika seizing his hair, forcing his mouth down towards her chest and Bill pulling up her clothing to reveal as much pale skin as he could. He never bothered to undress Marika, preferring to pin her back, exposed and vulnerable, beneath him. Eventually she would always break free. She was a strong woman and determined to wrench down her own trousers. And his. Bill had never known anyone like Marika for being instantly aroused. Foreplay as he understood it didn't seem to matter. She was always ready for him and always emitted a series of deep groans whenever he moved inside her. Bill was sure they frightened the cattle at times. Their first coupling was always quick. Then they would drink more wine and start again. There was nothing else to do in Tredessor.

This time however things did not work. "I'm sorry," he said. Marika lay there on the hearth for a moment and then sat up, pulling her sweater down so it hung like a dress over her scrawny knees. She reached to where she kept her roll-ups tucked against the fender.

They didn't normally talk after sex and usually that was fine. They were both happy to centre on their own sense of pleasure. This time however Bill wanted to talk. "Try again a bit later," he said. He put an arm round Marika's shoulders but she continued to roll her cigarette as if he hadn't. She wasn't angry. She just didn't know what to do with gestures like that. To Bill it felt as if he weren't there.

❖ ICARUS BLINDED

BILL HAD FOUND a place to eat near the Rialto and chosen to sit out of doors. Venice was not warm but the Perspex windbreaks of Ristorante Sommariva made dining *al fresco* just about possible for tourists. No Italian would be so foolish.

He looked at the view. He ought. That was what he was paying for really. It was a panorama that should have been truly splendid – this was the Grand Canal very much as Caneletto knew it – but whichever vista Bill tried, his view was partially obstructed by dredgers and the disgusting black barges that sludged closely behind them. How would the little Venetian have painted his way round that? Bill wondered.

He hadn't been here for years. Not since finding out that Libby Ziegler had some sort of job in Venice. He couldn't help loving it though. Venice was the only city that looked just as one imagined. It stepped straight out of all those wonderful paintings, or rather you stepped in. Not a building had changed unless you counted a nineteenth-century Post Office erected behind the Rialto. But even that had escaped a 1930s makeover, *stile fascisti*. Its sorting room still faced on to the canal through plausibly gothic arches. It was good to be back.

Bill had ordered a half carafe of the house prosecco and a starter. He wasn't interested in food. He just wanted somewhere that felt comfortable where he could collect his thoughts. The hotel was tiny. It was also central, but Siobhan had obviously booked him into the cheapest place on her list. He had been given a room on the ground floor, just behind Reception, which was probably the '*la camera meno 'spendiosa*'. Bill had not wanted to stay in there long. He left his suitcase and picked up the list of numbers and addresses Louis had faxed to Reception. There was a phone number for the family Maguolo, who did indeed lived in Mestre, also a telephone number and address for *Università degli studi di Venezia* where worked a certain Dotoressa Ziegler.

Bill could have made both phone-calls from Britain but of course Louis didn't want that. Louis wanted him in Venice, ostensibly to doorstop Felice Maguolo, ostensibly to review whatever La Fenice was performing, but mainly because Louis Montgomery wanted Bill and Libby to meet. It was quite bizarre. Bill felt that the man was taking an almost authorial role in his life. More surprising still was how little resistance Bill was putting up. He could have always told Louis to go to hell but he hadn't. Maybe he was surrendering the authorship of his own destiny.

Admittedly, he wouldn't have come were it not for the Wagner letter. It was true that Libby Ziegler could authenticate it. Her opinion was respected. Bill had seen her referred to more than once in articles on Wagner scholarship. Articles which over the last seven years he'd tried to avoid reading. One was even in the *New York Times*. To think that the erudite Vita would respect Libby Ziegler's opinion. How absurd to take Libby, the least responsible person in the whole world, seriously. She was a dangerous child, a wrecker of marriages. Nothing more.

Bill finished his meal and looked round to see if he could pay. The waiters were talking amongst themselves under the awning of the restaurant. The main perk of their job was an infinite amount of time to socialise, Bill thought. They had little interest in him.

But Bill was in no great hurry either. He wondered again about his unfortunate evening earlier in the week with Marika. That kind of thing wasn't easy to stop thinking about. Even in Venice.

Bill's sex-life since the break-up of his marriage had been sporadic. He had found many women dull after Libby, though he still wondered if what made her special was the absence of consumation in such a fraught, brief relationship. Nevertheless in the prolonged post-Ziegler period lunch had rarely led to dinner and dinner usually to nothing at all. Even when something had come of an evening in London, Antwerp or Helsinki the mornings were always disappointing. In fact the only constants in Bill's sex-life since Tamsin were those occasional vicious encounters with Marika. There was that one stray night – just over a year ago, just before the divorce was finalised – when he and Tamsin had been drinking Pimms in her garden and Bill had been digging out some saplings because Tamsin was thinking of extending the lawn. It had been hard work and she'd brought out a pitcher for the two of them and Coke for Reah who was reading under an umbrella. They'd talked almost like old times, Tamsin's eyes growing bright as the afternoon turned to dusk. He remembered her telling him about the successes she was having with autistic children at the local school and he felt a huge pride in her. Bill could not remember what else they'd talked about but he remembered now that Reah had put herself to bed by the time he finally stood up and found himself unsteady on his feet. Tamsin had laughed but when she stood up her legs were pretty useless too. Both she and Bill had been drinking on empty stomachs.

"I'll make you some supper," she said, touching him on the lips with her finger to pre-empt any dissent. It was the first physical contact between them for what seemed years. Looking back Bill realised that touch had broken a barrier they'd erected since his move from the farmhouse back to Holt's Cottage.

Later over supper he'd taken her hand, told her how marvellous she was in the way she'd coped with everything and they'd started kissing.

"Can we do this upstairs?" Tamsin had asked. She was already on his lap, pressing herself hard against him. The old hot habit of matrimony.

"What about Reah?" he'd asked. Tamsin had left the table quietly and quickly and come back almost immediately.

"Out for the count," she said, extending a hand to him.

Sitting in Venice now Bill wished he could recall the physical pleasure of being in bed with Tamsin. "I always did know what you wanted," she had breathed in his ear. "I always will."

Why had Tamsin said that? Words retain their potency, Bill thought as an unordered coffee arrived. He could always remember the thrill of things that had been spoken when making love, never the physical sensation. Not even that most unexpected night last summer. Afterwards he'd told her he must go. Her arms had made it clear she wanted him to stay but he'd said it wasn't fair on Reah. "If she finds me here she'll start thinking we're getting back together."

Looking back Bill wondered if he'd been too keen to get away. He had so much wanted to possess his wife again but afterwards he felt only the dread of being possessed in turn. Had he made some commitment by going to bed with her that night? The distance between Holt's Farm and the cottage was never so welcome. When Bill got to the gatepost, the one that Tamsin was gradually loosening with her bumper, he felt relieved. It was safer for Reah too. There was no going back, not over the scorched earth of their painful separation. Nothing would grow there again.

"*Il conto, per favore?*" Bill said to the waiter as he acquiesced over the unsolicited espresso. Over the years he had put together a basic Italian that did for restaurants and opera plots. "*Il conto*" was a line sung at the end of Act II in *La Bohème*, the moment when the bill is brought to Rodolfo and Marcello. It was one of the first Italian phrases Bill ever understood. Recognising it had removed some of the mystique of opera. An art form no longer posh and foreign if you spoke the language of Puccini.

But Puccini was no help with finding your way around Venice. Bill tried asking how he got to the *Università degli studi di Venezia* but the waiter could not follow his Covent Garden Italian. They quickly reverted to English. "The university is everywhere," the waiter said as if he were amazed that Bill could not see it before his very eyes. "Do you have the address?"

Bill explained that all he had was the *facoltà di storria e critica delle arte* and what looked like a postal code. The waiter looked at Bill's fax and went off to speak to one of his colleagues. That man in turn disappeared inside the restaurant and after a while Bill's waiter returned to speak to him. "My friend, he phones for you."

Bill tried to say that wasn't necessary. He may be English but he was still capable of picking up a telephone. The deed had already been done however and with uncharacteristic swiftness.

"You go to Dorsoduro," the colleague explained. "You look for the Calle Foscari. So from here you take the *vaporetto* to San Toma." But at this point a disagreement broke out between the two men over whether San Toma or Ca'Rezzonico was the better stop. Bill left a generous tip without waiting for the outcome.

He hadn't intended to just turn up at Libby's place of work but he preferred that to cold calling and, given that she was so close, it seemed absurd not to drop by. The *facoltà di storria e critica* was only three stops further down the canal from here. Or four. Depending on your waiter.

Dorsoduro was the student quarter. Although most of Venice had that wonderful run-out-of-paint-for-centuries feeling this bank of the Grand Canal had raised decrepitude to an art form. There were only a few shops, most selling Carnival masks – and one actually making them, but none of the instant tourist trivia that surrounded St Mark's. Bill enjoyed his walk in the late March sunshine.

Several times he stopped to ask "*Dove Calle Foscari?*" and tried to listen to how often he had to turn *destra* or *sinistra*. Bill couldn't help feeling it would have been a lot easier if they'd sung the answers back to him.

The Department of Art History and Criticism turned out to be in a long narrow alleyway which ran to the left off Calle Foscari down to a jetty sandwiched between two fairly substantial palaces. Bill walked its full length only to find Venetian pondweed lapping at his shoes. It seemed the only way to get in by the front doors of either of these huge *palazzi* was to arrive by gondola. He retraced his steps and found he had passed a small glass door with a number of brass doorbuzzers set into the wall. Against one was a plaque that read "*Storia del'Arte. Piano 3er*".

"*Pronto?*" answered a voice

"*La dottoressa Ziegler, per favore?*" said Bill, but he was completely unprepared for the implacability and fluidity of the reply. When in doubt repeat yourself, Bill thought. This time he added that his name was Bill

Wheeler. The woman at the other end of the mechanism was still being very emphatic about matters incoherent, but at one point he did hear her ask:

"*Ha un appuntamento?*"

"*No, signorina,*" he replied, "*Ma è urgentissimo.*"

There was a pause and then the glass door buzzed. Bill took the stairs to a surprisingly modern third floor that had been carved out of this old building. Here to his relief he found the secretary had drafted in a tall tanned young man with a smart blazer, slow languid manner and excellent English to do the talking.

"Mr Wheeler? My names is Bertelmann, Hauke Bertelmann. I am..." Hauke's lazy eyes rolled away as if he had forgotten exactly who or what he was. "I am a *colleague* of Dr Ziegler."

"Pleased to meet you," said Bill, shaking hands with the big German. "Is Libby around?"

"I'm afraid she is not," said Hauke giving nothing else away.

So this was where Libby Ziegler had washed up, thought Bill. It all seemed far too bright and uncluttered for her. It looked on closer inspection exactly like what it was: a small department in a moderately well-funded university with just that dash of chromium chic which the Italians can't resist, even in academia.

"Are you expecting her back?" Bill asked.

"I'm afraid I don't know her plans," said Hauke, his eyes now rolling to some other part of the room.

"Has she just gone out?"

"I'm afraid I don't know that either," said Hauke.

This was all beginning to sound a touch suspicious.

"Is she in the country even?"

"The countryside?" said Hauke, not understanding.

"I mean is she in Italy?" Bill asked.

"I could not be sure." Hauke was giving nothing away.

"But she does work here?"

"Sometimes. Yes."

This conversation was getting more and more bizarre. If Hauke had intended to be obstructive he couldn't have managed it better.

"I need to speak to Libby," said Bill, trying a new tack. "It's a personal matter. I'm a friend from many years ago when she lived in London."

Hauke's face remained impassive.

"I'm only here for a few days. It's quite important that I talk to her."

"I will surely tell her," said Hauke.

"When she gets back?" said Bill.

"Yes."

"So she is away at the moment?" Bill pointed out.

"I'm afraid I do not know where Dr Ziegler is at present."

Bill left his hotel number and also his mobile number without any conviction whatsoever that Libby would ever see them. He retraced his steps and, by checking the map, found that he'd been wandering round the back of some of Venice's best known waterfront properties. Ca'Foscari was a palace belonging to one of the doges, though it now seemed to be yet another part of the university while Ca'Rezzonico, currently a museum, was once the home of Robert Browning. As for Libby's office, that appeared to be at the back of Palazzo Giustinian which he was sure had some association with Wagner, who had lived in Venice on and off. But of course it was bound to have an association with the Meister. This whole thing kept coming back to Wagner. Time and again.

Bill walked back to his hotel across the Accademia's tall wooden bridge. Reaching its apex he looked back and glimpsed the low squat Guggenheim. Bill thought for a moment how he'd quite like to visit Peggy Guggenheim's truncated palazzo but he didn't enjoy art galleries on his own. He'd happily go to a film or opera by himself but he needed company when it came to looking at paintings.

Bill wished Reah was with him. Last year they'd gone round the National Portrait Gallery together because she was doing a project on the Tudors. His bright intuitive daughter had seen more things in the faces of people like Cranmer, Cromwell and Thomas More than Bill would ever have noticed alone.

Of course Libby knew about pictures, he recalled as he checked the route signs that led *Per San Marco*. He'd been round the London galleries with her hadn't he? One of the first things they'd done together. Of course. Bloody woman. So absolute in her views. He recalled how she'd dismissed Perugino in the National Gallery.

"Idealised," she'd said in that firm Boston accent of hers. "Wholly lacking in humanity. You can see how he influenced Raphael and Poussin." They were looking at some virgin or other. "Too much God on the brain." Her voice was unselfconsciously clear. "I mean *why* do a programme about him? It's so dead it's necrophiliac!"

"Oh, would you say so?" said an elderly lady standing ramrod stiff next to them, her eyes never moving from the martyr in question. It was an English rebuke, indirect but implacable, a stingingly subtle request that this oddly dressed American kept her views to herself.

"Oh yes," said Libby, with all too audible certainty. "Great draughts-manship of course but it's a priest's painting. You know the Pope wanted to make him a Cardinal? Him and Raphael. I mean it's like Stalin wanting to make some painter a Commissar."

"Do you work here?" said the woman with a stab of irony that Bill certainly detected even if Libby didn't.

"No," said Libby, with her sweetest smile. "I turned them down." Then they went in search of Fra Filippo Lippi.

"You don't care, do you?" asked Bill. He was slightly in awe of this slim 27-year-old who seemed to have a knack of being outrageous. Even though most of Bill's colleagues believed there were no more sacred cows left to slaughter, this young woman who had arrived from nowhere kept finding unsayable things to articulate. She'd done one interview for Bill's paper that ended up trashing the grand seigneur of British arts so completely that a written apology was demanded from the editor. From then on she was made. Suddenly everyone wanted Libby Ziegler.

"Care?" said Libby, leading them past a Mars Vanquished by Venus. "Yes, I care. Course I damn well care."

He'd meant about people. That was the thing with Libby. Everything she saw she saw with childlike clarity and intensity. People got in the way. They obscured the view.

"I know I'm right," Libby had told him once. "I may be out of step with my generation but I'm right." She was like a child at times, Bill had thought. Simultaneously innocent and ruthless.

He got in the way, didn't he? She'd wanted him, God knows why. Bill was still chasing bylines while Libby was creating headlines. But somehow he'd got in the way and the Ziegler juggernaut had simply rolled over his life. No it didn't actually. It beamed up to another planet. Disappeared. Everyone said she had a brilliant career ahead of her. TV has an insatiable appetite for iconoclasts. But Libby just got on a plane and went, leaving the mess that they were all in today. Himself, Tamsin, Reah. Not Libby of course. She had a very nice job and probably a very nice Venetian flat too.

Where the hell was he? Lost in his thoughts Bill had taken a wrong turning and found himself on the Fondamenta Delle Farine overlooking the Basin of St Mark's and not at all far from Harry's Bar. Hemingway territory. Honestly everything about this place either led back to Wagner or bloody Americans!

The afternoon was a write-off. Sitting on the bed of his curious hidden room behind Reception, Bill rang the family of Felice Maguolo to no avail.

The first time he got through to a woman and the second time to a rather breathless sounding man but neither spoke English or even Bill's kind of Italian. In the end he decided to take a taxi to the address that Bardini had faxed him. It seemed a shame to leave Venice and go to that giant railway shed that was Mestre.

Worse, getting from his hotel to Piazzale Roma where the taxis waited would mean catching a *vaporetto* and chugging all the way back down the Grand Canal. Taxis did not come to your hotel door in Bill's part of Venice. He contemplated the journey with a reluctance that could have easily have led him to kick the minibar. Damn Louis for sending him on such a fool's errand! He was wasting a Friday afternoon when he might be doing any of the thoroughly enjoyable things a tourist does in Venice. When he might be at home even!

Bill lay on the bed and rang the Family Maguolo again. This time there was no reply at all. Long depressing empty beeps followed, one after the other. Obviously his operatic Italian had left the Maguolos too frightened to even answer the phone now.

Damn it. He was here to work so work it would have to be. Leaving the hotel with a coat swung over his shoulder Bill suddenly decided that he would walk to Piazzale Roma. The *vaporetto* hardly moved any quicker than pedestrian pace anyway and it stopped all the time. If he followed signs *Per Rialto* and then picked up signs to Piazzale Roma on reaching the bridge he'd be fine. Get some exercise, see the city as Venetians saw it.

He got lost of course. Whoever planned the signposting of Venice seemed to take pleasure in sending Bill Wheeler off in one direction and then presenting him with a choice of narrow brick alleyways, with no subsequent signage to say which was the one to go down.

Bill improvised and after some furious walking reckoned he must be getting very close to the taxi rank at Ferrovia when he found himself back where he'd been twenty minutes ago.

"That's the Palazzo Vendramin Calergi," said a gazeteer-carrying Australian to his companion. "It's where the composer Richard Wagner died."

"I'm not surprised," said Bill, primarily to himself although audibly enough for the two men to turn and look at him.

In the end he took the *vaporetto* for the last section of the journey and found a taxi with reassuring promptness. The drive was not inspiring but long it certainly was. Evidently the family Maguolo wasn't too keen on being in Mestre either. As the driver zoomed relentlessly towards Verona Bill began to wonder if he'd have enough money to pay. He did, just. The driver then took off. This despite Bill's urgent request that he wait just *un minuto per favore*.

It was late afternoon and everything in the suburbs around Via San Polo was closed. Mind you it didn't look as if things would be much more lively when shops reopened. Underneath the concrete block of flats ahead of Bill was a hairdressers, a newsagent and a very Italian kind of shop that seemed to sell reconditioned old typewriters as objets d'art.

He crossed the road and found the appropriate buzzer to ring. To his total lack of surprise nobody answered. "I am ruining a perfectly good day," Bill said to himself. He tried the buzzer twice more out of a super-stitious belief that two more rings might summon into existence a family which had not been there when last he telephoned, nor when he pressed the buzzer less than a minute ago. For thousands of years humanity has deluded itself with the inexplicable belief that the third time will be lucky.

Then he tried the neighbours. They also seemed to have fled the country. No response on any buzzer until an old woman in black came and looked balefully over the plastic flowers on her balcony.

"Felice Maguolo!" shouted Bill pointing at the door buzzers.

"*Sono andati tutti alla stazione ferroviaria!*" she replied.

Great, while Bill had been making his way here Felice's family had been making theirs in the exact opposite direction. They were probably at Mestre station now. Bill asked when they would return but the old woman just shrugged. He asked where the bank was and was duly dismissed by a hand that gestured in the direction from which he had come. Maybe he could get some money out of an ATM and find somewhere to sit down and drink a coffee.

The bank was closed – worse, the ATM was located inconveniently inside a glass vestibule. To gain access to it you had to use your cash card and the door was adamant about not admitting anyone with English plastic.

Bill checked in his pockets. He had about enough euros left to buy a cup of coffee but he'd hardly be able to tip. Presumably he could find a cafe, drink his coffee, pay the bill and then make a run for it before the waiter noticed. God, I am wasting my life, he said to himself.

In the end he chose to go back to Via San Polo and tried Felice's buzzer again. To no avail. The old woman looked over her balcony a second time but communicated her disapproval in silence.

Bill developed a circuit between the bank and Via San Polo with occa-sional stops to look at the reconditioned typewriters and curse Louis. He did have one bit of luck however. Spotting someone gaining access to the bancomat Bill ran down the road and just managed to slip in behind him, making the poor man squeak in alarm.

Bill emerged with enough euros to book a suite at the Danieli and take a watertaxi back to Chepstow should it prove necessary. However the buzzer at 3/18 Via San Polo remained uncooperative. No Maguolo transpired. Bill made a mental note never to work as a door-stopping journalist again – ever.

After a while the tobacconist reopened and several old men arrived, from nowhere, to shuffle in and talk to the owner. Eventually a smart, tiny young woman in a Punto drew up and walked towards Bill swinging her hips and shopping as only women on the Continent do. For a moment Bill hoped that this might be Felice Maguolo but life had no intention of being that generous to him. Not today. The woman did speak English however. Felice's parents were virtually deaf, she explained. They had met and married when they were both learning to cope with hearing difficulties. They had a specially modified receiver on the telephone but it did not always work. Felice herself was in Rome and her parents were going by train that afternoon to see her.

"Is she singing in Rome?" Bill asked.

"No. Holiday," said the young woman. "Are you a friend of hers?"

"No," said Bill, feeling rather sordid. "No I'm not. Look, I wonder if it's possible to get a taxi from here? I have to go back to Venice."

"I will ring for one if you wish," said the young woman. She took out her mobile phone and dialled the local firm. Afterwards she took her shopping inside the block of flats, but not Bill. He gave her his mobile and hotel numbers in case Felice returned but he knew she would not. She was having a happy wholesome family holiday in Rome with her deaf parents. Had they ever heard their daughter sing? Bill remembered Reah's 'Oranges and Lennons' and wished he could be with her this weekend rather than waiting on this long dusty street for his taxi to come. He felt as if he never wanted to write another piece of journalism in his life.

The sun was dipping by the time Bill alighted at Piazzale Roma. Comparing his squalid afternoon with the sight of the Grand Canal at dusk Bill felt that God was a capricious bastard at times. Some days he casts heart-breaking beauty like this before us, just when we are resolving to never to commit to anything ever again. Bill wished he could feel more at one with the Easter holidaymakers and the opera-goers surging on and off the *vaporetti*.

In the event he got off one stop early, leaving at St Mark's and heading straight for Harry's. If ever there was a guy who understood how the broken spirit of a man must crashland in whisky it was Papa Hemingway. Icarus of the Malts, that's me, thought Bill.

The decor of the tiny bar was too bright, too Roaring Thirties for Bill. He had a double with ice, talked to no one, paid at the door, and then walked back to his hotel. So his life lacked shape and meaning today: that's because it was an interstitial segment sandwiched between Louis' and Felice Maguolo's.

The cheerful proprietress with rings on every finger took down a note for Bill as she passed him his key. Her arms jangled with the many metal bangles, equally cheerful, that she wore. Bill felt so world-weary he hadn't even noticed that for once his pigeon hole had contained something.

"Message for Mr Bill Wheeler." The words were written in a bold, open hand. *"Dotoressa Ziegler telephoned. She will be in the bar of Hotel Danieli until 8pm this evening."*

Bill looked at his watch. He had fourteen minutes. He left his key and ran. He knew the Danieli was opposite San Zaccharia where he'd disembarked on his arrival from the airport. It must be no more than ten minutes walk away from this hotel. Nevertheless he ran. Distances seem further in the dark. Pounding along Bill wondered why on earth he was so keen, all of a sudden, to see Libby Ziegler. He'd spent the last seven years avoiding her, cursing her, turning the page should her name crop up in something that he was reading. He'd actually made a point of *not* sending her the Wagner letter as soon as it came into his possession. Good Lord, he hadn't even wanted to come to Venice! Now he was running as if missing Libby would be the worst thing in the world.

Despite one wrong turning, Bill skeetered to a halt in front of the hotel with five minutes to spare. He drew breath and adjusted the collar of his jacket. Bill might not be sure how much he wanted to see Libby but he was damn sure he didn't want her to see him looking like a breathless scarecrow.

Once inside he was glad he'd smartened up. The Danieli had been purpose-built to answer the needs of nineteenth-century tourists. Its public areas were lofty, the staff uniformed and omnipresent and the music in the bar coming from a real pianist. Bill did a circuit of the sofas, wondering what Libby would look like now. Seven years ago her hair was shoulder-length. It might be short now. It might be dyed. What colour was it when he knew her? She dressed with outrageous eclecticism then. He could remember her in knitted ties, full length coats and boots. Was he right to be scanning the bar for a latter day new romantic?

But no. No one seemed to be Libby as far as he could see; no matter how hard Bill tried to bend the images of strangers before him. That might have been Libby over there, had she grown fat. There was another Libby near the bar, but only if she'd aged drastically. One proto-Ziegler had reverted back to her teens while another turned out to be a young man. Aware that time was getting on Bill did one more circuit, this time making sure that he took in the foyer's deeper recesses and peered behind its potted plants. Would it be like Libby to secrete herself and watch for him, unobserved in the foliage? He didn't know. Seven years had passed. Did Bill have any idea of what Libby was like now? Did he have any idea then?

It was eight o'clock as Bill made his way to the reception desk. Maybe she had had to leave early and had left a message for him. He explained his situation to a very young tanned Italian in uniform who spoke perfect American.

"No sir, we have no message for you, Mr Wheeler."

"The woman I'm meeting, that I was meeting. She's quite distinctive," said Bill.

"In what way, Mr Wheeler?"

"It's difficult to say... I haven't seen her for seven years but... she is quite distinctive."

There was no possibility that this man who wore his gold piping so well would betray the impatience he was entitled to feel. His demeanor – as well as his English – was derived from American hotel training. Nevertheless Bill recognised that he must be coming over like a total prat.

"Excuse me, sir," said another uniformed concierge from the other end of the polished reception desk. "I do apologise but from the description you gave I wonder if you might be looking for Dr Ziegler?" So Libby still created an impact, Bill thought. "Her party had to leave. She says she will contact you."

"When did she leave?"

"About five minutes ago."

Damn it! Libby must have left just as Bill entered. They might even have passed and not recognised each other. No, that was unlikely. People still recognised Libby Ziegler. Even if they didn't know who she was. Bill was sure he'd recognise her too.

Clearly it was going to be a night for raiding the minibar. He really should have known better. Talk about a wild goose chase! Here he was pursuing geese he didn't even want. Geese that only someone like Louis would find appealing. The Wagner letter had seemed a pretty oddball project to get involved in, but this trip! Why had he gone along with Louis' nonsense? Bill despaired. For goodness sake he didn't really want Libby did he? No. He just wanted something to go right that day, some connection to happen. Some reason to believe that the Universe did indeed have a use for him.

Bill walked back out, on to the broad Riva Degli Schiavoni, and saw the tethered gondolas lurching upward, battering into each other each time the Adriatic surged. Spiny black whales trying to beach themselves en masse. People were still walking about, although the night was far from warm. A fresh party of teenage tourists were disembarking from a launch. In the dark their voices scribbled loudly over the night air like so much joyous cosmopolitan graffiti. Bill felt old when he looked on those faces. Not because they were virtually Reah's age, but because they were so happy with their lot. Life had not yet denied them so many of the things they wished for. Maybe they hadn't got round to asking too much as yet. They just spilled out into the night and wondered what kind of place this Venice might be.

Bill's rule for several years now had been not to ask much of life. It was a conscious decision. Ask and you will be disappointed. Life will never be realised as you expect it. Accept. Certainly don't suddenly get seized with the idea that meeting Libby Ziegler will put right a god-awful day. Find calm through resignation. That was the philosophy to which Bill aspired. In some sense this was his own personal Schopenhauer. In practice, however, what he did was work furiously hard to try and avoid the disappointments that were always waiting round the corner to hit him. As they had done now.

And yet here he was in one of the most beautiful cities in the world! Life was out of kilter, Bill thought. A bell rang out from the distant cemetery island of San Giorgio. Bill said goodnight to its tall stark *campanile* and to the ridiculously optimistic gondoliers still trying to get a final fare that night. He went back to his hotel, entered the tiny room behind Reception and placed his armchair in front of the minibar.

"OK," he said, unscrewing a miniature whisky with ironic detachment. "Icarus, you bastard. You asked for this."

Bill was just unscrewing the second bottle when his mobile went.

"If that's my conscience, I'm out," he muttered, standing up and fumbling in his coat pocket.

"Dad? It's Reah."

"Hello, Sweet."

"Dad, I really miss you."

Bill sat down on the bed. This was strange. Reah rarely admitted missing him. Bill told her he missed her too.

"Mum's being all Jewish," said Reah. "She's saying I've got to go to Bristol tomorrow."

Bristol meant Synagogue.

"Well it is her religion and you're Jewish by birth," said Bill.

"I wish Mum could have an optional religion," Reah moaned. "Like everyone else. Why does my Mum have to be Jewish?"

"Too late to change that now." Bill tried to make it sound like a joke.

"Where are you?" Reah asked.

"Venice."

"Is that nice?"

"You must come here one day," he began to say but before he'd finished Reah had cut in.

"Better go," she said quickly. "We've got to sing the stupid blessing."

The phone went dead. Reah was obviously worried about being discovered. Poor girl, thought Bill. Bad enough to be caught between your divorced mother and father but to be caught in the divide between Jew and Gentile... He had talked to other Jewish parents and they had said their teenage daughters often objected to having to stay in on a Friday or wear a dress for Saturday morning synagogue. Reah's rebellion against Tamsin wasn't unique. It probably had little to do with the divorce but the divorce certainly made it more acute.

There were two more miniatures lined up on the arm of Bill's armchair. He got off the bed and put them back in the minibar. He was tired now. He wanted out.

When Bill and Tamsin had first separated he thought he'd use the time no longer spent arguing to read. There was so much literature he'd missed. Was missing. Poets did not abandon poetry and novelists did not cease turning out sequels just because the Wheeler marriage was disintegrating. But in fact all he had done since was merely to occupy his time. He worked, travelled, cooked for Reah, drank coffee in the morning and whisky at night and generally filled up the hours between waking and sleeping as best he could. He never regretted checking the clock and finding that it was half an hour later than he'd thought. Bill's waking hours were subdivided into activities that helped them pass. Distraction could stave off unhappiness. Nevertheless he did not read and he would not read now. Bill had developed an aversion to books; not to the things themselves but to the silent introspection that stole over him whenever he sat down to read. He did not wish to risk introspection. He wanted to sleep, maybe forever.

The next morning Bill was woken by a phone again but this time the room phone, not the mobile. It was Felice Maguolo, suddenly returned from Rome. Desperate to create headlines for Louis. Of course it was. But no.

"Bill – it's Libby Ziegler." What was the world doing to him? Her voice was exactly the same. Exactly the same but there was a warm laugh when she asked. "How *are* you?" He didn't remember Libby laughing before. His memories were of intensity. Since when did her voice have that honeyed quality?

"Hello," he said. "Hi."

"There's no need to translate," said Libby. "Bill, what are you *doing* here?"

Bill almost said "Looking for you". It would have been so easy. He was already intoxicated by the warmth in her voice. Bizarre that he hadn't remembered its sound till now. "Work," he said, trying to gather his wits. "I'm sorry I missed you last night."

"We had to leave," said Libby. "The boat was waiting for us."

"The boat was waiting?" asked Bill.

"Yes," said Libby, laughing at his incredulity. "There's a lot of water in Venice, Bill. What do you think we do? Catch the tube?"

Bill found this very strange. In all his fantasies about coming across Libby Ziegler one day he had never thought they would start by joking with each other on the telephone.

"Where are you now?" he asked.

"At home."

"You actually live in Venice?"

"It's a hell of a commute from Massachusetts," she replied.

"That guy – at the university – he really didn't want me knowing you were around," Bill told her.

"That's Hauke," she said. "He likes to protect me."

"Who from?"

"Married men?" Libby suggested.

"Who says I'm still married?"

"Who says I was talking about you?!"

There was a silence. Then Libby laughed again. They were flirting. But there always was something flirtatious about Libby. There had to have been a charm seven years ago. After all he had been charmed.

"Look, can we meet?" said Bill. This was outrageous. A woman whom he believed he had hated for so long. What was going on?

"Sure."

"I'm going to the opera tonight," he began to suggest.

"Don't," she said. "It's awful. American producer. Big concept, small brain. Look, let's meet for coffee in San Marco."

He noticed her Italian pronunciation was spot on. She was going to have a hoot with his.

"When?"

"Ten o'clock?"

Bill looked at his watch. It was already 9.15.

"Some of us have been working since six," Libby teased him.

"Some of us were sitting in the Hotel Danieli till midnight."

"*Really?*" She really did have a very honeyed way of drawling that word. Bill asked her where they should meet.

"It's a fine day. Let's sit out."

"Outside where?"

"In San Marco."

"But which cafe?" Bill asked. There must be at least half a dozen.

"I'll find you."

Libby put the phone down. That was it. Seven years of animosity were over. Incredible. Forty minutes later, having showered, dressed and grabbed a croissant from the stout Turkish lady preparing his breakfast setting, Bill was approaching the irregular columns that guard the Doge's Palace. As he turned into San Marco itself the Campanile was striking ten.

There were tables everywhere, each cafe marking out its territory in facile coloured chairs. Yellow. Pink. Green. And people. There were people everywhere too.

On one side of this enormous rectangle stood the Procuratie Vecchie and on the other the Procuratie Nuove and somewhere in between the Dotoressa Ziegler. Presuming she's on time. She will be on time. She will be, he thought. We are not late when life suddenly yokes us together like this. But why has it? And why is the sun shining? Why are the pigeons taking flight and arcing over Saint Mark's in such a beautiful formation? They block the sun. They block the sun like a great dark wing and their noise. Their noise!

Light stabbed into his eyes. Once the flock had passed the sun's rays had flashed cruelly straight into Bill's retinas. He staggered, hands clasped to his face, retinas glowing white and then yellow against his eyelids.

"Bill?"

Bill opened his eyes and, through a gap between his cautious fingers, saw a figure standing silhouetted before him.

"Are you all right?"

Shading his eyes Bill watched as her features emerged from this temporary blindness. It was as if she were being summoned up from his imagination and given form and flesh. Taller than he remembered but unmistakably Libby. The hair which had reached to her shoulders at first seemed to have been shorn. Then he realised it was swept back, longer, tied in a ribbon at the neck and disappearing an infinite distance down behind her shoulder blades. Now he could see, Libby seemed not to be wearing her mediaeval skirts and frock coats anymore but a vibrant orange and gold shift over what looked like black leggings and a black turtleneck sweater. The boots were Libby though. Oh yes. No boots had to be quite that tall.

"How extraordinary," he said.

"'Nice to see you' would have done," she told him.

He took in her eyes. They were the same. Oh yes they were the same. They were her. Tamsin's eyes were bright. They wanted you. They hated you. Pure and simple. But Libby's eyes were deep. They flashed, they mocked and then hid. You couldn't fathom them. There was a line around her mouth. The Libby of his imagination had no lines or creases but this one at 34 had a single weary notch cut by time – or disappointment – down to the right hand side of her jaw.

"I was dazzled for a moment."

"It's my effulgence," she quipped. "Shall we sit down?"

They didn't touch. Really he should have kissed her on the cheek but the time for that had already passed. Libby led them to the first set of tables and Bill made sure the sun wasn't in his eyes this time. Then Libby noticed that the sun was in *her* eyes if they sat like that and so they moved round again and laughed and then they talked, ordered coffee and talked some more. Oh yes.

Later that day Bill went to interview the artistic director of La Fenice out at the company's temporary home, Palafenice, an enormous Portakabin complex constructed on the waterfront while the old house itself was rebuilt.

All the way out to Palafenice he thought about his conversation with Libby; he thought quite a lot about it while he was interviewing the *direttore* too. She was different, he thought. And yet in many respects she was just the same. Damn, he wished he could be more specific. Any editor reading such twaddle would have flung it back at him and bawled across the newsroom about needing something that the reader could understand. OK, said Bill, trying to focus as he waited for a *vaporetto* to take him back. OK, she seemed happier. More fulfilled. Less intense perhaps. Not as obsessive about the arts as he'd remembered. She also seemed to be enjoying life more. The 27-year-old Libby he had known had been angry with much of the world, especially with the fools who thought they knew more than she did. Maybe that was it. Libby was now accepted as the authority she always knew herself to be. Yet was she also weary or disappointed in some way? That line down her jaw...

They didn't speak much about their private lives. Bill obviously had to say a bit more about the divorce, given that he'd referred to it in the first minute of their phonecall that morning, but Libby didn't ask him if she were responsible nor did he suggest she was. He told her about living in the countryside on his own and she was surprised that he could do without city life.

"It gives me more time to write," he told her.

"And *do* you?" she asked, her eyes meeting his provocatively over the coffee. That question, all of a sudden, seemed very personal.

"I write enough," he said. Libby looked disappointed. Was she with anyone, Bill had wondered, but not asked. She didn't ask this of him either.

"And what about your daughter, Thea?"

"Reah. She's thirteen. She's fine. Great fun. I think she's coped quite well with the divorce."

A thought had struck Bill.

"Aren't your parents divorced?"

She laughed. "I have no memory of parents, plural. I didn't see my Mom for years. My grandparents brought me up. Then my father took over. For a while. He used to take me on holidays with him. To places like this."

"You were lucky," said Bill. His father had never taken him anywhere. There wasn't the money. Or the inclination.

"Oh I didn't think about it at the time," said Libby. "I liked being with him. I didn't know whether it was the Uffizi or the Accademia. What the hell, that wasn't what mattered."

She'd stopped at that point as if she didn't want to disclose any more. Her eyes flicked away and the next minute Libby's soul was hidden from him. It was odd but Bill could recall her doing that in London.

He smiled. Bill had never known about little Libby Ziegler travelling Europe's art galleries with her Pa.

"So how did you get into Wagner?"

"Wagner?" said Libby.

"That was your big thing when..." He didn't quite know how to put it. "When you were in London. I've seen your name cited since."

"Oh well, I did some work on the letters," said Libby. "That was a long time ago."

It was extraordinary. Yes, extraordinary, Bill thought, as the *vaporetto* took him back towards his hotel. The thing that finally linked him back to Libby, a letter written by Richard Wagner, was something Libby no longer thought of as relevant to her life. To *their* life even. Time plays strange tricks. We not only go on to different futures when we part, we develop different pasts too.

When they'd got up from the table he'd found himself saying that he'd like to see her again. This to the woman he hated.

"How long are you here?"

"I'm flying back tomorrow morning."

"Shoot – I've got a party this evening."

"Yes and I've got the opera."

"Maybe next time you're over," she said, beating him to leaving some change on the little silver plate.

"Yep."

They found they were both walking back towards the Campanile.

"Are you ever in London?" he asked.

"No," she replied with a very definite shake of the head. Clearly never.

"Well," said Bill. "Maybe I'll be over again."

He did kiss her on the cheek when they parted. In fact she expected to be kissed twice, continental style. But not on the lips, sincere style. Why should Libby be sincere?

"Great to see you again," he said for something to say. But it was great. He stepped back and she walked towards the Giardinetti. When he looked round to see her again Libby had gone. Completely. Disappeared into the crowds. It was 11.15. A morning in the Venetian springtime. He might have imagined the whole thing.

Bill was still on the *vaporetto*, passing St Mark's on his way back to San Zaccharia and wondering if there might be someone in Libby's life. She had been very quiet on that score. On the phone she'd said that 'We' had had to leave the Danieli last night. 'We' had taken a boat too, probably one of those expensive water taxis. Clearly 'We' had money. 'We' might be going to the party tonight. And yet Libby had not made it clear to him that she was with someone. He had given her the chance to. Come to think of it, she hadn't in London all those years ago either. It was possible to be acquainted with Libby and yet know nothing of substance.

By the time he was back in his hotel room and thinking about where he was going to eat before the opera Bill was determined to see Libby again. He didn't know why. He just had to. He paced the narrow passage between his bed and the wall, positively consumed by a need for her.

She had given him her card. There was no address except for the university but she had put her home phone-number on the back.

He dialled.

The phone rang. Long Italian phone beeps. On and on. "*Pronto!*" said a man's voice. Bill's heart sank.

117

"I would like to speak to Libby Ziegler," he said, his Italian having deserted him completely.

She came to the phone, sounding less amused this time.

"Libby it's Bill," he told her even though he'd already had to divulge his name to *Pronto*-man.

"Hi, Bill," she said. Noncommittal.

"Listen I wasn't entirely straight with you," he began, extemporising. "I've got a letter I want you to look at. I believe it's written by Richard Wagner. I could really do with seeing you about it tonight."

"I see," said Libby. "Why didn't you mention this earlier?" It was a reasonable question. After all they had touched on the subject of Wagner's letters. That should have been his cue.

Could he really tell her the truth? That he'd never wanted to show her the letter. That he'd been bullied into coming to see her by Louis. That he was totally ambivalent about meeting her because he'd spent all these years believing that he hated her. That he'd made all that effort to see her last night simply because he'd had a wasted afternoon in Mestre and the possibility of something going right, even a meeting with the woman he most detested in the world, seemed better than watching CNN and drinking too much whisky alone in his hotel room?

Why? is the most difficult question to answer. Bill often found it possible to work out *how* things came to pass. Causality is discernible, but the great Why is an ultimate, and invariably shrouded from us.

"When I saw you this morning – when I could actually see you," he added – "I forgot completely about the letter."

Libby laughed. She believed him – or she liked his lie.

"Look, I'm going to feel such a fool going back to London without having shown you it. How about after your party tonight?"

"Too late," said Libby.

"Well what about–"

"Do you have a mask?" said Libby, cutting across any other ridiculous suggestions he might have.

"A mask?"

"For the Ball. It's not strict. You can come on right after the opera."

Bill thought she was joking.

"Where do I get a mask from?"

"You'll need a costume as well. Go to *Atelier Bosco*. Tell him I sent you."

"Atelier who?"

"It's the studio of Sandro Bosco. He knows the party I'm talking about. I'll make sure you're allowed in."

"You are joking," said Bill.

"And make sure you bring the letter this time!" said Libby, and then she put the phone down. She had a habit of doing that.

Bloody hell. A masked ball. Bill opened the door to Reception and asked his friend with the rings and bangles if she knew where the Studio of Sgr Bosco was. She did. Of course she did.

Strictly speaking Carnival was well over but that didn't seem to bother Sandro Bosco's assistants, who were busy making adjustments to a latter-day Marie Antoinette behind two screens. From what Bill could see of it, the costume was remarkably authentic, although he suspected Antoinettes were getting bigger these days. Certainly the assistants were making calculations over how much the queen's waistline would have to be let out.

Marie herself was from Denver and her partner, a Casanova in want of stockings, was from Michigan. Sandro's receptionist had introduced Bill to them because it turned out they were all going to the same function.

"Are you taking a water taxi?" asked Marie Antoinette over the top of the screen. "Only some friends of ours were here during Carnival and they tried walking and you know *nothing* is signposted in Venice and they got lost down these tiny alleyways and the whole evening was a disaster."

"I hadn't thought," said Bill.

This really was not his scene and yet he ought to talk to these people – he didn't even know where he was going tonight.

"Bill!" cried Sandro Bosco, a tall curly-haired man who looked more German than Italian. "Come here now." Bill duly got up and let himself be led into a sequence of enormously tall rooms crammed with costumes. Sandro placed an arm round Bill's shoulder. "You choose anything you want. Here we have the Renaissance. The next room is eighteenth century and then we also have fantasy – Mandarin, Tartar, Astronaut."

"How much does all this cost?" asked Bill hoping he couldn't afford any of it.

Sgr Bosco laughed. "Libby says to put it on the Baron's account. Don't worry about that."

"I've absolutely no idea what's going on," said Bill, feeling that he may as well confide in his tall amiable friend. Who the hell was the Baron? Was he the man who had said "*Pronto*" on the phone in Libby's apartment or had that been Hauke the Horrible? "I don't even know where this party is," he moaned.

"I'm sure Libby will send an invitation to your hotel," Sandro insisted. "So don't worry. Now I must leave you. If you want to try something ask the girls. And remember to give Libby my love OK?"

Bill was rather tempted by Napoleon's Coronation robes but in the end he settled for something traditional. Black cloak, black tricorn hat and a mask straight out of Joseph Losey's *Don Giovanni* film. Getting into all this gear after the opera wasn't going to be so easy though. He'd caught sight of couples wandering round Venice in fancy dress but he was damned if he was coming back from Palafenice dressed up like an idiot.

In the end Bill did his post-opera changing in a small bar not far from the Palazzo where Libby's masked ball was happening. First he fortified himself with a brandy. Then he stole into the lavatory and did the deed.

No-one seemed to notice as Bill walked back out through the crowded bar looking like he'd got off at the wrong century. He found wearing the mask helped. Helped other people ignore him and helped Bill not care. Maybe that's why Venetians adopted disguise for social occasions, he decided, so they didn't feel complete prats in all this get-up.

On Bill's map the Palazzo Trebbiani was very close to where the *vaporetto* had put him down. Bill was pretty sure he'd already seen it from the canal, its gothic windows ablaze, an eighteenth-century courtesan with walkie-talkie standing on the jetty greeting the water taxis. Finding the Palazzo from the landward side was not so easy however. A road of sorts ran behind all the waterfront properties but there were no entrances, only narrow brick alleyways hardly wide enough for two people to pass and very poorly lit. He headed down one only to find himself back at the Grand Canal. No entrances whatsoever apart from the communal door to several flats. Returning to the roadway, Bill chose another alleyway which turned and twisted and then stopped dead. Marie Antoinette had been right. Nothing was signposted. If this were Britain there would be announcements everywhere: *You Are Now Approaching The Palazzo Trebbiani. Welcome To The Palazzo Trebbiani. Thank You For Visiting The Palazzo Trebbiani. Please Call Again.* Frustrated, Bill tore off his mask and returned to the street.

A couple of Venetians in twenty-first century dress were passing and so Bill asked them if they knew where the Palazzo was. They tried to explain and, failing, took him down a third passageway which once again ended abruptly on the Grand Canal.

"*Questo è il Palazzo!*" announced the husband triumphantly pointing round the corner on to the canal itself.

"Yes but how do I get to it!" asked Bill, irritation creeping into his voice. The couple did not know. Bill thanked them but his "*mille grazie*" sounded considerably less than a *mille*. More like *uno* or *due*.

He returned to the street in exasperation and sat down in a shop doorway. This was like looking for Libby at the Danieli all over again. But worse. To be frustrated and thwarted was one thing but to be frustrated and thwarted while dressed like a total plonker was something else entirely. This was exactly the kind of thing that happens when one gets involved with Libby Ziegler, he thought.

Fortunately at this moment Napoleon came to his rescue. Slightly taller than one might expect, the French Emperor bore down on Bill at speed clutching his camera in one hand and gathering up his train with the other. "*Palazzo Trebbiani*?" Bill asked standing up. The man let out a curious spasm of noise which was probably "Yes" in some rather more obscure Romance language. Whatever native tongue Napoleon spoke he was in too much of a hurry to deal in commonplace pleasantries.

Bill followed the Emperor at speed down the maze of passages and recognised their route as the second of his blind alleys. What Napoleon knew, however, was which dusty old door to push aside as they neared the dead end. Once open, the door let on to a brick courtyard and beyond that a series of arches with the back of Palazzo Trebbiani beyond. They were entering via the servants' entrance but at least Bill had arrived.

Half an hour later he was still thoroughly mystified as to what was going on. No one had asked him to show his invitation or told him where to go. A meal was in progress upstairs, although a string trio continued to play Gluck in the marbled lobby below. Guests in costume came and went in leisurely fashion up and down the double staircase nodding at each other and taking photographs while dinner-jacketed waiters gave Bill champagne cocktails as they passed. No one seemed the slightest bit interested in this stray Don Giovanni hanging round the fireplace. At one point three people in Arabic costume turned up by boat and Bill saw the shivering courtesan, now wearing an anorak, informing someone of their arrival via her walkie-talkie. It seemed not to matter in the slightest whether you were in time for the meal. Bill decided to follow the Arabs upstairs. They bowed to him from behind their masks as he walked alongside and Bill did the same. It was like a secret society. Those in masks only acknowledged the existence of others in masks. A society of anonymous exhibitionists.

Upstairs on the *piano nobile* was a huge salon that presumably stretched from one side of the Palazzo to the other. People sat at the same kind of eight-seater round tables that Bill had seen at Press Awards dinners. Their masks and costumes were splendid but the ambience was altogether more humdrum. Take away the costumes and this could be the Grosvenor Park Hotel. Bill looked on the seating plan to see if he could work out where

Libby might be. There were a few individual names but most tables were blocked out in the host's name. Presumably one or more had been taken by the Baron but Bill was unable to find any place-name that matched that title.

As no one was challenging him, he entered the salon and made a circuit much like the one he'd made at the Hotel Danieli. At least this time he knew what Libby looked like. Still, the masks did an effective job. Mouths and cleavages were all that Bill had to go on and he had no idea how Libby might present in the latter context. She had always tended to wear layers of clothes that kept her actual shape a mystery. Which was not to say that Bill hadn't speculated about her breasts seven years ago, but he couldn't remember coming to any conclusion. This morning Libby had been enveloped in that amazing orange and gold thing. Who knew what lay beneath.

"Seven years later and you're still looking at other women's chests," said a voice next to him. Bill turned to find Libby dressed as a highwayman. Her costume wasn't unlike his own except that, whereas he had a doublet and cloak, she was wearing a riding coat and her mask was smaller, a diamond-studded Dick Turpin job. Her long hair, swept back in a large black bow, completed the illusion. How like Libby not to dress like all the other women.

"How was the opera?" she asked.

"Bad," he said.

"I told you so," said Libby. "Are you reviewing it?"

"Only if I'm feeling vindictive. This place is extraordinary. What's going on?"

"Oh they have them all the time now. For people who can't get over for Carnival," said Libby. "*Ersatis in extremis*. Come on. I'll show you round."

Libby clearly knew the Palazzo well. She took Bill up to the floor above and led him through a series of salons all heavy with ancient furniture, yet none of them seeming to serve a purpose. Suite after suite of reception rooms from the days when palazzi was comprised of people with nothing to do and lots of rooms not to do it in.

"According to local legend Casanova had a conquest here," said Libby, opening the door into a smaller room that might once have held a four-poster. "But then who didn't in Venice? It was where you came to get laid during the Grand Tour."

She flashed a smile at him that was almost a grin, a challenge certainly. Then she closed the door. "The story goes he escaped through a window that's now blocked up. You can see it here. There's another story, with more substance, that Wagner was going to take this place in 1883." She opened another door. "He and Cosima had even ordered children's beds for this room, I've seen the bill of sale. But when Wagner heard about the Casanova connection he turned it down, the old hypocrite. That's what they claim anyway. I don't believe it. Maybe Cosima objected. *Bürgerliche Wohlanständigkeit!*" Libby laughed. "Anyway who knows? Maybe it was just that the owners didn't want to pay for the privilege of having Herr Wagner to stay and he wasn't used to putting his hand in his own pocket. So they went to the Vendramin instead. Not too bad a place to die in." She closed the nursery door and turned round. They were facing each other in the corridor. "*So,* this letter..."

Bill had been admiring Libby's riding boots. It seemed she'd used the pretext of fancy dress to wear even more amazing footwear than the pair she turned up in at St Mark's.

"Are you looking to sell it or what?"

They were *very* face-to-face. This close up, Bill was thrown for a moment.

"Er, no. At this stage I just want it authenticated."

"Do you have it with you?"

Neither of them had stepped back which meant that they continued to stand very close. Closer than would normally be the case. Bill had thought they were going into the Wagner salon and he had taken a step forward. Libby, assuming they weren't going in, had turned back, to find Bill almost touching her. Yet neither moved.

"The letter?" he was saying. "Of course."

"Will you leave it with me?" she was asking.

Bill was unsure about this. He was also unsure whether she had been smaller seven years ago. Maybe it was the boots. He took a step back, intoxicated.

"It's not mine to leave."

"OK."

Libby thought for a moment, then led them out of the corridor back into the smaller salon where she went over to a Louis Quinze desk and switched on the reading lamp.

"Let's see then."

Bill took the letter out of his notebook and passed it over.

Libby opened the plastic bag, placed the letter under the lamp and removed her mask. Bill watched as she leaned forward on her palms to make a proper study. It was a very masculine pose, Bill thought. He caught sight of them in an overmantel and was amused by what he saw. Two eighteenth-century conspirators working by electric candlelight. The highwayman and the Don. Libby read page one and turned the letter over gently. Then she read page two. Bill watched her and looked again at her boots. It was difficult to resist someone who wore boots like that, regardless of what they had done to mess up your life.

This is an important moment, he thought. If she turns to me now and says this is a palpable forgery then I will have wasted a few days of my life. That's all. If she says it's authentic then this will be significant. I don't know why, I don't know in what way, but I know it.

Watching Libby Bill realised that he was no longer taking the letter at any value Katz might have put on it. This was entirely his own instinct now. Libby looked up, smiling. She entices me and alarms me in equal measure, thought Bill.

"Well," she said. "What do you think, Bill?"

He wished she hadn't asked him that. It seemed unnecessary, even cruel. "I came to you for what *you* think," he replied in tones sterner than he'd intended. He didn't want Libby to believe she could play with him.

"I think it's a significant find," said Libby.

"You do?"

Libby nodded, folded the letter carefully and put it back in its plastic bag. "Have you been told that it's significant?"

"Yes."

"But you don't know what that significance is?" She seemed almost amused by this fact.

"No. That's why I've come to you."

"So. What do you want to do with it?"

"Do with it?"

Libby was now right in front of him. She had been moving slowly across the room. The letter, still in her hand, was touching his chest. It connected them.

"I want to find out what it's all about," he insisted.

"Why?"

"I'm a journalist."

"And if you do find out what'll you do?"

"Look," said Bill, taking the letter with a clear show of irritation. "I came to see you for information. I'm not accountable to you for what I do with that information once I get it. If you're not willing to talk to me on that basis then I'll take it somewhere else." He could see they were both a little surprised by this outburst.

"OK," said Libby, as if she were weighing this up. She turned away from him, hands steepled together like a priest in thought. "OK. I think you'll find there's a lot of interest in this letter. I didn't know it existed. I don't know how you got hold of it but I imagine there are people who'd pay quite a bit for that letter."

Bill was amazed. Katz was right.

"Why?"

"Well there are lots of reasons," she said. "Have you eaten?"

He had. A pre-opera pizza. Several hours ago.

"What about you?" Bill asked. "Haven't you just eaten downstairs?"

"What, with that crowd of jackasses?" Libby looked shocked. Then she laughed. "I was only here to meet someone and it looks like a no-show tonight." She seemed disappointed but recovered immediately. "Look, what say we–"

One of the large double doors opened and a figure looked in. Bill somehow knew who it would be even before his eyes grew accustomed to the bright lights of the stairwell.

"Hauke..?" said Libby. There was a lot of meaning in that question. It asked something specific.

Hauke, not in costume, still in that damnable blazer of his, nodded. He didn't pay any attention to Bill whatsoever.

"Look we'll have to finish this some other time," said Libby to Bill, picking up her mask. She was in a hurry now. "I'll ring you."

Bill wondered what the hell was going on. "Shall I see you tomorrow? I can delay my flight."

"Sorry Bill I've got to go." Libby seemed very definite, very serious. He would have said excited but her eyes seemed anxious. Bill watched as she tied on her mask.

"I'll give you a call," she said.

"When?"

"*Soon.*"

What was in that look she gave him? He couldn't tell now the mask was in place. She was gone. Already walking to the door. Walking out of my life, thought Bill. As you always do. Going. It's what you do best. Being left behind with a mess that makes no sense. That's what I do.

Libby was already at the open door. Hauke stepped aside so she could pass. "Look after that letter, Bill!" she called back.

Damn you, thought Bill. Damn you for the stupid, self-indulgent, self-regarding spoilt little bitch you are. And yet he already knew what this feeling was. God, he was falling in love with Libby Ziegler again. Despite his best endeavour exactly what he'd always known would happen had happened.

Louis would be delighted.

❖ THE FIRST CASUALTY OF LOVE

BILL COULDN'T SETTLE. He had no wish to write meaningless articles for second-rate publications and all publications were second-rate today. Worse, his view down the Wye Valley seemed bland and rain-sodden after Venice. Bill hated the Wye. Its very name spoke volumes. Why the hell was he here in the middle of nowhere? No friends, no colleagues and an ex-wife who was taking his daughter to London. And as for Libby. Why was he anywhere that she was not? Yes he had let it happen. All Bill knew now was that Libby was somewhere out there, out of contact and desperately outside his life. Except she wasn't outside his life was she? Outside his ability to contact her, yes, but most definitely *inside* his life. That was the whole damn problem. He had no idea how it had happened but that moment when Libby had turned round and they found themselves face-to-face, closer than two people should be when those two people have no intention of kissing, part of him had been seized with the notion of possessing her.

She'd felt it too. He was sure. You don't get that feeling on your own. She'd started teasing him about the letter, hadn't she? She'd walked over to him holding it in her hand until the paper made contact between them. She had broken the touch taboo like Tamsin had broken it last year with that finger on his lips. They were connected and it had to be only a matter of time before her fingers connected directly with his, and his with hers and Bill pressed her down, back against that desk...

Bill got up and paced the room again. He'd written one sentence so far. One bloody sentence. That was all. One stupid sentence about the state of opera in Venice, when nobody was interested, not even the Venetians. All they wanted was tourism. They certainly weren't interested in his views – and neither was Bill. All he wanted to do was hold Libby and force her into the dimly lit salon, his mouth on hers. Nothing should have stopped them. They were ready in that moment. It was bizarre. What was it? Lust, it must have been. He hadn't felt anything like this for years. After that first evening with Marika he'd sworn he'd never go back to her farm, but three weeks later he'd had some intimations of desire and made a subsequent half-hearted visit. With Tamsin it had been familiarity and fondness that had drawn them into bed. But this was different. This was immediate. This was compulsion. This was hate turned bizarrely into desire.

Yet had he ever really hated her at all? Bill had left his office now and was moving to the sound system. He knew what he was doing: he was revising the past. Libby didn't trample his life down, Libby didn't create unthinking destruction wherever she went. She brought him alive. She had done the same all those years ago when he was just a jobbing journalist keen to move into the arts. She had opened up a world for him. He was sure of it. Maybe he'd just pretended to hate her all these years because he didn't want to admit how much he'd missed her when he found himself stranded in a world without her. Maybe he only hated her because doing so was the price of readmission to his marriage.

How much of this revision were true Bill didn't know but he knew he had to find her. He should have stayed in Venice and waited till she got back. Why on earth had he returned to Holt's Cottage? Bill opened the tape deck.

The truth was that the absence of Libby hadn't really hit him until he got in his Jeep at Heathrow and started to drive down the M4. Passing his regular service station Bill had suddenly remembered the cassette he'd bought on his return journey after that Israeli trip. It was still in the glove compartment. He had laughed in disbelief to think that he'd got Vita to send him some Wagner down the phoneline from New York when here was Siegfried's Death March "*as featured in John Boorman's Excalibur*". It had been sitting in his car all the time.

Squatting by the stereo now, Bill did what he'd done yesterday on the M4. He inserted the tape and rewound it to the Death March. In the concert arrangement it wasn't preceded by singing so there was no sound to be heard from the dying Siegfried himself. No clues to what was *neben* the *leitmotiv*, but Bill wasn't interested in clues now. He knew what he needed. There were angry hammer blasts in the funeral march, a sound that matched the blackness of his own desire for Libby, and yet, as he had discovered yesterday, there was so much poignancy in the opening. Yes, there were kettle drums which marked out the stunned silence that follows Siegfried's death. Yes, there was something very deep in the brass, something suggestive of a low mourning. But the whole thing opened in a much more minor key than Bill had remembered before he first turned the tape on yesterday. It was like the stunned but ominous calm that follows a terrible, terrible shock.

Then come the double basses notching up a series of ugly black notes like deep brutal sobs. Then the crashing, the first snarl of angry drums and brass. Then a theme of haunting melancholy from the horns. Then more drums and brass. It was like grief, Bill thought as he lay down across the sofa. A grief wholly inescapable, a grief that will not simply allow the bereaved to find peace in anything dignified or elegiac.

Now woodwind reprising the *leitmotiv* of Siegfried's love for Brünhilde. Now strings gathering in force and anguish. Now tubas gathering too. Now trumpets blasting in with another great crash, smashing down on the elegiac, like a wave bringing something violent in its wake. And finally the death march itself. Here was the roar of proto-fascism, Bill thought and, rising out of it, a theme of heroism, first on the trumpets, now on the horns. Heroism riding roughshod over everyone. Bill drew his legs up as the whole thing built, higher and higher, like a series of waves. As each one crashes so another builds, he thought. Building and crashing. Crashing and building.

And yet at the end Bill wasn't left with anger at all. At the end the final image in his mind was that of harp and woodwind and a return again to yearning as the strings ebbed darkly away, ebbing until Bill caught the plaintive cry of the Rhine Maidens lamenting their missing gold.

So much absence, so much missing. This march wasn't destruction; it was unresolved emotion and it wasn't at all what Bill had expected. Not the anger that Wagner might have felt for a cowardly death dealt out to his hero by Hagen, but loss. *Loss.* Bill knew all about that.

So Wagner did for him. It did for him now in Holt's Cottage as it did for him on the M4 as he returned from Venice. By the time he was crossing the Severn Bridge, Bill had played that march ten times over and in it he could hear his own yearning for Libby. He had seen her in the poignancy of the woodwind as she was summoned by Hauke to disappear into the light. He had seen Hauke's despicably handsome face swing its loathsome eyes impassively in his direction before departing after her.

And Bill's anger against this man was like the crashing chords that bore down repeatedly on the yearning within Wagner's music. He would be revenged on Hauke. He would find Libby. His was the cry at the end of the music. Loss. Such loss. Two people did not often feel as he and Libby had done in the Palazzo Trebbiani.

Bill got up from the sofa and stretched in an agony of expectation and frustration. He was unsure whether he was in love with Libby or with the music. As long as he kept clear of the *Vorspiel* from *Tristan und Isolde* he reminded himself. That was a dangerous piece of music, not for the emotionally vulnerable. Keep clear of *Tristan* and he'd be OK. Nevertheless Bill was playing Siegfried incessantly. And loudly.

"What the hell's that?" Lee had asked when he met Bill with the post that morning.

"Wagner," said Bill.

"Noisy bugger," said Lee.

"No that's me," said Bill. "Volume control."

"Ah," said Lee listening. "Gets to you though. Didn't he do that *Apocalypse Now*?"

"'Ride of the Valkyries'," said Bill.

"Ah love the smell of napalm in the morning," said Lee, in what might have been an impersonation of Robert Duvall had Duvall been a Brit intent on sounding like John Wayne.

It was now midday as Bill put the tape on yet again. He had still only written one sentence and he still hadn't shaved. He had to do something. He had to find Libby. Bill had already rung the University and her flat. There was no reply at home. Not even an answer-machine on which he could end up saying something stupid. Her direct line at the University did have a machine but Bill had chosen not to leave a message. Hauke would get to it first and make sure it wasn't passed on.

There had been an e-mail address on the card. Bill decided the time had come to go for that. He had a feeling that Libby might be assiduous about picking up her e-mails.

Next door the funeral march was beginning to gather its tortured momentum again as Bill typed in Libby's address and began the message:

> *Dear Libby,*
>> *It was good to see you again.*
>> *I'm sorry you had to rush off.*
>> *I think we have a lot to discuss.*
>> *Call me as soon as you can.*

He then typed "*Bill*" and his phone number with UK code. Was that line about her rushing off a mistake? Did it sound as if he resented her for doing so? He *was* sorry though. And he wasn't suggesting she'd had a choice in the matter.

He sat back and reread his words. They were so few. They suggested so little of what had been going on since she parted from him. Maybe he should head the e-mail *Turmoil* or *I Don't Hate You After All*. Or *Maybe I Love You*. In the end Bill settled for "*After Venice*." At least that way she might understand that he had hopes of a future beyond those few minutes which they had shared.

Who was he kidding? He had not been in Libby's thoughts for the past seven years the way that she had been in his. That meeting, the heady significance of their exchange upstairs, it might all be in his head.

Still if he didn't try now he'd never know. Bill pressed Send. Two things struck him as he did so. First, he had had his chance now. From now on his role was to wait, and waiting was almost as bad as no contact at all. Second, sending an e-mail would mean he'd end up receiving all the e-mails with which Vita's fact-checkers were bombarding him:

> *Dear Bill,*
>
> *We have found 57 references to the name Heinz spelt with a final zee but 1 reference with an 's' instead of a zee. Please confirm that the correct spelling is with or without a final zee...*

Was it ever worth writing for the *New York Times*?

Bill was making coffee when the telephone rang. He got to the phone in time to hear the receiver being put down. Not Katz's people again surely? Bill was just about to 1471 the call when the phone went again.

"Hello?"

"It's Timna," said a voice.

"Who?"

"Tamsin," the voice replied.

"You just said Timna," Bill told her.

"That was the name my parents gave me," she said.

"You're changing your name back?" Bill asked.

"I didn't say that. I'm just using it," said Tamsin. "I forgot you know me as Tamsin."

"For fourteen years," Bill reminded her.

"Please Bill, don't be difficult."

"I'm not being difficult!"

Why was it every time they were in contact she accused him of starting an argument? "Did you ring just a minute ago?" Bill asked.

"No."

"Oh, someone did."

"You asked me that last time I rang," said Tamsin sounding aggrieved.

"Yes. Well someone keeps ringing me and putting the phone down," said Bill.

"Why should you think that's me?"

"Because it's always you who rings immediately afterwards."

"Well I would have thought that suggests I'm the one person it isn't," said Tamsin.

She could be so logical and irritating at times, Bill thought. "What can I do for you?" he asked.

"I've got to go away just for a few days and Reah says she'd like to stay with you. I didn't know if you were back."

"Yes, sure," said Bill. "Where are you at the moment?"

"In London," said Tamsin.

"Ah," said Bill.

"Don't say it like that," said Tamsin. It was true. The word London as spoken by Tamsin did summon up unpleasant associations for Bill at the moment.

"I just hope you don't expect me to come all the way down there to fetch her," said Bill.

"No, Jess will bring her. She could bring her up on Wednesday if that's all right with you."

Bill said it was fine. It would be good to have Reah in the cottage again. She made it feel lived in.

"Tell Jess I can meet her on the other side of the Severn Bridge if you like," he said. "Save her paying the toll."

"No it's OK," said Tamsin. "She's got to feed Jethro and pick some things up from the house for me."

"OK," said Bill, wondering what it was that Tamsin needed so urgently. "When will you be coming back?"

"I'm not sure," said Tamsin.

'You're going away but you're not sure when you're coming back?" Bill asked.

"Oh just a few days," said Tamsin sounding flustered. "I'll be back before Reah's term starts."

"What about you?" Bill asked.

"What about me?"

"Won't you be starting back soon?"

"I've resigned," said Tamsin.

Bill was shocked. "I thought you weren't moving till the summer," he said, feeling the ground shifting beneath his feet again.

"I need time to sort things."

"What things?"

He heard Tamsin take a deep breath. "Bill I'm not willing to have this discussion. We agreed that anything to do with the move would be discussed through our solicitors."

Bill could feel an argument coming on. He was about to point out nothing had been agreed, that she had simply imposed, but why bother? On this occasion he held back. "OK," he said. "When shall I expect Reah?"

"I'll have to ring you back about that."

"Is there a number I can get you at while you're away?" Bill asked. This was standard procedure between the pair of them.

Tamsin hesitated. "You can ring my parents."

"I don't have their number," he replied.

Again Tamsin hesitated. "Oh, you can use my mobile," she said.

There was a silence. "Well have a nice time," he said at last.

"Bill don't. Please," she replied.

"Don't what?! I just said have a nice time."

"This is precisely what I wanted to avoid," said Tamsin and she put the phone down.

That woman is going crazy Bill thought to himself as he looked at the receiver. Then he thought about Reah's description of Tamsin's behaviour. He had never given much credence to her complaints before. Reah complained a lot about her mother, but she probably complained equally about him to Tamsin. Bill had always considered his ex-wife a good mother. Now however he felt uneasy with the thought that Reah might be on the receiving end of these peculiar mood swings.

With a sudden burst of irritation Bill realised that Tamsin had once again prevented him from running a 1471 check on the previous caller. Maybe she was in league with the mysterious heavy breather of Bristol.

Later in the day Bill was taking a look at that loose gatepost when he heard the telephone ringing. He checked his watch. It was 2pm, dangerously close to working hours in New York, so Bill took his time walking back in. Best to let the answer-machine catch all the flak from Vita's minions:

> Hi Bill, we have two references to Jaffa. One states that it is a settlement on the coast of modern Israel. The other that it is a make of jam. Please confirm whether you visited an Israeli town or a fruit preserve...

Bill arrived in time to hear the phone going down at the other end. He pounced across his office and seized the phone. "Hello! Who is this?" There was no reply.

He tried to trace the call but the machine's voice told him, "You were called today at 14.05 hours. We do not have the caller's number to return the call." Office, international or mobile. Damn.

There was a knock at the door. For a moment Bill was thrown. No one knocked at his door unless it was Lee with an overlarge parcel or ramblers who'd got lost. Bill walked through into the living room and saw two figures in the open doorway: a man and a woman framed against the light. From the way that the man was leaning into the cottage Bill could see that he was about to knock again.

"Mr Wheeler?" he asked on sighting Bill.

"Yes," said Bill, walking forward slowly.

"May we come in?" He was older than Bill, smart and dressed for travelling. He carried a dark navy mackintosh over his arm. His was a hefty presence; so much so that he all but obliterated his female companion from view.

"We would like to ask you some questions," said the man.

"Oh yes?" said Bill, getting to the door and closing the gap. "May we come in?" The man reached for Bill's door handle. "We'd rather speak inside if you don't mind."

"Take your hand off my door," said Bill, surprised by the sudden flood of cold anger within him. The man paused but he wasn't thrown by Bill's show of aggression.

"I have some identification," he said, reaching into his breast pocket.

"Do you have a search warrant?" said Bill.

"No," the man replied in an attempt to sound amused by the very idea. "We don't wish to search you."

"And you're not going to get the chance," said Bill, seizing the leading edge of the door. His visitor also took hold of the door, just below Bill's grasp. Bill could feel his strength.

"We simply want to ask you some questions, Mr Wheeler."

"Get out," said Bill. Sudden and inexplicable hatred was pounding through his veins now. "Get off my land."

"Please, Mr Wheeler," said the woman from behind. Bill had forgotten she was there. Glancing down at her he saw a face full of reason but hard-set and plain, framed by closely cropped hair. The accent had an unwelcome trace of the enemy in it. *German.* That did it. As if a spring was suddenly released inside him, Bill stepped back, letting the door fly open. The burly man stumbled for a moment and, as the door slammed back on its hinges, Bill had his shotgun down from its hooks. The man regained his footing and backed away instinctively.

"Go!" said Bill, making sure that the barrel was pointed straight at his uninvited guest. For one moment he could easily have pulled the trigger but the next found him checking in his own mind that the thing had not been left loaded. No he was sure. He was sure. He was sure. But he was frightened how easily he could have pulled that trigger a moment ago.

Bill advanced on the couple. He had never threatened anyone with a gun before and was amazed how totally people fell in with your wishes. It was like having a magic wand. "Go!" he shouted again.

The couple backed down the small pathway but the woman turned as she reached Bill's gate. "We only wished to ask some questions."

"I've had your sort of questions before," Bill shouted. "You usually wait till I'm out don't you? Well not today. You come back again and I'll blow your fucking heads off!" He slammed the door shut behind them, almost taking it off its hinges, then he leaned against it, knees buckling, and collapsed on the floor. He was panting. He'd had too much coffee, he told himself. And he was still suffering the shock of that burglary. And the shock of Tamsin taking Reah. But it felt bloody good to have struck back in some way. He crawled across the floor to the kitchen and ran a large glass of water. Bill knew that soldiers in battle got phenomenally thirsty. That was exactly how he felt now.

He half-walked, half-stumbled to the nearest armchair with his glass of water; his legs almost gave way again at one point. He drank deep and could have fallen asleep but the office phone began to ring. What he wanted to do was succumb, to drift away on this sudden soporific tidal wave but that bloody ringing was too insistent. Unable to wait for the answer-machine to catch it Bill picked up the kitchen portable.

"Hello?"

"Mr Wheeler. My name is Clements. Dave Clements."

"Ah." Bill tried to steady his breathing.

"At the moment I'm sitting in a blue Landrover outside your cottage."

"Are you?"

"I'm also a former constable, a sergeant, in the Mercian Constabulary."

"Really."

"In fact if you'll come to the door you'll see Miss Mertens and me." Bill was impressed. Clements clearly wasn't going to be put off by a shotgun. His curiosity got the better of him and he unbolted the door. "Well, so you are, Mr Clements."

"My companion and I are employees of a company with offices in the South West. Miss Mertens is an assistant to the UK Director and I work as company driver."

Bill regarded the vehicle and the two figures visible through its steamed-up windscreen. Clements in the driver's seat had parked halfway down the lane on the left. Miss Mertens seemed very small indeed. She had either shrunk or was trying to get something out of the glove compartment. Clements cleared the window with his hand to ascertain that Bill was indeed at the front door. His action made it look as if he were waving.

Bill was tempted to wave back. The two men made silent eye-contact.

"As I said, I am a former sergeant with the Mercian Constabulary," Clements continued. "If I were to report the fact that you turned a firearm on Miss Mertens and me a number of things would happen. You would almost definitely be required to go down to the station in Chepstow. You would almost definitely be handcuffed for the journey and you would almost definitely lose your licence to carry a firearm. You might get away with a caution."

Bill's mind was spinning. He had no fight left in him for the moment. The best thing seemed to be... what? He couldn't tell. He was unable to think.

"Mr Wheeler?"

"Yes?" Bill replied, summoning up his flagging resources of insouciance.

"Can I ask you why you pointed a gun at us?"

"I – I er, thought you were burglars," said Bill.

"Burglars don't normally knock at the door," said former Sgt Clements. "Why did you think we were burglars, Mr Wheeler?"

"Someone broke in here last week."

"Did you report this burglary?"

"No."

"Why did you think we had burgled you?" asked Clements. It was a good point. Bill ran the story quickly through his head and realised that in order to explain the connection between the German Miss Mertens and the loss of that Wagner book last week he'd have to refer to the fact that he was in possession of Martin Katz's letter.

"Um, well I think I may have overreacted. The stuff stolen was German material relating to Richard Wagner and she, your companion, she sounded German."

"My companion," said Clements. "Is an employee of a Swiss engineering firm trading in Britain, Mr Wheeler. I am also employed by them. I did offer to show you identification."

"Yes, I think you did," said Bill, his mouth dry. He leaned back against the door jamb feeling foolish, but Clements wasn't finished with him.

"You are aware, aren't you, that any defence of your property must not exceed reasonable force?" The voice was calm but laced with dislike. It was a very urban voice, curious in these surroundings, flat, procedural and worrying. "It can only be a matter of meeting force with equal force and nothing more. By pointing a firearm at Miss Mertens and me you are taking matters several steps beyond reasonable force. You could have seriously hurt someone."

"Yes, I see," said Bill. Not that he believed this engineering nonsense, but there were two of them and one of him; Clements, moreover, was a former police officer whereas Bill was an oddball, one of the English who lived in the hills, a man with no friends and a gun licence he'd forgotten to renew. Who were the Chepstow Police more likely to believe?

"I'm sure we don't want to discuss this at the station." Bill looked at where Clements sat. The man wasn't moving, his hand still holding the mobile to his ear. "Might I suggest you invite us in, Mr Wheeler?"

A few minutes ago Bill and his gun had ruled the world. Now he was at his victims' mercy.

Once inside, it was the woman who did most of the talking. Bill kept his eyes on Clements. It was a wonder that he hadn't spotted him straight off as a former police heavy. Those civilian clothes fitted Sgt Clements with the precision of a uniform.

Miss Mertens seemed to be a woman without charm. She accepted Bill's offer of tea with minimal grace and sat down, folding the pleats of her skirt. Maybe they'd got off on the wrong footing, Bill thought. Gunpoint doesn't bring out the best in any of us.

Mug in hand Bill sat down opposite Miss Mertens. Clements continued to stand however, so Bill explained that he'd be happier if they all sat. *Please*. It did no harm to try and set his own terms, to seize the initiative back.

"I wonder do you know a man by the name of Martin Katz?" asked the woman, once Clements had acquiesced.

Bill took his time. He had had a feeling that Katz, Israel or Wagner would crop up sooner or later. He wanted it to sound as if that name wasn't daily in his thoughts. "I wouldn't say I know him. I met him in Israel when I was last there."

"Have you been in contact with him since?"

"No," said Bill. This was odd. If they were working for Katz they would know this. Bill noticed that Clements was tapping his fingers on the arm of his chair.

"I should perhaps tell you that we believe Mr Katz is in possession of some material from a private archive," said the woman.

"Please," said Bill. "Could you stop doing that?" The big policeman looked up. Bill mimed a drumming action with his fingers. Having established himself as a somewhat eccentric – not to say overwrought – character, Bill had decided he should exploit this seeming oversensitivity. "I'm sorry," said Bill, turning back to Mertens. "Did you say he's been arrested?"

"No, but we are aware of numerous phone-calls he has made to this address."

"I thought you were in engineering," said Bill.

"Mr Katz has been working for our employer."

So he'd got it wrong. They weren't working for Katz at all. "What is the name of your company?" Bill asked, watching the small blonde hairs around the mouth of his interlocutor twitch as she took a sip of her tea. He wondered how old she was. Bill was finding it much easier to keep his cool than he had expected. He was a dangerous eccentric after all. The role was useful. "We are employed by a Mr Schmidt of Interlaken," said the woman. "I think that is all you need to know."

"Common name, Schmidt," said Bill, but she was not going to be distracted.

"According to a telephone log that is kept on all company phones Mr Katz has made a number of calls to this number."

Bill looked at her and she at him. "Not that I've been aware of," he said. It must have been obvious to her that he genuinely hadn't heard from Katz.

"As recently as yesterday," she replied, pointedly but to no effect.

"I haven't spoken to Mr Katz since he introduced himself to me in Tel Aviv," said Bill.

The woman clearly didn't like this reply. It left her with nowhere to go. She tried a new tack. "We checked out this number a few days ago from our office in Bristol," she said. "It connects with you."

That doesn't prove anything, thought Bill, though it did explain something else.

"We understand Mr Katz has approached a number of journalists with material from an archive," the Mertens woman continued.

"Yes," said Bill. "Wagner material. He talked to me about letters. Scandalous letters." Bill had thought it was probably a good idea to use the plural, get that detail wrong. Talk about one letter and it may sound as if he knew too much. May even sound as if he'd read it. "I checked his story out with a contact in New York," he continued. "They said that Katz has been spinning this yarn to a number of journalists but that he's never come up with any proof. I decided he was a waste of time. Can I ask you why you're asking me these questions?"

Bill saw Clements look away at this point. Maybe he was bored. He'd got them in. His job was done unless this madman menaced Miss Mertens again. The woman put down her cup of tea. It was a signal that she was cutting to the chase. "We are looking for a letter. One letter that Mr Katz has claimed to possess, but which he claims no longer to possess."

"So why do you come to me?" Had Katz told these people that Bill had taken it?

"Mr Katz telephones this number frequently. We think he thinks you might know where it is."

"Do engineering firms often tap people's phones?" Bill asked.

"It is common practice and quite legal to keep a log," replied Miss Mertens. "Our colleagues in Switzerland do not monitor conversations; our employer is, however, growing impatient."

"Look," said Bill. "Martin Katz hasn't phoned me. I haven't spoken to him since we parted company in Israel. That's the truth. I don't care what your bugging device tells you." Interesting, thought Bill. Katz either doesn't know what happened in the taxi or he's guessed and is keeping it secret from these two.

"We speak for someone who offers a reward for the return of that letter," the woman explained.

"I don't have it," Bill lied. Immediately he wished he hadn't. There was no stepping back from that kind of statement. He also wished he'd taken a different tack, asked who his would-be benefactor might be, but instead he talked on to try and distract Mertens. "I don't know Martin Katz. He did not give me anything when we met and I haven't received anything by post from him. Until now it never occurred to me that this Wagner letter really existed."

"You know then that it is from Richard Wagner?" asked the woman, hoping she had found a chink in Bill's defences. Bill hesitated a moment. Images of a letter he was claiming not to have seen, let alone possess, flashed in front of him. He tried to keep calm.

"Yes, Mr Katz told me that. Anyway I thought we'd established that it was a Wagner letter. He didn't say who to or what about. He just said it would create a scandal if it were ever published."

"And do you intend to publish it?" asked the woman. Her skills as an interrogator were surprisingly clumsy. This clearly wasn't her normal job. Maybe she really was Mr Schmidt's PA.

"I don't have it," Bill repeated.

"Then why is Mr Katz telephoning you?"

"He isn't!" said Bill. "Or at least there is someone who keeps ringing me and hanging up when they get the answer-machine. That may be him. I don't know." It was all beginning to make more sense now. There was Katz, working from a desk in Interlaken, wondering if Bill had the missing letter and suspecting that his phone was being tapped. Of course he would ring but not leave any message, especially one that might incriminate him. Clearly the same thoughts were beginning to fall into place for the woman sitting opposite Bill too. Even so, why would Katz be phoning Bill if Bill didn't have the letter? This question occurred to Miss Mertens about the same time it occurred to Bill. "I really don't know," he continued, "I don't even know if it is him."

"Have you tried tracing the call?"

Bill explained that he had, but that the British telephone system often didn't give out numbers if they came from a PABX or foreign caller.

"So these calls may come from Switzerland," said the woman.

"Yes they may come from Switzerland I suppose, but equally they may not. There's no way of telling and I've no idea why he's ringing me. He told me he'd spoken to a number of journalists about this letter. Maybe he's ringing them too."

"No," said Sgt Clements, suddenly peevish. Obviously he'd had enough. "He is only ringing you. Several times a day. He thinks you are important. Why is that Mr Wheeler?" Miss Mertens looked peeved. Clements had exceeded the brief of an office driver.

"Look," said Bill. "I really don't know." He stood up. "And I really think I've been very patient." But neither of them joined him. Bill may have succeeded in deflecting their enquiries but he wasn't free yet. "If you don't mind I'd like to get back to my work..." He walked towards the door, hoping to force the issue.

The woman rose and, to Bill's relief, Clements followed, but as she moved towards the door a thought seized Miss Mertens. "When we arrived, Mr Wheeler, you said 'You usually wait till I'm out.' Have you been visited by other people asking you about this letter?"

"No," said Bill, holding the door open and wishing like hell they would go. Neither tormentor moved. "But as I said, I was burgled, last week," he added reluctantly. "I assumed you'd come back."

"Why did you think we were the burglars?" asked Sgt Clements, the smile on his face immediately flustering Bill. Damn, he'd started too soon to think it was all over.

"I've already told you," said Bill.

"Remind me," said Clements.

"Because the lady here has a German accent."

"And you suspect your burglars to be German-speaking because..?"

Bill floundered. "Because the material stolen was German," Bill began. "I've already told you this."

"You have a lot of German material in your home, do you?"

"No, not anymore," said Bill, "Now I really think I've been very patient."

"You have a lot of German material," Clements continued. "Material relating to Richard Wagner, but you don't have Mr Katz's letter, is that it?"

"Look, we've had a lot of burglaries round here," Bill improvised. "I've seen you here before, both of you. On the edge of the woods, spying on this place. The same day as the break-in, in fact." He was surprised how well this was going. "Don't think I'm fooled by all this Swiss West Country engineering business and getting the police to back you up. You've been here before."

The man and woman looked at each other. "Now please will you go," said Bill, taking hold of the door. He was getting angry again. He could feel it. In his simulated rage Bill was stirring up genuine anger too. Moreover the heady possibility of escape was making Bill's heart race with adrenaline. "Just go!"

Clements wanted to tough it out Bill could tell but the woman decided it was time to walk. "We may have more questions," she said as she passed.

"Well I won't have any more answers," Bill replied. Clements followed her, glancing at Bill as he passed. It was a look of deeply unpleasant neutrality. "And you are *not* a driver," snapped Bill. He closed the door behind them, locked it and went in search of a large whisky.

Bill sat back in his old battered sofa and listened to Wagner. Whisky and Wagner – it was quite a combination. Bill tried to focus his thoughts on the people he was dealing with here. There was Katz who had had the letter. There were the odd couple from Switzerland who claimed to represent the owner or owners of the letter. And there may have been person or persons unknown watching from the wood the day Bill's book went missing, assuming they weren't PC Plod and the Mertens creature. People who had broken in and left him that distinctly Wagnerian clue. No doubt they'd be back.

Three groups, thought Bill. The question was... He'd had the question for a moment but when the alcohol bit he lost it. The question was... No, in fact there were two questions: firstly, who was the owner or owners? Secondly, who were the house-breakers working for? Did the owner(s) commission the housebreakers? If not, that made for a third question. Bill tried to assemble all the players in his mind: Katz, the owner(s), the house-breakers – and Mertens and Clements, don't forget them. Four groups. No, five if the housebreakers were working for someone other than Katz or the owners. He stared at the ceiling. What was everyone's interest in this letter? Four questions. Make that four. What was it about this letter that made up to five groups of people so interested in getting hold of it? Bill fished it out of his notebook. With all the folding and unfolding it was getting fragile along the crease. Not just five people. Libby had been interested too hadn't she? What was it she'd said? "Have you been told of its significance?"

What was its significance? Why were people willing to pay over the odds for this crinkly piece of Wagnerian scribble? Libby had suggested as much so it must be true. Katz had gone further. He had also suggested people would kill to get it off him. That Bill did not believe. It was a mystery. He returned the original to its plastic bag and went into his office where the three translations were now kept in the file sneakily marked 'Swalec'.

The answer-machine was flashing as Bill entered. When did he miss a call? How apt it would be if this proved to be the sound of Martin Katz's fat hand putting down the phone, but it wasn't. Bill clicked the machine to play while he fished out his translations.

The voice of Rory Llewellyn Goetz came on the line. "Mr Wheeler, Goetz here. I've been having further conversations with a colleague of mine..."

"I don't believe it," said Bill.

"I think this may be easier if I put something in the post to you... this word *neben* really is very imprecise... I'll write to you in the next day or so."

"You do that," answered Bill. He sat with the three translations on his lap and pinched his eyes wearily.

> *My worthy friend,*
>
> *What a brute I am to wait so long before replying to your solicitous enquiry! I must excuse myself on the grounds that many things have been happening here of a distressing nature, as you may imagine.*
>
> *That S—— is going around saying these things makes the suspicion sprout in me that he too might be a Jew!*
>
> *Dear Friend when I am in the midst of musical composition it is possible for me only if I am in a constant ecstatic state and behaving to all the world as a complete eccentric. In these moments who knows what I write?*
>
> *When I consider the phrase our friend refers to I believe he may be right that I did use that old song beneath the leitmotiv that accompanies the hero Siegfried to his funeral pyre but this does not mean that I intended the march to signify Death To The Jews. I merely drew on ABCGH because it served my purpose. The death of Judaism and of Jesuitry will be achieved by means greater than my music but if my*

music can play its part in this mechanism of wheels I would be delighted!

However if S—— speaks to you again I would urge you to ignore him. Having answered his letter once I see no reason to do so again.

Here however, my friend, things get worse. I had hoped, as you know, to endure no more special relationships of the kind that scars me still.

I have courted the affection of nobody, as you know, and I leave people to think of me as they please but if a finger of unconditional love is held out to me from anywhere I seize the whole hand and draw the mortal towards me.

I am such a child! I know no first or last midst those my heart belongs to. I've only one heart and whoever dwells there is sole tenant from top to bottom. You know dear friend of the one I speak of whose love for me was of the purest, noblest kind. This one however I love as my own child, as the All Father his daughter. Yet what hope is there for me? She cannot love me as I her. Siegmund had the love of his sister and Siegfried his Brünhilde but I am allowed no such consolation and will allow myself none. As for my wife, she refused this morning to embrace me. She knows my heart as well as I do. You will understand therefore why this matter of S—— has not touched me but I thank you, my friend, for concerning yourself with it on my behalf.

Bill stopped reading. It was just the stuff about the chambermaid going to visit her dad and further unsubstantiated despair. Why was this letter of so much value? He put the translations back in their file and turned his attention to the state of opera in Venice. After all the excitement of today, it would be good to get some routine work done.

Wednesday dawned bright. Bill, who knew little of these things, thought he detected fresh notes in the birdsong outside his office. At about 4.30 in the afternoon he heard a car stop outside. He was just about to get up to see who was there when the cottage door burst open and Reah bounced in. "Hi Daddy Boo!"

Bill tried to embrace his daughter and ended up with his face buried in hair. "I thought Tamsin was going to ring."

"Oh you know Mum," said Reah and she broke from him to lug her enormous bag into the cottage.

"Where's Jessica?"

"Gone to the house. She's got to pick up Mum's passport and fill Jethro's feeder."

"What's she want her passport for?"

"Search me, she's been so weird."

This was odd. Bill always told Tamsin when he was going abroad. They had an agreement. Then again he couldn't remember when Tamsin had last gone abroad on her own. Maybe they didn't have an agreement, maybe it was just an assumption.

Reah didn't want another hug. There was something she needed to see on TV. This seemed to be her routine these days, straight in and straight onto cans. Bill decided he'd wander down to the farmhouse and see Jessica.

He'd always liked Jessica. She was a little older than Tamsin and had also married out so she'd often acted as a cultural arbiter when Bill had attended family gatherings. Jessica knew the problems that such events posed for the *goy* spouse. He appreciated her willingness to translate, her awareness of all that could overwhelm an outsider.

He hadn't seen Jess for years, hadn't seen her third child, David, at all. David was an afterthought. A tragic afterthought, so Bill had heard. The day of his birth was virtually the last time that Jess had seen her husband. He'd been waiting before telling her that he'd found someone else. Another *goy*, another *yok*, so Bill had understood.

The Walken sisters had separated from their husbands at similar times although in Tamsin's case it hadn't been as dramatic as the desertion that Jess had suffered. He and Tamsin had spun apart slowly, finding more and more barriers blocking the possibility of reconciliation. Was it worse for Jess? Intense pain yet none of the distress that comes with false dawns. Bill wondered how she was.

He knocked at the open farmhouse door. The place was still pretty much furnished as he remembered although one or two paintings had gone. "Hello?" There was no sound. Bill wondered about stepping inside. He and Jessica were on good terms he felt, but he didn't want to overstep the mark. "Hello! Jess?"

Bill heard a noise of footsteps and clothing moving from the living room. The woman who appeared was still recognisably Jessica. She moved purposefully and straight past him towards the kitchen.

"Oh hello Bill, where's Reah?"

"Watching TV," said Bill, somewhat thrown by the way Jess had avoided eye contact. She no longer wore all those flowing clothes, he noticed. Maybe it wasn't that she'd put on weight. Maybe these days she was just dressing in a way that disguised it less well.

"Can I get you anything?" Jess asked, busying herself in the store-room that lay between the kitchen and the front door. She hadn't invited him in so Bill stayed on the threshold.

"No," he replied, somewhat uncomfortably. "No. I just came over to say hello. It's been a long time."

"Well. We all know why that is," said Jess closing a cupboard with pointed precision. She still wasn't looking at him.

"We don't have to be enemies, do we?" Bill asked. "Tamsin and I decided that a divorce was the best thing for both us–"

"Please Bill," said Jess turning. "I know what the story is but I also know what really happened." She looked not just angry but appalled, disgusted, as if she'd rather not even see him.

"I don't know what you're talking about," said Bill. The look in Jess' eye suggested she might hit him were he any closer.

"I think you'd better go," she said. "Timna wouldn't want you in this house and I don't want you here either."

"I don't understand," Bill repeated. He was out of his depth again. First Clements and Mertens, and now his sister-in-law.

"As far as I'm concerned you are Reah's father and we respect you as that. But that's all, Bill. Don't expect anything else from me, not from any of us. Not after what you did."

"We got divorced!" said Bill, stepping into the kitchen. "Divorced, that's all."

"All?" Jess repeated. "God, you make me want to smash something Bill. It's a good job this is Timna's kitchen, not mine!"

"OK," said Bill. "What else am I supposed to have done?"

"Get out," said Jess pointing to Bill's feet on her sister's floor. "This house belongs to my sister, not you. And I have not invited you in."

Shocked, Bill took a step back. "Please, Jess. Tell me. Look, Tamsin and I may have had our problems–"

"Timna," said Jess.

"OK, I gather it's Timna. I only found out the last time she rang me. You've got to give me a while to get used to that." Bill resumed his place on the threshold. "I got involved with someone. Come on Jess. It wasn't even an affair. And it was years ago for goodness sake–"

Jess cut him off with a laugh that was genuine disbelief mixed with outrage that he could be so obtuse. "Bill! How can you stand there? You who are the father of my niece. You who used to play with my children, whom I invited into my home... You who made those vows to my sister. How can you stand there and pretend that you didn't violate her?"

Now he *was* stunned. "Violate?"

Jess looked as if she were about to throw something at him. "You're going to deny it?!"

He tried to find his voice. "Of course I never 'violated' her! I might've knocked her glasses off once when she was kept hitting me, but that was self-defence. I never 'violated' her – whatever you mean by that."

"You're damn lucky she didn't go to the police," said Jess and she grabbed a large metal ladle. "I would have." Bang went the ladle on Tamsin's wooden work-surface.

"What the hell are you talking about?!" Bill demanded. Jess was advancing on him now. Clearly the next thing to be hit by that ladle would be made of flesh and blood.

"In this house, in this very house, while Reah was asleep upstairs, you got Tamsin drunk and then when she refused, you raped her."

The next thing Bill knew, the ladle had caught him a violent blow on the collar bone and was coming back for more. Too surprised to speak, Bill caught the ladle, ripped it out of her hands and threw it across the kitchen. It clattered with an extraordinary amount of noise on to the floor. Then Jess started hitting him with her fists.

"Cut that out!" shouted Bill as he grabbed hold of her wrists.

"Are you going to attack me now?" Jess yelled at him. "Me as well? Eh, Bill? Eh? Eh?"

Bill held her as still as he could and glared into her eyes. "Listen to me Jess. Listen! I did not rape your sister. I swear that. I swear it on Reah's life."

The oath had its effect but not the one he'd hoped for. "How can you bring Reah into this!" Jess hissed at him. "After all that you've done, how can you bring your daughter into this."

"Because it's true," Bill insisted.

"You're hurting my wrists," said Jessica.

"OK, I'm sorry," said Bill, and he released her.

Immediately Jess smacked him across the face. "Bastard!"

"Stop it!" Bill yelled back at her and he made to grab her wrists again. Jess retreated to the kitchen long enough to grab a vase of dusty dried flowers from the nearest work surface and throw it. Bill caught it, just. Then she was throwing more things at him. Bill put down the vase and tried to shield himself with his other arm, Jess shouting at him to get out. Bill did so. A cookery book whizzed by, its pages ripping free of the spine. There was clearly very little point in remaining.

He walked back slowly down the track that led to Holt's Cottage. Was that what Tamsin was telling everyone? Was that what Tamsin believed?

Bill simply could not understand it. Presumably Jess was talking about that evening last year, just before the divorce went through, when they'd ended up in bed together for the last time. But she had been so keen. How could Tamsin be claiming he forced her?

The world had been behaving strangely this week but now it had gone completely off its rocker. Bill felt utterly lost. He found himself longing for Reah and all she represented in his life.

"Hi," she said, looking up from where she was watching TV on headphones. "How's Auntie Jess?"

"Oh fine," said Bill, walking to the sideboard for yet another glass of whisky. Who cared if it wasn't yet six o'clock? He sat down in the same armchair used when Sgt Clements and the Mertens woman quizzed him. "So," he said after a while. "Did Mum say how long you're going to be here?"

"Depends when she gets back," said Reah, glancing up.

"From wherever she's gone," said Bill.

"Yeah."

Planet Bloody Mars, said Bill to himself.

Reah looked concerned, then switched off the TV and came and sat next to him. It was so good to feel his daughter snuggling up under his arm. "Hello Daddy Boo," she said.

"Hi," he replied.

"Boo Boo Bear," she reminded him. "Hello, Boo Boo Bear."

"Hello, Boo Boo," said Bill.

"How about we watch something old and black-and-white tonight?" she asked. Big smile. Nice girl. Normal world. Someone who is always happy to see me.

"Sure."

"And light a fire?"

"Of course." Bill exhaled and let the whisky do its job.

"Oh a lady rang," said Reah. "While you were out."

"American?" asked Bill. He'd been expecting a call from Vita's harpies.

"Yes, she said she'd call back."

"Great," said Bill.

"I asked her if she wanted to leave her name or if there was any message," Reah continued, giving a self-consciously detailed account of how efficient she could be on the phone. "But she just said she'd ring you back another time and that it was about Life After Venice. Does that mean anything to you?"

Bill tried not to react. He didn't even know if Reah had any memory of

Libby's existence all those years ago but this certainly wasn't the time to start explaining. "She didn't leave a number?"

"No."

"I'll just go and check 1471 in case I can ring her back." He got up. "*New York Times,*" he lied.

Of course 1471 would not have the number to tell him where Dottoressa Ziegler was. 1471 was in league with all the other little things that go wrong in life, all the irritations and instances of outrageous ill-fortune: flat tyres, PCs that crash before you've got round to saving, and women who only ring you back when you're out of the house being beaten and berated by a half-crazed former sister-in-law.

Bill sat down and wrote Libby an e-mail. In fact he wrote two. The first simply stated that he was sorry to miss her and gave her times at which she might more successfully contact him. He added that he hoped they could meet again. "*Soon?*" he typed, horribly aware of a silence that now hung in the air. The silence of Bill not talking to Libby. Even in anticipation the sensation of it was bleak. Bill sent his message in a somewhat gloomy state of mind. How often would Libby be able to check her e-mails from wherever she was now? It could be days.

Within half an hour the prospect of those days had got to him. Bill had just started preparing stir-fry veg when he broke off to write a long passionate e-mail about his own feelings having now re-met Libby and then seeing her taken away like that. Almost every sentence had to be corrected. He could so easily seem obsessive. Maybe he was, pouring out his heart in this way to a woman he hadn't seen for seven years.

Bill stared at the screen. What he wanted was for Libby to reply. He didn't need to write all this emotional guff. It provided no consolation for the fact that he had no idea where she was in the world, that as every silent minute passed he felt he had less and less hope of hearing from her.

> *I do not know if you have any feelings for me still, or even what your original feelings were. I cannot believe what has happened. For me feelings that have lain dormant have torn through me. I'm lost. I just need to see you, even if it is to find out that you share none of these feelings. That I'm imagining the whole thing. When will I see you? Ever?*

Bill was still staring. This was not an e-mail; it was an entry for his diary, were he the kind of person who kept a diary. As he reread it for the second time he couldn't help noticing how often he'd repeated the word 'feelings' But this was not a piece of journalism. It wasn't for publication. OK, so what was it for?

"Dad?" said Reah at the door. Bill swung round, fearing she could see the screen. He moved to click Save, then stood up to obscure Reah's view.

"Hi," he said as the machine whirred and produced shashy noises behind him.

"The rice has boiled dry," said Reah with a sad sad smile. "Poor rice. I rescued it at the last moment but it's feeling very dry and abandoned in here."

"Sorry," said Bill. "Coming." He turned back to the screen to put the machine in standby mode. A small box told him resolutely, *No New Messages*. How Bill hated e-mail. He hadn't even asked if he had any messages. Click, he told it. Click off. Go to Standby, just stop telling me how absent she is from my life. Annoyingly, the damn thing wouldn't move into Standby. It told him that he was connected still to his service provider. "I didn't want to be bloody connected," said Bill. Suddenly images of connecting with Libby flashed into his mind as he pressed her down on that Louis Quinze desk. Deeply disturbed, Bill switched the whole damn computer off and went back to finish supper.

Within fifteen minutes he was tempted to come back while Reah was laying the table, but he wouldn't give the machine the smug satisfaction of telling him *No New Messages* yet again. Now Bill was beginning to hate Libby. Part of him felt she was ignoring him. It was, he acknowledged, the lunatic part of him that made such an assumption. The sane Bill could believe that Libby was travelling, was in a hotel without access to the internet, was having problems with her service provider; but the person who was already in love with Libby was not his saner self. He wanted her, and his bastard screen liked telling him he couldn't have her.

"Dad, are you annoyed with me?"

"Annoyed? No," he replied, trying to focus on their meal together and immediately feeling guilty.

"You're hardly saying anything," said Reah.

"I'm sorry."

"When I said I hated my hair and my rotten skin you said 'Mmm.'"

Bill looked at her mimicry. He recognised the distracted expression currently on Reah's face from awkward photographs of him and Tamsin. *Silly Daddy thinking about his work.* He found himself smiling. "Come on, let's go down to Chepstow and get some really good videos for the weekend."

It was an act of will, Bill thought as they drove back with *The Third Man*. Love is surrendering and that is how it should be, but if you are going to cope while in love, particularly when you don't know where the person you love is, or whether you'll ever see her again, then you have to make a conscious effort to get on with life.

A canopy of trees darkened the road ahead. Bill checked his lights. How on earth could he be in love with Libby Ziegler? It didn't make sense. Maybe after the humiliation with Marika his subconscious was simply trying to restore his self-esteem. OK, so maybe his conscious and his subconscious were in love with Libby for different reasons. But he was still in love.

"What are we doing tomorrow?" Reah asked.

"No idea," said Bill. "I imagine you'll go on headphones."

"And you'll type."

"And we'll go for our walk after lunch."

"And I'll complain."

"And then we'll watch a video in the evening."

It was a good life he thought. The old team. Boo Boo and Daddy Bear. But of course this domestic bliss wasn't going to last. That was the problem, wasn't it?

Bill parked the Jeep and walked up to the ridge. Jessica's car had gone. It was almost as if she had never come down from London, as if he had never had that extraordinary conversation and had all those all-too-ordinary things thrown at him.

When he entered the cottage Bill had a prescient feeling that Libby had been in touch. He knew it was more than likely to be wishful thinking, but it didn't stop him making his way with slow deliberation to the office while Reah built up the fire.

Bill switched on his PC. He stared at the screen as it whirred and clicked. He so much wanted there to be a message from her. He didn't want to end up being angry with Dr Ziegler just because the screen refused to reveal where she was and what she was thinking.

Verifying user name and password, the screen told him.

Connected to host.

Checking for mail.

A quick flurry of graphics told Bill that the check had been completed and any mail in his Outbox had been sent. He looked down to see if there were any new messages.

No New Messages, the little box read.

Please, no, thought Bill. Please don't let this be the pattern of the next few days.

"Ready Dad!" came Reah's voice. There was only one thing to do. He had to think of Reah, to think of his relationship with the rest of the world.

Life could not stop because Libby Ziegler was mucking things up again. He mustn't think that either. She was not necessarily playing games with him. She was just failing to be in contact with him as he'd failed to be in when she rang. That was all.

"You're spending a lot of time with that machine tonight," said Reah, still at the door. Bill sensed she recognised a greater level of distraction today. Daddy thinking about his work was one thing, this was something else.

"Coming," he said. He would have another glass of whisky.

Reah hadn't seen *The Third Man* before. She was surprisingly hard on Holly Martens for betraying his friend.

"But look at all the awful things Harry did," Bill pointed out.

"But, like, he really cared for Holly," she argued.

"Is caring all that matters?"

"No," said Reah. "But he still shouldn't have betrayed him."

"Harry betrayed his girlfriend to the Russians."

"Well we don't know that, Dad. That's what Holly and the English soldier said he did. He made her happy, that's more than they did."

Bill got up and put his glass on the sideboard. "We can forgive people a lot if they make us happy," he agreed. Reah bridled in the belief that he was mocking her. "No, no, I'm serious. What is morally right and morally wrong is often difficult to know – that's what this film is about – but one thing we do know is when we're happy."

He wanted to check a review of the film that Reah ought to read. The writer was a Jewish American and far less forgiving of Lime. He saw Harry as the kind of person who let Jews be deported from Vienna because there was no profit in doing anything else.

The office was dark with very little light coming in through the chill, uncurtained windows. There was light coming from the screen however. Bill had forgotten to go Offline properly when Reah called him. He cursed himself for not disconnecting but as he drew level with the screen he saw he had two messages waiting, both from the same address: ziegler.409. Libby.

At the top of the screen was the second e-mail she'd sent.

> *Bill, you're still engaged. It's probably better that you contact Antonia direct on that number if you're interested. I'm going to bed now. Libby*

Bill clicked the second message. *What* number? In *what* might he be interested? The other message was headed "*After After Venice.*"

> *Dear Bill,*
> *I read both your messages. Of course they intrigued me. You ask if*

we can meet. And of course we can. We did. I'm sure we will again. You ask when. Well that is up to you. I am currently in contact with someone who would very much like to read the letter you showed me. As you review opera it was suggested that you came to the premiere of the new Götterdämmerung here. Did I tell you I'm in Munich? It opens this Saturday. Don't ask me who's in it. If you're interested phone Antonia Berg first thing tomorrow or you can get me tonight on...

Bill skipped the next bit. He scrolled past the fact the company would provide a hotel room. He wanted to see how she ended this e-mail.

"*I tried to phone you with this,*" Libby wrote. "*But your line is permanently engaged. If you get over ring me on the number above and we'll maybe have that drink!*"

It wasn't a drink, thought Bill. We were going for a meal. God, he was already getting petty. Yes this was genuine obsession. Bill could tell she was being deliberately light-hearted with him. Maybe she had fathomed the extent of his interest. She wasn't put off but she was holding him at arm's length. Maybe she had felt the same thing as he had in Venice. Had she invented this letter person? No. She had convinced someone at the Bayerische Staatsoper to invite him over after all. And they didn't often pay for journalists to visit. The scam was genuine. It involved someone else's money. It was a pretext but she'd probably had to have worked quite hard to get the Staatsoper to agree. Unless the letter really was that interesting...

Bill felt himself on the edge of something that he hadn't experienced for a long time. His travels had become mundane, an excuse to get out of the cottage. This however felt like an adventure. Libby always was that. And now it seemed they were going to meet up again.

"Dad?" It was Reah wondering where he'd got to with that book.

Bill glanced up from the screen. "Sorry, Boo. Bloody Americans again."

"Don't they ever stop working?" she asked.

"They're five hours behind us over there." But Libby wasn't in New York, was she? Why did truth have to be the first casualty of love?

"Dad," said Reah. "I've got an idea about our weekend."

"Ah yes," said Bill, snapping out of his daze. So had he.

❖ IN SEARCH OF AN AUTHOR

IT WAS SURPRISINGLY COLD in Nymphenburg. The last time Bill had been in Munich it was summer and he'd been unable to resist wandering through the Englischer Garten and browsing the beautiful young people who lay around on the grass, affecting ignorance of their own nakedness.

But in early spring Munich was surprisingly chill and the fact that the park was deserted only added to this sense of wintry desolation. As Bill crunched the gravel outside Adelaide of Savoy's huge towering villa he reflected on the monumental manner in which Italian ideas got translated into German. Libby had told him that the park had been a present to young Adelaide from Elector Max Emanuel when she gave him an heir. It was supposed to remind her of Italy, but, just as St Petersburg was Venice magnified out of all sensible proportions in the chill swamps of northern Russia, so this nominal 'villa' had also suffered North European gargantuanism. Five storeys high with a roof that held another two, this was no rural Roman retreat but a blunt monument to Max Emanuel's grandeur. The Elector had subsequently added a further four pavilions, in the French style, and connected them into an elegant, but daunting, crescent. No nymphs would have the temerity to disport themselves round this burg.

Libby had left him in front of the *schloss* while she went to get a key to the Pagodenburg. Bill missed her acutely. Ever since she'd met him at the airport there had been something in the air. Something more intense, more difficult, more frustrating. He'd gone to kiss her when she stepped out of the car to greet him, but Libby had avoided any real contact, placing her cheek against his in that damned continental fashion.

"You must be tired," she said as they sat back in the dark Mercedes.

"No," he replied, turning in his seat to get a better look at her.

"Michael, do you have the address of Mr Wheeler's hotel?" Libby had asked, addressing the screen behind which a figure in uniform sat. It was dark, both inside the car and out. Bill had hardly noticed their driver, even when he'd opened the doors for them.

"Whose car is this?" Bill asked.

"Mine," said Libby, not looking at him. Her hair was scraped back tightly into some fastening. Bill didn't like it. Libby laughed. "Do you really think I could afford a driver?" she said, and then glanced forward again. *"Lass uns so spät nachts nicht die Autobahn nehmen, Michael!"* She seemed very keen to keep contact with the man at the wheel.

Bill decided to try and concentrate on business. "Do you have anything on this production I'm seeing?" he asked.

"Oh it's dreadful," said Libby.

"Don't you like any opera?" he asked. Libby made a gesture with her hands.

"Wagner!" she said dismissively.

"What does that mean?" Bill was irritated. "I thought you liked Wagner."

"A lot can change in seven years," said Libby, and she looked at him. It was a strange, challenging look. Purposeful. She wasn't like she'd been in Venice, not at all. There she'd seemed happy and relaxed, humorous even. Here something was wrong.

"So you won't be coming with me?" he asked.

"Where?"

"To the opera."

"Oh no," Libby replied. "I'll be coming. We're meeting someone there."

"Who?"

"Ah," said Libby.

At that point her mobile phone had rung and Libby had answered it in German. She was fluent. Of course. Fluent and much less attractive. Bill definitely began to dislike the *deutsche* Libby. He had no idea what the conversation was about, but he felt distinctly excluded and he really didn't like the emphatic sound of her voice in that vicious, autocratic language. When the conversation was over she spoke to Michael, also in German, and then turned to him.

"So, what happened with your daughter?"

"Reah," Bill reminded her. "I arranged to leave her at her grandparents' this morning."

"That's your mother and father?" Libby asked.

"No," said Bill. Libby ought to remember that both his parents were long dead but he wasn't going to point that out now. He knew he'd only sound aggrieved if he did.

The whole business had been difficult to arrange. Reah had to go and get her address book from the farmhouse because she couldn't remember Tamsin's parents' number. But before that she had to find her key to the farmhouse because Bill no longer possessed one. Then Reah had to do the ringing. Tamsin's parents had not spoken to Bill for years. Now was not the ideal time for him to re-establish contact. But listening to Reah making the arrangements and taking the opportunity to present herself as doubly orphaned – first by Mum and now by Dad's work – had not been easy for Bill. He'd felt bad about jettisoning Reah. And what for? Oh yes, for this urgent 'work' in Munich? When on earth had the reviewing of opera ever been a race against time? Bill had tried to sound plausible to Reah but he'd not even convinced himself. For all his talk about this important production he had suddenly to review, all Bill had in mind as he pounded the Jeep along the M4 corridor were images of Libby Ziegler in that dark Venetian salon. Was Reah Wheeler convinced? He really didn't expect her to be.

At one point on the journey she'd suddenly wanted to come with him and Bill had begun to wonder about that. He'd certainly rather take Reah with him than leave her with Tamsin's parents.

"Have you got your passport?" he asked as they were passing Windsor.

"You've got it."

"Have I?"

"Mum wanted me put on her passport but they told her that there already was one issued to me in my own name."

"And I've got that?" Bill asked. He ought to know.

"Mum was really angry," said Reah.

"Must be in the cottage," said Bill. "I'm sorry, love. I can't turn round and get it now."

"That's OK," said Reah and she turned back to the music on her headphones. Maybe she'd just wanted to check he'd take her if she asked. It was a fact almost impossible for Bill to comprehend, but Reah Wheeler actually looked forward to being with her grandparents.

He dropped her at the house in St John's Wood before turning back to Heathrow. "Don't be sad, Daddy Boo," Reah said when she ducked back in to kiss him goodbye.

"I'm not going to lose you," he told her and stretched out a hand.

A flicker of discomfort crossed Reah's face. "It's only Gramma and Grandpops."

"I'll be back soon," said Bill. He was now embarrassed by his outburst.

"Yeah. And we'll go for walks and watch TV."

"Yeah."

Bill waited as Reah lugged that great overnight bag up the drive. A door opened and closed quickly, removing his daughter from sight. Deleting him from her life. No one waved. Tamsin's parents had nothing to say to Bill Wheeler. What the hell had she been telling them?

It was in this uneasy frame of mind that Bill had arrived at Munich's long, white shiny airport. The skies over Bavaria were darker than he'd expected but they matched his mood. Bill had hoped that Libby would lighten things, but she was on edge too. That drive to his hotel had not been easy and Bill began almost to regret what he'd done. Indeed were it not for the sight of Libby, her wide smile, her bright eyes and the sense of some dense intoxicating perfume in the car – an essence that he could not actually smell but which nevertheless refused to leave him in peace – he might have wished he were somewhere else rather than speeding Friday night away in a dark chauffeur-driven Mercedes.

That had been yesterday. Things were different now. It was early morning in Schloss Nymphenburg and enough had happened last night to keep Bill in Munich and, at this moment, make him desperate for Libby's return.

She had dropped him at the hotel. As Michael had opened the door he'd asked her up for a drink.

"I don't think so," said Libby with a smile that set limits: Reception and no further.

"You did promise me a drink," Bill reminded her as he received his keycard. He was trying to sound friendly. But it was forced. Bill was still prey to that dislike of Libby that had built up during her German phonecall. Nevertheless he knew that he was attracted to her.

"Surely you're tired, Bill."

"No. I'm not. How about dinner?"

He was being more direct now. Obvious in fact. She was denying him and so it became a simple matter of his wanting. No matter how much. No matter why. He simply wanted what was being withheld.

Libby paused and thought. Bill had no idea what she was calculating but after a few moments she said, "Not here." The way she said it surprised him. It was almost conspiratorial as if she were finally admitting something between them.

"Where?" he asked.

"I have to take the car back," she explained, although that explained nothing.

"Why can't Michael take the car back?" he asked. They were still in the lobby of this small but glittering and most unBavarian hotel. Libby looked around and then became annoyed. "Not everything can be changed because you've turned up, Bill."

He was surprised. This was the first time that her voice had suggested anything but goodwill towards him. The first hint of the emotionally complex Libby he could remember in London all those years ago. Then, however, she'd been difficult because of the passions that boiled within her. This sounded more like irritation. Bill had no idea what Libby was talking about but he did point out that she had invited him to Munich.

"Give me an hour," she said, preoccupied.

"OK." He looked at her. Libby was still calculating something. "Will you come back here?" he asked.

"No I'll meet you..." she answered. "Goddam it's so difficult."

"What is?" he asked. Silence. Then Libby laughed.

"Getting a table at this time of night. '*Absolutely bloody*' as you British say."

Bill knew she was talking about something else.

"I'll ring you. In 45 minutes," Libby decided. "I'll ring you in your room."

"I'll be there," he said.

Bill had had a bath and wrapped himself in a robe. He couldn't help wondering if Libby would in fact ring him. He imagined Hauke objecting. Hauke had to be around here somewhere.

But she did ring, sounding very much her old self. "Get a taxi to Pasing," she explained. "There's a Chinese restaurant there called Ming Garden"

"Why Chinese?" he'd asked.

"You're going to be eating a lot of *wurst* while you're over," Libby told him.

At the restaurant Libby was quite different than in the car. She'd relaxed. She'd changed her hair. She'd also changed from her top with leggings to something more like a dress. Libby's clothes were always voluminous and, as Bill now recalled, she tended to design them herself. Their many layers mystified him. As far as he could tell Libby might at that moment just as easily be wearing a loose trouser suit as a dress. Somewhere in all these folds was the essential Libby Ziegler. It seemed symbolic. The woman whose body he wanted kept from him in enigmatic layers of her own making.

"It's all in German," he said, passing the menu back to her.

"No it's not," she laughed showing him the English pages.

"What exactly is Fine Shark Soup?" Bill asked.

"Shark fin," Libby replied.

"Shame, I could do with some damn fine shark." She looked up at him to check it was a joke. There was a pleasure in her eyes that surprised him. "It's good to see you," he said. Libby paused before answering, then thought better of answering at all. "What?" he asked. Their table was hidden behind a pillar. Libby had chosen it. Given that the restaurant hardly knew they were there, Bill felt emboldened to push his question.

"Nothing," she replied, admitting something.

"What kind of nothing?"

"I just wonder why you're here," said Libby.

"Because you invited me." It was the wrong answer. He knew it as soon as he'd said it.

"You have the letter?" she asked, returning to business.

"Never mind the letter."

"But that's why you're here," she reminded him. Was she teasing? Libby flashed Bill another of her dazzling smiles. Complicit, appreciative. It was so easy to be distracted by her, particularly now that her hair was looser.

"Why was it difficult to come here tonight?" Bill asked. He had already imagined Hauke creating a scene, standing at the door, big, slow and difficult, preventing her leaving.

"It wasn't difficult," said Libby, closing her menu.

"It took you a long time to decide," he reminded her.

"As I said, restaurants get booked up in Munich on a Friday."

"I don't believe you."

"OK," she said, looking around provocatively. "Ask a waiter. They'll tell you this place is packed-out every weekend."

"*Libby*," said Bill. It was the first time he'd used her name. The effect was electric. Certainly on him. He was lost as what to say next. Then he realised she was looking at him. He could sense her breathing. Nothing audible and yet he caught its rise and fall. Suddenly in the spasm of that moment they were attuned.

"I don't know," she said quietly apropos of something unspoken which must have been said in the silence between them.

"Don't know what?" he asked. Silence. Bill sensed her breathing and nothing else. It was as if suddenly they were the only two people in the world.

"Nothing," she said dismissively.

"You don't know... nothing?" Bill asked. Libby put a hand to her throat.

"Guess that means I must know something," she laughed.

"Double negative," Bill agreed.

"We Bostonians," she joked. "Famous for them."

He looked at her hand. The small fingers. She seemed so capable, so much in charge of the world, and yet her fingers seemed so delicate. What on earth was he getting himself into with this woman? "Libby," he said again, more urgently this time. The waiter arrived with a platter.

"Saved by the spring rolls," said Libby over her menu.

That was last night. Now here he was kicking gravel in the chill baroque gardens of Nymphenburg. Where was she?

That hadn't been all of last night of course. They had laughed a lot. Bill was surprised that they laughed so much but Libby seemed to find him funny. Everything he said or did that was unfamiliar to her she took to be typically English.

"I'm not typical at all," said Bill. "I married a Jewish woman, that isn't typical. I live in Wales in a cottage miles from anyone. And I'm divorced. That isn't typical either. Not yet anyway, not even in Britain."

"I'm sorry about that," said Libby.

"What, the divorce?"

"I'm sorry for the effect it must have had on your daughter."

"Reah," he told her. "Yes. She's coped very well. I suppose her earliest memories are of Tamsin and me falling apart. She once caught us fighting. Well almost—"

Bill hesitated. He had just remembered that that particular argument had been occasioned by one of Libby's ten page faxes. Tamsin had rolled it up and hit him in the face with it and Reah had found her mother in tears, her father standing impotent and foolish, looking on. "It isn't fair, Bill." Tamsin had cried. "She's a single woman. She spends hours writing to you, impressing you, flattering you while I'm trying to bring up your bloody daughter. I'm *tired* Bill!"

Oh God yes.

"Mummy and Daddy are being silly." How often had he heard that when Daddy stormed out and Mummy thumped her fists into the pillows.

No, thought Bill. This was not the time to tell Libby about how well Reah had coped.

"I'd like to meet her sometime," Libby was saying. "She sounds great."

Bill smiled. He liked the thought of that. "I almost brought her with me," he said.

"Really?" said Libby, suddenly looking at her food. "That would have been nice."

"It was looking difficult at one point," Bill explained as he had in his subsequent e-mails to Munich. "But, to be honest, I'd rather it was just you and me."

Now Libby looked away. Bill felt that there was an inner dialogue going on for her of which he only caught occasional impenetrable glimpses.

"You haven't changed," he said, and wished immediately that he'd kept his mouth shut. The one thing they could both be certain of was that Libby Ziegler had changed. She was more sophisticated, more successful and possibly more content. Seven years ago Libby's face was still young enough to be unclear and indefinite. Now she had arrived. She had become who she was going to be when Bill had known her. And she was, in certain lights, at certain angles (and when her hair wasn't scraped back and her language wasn't German) most definitely beautiful in his eyes. But that wasn't what he meant to say either. And it was a good job he didn't. What Bill had actually meant was 'I am still attracted to you.' But such words have consequences. Said at the wrong time they can sound louche. Said at the right time they can precipitate too much too soon.

Libby was looking at him now with an indulgent half smile. It was as if she knew he wished he hadn't paid that limp compliment about not changing. "Oh I hope I have changed," she said.

"Yes but you're..."

"I'm..?" Libby replied when his silence had hung in the air for too long.

Bill lifted his hands. He didn't know what to say. He hadn't had this kind of conversation for so long. He wasn't even sure what he was doing here, whether he had a chance. The truth was that he had wanted to possess Libby as soon as they were in close contact. Something in the air between them had driven him to that conclusion and driven out his belief that he hated her. Here he was now, responding to an invitation that was supposed to be professional when, in reality, he was responding to the most powerful physical urge he had felt in years, an urge which had driven him to abandon his daughter and fly to Germany to review something dubious at the Bayerische Staatsoper.

"Let me put it like this," Bill took a breath. "I thought I was fortunate to stumble on that letter but the fact that the letter has led me to you..." And again he paused. Bloody hell! Bill looked at Libby for help. "I'm supposed to be reasonably good with words," he conceded.

"Tell me about the letter," she said kindly.

"To hell with the letter," Bill sulked.

Libby pushed her bowl to one side. "The rest can wait," she said. "Till you've found the words. Come on."

It had been a good meal after that. Bill as good as told Libby the full story of Katz although he lied about how he came to appropriate the letter. Initially he hoped just to obscure the facts but in the end he found himself claiming that it had been lent to him. That was a significant lie but Bill wasn't sure how much he could trust Libby yet. About the rest – how he got the translations, the puzzling business of the *leitmotiv* being under, above or before Siegfried's Death March, the Swiss PA and her pet cop – he was quite open although he did omit the bit about the shotgun. Nevertheless realising just how much he was leaving out shocked Bill. He had never thought of himself as a gun-toting thief. Telling any more of this story would make it less a question of how much he could trust her and more one of how much she'd trust him.

"*Schmidt?*" said Libby.

"I'm sure it wasn't his real name," Bill replied. "But what I don't understand is all this interest in the letter. Four or five people. It's crazy isn't it? Do you really think that this ABCGH thing could damage Wagner's reputation?"

"May I have a look?" Libby asked. Bill took the letter out of his notebook and passed it over. She reread it with an amused smile.

"*Bürgerlicher Anstand*," she said, turning the page.

"You said that last time," Bill pointed out. "What's it mean?"

Libby sought for a translation. "I suppose it's 'bourgeois respectability', but it has nineteenth-century connotations, particularly to do with marriage. The way people like Wagner and Victor Hugo – revolutionaries in their youth – invented the perfect respectable marriage as the crowning glory of their success."

"You've lost me," said Bill. "I thought Wagner considered marriage a utility. Wasn't that the word?" It certainly was, he was sure of that. "Marriage reduces love to property and utility." Libby Ziegler had said that, even if Richard Wagner hadn't.

"*Zweckgemeinschaft*," said Libby, putting the letter back in its plastic wallet and holding it up. "But that was years ago during his Bad Boy period." She passed the envelope back. "When Wagner made it, he chose to project this image of perfect domestic union. Nietzsche thought it stank. The artist and his helpmeet in total harmony surrounded by their children. You've heard the tedium of that Siegfried Idyll haven't you? Children who never get in the way. Never interrupt Daddy working or need Mom to breastfeed. Wagner even dressed his kids up to be photographed as characters from the Ring Cycle. It was a religion of the family," she explained with distaste. "With everyone worshipping Papa's genius." Libby gave Bill a significant look. "Of course it was phoney. But it was fashionable. You get the same with Victor Hugo. No wonder Baby Siegfried went gay."

"And you see that in the letter?" Bill asked, somewhat at a loss.

"No I can see just a few cracks, can't you?" Libby asked. "*Was meine Gattin betrifft, sie verweigerte sich mir heute morgen.* This morning my wife refused to 'embrace' me. I think we all know what 'embrace' means in that kind of context."

"I hadn't realised," said Bill.

"Marriage!" Libby scoffed.

"You've never..?"

She shook her head lightly. "Once was enough."

"What happened?"

"I was drawn to the family, but he was a boy. So –" A hand gesture. There was clearly no more to be said on that particular subject. Libby closed the window.

"Well," said Bill. "What about this ABCGH thing?"

"Ah yes, it rings a bell," Libby said. She thought for a moment. "There's someone I know who may have the dirt on that. He's in Munich during term time. I'll try and find him."

"What dirt?" Bill asked, pouring himself another glass of wine.

Libby shook her head again. "I need to talk to him. We can meet him in fact. That would be good. Would you excuse me?" With that she fished into her bag and brought out her mobile. Bill sat back and sipped his wine. Drinking with Libby was a somewhat lonely experience because Libby didn't. He'd forgotten that. Seven years ago he hadn't noticed but then seven years ago he probably didn't drink much himself either. A rocky marriage has many effects and one of them is a fridge door invariably open at 6pm. At first Bill and Tamsin used to hit the white wine together. Later they drank apart. Now Bill drank on his own.

"That's fixed then," said Libby, switching off her phone. "Remarkably succinct for once," she added, looking at the phone in case it could explain why the call had been so brief. "Tomorrow at nine. Do you know Nymphenburg? Josef has an apartment there."

"Who is Josef?" Bill asked.

"Bring the letter," she replied. "You'll find out."

Libby didn't have Michael and the car with her in Pasing so they'd gone their separate ways by taxi after the meal. "Don't forget the letter!" she said, and this time let him kiss her on the cheek.

Bill had returned to the hotel by taxi, consumed by his fascination with Libby. It was like the day he'd gone to interview the *intendante* at Palafenice. He was now unable to think of anything but her, except that this time his mind was more troubled. She was not making it easy for him.

This morning he had met her at the gates of Nymphenburg just before

9am. His taxi driver had pointed Bill to where the main entrance lay off Notburgastrasse. Libby was already there finishing a phone conversation on her Handy.

"Josef says his apartment is a mess," she said with a smirk on her face. "Between you and me I think he's got a woman up there and had forgotten all about us. He says he'll meet us in Pagodenburg. Wait here," she said. "I've got to go and pick up the key."

That was five long minutes ago. Bill had been intoxicated by the sight of Libby that morning. She'd been dressed up in some huge quilted thing against the cold, but her hair was loose and seemed to have an unexpected hint of blonde as it blew out in the crisp morning sunlight.

"You look great," he'd said.

"Thank you," she replied. She knew she looked great too. Bill could tell she did. It was impossible not to fall for her this morning. And now here she was coming back from one of the further French pavilions, right hand lifted to show the key. Bill watched her approach and Libby did not for one moment seem self-conscious to have his eyes upon her all the way.

She was laughing. "He looked terrible. I don't think Josef got much sleep last night!" And with that they began walking down the main canal following 'Pagodenburg' signs. "No wonder he was so short on the phone yesterday."

Seeing what Max Emanuel had done with an Italian villa, Bill wasn't at all surprised to find that his son had built himself a very statuesque Japanese lakeside pavilion. Repeating a rectangular design of balconies, balustrades and Corinthian columns the Pagodenburg did not look remotely oriental. The Wittelbachs were like Teutonic Midases, Bill thought. Everything they touched turned to German.

Inside the Pagodenburg proved slightly more convincingly Japanese with some black lacquered furniture offset by blue and white delft tiles. To Bill's surprise the room was heated. Libby led him through to the connecting salon where an exhibition was set up.

"Josef has this space for six months," Libby explained.

Bill was shocked to see familiar black-and-white images of the Holocaust on the exhibition screens. "If they can't forgive themselves, how are we supposed to?" he asked, looking past the gaunt monochrome faces in the foreground and nodding at those dark uniformed figures, caught in a blur in the background. One helmeted guard was raising a rifle butt and damning his nation for all time.

"Oh, each generation has to *learn*," said Libby, with an ironic lilt. "Or else the horror will happen again."

"Can't the genie go back in the bottle?" Bill asked.

"I think the idea is that now we know how to commit mass murder we have to keep reminding ourselves of its hideous consequences or we'll forget and do it again."

"Do you believe that?" he asked.

"Me?" said Libby. "It's total naivety. *Lest We Forget*. Isn't that what they wrote on your Cenotaph in 1919? Supposedly the idea of commemorating the Great War on an annual basis was so everyone would remember how awful it had been and that way there'd never be a Second World War!" She snorted and Bill remembered the schoolgirl iconoclast, for whom clarity of thought and expression outweighed any other consideration. "People don't weigh up the pros and cons of genocide, Bill. They don't decide 'Well no one can remember whether it was a good idea or not last time so, hell, let's try it and see.' It doesn't happen like that, whatever the Germans and Israelis may claim. D'you think they didn't know about this in Rwanda and Cambodia?" she asked, pointing at the display. "No, this is self-laceration. The Germans are still having difficulty coming to terms with the fact they're not perfect. Now, if you were to ask me, the more interesting question is why the Jews keep commemorating it. What's in it for them, eh?"

Bill chose not to be drawn on that one. "I always thought you might be Jewish," said Bill. "With a name like Ziegler."

"My grandfather married out. Neither of my parents were. I don't know a word of Hebrew. I'm just your basic New Englander but I can still understand something of the mindset. They may forgive but they'll never forget. Still I'm just a woman," she said. "We have no sense of justice." He gathered she was being ironic but didn't get the reference. "*Schopenhauer,*" she rebuked him. "I thought you'd remember that. Didn't we used to talk Schopenhauer in London?"

"You used to," said Bill. "I listened."

"God I was naive in those days," said Libby with a laugh. "He's a great philosopher for adolescent pessimists. '*Every parting is a foretaste of death.*' Still, I kinda go for his views on art. Don't you?" Libby was puckish this morning, delighting in her own attractiveness and erudition. "As for this..." she said, nodding at the nightmare before them. "Arthur would find it unremarkable, I reckon. I'm sure he'd say the only remarkable thing about the Shoah was that it hadn't happened before and that the only thing that distinguished the Nazis from any other group of thugs was that they had technological advances that made the nightmare more effective. Trains, Ovens, Zyklon B. But the desire to destroy, to eradicate The Other has been with us ever since we became tribal. Strife is inevitable."

"What's the answer then?" Bill asked. They were standing shoulder to shoulder now, looking, yet no longer looking, at the display.

"Renunciation," Libby said, "if you believe Schopenhauer. The pursuit of art, finding renunciation through something higher. Otherwise we're just ruled by the Will. Being nice is irrelevant. It's like being cute. I'm sure there were lots of very cute Hitler Youth."

It was an odd conversation. Bill wanted to ask Libby what she believed herself. Was she a 'nice' person? It was a question he'd asked himself since Venice. Having a daughter meant one frequently sojourned in the world of nice. Whether people were or were not, had been Reah's obsession ever since she went to school. But did nice actually matter? At the end of time, when humanity is weighed in the balance, will the scales really be tipped by an accumulation of niceness?

Libby was already elsewhere. "But don't confuse our friend Wagner with Schopenhauer! He wasn't as bright as he thought he was."

"No?"

Libby turned to Bill and placed a finger on his chest. "No one respected Wagner's genius more than Wilhelm Richard. Nothing else mattered. And yet the man was petit-bourgeois when he died. He wanted the ultimate respectable marriage once he'd made it. And anyway Schopenhauer always preferred Rossini!" she laughed. "He thought Wagner's operas were too long." Libby turned away to glance outside. "Mind you, they were both agreed on that. Oh here's Josef. Now Bill, all this," she said, indicating the display boards. "It means a lot to him and we did get him out of bed this morning."

Bill liked Josef Steiner. He was gentle yet lively, almost femininely dainty but very handsome in a miniature way. He carried with him a thermos of coffee and had milk and sugar in his coat pockets.

"For our English guest!" he chortled, kissing Libby. Bill's assurances that he was happy to drink his coffee continental fashion were ignored.

"So," said Josef sitting down on a step. "You have a letter for me from Meister Richard, eh?"

"I've brought a photocopy which I did in the hotel this morning," said Bill. "The original is getting rather frayed."

Josef accepted the letter from Bill and started to read. From time to time he laughed to himself but Bill was unsure whether this amusement was specific to the letter. Herr Doktor Steiner seemed to be one of those people who found the everyday living of life an irresistibly comical experience. "What an old devil!" he said when he finished the letter and handed it back to Bill. "Outrageous, no?" he said to Libby.

"What do you see in it?" Bill asked. "I'm told there's something controversial in there, but Libby won't tell me what it is."

"Oh *Liebchen...*" said Josef reproachfully.

"It's not my area, Jo," Libby protested, taking a step back. "I just had a hunch."

"Well!" said the young man standing up. "Let me try not to be tedious and academic. That is innate with me. You are a journalist, Libby says, so I will try and be succinct for once." He paused as if he were thinking in one language before translating into another. "What I see in this letter is a reference to a song, an anti-Semitic song that may well have been around in Wagner's day. It was a musical joke really. If you take the notes A, B-flat, C, G and B natural you get a tune, I assume you do. Isn't that true Libby?"

She nodded and Josef giggled. "Who knows why the letter H was roped in to represent B-natural but it was. It's a German thing, I believe. Don't believe the Prussians have good reasons for everything they do, Bill! Now I am not a musician but I have made a study of the relationship between this country and my people. You may say I'm just another Jew obsessed with the past. Well, yes I am, but I take a slightly longer perspective. I like to look back to the beginning of the nineteenth century when we were just coming out of the ghetto and Germany – well it wasn't Germany then, but many German-speaking states, most notably Austria and Prussia, were in the forefront of emancipation." Josef paused. Bill noticed how tired his face did indeed look. "Libby, I can see I'm going to be long-winded. Please let's take Bill for a walk so he has something to look at while I do all my rattling on!"

They set off, despite Bill's protests that he was happy just to listen, on a walk around the lake and over a low bridge that ran across the main canal. Josef made a point of asking Libby which of the many *burgs* with which Carl Albert had littered these grounds Bill might enjoy. "We have the Badenburg for bathing, the Amalienburg to hunt from and the Magdalene's Retreat for whatever Magdalenes did when resting! Actually I joke, it is a chapel, very coy I think. And of course the Pagodenburg where the state lets me brood upon the nightmare. Come, let us flee."

Away from the Pagodenburg Josef became even more animated, as he explained how until the end of the eighteenth century his people had lived in self-enclosed rural communities or urban ghettos. "Partly because your law could not forgive us for failing to recognise Jesus of Nazareth as the true Messiah, but mainly because of the Torah, that's our law, which required us to isolate ourselves. The Enlightenment changed much of this, so did the revolutions of Europe, and there began what has been called The German-Jewish Dialogue. I hope I'm not boring you, Bill, but you must understand that we Jews have very long memories. We're still debating whether Sabbatai Zvi was the true Messiah. Isn't that right Libby?"

"Not my subject," she insisted, a few steps behind. But with a winning smile.

"Anyway foremost in this period, dominating the Berlin Enlightenment," said Josef, pausing by an oval basin, "was Moses Mendelssohn, you'll no doubt recognise that name. He was the grandfather of Wagner's bête noire, Felix. Also foremost, and I really should have mentioned him first, was Gotthold Ephraim Lessing, a journalist like yourself, and the founder of our German theatre; his play *Nathan der Weise* was seminal in the creation of a tranche of what might be called Philo-Semitic writing, works which held up admirable Jews for public approbation. Because of the enlightened views of the Germans – the Austrians and Prussians in particular – Germany had many Jews at this time. In fact these curious compound names which so many of us hump around – Rosenburg, Goldstein, Rosenblum – were chosen for us by Frederick William I of Prussia who wanted the Jews to be assimilated and thought that poetic family names would be an incentive! Thank God my forefathers were being persecuted in Cologne at the time or you might be listening to a Rose-Blossom or Gold-Water!

"Anyway Mendelssohn, that's the grandfather, he in particular paved the way for Jewish integration by asserting in his treatise *Jerusalem* that what was revealed to Moses on the Mount was not doctrine or dogma but a rational way of living in the desert. Note the use of the word 'rational', Bill. A word designed to appeal to the great thinkers of the Enlightenment. Thus the 'rational' Jew was born. And accepted. And from the Patents of Toleration issued by Joseph II of Austria – that's Mozart's patron, Joseph – all the way through to the restricted civil rights granted to Jews in 1812 by Frederick William III of Prussia – grandson of our Rose-Blossom monarch – the Jews moved wholesale into German society.

"The result of this was dramatic. Within a generation the ghetto walls were down. Jews were in business and the law and medicine and, as I'm sure you're glad to know, journalism. There were still restrictions. We weren't allowed to be postmen or civil servants. We couldn't deliver letters in case we stole state secrets! And we couldn't teach in universities and schools unless we converted, but we had arrived and we made a big difference. Let's turn across here."

Taking Bill's arm Josef led them over the bridge and through a screen of dark trees. Libby trailed behind, kicking the gravel. When Bill caught sight of her she looked happy enough yet slightly distant.

"Of course, not everyone welcomed this influx of rational, moneymaking Jews with their bourgeois ambitions, these Jews who forsook the clarinet and violin for the pianoforte. You see the symbolism of that, Bill? Relinquishing two eminently transportable Jewish instruments for the solid, respectable permanence of a grand piano in the drawing room. But the arguments against us were primarily economic. We were taking jobs away from Christians. Not Christian postmen, of course! But we were creating unfair competition for doctors and lawyers. And unfair competition for German businesses too. Some of us were obviously growing rich and in those days many people believed there was only a finite amount of money to go round. The Jew was making progress of a kind. We were still hated. But the reasons were different!"

They were crossing an expanse of open ground where geese waddled and the Badenburg rose up in front of them. A much larger structure than the Pagodenburg, the bathing house had glass doors at the top of a flight of steps guarded by two lions.

"Take a look!" Josef urged. "I'm afraid it's closed for refurbishment. Such a shame, it's a fine building, don't you think so Libby? Hot and cold water even in 1750. So now where was I?"

Bill, peering in as best he could, was beginning to realise why Libby had been surprised at the brevity of Josef's conversation with her on the phone last night.

"At this stage the intellectuals sat somewhat on the fence, as we intellectuals often do. It has to be said Kant had never been philo-Semitic. Hardly! Fries, that's Jakob Fries, Bill, he called us 'a commercial caste'. Marx said we were 'the agents of capitalism' and Gutzkow, another playwright and journalist, he said that with the creation of Christianity we had outlived our purpose. So we were tolerated. Just. But there was a growing sense of disquiet, right up until 1848 and the revolutions. What so upset everyone about the failed left-wing revolts was that Jewish bankers had supported the status quo. Well bankers do, don't they? There were various things written against my people at that time. The serious Meister Richard himself wrote *Das Judentum in der Musik* circa 1850, isn't that true Libby?"

She nodded.

"Published under a pseudonym. I'm right aren't I?"

"And republished in 1870 under his own name," she agreed absently, looking at the morning sky. Libby remained detached but Josef forged on, addressing Bill across a dusty pane of the Badenburg's glass doors. "Now, not all this anti-Semitism went into works as dense and 'scholarly' as *Das Judentum*. There were songs, graffiti and... what is that lovely English word of yours..? *Doggerel*. Included in which – and here I thank you for your patience, Bill..."

Josef removed the glove of his right hand.

"Included in which was:

Abraham, Benjamin, Chaim, *geht heim*.

Abraham, Benjamin, Chaim, *geht fort*."

He was writing the first letter of each word of the window-pane.

"Abraham, Benjamin, Chaim, *aus Deutschland fort*.

"Do you see what I'm doing here? Abraham, Benjamin, Chaim is ABC. Then you get G and H for '*geht heim*'. G and F for '*geht fort*', AD and F for '*aus Deutschland fort*'. I forget how well you follow German, Bill. You see this charming song addresses the Jews in general, Abraham, Benjamin, Chaim being typical Jewish names, and it tells them 'Go Home' (that's '*geht heim*') 'Go Away' ('*geht fort*') and 'be away from Germany', that's '*aus Deutschland*' as you can imagine. Dear me, I'm running out of window. Finally it concludes '*haut ab aus Deutschland*', H, A, A, D. A truly charming phrase that we might translate as 'Bugger off out of Germany' and of course let us not forget finally '*haut endlich ab*' – A, B, C, H for '*haut*', E for '*endlich*' and A for '*ab*'. 'Bugger off at last.' One might even choose to translate '*endlich*' as 'finally' and be forgiven for making a link there with all the obvious connotations of any German solution that might call itself final."

Josef seemed to have run out of breath as well as window. "So!" He stepped back, as if pleased with his work. "So, as you can see, we have here, in my opinion, only in my opinion of course, well Bill, do you see what we have here? Each letter of that song corresponds to a musical note. I know this tune. I have heard it. And I know that it was enough for people to whistle it in front of a Jew. It was a joke, a way that even in the most civilised drawing room, even in front of your rich Jewish banker host, that you could tell him to bugger off out of Germany. Everyone else would know. You might even sit down to play the piano at one of his damnable soirees where the Jew put on his Gentile airs and graces, his wife in her black bombazine and jewels, his daughters dressed for their first season, with the gall to pass themselves off as decent Christian girls. But before you played something suitably respectful for your host, some Bach or Spohr or even Jakob Felix Mendelssohn-Bartholdy, you could trill these few notes on the piano, or pick them out in the bass clef, and everyone would laugh. Everyone except the foolish Jew with his ridiculous Christian airs and graces and his ersatz German *hausfrau* of a wife and his daughters, stood in a line waiting for their partners at the Emperor's ball. What a joke, eh? What a joke, Bill!"

Bill noticed how white Josef's face had grown. He nodded and waited for the young man to regain his composure.

"So Wagner is admitting..."

"Absolutely," said Josef and he began wiping the window vigorously with the glove of his left hand. "Absolutely, what a joke. Herr Meister Richard used the tune, so he admits, somewhere in Siegfried's Death March. What a comic genius, eh? What a joker, eh? What a joke."

"He's a great fan of the music," Libby said as they left Nymphenburg. "It's hard for him."

She had spent some time talking to Josef during their walk back. Ostensibly Libby was thanking him for taking so much trouble but in fact she was trying to calm her friend down. Bill, walking a few steps behind, had heard Josef say. "It's nothing. I make myself ridiculous, dear girl," and then the two of them lapsed into German. Bill thought of all the Jews who admired Wagner. Of Mahler, Barenboim and James Levine who'd conducted at Bayreuth. It must be hard for men like them to accept how much casual hostility could underlie a work like *The Ring*. What was it Wagner had said? "When I compose who knows what I draw on?"

The sun glimpsed down through the trees as Bill fished out his translation and the photocopy of Wagner's original.

> *Theurer Freund, wenn ich mitten im Komponieren von Musik bin...*
> *it is possible for me only if I am in a constant ecstatic state and behav-*
> *ing to all the world as a complete eccentric. In these moments who*
> *knows what I write?*

Bill slowed his pace so that the couple wandering ahead of him down these intersecting avenues did not see what he was reading.

> *When I consider the phrase our friend refers to I believe he may be*
> *right that I did use that old song beneath the leitmotiv...*

Here Bill had put an asterisk on his copy of the translation: *Beneath? Before? See Goetz.*

> *... that I did use that old song beneath the leitmotiv* that accompanies*
> *the hero Siegfried to his death.*

So was that it? Wagner used that nasty little tune in or around or some-where in the vicinity of Siegfried's Funeral March. Ironic that he should be booked to hear *Götterdämmerung* this evening.

"I'm sorry," said Josef as they passed under the schloss and back out into the public grounds which led down to Notburgastrasse. "I'm sorry Bill, if I seem emotional. It must be very embarrassing for an English man like you."

"Not at all," said Bill.

"We Continentals..!" Josef tried to joke.

"No really," sad Bill. "I can understand how upsetting it must be for you."

"It's not upsetting," the young man suddenly insisted. "Not upsetting, God!" Josef looked to heaven. "Six million, now that is upsetting." He seemed angry with Bill. "This is just... well it's not even disappointing. It's what one should expect..."

"From Wagner..?" said Bill, completing the sentence hesitantly for him.

Josef snorted, dismissing the idea. It was a gesture that shocked Bill. *From all of you*, it seemed to say. A taxi drew up at Libby's command.

"*Liebling*," Bill heard him say as he moved to open the door for her. "*Es tut mir leid*." When Bill looked back Josef had his hand on Libby's shoulder and seemed to be saying goodbye. "*Ich versuche zu verzeihen. Ich versuche es. Nicht ihretwegen, sondern meinetwegen.*"*

He was shaking his head. Bill saw Libby try to say something to comfort him but Josef stepped back. "*Aber ich kann nicht! Ich kann es einfach nicht.*"†

"What can't he do?" Bill asked as he joined her in the taxi.

"Oh, forgive," she replied. "He's upset. Don't take it personally."

"Me?" said Bill. "No. It comes with the job. Besides, I was married to the state of Israel, don't forget."

"He's changed," she said, gazing absently at the roof of the taxi. "He's been doing this job for nine months now and he's changed."

"What is his job?"

"It's a reconciliation project funded by the city of Munich and the state. You know the Nazis had a powerbase here. Josef's working on original documentation, looking at the history of anti-Semitism before Hitler. That's why I thought he'd be your person. The idea is to put it in a longer context. He was saying to me just now that trying to explain the horror isn't making it any easier. The more he knows the greater the nightmare. He knows it's doing him harm. Oh," she added. "I was wrong about the

---

* I try to forgive. I try. Not for them but for me.
† But I can't. I cannot do it.

girl. It seems he just doesn't sleep too well these days."

Bill wasn't surprised. What room is there for love when your heart is traumatised like that? Maybe you can't explain it, Bill thought. Maybe that was the mistake. Maybe you just have to accept that it's in all of us. But he didn't say so.

It was odd how different he felt sitting next to Libby now. When they'd met outside Nymphenburg his senses were so attuned to her that he'd craved physical contact and could not bear to be separated from her. Now his thoughts were absorbed by Josef. Libby's were too. That man, so charming, so troubled, had come between them. Bill felt comfortable alongside her but that was because coexistence was easier now they had lost focus on each other.

"Well," said Libby. "Shall I drop you at your hotel? The performance starts at five."

"I was hoping we could perhaps go somewhere for coffee," Bill said, but he was aware that there was none of the urgency, none of the audacity behind that request as had been behind his entreaty to dinner last night.

"I have work to get through," said Libby with a smile. Bill sensed she was a little disappointed too. Not so much with him but by the way they seemed to have lost it. This morning Libby had seemed so full of herself, so turned-on by her own charisma.

"Can we have dinner afterwards?" Bill asked. Even if he wasn't desperate for Libby's body now he knew he would be by 5 o'clock this afternoon. He had to put in some spadework here or else the horny Bill of 5pm was going to be facing a very frustrating night at the opera.

"There's a party after the opera," said Libby. "If we meet this person I told you about, we'll be going on to that I think."

"But if we don't..." said Bill, already provoked to the chase by Libby's habit of evading him.

Libby took a moment and looked at him. She seemed to be saying, "What is it with you, Bill Wheeler?"

"I've come a long way to see you," Bill insisted.

"And I thought you'd come for the letter..." Libby replied, teasing him yet again. Did she used to tease him seven years ago?

"Well I've got my answer now, haven't I?" said Bill.

Libby paused before nodding. "Uh-huh."

"So... even after *Götterdämmerung* the night will still be young. OK, who is this person you want me to meet anyway?"

"I'll tell you later."

"Why can't you tell me now?"

"I'd rather tell you later."

Bill didn't believe her. There was something strange in all this. What could be worth keeping secret about the person he might be meeting? "This person is to do with the letter?" he asked, realising something significant.

"Maybe," said Libby, glancing out of the window.

"So why can't you tell me his – or her – identity?"

"I can," Libby insisted. "But in case it doesn't come off I'd rather not."

"Why?"

Libby shrugged. "That's the way I work," she said. "It pays to be discreet. Godammit Bill, you don't have to come tonight."

"I'm reviewing *Götterdämmerung*," said Bill. "I'll be there. Besides, I'm going to have to listen out for that blessed tune. Have you any idea where I can get a score and have a look for those notes?"

The subject had changed and Bill noticed how Libby suddenly became helpful again. She wouldn't be able to find any academic to help out on a Saturday, she said, but she could drop him at Hieber in Marienhof where he'd be able to pick up a full orchestral score.

"There must be 20 parts though. How are you ever going to find that tune?" she wondered. "Really it's the kind of thing you need a computer to do. There must be an equivalent of Word-Search. 'Note-Search' or something."

Bill said he'd take a chance on getting lucky and got out where the cream-coloured taxi pulled up. "Will you pick me up?" he asked, closing the door. "Or shall I see you there?"

"I'll meet you outside!" she called, winding down the window.

"How will I recognise you?" Bill joked.

"I'll be looking wonderful."

Bill laughed and made his way to Hieber. He was about to go in when something made him divert to the nearby Ratskeller. And it wasn't the idea of alcohol. He needed to sit down and get out his notebook. Thoughts that had begun to form were finally crystallising.

There was more in this letter than Libby was letting on. There had to be. Whatever she had seen in those two pages, it wasn't what Josef Steiner had, with such discomfort, expatiated upon in front of the Badenburg. No doubt Wagner was indeed alluding to that piece of anti-Semitic doggerel when he wrote to his worthy friend. No doubt, if it could be proved that the mysterious S—— had been right to discern a reference to that tune somewhere in *Götterdämmerung*, it might put back the cause of a Tel Aviv Ring Cycle by several years. But would the great opera houses of Europe and America really throw out the entire Wagner canon just because he'd quoted, blithely but unconsciously, from an anti-Semitic song of his youth? It was no secret that Wagner blamed the Jews for the spiritual poverty of the century in which he lived. But to suggest that he'd used part of the Ring Cycle to put this message over in code was nonsense. Wagner had already written and publicly owned up to the authorship of *Das Judentum in der Musik* by the time *Valkyrie* was performed. What would make him hide a coded attack while orchestrating *Götterdämmerung*? Besides, like him or loathe him, Richard Wagner was a serious artist. He wasn't going to sully a work like *The Ring* just to take a swipe at Judaism down in the sousaphones, just in order to make his old drinking-buddies laugh. *No.*

Bill sat back and looked up at the barrel-vaulted ceiling. A woman in folksy Bavarian costume took his order for coffee. No, he told the ceiling, he would not be buying a score. That was a blind alley. Bill felt sure of it. And Libby wasn't stopping him from pursuing it. Why? Uncertain what to do, Bill got out his pen. The world always made more sense when written down.

"*Question 1:*" Bill wrote. "*What does Katz believe is the impact of this letter?*"

After all even if Martin Katz were exaggerating the business about his life being in danger, he certainly believed that the letter was sufficiently important for people to want to get it off him.

> *Question 2: Assuming Katz believes it's ABCGH that is so explosive, is he right to think Wagner's reputation would be wrecked by it?*

Bill could think of one or two *intendantes* who might even relish the whiff of scandal contained in those notes.

> *Question 3: OK, that was his sales pitch. He's not right. So why did Clements and Plod break into my cottage to try and get it back?*

This was the paradox. Yes the Katz letter was clearly *something*, but not necessarily what anyone claimed it to be.

"*Did Libby see something else in that letter?*" Bill wrote. "*What?*" He stared at the paper and began to circle Libby's name with his pen. When he did that he began to imagine her mouth, the circling motion was his tongue, the circle it created her lips. Bill took a breath and tried not to have those thoughts.

Why won't she tell me who I'm supposed to be meeting tonight? he wondered. The word *tonight*, even spoken inside his own head distracted Bill for a second time. He wrote it down as he remembered the two of them in the dimly-lit Venetian salon. *Tonight*. It has potency, that word. Yet something called him back from heady fantasy. What had she said to him? "That's the way I am, Bill."

That's the way I am.

No. Looking at his notebook, Bill realised that wasn't what she'd said. Try as he might he couldn't recall Libby's exact words in the taxi. He was getting a distant echo of them now, as if his mind had measured those words on the page against some fading memory and barely noticed the discrepancy before everything blanked out forever. "Work," he said aloud. "That's the way I work." *That* was what she had said.

So. What was Dr Ziegler doing in Munich? And where did he fit into her work? Bill suddenly felt very peeved with Libby. He had used his work as a pretext to visit but here she was using his visit to work! Damn her, he thought. She had an ulterior motive in all this. So did he, of course, but his was the right kind of ulterior.

Bill paid his bill and decided to wander down as far as the Hofgarten. He had a perverse desire to maybe walk as far as the Englischer Garten to see what it looked like without all the bodies and haze of recollected summer. Surely no one would be sunbathing today, even if the sun itself was now flattering Munich with a slightly brighter light.

Bill walked down Dienerstrasse and past a string quartet of Russian buskers. At Max Joseph Platz he was shocked to see that someone had threaded a gigantic bright yellow hoop through the Staatsoper's neoclassical facade – a gesture, presumably, towards making the art-form more accessible. Coming from a home where the only music emerged from transistor radios, Bill was suspicious of such inducements. He'd discovered classical music relatively late in life, was twenty before he went to his first concert. No amount of lurid plastic hoopla would have got young Bill Wheeler or his dad into an opera house. It had taken Bill time to care about music and the people who made it, and when he was ready the music was there, where it always had been.

Bill had never been to a performance at the Bayerische Staatsoper before. When reviewing he always liked to case the joint so that, come the performance, he was no longer concentrating on his surroundings. It was a fine monolith. Built in 1818 so his guide said. Then rebuilt after the war. You'd never think that Allied bombs had blown this place up though. The Bavarians had replaced every stone. A fastidious people, Bill thought. Stupid hoops aside, there was no way of telling from the outside that this wasn't the very place where von Bülow had conducted the world premieres of *Tristan* and *Meistersinger*. Now there's a guy, thought Bill. His wife dumps him for Meister Richard and he still champions the man's work. Did he continue to conduct Wagner, though, after Cosima sought perfect union with 'Our Friend'? What do you do? Bill thought. Good art is good art even if the man who writes it buggers off with your wife. Even if he hates Jews and steals from virtually every home he stays in. Wagner, for all that we might loathe him as a man, never wrote a bad note. Not as far as Bill knew anyway. Maybe he should have looked at that score after all.

Bill skirted the Feldherrnhalle, a monumental triple-arched building clearly modelled on the Loggia dei Lanzi in Florence which became a Nazi shrine after the failed Putsch of 1923. As a schoolboy Bill had seen colour photos of its pillars draped with red flags, a white circle in each and within those circles the crooked black cross of our nightmares.

Swastika.

How do we ever escape the past, he wondered. Does Reah see those same photos? Of course she does, and she probably goes to exhibitions of the kind Josef Steiner was organising. Most definitely in fact, even if her school didn't teach the Holocaust, she'd get it from her family. And to what end? Was she going to end up with nightmares like the ones that plagued Josef? What good does it do? Bill asked himself. Was Libby not right? Do we really prevent the recurrence of horror by dwelling on it? There had been a time to honour the dead, a time for the surviving generation to grieve, but this was a new century. Most of those who were killed by gun and gas would in any case be dead from natural causes by now. When does history begin?

And yet he couldn't look at the Feldherrnhalle without seeing those long red banners, one down each column.

Bill entered the Hofgarten at a pace. Bavarians wrapped in expensive green lodenmantels and furs were sitting at tables under blue umbrellas. The Germans really are our cultural cousins, thought Bill. The Italians wouldn't dream of sitting out for another two months but the Germans are like us, going to any lengths to pretend we have a Mediterranean climate.

He ordered another coffee and took a long look round at the elderly clientele. It was odd to think that these portly old burghers in their layers of costly clothing would have seen those banners on the Feldherrnhalle and thought nothing of them. The day-to-day presence of swastikas in one's life. As children they probably had school exercise books with the emblem printed on it, considered it noble even. Or possibly mundane.

Extraordinary. There are times when the world's perception of itself is radically altered. The fall of the Berlin Wall proved Communism could not destroy the human spirit. Landing a man on the moon proved we could journey beyond our own world. And the opening up of the concentration camps brought all of us face-to-face with humanity's extraordinary capacity for cruelty. When the camps were opened, these Bavarians here, youngsters in the days when one always saluted the Feldherrnhalle, they must have learned quite suddenly to look on the swastika in a different way. Now it was illegal, as was the salute. How long does it take the human mind to effect a fundamental change in its perception of the world? Probably less time than we think.

Bill felt uncomfortable. These people, so courteous and kind, they were the enemy still. They would barely have registered the destruction of his daughter. God, if *he* felt like that, what chance did the state of Israel have?

Bill wished he had a book with him. Today would be a good day to read that Wagner biography, especially so after this morning's conversation, but Mertens and Plod had that didn't they? Or one of the many other interested parties trying to get their hands on this letter.

Fortunately his coffee came quickly. Bill sipped it and immediately regretted he wasn't in Italy. What was it with these Schwarzer coffees that was so unappealing? He sipped from the glass of water and felt tiredness overcome him. Getting up again would prove the most enormous undertaking. Was his languor caffeine-induced or something more existential?

Of course he had a hotel room to go to. He'd been up late with Libby last night, hadn't he? And he'd got up early this morning to meet Josef. Not to mention the long Wagnerian night ahead of him.

Bill slept through the afternoon, but as he did, images kept flashing up before his eyes. The dark mournful pinnacles of coniferous forest against a grey implacable sky. Rain and the child in his arms. Bill woke up missing Reah badly and feeling guilty for leaving her with Tamsin's parents. And for what? For his so-called work? Bill knew why he didn't bother to decorate Holt's Cottage: if he did he'd have to ask himself the question 'Why?' Why was he decorating? For whom was he decorating? No. He woke every morning in the cottage, made coffee and worked, because in that way the question and the prospect of emptiness were always avoided.

He wished he could ring Reah. He'd taught himself to miss her less but whenever he was low like this his thoughts turned to her. Sadly he didn't even have her grandparents' number. And would Mr and Mrs Walken let him speak to her after all this time? After all that Tamsin had been saying?

Bill bathed and dressed for the opera. As he did he looked at himself in the mirror. These days he didn't look entirely comfortable in suits, but at least he didn't look like the mad gunman of Holt's Cottage.

He heard music, or thought he did.

As he glanced back into the mirror Bill caught the sensation of an orchestra tuning up. Not so much the sound of an orchestra but that unmistakable tremor of expectation that comes from the pit. Life was tuning up, not for tonight's opera but to prepare the players in the real drama of this special evening.

And what was the drama? It was his life, wasn't it? He hadn't been aware until now how much the whole of this day had felt like waiting in the wings. To go on with The Bill and Libby Story, Part II. He should have known that when he felt so unhappy to be parted from her at Nymphenburg. There hadn't been a story till now, had there? Looking back Bill felt as though he had been living in an entirely plotless way these last few years. Getting up. Drinking coffee. Working. Drinking whisky. Travelling when the isolation got too much for him. There had been no story, no plotline, unless Louis or Tamsin devised one. He had been a character, one character in search of a drama, a lost soul in search of an author to make sense of all this.

More than that, he'd been one character, one soul, in search of another. Bill's one man show had suddenly become a two-hander.

❖ VERY SPECIAL PEOPLE

THEY APPLAUDED, Bill watching Libby's hands out of the corner of his eye. How did she applaud, he wondered? Not wildly or aggressively like some of these Wagner-acolytes around them. Not half-hearted either. He wanted to know how Libby clapped, just as he wanted to know how she made a bed, or made love in one. Oh yes, this obsession was becoming stronger. Everything about her was fascinating until she did something he did not like. Then everything was hateful. What was going on?

The performance had been good. The singing was audible (no mean achievement in Wagner), the costumes historical yet timeless and the producer had taken a sensible middle path, neither ignoring nor carrying out to the letter Wagner's over-demanding stage directions. It was only when Brünhilde lit the funeral pyre (a large piece of red cloth) and the Rhine burst its banks (an even larger piece of blue) that Bill began to feel short-changed. This was not the Gods' Apocalypse. It wasn't even symbolism, for those pieces of material symbolised nothing. It was a cheap way of gesturing at an effect that was beyond the producer's stagecraft. A cop-out.

"I've yet to see a production where she actually rides her horse into the flames," he said to Libby as the applause dimmed.

"And what would that achieve?" she asked.

"The composer's intentions."

She stood up to leave with everyone else. Libby was wearing something voluminous that was half dress, half toga, with her hair in a headband. "Wagner should have been working with George Lucas or Spielberg," Libby insisted. "You can't do all that stuff on a stage today. We just won't buy two dimensional rivers and Rhine Maidens on string. They tried it in Seattle," she declared, as if that said everything.

"But if we don't go down the literal route you've got to interpret," Bill replied. "What did all the red and blue duvet covers stand for?"

Libby looked at him, amused. "Listen, I'm the one who warned you that it wouldn't be any good."

"You look wonderful," Bill said. He hadn't meant to say it then, but she did. He wasn't entirely sure Libby heard. The rising of a 1,700-seat opera house would drown the last trumpet.

He wished he'd said it when they'd met that evening. One look beyond the toga and into her eyes had reminded him why he had forsaken Reah for Libby. But Libby had been busy, taking his arm and guiding him past the hordes of people who'd congregated under the eight enormous Corinthian columns of the Staatsoper's portico. She'd spoken to a few but never for long. Bill's introduction to the press officer who had moved heaven and earth to get him a ticket was briefer than heaven and earth deserved. It was as if Libby had no wish to be drawn into the lives of others or be noticed – curious for one who dressed so extravagantly.

At the first interval Bill had had no chance to talk to her. She'd left him alone while she used her mobile. In the second they had been joined by a University party who had some claim on her. Before Bill could begin to do justice to Libby's loveliness they had been appropriated by an unusually tall Canadian, an authority on anti-Semitic imagery in Wagner's operas who was clutching a vanilla cup.

"Moreton, this is Bill Wheeler," Libby announced, adding something under her breath that Bill didn't catch. Looking remarkably angular in his Italian suit, Moreton had resolutely barred the way out of the niche into which Bill and Libby had found themselves thrust by the crush of people. He visibly relaxed once he realised that Bill was not a fellow academic, but he continued to hem them in.

"Bill's writing an article," said Libby, attempting to escape sideways into the crowd. It was useless; they remained shoulder to shoulder in the press.

"*Help*," said Libby quietly and Bill realised this was the second time she'd whispered that word. Moreton however was already into his stride.

" No, no, Wagner's anti-Semitism is integral to an understanding of his mature music dramas," he insisted in response to Bill's polite suggestion that you could differentiate between the man and the musician. "You may have read my paper on Corporeal Images in his Dramatic Works?"

"I might have," said Bill, beginning to dislike the man. "But I really can't remember."

"It's brilliant," said Libby. "Quite brilliant. Would you excuse me?"

Moreton went through the motions of standing aside but the throng beyond gave no quarter. The flow of people intent on champagne and beer had formed a log-jam with those who were refusing to move out of the only designated smoking area on this floor. Libby remained.

"I have proved that bodily images such as the elevated, nasal voice, the hobbling gait, ashen skin colour and *Foetor Judaicus*–"

"The what?" said Bill, disconcerted by the fact that Libby was now trying to squeeze a way out behind him.

"The Jewish Stench," said Moreton. "It was a common cultural cliché at the time, that Jews smelt. The *Foetor Judaicus* – that, along with ashen skin colour, deviant sexuality, hobbling gait etcetera. These were stock anti-Semitic clichés of the time and you'll find them in Alberich, Mime, and Hagen."

"What?" Bill was wondering where it was written that Hagen stank.

"Yes indeed, you should read my paper."

"Oh I'm sure I have," Bill bluffed, out of firm resolve not to appear impressed.

"Excuse me," Libby tried again.

"There is no doubt in my mind," Moreton continued in the tone of one who considers his mind the only arbiter of any consequence. "No doubt that Wagner used stock anti-Semitic imagery in his operas. Similar characteristics can be found in Beckmesser in *Die Meistersinger* and Klingsor in *Parsifal*. Of course Libby doesn't agree with me," he added in what he clearly believed was his joshing mode.

"No, Libby agrees with you," she rejoined reluctantly and still no further off. "I simply said that those were some of Wagner's most richly complex and enigmatic dramatic characters, and the music associated with them is some of his most haunting. They are not second-rate characters, therefore I think what Wagner is doing with them is not a simple matter of Jew-baiting." She was having to raise her voice to be heard and Bill was quietly thrilled to hear the Libby he remembered coming through hard and loud in that exchange. "Your evidence is brilliant, Moreton, it's the stock liberal self-exculpation and naivety of your conclusions that bug me!"

Moreton laughed. "We are sparring partners of old," he told Bill with unwarranted pride.

"No we're not," snapped Libby and she tried again to move again. Bill was just about to ask Moreton why on earth he came to *The Ring* when Libby started speaking loudly in German. "*Ich muss dringend auf die Toilette!* I have to go to the bathroom, would you excuse me?"

Moreton smiled down blankly at Libby but fortunately someone in the crush admitted her and she backed out of the crowd, repeating her need in German. Moreton smiled at Bill in a fixed and uncomprehending way. "Poor Libby and her bladder," he said. "It seems to be a constant problem for her."

"Only when he's around," Libby told Bill when they were back in their seats for Act 3. "I'd fake cholera if I had to."

Now as everyone made their way out of the stalls Libby spotted

Moreton again. "We've got to find another way out," she hissed but there was laughter in her voice.

"Who is he?" Bill asked.

"Visiting professor. He helped me with something I did here a few years ago. I don't know why the Germans haven't deported him. He's the most undesirable alien I've ever come across. Seems to think we have some witty badinage going on. Fortunately he's never realised how much I loathe him – well, fortunately for him, anyway."

"He's Canadian," said Bill. "You can hardly call him an alien."

"North Americans," said Libby with a visible shudder. "OK, down here."

It was an adventure squeezing through a queue of Wagnerites set on going the other way. They both laughed when they made it to an exit door lower than the one they had shared with Moreton. Bill was just about to return to the subject of Libby's attractiveness when she announced, "There's Hauke, thank goodness!"

They drove for some time out of Munich along Dachauer Strasse. The road signs made Bill feel uncomfortable. Hauke sat in the front with the same driver Libby had used when they'd met at the airport. Bill felt it was an achievement of his that Hauke hadn't prevented him riding in the back with Libby. Nevertheless he resented the young German's presence massively.

"Where are we going?" he asked Libby.

She smiled. This was evidently all part of the plan. "Someone wants to meet you."

"Who?"

"His name is August. He has a title but he likes to be known as Willy."

"*Baron* August?" Bill asked. The Baron had been in Venice with them. Libby nodded, pleased and impressed.

"Baron August *What*?" Bill felt like being difficult. Insisting on every detail seemed a good conduit for his mood.

"August Wilheim Louis Bomberg de Something von Meck," said Libby.

"And we came here to meet him?"

"He said that he might meet us at the opera or afterwards. It depended."

"On what?"

"On other people."

"Libby this is all very mysterious, does it have to be quite so..." In his exasperation Bill was uncertain what adjective to use. "Why is Hauke coming?" he asked. It was an irrelevant question but Bill wasn't inclined to be logical at that moment. He wanted to provoke her, to see if she'd admit that this lugubrious sensualist was her lover.

"He's involved," she replied, refusing to be shocked at Bill's rudeness.

"With whom?"

"With what I do."

"And what *is* it you do, Libby?" Bill asked.

She paused a moment before being replying. "Why am I getting all this hostility, Bill?"

It was a good question. "Because I'm confused," he admitted. "I don't know whether I'm part of your work or whether you're helping me out or whether we're out on a date."

Libby was looking ahead as if she were concentrating hard on the back of Michael's head and about to give instructions on their route. She shot Bill a sideways glance. "Does it have to be a choice?"

"No..." said Bill, and now his eyes were also on those heads in front. He watched Hauke's ears either side of the neck rest, his hair given a silvered halo by the glare of oncoming traffic.

Knowing where her gloved hand lay on the leather upholstery, Bill extended his own. Though he kept his eyes on Hauke, he knew exactly when his fingers were within range. Neither of them glanced at each other as the Mercedes slowed and executed a left turn signposted *Obermenzing*. Bill's fingers closed round two of hers. He felt the softness of that dark kidskin glove and the slimness of her fingers within. The noise of the car seemed intense. Libby did not look his way, neither did she withdraw her hand. Bill pressed her fingers, felt them move closer together, inert yet yielding to his pressure. Releasing, he waited a moment then squeezed them again, trying so hard to communicate the need he was feeling for her. He waited to see if her fingers would reply. All he wanted, just for a moment, was to feel Libby's fingers tighten on his, but they remained still, receiving him but not responding. Bill was aware that he was breathing ridiculously fast. What did he make of her words, and of her accepting his touch in this way? He was just thinking of withdrawing his hand when suddenly hers had gone. Libby was sweeping back an imaginary strand of hair as she said, "Hauke can we telephone ahead and make sure there's a fire in the *Arbeitszimmer*."

"*Kann ich dein Handy haben?*" asked Hauke, and he slid back the glass partition. Libby passed her mobile phone to him and Hauke tactfully sealed them off again. Bill could feel his heart pounding. He was not normally aware of his heartbeat. Was Libby distracting Hauke? Strange, that it took something so little for his heart to thump like this.

Stranger still that it had begun to do so even before he'd realised the significance of what she'd just done. Libby could have rung ahead herself. Clever girl, thought Bill. And yet he knew he'd felt the kick of that moment, felt the rise in their body temperatures long before his brain had worked out what was going on.

She leaned back, her shoulder possibly a little closer to his than before on the leather upholstery. Bill could sense she was trying to find the right words and when she spoke, they surprised him. "This is not easy for me, Bill." Libby said those words with the utmost seriousness. It was as if she had told him everything he needed to know. And yet Bill felt he knew nothing.

"I don't understand," he replied, equally seriously and just as quietly. He was facing her now, but Libby wouldn't be drawn. Her eyes remained on Hauke as he talked into the mobile. Bill watched her speak. The moments before her next words formed seemed an infinity.

"As I said, Bill, I read *both* your e-mails." Her voice was quiet. "Wouldn't you be surprised if I weren't taken aback by the second."

"The second?" Bill was surprised, uneasy. He was aware of significance in the air.

"'Feelings that have lain dormant have torn through me,'" Libby quoted. Her eyes still not on him. Words from the e-mail he hadn't sent. "Bill, you told me you were coming over to see if I shared those feelings."

She remained in profile to him. Oh my God, thought Bill. I did, I said that in the e-mail I saved but didn't send. But then, when I came back to the machine it told me I was online. Bill remembered the cursor blinking away at him. *No New Messages.* Hell! Reah had come in and he must have pressed Send rather than Save. What else did it say for God's sake?

At this point they turned off through some electronic gates that had opened for the car in front. My God, thought Bill, Louis is going to have a field day with this.

The house of Baron August Willy de Whatever was, contrary to Bill's expectations, a modern construct, although it followed a baronial floor-plan. Guests entered into a large, tall hall. It was as spartan as any modern architect might wish, but there were galleries running round at first-floor level where latterday minstrels might strum their electric lutes. A small group of people was already congregating around the twin flame-effect gas fires which had been mounted either side of a large central fireplace. Someone had been here and designed with a capital D, thought Bill as he sat down on a low concrete bench. He felt like Siegfried in the hall of the Gibichungs. This was a world beyond his previous experience.

"Hello," said a woman of advanced years with remarkably long blonde hair. "I'm Heidi. Let me give you a drink."

There were quite a few guests, men in expensive suits, their wives in varying shades of oyster, ecru and champagne. The opera had obviously been an excuse, a prelude perhaps, for tonight's party.

"I'm with Libby," said Bill as he rose to shake hands. He felt he had to say something to explain his presence, for Libby had disappeared. Another annoying habit of hers.

"Of course," said Heidi. "It's so good to see our Libby with someone." Bill didn't trust her one inch.

"Tell me do you like *art*?" Heidi asked, offering up glass of champagne.

"Dare I say otherwise?" Bill replied. What kind of question was that?

"I think you like art, Bill," the woman said. "Let me show you round."

"Why don't you tell me who you are?" said Bill, taking more than a sip from his glass.

"I am the Baroness de Teisier von Meck," she replied, her hand on his arm. Bill swallowed quicker than he'd intended. "But you can call me Heidi."

"So," said Bill. "This is your house." Such a lame thing to say.

"It's somewhere to stay when we're in town."

"You have a *schloss*, I presume," he enquired, hating the way that everything he said came out facetious. No one in Bill's family had ever talked to the aristocracy. Now here he was, face-to-face with *Junkers*.

"It's in the wrong part of Germany," she told him. "My husband's family transferred most of their money over here in 1957."

They had walked up some steps and were now heading down a wide corridor that seemed to double as an art gallery. Photographs, mainly portraits, lined the walls.

"That's Horst P. Horst," Heidi explained looking at a monochrome fashion print of some woman in a 1950s swimming costume.

"Nice girl," Bill replied. "Shame about the name. Have you been sent here to distract me?"

"I thought you would not wish to sit all alone."

"I'm a journalist," he replied. "It's what I do best." Heidi affected to be amused. "Where's Libby?" Bill decided to try the direct approach.

"She had to telephone someone."

"She's always telephoning someone or meeting someone."

"That's our Libby," said the Baroness indulgently.

"But *who?*" Bill didn't like being messed around with in this way.

Heidi pointed out another photograph to him. "You know if you are a journalist you really should know about Horst. He succeeded George Hoyningen-Huene at *Vogue.*"

"No, I've never heard of him either"

"Baron Hoyningen-Heune. No? Principal fashion photographer at *Vogue* until, I believe, 1934."

"You barons do get around," said Bill. He felt he was behaving like the least likeable of adolescents. His inclination was to return to the main hall of Schloss Bomberg with its brutalist concrete blocks and hideous purple scatter cushions and look for Libby, but in fact at that moment Bill felt a welcome sense of movement behind him, something that could only mean Libby was nearby. Before Heidi spoke, he knew it was her.

"*Herzerl!*" said the Baroness. "Bill has been inconsolable."

"*Es tut mir leid, dass ich so lange weg war,*" said Libby. "Sorry." She kissed Heidi, who seemed to melt away with the ease of a truly professional hostess. "Well," said Libby, smiling. Her eyes seemed to be trying to convey an impression of excitement. Here they were after all. This was it. Bill did not believe her eyes.

"Well?" he said.

"Have you got the letter?"

"Of course," said Bill.

"I believe Willy has someone who wants to meet you," said Libby. Bill didn't like the German way in which Libby pronounced the Baron's name.

"I thought Villy *was* the person who wanted to meet me," he quibbled. "Libby, why are you doing all this?"

They were standing alone in the gallery now, monochrome prints on white concrete, Libby's black boots on white marble flagstones. She looked as if Horst B. Flagpole might well have snapped her on Rhode Island, Summer of '43. "That letter..." said Libby. "You wanted to know about it." The point was made. She turned to go.

"And us?"

"That's difficult," Libby said, not looking round. "We can discuss that later."

"No, we can't," said Bill. Libby turned. She looked surprised. "You know why I came here," he told her. Boy did she know that.

"*Bill,*" said Libby, with the indulgent smile of someone speaking calmly to an over-demanding but charming child. "Bill, you can't just walk in here..." She didn't quite know how to complete that sentence. She was not at ease. Bill took her arm.

"You said that before," he told her. "What does it mean?"

Libby wasn't looking at him, she was looking at Horst's handiwork. Bill squeezed her arm. "It's complicated, that's all."

"By what?"

"Not by what," she turned to face him. "By *whom*." Bill felt the earth fall away.

"Hauke?" he said flatly.

Libby laughed in genuine surprise. "Hauke? No. He's like my kid brother."

"The Baron then?"

"Does it matter who?" She looked him straight in the eye. Not challenging. Brave. Wow, thought Bill. She is waiting for my reaction. He reached out and took her other arm.

"It matters to me, Libby, surely you can see that."

"I'm a private person, Bill," said Libby.

"I want you," he said simply. "That's all I can say." He could forget who this other man was. This man was not important. She was. In the silence that followed he could sense her breathing as he had in the restaurant.

"How can you say such things?" she asked and moved suddenly away. It was almost as if she were trying to step aside to avoid his words. "How can you say things like that now?"

It was easy, Bill might have said, because he was at that moment unaware of any motivation save that of wanting her.

"Do you want me?" he asked.

Libby looked away. "It's too soon," she said. "I don't know. Maybe it's too late."

"*Tonight*," said Bill. She was determined, but his will was greater than hers. He could not attempt to understand at this stage. He just had to take every cue to possess her.

"Will you come back to my hotel tonight?" Libby didn't reply. "Is he expecting you?"

"He's out of town," she replied looking down. "In any case it isn't like that."

Bill didn't like the idea that 'he' – whoever he was – existed in the same world as them. Determinedly he tried to see into her face. Recognising this, she met his eye. Never had latent tears shocked him so. There was a candour about her eyes that was beautiful and alarming in equal measure. I am stronger than she is at this moment, he thought. "I didn't know you cried," he said to her, stupidly. He wished to be kind. Even as he rode roughshod over her feelings.

"Yeah well," she said. "I'm human. American but human." Bill was suffused with tenderness for her. "God knows what you are, Bill Wheeler."

"I don't want to hurt you."

"Nobody ever does," she replied. "Not at this stage."

"Is this a stage?"

"*Christ*, Bill," said Libby. She leaned towards him. It was as if she were conceding. Her shoulder touching his. She was his prisoner – for the moment anyway. He was about to put his arm around her when a shadow fell on them from further down the gallery. Young Hauke. On cue as always. The Baron required them both.

"Does it matter that he saw us?" Bill asked as they walked back down the corridor.

"Hauke? No," said Libby.

"I thought in the car you were making sure Hauke couldn't hear us."

Libby shook her head. "No," she said with what was almost a laugh. "That was so Michael was distracted."

"Why Michael?"

They were approaching the steps down to the library. Libby stopped and turned to Bill. "This man, the one I spoke of, it's his car we used tonight. Michael's his driver. He might report back. I think that's why I get so much use of the car. This other man, he can be very jealous. I think it's his way of keeping tabs on me when I'm in Germany."

Bill felt things were happening too quickly for him. First Libby divulges that she's read that excruciatingly personal e-mail. Now she tells him she's involved with some man who pays uniformed spies to ferry her round Munich.

"Don't get me wrong," said Libby. "He's a good man–"

"But he checks up on you," Bill completed her sentence with saturnine precision. "Is that why it was difficult last night?" he asked. "Because he was expecting you? Is he here now?" Jealousy was seething within Bill. He needed someone to punch, preferably this plutocrat with his Mercedes Espionage Machine.

"He's gone out of town," said Libby. "I told you. I thought he was coming but he's gone away. He's paying me back for last night."

"What? To leave you with me?"

Libby was not looking entirely happy. "He doesn't know about you. He just thinks you're part of my work. We're not together in the usual sense of the word, Bill, but he doesn't like it when anything gets in the way, like last night."

"Oh sounds like a really nice guy," said Bill. He felt nothing but animosity towards this creature – whoever he was.

"I don't want to talk about him," said Libby. "I never meant to. He's kind and he's brilliant..." She paused. "I always get mixed up with the impossible ones."

Hauke had opened two polished aluminium doors ahead of them.

"We have to talk," said Bill, taking Libby's arm. He took it more gently this time, not to bend her to his will, as he did before, but to show support. They were in this together.

"Later," said Libby. Bill loved the sound of that word, the image it created of half-lit rooms and intimacy.

The library was darker than Bill expected and wood-panelled too. That he really had not expected. After the concrete chic of the entrance hall, this room seemed positively Victorian – not at all Teutonic. It was curiously lit, hardly bright enough for reading, more a room to brood in. Those few spotlights in the ceiling illuminated sculptures and a polished metal table with bottles of mineral water, but of books there seemed to be precious few.

A middle-aged man as broad as he was tall was rising to greet them. He was dressed in an Austrian cardigan and Moorish slippers. He looked faintly ridiculous, Bill thought, but his voice was deep and resonant. This had to be the Baron. If former Sgt Clements had been a policeman out of Central Casting so this was Hollywood Bavarian Baron Mk I.

"Libby," he said warmly, clasping her hand and kissing her wrist. "You see the fire is lit, just for you. Bill!" He had finished with Libby's hand and was now clutching Bill's in his huge paw. "Welcome! Come and sit down, we're all very excited about this letter you've found."

They sat round the fireplace in leather sofas of unbelievable comfort as Hauke closed the doors and withdrew. There was no one else in the room. Bill looked around and wondered who exactly he was supposed to be meeting here.

"You like the room?" the Baron was asking.

"Remarkable."

"And what did you think of the opera? Is this the first time you have seen Wagner?" Bill was slightly put out that the people who had invited him over thought this British reviewer such a philistine.

"No, but it's the first time I've seen it in Munich."

"I think the producer had nothing to say and the conductor was out of his depth," said Willy. "Siegfried was straining and the chorus under-rehearsed but I am no expert," he added. "I shall look forward to your review. Now, to the business of this letter," he announced with sweeping authority and producing a pocket book as if from nowhere. "I am authorised to offer you a sum of money for the letter currently in your possession."

"What?" said Bill.

"Assuming that it is yours to sell," the Baron added. "But then we both know that is a nicety."

"I don't understand what you mean," said Bill.

"Please," the Baron insisted. "I do not mean to insult you. Forgive my clumsy use of English. I am just saying that, in order to have left the Archive in the first place, it has to have become stolen property, so the question of whether you are legally the owner is a technical point we can dispense with. The true owner of that letter, a man of my acquaintance, who wishes to remain anonymous, he is willing to overlook the question of how it came into your hands and to repay you for your trouble."

Bill was astounded. He had had no thought of selling the Katz letter when he entered the Baron's library. Although he had not finally decided what to do with Wagner's missive, it had never once crossed Bill's mind to flog it. If he had imagined a future for these two sheets of paper, it was that they be returned to Katz or whoever the true owner might be. He shot a glance at Libby. Of course she'd mentioned the business of selling when they first met but did she really think..?

Libby was looking at the Baron and seemed impenetrable. This was between Bill and the big man.

"It's not mine to sell," Bill began.

"Please," said the Baron. His hand gesture was open and generous, as if they were all too grown up for this kind of game and he wanted Bill to understand they could dispense with such prevarication.

"I have no interest in selling," Bill explained. "Besides, the letter isn't mine."

"We know it isn't yours," the Baron repeated. "How could you come legally by such an artefact?"

"I was lent it," Bill lied, realising that he was moving on to shaky ground.

"By someone who had no right to it, no doubt," the Baron pointed out. "Bill, I am speaking to you on behalf of the owner. He is willing to drop any possible charges, he is even willing to pay you for your trouble, subject to certain conditions. But he does want it back."

"Who is the owner?" Bill asked.

"That is one of the conditions," said the Baron. "Do you have the letter with you?"

"No," said Bill.

"*Bill...*" said a voice. Libby. A kind but patient voice with a note of disappointment in it. "Bill, you told me you'd brought it." She made it sound as if he were a difficult child. And not necessarily hers. He really did not like that tone.

"I've brought the photocopy," Bill told her, fishing it out of his breast pocket.

"You said–" Libby began and Bill heard the Baron snort. He was clearly not pleased.

"The photocopy I made at the hotel this morning. The photocopy I showed to Josef. You never said to bring the original."

The Baron stood up.

"*Ich glaube, das Interview ist jetzt beendet,*" he said to Libby.

"I'm sorry," said Bill, peeved by the rudeness. "What was that?"

"I said, this interview is over," the Baron informed him. "I advise you, Bill, if you want to avoid criminal charges to have that letter with you tomorrow."

Bill stood up to square with him. "I'm flying out tomorrow."

"Are you, indeed?" said the Baron with veiled menace. Then he snarled something else in German to Libby which Bill didn't catch and was gone. The door closed. They were alone. There was a pause between the two of them. Libby hadn't moved from her side of the fireplace.

"What the hell was that all about?" Bill was nearly shouting.

"You said you had the letter with you," Libby reproached him quietly. She was looking at the fire.

"And if I had, would that thug just have expected me to hand it over?" Bill demanded.

"God what a mess," said Libby, getting up and smoothing down the folds of her toga.

"What was that man talking about?!" Bill was still shouting, gesturing towards the library's double doors. "Was he threatening me?"

"Oh come on Bill," Libby argued. "We all know you didn't come by that letter legally."

"Oh do we?" he retorted.

"Yes we do," said Libby. "Wouldn't you be surprised if I hadn't picked up on how vague you were about its provenance?"

Bill felt deceived. True, he had not been straight with Libby but she hadn't been straight with him either. She'd suspected something about the Katz letter all along and never told him. That seemed worse than his theft...

"Oh, its *provenance!*" Bill replied, resorting to sarcasm. "Look, never mind its *provenance*, I came to you because I wanted the letter authenticated, not because I wanted some shady deal to blag it on the baronial black market."

"Oh really," Libby glared at him. "And I thought you came to me because of 'feelings that had lain dormant'".

"I never meant to send that e-mail," Bill snapped.

Libby stepped back as if he had hit her across the face. "You mean–" She paused and tried to smile the awfulness away. "You mean – those *weren't* your words?"

"No, they were my words."

"You didn't mean them though."

No. He couldn't deny those words. "Of course I meant them," he admitted. "They're even more true now than when I wrote them."

"The truth can't become more true, Bill," Libby snapped at him and she walked over to where bottles of spring water shone under their spotlight. "Truth is an absolute. Something either is or isn't."

"Oh come on," said Bill. Her sudden pedantry told him she was hurt, that she had been building castles on the foundation of his words, words that she now discovered were never intended for her to see.

"I meant what I said Libby."

"But you wouldn't have said it if you'd known I might hear you. What kind of truth is that, Bill Wheeler!"

"Listen," he said. But to be honest he had no idea what he was about to say. "Listen, we've both been less than direct with each other. You didn't tell me about the guy with the Mercedes–"

"I did tell you," Libby retorted.

"Yes but you admitted you hadn't intended to," he reminded her.

"Do you think that kind of thing's easy?" she said, turning to him, her glass full.

"And you certainly didn't tell me that you were fixing to flog the letter," he continued.

"But I thought that was why you'd come to me," Libby replied angrily. And honestly. Yes, she clearly had been surprised.

"I mean who is this mystery purchaser?"

"I don't know."

"Just what kind of business are you mixed up in?" Bill continued.

"That's nothing to do with you."

"Libby, look–" Bill began.

"You came to me and I acted in good faith!" It was her turn to shout now. "Have you any idea how foolish that made me look just now? That man believes I have credibility."

"Libby, you knew the letter wasn't mine," Bill insisted. Reason was surely on his side.

"So if I knew you were willing to steal someone else's property you can't blame me for thinking you were also expecting to sell it on!"

Libby could be very harsh, Bill realised. He also realised reason wasn't quite so firmly on his side after all.

"I think we've both been less than direct with each other," Bill admitted, hoping to heal the rift. He walked over and put his hands on her shoulders. "Mm?"

"Just don't criticise what I do," said Libby grudgingly and she shook herself free of him. Bill was used to Reah doing that. He placed his hands on her shoulders again. Libby let him this time, sipping sulkily at her water. After a while she admitted, "I thought I was helping you."

"OK," said Bill, "I understand. And I won't criticise what you do." But he felt an unpleasant aftertaste nevertheless. Who was that titled thug? And who was the anonymous 'owner' he was speaking for?

Libby dropped her head towards his chest and leaned there like she had in the Hoyningen gallery. Then Bill put an arm around her. They stayed like that a while, Bill listening to the noise of the party next door. He realised that this ought to be his chance to kiss her, but he no longer felt such an urge and she was cradling a glass of mineral water anyway. His whole body felt tender, hurting on the inside but also feeling the hurt in her. Poor Libby, she was obviously deeply embarrassed. That unfortunate e-mail hadn't just betrayed his feelings, it had betrayed hers too. She'd been acting on it, acting on words he'd never knowingly uttered. Ever since he'd arrived Libby had been working to a much more direct agenda and now he knew about it. Knew she had been considering the depth of her feelings for him all this time. That was embarrassing. And now he'd made her look a fool in front of the Baron, a man whose good opinion she obviously valued, though God knows why.

"What shall we do about the party?" he asked. "I think we've rather blotted our copybook."

"Let's go somewhere," said Libby. "Hauke can get us a taxi."

"What about Michael?" Bill asked.

"Michael can screw himself," said Libby wearily. Then she laughed. "I can't leave him sitting out there all night, can I? I'll tell him to go." She sniffed.

"You're not crying again are you?" Bill asked, looking down at her face and smiling.

"Me? No," said Libby. "Tough Bostonian cookie. Surely you knew that."

"Let's go back to my hotel," said Bill.

Libby shook her head. "I'm not ready for that, Bill."

"We don't have to do anything," he said. "I just want to be with you where we can talk without Michael or the Baron, or Moreton or even dear old Hauke."

"You really under-esteem my Hauke, don't you?" she joked, fetching a tissue from her bag.

"Well now that I know he's not the one I have to be jealous of I may start to warm to him."

"My big polar bear," said Libby. "He looks after me. You've no idea."

"I want to look after you too," said Bill. He had never had this idea before but it certainly occurred to him now. There was in Libby, despite her strength and abilities, something that brought out the father in him.

"Not your hotel though," she said.

"OK," he agreed. "What about your place?"

"Worse," she shuddered.

"Is that where you live with him?"

"I don't live with him," said Libby. "Just stay there when I'm in Munich."

"Well where then?"

"Couldn't we go somewhere that isn't your hotel?"

"Libby, it's pretty bizarre to have one hotel room booked and go and stay in another."

She laughed.

And because they had laughed together, Libby went with Bill to his hotel in a taxi that cost them all their deutschmarks combined. And in the taxi Libby had laughed openly at her own folly and admitted that the one thing she had said to herself she was not going to do tonight was go back to Bill's room. And here she was doing so. They had laughed at that too and then Libby had grown serious again in the narrow lift with its polished mirrors and gilt fittings.

"The people here know me," she said. "Damn."

"Does that matter?" he asked.

"I like to live my life privately. This other man. No one knows. This isn't the kind of thing I'd do with him," she mused. "He's very discreet too."

"Is he married?" Bill asked. It was the obvious question. Libby hesitated before replying.

"Ah, Jesus," she said, conceding. "I won't go into all the usual stuff about his wife and him leading separate lives, that he hardly lives with her, all the familiar arguments to justify an old familiar situation."

"He stays with her for the children?" Bill asked.

"They don't have children. He's Catholic, that's why he won't leave. The children thing's a real shame. He'd love kids."

"Then I don't see the problem..."

"The Church, Bill. He's, well, if I tell you any more about him you'll probably guess who it is and I don't want that. The religion thing is important to him, believe me. Godammit, I've wished it weren't."

Their lift came to a halt.

"He's well-known then?" Bill asked. He could not help but be morbidly intrigued.

"I'm not saying any more," she replied.

"But in the arts?"

"Stop it," said Libby sharply. They were walking down the corridor now. She took his arm gently. "Bill, you must respect me on this. Please."

"OK," he said, reaching for his keycard. "You're so secretive. Just tell me one thing though. Was he with you when you were in Venice? Was he the one who answered the phone?"

"I'm not saying anything more about him," Libby insisted. "And if you don't let it drop, I'm going straight back out and getting another bloody taxi I can't afford." Bill closed the door behind them.

"All right. One last question, but not about him."

"OK," said Libby, as she unbuttoned her coat.

"When you were in London all those years ago was there someone then?" Bill asked. "You never gave anything away about your private life. I had no idea. Was there someone?"

They were standing close again, as they had been in Venice. Libby looked up at him. Bill was struck by her total candour. It was a quality that made her seem almost childlike.

"Yes," she said, and she reached up, her arms around his neck, lips on his, her mouth suddenly, incredibly, moving effortlessly within him. Bill was swept away. Warmth and softness of a kind he had never known overwhelmed him. When he regained awareness of his place within this material universe his arms were inside her coat circling her waist. He wanted to move her backwards towards the wall or the bed or down to the floor even, but her kiss, which had no place in space or time, paralysed him. He just lost himself and his self was more than happy to disappear.

When the kiss was over Bill leant back against the wardrobe door. "I'm

194

sorry," he said, wiping his mouth. "I've got to sit down." He remained completely unaware of Libby's presence until he found that she had taken off her coat and was sitting on the bed next to him, her hands holding his. "I'm sorry," he repeated. "I guess I've waited years for that. Libby look..." He wasn't sure what to say and words would have been so useful at this stage.

"I won't sleep with you Bill," she told him kindly but firmly.

"You won't..." Bill repeated, his world still failing to make sense. "OK," he said. "Yes, OK, but–"

"It's not a moral thing," she explained. "It's just that I cannot. Not while there's him."

"OK, get rid of him," said Bill, surfacing at last into reason.

Libby laughed quietly. "I can't, not just like that."

"It's going nowhere," Bill insisted, squeezing her hands. "I love you and I'm not married to someone else."

"How can you say you love me?" Libby asked. It was a fair question. Were he not so caught up in his desire for her Bill would have thought the same thing himself. As it was, he'd probably think it tomorrow, particularly if he woke up with Libby's face on the pillow beside him.

"Seven years ago..." Bill began.

"Seven years ago you gave me up for your wife and child," Libby reminded him. She stood up and turned to face him. "Have you any idea what that felt like? I didn't want to take you away from them, Bill, but I had feelings for you in London and to be told *that* by another of your damn faxes."

Bill remembered that fax. Tamsin had never forgiven him for it. "Please, that was then," he insisted. "I was confused. I couldn't let Reah down. I was, I am, her father."

"I know," said Libby. "Tamsin had the trump card there, didn't she?"

Bill recalled the arguments. Tamsin's rage when she read his final letter to Libby. Maybe he'd been a fool to keep it but it was important to him. It contained his truth. "*For the sake of Reah we have to end this relationship.*"

One month into their reconciliation period, during the move to Holt's Farm, Tamsin had found that fax. Maybe he had been a fool too, not to hide it.

Her rage was terrible to behold. "You told her that! You told her that if it weren't for Reah, you'd be off with her tomorrow!"

"I didn't say that," Bill insisted, but Tamsin was wounded beyond recovery. She smashed things, she moaned, she screamed, she threw books at him.

"She'll always have those words, the bitch! Wherever she is and whoever's marriage she's wrecking next, she'll always have those words. *He loved me, I was his true love. He would have left his dreadful old wife if it hadn't been for his daughter. What a great man he is.* What a great man you are Bill! What a great fucking bloody man you are staying in your bloody fucking boring marriage for the sake of your wonderful bloody daughter!!"

He could still hear Tamsin's screams in his mind. He wondered if Reah could too. Probably. They imbedded in the rafters of Holt's Farm and hung on the dank coniferous trees beyond. Holt's Farm had always been cursed.

"Libby, I don't believe in fate," Bill said as he reached for her hand. "Or at least I thought I didn't. But I don't believe that it's an accident your coming into my life like this, or me into yours. I don't think it was an accident that I was sent to Venice when you were there."

Too right it wasn't an accident, Louis had arranged it. That was his editor's piece of mischief-making, squandering company funds before the financial year ran out, taking vicarious pleasure in Bill's sex-life.

"I know," she said, coming over to kneel down in front of him. "Do you not think I've thought of that too? Tried to puzzle it out. You disappearing so completely from my life and then, suddenly, there you are again, just when I was thinking that I must leave this guy, really get him out of my life. Maybe lead a celibate life from now on. And suddenly there you are and so sure of everything, when at the time, in London, I had no idea you reciprocated. We never spoke of feelings then did we?"

"Just Schopenhauer," Bill reminded her with a smile.

"Did you love me then?" Libby asked, but before Bill could answer she put a hand to his mouth.

Bill was glad she'd kept him from answering. He couldn't remember now what his feelings had been for the tough young Massachusetts iconoclast whose company had shocked and fascinated him when they were both in London and whom he'd learned to hate in the years that followed. All he knew now was that he wanted her. There could be no price he would not pay.

"Please, stay with me tonight?" he asked and he tried to kiss her. She avoided the kiss but leant forward to hug him. Bill held Libby and stroked her head. He had never touched her hair before. It was so fine and there was so much of it. Was her hair like this all those years ago in London? He would never know. That made him sad. He could feel her arms around his neck beginning to let go.

"I need time to think," said Libby as she stood.

"What?" said Bill, and he stood up too. "Libby... love, you don't need time to think." Why was it that whenever Libby fled from him he gained confidence and clarity about his feelings? "You know you want me, you just feel you need time to get used to the idea. What good will going on three or four dates do? It'll only confirm what you already know. It's a ritual that we haven't got time for. Libby my flight is in the morning, we need to decide what we're doing."

He had her by the arms again. He wanted so much for her to be swayed by his arguments. Words were never more important. Yet, even more vital than having Libby for the rest of his life, was having her now. Tonight. In this room.

"It isn't that simple for me, Bill."

"You know that you wanted to meet to see if you had a life with me instead of with him," Bill said. "Have you decided?"

"I think..." Libby began.

"Never mind what you think," Bill insisted, shaking her gently. "Do you *know*?"

She looked into his face. Her eyes, grey and mysterious, seemed to peer right into his soul. God, she frightened him when she looked that deeply.

"Do you know?" he asked again but with less confidence now. Could his inner life withstand the scrutiny?

"Yes," she said, and nodded. "I knew tonight when you said that you hadn't intended to send those words and it hurt, I knew then that your love had come to mean so much to me. So much. So soon. Bill, it was just difficult to take in." She paused and breathed slowly. In and out. "Yes. I had hoped that I'd never want another man in my life. But now I do truly believe your feelings for me."

How can she be so sure? wondered Bill as she took his face in her hands and kissed him. When she looks at me it seems as if she knows everything and yet she has no idea. How can anyone look at me and be that certain? Wrapped with these anxieties Bill found he'd failed to respond to the kiss this time. *Bed*, he thought. If only we can go to bed together I'm sure it'll all come clear.

Libby was saying something. "Thank you for understanding." What was it he understood? She was already stepping back from him.

"What are you doing?" Bill asked.

"I'm going to see him," Libby explained, picking up her coat.

"What – tonight?!"

"No, tonight I'm going home. Then I'm phoning him first thing tomorrow and I'm going to arrange to see him. He has a *hütte* in the country, a sort of *dacha* where he works. It's in the mountains. I know that's where he's gone."

"But tonight," said Bill.

"I told you," Libby explained putting her hand on his cheek. "I can't sleep with you tonight. I've got to speak to him first."

"Tomorrow, then," said Bill. He suddenly couldn't bear the thought that he wasn't going to possess her.

"You're going back tomorrow."

"I'll stay."

"Bill, if we're right about this, we've got a long time ahead of us," said Libby, stroking his cheek. "I want it to be right."

Bill took her hand from his cheek and kissed it. "I can't bear to go off not knowing when I'm going to see you again."

"I have something to arrange with the new director of the *Instituto Cultura* in Belgrave Square," said Libby, fishing out her diary. "We were going to meet in Munich next time he visited. I'll come next week."

"Next week?"

"Yes."

"And you'll come to the Wye Valley too?"

"It sounds heavenly," she said. Clearly her mind was made up.

Bill could hardly believe his luck. "Oh it is," he agreed, imagining Libby in Holt's Cottage. "Beautiful. Actually though, I can't quite see you in muddy fields and river banks."

Libby laughed as she flicked through her diary. "I'll have you know my father's family had a cabin in Maine. We did the backwoods stuff. Well at least till my Dad got hold of it and put in central heating and a jacuzzi."

The humour of the moment helped them both. Bill felt less desperate about letting her go. "Will you ring me?"

"Give me your mobile number. I'll ring you as soon as I've spoken to him."

"Do you think I'll get out of the country?" Bill asked as he wrote it down on a piece of hotel stationery. "Our friend the Baron sounded like he wanted me stopped at the border."

"Willy likes to think of himself as a fixer," Libby replied. "You know we're going to have to talk about that letter, Bill. Tonight wasn't funny."

"For either of us," he said, pressing the number into her hand. Already the small black gloves were on again. "I'll see you out."

"No," she insisted. "I'm already making a spectacle of myself coming here with you. I don't want to leave with you as well, as if we stopped off for a quickie and now it's time to go."

"You'll ring me tomorrow?"

"I warrant you."

Bill tried to kiss Libby again when they got to the door of his room. She yielded for a moment but it was not a kiss like their first. It was a kiss for leaving. Frustrated, he pressed her to the wall. She lifted a hand to his chest to stop him. "Bill, when I give myself to someone I do so 100 percent."

He dearly wished for 50 percent on account now.

"Can you wait?"

"No," he admitted and laughingly banged his head twice on the wall behind her shoulder. Better that he hurt himself.

"Well you're just going to have to," said Libby. Fond. Amused. Unaware of the violently conflicting passions within him. She squeezed his shoulder and kissed him on the cheek.

"I'll call you," she said, as she opened the door. "I promise. Oh–" Libby was almost gone. She turned. "Did you find that tune in the Death March? The Abraham, Benjamin, Chaim motif?"

"No," he replied, simply. "It doesn't matter. I meant to listen out for it tonight but I was looking at you the whole time. I hardly noticed."

Libby smiled at the flattery. "I too shall read your review with interest, Mr Wheeler."

When Bill woke up he couldn't believe any of it. He remembered the odious Moreton whose Adam's apple now figured preternaturally large in Bill's imagination; he remembered the Baron, snarling in his slippers, and Heidi with her long, artificially-blonde tresses. And he remembered Libby's fingers, how he had clasped them in the taxi. Most of all he remembered that kiss in this room. This very room. And Libby's other man, of course, this anonymous international Catholic celebrity. Bill was sure he was a conductor. Or a pope. He tried to think which famous conductors lived in the south of Germany. Of course this guy could also be in Salzburg. He could be Austrian. Who the hell was it? Unable to come up with a name, Bill got out of bed and took a shower. He had to leave for the airport in an hour.

Over breakfast Bill checked his watch and laid his mobile on the table. Libby had said she'd ring him. Would she really? Would she really come to London next week? Oh come on. He'd got the impression she hated the place. Wasn't last night just a fantasy?

Later in the taxi Bill began to worry that, even if it had really happened, Libby had only said those things to fool him into letting her go. She'd panicked in his room and used this ruse of having to find Vatican-man first, so that he'd stop trying to get her into bed.

By the time he was checking in, Bill was convinced the whole thing had just been a ruse. He even re-checked his notebook to make sure the original Wagner letter was still in its envelope. Libby might have come to his room last night to steal it for the Baron and then fled with that ridiculous story about having to get a Papal Dispensation first. But the letter was there. So what had last night been all about?

He looked at his mobile phone.

"Aisle or window?" said the man from Lufthansa. Bill couldn't care less. He put his phone back in his overcoat pocket. "Aisle seat or window seat?" Were there really people in the world to whom such things mattered? People whose day was affected by where their bottom was located in relation to a porthole? Was life so tedious and empty as this?

"I'm not sure I'm getting on," said Bill.

"I'm sorry sir?" That's right, he wasn't getting on. A wild thought had seized Bill. He was going back to Munich. He was going to find Libby – even if he didn't know where she lived, even if getting to her meant killing Hauke, the Baron and The Other Man.

"This is your flight, sir," the Lufthansa man was explaining in his perplexity.

He'd left Venice without her and that had been awful. He'd left London without her, hadn't he? He'd followed Tamsin to the Wye Valley and that had been awful too. Why did he keep making the same mistake over and over again? How often was he going to let Libby escape? The memory of last night's kiss suddenly overwhelmed Bill and with it came a frantic desire to be inside her. The image of Libby's thighs parting to admit him hit Bill, hit him to the core. His legs grew weak, there was a roaring in his ears.

"Sir?" said the man from Lufthansa.

"No, no I can't," said Bill, gathering up his passport and ticket and trying to pull his bag and coat off the scales. They didn't move. "You go on ahead of me," he said to the woman behind. "Have my seat, have them all, stretch out, sleep in the aisle. I'm not going. Can't."

Then his mobile phone went off. It was in his coat and his coat was over his bag and his bag was with the check-in clerk. Bill leapt to floor-level in order to save time. He pulled his coat free. The phone was still ringing, but this coat had a thousand pockets and whichever way Bill turned it, the damn thing was always on the other side.

"Don't ring off. Don't ring off," he begged the phone, grabbing at it with such force that it shot out of his hand. Bill scrabbled after it across the airport floor, convinced that the phone's battery would have broken loose and the call would be lost. But no, it was still ringing as he rugby-tackled it, his feet tangled in the strap of his dislodged shoulder bag. Bill hit the ground and the OK button simultaneously. "Hello!" he gasped.

"Bill?" said a voice. Female. American. Libby.

Thank God, he wanted to say, but he managed "Hi."

"Is it OK to talk?" she said. "Are you not on the plane yet?"

"No," said Bill, lying full-length across the highly-polished floor. "Just checking in. How did it go?"

"It's going to be all right, Bill," she said, quietly and close. Her voice held significance like a precious jewel.

"You saw him?"

"Yes, and I told him. He was upset. We talked for some time. I don't want to say anymore but, Bill, it's going to be OK. I've told him and now I can be with you."

Bill was lying on his back next to the check-in queue. "You can?"

"Yes," she said.

"You can?"

"Yes."

"Sorry. I want to keep asking so I'll keep hearing you say yes."

Libby laughed.

"It's wonderful news," said Bill, gazing at the bright, white ceiling of Munich's mile long departure zone. "When are you coming?"

"Tuesday."

"Come tomorrow," said Bill. No, come today. Come now!"

Libby laughed, it was a deep honeyed sound. He loved to hear her laughter. "I have things to clear up here, Bill. I need to move my things out. He said I could keep them here. But I wouldn't be happy. It wouldn't be appropriate."

"Where will you go?" Bill asked, basking in the conversation and unconscious of the looks he was receiving.

"I'm sure Hauke's parents will let me store things. They're in Nürnberg. I know them well. I'll call them when I get off the phone from you."

"How can I contact you?" Bill asked.

"I'll still be able to pick up e-mails and you've got my mobile number," she said.

"I want to talk to you every minute of the day." Bill felt quite besotted.

"Write to me," she said. "I like your e-mails."

"Thank God for e-mails," he said, particularly mindful of the ones that send themselves. "I love you Libby," he told her.

There was a silence at the other end. "Are you still there?" he asked.

"Bill, I... I find it easier to show my emotions than to put them into words," she said. "Do you mind?"

"I understand," he told her kindly. She didn't need to say she loved him. She was coming to Britain, she was coming to the Wye Valley, she was coming to be with him in Holt's Cottage and they would make love tenderly by the fire every evening.

"You're going to miss your flight," she told him.

"If I knew where you were I would. I'd come and get you now."

"Bill," she said. "Bill you're... a very special person. You always have been."

Bill was aware that two security guards were now looking down at him. One was wearing a bullet-proof vest and carrying what looked worryingly like a submachine gun.

"I've got to go," he said, realising for the first time that there was something unorthodox about his check-in technique. "I think I may have upset the *Polizei*."

"How?"

"It seems I'm lying on the floor of the airport," said Bill. "It's OK, I'm getting up. Thank you officer."

"Why are you lying on the floor of the airport?" Libby laughed.

"I'm a very special person," said Bill, gathering up his coat and bag. "That's what we special people do."

❖ TAKING THE PLUNGE

"DEAR BILL," Libby began.

Bill had gone straight to his Inbox without even removing his coat. He was sitting in his office, wholly unaware of the sun casting its glories down the River Wye. Now the rain had stopped, the colour scheme outside Bill's window had gone positively Van Gogh with vibrancy but what did he care? While the machine downloaded all the irrelevant e-mails he'd received during his absence, Bill shuffled off his coat and kicked his bag underneath the makeshift desk. All the time he was praying that Libby would have written to him. Driving down the M4 Bill had begun to fear again that this had all happened in his imagination. The course of our lives does not suddenly change direction this dramatically. Or, if it does, only for the worse. Bill almost rang her on his mobile but no. He wanted to trust to love. He had to try.

Here came the messages, chugging up the page. One. Two. Three. Seven in all. *New York Times*: Boring. *Opera Now* magazine: Boring. *Vlaamse Opera*: Boring, boring. *Malmo Opera*: Boring in a way that positively redefined boring. And two from ziegler.409@aol.com. Bill was about to open the uppermost of these when he saw that it read *Further To Last*, so he clicked on the e-mail below, entitled *After Munich*, and endured with acute impatience the fraction of a second that it took for Libby's words to be displayed before him. His instinct had been to read both e-mails simultaneously. He was greedy for her and this was like being presented with two breasts of equal perfection. Which to kiss first? Fortunately in the saner, less aroused part of his brain (currently a very small part) Bill did recognise that he wanted to experience Libby's life as it had unfolded since they last spoke. Sequentiality would heighten the intimacy.

> *Dear Bill,*
>> *It's two hours since we spoke...*

Two hours, thought Bill. What can she have been doing for two hours that's more important than this?

> *...As I said a lot has happened. I came home to pack those things that could be packed easily and Hauke is coming in an hour to help me with the rest. It has felt very strange and sad to be here, finally folding up my*

life in this place. I have left many times in my mind but only now am I truly leaving in my heart because I am coming to be with you.

Bill sat back in his chair, hot and suffused with happiness. There were words of the kind he needed. *"Heart" "You"* and *"With"* all in the same sentence. It was no dream, it was wonderful, wonderful reality.

A lot has happened since last night when I left your room. I did not tell you it all on the 'phone this morning.

Bill was struck fondly by Libby's use of an apostrophe to indicate abbreviation, then more urgently struck by the fact that there were things she hadn't told him. Don't let it be bad news. As long as she were neither dead nor married, he thought. Anything but those two.

Before travelling to see this other man (I hope you do not mind that I don't reveal his name) I telephoned to say that I needed to see him. He is always working by six in the morning so this didn't seem monstrous. Although we both rise early, I have never set out at such an hour to see him. I thought by his tone that he understood why I wanted to meet. As I explained to you, our relationship – his and mine – has been unravelling for some time although we have remained friends. I admire him enormously and in many respects he has been like a father to me, but for the last year, while remaining emotionally close, ours has not been a sexual relationship.

Wow, thought Bill.

This has hurt him I know.

Yes, it bloody would.

Initially it hurt me too but that is the person I am. While I admired him no less, I could no longer accept him as a lover. I believed we had both come to accept this. When I told him that I had met someone else, he was at first resigned, gracious and wholly admirable, even though I could see that this hurt him greatly. We discussed arrangements for removing what remained of my things from his apartment and he was kind enough to say that I could stay there until I had found somewhere else. He would stay out of my way in the country. This is the kind of man he is. I did not tell him about you but some fragments must have emerged. It is likely that I became more relaxed. We – he and I – had coffee on the terrace where he works before my return...

I bet he's a composer, thought Bill. Gustav Bloody Mahler that's who it is. Bloody hell, they had coffee together, slapping each other's lederho-sen and drinking a toast to Tyrolean sang froid.

> ... *this was a place where I had been very happy in the past and, remembering those times, I can only assume I relaxed and said some things about you. Stung by these details – I cannot recall them now – he changed completely, became wild, alternately angry and passionate, cursing me for ruining his work then begging me not to ruin my own life and my work too. He believes that you are evil and that the suddenness of our relationship proves that you have cast some kind of spell over me. This may sound absurd to you, dear Bill, but I can assure you it was terrifying. I fled the hütte and telephoned you as soon as I returned to Munich, by which time my heart was no longer racing. It was so good to hear your voice. I have always loved your voice and you sounded so happy and sane – even if you were lying at the check-in desk (I wish I had a picture of that). Bill, I so much want to be with you, to reconnect with those feelings of seven years ago.*

Bill flopped back in his chair again. This was strong stuff. He needed a glass of water.

> *I look forward so much to your touch.*

Bloody hell, definitely a glass of water.

Bill scrolled down the screen. That which is written must be read, particularly when a woman is committing herself to your bed.

> *I have now packed all there was of my life in this apartment and am looking forward to starting a new stage of my life with you – though how we do so when I work in Venice and you in Wales I cannot imagine. I believe these things do not matter however, if the heart knows where it resides. I have never felt comfortable with 'the boy next-door'. The boy in the country next-door might be a tad more convenient but I prefer men to boys anyway, and at least we're on the same continent. Imagine if I were living in Massachusetts! That's the entryphone. Hauke is here. I'll write you again later.*
> *Libby*

Bill wanted to print the letter out and carry it around with him and fax it to God. What was he doing obsessing over Richard Wagner's ramblings in his notebook, when the world was as bright and fresh as this? The woman he loved had said she wanted to start a new life with him, she longed for his touch, she loved the sound of his voice, she so much wanted to be with him, just as she had been emotionally with him all those years ago in London. It was not right to dissect and anatomise Libby's letter like this. It had integrity, it was an expression of her emotional state in its entirety. It should not be plundered for titbits and emotional soundbites, but he loved each of these cadences and had run his emotional highlighter over them. No matter that Libby had not intended them to be heard in amorous isolation. Besotted, Bill cut and pasted her honesty into nuggets that left him reeling with delight. He was loved! Not since the sixth had God done a better day's work.

He had to have some coffee.

It was afternoon now and the sun had moved round Holt's Cottage which meant that light was positively streaming in through the kitchen window. The swollen clouds above looked black and bruised, but light was bursting across what remained of the sky. Bill couldn't tell whether it was Spring or Love that was lending his home such Technicolor hues. All his senses were heightened. He wanted music, no, he wanted coffee first, then music, then he had to make love to Libby. He looked at the fireplace. *There.* Could they make love in front of it? That would be wonderful! It couldn't help but be wonderful. What did she look like without her clothes?

Suddenly Bill realised that in his distracted state he had done something wrong. He lifted the machinetta off the hob and realised that he'd forgotten to put any water in. He was in a state. My God, he needed calming down. The kind of calm that comes in the wake of penetration and ejaculation. There was no alternative at this stage. Refinements to the process of making love could come later. Please God she doesn't have her period next week, he thought.

Bill put water in the machinetta and returned it to the hob then decided to read Libby's second e-mail, *"Further To Last"*. Reaching his desk, Bill clicked it open just as he remembered he hadn't put cups under the machine's twin spouts.

> *It wasn't Hauke. It was Him. He had followed me back. Bill, this is bad. It is painful and difficult and I have never been more upset.*

Oh God, thought Bill. She's ditching me.

> *We have just had the most horrendous fight. I have never seen him like this.*

Bill could hear the coffee beginning to splutter and gurgle next door. He rushed back to the kitchen, looked for the cups but failed to find them in the scree of crockery stacked up on the drainer. Anxious to get back to

Libby's e-mail, he grabbed the machinetta off the hot plate and shoved it in the sink, then realised he'd blistered his hand in the process. Buggering hell!

Bill waved his wounded hand around and ran the cold tap. Steam hissed from the machinetta and Bill saw red marks forming on two of his fingers. He picked up a dishcloth, wet it with cold water and wrapped it round his hand, then he ran back to his office.

> *We have just had the most horrendous fight. I have never seen him like this. He says that if I leave him now I will ruin his work forever and I will probably ruin my own life too. He says such awful things about you, that you didn't care for me seven years ago so why should I believe you now? I'm afraid I have told him more about you – about what a good father you are and how you have lived on your own since your wife left you – but somehow everything I say he is able to twist round to depict you as an opportunist and me as some foolish desperate woman. When I tell him that you only sought me out once you were divorced, which I feel to be an honourable course, he says that you only sought me out because your wife would no longer tolerate you. That you always chose her over me but hid behind your alleged concern for Reah, that if she came back to you, you would break up with me again.*
> *Bill, I am very confused.*

Bastard, thought Bill. What a bastard. He's had his chance. No doubt he'll be saying next that he's leaving his wife after all.

> *I want you to understand that my feelings for him have died naturally over the last year. This he cannot believe. He thinks you must have done something to undermine him and me. Bill, I cannot return to him. I no longer have those feelings. Because I admire this man and love him like a father...*

I wish she'd stop saying how fucking wonderful he is, thought Bill.

> *... I was happy to continue to live a life alongside him. That is no longer possible now that I have met you again, but I realise now that while he accepted the distance that had come between us, and regretted it as much as I, he always believed that we would reconcile eventually. Bill, he was wild. I fear that he will try and do something to you (don't worry he won't try and harm me). He was even talking about leaving his wife...*

"I bloody knew it," Bill said out loud.

... which shows how desperate he is for I know that such an action is not possible for him. He has now gone...

Thank bloody God, thought Bill.

... and he will not be coming back until I leave. I've told him when I am flying out. Bill, I wish it were today.
Sorry about that...

Bill was thrown for a moment.

Libby was in such a state she'd forgotten that an e-mail didn't register the fact you've broken off and resumed five minutes later.

... Hauke has just rung me on my Handy. He's been outside for ages. When he (The Other Man) left I locked all the doors and disconnected the sprechanlage (what the hell is the English word for phone that connects with a door bell?) Anyway Hauke's here now. My big bear cub. I feel so much better when he's around. Bill, I can't wait to be with you.
Libby

Bill sat back nursing his injured hand. What on earth had he got himself into? Wow, he'd better check that she hadn't sent any more e-mails since he downloaded these two. The machine whirred and shashed to Bill's command. *No New Messages*, it said.

Right, thought Bill, clicking Reply.

Dear Libby,
I was delighted then very worried by your two e-mails. You poor thing. It is awful that he has done this to you. I wish I were there to bop him on the nose. Whoever he is, I realise you must have loved him very much, once upon a time, and I can believe that he must find the loss of that love very difficult to accept. I'm sure I would.

Bill felt obliged to be reasonable. He wanted to say something that might help Libby feel better, but he also wanted to reinforce the notion that she no longer loved this man. She loved him.

I believe we can absorb the sensation of love dying away without being aware of its process until someone else comes on the scene. It is only then, when we see the person we have loved – someone whom we might have thought no longer capable of love – loving someone else that we realise truly what we have lost. Then it is that the pain suddenly takes hold.

Bill would be infinitely generous but he would fight as well. His tactics might be subtler than those of this boorish religious egomaniac with his chauffeur-driven spymobile and pretentious *dacha*, but Bill would fight just as hard and just as dirty to beat him off. Words, after all, were his medium. He would make them work for him. Libby needed to be reminded at every stage that she loved him and no one else.

Suddenly Bill felt unsure how to continue. He looked at the screen, its cursor blinking impatiently. *Well?* the cursor said. But Bill's flow of words had gone.

What was wrong with him?

Yes, he wanted Libby. He had thought of nothing else for two days but somehow, in an instant, that desire had curdled. Maybe it was because Libby was finally using the words he wanted to hear. No, it was more. For a moment, inexplicably, Bill had wanted out. He flung himself back in his chair and scowled at the monitor.

"Bloody hell."

Suddenly he resented Libby's power over him, the way she had compelled him to go over to Munich. Damn it, he even resented the words he'd written, the lies he'd told. And for what?

Bugger! This was not a good time to develop ambivalence.

His mind was filling with images of Reah, silent and traumatised, standing in the doorway. Not his doorway. No, the doorway of Tamsin's bedroom. And Tamsin was there, Tamsin and some other support teacher under the duvet, thrashing around, attending to each other's special needs. Was that what this London move was all about?

Suddenly Bill wanted his daughter with him. He was angry. Why hadn't he picked up Reah when he'd arrived back at Heathrow? He should have driven into London to get her. What the hell was he playing at coming straight down here just to collect his e-mails? This was Libby's doing.

No it wasn't. It was *his* doing. And the sad thing was, he couldn't have rung his daughter to arrange collecting her because she was with her grandparents and Bill didn't have their number anymore.

Bill wondered about ringing Tamsin. At least he had a mobile number for her. Maybe she was back in the country. As he reached to dial, another image arose. His ex-wife with a man behind her, shadowy, dark, his arms around Tamsin's waist, his groin fast into the cleavage of her buttocks, those buttocks so visible in that ridiculous, overtight skirt of hers. An unknown man. *Hauke.* The bear cub had a lazy sensuality about him. And he was irritatingly young.

Bizarre. Bill hadn't bothered greatly about Tamsin finding someone else until now.

Tamsin's mobile began to ring. At least she was accessible even if she were in some distant country, face down in the sand while Siegfried von Blazerman sated his lust. The phone went warbling on, unanswered, and Bill's mind, unfettered, went on a rampage. Tamsin, buttocks and legs spread wide, stretching for her tote bag, responding to the mobile's shrill command as Hauke, swearing apoplectically in his best Wagnerian German, climaxed noisily behind her. "*Oh, oh mein Werther, Werther Freund!!!*"

Despite himself Bill laughed. With all this longing for Libby he was clearly cracking up. The ringing had stopped and here was Tamsin, not face down in the sand at all but in a Greek restaurant, by the sound of it. "It's Bill," he said.

"Where are you?" she asked without formalities.

"I'm home," he replied. "Where are you? It sounds like bloody Crete."

"We're in Muswell Hill at a Greek restaurant."

"Who's we?"

"None of your business," said Tamsin, sounding surprised and peeved. "Listen Bill, you were supposed to be looking after Reah."

"I was," he said. "I had to go abroad for my work so, as you had left me no contact number, I took her to your parents." He could be just as awkward as she. "Where's Reah now?" he added.

"Gone outside to buy a magazine."

"Outside where?"

"Outside the restaurant."

"In Muswell Hill?"

"That's right. If you don't mind now, I'd like to finish eating."

"Are you bringing her back down?" Bill asked.

"I'll bring her back down at the weekend if you want."

"Of course I want," said Bill. Angry if paradoxical.

"I don't want her suddenly abandoned," Tamsin reproached him.

"You mean you wouldn't like it if I suddenly buggered off refusing to leave any number where I can be contacted," Bill retorted.

"We are not married any more," said Tamsin, willing to give him a fight.

"We are both still her parents though," Bill replied. He'd said it without premeditation but it had the positive effect of cooling things down. In the silence that followed he added. "She needs us both." More silence.

"I'll ring you later with the details," said Tamsin quickly and she switched off her phone.

Bill went to put a proper dressing on his blistered hand. When he came back, he wondered about completing that e-mail to Libby but instead went through his phone messages, paying them little attention until he got to Vita, who finally seemed happy with that Israeli piece.

"I'll be authorising a cheque later today, Bill," she confirmed.

"My kind of woman," Bill said aloud. Anyone who paid on time was automatically in his good books. People like the *New York Times* who actually paid ahead of publication deserved a Pulitzer.

"*Hi Dad*," said Reah and Bill felt his heart open and sing as it always did at the sound of her voice or sight of her outrageous mass of hair. "Hope you had a good time in wherever it was, oh yes, Germany. Gramma says her parents used to go to the opera in Munich. Before the war."

Oh dear, thought Bill.

"Anyway there was this really good programme on last night, I really think you would have liked it but, anyway, I'll tell you about all that next week. Am I coming to you for the weekend? I think it's your turn. Mum's back and she says she'll drive me down on Saturday. Then it'll be the last week of my holiday which really sucks..."

Bill found himself switching off. Reah's burble could occasionally overwhelm. He breathed out and found he could return to that uncompleted e-mail. Strange how Reah's presence, even on a recorded message, settled him.

"*When you speak of our touching, I can still recall the sensation of your hand in the taxi*," Bill typed. 'Fingers' sounded too specific, he thought; 'Glove' insufficiently romantic. A lover held your hand. He didn't squeeze two of your inert digits through kidskin. Bill let the sentence stand.

I can also recall sitting on my bed in Room 113 stroking your hair...

Most of all he could recall their kiss but it seemed best not to get too graphic at this stage.

Your hair and your skin intoxicated me from the time we met at the airport...

Should he not say Venice? Bill wondered, wincing at the pain in his hand. Actually it was only once they were in the Mercedes that he began to feel intoxicated by her. And to be honest he soon lost contact with that sensation once she started speaking German on her mobile. Bill took the cursor back, deleting his last three words. A few clicking noises and the truth suddenly looked much better:

"*Your hair and your skin intoxicated me from the time we met*" Full Stop, he decided. Definitely better but less true? Truth might be an absolute,

Libby, but the manner in which it can be expressed is infinitely variable. This, though, was neither true nor precise. What did he mean "the time they met" When? In Munich? In Venice? London? Yet wasn't its very imprecision the best thing about it? Libby could make of it what she would.

I am so looking forward to being with you. To picking up where we left off.

Again Bill stopped. Would she assume he meant where they'd left off in London or in Room 113? If the latter, his words did seem overtly sexual. He didn't want to frighten her away.

Damn, thought Bill. Why was it so complicated? Presumably because truth at this stage of a relationship was not an entirely palatable thing. It had to be dressed up and edited. Particularly edited.

I am so looking forward to being with you. I have missed you since we parted, sometimes it feels as if I have missed you for seven years.

Now that last bit was surprising, but he liked it. It had felt absolutely right as he wrote it, but what on earth had made him do so? It was hardly true. In fact when Bill looked back over the words on this screen, very little seemed to be true. He had omitted things he really felt and invented things he didn't. In fact, his desperation to catch up with Libby in Venice had nothing to do with love at all and everything to do with life going horribly wrong that day. And when they did meet his reactions were ambivalent. True, he was consumed by feelings for Libby, but what exactly were they? Was this love or simple lust? Was Libby's Other Man right that he was just clutching at the first available woman out of loneliness? Would he actually go back to Tamsin if she'd have him? *No.* And yet if he did, he wouldn't have to lose Reah. Hell! About the only thing Bill knew for certain was that now – and for the last week or so – he had been in the grip of an extraordinarily strong desire to have penetrative sex with 34-year-old Libby Ziegler. Christ, when he compared literary illusion with sexual reality Bill felt somewhat ashamed. But what should he write? What was the purpose of this letter? To help him feel in contact with her still, to sustain their relationship over the next few days, to keep Libby in contact with him and, above all, keen? The message in front of him served that purpose, that was all. It was neither great art nor honest. It used the palpable hyperbole of love as an inducement for bed. Bill wanted to get laid.

It did serve one other purpose however, Bill reflected. He was concerned that she should feel his support if things were difficult over there. Genuinely concerned.

I imagine taking your hand. Too overt. He back-spaced.
I imagine taking you by the hand. Better.
and showing you my world. Good.
I simply cannot wait...

Damn, if he completed that sentence, the word 'bed' was going to erupt on to the page and wreck everything.

"*The river is so beautiful today.*" That's right, change the subject. "*The sun has broken through.*" Oh Christ, she wasn't going to stand for his waxing lyrical like this. Bill deleted any reference to what the sun was doing today. Libby was a New Englander. She'd seen plenty of weather in her time.

Bill went next-door and poured himself a glass of whisky. It was way too early in the day but he needed something to effect a change in himself. To run the cursor over this mind-numbing self-consciousness and delete his own ambivalence. True to form, the spirit in the water reached inside him, reassured him, warmed him and sent him back to the keyboard.

> *The river is so beautiful today. I always see it from my office but the forest that is visible from my bedroom is never anything but sad. I cannot understand why it has that effect on me. Those trees have been there so long, I am sure that they have witnessed too much sorrow. Probably if they could speak they'd disagree with me. They'd talk of winter giving way to summer with such reassuring regularity that we should never be sad for long. Nevertheless I imagine. I think. I project on to them my own feelings of life in this fractured place. Libby, I do hope that when you come here the trees will forget their winters and that we can look forward to sharing summer with them.*

Bill took another sip. He'd got rather carried away there. These were ideas he hadn't had before. Or at least they were ideas he had not known he'd had. It was true the forest did spook him and yet he walked there every day. Maybe he should move. Bill hadn't had that thought before either. He looked at his whisky glass, bright sunshine outside the window delineating its every smear, evidence of Bill's inadequate washing-up technique. The spirit washed around, amber and potent.

Bill read that last paragraph over. It worked rather well, he thought. It confided. It spoke of loneliness and suggested she was the one who could put his life right. It alluded to bedrooms in a way that was not overt. Libby would get the message, but she could choose to ignore it if she wasn't ready to deal in those terms. He had even suggested that when they were in his bedroom they might spend some time looking at the trees. He wanted her to know this wasn't just about sex. Now his conscience pricked him. Was he only bent on seduction?

This was the problem with writing when you write for your living, Bill thought. You become too aware of how words can manipulate. But in fact all words manipulate. Only Wittgenstein wrote in a language that didn't rely on hidden potency, but then he never had a girlfriend. Outside logical positivism the innocent sentence was an impossibility. All words corrupt. Bill decided he shouldn't give himself too hard a time. Paid to create an effect in the reader, we all become accomplished whores in the end. And grossly underpaid whores at that, he thought. Unless the *New York Times* is punting of course.

Bill wrote a little more and then wondered how to sign off. She had just written her name. He would do the same. Professions of emotion should be used carefully at a time like this. He and Libby had passed the point where the words 'with love' had simple honorific value. The second of those two syllables was now of critical importance. They would both be testing out its existence in the next few days. Such words should not be thrown in lightly.

Bill was about to press Send when he remembered that Libby had referred to the fact that she had always loved the sound of his voice. So should he perhaps make an oblique reference to the verb after all? No, she had said "*touch*", he'd said "*skin*". That was upping the ante. He had also yoked in bedrooms. That would do.

Bill sent the e-mail and went out for a walk. *Phew*. He had to get that opera review written when he got back. In fact he had to try and order things so that none of his journalism intruded on the two of them for the few days Libby was here. He would clear his mind with a twenty-minute stomp through the woods and then come back and not even check his e-mails until he'd done a good hour's word-whoring.

He had hardly reached the gatepost when the thought occurred to Bill that he would not be able to come back without checking for e-mails. Who was he kidding? Nevertheless he'd try now to get the review written in his head. That way he might be desperate on his return to get stuck in, filling the screen with words that encapsulated the problems inherent in any staging of *Götterdämmerung*, rather than attempting to make love over the internet.

Instead of heading east, directly into the forest, Bill turned north for a change and stalked across the no-man's land that separated his cottage from the Forestry Commission boundary. He rarely came this way with Reah because it was boggy, and indeed after so much rain Bill soon realised his boots were heavy with mud. There were tracks leading through the forest that would take him, if this fresh growth of brambles weren't so thick, down to that rock which held stunning views over Tintern. Satan was supposed to have preached to the monks from here, but the foliage had grown up a bit since his cloven hoof made its hairy way along the Wye. Bill was soon lost and was about to turn back when he noticed someone observing him.

"Hello?" he said to the figure. Whoever it was had been moving towards him but had stopped now, twenty feet or so away, half obscured by saplings that were trying – and failing – to reach up to the sunlight. There being no reply, Bill squelched forward a few steps. Strangers in the city we ignore all the time, but there is something primitive in our response to a solitary stranger *en plein air*. He is either friend or foe and we cannot pass without discovering which. As Bill stepped out round a particularly vicious holly bush he found that this was neither. It was, hugely to his surprise, Marika.

"Oh hello," he said. Bill had never seen Marika anywhere but at her farm before.

She made some indistinct rejoinder.

"Don't normally see you round these parts," he said, with forced jocularity. He had to say something.

"I get out," said Marika tersely and she fumbled in her pocket for tobacco. "You got a light?"

"No," said Bill, surprised she hadn't remembered that he didn't smoke.

"Oh."

"How's things?" he asked. It seemed odd having a conversation with Marika that wasn't taking place on the way up to her derelict bedroom.

"I got a few to sell," she replied. "One's lame again." She was referring to the herd. Marika never actually used the term 'cow', Bill remembered. Occasionally she'd talk about "the bloody things" or "the buggers", but usually she'd just take it as read that the topic of conversation was bovine by default.

"I've been away," said Bill. "Venice and Munich."

"Nice," she said. Her look was noncommittal yet at the same time resentful. Bill wished he hadn't told her this now. It had somehow sounded as if he were apologising, making excuses for his absence. As if, were it not for all those trips abroad, he would have been round by now. Whereas at this very moment the only desire he had was to get away. Marika with her battered wax-jacket, her preternaturally lined face and disintegrating pullover was the last person in the world he wanted to encounter. She was the antithesis of Libby and yet Bill couldn't help wondering whether, should they fall to it here, he'd be more successful than before. There was a patch of what looked like dry ground behind Marika. Incredibly he was tempted, though he didn't know why. What a sordid event it would be, yet how perversely appealing was the idea of laying bare her skin in this damp atmosphere, fixing his teeth on her breasts, seeing if he could make her shudder as he used to.

"I'll give you a ring," he said, taking a step back in more ways than one.

"Yeah," she said. "You do that."

Bill was shocked at himself. When he thought of the sweetness of that one kiss with Libby and compared it to the squalor of his couplings with Marika he couldn't imagine how on earth he could even be tempted. In fact he wasn't, not in any positive sense. Maybe it was just that once the taboo has been broken, it proves impossible for a man not to make presumptions about his access to a woman's body. Maybe that was what happened with Tamsin last year. Bill shuddered inwardly as he retraced his steps. He did not want to go down that route again. He wanted Libby and all the hope that she represented for the future. Together they would talk and make love gently in front of the fire. A kiss with Libby was about melting into the sublime moment. With Marika it was about stale cigarette smoke and worse – much worse.

Bill returned to Holt's Cottage at a pace. He wanted to shake off the encounter with Marika, particularly so close to where he lived. When he drove down and up again in order to get to her farm, he was able to imagine that he lived at some considerable distance from the cesspit that was Tredossor but in fact she was not far away at all. She could infiltrate his world more easily than he had imagined. The dank poison of Marika's world seeped towards him through the boggy stretches of that forest. Maybe it did every day. She might even reach the woodland's edge and be able to see where he lived. Like a vampire, she would not cross open ground, Bill thought to himself, but he didn't like the idea that Marika could be so near. Especially given that Reah spent time with him at the cottage.

When he got back in, Bill strode straight to the computer and switched it on. He hadn't even removed his muddy boots, so while the machine whirred up to speed and sought out its mailbox Bill pulled them off under the table. God, he had prayed as he returned from Heathrow that Libby would be there when he clicked Connect, but now he really did need her there. Really, really. She alone could take this taste from his mouth. Smoke. That dry stale smoke and emaciated skin, that was Marika. Something akin to the taste of death. Her whole body was desiccating except for those remarkable breasts and the excessive moistness between her legs. Without those she was cadaverous. What the hell had he been doing with her all this time?

Receiving list of messages, Bill's screen said, and a little blue arrow indicated that something was connecting with his Inbox.

"Come on ziegler dot 409," said Bill, and she didn't disappoint. Two more messages. One headed "*Trees*", the other "*Ciao Giorgio!*"
"*Dear Bill,*" said "*Trees*".

> *You write to me about touch and about trees. I share your feelings about these. Like you I am remembering moments from when we were in Munich and Venice. We seemed so close I believed we could easily be touching. When we did, I believe it was no more than a confirmation of all that had already happened.*

That wasn't how it had felt to him. Either Libby also revised the past, or things had been going on in her at a level deeper than anything she'd admitted hitherto.

> *After I wrote to you last I found myself sitting here alone again. Hauke left, taking some things with him to his parents. I had work to do so I decided not to drive with him to Nürnberg. Inevitably the words of The Other Man came back to me and I had a moment of panic, Bill. What am I doing setting off to go and spend several days in Wales with a man I hardly know? (Bill, is Holt's Cottage in Wales? I can't tell. I looked on a map but it seems the border runs down both sides of the River Wye in different places.) It is not that I don't know you in some respects. We talked a lot all those years ago and although we did not talk about our feelings then, I find, as we talk now, that you are exactly as I imagined you to be all that time ago. But I was a girl then. Maybe at 27 I should not have been but when I look back seven years it is to an ingenue, a girl so incapable of commitment. If that young woman thought she was committed, how much credence should we give her judgement? And yet if we take away her past, my behaviour now seems reckless in the extreme.*

Bill was beginning to worry but Libby's question about the Welsh border had reassured him still. One didn't throw in jocular geographical asides when intending to pull out.

> *And then of course I read what you wrote about trees. You wouldn't know but my father's cabin in Maine is surrounded by trees. I have gone there on my own for years, particularly when I've needed to write. There is a lake in front of the cabin and a forest on its other sides. It is a very knowing forest. When I was younger it quite terrified me.*

How bizarre, thought Bill, both of us spooked by the foliage.

> *As I have grown older I have learned to be more at one with the forest.*

I know that it cannot share my joys but I've also learned not to attribute anything malign to its silence.

Good point, thought Bill. He was enjoying this e-mail. No longer looking for clues to their chances of making it under the duvet, Bill was excited to be in touch once again with the Ziegler whose mind he had so enjoyed in her faxes of long ago.

I, of course, have the lake, rather than the River Wye, in front of me and whereas I think you say the river is over a hundred feet below your cottage, the lake is only ten feet or so beyond the porch where I can sit with my laptop. The lake is dark and very cold all year round. As a child I learned from my father that if you are going to leap in you have to do so without another thought. I was brought up to value thought but never at the expense of action. The circumstances dictate which is appropriate. There is a small jetty in front of the porch with a two-foot drop and I remember once standing on it in my bathing suit, trying to reach down my toe to test the water and reassure myself. My father was so annoyed as he watched me endlessly resolving to go in and then retreating! Eventually he came on to the jetty himself and told me that if one is going to jump, there is never any point in checking, preparing and vacillating. All the time one delays, fear grows more acute and so does the eventual shock of the water because we have anticipated too much. Then before I knew it, he suddenly seized me by the waist and we both went in. I cannot remember that plunge now except that it was over before I even realised what was happening. "Now Miss Bonnie-Blue," said my father. "The next time I expect you to come down here and straight in and I don't want to see any namby-pamby toes dipping in the water." Ever since, when I go to the cabin I make straight for the lake as soon as I wake each morning, and simply run off the end of the jetty. The shock is sometimes acute but it is nothing to the pain of vacillation.

Bill had become so interested in this incongruous backwoods story from Libby's curious upbringing, that he'd ceased to assume there was a relevance in her narrative. He speculated on how badly Reah would take to such manhandling.

I feel the same about life. If one is going to take a step then it must just be taken. You yourself asked me what point would be served by our going on numerous dates. I have made a commitment to exploring this relationship. If I hadn't done so I would never have ended things the way I did with T.O.M. (The Other Man). Having made that commitment I will take the leap. That is the kind of person I am.

Bill sat back and admired what he had just read. The image of Libby running down a whitewood jetty towards the chill black waters of Maine arose before him. She was naked, her body white and girlish. He wondered if she were naked in reality when she leapt? Surely if she got straight out of bed and ran down to the water's edge she wouldn't pause to pull on a swim suit. Not if she were staying there alone... Bill was growing tired of his own carnal obsessions, and yet he couldn't help wondering if Libby knew she was presenting him with such images when she sent that e-mail. He had never thought of her as coquettish but at the same time words were her forte too. She knew what she was doing with them.

Libby spent the rest of the e-mail explaining that she was going to try and sort-out flights although she couldn't confirm anything until she had spoken to her friend Giorgio at the Italian Cultural Institute in London. She would get back to him soon.

> *I am looking forward very much to when you do take me by the hand and show me your world. I'm sure I can reconcile you and your pine forest.*
>
> *Libby*

Bill was touched by the way she had used his own words back to him and by the promise of reconciliation. She had not balked at the reference to his bedroom. She had developed the illusion.

Optimistically he clicked the e-mail headed *"Ciao Giorgio!"*

> *Dear Bill,*
>
> *Extraordinarily, as I sent that last e-mail from you I found I had received one from Giorgio with his home number. We have now spoken and I have arranged to see him on Tuesday morning before getting the bus to Chepstow. Can you tell me what time the buses for Chepstow leave London Victoria? Do I need to book? How do I pronounce Chepstow? I will need to know this when purchasing a ticket. I know how the English like to spell a word one way and pronounce it quite differently. The producer who canned me from the BBC was called Featherstonhaugh but pronounced it Fanshaw. This is a form of linguistic perversity that my countrymen abandoned after pretending that Arkansas should be pronounced Arkansaw.*

Libby was having fun.

> *Back to Giorgio. He was surprised that I was coming to London when I'd told him only a month ago that I never did. He was even more surprised when I explained I could not stay for lunch because I had to*

travel on to Chepstow. When he asked me why, I was at a loss to answer (not something that often happens to me!) I told him I was taking a short holiday there. I am absolutely sure he suspects. The Germans would not, but the Italians and French always know these things. Please let me know bus times as soon as you can. I'm going to ring Lufthansa and British Airways now. Can you believe that we are doing this? I feel as excited as I used to when we (my father and I) would drive to the beach. I'd never stop asking "Are we there yet? Are we there?" We almost are, aren't we?

Libby

A thrush was singing outside his window in gorgeous liquidity. Bill clicked Reply. *"Almost There"*, he wrote in the subject box.

Dear Libby,

I have been in the forest this afternoon. I wish you had been with me. It feels at times like a place of death. Does that sound extreme to you? I realise when I tell you about my life on this cliff edge that that is what it is. Below me is the drop, behind me the forest. I am literally on the edge. You say that the forest cannot share our joys but that you've learned not to attribute anything malign to its silence. I have not learned to be at peace with it yet. It haunts me still.

This was not going where he'd intended.

The forest is where humanity's darkest deeds were done. It is where Grendel and all our torments were born. In the forest trees and saplings obscure those who lie in ambush for us and their roots grow down through the unconsecrated remains of children shot in the back while humanity looks the other way.

Where the hell was this coming from? What in God's name was he writing? Despite himself Bill ploughed on.

You know what I am writing. The bullet in the neck, sweep back the hair, press the cold metal into the tender nape and squeeze. Watch as she falls. Flick the stray globule of blood from your lapel. There are plenty more standing in line to take the drop.

Now he was cracking up. Definitely.

It happened in fields and woodland that you and I drove past as we motored from Munich to Schloss Villy. Ask Josef, ask the ghosts of six million.

Hell! He couldn't send an e-mail like this. Why was he turning into Lev Davidov? She'd never come. Bill pressed Delete and made damn sure to keep away from the Send key.

What did he say to Libby now that she was on her way? Help?

Help keep the nightmares from my door.

Later, before turning in, Bill stepped up to where he'd parked the Jeep. He glanced at Tamsin's farmhouse, dark with the trees behind it. With Reah gone he would definitely want to leave this place. The woods seemed darker than ever before. Bill went inside and stoked up the fire. Like every generation before him he felt more secure when kindling warmth and light in the forest.

He checked his e-mails one last time and was almost weary to find ziegler.409 there again, just the one this time. What Bill had finally written to Libby was much more lightweight, but it had taken an effort of self-control. In the end he had spoken of the stars he could see from his bed:

> *I have not learned to be at peace with the forest yet but I know that the roof light over my bed looks directly up at the stars. After living here I don't think I could ever live in any city where the orange smear of sodium streetlampery robs us of the stars. They represent calm and order. If we fix on them then the night is not so frightening.*

"Dear Bill," Libby replied. She had entitled this e-mail *"The View"*.

> *I can see the stars from our cabin. At night on the porch, if the moon is not making too much of a spectacle of itself over the lake, they hang there revolving slowly in the massive silence. How curious that there may have been nights when you and I have gazed at the same stars (always allowing for time difference of course).*

Libby went on to explain that she had just had a call from The Other Man.

> *He wanted to meet to give back some things. He sounded so much calmer. I feel relieved.*

Bill didn't trust Gustav Mahler. He'd probably knocked up a symphony that afternoon and wanted to present it to her, that and the divorce papers from childless Alma.

> *I've also had a call from Heidi, clearly wanting to be friends again. She was probably digging for gossip (about you and where we disappeared off to on Saturday). Bill I've no head for intrigue like some of these women. They seem to thrive on information; it is their currency.*

A certain kind of female trades tittle-tattle. I sometimes think that being brought up by my father left me with no skills in this area. I am not subtle (you may have noticed), consequently I either share every-thing or nothing. My normal rule is nothing, as you may recall. I have found it necessary to be a very private person. Heidi does not even know about The Other Man. No one does. What she would think of my travelling to Wales to gaze at the stars with a disreputable jour-nalist I do not know. Are you disreputable Bill? When are you going to write your book? There is one in us all. I was sure when I met you in Venice that you were going to tell me about some book. Not the kind that I have written, but a real book.

"Too busy getting divorced," Bill told the monitor. He was still savour-ing Libby's reference to joining him, looking at the stars. They were visible from his pillow. Surely she would not have missed the fact that these e-mails were getting horizontal now. A commitment existed, a compact, contract and promise. For a moment he felt rather squalid. Libby was sharing her heart and all Bill could do was concentrate on a lower part of her anatomy.

We must also do something about the letter when I'm over. If you do not intend to keep it, I may be able to help you restore it to the rightful owner.

"*Dear Libby*," wrote Bill. He had clicked Reply with some reluctance. This correspondence had left him unsettled.

I'm going to bed now. You seem very keen on Herr Richard's letter. I hope it is not the only reason you're coming over and that while I'm gazing up at the stars you won't be winkling it out from under my pillow and mailing it to the Baron. What was that old rogue up to on Saturday? I have no wish to hang on to this letter, but I'd like to know why everyone wants it. Who exactly is the rightful owner? Or at least the person who's willing to shell out for it. How much do you think the Baron was about to offer for it? In a few hours it will be tomorrow. Only one more day and you will be on your way. I can't believe it. Are we there yet? Almost.

"Seven years too late," he thought. "But almost."

On Monday their e-mails became more frequent. Libby had so many questions: what would she be seeing, what clothes should she bring, what kind of food would they eat, did he have a diningroom table, was there anything she could bring from Munich?

"Not much post today," said Lee who had a small package of complimentary CDs to hand over, which needed a signature.

"Don't you believe it," Bill replied. Libby had been a frequent correspondent in their London days but that was nothing to this. It seemed that every time he checked his e-mails there was something from her. And he checked his e-mails pretty frequently.

She had found a CD of *Salome* which had been given to her and never opened. Did Bill want it? Would it help with his piece on Bardini? The Other Man detested opera. What did he think she should do with all the food in the fridge? The Other Man had arranged for it to be stocked pending her return, and now there was too much to eat. To take it with her seemed greedy, to throw it away profligate; but to leave it would only distress him, she was sure. She'd give it to Young Hauke. That's what she'd do.

Libby was sharing her life with Bill and it was something he'd never experienced before. That evening she was going out to meet The Other Man. She hoped he didn't mind:

> *It feels outrageous that he should not come to his apartment to see me, but that is his wish. Bill I feel so sorry for him. He is such a decent man you have no idea.*

Yeah, yeah, thought Bill, but instead of arguing he reminded her about the Wagner letter. "*You still haven't told me who the owner is. Do you have any idea?*"

"*Jeez, this is complicated,*" Libby wrote, her plain bold font suddenly appearing in the midst of Bill's previous message. Libby had recently started clicking Reply and typing in on top of what Bill had written. At times it gave their e-mails the appearance of dialogue – a dialogue in which she always had the last word.

> *If I don't finish now I'll tell you more when I get back. We know that on Wagner's death all his papers passed to Cosima who became guardian of the sacred flame. She also set out to acquire the rest of his correspondence. After a few weeks lying on his tomb and begging for death Cosima suddenly sprung into life demanding all Dear Richard's letters back. She harassed enough people to acquire over 6,000 (that's the number extant) How many she got and destroyed we don't know. She certainly did censor them. One of her reasons, without a doubt, was for the purpose not just of preserving an untarnished memory of Wagner but of creating a legend – Bürgerliche Wohlanständigkeit. Anything that was critical of the family was destroyed. For example, Wagner detested his mother, Johanna, for much of his life but virtually all negative references to her*

were removed. Glasenapp's 1907 edition, put together under Cosima's watchful eye, omitted all the poisonous stuff he'd written to his half-sister Cäcilie about their mom. Those few letters that did escape Cosima Wagner paint a very different picture. The Wagner house-myth of supremely successful artist, perfect family man and German patriot needed bolstering in certain places and from the few letters about Johanna Geyer that survived Cosima's wholesale suppression, it's clear that he thought her a dreadful old harridan, petty, vulgar and hardly the holy Sieglinde whom Wagner claimed, passim, *to venerate.*

A further cull of the letters took place in 1930. I tried to find out the exact details but the family closed ranks. What we do know is that after Cosima's death her pliant daughter, Eva, removed a whole tranche known as 'Correspondence with C' from the archive and destroyed it. Owning up to this four years later dutiful Eva claimed that she had been acting on the express wishes of both Cosima and Wagner's son Siegfried. What survives is pure Bayreuth Pravda, painting a rosy picture of Cosima's life with the person she refers to as 'Our Friend'. There's one glutinous letter she wrote to her children (I don't have the reference here so this is only something like it, taken from memory):

"Dear Children, Today I committed a dreadful error. I offended Our Friend over the tempo of Beethoven's C Minor Symphony. Wilfully I insisted on a tempo which I felt to be right and now we are both suffering, I for having done it, he for having experienced such wilfulness at my hands. I wish never to do so again..."

Of course this cultivation of the perfect marriage wasn't wholly selfless. Cosima exercised tremendous power after Richard's death. She outlived him by nearly half a century and insisted that everything was done his way (which was of course also her way for theirs was the Perfect Union). Ergo Cosima could do what she liked. This is why Bayreuth fossilised artistically under Siegfried Wagner. His mom controlled everything. 'Papa' Wagner fell hook line and sinker for the Bürgerliche idea, but I think it's also wholly in keeping with Cosima's character that she chose to suppress letters or diaries that suggest their marriage was anything less than blissful harmony. The woman rewrote history by a process of editing and invention. However, some letters did survive the holocaust –

Bill winced at Libby's appropriation of that word. She had no concept of censoring herself in order to protect the sensibilities of others. He remembered it was one of the reasons she'd had such a battle with the BBC during her time in London. Two producers were very keen to have her present a personal view on one of the galleries, possibly the Tate, but on the first day of filming Libby was asked not to refer to a servant in one of the paintings she was talking about as 'black'. "They wanted me to call him Afro-Caribbean, which is asinine! There was no such concept at the time. In 1600 the Caribbean hadn't been populated by slaves!" she told Bill. The film hadn't been made.

> – *However, some letters did survive the holocaust; they turn up from time to time. Where they come from I don't know. Maybe some people were resistant to Cosima's imperious commands. Or maybe these were correspondents that she didn't know of. Often collectors try to get hold of these letters. The Wagner Archive clearly would like all of them back. I don't think their motive is to suppress, simply not to see the Wagner legacy sold off piecemeal like that. I assume that when Willy talks of offering you a reward he is not speaking of much money. I think he means just some recognition by Bayreuth of its gratitude that one of these letters can be returned. Mind you, Bayreuth's a crazy place. There's a lot there you can't get access to. The Americans closed it down for six years after the war to 'decontaminate' the shrine of its Nazi associations. I know quite a few people who believe that more is to come out about the association between Hitler and the family. They're very secretive up there and there's no knowing that if you hand that letter over anyone will ever see it again. My advice would be to publish it, then hand it over. That way scholarship gets its due and the archive gets its letter back. I assume that the Archive is the 'friend' that Willy speaks of although you can never tell with him. He has a wide circle and likes to play Capo di Capi, as you noticed! Where did you get that letter, by the way? Damn it Bill, you've let me rattle on and I'm going to have to run now. I'll be back in touch after.*
> *Libby*

In a way Bill was pleased that Libby was going to be out for an hour or so. He did not trust this musical Nietzschean Supercomposer of hers one bit, but he welcomed the chance to get on with his work. The temptation to check for e-mails was constant these days. He reckoned he spent no more than fifteen minutes at the PC before looking to see what Ziegler Dot 409 was up to. Invariably she'd sent him something and her self-absorption was itself wholly absorbing.

Bill finished his review of *Götterdämmerung* and sent it off. It was odd as he watched it wing its way to Louis to find *No New Messages* on his screen. Reflexively he clicked New Mail and began to write to Libby. He was becoming addicted too.

I cannot help wondering where these letters are coming from? Is there a steady trickle of them do you think? Has someone got a whole collection and is selling them slowly to make maximum profit? How much do you think one would be worth? How did they survive the cull in the first place?

Libby was not a journalist. As far as Bill was concerned the interesting thing about that letter was not the fact that it confirmed Wagner's marriage had its rocky moments. That was musicology, that was history and hardly surprising history at that. The story was that someone was manipulating the market in this way. Who was selling? Moreover, who was buying? When they'd gone to see the Baron, Libby had said "Willy has someone who wants to meet you." This person was never produced, only the Baron's cheque book. Bill suspected that if he had handed over the letter he might well have met that night's mystery purchaser. One of the Wagner clan? Maybe he – or she – was actually at the party that night.

Do you have any idea who the Baron's contact might be? Who's doing the buying? I'm not convinced it's the Archive.

Bill deleted those last two sentences. His suspicions had only formed as he wrote those words. But it was not good to fire off every thought to Libby. He loved her, he wanted to be with her, but did he entirely trust her?

"*Dear Vita,*" Bill wrote.

I'm thinking there may be a story in this Wagner letter we spoke of after all. I believe someone has a whole collection of letters and they may be releasing them slowly on to the market, selling them privately. In this way scholarship is being denied a valuable asset. It's like the stolen Picassos that disappear forever into bank vaults. The greater crime is not the initial theft from one person, but the fact that these things are denied to all of us long-term. Is there a piece for you in this? I am currently in possession of one of these Wagner letters and have had it authenticated. This will take some investigation. Let me know what you think.

Bill

His back was stiff. Bill wandered into the living-room, checked the time and poured a glass of whisky. He took a sip and, from an old, old habit, pulled out his notebook.

New York Times
(1) Where does Katz fit into this? Is he:
  (a) the owner of an archive

(b) a thief of one or more letters

(c) a salesman who has bought one letter from (a) or (b) and is trying to make an 'honest' profit?

Maybe he's the great grandson of Wagner's *Werther Freund!*, Bill thought. No, he doesn't behave like a man who has inherited these letters.

(2) If I could get to see another letter what pattern might be visible? Are they all to the Werther Freund? Are they all about Jews? All about domestic strife with Cosima?

Any pattern would help identify the owner.

(3) Do I trust Libby? Why is she so secretive about her 'work'?

He wished he hadn't written that. The woman who had been writing to him since he came back from Munich was someone he now trusted but she was still the same Libby of whom he'd grown suspicious even while he was in Munich on his way to buy a score of *Götterdämmerung*. Someone he thought he'd hated for the past seven years.

Bill decided to go and clean the kitchen. It wasn't something he often did, but he rarely had guests. Only Reah. A clean kitchen was the least he could offer Libby. He also ought to put clean sheets on the bed, but that could wait till tomorrow morning. Bill wished it could be Tuesday now. In the meantime he'd be domestic.

About nine o'clock that evening the telephone went. Bill had been thinking of Martin Katz as he vacuumed behind the cushions of his sagging settee. Long, unmistakable strands of Reah's hair, sweet wrappers, seven pence in change and a library card with a wad of gum attached had come to light in the long-congealed detritus. No sign of her missing guide to the countryside or Anne Frank. Just the sticky souvenirs of parenthood. Bill picked up the receiver just before the answer-machine clicked in.

"Bill –" It was a woman's voice, not Libby, not Vita. How odd that it should take him a moment to recognise Tamsin. "Have you got Reah's passport?" she asked. Odd, too, that these days she never said her name.

"I'm not sure," he replied. "She thinks I have."

"I know, that's what she told me. Could you check?"

"Why?" Bill asked.

"Because I need to have it," Tamsin said, bristling.

"You're taking Reah out of the country?" Bill asked.

"No, but I might."

"You do know that you're not supposed to take her out of the country without my agreement," Bill reminded her.

"Yes," she said in a peeved voice. "I do know that. All I want at this stage is to have her passport."

"Why?" said Bill. "She's just as much my daughter."

"But you're never *there*, Bill," said Tamsin wearily. "If I suddenly needed her passport, I'd have to track you down wherever you are and then come down to Chepstow to get it from you. Assuming you're in the country. If I have it in London you'll be able to pick it up with Reah on your way to the airport, if you were taking her with you."

"So," said Bill. "You are moving to London." He realised Tamsin was putting a sensible case to him, but he still resented the idea of her having the passport. It was like a legal document of ownership. This was why he was being awkward, he knew it.

"Yes, I'm moving to London," said Tamsin heavily.

"Only this is the first time we've actually discussed it," said Bill. "We haven't discussed schools either, as far as I know."

"Bill," said Tamsin, as if this pained her.

"Tamsin," said Bill.

"*Timna*," she countered. This was getting worse.

"It's only causing more problems, not having a dialogue," said Bill. "If we discussed Reah on the phone or in person like we used to–"

"For God's sake Bill!" Tamsin exploded. "That is... that was what I was doing tonight, asking about her passport and all you can do is, is – score points about the fact that I'm not supposed to take her out of the country without your permission!"

Bill heard her starting to cry – ugly, unexpected sobs of anguish.

"OK, I'm sorry," he said. "I'm sorry, Timna." God, he found it hard to say this new name.

"You can call me Tamsin," she replied. "I don't expect you to change just like that."

"I'll look for the passport," he promised. "Are you OK?"

No reply, just gulping.

"Did Reah say where she thought it was?"

"In her room." Tamsin was recovering now. "You know how vague Reah is."

"Yes, I've just found her library card," said Bill. "Under the sofa cushion. With gummy attachments."

"I've got to go," said Tamsin.

"Have you got e-mail?" Bill asked. "It may be easier if we sent each other messages. We could deal direct without the upset."

"No," she sniffed. "I'd rather deal through the solicitors."

"Listen love, everyone says they'll cost us a fortune and just turn us into enemies."

"I'm not your wife anymore, Bill," said Tamsin. Harsh, as if that were the only way she could cope with the fact.

"But you don't have to be my enemy do you?"

Silence. Tamsin was still there but not speaking. Bill almost said her name but now he felt self-conscious about which one.

"Sometimes it's easier that way, Bill."

"What, to be enemies?"

"Do you think I could ever live there now?" She put down the phone.

Again he was left wondering what was going on in the world, particularly the part of it occupied by Tamsin. Bill wondered about having a drink. No. He didn't need one tonight. The phone went again. Bloody hell. Maybe he did.

"Bill?"

"Yes?" It was Libby. She too was sounding strange.

"Did you get my e-mail?"

"I don't know. I've been on the phone to Tamsin."

"Please read it," said Libby. "You don't have to ring me back."

"What's the matter?" said Bill. Two women in distress. This was crazy.

"Please just read it. If it's not there send me an e-mail to say you haven't got it and I'll send it again."

"Libby—" said Bill, but she'd gone. Why the hell did women keep putting the phone down on him?

Dear Bill," the e-mail read. The heading was "*Despair*".

> *This has been a terrible evening. I don't know how to describe it. I went to meet him at a restaurant. It was strange for us to be at a restaurant together in Munich. We have always been very discreet here, only eating out together when he has come to Venice and then only with a group of people. Bill, you have no idea how bad he looked. He said he hadn't slept. He looked like a man who had not slept. Worse. He said that he had argued with his wife, that he realised now that he had made a terrible mistake in not leaving his wife for me before and that he had been unable to work since I told him about you. I told him that he must look after himself, that his work was important and that he must not let this get in the way of it. He told me that he is going to destroy the thing that he has been working on.*

I don't believe this, thought Bill.

"*I couldn't bear that,*" she wrote. "*It is a work of great beauty.*"

"He is a bloody composer," Bill muttered.

He said that only if he did that would I realise what losing my love meant to him. I think this is like Van Gogh's ear for him. He says he is willing to go against the Church and divorce his wife, he is willing to leave Germany to live with me (I have never asked him to do this), he is even willing to give me children. I felt at that moment that I should cry, Bill. This man was offering me everything that I had asked for over the last three years. Everything that I desired was being presented me.

"Don't believe him," Bill said to the monitor. "The moment he's got what he wants he'll start withdrawing, changing his mind, saying it's too soon. Come on Libby!" He was genuinely worried now. "For God's sake. Don't fall for it!"

I had to tell him that it was too late. I no longer loved him. Bill, he went crazy. Fortunately we were in a very noisy restaurant so very few people noticed, but still... I felt so sorry for him. Worse was to come however.

Bill's heart sank.

He told me that he had done some investigating and discovered that you have a criminal record.

"What?!" said Bill.

He knows about your approaching me with the Wagner letter. He says you are well known for dealing in stolen property. That police in several countries have you on their records and that you only came to me because you are trying to find someone with a respectable reputation who can act as an agent.

According to him your previous partner – another gullible woman – became so sickened by the work you were doing that she received an amnesty in return for giving information on you. He said many things, worse even. That you are always posing as a New York Times journalist but they have never heard of you there, that you had abused your wife – he knew her name – how would he know her name, Bill? – and that was why she had divorced you. He even said that Tamsin was taking Reah away from you because she feared you might abuse her too.

Bill I don't believe this but where did he find out all this about you? I am so unhappy. Please tell me the truth. I cannot believe this about you. I believe you are a good man, but he even knows that you have a cottage in the Wye Valley. I have told these things to nobody. How could he know these things?

Bill was dumbfounded. Then he flung a telephone directory across the study. Bloody hell! Fierce emotions boiled in him. He felt betrayed, betrayed by Libby for believing these lies. Then livid that this man had said such things, particularly about Reah. He wanted to smash his face, to beat it into a pulp. Finally he began to worry. Despite himself, Bill began to wonder: what if some of this were true? Tamsin might hold such a view of him. He had in effect stolen the letter. He had been visited by some Swiss investigator and her tame ex-cop. Maybe there was a file on him somewhere. Who knows what data gets stored and distorted? This man may have looked Bill up on the web, tracked down Tamsin. Was this why she wanted Reah's passport? To spirit her out of the country? Maybe Tamsin told him about the alleged rape. Bill slumped on the floor, flooded with anxiety. Were there really files that gave such an impression of him? His own sense of identity was under threat.

No, it was ridiculous. He had cheques from the *New York Times* that proved they employed him. And who could be this mysterious 'partner' who'd gained an amnesty – that was a total fiction and in any case if she'd given evidence good enough to get an amnesty, why was he still at large? Of course it was nonsense. Look at the man's motives for goodness sake. If this were all true why didn't he straightaway tell Libby – this was alarming stuff after all – rather than try to get her back by other routes? The man had a duty to warn Libby, whether or not she decided to go back to him.

No, he had left this to last because it was a desperate gamble. She might believe that he'd leave his wife, she might believe that he'd tear up his new symphony, or whatever it was, but it was most unlikely she'd believe these fictions about Bill's criminality. That's why he'd left them to last. Anyway, if he was some criminal mastermind what was he doing only just managing to pay his mortgage on a two-up two-down cottage in the Wye Valley?

Bill got up off the floor and went to get himself another whisky, but he came back before he'd even reached the cupboard. Something still bothered him about this. He stared at the monitor's luminescence. Why did Libby believe that nonsense? She believed it because of all the corroborative details this man had been able to supply. Things she hadn't told him. And how had he got hold of those?

"Fucking hell," said Bill, transfixed by the flashing cursor. He quickly copied down Libby's accusations into his notebook. Then he clicked on all his Sent Items to Libby and pasted them all together in one document.

"Clever, clever bastard," said Bill as he started Word-Searching for the key words in each accusation. Very soon he had his answer. Every phrase Libby had used just now, every bit of corroborative detail that this Other

Man had given her about Bill, had been contained in the e-mails Bill had sent her. The bastard had been hacking into her Inbox. So the Pope wasn't so pure after all.

Bill highlighted each phrase and then pasted the document he'd created into an e-mail.

> *Dearest Libby,*
>
> *This is a terrible thing he has done to you but it is all lies. If I were a criminal why would I be (1) poor, (2) still at liberty. As for the 'evidence' he presented, look at what I have highlighted below. Everything that he claims to know about me which is not something you have told him, he has found in e-mails that I sent to you. This is a horrible thought, my love, but this man has been intercepting our correspondence. He is probably reading this e-mail right now. If he is, I want him to know two things. Firstly he can be prosecuted for what he has done. You only have to give me his name and I shall make sure that happens. Secondly I want him to know that I love you, that I want to be with you and make love to you. That I believe we will make each other happy.*
>
> *Bill*

He pressed Send and went back to the living room to put the vacuum cleaner away. All was clear. All was right. When Bill returned there was already a reply from Libby. The poor love must have been online all the time waiting for him.

"*Darling*", it was headed. Libby had not written a new message just inserted her reply into the second paragraph of his covering letter. Where Bill had written "*I want him to know that I love you*", she had added in her bold font "***And that I love you too Bill***". Where he had written "*I want to be with you*", she had inserted "***You will be***". Where he had added "*and make love to you*", her response was "***Definitely***". Finally at the end where Bill had written "*I believe we will make each other happy*", she had typed the simple words "***We Shall***". A postscript followed: "***Tomorrow evening cannot come soon enough as far as I'm concerned.***"

❖ STARS IN THE AFTERNOON

"HELLO," said Libby, as she stood there, absurdly, deliciously, real in the narrow, squalid back street which doubled as Chepstow's bus station.

"Hello," said Bill. She was like a film star who had stepped into his reality. Libby Ziegler still in glorious Technicolor despite these mundane surroundings. Bill took in her designer clothes, her perfect complexion, her American teeth. All in contrast to the steps of Somerfield supermarket where she stood now, as the bus moved off. He advanced to kiss her.

"I never thought... I'm amazed," he said, brushing her cheek with his lips. Chepstow didn't deserve this. "How was Belgravia?"

Libby laughed. "He was teasing me about Chepstow all the time. He said Turner painted the castle but since then it's been of no interest."

"Very true," said Bill, picking up her bag from where a heavily perspiring driver had dumped it. "We'll have to try and do something about that won't we?"

Libby seemed delighted with it all; she laughed at Fatty's Breakfast & Burger Bar and was intrigued by the subterranean squalor of Dominion Records, the Home of Second Hand Vinyl. And Bill delighted in her delight. Before his very eyes she was transforming what he had always thought to be mundane at best. She seems so young, so hopeful, he thought. Seven years on she still looks so fresh. She looks happy too.

"The castle's down there," Bill said pointing through the windscreen of his Jeep as they approached an arched gateway into the old town.

"*Really?*" she said, charming him anew with the way she drew out that word.

"But we go to the left now. You don't want to see it, do you?" he asked, stopping at the junction before them.

"I don't want to see it?" Libby asked as a car horn pointed out that the lights were green. "Why should I not want to see it?"

"It's down there, say the word."

"Consider it said," said Libby, leaning back in her seat and gazing up at him.

Bill put the Jeep into gear and they shot forward. "Welcome," he said. "To the Norman fortress town of Chepstow. Pizza Express on your left. *Chep-stow*, meaning market place, is built on a spur of limestone that overhangs the River Wye. It was used by Edward the Something or Other – we had several – to keep the Welsh in their place, their place being the bits of Britain no one else wanted, i.e. Wales. A land that exports rain, rugby-players and writers who drink. That's if you believe the national stereotype which, personally, I do. Let me show you the impressive sixteenth-century bridge that links Chepstow back to England." They were forking left past his solicitors now. "Built by the equally impressive John Rennie over the site of an original Roman ford. We trust you are very impressed."

"I am," said Libby. "How long did it take you to learn all that?"

"Did it while I was waiting for your bus to get here," said Bill, decelerating. "If National Express had been any later I could have also given you Offa's Dyke, Owain Glyndŵr and Llewellyn the Last-But-One. There!" he said, slamming on the brakes again. "Behold Mr Turner's castle."

Libby was entranced. She had never ventured further west in the UK than Windsor. Chepstow was an Arthurian Neverland to her, rather than the place where buses arrived notoriously late, the Indian was OK and the video shop also sold popcorn. During the journey to Holt's Farm she was in positive raptures. "It's so green!" she exclaimed as they passed the manicured race course, the remains of Piercefield House, the long tunnel of trees that led up to Holt's Farm and finally the cottage itself. "You live here..." said Libby, stepping down from the Jeep.

"I call it living," he replied. "I'm sure you wouldn't."

"Oh no..." said Libby, and she sauntered round the boundary of his small front garden, trailing her hand over the hedges, rocking the loose gatepost and caressing the poor broken laurel bush Bill had intended to replace but had not because this place had never quite seemed permanent enough for serious DIY. "So this is you," said Libby.

"There's more of me inside," he told her.

"Yes please."

Bill had offered Reah's bedroom to Libby. He had felt it right to suggest, obliquely, that she shouldn't feel obliged to sleep with him. He was desperately keen that she did not take him up on this gallantry though.

"It's so much as I imagined," said Libby, walking round his living room.

"The office," said Bill, opening the door. Libby was keen to see his river. "You have to employ poetic license if you want a really good view," he explained. "Or the sofa."

Libby chose to stand on his desk instead. He saw tall black boots as she lifted her loose black jerkin to ascend. And a momentary glimpse of leg. Black of course. Black boots, black leggings too by the look of it.

"That's Reah's room," said Bill, opening the door at the top of the stairs, but not too wide. "And this is mine."

Libby took longer than he would have wished to look in Reah's room, then she came to join him in the doorway of the one decent-sized bedroom in Holt's Cottage.

"And this is where you find the nightmares?" Libby asked. They were standing on the threshold of his room.

"Where they find me," he told her. "Yes." Libby took his hand in hers.

"Not any more," she said.

"No?"

"No."

Where they stood the bed was unavoidable and far too visible. Bill felt his heart pounding. He simply didn't know what to do next.

"Show me the trees," said Libby. Her voice, so quiet, had a tenderness that he had not expected. Bill took Libby by the hand to a small low window underneath the eaves. Libby dipped down to look but said nothing. Bill stood behind her. He could see now how this loose black thing of hers draped around her shoulders and delineated them. Not wide, her shoulders. Narrower than Tamsin's certainly. His eyes followed her hair as it slid down the back of her neck and between her shoulder blades before disappearing within the folds of that jerkin. Now Libby was standing again, turning to him, her face frank, yet flushed. "And the stars?" she said.

Bill nodded to the skylight over his bed. "I thought I'd show you tonight."

"Now," said Libby. She lifted her arms around his shoulders and kissed him, not the social kiss of the bus stop but as they'd kissed for the first time in Munich. But this time it didn't stun. Instead, to Bill's dismay, it drove him forward. His hands. Her waist. He had to take hold of Libby, to get his hands on her skin, yet however hard he pulled at the loose black jerkin that enveloped her it held fast. Libby broke from their kiss, laughing.

"Just a minute." She unhooked something and looked up at him again. "There we are."

They moved to kiss for a second time and Bill was able to run his hands up her leggings and find the thick elastic waistband. Here clothing should end and skin begin. All this time he was melting. What was it about the way that Libby kissed him? It went on forever and he grew molten within it. But skin evaded him still. Bill's hands sought but only encountered more layers of clothing. Libby's flesh was something he no longer believed in.

Who had ever seen it? Mariners and travellers from distant lands talked of having heard tales of it, late at night, in old bazaars while oil lamps flickered and the Sirocco blew. Frantic, Bill's hands searched upwards for flesh as if it were some sensual Holy Grail. Preventing him there was a tightly-buckled turtleneck and beneath that some form of tank-top – black no doubt. It snagged on his fingernails, dammit. He tugged at the thing, incensed by yet more delay. Then the turtleneck broke up from her belt, and with it the other thing and suddenly this was her skin. Bill plunged his hands up and down her back. He found underwear, tight and unyielding, and skin that did yield, skin warm and smooth. He had to have her.

Bill forced that voluminous outer garment up to Libby's armpits. For a moment she stopped kissing him and adjusted the neck to one side. It came off at an angle over her head, catching briefly on the ribbon that held her hair. Libby, more used to this than he, freed the ponytail with a shake. Bill took the jerkin and threw it to one side. She stood before him. Black leggings, black boots and that tight black turtleneck, still tucked into the waist in places but crudely displaced elsewhere. To Bill, for whom her figure had always been wholly elusive, this was as great a shock as seeing her naked.

Her eyes were on him. Her face reddened. Bill had never seen such candour. He had to have her now before the challenge in her eyes unmanned him. Seizing Libby by the shoulders he threw them both on the bed.

It was later now. "Bill," said Libby. "That hurt, you know."

"I'm sorry," Bill said into her ear.

"It's OK," she said softly. She didn't mind the pain as long as they were in it together.

They were lying on the wrecked bed, Libby had drawn herself up close against him. Now she smoothed the hairs on his chest with one hand and burrowed her head into his armpit. She wanted him to hold her.

Bill stared at the ceiling. He felt very bad. He'd not intended to be so violent but something had come over him. His need to possess her was like anger. There had been a moment when he felt that if he could not have Libby he would destroy her. He'd hardly heard the rip of the strap on her tank-top or the cry when he'd held her down and pushed inside. This was not as he had intended.

"I'm sorry," he said. He was wretched. Bill stared at the skylight but no stars looked down. The afternoon still hung there, bland, unfocused and remote. What had he done?

"Don't be," she said.

"I love you," said Bill. "It's just–"

"I can get used to that," said Libby, and she lifted herself on top of him, pulling the duvet over them both. "I can get used to anything."

"You don't hate me then?" Bill could feel excitement again between his legs. He sensed first the press of her pubic hair on his penis and then the firm pressure of her hands.

"I don't hate you," said Libby. "Though next time you need to give me some time to be ready."

"I'm sorry," said Bill. He felt sick in his heart – but aroused elsewhere.

"Don't be," said Libby. She inched forward up his body until her breasts were just in front of him. Libby moved to place first one then the other against his lips. "This kind of thing goes down rather well," she said. There was a honeyed warmth in her voice. "Lips and tongues, you know." Bill was intoxicated by her voice and by her body. He found himself growing erect again. He tried to close his teeth around one of her small hard nipples but Libby withdrew. "Gently," she told him.

"Sorry," said Bill.

"Don't be," Libby told him again. "Look what happens down here when you're sorry."

Bill couldn't help but laugh.

"Now I'll have to start all over again," she said, clasping his penis while keeping her breasts only just out of range of his mouth. "That's better," said Libby, working his foreskin harder now. "Now," she whispered, her hair falling over his face. "Now let's take our time."

They ate that evening in front of the hearth. Bill went down to Chepstow for an Indian takeaway while Libby prepared the fire. "One thing I'm damn good at, Bill Wheeler. Our cabin is freezing in winter until you get the furnace going. And when I say freezing I'm talking subzero."

When he got back, the whole cottage was glowing. Bill realised he had never actually come home to a fire before. They hadn't had one in Chiswick and life after the move was so difficult that the last thing on Tamsin's mind had been preparing a warm welcome for her husband when he returned.

"Are you're OK?" he asked Libby as she greeted him, her face upturned for a kiss. Hell, he was still scrabbling for reassurance since that afternoon.

"Sure," she said, taking the first plastic bag from him. Bill didn't want to let her go. If he didn't hold her she might hate him. "Bill," said Libby, indicating that her hands were full. Two plastic bags of tandoori were quite an impediment to intimacy at this moment.

"Are you *sure* you're OK?" he asked.

"This afternoon was a surprise," said Libby, moving to put the plastic cartons down on Bill's kitchen work-surface. "But I said to you when I give myself to a relationship I do so 100 percent. That's the kind of person I am. Besides, I think I gave as good as I got second time around." It wasn't true. Bill knew he'd hurt her, but in his wretchedness he appreciated the gesture.

Now Libby inclined her head against Bill's chest. Before he knew it Bill had his hands around her waist again. Her proximity outraged and overwhelmed him. "Bill!" Libby cried as she landed on the sofa. He was already yanking down her leggings. The preternaturally white skin of her thighs against those tall black boots drove him wild.

"Please, take your time!" Libby was laughing and yet excited too. When it was over she stroked his head. Bill couldn't look at her and yet he felt marvellously sated. This was a madness.

"Can you love me?" he asked.

Libby looked down at him with overwhelming compassion. "I do."

"Can you keep the nightmares away?" He buried his head in her stomach.

Libby continued to stroke his hair. "Uh-huh."

Bill began to kiss her skin again. He had to lose himself in her.

"Bill?" she asked.

"Mm?"

"Where are the books?"

Bill looked up at her. "Books?"

"I'd always imagined you read a lot. I was looking round while you were away. It's mainly reference in your office."

Bill turned on his back and exhaled. "Tamsin had the books. I left them with her in the farmhouse. We were all going to live there." Bill gazed at the ceiling. "In the farmhouse. All three of us – and the books. I didn't want to take them away from Reah. Or the paintings. Besides, this move out was supposed to be temporary. And so it is. My life is temporary, permanently so."

"I'm glad you had paintings," said Libby. "This place though..."

"What?" he asked.

"It just isn't a home. Not yet."

Bill wanted to disagree and yet he knew she was speaking the truth.

"I was thinking while you were away," Libby mused. "Not just the books and the paintings but where are the friends?"

"Tamsin took those too," said Bill with a rueful smile.

"It feels as if you camp-out here." Libby told him. Bill stretched. Yes, he knew.

"I like it though," she added, her hands still within his hair.

"I'm glad you do," Bill replied. "And thank you for the gracious living!" He pointed at the kitchen-roll place-mats Libby had prepared on the coffee table. They both smiled. He'd joked. Joked because at that point he'd wanted to say something else and couldn't.

"You don't mind my playing *hausfrau*?" Libby asked.

"*Burgischerwhatsit*," said Bill, teasing. Teasing because he'd almost said that which he shouldn't.

They were quiet for a moment. Bill could hear the blackbird in its final effort for the evening. No wind, no rain, just the sound of Libby breathing and the warmth of his head in her lap.

"It feels like a home tonight." There, he had said it. Finally.

Silence.

Her hands.

His hair.

"Yes," she said. "Bathtime?"

They ate their re-heated tandoori by the fire, wrapped in towelling robes, a couple of blankets each and Bill's duvet, which he spread over Libby's legs. They ate in silence, Bill's hand resting on Libby's. Eating single-handedly was a slow process but it didn't matter. Time had stopped. Eating single-handedly proved clumsy too. Inevitably the tandoori spilt, and when Libby moved to avoid it the mound of blankets parted and red sauce dripped on to her navel. And when Bill moved to wipe it up his hand remained and soon her legs were apart again.

It was a night like nothing either of them had known. Libby became increasingly aroused. "I was so close!" she laughed, rolling back on the rug again. "I'm not finished with you yet, Bill Wheeler." They would sleep briefly in front of the fire but the moment one of them stirred the other would want to begin again. Their coupling trailed happy destruction late into the night and even into the kitchen area. Bill, his head against the fridge, was exhausted by now but Libby wasn't, not by any means. Reaching up she took a carving knife from the cutlery rack above and pressed its tip against his scrotum.

"Do you trust me?" she asked, with a look of disturbing intensity – half vicious, half-desperate. Bill felt almost disconnected from himself. "I trust you," he said abstractly. He was fast abnegating all responsibility for his body. He wasn't there.

"Do it to me," said Libby.

"What?"

She pressed the knife into his hands and lay back on the now grubby duvet, her legs not exactly open. "Do it to me, Bill."

Bill took the knife from her hands but when he moved closer with it she flinched. "It *is* dangerous," he told her, trying to reassure.

"But you trusted *me*," said Libby, disappointed.

Later that night when the fire had gone out and they found sleep in a pile of cushions and blankets, Bill thought again about that curious moment by the fridge and Libby's bizarre sense of inadequacy. What she didn't realise was that he failed to flinch not because he trusted her but because he didn't care. That was the awful thing. At that moment he would have surrendered to anything. Or rather to a vast and infinite Nothing. Anything not to feel anymore. As sensation returned to his spirit Bill realised that daily life presented him with so much pain he could easily slip away, out of time altogether.

The way Libby's presence was transforming this cottage made it abundantly clear how empty his life had become. Waking alone Bill would view the day stretching ahead of him, dividing it up with coffee-breaks just as he divided up the months ahead with plans to travel. The very act of moving on kept him occupied. Only when Reah was with him was there any wholesome sense to it all; the rest of the time he just passed the hours with work and tried not to reach for the whisky as evening approached.

Bill looked at Libby, or rather at the mound of bedclothes, cushions, rugs and hair where she slept in childlike innocence. If only he could love her, this would be the answer. She could be with him. He would not wake alone and when he came back in the evening the cottage would be bright with light and life. If only I can love her, he thought.

Bill got up to go to the lavatory. It seemed too much of an effort to climb the stairs so he opened the front door and stood in the garden to urinate. A small luminous smear above the treeline suggested that dawn was not far away. Bill felt sadder than he had ever felt before. Yet why? Here was a beautiful, intelligent woman who, amazingly, wanted to share her life with him. She clearly loved him. She had even accepted the violence that had erupted from him. She'd be a great friend to Reah too, thought Bill. Libby was less than twenty years older than Reah. He could imagine their teaming up like sisters. The idea cheered him, but something was wrong still. Bill looked up at the stars as grey daylight limped in from the east. What was it that was wrong? Bill asked himself. He winced. Good grief, he was sore from so much penetration. Had it been like that with

Tamsin? Bill wondered. No, surely they had been much more conventional when it came to sex. Maybe it was routine, but they had always known what each other wanted. God, how close he and Tamsin had been fifteen years ago. How on earth had they lost that?

That was it, Bill realised as dawn finally broke. And with it some illusions. What had he said to himself as he watched Libby sleep? "If only I can love her." He didn't. He doubted now that he could love anyone. It was the saddest dawn.

Bill awoke to hear Libby battling with the shower but decided to sleep on. He woke a second time to the sound of Libby making coffee. From where he lay crashed upon the sofa Bill could see her grinding the beans and putting his machinetta together, wet hair hanging loose. The long, dark strands flicked about as she moved quickly round the kitchen. Bill was impressed to realise that Libby had figured out where he kept everything.

He stood up. "Hi," she said, smiling. She seemed very bright and light. His stillness arrested her. She looked at him, wondering.

"Hello," he said, remembering that it can be nice to wake up to someone. Bill walked over and kissed Libby on the forehead. "You OK?"

"Stop asking me that," she teased him. "I'm fine. I just need an adaptor for my blow-drier. Listen I've made coffee and I've made a list of food you seem to be out of – which is a lot. What exactly do you eat for breakfast?"

"Just coffee," said Bill. He liked what she was wearing. It was a bright red and orange jacket over the inevitable black turtleneck but instead of the usual leggings, a long black skirt had materialised. Libby was talking to him about not wanting to be the stereotypical female who comes in and fuss-budgets. "But you have to have more than that for breakfast. Look at you. There's no weight on you. Well there I go!" she laughed. "That's the Jewish ancestry coming out in me. Never mind the books, where's the bagels?"

Bill felt at a loss to know what to do or say. Yesterday it had been fine. After all that longing there was only one thing to do and they'd done it, many times. Now he seemed to be stuck with Libby. Obliged to have a relationship with her. He liked Libby. She was very decorative, but what exactly did one do with her?

"How about coffee outside?" she said. He never had coffee outside. He had coffee in his office, pretending that it overlooked the river. That was what he did in the morning.

"*Great*," said Bill. "I'll just go and put some clothes on."

"You owe me for a camisole!" said Libby. "That strap really did break, you know."

Bill didn't know what to say.

"I'll buy you another." He was standing on the stairs now. "We could go into Cardiff or Bristol."

"I'd rather stay," said Libby, leaning back against the sink and regarding him archly. "I don't seem to need much underwear while I'm here anyway, do I?"

Bill went to the bathroom in something of a panic. He'd been on his own for too long. He'd never woken up with Marika. He hadn't even done so that last time with Tamsin. What the hell did he do now? He closed the bathroom door and locked it.

"What?" he thought. "What do I *do*?" But the only idea that occurred to him was to sit on the lavatory and put his head in his hands. This is ridiculous, he told himself. You are not under arrest. You haven't been diagnosed with terminal cancer. You simply have a young woman downstairs who seems to be in love with you and who thinks you are with her. It's not the end of the world. But what to do?

Think daughter, Bill said to himself. That was the answer. He knew how to handle Reah. She was his little girl. Libby was the same except that she had a dozen PhDs and more stylish footwear. Think daughter, he said to himself as he showered. Goodness he was sore.

"Coffee then!" he announced in noisy anticipation as he came downstairs.

"Bill," said Libby. "Are you all right with my being here?" she was sitting on the edge of the sofa, having put all but the last two cushions back. Obviously she had not just been tidying up. She had been thinking. Now she looked up, very lost.

"Yes," he said, all but scooping her up in his arms. "Yes! Absolutely! I think you're the best thing to happen to this house since I stopped buying sliced bread."

It wasn't difficult. Libby broke into a smile again. She is so much the little girl, thought Bill. As long as I think 'daughter', I can cope and if I cope she's happy.

They took two chairs out into the spot of garden just in front of his office window.

"I did think of putting a door through so I could sit out here in the summer" admitted Bill.

"Do it," said Libby. "And if you get a table and some chairs and you stand on the top of one of them you might just be able to see down to the river. Poetic licence!" she mocked.

Lee arrived in his van and Bill introduced them. Libby's accent suddenly seemed very rich, very cosmopolitan, like a fragrant musk that changes our very perception of everything around us.

"Oh aye?" said Lee shaking hands. "Where you from then?"

"Venice," Libby replied playfully.

"That in Little Italy then?" Lee considered himself a bit of an expert on American popular culture.

"No, Big Italy," said Libby.

"Oh."

"The one next to Austria."

"Ah," said Lee. "Only pardon my asking but you do have this accent." His eyes gleamed. Clearly he had always had Bill down as a sad old recluse.

"*Really*?" Libby drawled, using the word with relish. It made her sound even more exotic. As far as Bill was concerned she could say that word all night.

"You stopping long?" said Lee who obviously felt the same.

"Wouldn't you like to know," Bill interjected stepping forward.

Lee laughed. Time for him to go. "Well, see you tomorrow," he said, never once taking his twinkling eyes off Libby.

"I think you've got a fan," said Bill as they watched Lee's van depart and he ran his hand down Libby's back, resting it pleasurably on her buttocks. Seeing how taken Lee was with Libby Bill had been fired with desire for her again. He squeezed his hand between her thighs, opening her up.

Libby turned to face Bill. "You haven't attacked me in the shower yet," she suggested. But they never got to the bathroom. At the bottom of the staircase Bill couldn't resist her any longer. He grabbed hold of Libby and pushed her roughly on to the bare wooden steps, pulling up her skirt. Libby spread her legs and hung on to the stair rods. She cried out as he entered her and tore at his shirt with her nails.

Later Bill made them more coffee but he limped as he brought it to where Libby was sitting on the sofa, hugging a spare cushion.

"I think I did my knee in," he admitted.

"You're going to have to get those stairs carpeted," she told him.

"How's the back?"

Libby rolled face down on to her cushion and pulled at the waistband of her skirt. A significant bruise was forming at the base of her spine from where she'd hit one of the wooden steps.

"I'm sorry," Bill started to say, but he found himself laughing. Libby turned around and she was laughing too.

"Bill we have got to stop this. Can't we just do something nice and gentle like bestiality or flagellation?" They were laughing together now. It felt so good. Bill put his arms around her and they hugged each other.

"I love you," said Bill, and at that moment he truly did.

Those few domestic days proved to be the nearest thing that Bill had known to happiness for many years. Libby, despite her resolve to the contrary, did organise the cottage. She even cleaned out two of his cupboards.

"What are you doing?" Bill had shouted. "You're UN cultural advisor to God knows where and a PhD in twelve different languages. You can't clean out my cupboards!"

"Let's always live here," Libby said later as they watched television together, a thoroughly domestic scene except that Bill had opened the shirt she'd borrowed from him and was lying against her breast again.

"What about Reah?" he asked.

"Don't think about the future," said Libby. "Kiss," she commanded guiding her nipple towards his mouth. "Don't think about the future. Just think about forever. There don't have to be practicalities in forever."

Their love-making was becoming more tender. Bill even began to find that he could talk to Libby in the silent aftermath while the stars looked down on his bed. She always wanted to talk after sex but Bill felt an acute need to separate off. Even thinking 'daughter' was of no help then. If he even put two words together the emotional wound rubbed raw.

"Bill," said Libby once in the silence. "Can I touch you?" It was night and he was staring at the silent cosmos.

"Of course," he said, wishing she wouldn't.

"Where do you go?" she asked, snuggling up alongside him. "When we make love, I lose you."

Bill thought for a moment. "I lose myself too," he said.

"Why?"

"I don't know." Bill would rather not have this conversation. He felt that it might turn dangerous and negative at any moment. She was intruding on him.

"Isn't that what we all seek in sex?" he asked. "To surrender our sense of self?"

"But you don't surrender it to me," said Libby. "I feel you lose touch with us both. You just *go*."

"I'm sorry," he said, turning slowly on to his shoulder away from her.

"Don't," Libby cajoled. "Bill, you don't have to apologise. I'm just concerned for you."

He didn't reply. He didn't want her tugging at him, he didn't want her concern. He wanted her to disappear. He was tempted to say, "If you don't like the way we make love..." but he didn't. What he said was "I'm fine." and after a moment "I thought you were OK too."

"I am OK," said Libby, holding on to him now and trying even harder to turn him to her. "Anything you want Bill. I'm OK with anything you want. But I'm worried that you aren't."

Bill responded to her entreaty and saw in the halflight of his room how bright her eyes were. He owed her something.

"I feel uncomfortable," he admitted. Yet he was scared to admit it.

"What, now?" she asked.

"Yes," he replied shamefacedly. "When we make love I go somewhere. I switch off. It's..." He had a feeling he was about to say something truly awful here. "It's like I can get out of me, stop thinking, just be. Then when it's over I'm me again. Only I'm not just me. There's also you..." Was that why he hated her in those moments?

"It's OK," said Libby, pressing herself against him. She sounded so compassionate. Her eyes showed so much concern. God I must look needy, Bill thought. He hadn't expected this reaction from her. Libby held him in her arms and stroked his head. "It's OK," she kept repeating. Bill nuzzled her breasts.

"I want to make love with you," he said.

"We are making love," said Libby gently. What was it with men that they had to have their penis engaged before love-making could commence?

"No," said Bill. "With you, the way you Americans say it. *With* you rather than *to* you. With you, not against you."

Afterwards Libby rolled back to her side of the tangled bed, adrift in a world of warmth and moisture. "That was the best ever," she thought to herself. She was delighted. Bill had never stopped looking at her. That was why she had climaxed the way she did. He hadn't gone away, not for one moment. But she didn't tell him this. "Sometimes you talk too much, Bonnie-Blue," she said, but only to herself.

For Libby time floated while she was at the cottage. She had no idea how many mornings she met Lee, how often they sat and drank coffee looking at where the river was supposed to be if you stood on enough tables, how often they made love, how often she saw that look, that needy, angry look come in his eyes. It was her honeymoon. Nothing intruded as nothing should on a honeymoon, except for two stray calls to her mobile, and the irritation she felt when her Breughel catalogue disappeared.

"You know, I can't find it," Libby said. It was morning and she was repairing the damage they'd done to his sofa.

"What did it look like?" he answered from the sink.

"It's a Sotheby's catalogue from 1938, black-and-white plates."

But Bill hadn't seen it either. "It'll turn up," he said. "Books have a habit of walking round here. I've accused Reah of taking things before now. She's lost all sorts of stuff."

To Bill's great surprise this was the only conversation they had about art the whole time Libby was staying. He had imagined that sharing his cottage with Dr Ziegler would be a pretty erudite experience, that they'd have the kind of debates he remembered from London, in the days when he was married and she kept her clothes on.

Libby had laughed at his idea. "I don't know why you thought we'd discuss poetry and Nietzsche!"

"Well you're such a heavyweight," he admitted. He was lying in bed looking at the stars again. This time she was sitting astride him, the duvet round her shoulders.

"I am not a heavyweight!"

"I only mean intellectually speaking."

"Bill I can take most things from a man but I draw the line at puns. I *assumed* you meant intellectual heavyweight."

"OK," said Bill. "But are you really saying you're not? How many universities have got you on their books?"

Libby insisted you didn't have to be heavyweight to work for a university. "You just have to look good on paper. Before I got out, I did a lot of work on authentication, and I consult, that's all. It's a skill really. Detective work. Not intellectual in the slightest."

"You're not lightweight though, c'mon," said Bill. "Most women don't carry catalogues of Flemish painters round with them as airport reading."

"I'm middleweight," said Libby. "Believe me. The only reason you think I'm anything more is that there are a lot of lightweights around – particularly in Britain – airheads who pass themselves off as heavyweights. The people on your radio. Sometimes I wonder what's happened to the collective brains of Radio 4."

It was getting cold. Bill pulled the duvet down to cover his shoulders and Libby with it.

"So why are you carrying an old Breughel catalogue round with you, mm?"

"It's part of my work," said Libby, squeezing in alongside him and rolling on to her back. She wanted him inside her again. "That's Orion," she said, pointing through the skylight. "My dad told me how you can always see a nebula when Orion's in the sky. See the belt? The middle star in his sword is the Great Nebula, streams of matter swirling in chaotic currents reflecting light from the stars all around."

"And this is the woman who says she's not heavyweight," Bill teased her.

"Don't you remember things your parents said to you?"

"My father was a man of few words," Bill told her. "He kept us going when things were difficult. I admired him, but we didn't talk much."

"What about your mom?" Libby asked.

"She was the reason things were tough," said Bill.

"What happened with her?"

"She died. When I was eight."

Libby was shocked. How had she not known this? In all that they had said, all those years ago, had Bill never spoken of his mother's death?

"Anyway," he said. "You still haven't told me why you're reading an old catalogue from when..?"

"1938," she replied. "And you've changed the subject."

"So?"

"So... it was a good year," She conceded. "The few illustrated catalogues there are from 1938 contain some of the last sightings of certain works."

"Things that got destroyed in the war?"

"Or carried off," she said.

"Looted?"

"Looted, misappropriated, rescued and then abandoned, lost, filed away by people who didn't know what they were. It's a complex issue. Europe's still in a mess but nobody knows. Now listen Bill Wheeler, why don't you want to talk to me about your mother?"

Bill furrowed his brow then kissed her lightly. "I don't know how to."

"Why?"

"That's a complex issue too," he explained.

On the Friday night they were going to have dinner in Bristol. Bill thought Libby was taking a bath but he found her sitting naked on the edge of the tub, her elbows on her knees, her chin resting on her palms.

"Anything the matter?" he asked. She seemed not to hear him at first.

"No."

Bill sat on the lavatory lid and put his arms round her.

"Is it because you're leaving tomorrow?" he asked. Bill had worked out that he could drop Libby at the bus station half an hour before Tamsin arrived at the Severn Bridge with Reah.

Libby shivered.

"Don't then," said Bill. "Stay."

Libby began to tie up her hair. "Reah's coming. She won't want me here."

"She's going to love you," said Bill, though he wasn't entirely sure about that. He looked at Libby, as she paused before getting into the bath. The whiteness of her body delighted him even when she was unhappy.

"It's not going to be the same," said Libby.

"What isn't?"

"Us."

"What do you mean?"

She looked away, unable to explain. "I'm being stupid," she said, getting in. Bill put his arm around her but Libby had already found a hiding place.

They got as far as the Severn Bridge before she asked if they could just get a takeout from the Indian in Chepstow and return to Holt's Farm.

"Why?" said Bill, pulling over.

"I just feel that I may not be coming back. I want to have one last night in the cottage." Bill was looking at her uncomprehendingly. "It feels like home Bill."

"It is your home," he said. "If you want it. Libby, of course you're coming back. You want to come back, don't you?"

Nothing he said shifted her sense of foreboding. As Libby looked down at the long white arch of the bridge reaching out to England she felt that once she crossed it she would never return. A terrible conviction had grown in her that evening: this was as far as happiness went.

"I'll come and see you in Venice in two weeks time," said Bill. "And then we can really start to plan." To be honest, he had been a bit worried about her eagerness to rearrange the rest of their lives, but had gone along with things as positively as he could. What Bill wanted now was a calm few weeks. He wanted to discover whether he wanted Libby as much when she was absent as he did when she was in his bed. All this passion was confusing. Part of him feared that when the heady atmosphere of Holt's Cottage cooled he'd be left wondering what on earth this had all been about. Theirs had been a rapid coming together. Were they desperate people fooling themselves or was this real love, something of which his time with Tamsin had been a mere foreshadowing? If they did still feel the same then there was a lot of thinking to be done.

He hadn't asked Libby to move in with him, but he imagined he wanted her to. She'd continue to travel the world. She was supposed to be going to Finland shortly. He would continue to travel too, that would give them both freedom, but Bill believed that he wanted Libby to come home to him when she came home, not to an empty apartment on the outskirts of Dorsoduro. And he wanted to come home to her. That image of returning to a warm fire had stayed with him. It was the nearest thing to happiness he had known.

Even if his heart could not fully comprehend what had happened, Bill felt sure this was more than two lonely people cramming the maximum amount of sex into a few isolated days in the Welsh hillsides. Given time, Bill felt sure that he'd want Libby at Holt's Cottage for good.

On the other hand there was Reah. If Reah was going to London maybe Bill should go too. Unfortunately Libby had been adamant that she wouldn't live in London again.

"I left there seven years ago and I said I'd never go back," she'd told him. "I hated it when I went to see Giorgio in Belgravia."

"But this time we'd be together," Bill had told her.

"I like it here, Bill!" Libby had insisted. They were standing in the kitchen. "Why can't we live here?"

"Of course we can," said Bill, and he kissed her and told her it was time to go for a bath if she were having one, they had a long journey to Bristol. That was before he found her sitting on the tub, silent and staring.

"It's all going to go wrong," said Libby. It was night now as she stared at the long white bridge. "I can feel it, Bill. You know how you feel about the trees outside your cottage. That sense of foreboding."

"But I'm wrong about the trees," said Bill. "You convinced me."

Libby wouldn't be mollified. "Sometimes you just know," she said. "Let's go back and make love in front of the fire and watch TV."

But when they got back the fire wasn't there to welcome them as it had welcomed Bill that night he'd gone down to Chepstow. Suddenly neither of them felt remotely sexual. Bill put his arm round Libby as she slumped on the sofa.

"Don't go," he said.

But she knew he didn't mean it. He wanted to be nice to her. He cared for her. She knew these things, but she also knew he wanted her to go now. So she clung on to him. She couldn't understand why once again everything she wanted was being taken away.

"Will I see you again?" Libby asked as the bus pulled in on Saturday morning below the Somerfield steps.

"I'm coming over" he said, this man who thought he loved her. "In two weeks. Can you wait that long?" His tone was avuncular. This man who thought he loved her. She had welcomed him as father and lover, she wanted him inside her now more than ever but every word seemed to reinforce the fact that he was desperate for her to go now.

"You'll just get on with your life," said Libby. "You don't need me."

"Hey," he said. "Hey, listen, let *me* know what I need. I'm going to miss you like hell."

She didn't believe him. She wanted to but the truth was that she knew him better than he knew himself, and that would always worry her.

When Libby arrived back at her apartment in Venice she told Hauke that she was tired. He didn't ask her how things had gone in England but he could recognise the old sorrow.

"I have brought many letters," said Hauke, standing near her, tall and reliable. If cripplingly incurious. "And there's one phonecall you must look at. Nothing from Him, don't worry."

"You don't have to speak English to me," Libby muttered into the cushions where she lay. "I'm not sick."

"This Bill," said Hauke sitting down. "He rang for you."

"What did he say?"

"He said he had sent you an e-mail and that he hopes you have returned OK."

Libby sat up, clutching the cushion to her abdomen.

"I love him Hauke, I know this is not the best time... but I do."

Hauke looked at her, bland but benign. She knew he could not understand the things she went through but he seemed to be saying write and tell this English man that you love him. Go back to his cottage, Libby Ziegler. Live your life.

"I must go," he said, standing up and rebuttoning his blazer. "It is a four hour drive."

"OK," she said. "Take care. Call me when you've had a chance to look round."

"Sure."

"I'll just check the e-mails," she said with a sniff.

"Yes, you check," said Hauke.

"Thanks, Big Man."

❖ HAGEN

BILL WAS FLOATING in memories of the last few days. He could still sense Libby's words hanging in the air. More distinctly than he had ever smelt her scent, tasted her skin or heard the rise and fall her breathing, he could feel her words around him.

"Let's do something you've never done with anyone else," she'd whispered in his ear.

"No," he laughed.

"Bill I *want* to, I want to know that this is just you and me. That you've never experienced anything like this with anyone else before."

She was amazing, he thought. She had known the violence within him and not flinched. Had she tamed it or exhausted? He did not know but he was amazed to feel so at peace. Within minutes of her going, Bill had had his answer. He loved her.

It was true that she'd been sad when they parted, but Bill was sure that Libby's sudden pessimism would pass. Certainly it should once they were together again. That time could not come soon enough. He'd been in a daze ever since the bus station. As for picking up Reah from the Severn Bridge, he couldn't remember what he and Tamsin had said. Not very much in all probability.

"Dad?" said Reah. "You've been looking at that screen for ages."

"Oh, sorry. Just thinking."

"Only it's not switched on," said Reah.

"Right," said Bill. "Sometimes, you know, I think better without a computer."

"But why do you have to sit in front of it?"

"No reason," he said, getting up and tousling her hair.

"You're in a very strange mood, Daddy Boo."

It was afternoon. They went for a walk. Spring seemed to be all round Bill. He drank it in. For once Reah was walking ahead of him. "Dad!"

"Sorry. I'm... I'm just a bit tired," he said. "Let's sit down."

"You sure you're OK."

"Isn't that view just amazing?" as they settled on a rock looking down to the Wye.

"S'pose," she replied.

"God knew what he was doing when he created this place."

Bill wanted to talk to his daughter, to ask her what she thought it was all about. Life's great mystery. Was the answer nothing more than feeling love for somebody else? Opening up a little and letting the light flood in? Connecting across a vast cold Universe? Was that it? Not being loved, as he had thought, but feeling love for someone else. Bill's emotional central-heating system was stoked by the certainty of his feelings for Libby. He was suffused as never before.

"What do you think you'll do with your life?" he asked his child, full of paternal glow but resisting the temptation to tousle. Bill could see the decades stretching pleasurably ahead of them both.

"Me?"

"Only daughter I've got."

Reah thought for a moment. "Go to University, get a job," she said. "Get married, stay married." Bill put his arm round her. "Have you been drinking?" Reah asked. She was used to the six o'clock J&B but this was three in the afternoon. Ever since Bill had picked her up he hadn't been right.

"No, why d'you ask?" Bill asked.

"You're all fuzzy round the edges," she said. "Like you're not so both-ered about things as you usually are."

"Do I get bothered about things?"

Reah took an emphatic breath. "*Yes Dad.* All the time. Did something happen in Germany?"

"No," he replied, surprised at his daughter's intuition. It wasn't like Reah to think so far beyond her own self. She was the wrong age for that kind of perspicacity.

"Maybe it's springtime," he said. They were silent for a moment. Bill looked at the view again. "You know I haven't always been happy here, don't you?"

"Yes," said Reah cautiously.

"There have been times, you know, when you haven't been with me..." He noticed Reah was shifting uncomfortably.

"Can we go back?" she asked. Bill smiled. Maybe this wasn't the time to tell her that he wasn't going to be so lonely in future.

"Don't you want to stay and look at the view?"

"The view? It's always the same, Dad. Trees, water. Water, trees."

"But sometimes the leaves are green," he pointed out.

"Oh yeah," said Reah choosing to sound her most disenchanted and teenagerish. "Green leaves, *right.*"

"They stand for hope," he said, stretching back on the rock and looking at the sky.

"Oh God, Dad's turning into a hippie," Reah grumbled. "I'm going back, OK? You can stay here and do your green leaf thing if you want."

"No, wait," said Bill. He didn't want Reah walking back through the woods on her own. There was poison in the wood. Dampness and corruption, stale and smoky.

"Mum wants me to find my passport," Reah told him as they were approaching the cottage.

"Do you know why?" Bill asked.

"She says we might go for a holiday in Israel at Whitsun. Dad, it's not fair. I thought I was moving schools *now*. I don't want to go back to the Comp for another term."

"Your mother and I have to agree about the school move," said Bill. It was true. He'd had a letter about it that morning from Aaronovitch. Tamsin was being reasonable, if formal. Bill was so loved-up he hadn't even been alarmed by the legal-looking envelope. He just couldn't get worked up about anything at the moment. Israel sounded like a nice idea.

"I told her I don't want to go. Israel's full of Jews with guns killing Palestinians and claiming it's not their fault." Bill wondered how that view went down in the Walken household. It wasn't like Reah to be political about anything other than animal rights. People were not the usual recipients of her sympathy.

"You should go," said Bill. "It's part of your heritage."

"I didn't ask to be Jewish," said Reah moodily.

Bill wondered whether his role was that of sole repository for Reah's ambivalence about Judaism. He'd seen her happily clapping and singing along with her aunts round the table.

"Are you going to put this place up for sale?" Reah asked as Bill opened the door.

"Maybe," said Bill.

"Mum said you might not move to London." Reah was standing there, hands in coat pockets. She wanted an answer.

"It's all money," Bill told her. "I don't know whether I can afford to."

"I want you to," she said.

Yes, thought Bill as he kissed her forehead. And Libby doesn't want me to.

He needed to be in contact with Libby. The cottage reminded him painfully of her absence. All the places they had made love, all the things they had said. Most of all Bill remembered lying on the sofa watching TV, Libby's shirt open to suckle him. He could not be without her.

"I just need to check my e-mails," he said.

"Then can we go down to Chepstow and get a video?" Reah asked.

"We should have got one on the way up, shouldn't we?" What a daze he must have been in. "Sure. I'll just check and then we'll go down."

The answer-machine was flashing in Bill's office so he attended to that first. It might be Libby, given that he'd rung and left that message with Hauke. But it wasn't, it was Vita.

"Bugger," said Bill once he'd realised this was the wrong American in his life.

"Sorry to call you on a Saturday, Bill, but I thought you'd be interested to know that one of those Wagner letters has come up for auction over here."

Interesting, he thought.

"They're only revealing a fragment, or rather the second page of a two-page letter, but it's in today's *Boston Globe* with a translation. I think you should read it, Bill. Then maybe we should talk, see if there is something to be investigated here. The article I've been reading says nothing about its provenance." Funny to hear Vita using the same vocabulary as Libby. "I've asked Lyndon to scan it and e-mail it over. Let me know next week how you plan to proceed."

Bill switched on his computer. Now this was interesting. Would it speak of *S——* and the Jews? Or of Cosima refusing to embrace him again? A second letter would help him home in on the identity of the *Werther Freund* and the significance of that cache.

His machine told him that he had two new e-mails. One was from a press office in Vyborg, the other from ziegler.409. Bill forgot Vita, Wagner and Vyborg for a while.

"Missing You" the e-mail was headed, although Bill remembered with a tinge of disappointment that his to Libby that morning had had the same heading. She'd obviously just clicked Reply.

> *Dear Bill,*
>
> *It was wonderful to receive your e-mail. I rushed to the machine as soon as I got in and was so pleased to find something from you. Venice was beautiful in the afternoon sun today but my heart is still very much in the Wye Valley. Please can we live there forever? My father's cabin was like your cottage. He and I spent many weekends there in the time BC.*

What was BC? Bill wondered.

Now I must go about the hundreds of tedious small things waiting for me. Hauke has kindly driven down from Munich with as much of my stuff as he could fit. My apartment is not big, so I must find space for it all. Bill, I so look forward to your being here, but most of all I want to be in Holt's Cottage again. Will you think me crazy when I tell you it feels like home to me now? Promise me you'll never sell it, not until there are no corners left for us to make love in! Must go now. Write soon.
 Libby.

He did feel disappointed by her e-mail. His to her that afternoon had been constrained by the fact that Reah was next-door. Now that they had lain together watching the stars, maybe the written word wouldn't suffice anymore. Bill pressed Reply.

Dear Libby,
 I feel lost without you.
 And wish to lose myself within you.
 Again.
 And Again.

It looked like a poem. He was surprised at himself.

I remember your writing to me about the Siegfried Idyll, that dirge which holds up The Ring so that Wagner can tell us how bloody happy Siegfried and Brünhilde are now that they have found each other. I think we agreed how interminable it is. Well it is, yes, (the concert version anyway) but that's because we, as an audience, want drama. I don't imagine that tranquil interlude was at all boring for Siegfried and Brünhilde, nor for Wagner and Cosima for that matter (didn't he write the concert version as a thank you present when their son was born?) I have felt the whole of today that I have been walking around in my own Siegfried Idyll. Reah thinks I've gone soft. Libby, love, I hope our own concert version will go on forever. I don't want to stop feeling like this. I don't care if the rest of the world thinks we're boring. In fact I want them to shout "Stop this soporific saccharine content-ment! Bring on Hagen, black revenge and the curse of the Ring! Let's have a few plot-twists and disasters!" But if we keep true to what we found in the night there will be none of this. I am sure of it because I knew you in the night and you knew me and now the night is no longer dark.

He had not intended to write any of this, but it was very much what he felt. Bill pressed Send without another thought. His machine whirred and clicked away. The shash of a thousand tiny commands exploding sibilantly down the telephone line. Bill saw that he had 1 New Message. He went offline and clicked to open it. Sadly it wasn't a postscript from Libby in Venice. It was from the *New York Times*.

> *Dear Bill Wheeler,*
> *Vita has asked me to enclose the following. If you have any trouble opening this attachment please contact me directly.*
> *Lyndon Luberman*

Bill double-clicked to open the attachment without too much optimism. He wasn't at all surprised when a mass of geometric symbols hit the screen. Bill scrolled through them. No discernible text. He might have guessed.

> *Dear Lyndon,*
> *I'm sorry, my machine can't open your attachment. Can you paste in and retransmit?*

Bill pressed Send.

"Dad?" said Reah from the doorway. "Are we going yet?"

"I'm just trying to get a document opened from New York," Bill replied. He'd really spent far too much time in this office today. It wasn't fair on Reah, but it was where he felt most capable of being in contact with Libby. Were Reah not with him, he would probably have sat in the office all day, tinkering with articles and checking for messages. He must get on, give her the time she deserved.

"Dad my programme will be on soon!"

"OK, coming!"

Bill had waited to check that the message to Lyndon had gone through and was just about to switch off when he saw he had yet another New Message. Maybe it wasn't important. He clicked and it was. Ziegler.409 was back in his life.

"Sorry Boo," he said, appearing at the doorway. "Can you give me another five minutes?" Reah grabbed a cushion and turned her back on him. It wasn't going to be easy juggling Libby and Reah. They could both sulk. Still Libby did have a certain claim on him.

The e-mail was headed "*Bill!*" At first sight he thought it a cry for help but, no, it was more likely an exclamation of passion. That was what he had wanted from Libby. After all he had written of his wish to lose himself within her. Maybe she had taken up his cue.

Bill, this is the worst thing that could happen.

He went cold. Bill could not imagine what would be the worst thing. She was alive. He was alive. They could be together.

Bill, half an hour ago I had a phonecall from Heidi Von Meck. You remember Baroness Heidi? She said she thought I ought to know that they had received an e-mail about me. She sounded formal but concerned. I couldn't think what it might be. Heidi said she would rather not speak of it. She had forwarded the document in its entirety to me and was at pains to point out that she had not read beyond the first few sentences. I have just gotten to my mailbox and found it.

Bill could tell that something was very wrong but he had no idea how a document relating to Libby could do harm. What harm could flourish in this world when two people loved each other?

When I opened it I saw most of the e-mails that we have sent each other. Someone had copied those e-mails and pasted them into a single document Bill, a document headed "Dealings between Libby Ziegler and an International Art Thief". Bill, it contained all the intimate things we had said to each other, even down to our wish to make love when I came to the Wye Valley. Worse, when I looked at the list of recipients I saw that those things we had said to each other, those most intimate things, had been sent to everyone I know in Venice, Munich, Prague, New York, just about my entire address book. People who employ me. People with whom I've had very sensitive dealings. Ambassadors, editors, professors, even friends of my father and Carey.

Bill was stunned. Who would do such a thing and why?

Of course it is obvious who has done this. We know he had access to my e-mail. He probably knew my password. I had no secrets from him, but he knows how private I have always kept my life, how privacy has been of paramount importance to me, how I can only give myself to someone by doing so 100 percent and that in order to do so I have to know in our relationship that I am protected.

Bastard, thought Bill. Worse than bastard. Much worse.

Bill I cannot move. I cannot even reach for the telephone. Hauke is in the Czech Republic. I am all alone. That these people know my most intimate feelings for you.

The e-mail seemed suddenly to have stopped, the e-mail went blank but it then resumed at the bottom of his screen. Libby must have hit the return button unknowingly. Clearly she was writing and not even checking what went on to the screen.

> *Sorry about that. I have just been sick. In fact I've just been sick again. I can't stop vomiting. Bill this feels worse than being raped. I need you to come to me now. I enclose my address. It's quicker to get a taxi from the airport. I am going to try and go to bed now. I'm taking some pills to help me sleep. I threw up the first ones. I'm taking the phone off the hook. I can't bear anyone to be near me. Please come. Please. I have never been more unhappy nor more alone.*
> *Libby*

Hagen, thought Bill. Stalking the forest with his long cold spear. Evil was back in the world.

He clicked Reply. He wanted to write back to Libby and reassure her that all would be well. Then he thought it would be better if he knew what flights to Venice were available. He picked up the telephone and began to dial.

Reah walked in, big and angry. "Dad, I'm getting really fed up with this," she complained.

"Just a bloody minute, for Christ's sake!" Bill shouted.

Reah turned on her heel, shocked, and walked out.

It wasn't a good flight over. Reah Wheeler made it clear to her father that she was not interested to know who they were meeting or why.

"Boo Boo, please," said Bill. "This is a very dear friend of mine. She needs help."

Reah studied the view from her portal.

"Oh for goodness sake," said Bill. "Aren't I allowed friends?"

"Is she someone you met in Munich?"

"No," said Bill, economising on the truth. "I've known her for ages."

"Is she the one who split up you and Mum?"

"No one split up me and Mum."

"Oh come on Dad," said Reah turning to him. Her face was white, her eyes deeply unhappy. "What kind of *klutz* d'you think I am?"

"If you must know," said Bill, making a virtue out of ambiguity. "If you must know she is someone I met again recently in Venice. She needs my help. Is that so awful?"

"S'pose," grumbled Reah.

Bill had felt bad about depriving Reah of yet another of their weekends. He also felt dubious about taking her to Venice with him. Bill had had images of how she and Libby would meet. Pleasant images. It would be a special place, somewhere Reah had very much wanted to visit. That way she'd associate a good day out with Dad's new friend. That was the fantasy. This was reality: the aeroplane engine droning while Bill hoped to hell that Reah liked Venice. He dreaded to think what state Libby would be in. Not at her best for certain. This was bad timing but what else could he do? He couldn't take Reah back to her grandparents again. Where was Tamsin? But even if he knew, Bill would have been loath to hand Reah back. He was supposed to be keen to spend more time with his daughter, to be fighting to keep her in the Wye Valley. How credible was that, if he dumped her every weekend they were due to be together?

At Marco Polo airport Bill decided to take Libby's advice and splash out on one of the long water-taxis moored just outside Arrivals. Besides, travelling at speed across the lagoon might be something of a treat for Reah. It was certainly something that Bill had always wanted to do. Unfortunately there was drizzle in the air and quite a lot of spray hitting the boat. Reah slouched back in her seat sullenly, hands thrust in her pockets, just like Tamsin.

"Venice is the most beautiful city in the world," Bill told her. "I've always wanted you to see it." Reah looked at him with a suspicion that bordered on hostility. "We can have fun here," he continued. "I'm sure it won't all be looking after Libby."

"Why can't someone in Venice look after her?" Reah asked, fiddling with the white leather seats.

"She's not from Venice. I don't suppose she has many friends here." Not exactly true, Bill thought. Libby seemed to have friends everywhere. Acquaintances anyway. "Look we'll go out to dinner tonight. Venice is supposed to be the most romantic place in the world." Bill wasn't impressing her with his leaden superlatives; most beautiful buildings, most romantic restaurants, most compromised father.

Reah shuddered. He asked her what the matter was. "I just don't like the idea of you two going out for a romantic meal and me having to tag along."

"I don't mean romantic in that sense," said Bill.

He stood up to take a look at the view. "There's a wonderful island over the other side of the lagoon, Torcello. We should go there."

Reah said nothing. Bill got the impression all local excursions would cross over a territory known as Reah Wheeler's dead body.

He took out his mobile and tried Libby's number again. Ever since last night her phone had been off the hook. This time it rang but she didn't pick up. After a while Bill got through to the answer-machine. He was just starting to leave a message to say they were on their way when Libby's voice cut in. She'd obviously been screening calls.

"Bill–"

"Hello, how are you?" he asked, straining to hear her voice over the noise of the boat.

"Well, I took some stuff," she said. "It seems to have helped. Did you get my e-mail?"

"I just got the one you sent yesterday with all that news."

"I sent you one this morning," Libby explained sounding slightly aggrieved. "After I got yours. Is Reah with you?"

"Yes."

"Oh."

"Is there a problem?" Bill asked. He didn't feel he could say anything more in front of Reah.

"I..." Libby seemed lost for words. "I just don't feel it's appropriate. I don't have much space here." Bill hadn't thought this through. He could see that it was a going to be a bit of a crash course for Reah: discovering Dad had a 'friend', then meeting that friend and finding that the friend intended to spend the night in bed with her father, all in the course of 24 hours. But what else could he do? This was the woman he loved. Reah would have to come to terms with that. Libby had gone silent.

"Would you prefer it if we booked into a hotel?" Bill asked. He could see Reah's mass of dark hair twitch as if her ears were homing in on the conversation.

"No," said Libby. "You stay here, I'll go to a hotel."

"Look, let's get to you and see how it goes," said Bill. "We should be there in twenty minutes or so. What about you? Are you OK?"

"I'm coping," said Libby. "No one else has phoned. I don't know whether that means people are deleting that document without reading it or whether they're sitting down with a glass of wine and enjoying every word."

Bill didn't want her to start down that avenue of morbid speculation. "Don't think about it. Look, your friends aren't going to care two hoots. What do those e-mails say other than –" He was about to say 'You've got a boyfriend', but given the proximity of Reah he changed tack "– than something perfectly normal and natural. They'll probably be pleased for you."

"What about the art thief thing?" asked Libby.

"Well that's laughable, "said Bill. "It's obvious he's just trying to give people a more serious reason to read through the e-mails other than scurrilous gossip. He's saying 'Look, this is dangerous ethical stuff, not just tittle-tattle. We must stop her.' It doesn't bother me."

"But it does me, Bill," Libby insisted. "People trust me. It's essential that they do for my work. Oh god–" She went silent, worryingly so.

"Let's talk about it when I get there," Bill told her.

"OK." She sounded very quiet.

"Put the coffee on," he said.

"Well, at least she's answering the phone now," Bill said to Reah, who made a point of turning away further. "Reah, love, what is the matter?"

"She doesn't want me there. I know what she was saying."

"She wasn't saying anything of the sort. She was just saying her flat wasn't very big and that she'd go to a hotel to make room for us. She's looking forward to seeing you."

"Did she say that?"

"Yes. She thinks you sound great." Bill was amazed how easy it was to fillet their conversation in order to present Libby in a better light. Sadly, Reah's version of events probably was the more accurate, but by using words that Libby had said in Munich and putting a more positive spin on her talk of hotels, he had been able to make her sound much more welcoming and generous. "You are great," he said, sitting down and putting his arm around her. "And we're going to have a great time. Think of all the films that have been shot in Venice."

"Like what?" said Reah, lumpishly.

"Well, there's *Death In Venice*," said Bill, suddenly struggling.

"Oh. Wow."

"And... *Don't Look Now*."

"Does someone die in that too?"

"Yes," he admitted "There's also *Decapitation in Venice, Suicide in Venice* and *Really Nasty Cold in Venice*. They're all of them great films." Reah began to laugh, despite herself.

"And *Ingrown Toenail In Venice*?" she suggested.

Bill found them a cafe on the Campo Santa Margerita and ordered Reah pizza and a Coke. "Will you be OK here while I go round the corner and see how Libby is?"

"Sure," she replied.

"Don't eat it all at once, we may be back to join you. Depends how she is. Whatever happens, I'll be back in ten minutes, OK?"

"Sure."

He made his way quickly towards Calle Del Magazen where Libby lived. Twice he turned back to check that Reah was still OK under the cafe awning. When he saw her sitting alone at the table in her bulky coat and mass of hair he was sorry to see how still she sat, almost as if she were trying to avoid detection. What a shame. What a shame to be in Venice for the first time in your life under these circumstances. He wished he could have brought her as he intended, when the weather was better, when the three of them could have walked around together, Reah in that dress with straps she'd worn last summer. Libby introducing her to Italian style. Sunlight on the canals, ice-cream to die for and gondolliers telling her how beautiful she was.

Bill found the apartment with no great difficulty. "*Ziegler*", read the third bell down. *Buzz.* "It's me."

"Come on up."

The stucco was faded to an organic pink. Only Venice could decay with such self-confidence.

Buzz and click. The door fell open. Bill saw a narrow hallway with a floor of cracked tiles, tilted by years of subsidence and flood. Anywhere else and this would have seemed scruffy. In Venice it was Renaissance chic. He passed a marble table with a gilt mirror that had lost some of its silvering. He couldn't help wondering if this was Libby's style. Would she choose to live like this wherever she was, or was it only how she chose to live in Venice? He felt an acute sensation of anticipation.

At the top of the second flight of stairs a door opened, one of a pair that were hugely tall and scarcely painted. Libby stepped out, wonderful still. "Where's Reah?" she said, looking round him.

"I left her in a cafe round the corner so we could talk first."

Libby's eyebrows furrowed. "Is she on her own? She'll get pestered by boys." Libby went back into her apartment and emerged with a coat.

Bill was pleased, if surprised, at this show of concern. Nevertheless he couldn't help wondering if it were displacement activity: Libby focusing on Reah because that was easier than everything they had to discuss, easier than being with him, in fact. In the hallway he took hold of her by the arms and asked her if she were OK. "Please, Libby. We have to be together on this. He's trying to split us up. You haven't kissed me yet."

Libby looked at him. It was as if she couldn't bear to be open to anyone ever again. Bill thought he saw her fight down the feeling. "Oh *Bill.*" She put her arm round his neck and pulled them close. She could not kiss him though – not yet. Bill felt uneasy. Certainty is so fragile, so temporary.

*

Reah was sitting there absolutely still, as before. Her Coke hadn't even arrived.

"Hi," said Bill. "This is Libby, Libby this is Reah."

"Hi," said Libby.

"Hi," said Reah.

"I love your hair," said Libby, sitting down. Reah looked suspicious of the flattery. "No really," Libby continued. "You're so lucky."

"Did he tell you to say that?" Reah asked, looking more at the table than at Libby.

"No your dad didn't, but anyone would love your hair," said Libby. "And thanks for coming really. I don't know what I'd've done without him."

"I didn't have any option," said Reah shooting a sideways glance at Bill.

"Reah," said Bill.

"Well I didn't, Dad," she replied, happier to argue with her father than make small talk with this American with her bright teeth, white skin and tired eyes.

"Well I appreciate it anyway," said Libby. "Shall we go and have lunch?"

"You've already ordered me a pizza," Reah told Bill.

"That's all right," said Libby. "I know the people here, I can tell them we'll come back another time. There's a lovely place just the other side of the Rio Di Ca'Foscari, Bill, you'd love it, I know." She reached up to touch his arm. Libby was beginning to reconnect with the world again, getting back to being more like Libby, less like a ghost. Spending the last twenty-four hours vomiting wouldn't have helped. Oh, she would convalesce with him.

"I like it here," said a voice. *Reah.* She had seen that touch and no way was she going to be budged to suit the American.

"She hates me," Libby said sadly as they walked back. Reah was dawdling behind.

"I'm sorry. It's all been rather a shock for her. I hadn't mentioned you before. She hasn't had any time to get used to the idea that I've got someone."

"Damn it, I shouldn't have asked you to come," said Libby, looking down at her feet.

"Hey – we're in this together," he told her. "Look, I'll take her to one side. Tell her to stop being so bloody awkward."

"No," said Libby. "I know what she's going through. I had something like this with my Dad. She needs time, Bill, but she also needs to see that we haven't got anything to apologise over. I just wish this weren't all happening now! I need you to hug me."

Bill put his arm around her but after two steps he turned round on instinct. Reah had stopped walking. "Oh good grief," he said

Libby's apartment was wonderful, Bill thought. Reah obviously thought it old, smelly and in need of central heating. She sat down on a glorious, if slightly damp, chaise longue and refused to take her coat off.

"I'm afraid I've been away a lot recently," said Libby, moving aside boxes and turning on what heating she could find. "It hasn't properly warmed up yet."

"Dad," Reah appealed to him quietly, as Libby disappeared into the bedroom. "Can we go to that hotel?"

"Can you wait a while?" Bill asked her. "You two have only just met."

"It's not *her*, it's so cold and horrible here."

Bill could see Reah's point. Libby's apartment was magnificent – if you didn't mind an eighteenth-century lifestyle. The ceilings were very high, the rooms disproportionately narrow, and only partially carpeted with rugs. The whole place had clearly been left unpainted for years. There were only four rooms: a very long salon with a desk and various painted cupboards all crammed full of papers, a bedroom off the salon, which Bill hadn't seen yet, and a third room which might once have been for a servant but which had been divided in two to make a kitchen and shower/wc. This alone was modern. Libby had stacked the tiny kitchen with shining chrome appliances and obviously kept it clean.

Fortunately this Reah did like, although Bill had to call her in to look. She sat there at the tiny two-person table while Libby fixed her some orange juice. Reah was taken with the press Libby used for squeezing the juice but horrified with the result. "It's got bits in it."

"Bits?" asked Libby. The kitchen was sufficiently narrow that Bill could only see what was going on by looking over Libby's shoulder.

"That's just fragments of orange, love," he said. "It's what you get in Natural Orange Juice, like at the supermarket."

"But I don't like Natural Orange Juice," said Reah. "You know that, Dad. We never buy it at home."

"She doesn't like bits," said Libby. "OK. I'm going to have to go to the store but they'll be closed at the moment. What else have I got?"

"It doesn't matter," said Reah gracelessly.

"Can I have a word with you?" Libby asked Bill.

They went into the bedroom which was small and wood-panelled with shutters at the window. To Bill's eyes it was a veritable bower. Unfortunately for the moment it had to double as a council of war.

"I'm sorry Bill," said Libby. "Any other time I could cope with this. I know what it's like for her. I used to pull all the same stunts with my Dad and Carey."

"They're not stunts," said Bill. "She really doesn't like bits."

"I'm sorry," Libby insisted. "But they are, Bill. I know what girls are like. I could have anticipated this. I did anticipate this." She was pacing now, much more animated even than when they'd argued in the Baron's study. "I'm sorry Bill, but at the moment I've got enough happening in my life. I don't think I can cope with someone in my apartment who hates me."

Bill tried to insist again that Reah didn't hate Libby, that she wasn't that kind of person.

"OK," said Libby, waving her hands. "Maybe she doesn't hate who I am, but she sure as hell hates what I am."

"What d'you mean?"

"Our relationship. Not that I blame her if this came as a total shock—"

"Look," said Bill, aware that Libby needed someone to be angry with. "Look, I was just thinking about how I might begin to introduce the subject when I got your e-mail asking me to come. I had no time."

"I know," said Libby. She'd stopped pacing now. "I should have remembered. I shouldn't have asked you to come." She touched his face. Bill valued the contact. He put his arms around her. "Bill," she said into his shoulder. "I need looking after. I really do. Whenever I think about what he's done..."

"Don't," said Bill, holding her tight.

"It's like standing there in front of all those people, naked."

"Dad?" said a voice from the salon. Bill felt Libby freeze in his arms.

"Just a minute, Boo!"

"Can you go to a hotel?" Libby whispered. "Find somewhere she'll be happy."

Bill didn't want to admit that the cost of Venetian hotels worried him.

"I came here to be with you, love."

"Get her somewhere with Room Service and a choice of movies," said Libby, squeezing his arm and slipping away.

It took a while to find somewhere. To save time, Libby rang round. Bill and Reah sat in the kitchen.

"You know I would prefer it if you'd be nice to Libby," Bill said. Reah didn't reply. "Boo, this isn't like you."

"Well it isn't like you either," said Reah. "You never told me you had a girlfriend."

"She isn't a girlfriend, as such," said Bill. What an asinine thing to say.

"What is she then?"

"She's someone I'm very fond of who's going through a bad time."

"She seems OK to me," said Reah ungenerously.

"That's because she's making an effort!" Bill told her quietly. "I wish you would."

Reah didn't know how to reply to that. She hated him for comparing them, especially as Libby came off better. All she could do was remain uncommunicative, even on their walk to the hotel. When they stopped outside a rather old looking building with a single glass door she told Bill she wanted to go home, back to Chepstow to watch a video. She was chewing her bottom lip. Bill felt terrible. They went inside and checked in in silence. The pleasant but matronly woman looked rather surprised at the sight of Bill with Reah and tried to explain that it was *una camera doppia*.

"*Si*," said Bill. "*Doppia*, me and my daughter."

"*Non ho fatto la camera condue letti*," she told him.

"*Si, doppia per due*," said Bill. The woman shrugged and gave him the key. Then she seemed to ask if they needed any help with the cases.

"No, we can manage," Bill told her, although they had difficulty even squeezing into the lift, given the size of Reah's overnight bag. Not to mention the fact that the lift was no larger than a broom-cupboard.

The room was much more pleasant, and modern, than either of them had expected, but to Bill's surprise it contained a double bed.

"I asked Libby to reserve a twin room," he exclaimed, gazing at its padded headboard and remembering suddenly that *doppia* meant double.

"It's all right," said Reah looking at the TV.

"Are you sure?" he asked.

"Sure." Reah seemed much happier now and decided she wanted to take a shower.

"Now look," said Bill to the bathroom door. "I need some time with Libby. Are you going to be OK here for an hour or so?"

Reah popped her head round the door.

"Sure," she said.

"Don't answer the door. Ring Room Service if you need anything and I'll leave Libby's number on the desk."

"OK," she called. Bill went to pick up his coat from the bed. "Oh Dad," said Reah, peeping round the door, a towel under her armpits. "Er, would you mind?"

"What?"

"Well, *Psycho* – you know. Would you mind waiting till I finish my shower?"

Bill sat in the window with his feet up on a small reproduction eighteenth-century coffee table. Surely there had been no such thing in the days of Casanova? But if there had been, this represented a pretty good stab at what it might have looked like. He held in his hands a print-out from the second e-mail that Lyndon Luberman had sent him. It contained fragments of an article about a letter signed by Richard Wagner that was being offered for sale. There was also a photograph of the letter itself and a translation. The type had reproduced in a very small font, so Bill had brought along a magnifying glass. He peered first at the text that surrounded the letter. Much of it had distorted but Bill did note an interesting reference to the fact that two more Wagner letters had been offered for sale over the last three years, one in London and one in Berlin. Each had been bought anonymously over the phone without the new owner even having seen them. Then there was half a paragraph devoted to when it might have been written. "*Given that so much of the material contained in this letter is of a personal rather than professional nature,*" ran the article, "*it may never prove possible to date it within 10 years, unless other similar letters are discovered.*"

Little do you know, Bill said to himself. He opened his notebook and transcribed details of the Berlin and London sales just below "*Do I trust Libby?*" and "*Why is she so secretive about her 'work'?*" Above that question he noticed that he had written,

> If I could get to see another letter what pattern might be visible? Are they all to the Werther Freund? Are they all about Jews? All about domestic strife with Cosima?

Well now he was finally getting his first chance to find out.

> ... that she is in Venice is a great trial to me but that she will from there go to Berlin I find unbearable.

It seemed typical of Wagner that he should launch in so directly like this. Bill had to remind himself that the article only reproduced page two. The letter itself would have started off more formally, and yet bursting on to the page like this with such overweening self-importance, not even waiting for the reader to get up to speed, seemed inherently Wagnerian. So he and

Wagner had something in common. Women in Venice who were a trial. Bill wondered if this were the same Brünhilde of whom the Meister complained. Was she the woman who occupied the spiritual attic of Bill's letter?

Oh my dear Friend...

Aha. Bill leant forward, the reflex of a man who has uncovered something important. Well now, it seemed he had the answer to at least two of his questions. In all likelihood the woman in Wagner's attic and the woman in Venice were one and the same. And these letters were probably from a collection of correspondence with one man, *Mein Werther Freund* – whoever that might be. At this moment he – and Katz – probably knew more about these letters than anyone else in the world, apart from Miss Mertens and Policeman Plod perhaps. How did they fit into this? Were they working for Bayreuth? Supersleuths assigned to the *Freund* file? Surely these scribbled notes of despair were hardly worth a detective agency's fee? It was odd.

> *She is the fruit of entwined roots. When I gaze upon her I feel like Siegmund gazing for the first time on his Sieglinde, his but yet another's.*

But what actually was the problem? Bill wondered. Wagner had never balked at taking another man's wife away in the past. One thing we could be sure of, he wasn't afraid of Cosima. He could be very harsh with her, particularly if another man ever came near her. The Meister even managed to create a distance between Cosima and Liszt, because he was jealous of her father's intimacy.

Bill tried to think back. That missing biography had said something about Wagner's death in Venice; it was after he and Cosima had had an argument about Wagner fooling around with some flower girl. Was this her? No. There was another woman, a Parisienne with whom he held hands during the second season at Bayreuth. Maybe it was her? Bill wished that bloody book hadn't been stolen.

> *I have dared but now I may dare no more. I have known what it is to be Siegmund. In my youth I was brave enough to be Wehwalt, son of Wolf, hunted in the forest, an outcast and ill-fated one but no more. It is not just my own bravery that would be tested but hers. This I cannot do. No man must know what I have done. My worthy friend, I ask you to destroy this letter and with it all knowledge of the deeds of which I spoke to you.*

So much for the freund's werthiness, thought Bill.

All this costs me more than tears, but what afflicts me greatly is this creature who has given me such pure love, such noble sacrificial love.

Yeah, right, as Reah would have said. Bill was beginning to feel tired of Wagner's relentless histrionics.

I have prayed that my Sieglinde should love me as I her but I know that she must not. I send her from me with so many sobs.

Oh give it a rest, thought Bill. He scanned the columns surrounding this translation. There was speculation about the various wives with whom Wagner had been linked and the name of the young French floozy, Judith Gautier, whom Wagner had seen as the new incarnation of his soulmate. Clearly American interest lay not only in dating the letter, but identifying the woman Wagner was dating.

Mention was made of someone Bill hadn't heard of before: Cäcilie Geyer, Wagner's half-sister. Was it possible, the author suggested, that she was the Sieglinde of whom Wagner spoke? No, now that Bill thought about it, Libby had mentioned Cäcilie in one of her e-mails, something about Wagner confiding his hatred of their mother to her. But was she in Venice, before travelling on to Berlin, at about the time Herr Richard was finishing *Parsifal?* It shouldn't be hard to find out.

Bill made a note to this effect in his book and folded the letter back in.

"Dad?" Steam was escaping from the bathroom as Reah, wrapped in towels, looked round the door. "I've finished now. You can go."

"Thank you," he said.

"Dad, is Libby her real name?" It was the first time Reah had acknowledged the existence of Libby by name.

"I suppose it's short for Elizabeth," said Bill, putting on his coat. "I'd never thought."

"Well, tell her I hope she's feeling better," said Reah.

"Thanks," said Bill. His heart lifted. If those two could be friends, all would be well in the world. They would eat ice-cream under Italian stars and glory in God's bounty.

Bill and Libby lay on her bed. They had not made love. The world was not like that anymore. She lay curled, foetus-like, in her black leggings and black lycra top. He encircled her, his arms holding on tight.

"I want to get away from here," said Libby. "From everyone. I can't stay somewhere where I've been really unhappy."

"Don't let him beat you," Bill said quietly into her ear.

"Bill, you've no idea," said Libby. "I'm a very private person."

"I know that," said Bill. "But what is so awful in those e-mails? What do they say except that we love each other and want to make love?" He felt Libby stiffen. "Is that so awful? Or is it that I'm supposed to be this international art thief? Do you really think anyone will believe that?"

"You don't understand," said Libby quietly.

"No I don't," said Bill. "But I do understand that this man – whoever he is – had a damn good idea what would really hurt you and what would threaten our relationship, and I don't want him succeeding. Do you?" Libby was silent. "Do you?"

"No," she said. After a while she added quietly, "Bill, it feels like rape."

"I know."

He knew too that she needed this time. She needed to grieve. It was like Reah complaining about the divorce or the size of her thighs. He shouldn't try to convince by argument that there was nothing to be done now, that life had to continue. All he could do was give her time.

Bill watched the light that bled through Libby's shutters. The sun must be low now. A series of diagonal orange lines cut across the wall opposite. As he watched, they seemed to inch gradually up the panelling. Outside he could hear the footfall of Venice. A whole city going home and not a single car to be heard. This must have been what cities sounded like for hundreds of years, thousands of years, right up until the last century in fact. A thousand footfalls of strangers passing their daily lives, unaware of Libby and Bill lying on a bed, fully clothed, nursing her broken life.

Now the sun was gone. Those orange bars had been extinguished one by one. Bill looked at his watch.

"I wish we could make love," said Libby, face down in the pillow.

"I don't think we've forgotten how to," he told her, trying to sound fond. He heard himself. He did sound fond. Maybe that was all it took. Love leading to the expression of love and the expression reassuring us. Bill had been thinking of leaving and had prepared something about needing to go and check on Reah, when Libby said a strange thing:

"Bill, will you make me pregnant?" She corkscrewed round to face him, her eyes bright. It was as if she had just discovered the answer.

"What?"

"I've stopped taking the pill. After I was throwing up so much there didn't seem much point carrying on with it this month. What if I don't start again? Would you make me pregnant?"

Bill was shocked. He had absolutely no idea where this was coming from. All he could manage to say was "But–" and he didn't even manage that very convincingly.

"I want to have a child," said Libby. "All the time I was with him, I knew I couldn't. That's why I kept on taking the pill, but now..."

"I thought you said you and he hadn't had sex for over a year," said Bill. He was confused.

"We hadn't."

"So why were you still taking the pill?"

"That's not the issue here," she said, and then turned suddenly away from him, hurt. "OK, fine, I get the message."

"No, Libby, stop," said Bill, trying to turn her back towards him. "Don't go away from me. We need to talk about this."

Libby came back to face him. "A child would make it all right," she said.

"This needs thinking about," said Bill. "If there's one thing I know it's that children lock you together for life. Look at Tamsin and me. We're divorced but we're still fighting. That's because we have Reah."

"Don't you want to be with me for life?" Libby asked.

"Yes," said Bill, but his tone was measured. "I think I do but I'd like us to consider all the implications before we go into something like that."

"We didn't think of implications when we were screwing around in Holt's Cottage," said Libby.

"That's because you said it was safe," Bill insisted. "And we weren't *screwing*."

"What were we doing then?"

"Making love," he told her.

"And when two people make love," said Libby. "There are implications. Consequences. Bill I want us to be together. I want your child. OK, I may not be pregnant at this moment but logically I could be. It's a consequence of making love."

"I know," said Bill.

"Will you promise me we can talk about it?" she asked. "One day."

"Yes."

They were quiet in the darkness. Then Libby moved closer.

"Now," she whispered in his ear. "Make love to me Bill. Please." Her grip on him was hard.

"I can't," Bill said but Libby wouldn't let go.

"Libby, this isn't how it should be." He tried stroking her hair. She squirmed out of his grasp and flung herself away from him with a cry of frustration.

"Libby I want to make love to you," said Bill, following her across the bed. "That's one of the things I came here for but not like this. You're confused. You're upset."

The bedside phone began to ring. Libby turned round and glared at Bill. "It's your daughter," she said. There was pain in her voice.

"You don't know that," said Bill.

"You gave her this number," Libby reminded him, getting up and pulling on a calf-length black cardigan.

"It could be Hauke," he said. "It could be anyone."

"But it isn't," said Libby, and she stalked out of the bedroom. Bill thought about Reah hanging on at the other end. He picked up the receiver.

"Hi Dad," said Reah's sad voice. "I was wondering when you're coming back."

"Half an hour," said Bill.

"Can't you come any sooner? It's getting lonely here."

Bill paused then said. "No. Get yourself something from Room Service."

"I already have. I had a Coke and some ice cream. I feel sick."

"OK, don't get yourself something. We'll be going out to eat later. Watch TV or read a book or something. I'll be half an hour."

"OK," said Reah. "Can I get a video?"

Bill walked into Libby's kitchen where she was drinking the juice that Reah had rejected earlier that afternoon.

"I'm sorry," she said, not looking at him. "I know what it's like. Mind, it was worse in my case–"

"I've told Reah to wait," he said, and took her by the arms, tight enough to bruise. Libby winced. "I want you in that bedroom."

"You don't have to–" said Libby.

"Yes I bloody do!"

It was a different way of making love that time. Before, the passion had been on his side and she had surrendered to it. This time Libby was the desperate one but her wildness came from need rather than anger. For Bill to climax inside her became the only thing that mattered in the world to her. That desire, that longing, was more powerful than even her own identity. When Bill withdrew to put on a condom the hunger inside her was intense, her whole body begged for his return, and when he came back inside joy suffused her.

"That's what was needed," said Libby, watching Bill dress. She was still floating. She didn't want him to go but wherever he went she knew that she was with him.

"Shall we eat in or should Reah and I meet you somewhere?" Bill asked. Libby was drawing her fingers pleasurably across the pillows.

"Bill, have you seen the size of my kitchen? It's big enough to make coffee, that's all!"

"How about we call for you?"

He had never been so desperate to get away.

"Come back to bed," she said.

That meal was an improvement on the first, at least to begin with. Reah displayed a rather obvious desire to talk to Bill about their life in Chepstow, leaving it up to Bill to translate. He and Libby had agreed in advance that they'd not divulge she'd been to the Wye Valley already. As they walked over the Rio di San Barnaba it had suddenly struck Bill that Reah would think of Holt's Cottage very much as territory that she alone shared with Bill. It was too soon for her to concede her home to another, so he'd taken Libby on one side as they stepped down from the bridge and asked her if she'd mind such subterfuge, should the need arise.

"Of course not," said Libby. She was holding his arm and clearly very happy. Bill was relieved to see the smile on her face. To anyone other than Reah, it must be totally obvious what they'd been doing a couple of hours ago. Everything would be OK now. Libby was happier. Reah was happier. As for Bill, well he just needed a little time. Maybe then he'd be happy too.

Their deception had not been hatched in vain. Reah was full of Jethro and how she had to programme his seven-day feeder when she went away because Dad couldn't be relied on to feed him, of the gatepost that Mum kept bumping into and Dad never got round to fixing, and how she and Dad hired videos on a Friday night. None of this was addressed to Libby. It tended to come out in rhetorical questions.

"Dad, you remember that walk we always go on in the afternoon?" Or "Dad, what's Lee going to do with all your mail while you're away? Won't your mail box fill up?" To round the conversation off Bill would throw in explanatory asides for Libby's benefit, telling her things she already knew but was supposed not to. After a while, though, Reah started to open up and include Libby in the conversation too.

"Dad makes this really awful coffee," she said. "Every morning I wake up to it."

"I know!" said Libby, laughing and clearly pleased that the conversation had widened to include her now.

"How d'you know?" Reah asked.

"He writes and tells me about it," said Libby. Bill was impressed how effortlessly Libby carried that off. There wasn't a moment when her face betrayed the fact that she'd nearly dropped them both in it. "*Dear Libby, I've just made coffee. Dear Libby, I've just made some more coffee,*" Libby recited.

"*Dear Libby, this place stinks of coffee!*" Reah added, and they both laughed. It was a sublime moment for Bill. The woman he loved and the daughter he adored united in teasing him. They were happy.

Libby had got them a window in the Taverna San Trovaso, a place she thought Reah would like for its cheerful atmosphere and reliable pizzas. Once the food arrived, Bill took the opportunity to ask Libby about the possible identity of that woman Wagner was writing about.

"There's another letter come to light in New York," he said. "One of the commentators over there reckons it might be referring to Judith Gautier. Do you know about her?"

Of course she did. "No I don't think it would be her. Wagner dumped Judith summarily. She was around when he was writing *Parsifal*, that's true – she used to buy the satins and velvets he needed in Paris – their letters are full of eroticisms and curtain measurements – but when Cosima put her foot down, Wagner wrote and told her '*from now on my wife will be dealing with you*'. No agonies as far as I remember. Mind you, he did tell her more than once that she was his other self, his female counterpart!"

"That's not very nice," Reah observed.

"What isn't?" Bill asked. The wine had left had left him unfocused.

"Telling someone else she's your female – what's that word?"

"Counterpart," said Libby.

"I mean he was married, Dad, right?"

"He was an unusual man," said Bill. He noticed that Reah suddenly looked far less happy.

"Did he have children?" she asked.

"Yes."

"Well imagine how they felt," Reah was hurt. "Knowing their Dad preferred someone else over their Mum."

Inexplicably, unexpectedly, the subject seemed to have been hijacked.

"I don't suppose they knew," said Libby in the silence that followed. "Richard Wagner was always in love with somebody. I imagine their mother kept it from them."

"That doesn't make it right," said Reah. "I think it stinks." She was looking coldly at her plate. Libby glanced up at Bill as if to say 'sorry'.

Maybe they'd relaxed too much. Bill tried to say something sympathetic but it petered out in indecision. Libby took over.

"My parents split up," she said gently to Reah.

"I don't care about your parents," said Reah and she got up abruptly from the table and left.

"Reah, sit down," Bill was shocked at her rudeness. "I'd better go after her," he said, feeling there was an awful, tedious inescapability about his new role of compromised parent.

Libby nodded.

"She can't be rude to you like that," said Bill. And to Reah, when he found her silent on the quayside, he said that it really wasn't fair to blame Libby for the break-up of her parents' marriage.

"But she's pleased about it, Dad," said Reah at last. "I don't know whether she split you and Mum up or not but she's laughing about this man telling someone else she's his female counterpane."

"Counterpart," said Bill, finding it much easier to understand and forgive the malapropic Reah. "Look, Boo, firstly Wagner and Cosima had a great marriage even though he had girlfriends. Secondly Libby and I weren't laughing about this mystery woman. I need to work out her identity for this piece I'm writing, that's why we were discussing it."

"I bet they would have had a better marriage if he hadn't had girlfriends though." Reah was a bright girl, he thought. She could talk a lot of sense sometimes.

"But listen, Libby isn't pleased Tamsin and I got divorced. When I told her, she was sorry and surprised it had happened."

"So she knew you before you split up?" Reah asked.

No, sometimes she was too bright this girl. And he'd had too much wine. "Yes. I knew her ages ago, when I was married. Then we lost touch."

"But she's not the one who split you up?"

"No one split us up, Boo. The only people who are responsible for two people splitting up are the people themselves."

"There was someone though," Reah said. "She used to write to you. That's all I can remember, but I know there was a time when you two were fighting over someone who used to write to you. Mum's never said who it was, but I remember that. Was it her?"

God, this was an awkward moment. If he told Reah it was Libby who occasioned those awful arguments, then the possibility of his daughter accepting Libby was gone forever. If he lied now and she found out later, then things would be even worse. In the instant it took his thoughts to crystallise, Bill remembered Louis' words many years ago when Bill had first told him the sad story of his involvement with Libby Ziegler.

"Bill, for goodness sake why didn't you use a little subterfuge? Why did your wife need to know that you were spending all night faxing this woman?"

"I suppose I didn't realise I was having an affair," Bill had replied. "I'd just found someone... more interesting, more interested in what interested me. I didn't expect it to last, or even to amount to anything in the end."

"All the more reason to be secretive!" Louis had pointed out as if secrecy were a virtue. Which perhaps it was at times. The big difference between Bill and Louis seemed to lie in the fact that Bill believed one took a decision about what one *didn't* tell people and Louis about what one *did*. Now, as Bill opened his mouth to reply, an even more Machiavellian thought struck him. If things worked out with Libby then it was true. Long-term he would have to reckon with Reah's outrage at being lied to. Tamsin was bound to tell Reah who Libby was once she'd discovered that "the American bitch" was back in his life. But that was way off in the future. Why hurt everyone now when it was always possible that things might not work out with him and Libby?

"*No*," he said. "She wasn't the person we argued over when you were little."

"I'm glad," said Reah and she hugged him. A gondola passed only a few feet from them, like a long black shark heading home silently for the night.

"Let's go back inside," Bill said, but he didn't feel too good. Not only had he lied to Reah – a lie with huge long-term implications – he felt he had betrayed Libby by admitting his uncertainty about their future together. It seemed only minutes ago he was so sure, so happy to be seated between Libby and Reah.

Why was it suddenly possible that he and Libby would not work out? Was it because she now seemed so certain, talking about where they'd live and bring up children? Was that why he, by contrast, could envisage them separating?

"What's up?" Libby asked. Coffee had been drunk and she was guiding them back towards her apartment and the hotel.

"Oh, I'm sorry we're not sleeping together tonight," Bill lied.

"Me too," said Libby, slipping her arm pleasurably through his.

"You know, they've given us a double bed," said Bill.

"No! I didn't say *letto matrimoniale*. I'm sure I said *doppia*, that means double room. Shoot, what are you going to do?"

"Well we've shared beds before," said Bill. "Reah's quite happy."

"Now I am jealous," said Libby.

"Is that a joke?"

"I'm not sure," she admitted. "I really don't like it, but I'm not sure why."

"She snores," Bill said, trying to make light of it.

"Bill don't," said Libby. "Not funny."

They'd stopped. Reah was a little way ahead looking in a shop that sold marbled paper and handmade books.

"Reah always sleeps late. I'll come round first thing," said Bill.

"From another woman's bed," said Libby.

"Don't be ridiculous," he laughed. Libby gave Bill a small but very hard punch in the ribs.

"Don't laugh at me."

"OK," he said. "I'm sorry."

"Dad," said Reah as she got into bed in pyjamas, dressing gown, socks and slippers.

"Yes," said Bill as he emerged from the bathroom clad in a similar number of layers.

"Libby hit you, didn't she?"

"Not really," said Bill. "I made a joke that she didn't think very funny, that's all."

"If I did that every time you made a bad joke..." Reah scoffed.

"I know," said Bill, getting into bed. "Now rules: No talking. No snoring and no midnight snacks."

"And what about me?" said Reah.

"Very funny. Look, I've set the alarm for six. I'm going over to the Rialto Market with Libby. I'll be back in time for breakfast, OK? I assume you won't want to come."

"No," said Reah, turning on to her side.

"So I'll see you back here, say 8.30, nine at the latest."

"Sure."

"Goodnight then." He kissed her hair and rolled over in the other direction, thinking of 6.15 tomorrow and parting Libby's thighs. Part of him very much wanted her, but at the same time he felt uncomfortable about the extent to which he had lied today. Why was it so necessary to lie when one loved? Might it be because we require certainty in love but only rarely feel it? Didn't every woman that Wagner fell for believe that she was his other self, his female counterpart? Did he ever tell them, 'Look I'm not leaving my wife, this is just me getting a bit carried away; when I've spun you lots of hyperbole I'll probably dump you...'? He probably used the same technique to Judith Gautier and poor old Marie Wesenbonk and the mysterious attic woman who travelled from Venice to Berlin with Wagner's sobs ringing in her ears. Except – and here Bill found himself grappling with a new idea that had some significance – except Wagner wasn't making all these florid professions to the woman herself, was he? He was making them to his *Werther Freund*. So either the Meister, for whatever reason, felt unable to tell this Sieglinde of his passion – and Werther was getting it all – or this woman *was* the genuine article. After all, he had said those same words to Cosima while she was still married to Hans von Bülow. He had said those words so persuasively that she had left von Bülow, Wagner's greatest supporter. So persuasively in fact that she had taken von Bülow's children from him, and devoted herself – and them – to the service of Richard Wagner.

Maybe this was another woman in the same mould as far as Wagner was concerned. Another Cosima. Richard Wagner's last – and most lamented – lost love. Who was she? Did Cosima know? And if she did, how was it that the widow Wagner never got her hands on all these letters?

❖ BACK FROM THE ABYSS

"MAYBE BECAUSE SHE NEVER KNEW," said Libby. "After all, if Wagner could lie with a clear conscience to everyone he met, why shouldn't he lie to her as well? If this were a truly great love he might have kept it from her. The norm was that Cosima was abreast of his affairs. That way he could use her to put an end to them when he became bored."

They were lying in Libby's bed and talking. At first it had been diffi-cult. Bill's walk through the early morning mist and half-light of Dorsoduro had been magical and serene, but Libby had been prickly when he'd arrived. At first she'd even given the impression that she didn't want to make love. Later however she became wild, digging her fingernails into his back. Bill knew that it wasn't him she was trying to hurt. Last night's sulk was to do with him, yes, but this – this was beyond him. She was desperate. It was like a fight to the death and yet she couldn't climax. Bill stroked her face. He felt relieved she had given up. It had been getting pretty painful. "Oh dear." Libby could see where she had scratched him. She kissed the red marks better.

"It wasn't *us* was it?" He was facing away from her now.

"*Him*," she kissed again, burying her face in Bill's back. "When I think of what he did."

Then they slept for a while. Perhaps it was only for a minute or so but Bill felt himself drifting away forever. Forever seemed a very nice place to be.

"My Dad left me." He heard the words and for a moment thought it was Reah speaking. Surfacing in a panic Bill was surprised to see Libby sitting up and smoking, something she had never done before in his presence. "Sorry," she said, putting down the cigarette. "I thought you were awake."

"You said your Dad left you?" Libby lay down alongside Bill. He smelt a staleness on her that he associated with Marika. "You mean when your parents split up?"

"No, *later*," said Libby, looking up at the ceiling. "I was thinking about Reah. When my parents split, I lived with my grandparents and he would visit all the time. Then one time there was a fight. My Dad was a big man. He usually got his own way. Nobody told me there had been a fight but I could see my Grandpa had retreated behind the *New York Times* and my Grandma was outside attacking the rosebushes."

Libby had never told Bill about her family before. He hardly dared prompt her for more. "What happened?"

Their voices were very quiet now in the early morning silence. No one, not one person, was moving in the world beyond this bedroom. "They told me I'd be living with him for a while. That he'd finally paid my Mom off and gotten himself somewhere to live. And –" Libby leaned over to the ashtray. "And he wanted me."

Bill watched the smoke issue from Libby's lips. His eyes took in the pallor of her skin. "How old were you?"

"Twelve."

"And?"

She stubbed out the cigarette. "And, you know what? I don't want to talk about it."

"But you introduced the subject."

"Yes, and I wish I hadn't."

Bill put his arm around her. "You said he left you, though?"

"Let's talk about Wagner."

And now the city was beginning to stir. Bottles being taken out from the *trattoria* at the end of the street and Bill was discussing Wagner in Venice with Libby Ziegler. "Is it likely that he could have an affair and cover all traces?"

"No," said Libby. "He'd consider himself above subterfuge. And besides, he wrote so many letters, I'm sure there'd be some cross-reference somewhere."

"Unless Cosima destroyed anything that made even the tiniest allusion to this affair so it only exists in the *Werther Freund* archive which, presumably, she never found."

Libby thought about this. "He's so full of himself though, Bill. He just marauds through those letters. There are some artists you can imagine having a wholly secret side to their life – Magritte, Henry James, Ravel – but not Wagner. No, she must be someone we know about and if we don't, he had very special reasons for keeping it quiet. Have you got the new letter with you?"

"It's stapled into my notebook," said Bill, reluctant to disturb the sense of inner stillness he had finally reached. He watched as Libby stretched across the bed towards his coat. Looking at the full girlish length of her, he felt himself invaded by desire. Libby couldn't quite reach. She was about to get off the bed and step over to where Bill's coat lay but he caught her before that, seizing her body and throwing her back on the pillow, his hand already in her groin. Libby looked up at him in anticipation. Bill had been in two minds about responding to that sudden return of desire but now he knew only one thing. They would have all eternity to find stillness and only a finite time for orgasm. This time there'd be no doubt about her climax, he'd make sure of that.

The phone rang. They looked at each other. "I don't think it's Reah," said Bill, refusing to remove his hand.

"No I don't think it is either," said Libby, but she kept an eye on the phone, trying to decide. "I'm sorry Bill," she said suddenly and rolled away to reach for the receiver.

Bill felt annoyed. He was even more annoyed when Libby started talking away in German. *Der Junge Hauke*. Bill went to the kitchen wearing her towelling robe. He objected to hearing Libby in bed with another man. Particularly one to whom she spoke German.

He was fixing coffee when Libby came in. She was wearing that full length cardigan which he'd watch her struggle into yesterday when Reah was so awful. But nothing else. Bill was drawn to the way it hung open. "Sorry *Liebling*," she said. "That was important. Come back to bed."

"Time's getting on," said Bill, working the coffee machine – and yet he knew he was tempted "I ought to get back."

"I'm sorry Bill," said Libby, nestling against his back. "We all start work so early over here. Hauke couldn't know."

Bill turned round. "If I go now there's no problem. If I stay I might be back late. I want Reah to know she can still rely me. That's important."

"You're not annoyed with me?" she asked.

"No."

Libby asked him to kiss her. "Bill that is not a kiss!" They tried again. "Bill, you kiss like a man who is halfway out the door."

"I'm sorry," he said. "Somehow the world intrudes on us here. It isn't like the cottage."

"OK," she said, giving up. "I'm going to take a shower."

They discussed the day ahead while Libby used the bathroom and Bill finished making coffee. He rather liked this illusion of a shared domestic life. Oh how he'd love to live in Venice with Reah and Libby!

"Godammit, my period's started," said Libby, her head round the bathroom door. She began to inveigh against the burden of womanhood. "Why does this always happen when I've got to travel!"

"Have you got to travel?" he asked. The coffee was now ready.

"Yes!" she continued unseen. "Hauke wants me to go over to Karlstein."

"When?"

"Tomorrow. Tonight. As soon as possible really."

"Why can't he come here?" Bill asked. Libby put her head round the door. "That's a joke, right?"

"No seriously," said Bill. "What so urgent about going to... where is it?"

"Karlstein. It's about 25 miles this side of Prague."

"What?" said Bill. "That's... that's, well, I assumed you meant somewhere near the Austrian border." They fell to discussing how long Libby would be away for. Too long was the answer.

"Why don't you come with me?" she said, emerging in a hooded dressing gown.

"There's Reah," Bill reminded her.

"Bring her with you. We're staying by the castle, she'd love it. Train journey through the Alps to Prague."

"No, she wouldn't." This was true. "Do you have to go straight away?"

Libby explained that she and Hauke had a window of opportunity to go through some documents at the castle. Even better, there was someone who'd asked to meet her. A someone who was important for her work. She couldn't afford to miss this.

"What is it that you do exactly?" Bill asked. Libby didn't seem to live like other people.

"I'm an art historian. You know that. I always was. The Wagner letters were a joint project, a labour of love. Well it started off that way. Then marriage wasn't what I thought it would be. He was just a kid. Labour of increasing disenchantment, I suppose you could call it."

"But why are you going through documents if you're an art historian?" Bill asked as Libby wandered into the bedroom. "Why aren't you looking at pictures?"

"Pictures are only half the story. You don't just authenticate something by saying 'Jeez that sure looks like a Vermeer'. You try and trace how a Vermeer could be there, in that particular place, today. Finding out if Vermeer could actually have had the time or the commission to paint this thing that looks like a Vermeer. Tracking down ownership documents even, that can make all the difference. Part of my job is to see if it's possible for a work of art to be what and where people are claiming it to be. You have no idea how much stuff went missing during World War II – and the Cold War. Everyone knows Eastern Europe's a mess but believe me things aren't much better over here. There's a lot of material in private hands that no one knows about and because no one knows about it, nobody gets to catalogue it."

Bill put his coffee down and put his head round the bedroom door. "You mean Nazi stuff? Things that are still in Swiss banks?"

Libby shook her head as she sorted tights and leggings. "It's much more complex than that. Basically, any major period of upheaval means that people loot. The Finnish Civil War in the '20s, the Spanish Civil War in the '30s, the Dublin Easter Rising, Iraq for goodness sake. Any time people fight, they steal. Soldiers retreat, other soldiers move in. The new people have no idea how long they're going to be winning, let alone stay alive. They want something, anything, to tell them that the danger is being rewarded, or at least compensated, so they carry off what they can and nine times out of ten they have no idea what they've got. Fifty years later their families are going through the attic and–"

"They find a Vermeer," said Bill.

"Maybe."

"And what do they do – call in you and Hauke?"

"No we tend to go in first. You get ideas about the kind of place you want to look at. Then it's a question of working away, convincing people they can trust us, getting them to let us have a snoop round. That's how I met Josef. When I heard he'd got permission to go through some private collections in Munich–"

"But who pays for all this? The Universita di Venezia?"

Libby looked surprised. "Oh no. They know about my work obviously. But no, this is private. Hauke isn't part of the University."

"But it must cost you a fortune the two of you, travelling round Europe. What do you do? Charge an authentification fee?"

Libby was regarding him in an uncertain way. Why the sudden interest? She shrugged. "I get some funding from the Commission for Looted Art in Europe," she said.

"There is such a thing?"

"Oh yes. That's how I started off. After London I did some work on authentication for them. These days it mostly finances itself."

"But do you work for claimants, people who are saying, 'My family's painting is in that castle'?"

"No, if anything we get called in by people who want to dispose, people who don't want the embarrassment of handing-on something that really isn't theirs."

This intrigued Bill. "There are such people?"

"Don't underestimate guilt," said Libby. "There are a lot of respectable people around who may not want their children to find out what's up in the attic. Think about it: would you want to pass something like that on to

Reah? Imagine ten years after you're dead, she opens the door and there are investigators who want to get her into court as the daughter of a crook. Or worse. They might be Israelis from the Simon Wiesenthal Centre, they might be private detectives working for someone with a very long memory. Think of the publicity, the hurt to her and what she'll think of you when she finds out." Bill remembered Mertens and Clements. "Believe me there are a lot of old men who in the last ten years have been trying to make their peace with posterity."

"So why don't they just destroy what they've got?"

"Some do," said Libby. "That's the sadness. Who knows what's gone up in smoke? A lot of the stuff that was seized during the Russian Revolution wasn't destroyed until Stalin started his purges. Beautiful works of art – Poussin, Breughel, Canaletto – incinerated by anxious appa-ratchiks who didn't want to be caught with spoils of the Civil War."

"Canaletto?" said Bill.

Libby nodded. "I met an old guy who helped his father destroy what he thought was one. They were living just outside Minsk, God know how it got there. They sawed up the frame, ripped out the canvas and poured petrol over everything." Bill was stunned. Libby got up to get dressed. "Don't run away with the idea it's glamorous. I don't go around saving Canalettos every day. We're not just talking about paintings either. There are rare books, maps, manuscripts – those are particularly valuable. Basically, it's anything I can bring back from the abyss." She paused, half naked, completely wrapped up in what she was saying. "This is a critical time, Bill. In ten years time anyone who was around during the Nazi inva-sions of Europe will be dead or *non compos*. That's why I pursue every lead we get." She picked up her leggings. "Can you see now why it was so awful, that accusation about my associating with an art thief?"

He took her hand. "Yes."

"He knew what he was doing. These people need to feel they can trust me."

"And the people who are left in a quandary, wondering what to do with their ill-gotten gains," said Bill. "These old guys actually *pay* you to return these things to the rightful owner?"

Libby laughed. "What is it with you and money, Bill Wheeler?"

"I'm a journalist," he said. "We recognise only two motivations in people. Sex and money."

"Well I sure don't do it for the sex," said Libby. Now she was dressed.

*

Bill was relieved to find that Reah wasn't already down for breakfast. He used his key to get back into their room and knocked on the bathroom door. "Reah?"

"Don't come in! Don't come in!" she shouted.

"Breakfast finishes in twenty minutes."

His daughter seemed to have enjoyed having the bedroom to herself. She was in a sunny mood and even asked how Libby was.

"She's got to go to Prague," said Bill. "So I thought we'd go back tomorrow."

"I thought we *were* going back tomorrow," said Reah, on to her second croissant now and belabouring it with jam and butter.

"Yes we were but..."

"But what?"

"Well I thought we might stay longer if it worked out, but in fact as Libby's not going to be here we'll go back anyway. Is that OK?"

"Sure." Reah was cool today. Nothing was going to bother her.

Bill fell to wondering what to do with the day. Venice was a wonderful city for lovers but what would a thirteen-year-old do here on Sunday morning – except shop herself to death around St Mark's of course, which Bill wasn't even going to begin to countenance. Libby had suggested meeting at the Guggenheim which was within walking distance. "It's full of second-rate Magritte – and the Picassos that nobody else wanted – but you do get a broad sweep of art in the twentieth century. And the post-cards are good."

Reah said "Sure" to the Guggenheim too. It was a word that came pre-packaged with blasé shrugs. Bill, already on his second injection of coffee that morning, felt rankled that she had no measure of her own good fortune. When he was thirteen he hadn't even been abroad, let alone round an art gallery with his father. Then again going around an art gallery with Bill's father would not have been fun. Mr Wheeler had been a man of few words, and most of those related to the venality of whichever political party was in power.

Libby's coffee was strong but this was stronger. Bill could feel his heart racing. As they walked to the Guggenheim he could also feel himself dangerously close to irritation with the slowness of Reah's pace. "About tonight," he said. "There's this restaurant Libby wants to go to."

"Sure," said Reah.

"I didn't ask you if you were *sure*," said Bill. "I was going to ask you if you'd prefer to do something else while she and I went."

"Like what?" said Reah. Bill wished he felt less ratty.

"Well, go to a film..?" To be honest he hadn't thought this out, and when he'd raised the idea with Libby she hadn't thought it a good idea to send a girl Reah's age out on her own in Venice. Nevertheless, the restaurant Libby had in mind sounded overtly romantic. Reah might well object to the ambience of their *tête à tête*.

"It's not very nice being made to feel like you're in the way," said Reah.

"You're not 'in the way'" Bill replied. "I just don't want you pulling a stunt like last night."

At which point Reah informed him that she did not 'pull a stunt' last night, so Bill informed her that he hadn't much cared for the way she'd walked out, and Reah replied that she thought she was being pretty tolerant, considering.

"Considering what?"

"Considering that I've just met my Dad's girlfriend."

"And that's a licence to behave badly, is it?" The caffeine was doing the talking now, pulling him on to a collision course with Reah.

"It's not exactly nice is it?" She wasn't conceding any ground.

"Oh yes, and what am I supposed to do with the rest of my life? Live on my own until you leave home? Oh no I forgot, you're already leaving aren't you? Have you any idea what that's going to be like?" It had been a cruel thing to say and Bill hated himself immediately for taunting her. None of this was Reah's doing and the look on her face made it clear how much the injustice had stung her. "I'm sorry," said Bill, moving forward. "I'm truly sorry."

"It's not my fault you two split up." She resisted his embrace.

"I know," said Bill. "I'm so sorry. If anything it was you who kept us together. Really you did."

"Don't make me responsible," Reah said fiercely.

"I'm not, love, honestly." He put his hands on her arms and felt the surprising sturdiness of his daughter.

"Didn't make a very good job of it, did I?" she grumbled.

"You were gorgeous. Neither of us could bear to lose you. That's why we moved to Holt's Farm together, you know that."

Reah inclined towards Bill's chest and again it all came back to him. The pain, the fumbled choices, the compromises and guilt. Nothing clear except for the fact that Libby had gone. Bill remembered his anger against her. That came back to him too. She had just disappeared. When he rang they said she'd left London. His life laid waste. Libby Ziegler in an aircraft miles above looking down on the devastation. And Reah one of the victims. Little Reah Christabel telling Mummy and Daddy not to be silly any more, to kiss and make up. Putting her faith in woolly lambs, catkins and country life to restore the family. Catkins, lambs and the little sister Bill and Tamsin had promised her when they moved to the Wye.

"I will never leave you," Bill whispered now to Reah, holding on to her, hugging her as if he were desperate to keep out the cold on this bright spring morning. "Never, never." Inexplicably his eyes were filling.

"*Da-ad*," said Reah. She sounded embarrassed and uncomfortable. Could she hear the tears in his voice? Bill felt as if he were holding her for the last time.

Libby was waiting in the garden of Palazzo Unfinito, Peggy Guggenheim's single-story palace on the Grand Canal. "Hi Reah."

"Hi."

"Do we want to get some coffee?" she asked.

"I think I've had enough," Bill told her.

Libby was fine with Reah when they were talking about pets, hairstyles or clothes, but inside the gallery she clammed up. It was as if she only knew one way to speak in the presence of fine art and that wasn't appropriate in front of her lover's daughter. If Bill had retained fond memories of going round the National Gallery and Tate with Libby, those recollections soon became jaundiced. When Reah commented that something by Max Ernst looked 'pretty scary', Libby made no reply. In the silence Bill felt it incumbent on him to suggest that people like Ernst and Dali sought to give expression to landscapes of our subconscious, the place where order and reason break down, or maybe fail to exist in the first place. But he didn't feel he put it very well.

Still Libby said nothing. They paused at a Magritte: 'The Empire of Lights', a house with some dark trees and a street lamp. "That's nice," said Reah. Bill winced. Still Libby said nothing, so they passed on to another Magritte. Bill actually found himself disliking Libby for that nothing. It seemed that she was using her silence to reject Reah.

"The thing is, the landscape is in darkness as if it's night," Bill pointed out. "But the sky is blue. See. Like day."

"Oh." Reah was underwhelmed. "So, like, you're saying it's a mistake then?"

"Well actually this is Libby's subject area, really," Bill replied, trying not to make it too obvious.

Reah glanced across at her. "Did you like it?"

Libby thought for a moment. "Yes," she said.

"It's not his best though is it?" Bill was flailing, failing hopelessly to bridge the gulf between daughter and lover.

"No," said Libby. "But I do like it."

"Really?" Bill asked.

"Uh-huh."

"I don't think you mean that," Bill said, fixing Libby with his eye.

"No, I think it's pleasing," said Libby.

"You do?"

"*Yes*," said Libby, with a look that seemed to say, 'What is going on with you?'

"It's only a picture," Reah remarked as she moved on. "And anyway I don't think it's *that* wrong, Dad."

"Will you stop being so condescending," Bill whispered to Libby once Reah was out of earshot. Libby looked up at him, surprised. "Reah is thirteen, she can talk about pictures."

"She is talking about them," Libby told him.

"Then why won't you talk back to her?"

"I am." Reah glanced back at the two of them, suspicious of the delay.

"You're not taking her seriously," said Bill.

"She asked me if I liked the picture, I said I did," Libby insisted. "What d'you expect? A lecture on Surrealism?"

"You might try outlining the idea to her."

"Sorry," Libby muttered. "It's my day off."

"What is the matter with you?" Bill asked, taking her arm. The gesture wasn't harsh but it wasn't gentle either.

"Me?" said Libby. "I'm just looking at pictures with your daughter–"

"She's called Reah."

"You're the one who's got problems," said Libby with finality.

"Look Reah's had to put up with a lot," Bill told her. He found it difficult to complete that sentence.

"Well I don't think that me rattling on about Surrealism or Dada or Max Ernst's collage techniques is going to compensate for her parents' divorce."

"You're being very cold," Bill told her.

"What?"

Challenged, Libby withdrew further. When they traipsed outside into the sculpture garden she separated from Bill entirely.

"Look, I ought to have a word with Libby," said Bill.

"OK," said Reah and she sat down to write some postcards he had bought her.

"You'll be OK?"

"Sure."

There was a small white pontoon bobbing in front of the gallery. Bill and Libby stood at the top of a flight of steps that led down to it, flanked on both sides by a tall sculpted hedges. They were in effect in a corridor of topiary, a secret tunnel down a watery escape route, hidden in momentary seclusion.

"I'm sorry," said Bill. "It's not easy," he admitted ruefully.

"I know," said Libby, tearing distractedly at a leaf.

Bill gazed across the Grand Canal. How sad to argue in this place. With these people. "I feel that we can't just be Us here," he began. "Like we were at the cottage. I'm balancing you and Reah and you're balancing me and your career."

"I'm just trying not to intrude," Libby told the hedge.

"I'm sorry," repeated Bill.

"Are you jealous of my career?" she asked.

"No!" He felt sure of that. "I just wish you weren't going away tomorrow, I wish that that man – whoever he is – hadn't done what he did with our e-mails and I wish Hauke didn't ring up every time we're making love!"

Libby smiled. "Don't you think I wish all those things too? I feel just the same as you about tomorrow, but it doesn't make me angry."

"Well it's an aspect of your life. You're used to it. In the way that Reah doesn't bother me. That's the problem, it's your intrusions bothering me and my intrusions affecting you. Lovely though she is."

"Reah doesn't bother me," said Libby.

"Really? Don't you wish I'd come on my own?"

"Of course," she said. "But she doesn't bother me. She's fine."

Bill felt that there was something of a protective shell over Libby at the moment. He didn't like the way she failed to engage. "I want to be as we were at the cottage," he said. "I feel we're different people here."

"We can go to the cottage again," said Libby. "*Can't we?*" Now that was genuinely meant. It cheered him for a moment.

"I want you to live there," said Bill. He felt extravagant but unfortunately Libby's mood was still circumspect.

"Do you? Do you *really*?" she asked.

"Why do you doubt me?" He put his arms round her waist. He wanted to turn her to look at him. He wanted to see her face as he'd seen it two weeks ago in St Mark's, as he'd seen it at Baron Willy's soiree, as he'd seen it in the cottage when she had been so incredibly open to him.

"What happens when we're in the cottage and Reah comes to stay?"

Libby asked. "Or Hauke rings up? We can't cut ourselves off from the world, can we?"

"I'll get used to having the two of you occupying the same space," he replied, pulling her closer to him. "And I'll make sure the phone's off the hook. Permanently. Please Libby." He tried to kiss her but only got a cheek.

If he were honest with himself it wasn't just that the outside world had intruded. It was disappointment too. Bill had wanted Libby to shine for Reah, as he knew she could, as he'd known her to shine when they went round galleries together seven years ago. She genuinely could illuminate art. She could throw the switch that made life beautiful. He had wanted to show her off and Libby had not performed. None of this was worth saying however.

"Once I give myself, I'm easily hurt, Bill," Libby was saying into his overcoat. "That's the kind of person I am. Most people never get the chance. I've let you in. Maybe I shouldn't have but I couldn't help it. Please don't talk to me like that again." She could take his violence in the night, she enjoyed the extremity, but she couldn't take his anger.

"I'm sorry," said Bill. After a while he asked her, "Do you blame me for those e-mails getting published in that way?"

"No." No, no that wasn't what she'd meant at all. He could be so obtuse.

"But by association? Has it soured the experience of Us?"

"The experience of Us," said Libby, relaxing a little, resting her head against him as she'd done in Munich, as she'd done in Holt's Cottage. "The experience of Us was so special that I couldn't bear the way it was warped and twisted by that man. The way our words were perverted and turned into pornography..." She paused and stepped back to look at him. "What happened was so painful, Bill, that I know I've withdrawn a bit. That's true. I can't help it. I told you didn't I? I told you something was going to go wrong." They had drawn apart but their fingers remained in contact.

"Don't let him win. Don't let any of them win," said Bill.

Libby seemed to take a long time to consider this. "I told you my Dad left me," she said.

"Reah knows I'm not going to do that," said Bill.

Libby looked down towards the canal. That was not what she meant. Not at all. "She's lucky," she said.

"I love you," said Bill. He loved me too, thought Libby.

"Girls can be too close to their fathers, you know," she said, keeping her eyes on the subtly shifting water.

"What do you mean?"

"My Dad made me feel special. We used to go to galleries. And concerts. You know how damn cultured Americans like to be. He used to talk to me. *Really* talk. I was twelve."

"What happened?"

"We had three years together and one day he left. He'd met this other person..."

"This is Carey?"

"Yes. He was one of My Dad's grad students. Can you believe that? But they've both been really happy ever since."

"I hadn't realised Carey was a man."

"It's not an issue," said Libby. "My dad was unhappy on his own. Now he's not."

Bill smiled. She smiled back. "Well I promise you something. I'm not going off with another man." They were silent for an empty moment. "Lunch?" he said. "We could go to Torcello. It's the perfect place."

"It's perfect in summer," she replied. She could still talk to him. She could still live alongside him, this man. It was just that they were no longer in the same world. Libby wanted that world back. More than he did. More than he would ever know. She wanted to be magical again.

"Isn't there a restaurant, the Atilla Something?"

"*Al Trono di Atilla*," She had all the information. "His throne's supposed to be on the island. It's an old fisherman's inn." Oh yes, she had the facility.

"So how about it?"

"The Number 14 *vaporetto* goes from San Zaccharia," Libby said. That wasn't agreement but he took it as such. She felt an old sadness overwhelm her as Bill went to find Reah. Libby knew the more she probed this wound the deeper it would prove to be. She had to keep him happy, stop him worrying her so that, in time, her heart could heal. He had no idea, she realised that now. This man, he could not be expected to know where the wounds lay deep. She was sure she could heal, though, and when her heart was whole again she could give it to him once more. But not now.

On the boat to Torcello Bill and Libby discussed the two Wagner letters again. "I think the importance of them really lies in the identity of this woman he's obsessed with," Bill insisted.

"What about the Jewish connection?" Libby asked.

"Do you think that's really the reason someone wants to buy this letter off me?" Bill asked. "To stop Israel banning Wagner forever?"

Libby thought for a moment. "No," she said. "Not at all. But don't assume that just because you've come across two letters that refer to Wagner's Sieglinde, this mistress figure is the vital link. A third letter to the Friend might not mention her at all. Then again Wagner was always in love with someone. It may be that we're bringing tabloid criteria too much to bear. There may be other references, seemingly insignificant, that we're missing because we're assuming that any scandal has to be racial or sexual. He lived in a different time from ours. Can you show me the letter now?"

"It's a blow-up from a scanned image via my e-mail," said Bill, drawing the notebook out of his pocket. "They've only sent me the translation and the quality is poor. I don't have the original German."

"I bet I could reconstruct it," said Libby. "Or I could have once. He's unmistakable."

Bill passed his notebook over to Libby and kissed her. "I'll just go and see how Reah's getting on up on deck."

"You do let her out of your sight too much," said Libby. Bill liked her concern. It gave him a warm feeling when Libby scolded him for neglecting Reah or when Reah asked after Libby. Boy, he needed that warmth when he got up on deck, the spray and mist made Bill shudder momentarily.

Libby watched him go and opened the notebook where Bill had stapled the letter in. As she was easing it flat with one hand she saw her own name, written in his hand. A stray gust of wind from the door had flipped the previous page over and into her line of vision. "*Libby.*" A page where he had also written "*New York Times*". This man, her man. He was, wasn't he? And he had written her name. Momentarily she lost where exactly in the book, but what remained was the shock of something intense, exciting and disturbingly narcissistic. She had to see her own name spelled out in his script. It was a primitive and magical desire, seeking the rune that represented the bond between them.

> *Where does Katz fit into this?*
> *If I could get to see another letter what pattern might be visible?*
> *Do I trust Libby? Why is she so secretive about her 'work'?*

She froze. Even before she fully understood the meaning of the words and the full nature of the shock, Libby knew herself to be deeply, bitterly wounded. He must have written this after they had spent those honeymoon days together in the cottage. He must have written this after she had appealed to him to come and rescue her in Venice. After that man had betrayed her in such an awful way. Libby studied the words. Another betrayal. Now she was calm. She knew herself to be calm. This was how it always happened. This was how it all went wrong. She was not feeling well. With the rising and falling of the boat she was pretty certain she would vomit any moment now.

Bill had remembered Torcello for the din of cicadas but that was in the summer, a summer many years ago. Their walk down the one canal not entirely silted up on this deserted distant island, was therefore strangely silent. The drizzle had stopped, but fewer than ten people had disembarked from the pitching *vaporetto*. One couple looked as if they'd come to see the basilica, a few more had probably turned up to sample one of the island's three restaurants. The rest were locals, small squat people with handfuls of baggage, dressed in layer upon layer of cheap clothing. "This was where the people of Venice first lived," Bill told Reah. "But the Huns attacked and it became unsafe. They withdrew across the lagoon. Then there was malaria in the swamps and the population fell to... do you know, Libby?"

"Not my subject," she said with a quiet smile. She was two paces behind and seemed happy enough. "Well, they say there are more cats than people here nowadays."

Reah was delighted to see evidence of the cats as they walked along the paved embankment. She turned round and told Libby about Jethro but then stopped mid-sentence when she was actually able to pick up one of the kitties.

Bill waited for Libby and they walked on together. "Are you happy to eat here?" Bill asked when they reached Al Trono.

"Sure," said Libby.

"I came here once to do a restaurant review on the island," Bill told her. "I didn't have much time so I just went to the first place that was open. But I liked it. Typical journalist," he grinned.

They sat out in the garden under a huge canopy of reeds, surrounded by empty pink tablecloths. The waiters obviously thought they were nuts. The only other clients – a smart looking French couple – were eating indoors, watched from the bar by two silent friends of the *padrone*.

"What about Cäcilie?" Bill asked. "Do you think that she could be our Sieglinde?"

Libby shook her head. She was wearing sunglasses, a rather incongruous thing to do, considering the day was far from bright. Aggravatingly distant, she was. "No he'd known her for years. This sounds like a new passion."

"He does talk about her being in the house though, doesn't he?"

"Yes but Cäcilie didn't live with them I'm sure. Besides, the Wagners had a whole entourage. There were five children, nannies, governesses – Cosima was very concerned that her children got all the education she'd missed out on when she was trailing round after Liszt. Wagner lived in a world surrounded by women, it could have been any one of them."

"Imagine that, Dad," scoffed Reah. "Being surrounded by women."

"Two's enough," said Bill. It should have been a moment for teasing, for raillery between the genders and solidarity between the girls but instead it felt awkward, a curt response in a tense situation. "What about young Siegfried?" he asked.

"Oh he'd be there too but just think of it: until Blandine got married and Daniela went to live with her real father, the kid had four elder sisters, plus all the servants, the seamstresses running up silk drapes for Wagner and the women like Judith Gautier who hung on his every word. And Cosima who was so wrapped up in her husband that Siegfried would never have gotten any attention at all. No wonder he turned gay."

"I thought gay people were born that way," Reah chimed in.

Libby seemed uncertain how to respond.

Fortunately some food came at that point.

"Oh God, octopus," said Reah as Bill's plate passed her.

During the meal Bill felt something was wrong, more wrong than even before, but he didn't know how to deal with it. If Reah hadn't been there he might have just asked outright, but Reah *was* there and he couldn't keep taking Libby on one side. He felt very rusty at relationships. It had been four years now that he'd lived on his own and before that he and Tamsin were falling further and further out of a relationship rather than being in one.

As Bill drank the sparkling *prosecco* he began to wish that he and Libby could swim into a mood of warm sensual indulgence this afternoon. He was feeling easy and fond of her now. He remembered the sensations of desire that had been there only this morning. Sadly, however, he had no idea how to return their relationship to where it rightfully belonged. He offered Libby some wine. She refused gently.

"Are you sure?" he asked. He didn't usually need to drink when they were together but at this moment he really felt it would do them both good. It would short-circuit the distance that had built up between them.

"It gives me a headache," she said from behind her sunglasses. She was speaking in all honesty but choosing to ignore the underlying malaise.

"Dad," said Reah. "If you write and say this is a really great restaurant, will they give us a free meal?"

"It doesn't work like that," said Bill.

"Sometimes Dad gets free meals," Reah explained. "If they know he's a journalist."

"Sometimes I'm invited," said Bill. "There's a difference. I don't just turn up, show my press card and ask for a free plate of chips."

"That's what I'd do," said Reah. "And I'd say that if I didn't get champagne, I'd trash them."

"There's more to journalism than that," said Bill, attempting to sound jolly.

"Not much," said Libby. Bill looked at her and Reah looked at them both. Libby avoided them both.

"I'm sorry," said Bill. "Is this something you want to share?"

"It doesn't matter," said Libby.

"It obviously does," said Bill. He could feel his own tone growing icy as he spoke.

"There's nothing wrong being a journalist," Reah began to say, but Bill gestured for her not to get involved.

"Was that a joke?" Bill was trying very hard not to sound annoyed.

Libby took off her sunglasses. Bill saw how dull her eyes seemed now. They were unhappy eyes, bruised even. "Well if you must know, I feel – I always have felt – that journalism corrupts. How can there be any truth in an intellectual activity whose primary tenet is to encapsulate any given subject in no more than 1,000 words?"

"You can do a lot in 1,000 words," Bill argued.

"And do you? What about that piece about Wagner in Israel?"

"That was 1,500," said Bill.

Libby was not deflected. "Did you really get to grips with the issues of forgiveness, remembrance, bitterness, guilt and expiation, Bill? Or did you just round up the same bigots and let them restate their sound-bites. Seventy words each, 'Bill Wheeler reports that nothing's changed in Tel Aviv', two photos, a line drawing of Richard Wagner, the same tired old images of Holocaust faces and a bit of glib editorialising." Libby obviously read him.

"That's hardly fair," said Bill. "You know that's what the *New York Times* wanted. Just enough words to keep the debate going."

"And didn't you ask yourself why? Might it not be to do with the fact that New York Jews like to keep presenting the image of their people as martyrs?"

"No," said Bill, getting angry now. "No, I didn't ask myself why. I did the job because I was asked to do it, because I was capable of doing it and because I needed the money. I think if you ask 95 percent of the working population they'd say the same thing. Is that so bad?"

"I think you're worth more than that," Libby said, simply but not generously.

Bill didn't know how to reply. This was a day for inexplicable arguments. "*Thank you*," he said, not without a hint of irony.

"I think people should remember the Holocaust," said Reah.

Libby didn't even hear her. "I mean, look at this Wagner letter," she said. "You have come across something unique, something that no one has read in fifty, maybe a hundred years. Something that might give us an insight into one of the great creative artists of the nineteenth century, if not *the* greatest. And what do you do with it? First of all you look to see if there's some scandal attached to the Jewish references. Knee-jerk journalistic reaction number one: play the race card. "Was Wagner an Anti-Semite?" As if it matters–"

"It matters to some people," said Bill.

"Yes and we all know who," Libby snapped, quite unconscious of Reah's stunned reaction. "And when that doesn't tell us anything new," she ploughed on, "anything that might not make a front page by-line for Bill Wheeler, what do we go to next? The sex scandal. Knee-jerk journalistic reaction number two: "Did Wagner have a secret mistress?" As if that matters either! And don't say that it matters to some people, Bill, because we know what kind of people. The kind of people who believe that art is only of interest if you can turn it into posters, movie soundtracks or fodder for the scandal sheets!"

Bill couldn't believe what he was hearing. He was angry, embarrassed on Reah's behalf, and deeply hurt on his own. He had no idea Libby had been harbouring these thoughts.

"Dad writes for all sorts of papers," Reah protested, clearly distressed.

"I thought you were worth more than the artistic gossip columns when I met you," Libby continued. "I thought that seven years ago and I still think that now. What have you done with your life, Bill? What have you done since London? You just go round the world digging up bits of dirt for people who don't have the intelligence to appreciate opera – or music – as an art form. They just want to know who is having sex with whom. Art for them is glamorous divas, crazy composers and big egos having a better time in the bedroom than the poor pathetic individuals who read the kind of scandalsheets you write for!"

"Stop it!" said Reah, but Libby couldn't hear her.

"And what's in that letter Bill? Maybe nothing, but have you actually read it? Read it in the sense of trying to *understand*? No. You've just run a scandal-detector over it. Have you ever tried to find the *truth*?"

Why wouldn't she shut up? All Bill could feel inside himself was steel. He had no arguments. It seemed at that moment that Libby was right. What was he but a glorified muckraker for the likes of Louis and a political pawn for people like Vita?

"Enough," he said, but it wasn't. Libby was still talking. He didn't know what she was saying, he just wanted her to stop. The next thing he knew he had slammed the letter in its little plastic bag down on the table and shoved it over to where Libby sat. "OK, you tell me how I should read that letter. You have the benefit of not having had your sensibilities corrupted by the need to earn money! You tell me how a Fullbright Scholar reads that letter, you tell me how the Baron's friend reads that letter, how someone with the free use of apartments all over Europe reads that letter."

"Stop it!" said Reah. She was crying and holding out her hand to him. And Libby stopped. The blur had gone. Her eyes focused again. It was as if she hadn't been able to see him while she was talking. Now that she looked anew at the scene in front of her, there was nothing but devastation. This man in pain. His daughter in tears.

"I'm sorry," she said, picking up the letter and then standing. "I'm sorry." Now she could see him again, the man and his daughter. He had his arm around her now. She wanted to say sorry to the child but at the moment she couldn't even remember her name. She had to say something.

"Bill, I'm sorry. I didn't mean to hurt you but now that it's said, what can I do?" There was a horrible logic to all of this now. These were the final moments. "Seven years ago I thought you were worth more than journalism. I still do. I respected you for staying with your wife and child." She couldn't even think of the girl's name but still she spoke. "I couldn't respect you for the way you earned your living, though, and I still can't. I wish you didn't do what you did. I'm sorry."

It was all hopeless, Libby knew it now. "I love you Bill," she said, ploughing on in her misery. "I love you, but I'm sorry, I can't love what you are."

Bill glared up at Libby. He was defending his daughter. He was not engaging with her anymore. 'This is my child,' he seemed to be saying. 'I do not owe you anything. I owe you nothing because you are nothing and you have upset this child.' Now he was speaking to her, this man who had held her in the night. What was he saying? "*We can't all write symphonies.*" It was so like him, so like him to make a cheap remark about another man in that way.

"I think I had better go," said Libby, and she did. She walked out of the garden and back through the restaurant. She walked in cold silence down the towpath and headed towards where the *vaporetto* would come to rescue her. She was almost there when suddenly nausea overcame her and she was nearly sick against the wire that fenced this route. Wiping her mouth, Libby tried again to get to where the *vaporetto* would be. She knew if she could get there, the ferry would come and rescue her. It would take her home. Then she would board a train and go tonight to where Hauke could look after her in a way that none of these men could.

"I've lost him," she said aloud, as a fresh wave of nausea came over her. She stumbled, held on to the fencing. It was a journey through pain, a journey that seemed to take forever.

She was now within a few feet of the pontoon and, just as she knew would happen, the ferry arrived, at the very moment that she reached the little black and yellow floating shelter that bobbed up and down with the swell. The railing opened. No one got off. Why should anyone come to this desolate place? Three people got on. Libby stepped down on to the pontoon. It lurched and the movement almost drove her back, back to all that devastation. A man in uniform, the one who had pulled back the railing to allow those others on, asked Libby if she wished to get on too but she couldn't understand him. Her Italian had deserted her completely. She should go back and make her peace with Bill. She had let him think that she despised him when all she felt was hurt, was pain. The pain that came from knowing that he despised her, like all the others. He whom she had admitted deep within her, filling her soul with gratitude and love for the children they might have between them, he had no trust in his heart, no love for her. She held out a hand to Bill. They must love each other. What else mattered in this world? But her hand was taken by the man on the *vaporetto* who helped her on board. The boat roared, pitching alarmingly, and the railings clanged shut behind Libby. She was gone.

Bill came round the corner at speed, his coat-tails flying. He had seen the *vaporetto* arrive as he came out of Al Trono Di Attilla. He had run to catch Libby and stop her departing. Now he could not see her as the *vaporetto* drew away, but he knew she was on that boat. Out of breath, he dropped down, swore, and then returned slowly to Reah. There wouldn't be another boat now for an hour, the waiter said helpfully, but Bill already knew.

The French couple inside the restaurant took no notice of his return but the *padrone*'s friends had transferred their interest to the table in the garden where the English couple had argued, where the woman with extravagant clothes had left with tears on her face and the girl with the hair rose up frightened as her father returned.

Bill sat down next to Reah and squeezed her hand. "Sorry about that."

"I'm glad she's gone," said Reah

"She's not entirely wrong," said Bill. "There is something in what she says. Stay in this business too long and everything is either a headline or a non-story."

"She's the one who broke you and Mum up, isn't she?" Reah asked. "She said seven years ago she respected you for staying with us rather than going off with her." Bill sat down and took her hand. "She's the one who used to write to you, isn't she?" Reah was relentless. "The one who made Mum cry."

"Yes," said Bill. What was the point now? He'd lost her. All he wanted to do was to sleep. There was no point in building castles in the air anymore. They all came tumbling down.

"I hate her," said Reah turning away from him. "I never want to see her again."

"I don't suppose you will," said Bill.

The waiter came and asked whether they still wanted the main course. Bill shook his head. "*Il conto, por favore,*" he said. It was the only Italian a journalist needed to know.

❖ THE LOVE OF YOUNGER WOMEN

BILL STARED AT THE SCREEN. He seemed to have done a lot of that recently. The dark rectangle before him could hold his attention indefinitely, it seemed. Within it, Bill had finally found stasis. Reluctance overwhelmed him and he embraced it. True, he could use this thing to write journalism. True, he could use it to write to Libby. But both activities seemed pretty pointless now.

So Bill did neither.

The coffee in his cup was bitter and cold. Maybe he was finally developing an aversion to it. He had sat here this morning for over a quarter of an hour, unable to decide even whether or not to switch the computer on. He knew there would be no message from Libby, but perversely, his heart still tempted him. It tortured him with possibility.

He ought to get on and work, to commit his vision of the world to 1,000 words of journalism, words that would be meaningless tomorrow if they weren't already today. What was the point? There was something chill within him, and had been ever since Libby left them on Torcello, ever since he'd said goodbye to Reah the following Monday afternoon. Something that felt like death. Today was Tuesday. He had woken into a state of icy stasis. Riven with indolence he had lain there wondering if he might ever rise again. His sleep, after returning from Venice and after delivering Reah up to Tamsin, had been very deep. But it was not the kind of slumber in which a man can find repose. It was the cold embrace of shock. Somewhere inside, Bill Wheeler might be hurting, but his ability to feel that hurt had been switched off. Bill had risen, walked about and found himself surprised to discover that his body still functioned, that he had all his limbs still, could dress and make coffee and look at the view. What he couldn't do, however, was enjoy his coffee.

Yesterday had not been good. Neither had his last evening in Venice. Reah, when she wasn't hating Libby, was hating him. She would not forgive her father for lying to her about who Libby really was, nor for taking up again with the woman who destroyed the childhood of Rachel Christabel Wheeler. Bill had sat in the armchair of their small hotel room locked within the pain of his own heart while Reah sulked on the bed. Theirs were two different silences. Hers flowed towards him in angry waves. His imploded within him.

"I want to ring Mum," Reah had said.

"OK," he replied, resignedly. "It's a hotel phone. Can you keep it brief?"

He had hoped that she wouldn't ring Tamsin. At that moment he still believed in the bond between them. Reah had never rung him to denounce Tamsin while she was with her mother. She would not do this, surely.

She did. But indirectly. "I'm really not getting on with Dad's girl-friend," said Reah using her miserable voice.

Bill, sitting in the chair by the window, wondered if he'd ever find the energy or inclination to get up again. He ought to remove his coat, but that would require movement. So he supported his cheek with one hand while Reah spoke to Tamsin. It was a pensive pose, but thought was beyond him. His mind could not move forward. He was remembering that argument. He was remembering her boat drawing away. He was remembering their arrival in Dorsoduro to find Libby gone. She had left a message with a neighbour downstairs. She was no longer in Venice. She had known he would call.

Now Bill was remembering the neighbour's kind face, the face of a woman who clearly loved the daughterliness of his charming *Dottoressa*. She had had no idea what was going on, this sweet woman with the open face. She had not known Libby in the night begging him to give her a child, or digging her fingernails into his skin. She knew nothing of their strange communions.

"She doesn't like Jews either," Bill heard Reah say.

He gazed at the nothing outside their misty window and remembered the *vaporetto* trip back from Torcello. Reah would neither sit by him nor accept his embrace on the boat. Bill remembered his words to her: "*there is much that you do not understand.*" And hers to him, that she was old enough to know you don't lie to your own family.

"Mum, I really want to come back."

Libby had said it would go wrong. Was that why it did? Had Libby willed this disaster or was she genuinely wiser than he?

Bill had tried ringing Libby's mobile but it was only taking messages. Of course. She was disappearing again like she did seven years ago. Invoke chaos, pull down the world and then fly away.

"Dad, Mum wants to talk to you," said Reah offering up the phone to him.

Just what I need, thought Bill. Slowly, he stood up to collect the phone from his daughter.

Reah, tired of waiting, left the phone on the pillow and went to the bathroom. Bill removed his coat and lay by the receiver. Then he picked it up." Hi," he said. "Look–"

"This obviously isn't anything to do with me," said Tamsin.

That wasn't what Bill had been expecting. "She's upset," he said. "There was an argument."

"Bill, I don't need to know," said Tamsin. She sounded almost hasty.

"No," said Bill. Maybe she didn't. He was completely confused at the moment. Emotional upheavals left Bill adrift. It had been the same when they had divided up the matrimonial home. There were no parameters that he recognised. Other people knew how to focus, knew where right and wrong resided. Bill only knew that he felt ripped apart and unable to calculate.

"I've told Reah it's between the two of you," said Tamsin.

He didn't know what to say. It seemed generous.

"That's... good of you."

"And I don't want to know the details."

"OK," said Bill. Even in his stupefaction he knew this was not how he had imagined the scene playing. Tamsin had not screamed at him, 'What are you doing taking Reah to visit your tart!' But then Tamsin wasn't like that, was she? No, of course she wasn't.

"Have you decided when you're coming back?" she asked.

"Tomorrow. I'd booked return tickets for tomorrow. We'll be getting a morning flight."

"Can you drop Reah at my parents' house? I'd like to talk to you about schools."

Bill was completely thrown by this. Even more surprising than Tamsin's moderate tone was all this getting on with normal life stuff. It was as if she had put this idea of 'Dad's girlfriend' to one side, to behave as if his life, the life of her ex-husband, was nothing to do with her. Bill made some vague noises about when he thought he'd be able to pick up the car from Heathrow and added an hour's travel time to that.

"On second thoughts, how about meeting in Highgate?" she said.

"Why Highgate?"

"There's a school there I'd like you to see."

"For Reah?"

"Yes."

Something seemed to have occurred in the few days that separated his making love to Libby in Holt's Cottage and the present moment. What had happened to his attempt to keep Reah and Tamsin in the Wye Valley? Here he was in a discussion with Tamsin that seemed based on the agreed inevitability of this move. He'd obviously conceded, hadn't he? At some stage when Bill and Libby, lambent with desire, were rolling naked in front of the fire, Bill had recognised that he had to work within the bounds of what was possible rather than what felt just. It seemed he had accepted the loss of his daughter because life had offered him the possibility of coming home every evening to a warm fire and the youthful, accepting flesh of Libby Ziegler.

"It's such a shame," he found himself saying. "Her first trip to Venice. I wish it hadn't worked out like this."

There was silence at the other end of the line. Tamsin might be willing to be reasonable but she wasn't going to comfort him. "You'll ring me when you're on your way, then?"

"Sure," he'd said. Reah emerged from the bathroom. "OK?" said Bill.

"What did Mum say?"

"She wants me to go and look at schools with her tomorrow. Schools for you."

"Oh," said Reah, as if this was not quite what she'd expected either. The need for drama seemed to have been obviated. "Can I come too?"

"I suppose so," said Bill.

"Cool."

And so Bill looked at the screen. Reah was in London now. True, she'd be coming down at the weekend but a transition had been made. She was with her family now. She was leaving him.

Reah had liked the school, this new place. It was fee-paying but Tamsin's father had offered to help. "I'm not happy with that," Bill had said.

"You've got to pay for good education in London," Tamsin told him, short jacket, short skirt, her low black boots shuffling with the cold. "It's not like Chepstow."

"No one's asking you to move," said Bill. The thaw in their relations hadn't lasted long.

"Goodbye, Dad," Reah had said as she was about to get into Tamsin's car to go back to St John's Wood. She actually came back and hugged him. Bill tried not to hold on to her for too long. "See you at the weekend," she whispered into his ear.

"Yeah."

She wanted to be friends again, he could tell. Sulking was a useful weapon for daily conflicts around the house and the petty altercations of school, but this was the big stuff. This was Reah and Bill. This was the two of them, always close. Forever friends.

"We can watch a video," he said.

"Ooh but I'm supposed to be eating with Mum," said Reah.

"Sure," Bill said, retreating. "That's OK."

"I can come over," said Reah. "Can I Mum? Can I come over to Dad's at the weekend?"

Tamsin looked unsure. "Oh," she said. "Well, on Saturday afternoon I suppose."

"On no, please, Mum, Friday?" said Reah. "All the best programmes are on Friday."

"But–" said Tamsin. "No, not on Shabbat."

"Please Mum."

"Well, maybe after the blessing," said Tamsin. Reah looked as if she weren't entirely happy about that, but she'd let it go this time.

"Saturday morning with me, though. All right, *bubbeleh*?"

"Sure," said Reah. "Bye Dad!"

Now it was Tuesday afternoon and the screen before him was blank. As blank as the week before him. What the hell was wrong with this coffee?

When he'd got back on Monday night Bill knew there would be no message from Libby. He hated the way that the hope kept rising in unbidden and unwelcome surges within him. Eventually he had sat down in front of the screen with the resolution of writing to her. He had to write even if she never read his words. Writing was how he fashioned the world into something that made sense.

So, finally, Bill switched the damn thing on. The brightness of its screen told him that dusk was gathering outside. His office had suddenly seemed very dark indeed. "*After Venice*", he typed in the subject box, then amended it. "*Once Again After Venice*".

"*Dear Libby,*" he wrote. Each key seemed such an effort. Life seemed such an effort. Driving down the M4 had not helped. Leaving Reah with Tamsin and the Walkens had only accentuated how completely alone he was now. What was once his way of life now seemed no life at all.

> *Dear Libby,*
>   *I don't understand what happened on Torcello. It was a time of great strain for both of us. For Reah too. I can't bear the thought that I have lost you again from my life. Please write to me. We need to talk.*

He had looked at those words. They were stark in their honesty. Yet how could he express himself other than with total honesty? No longer merely the first casualty of love, it was now its last resort.

Please don't throw this away. I'm sure we can work something out.

Bill wondered about typing 'I love you'. It wasn't his pride that held him back. He was wondering how genuine this love of his might be. He had felt such anger towards Libby since Torcello. The old dark anger. Could this really be love? Was the intensity of his current feeling just the rage of some child whose plaything has been snatched away? But in their love-making he had known himself growing closer to her, opening up even. There had been so much he had wanted to share with her in the silence of the night. This pain he felt now was not just frustration, one lonely man's fear of coming home to an infinity of silences. No, if this were not love what was it?

But Bill sent the e-mail without telling Libby that he loved her. Afterwards he worried that he had done the wrong thing, but he went instead to unpack. In half an hour he was back switching on, foolishly, to see if she had responded. *No New Messages,* his machine told him. Bill stared at the screen. Libby was out there beyond him. Her silence screamed at him. He had never known emptiness prove so horrifying. Bill understood why we are wary of silence: out of it we may suddenly hear the noise of something malevolent, like the twig that snaps and warns us we are not alone. But this, this was different, this was the silence that babies fear, the silence that mankind struggles to ignore, the silence that tells us we are alone in the world, that the world is unknowable, empty, devoid of kindness or reason. We speak. We struggle to communicate, but no one hears. Maybe God Himself is no longer up there.

Now it was night. Bill had switched off. The screen died. He could not bear such silence any longer. In the end he reached for the telephone. "Hello," said a voice at the other end. A dull, late-night voice.

"It's Bill."

"Hi," said Marika.

"I've been in Venice."

"Nice," she said. "I've been here."

"I was wondering about coming over tomorrow," Bill said.

Bill spent Wednesday trying to sort out his life. He had to earn some money now. Taking Reah to Venice on top of Munich had dented his finances. The post contained no cheques. Louis could have done something to help, damn it.

In the cooler light of evening, Bill had to admit that he had accepted

305

Reah was moving. And that meant he himself had to move on now. There had been a brief time when Bill had been torn between keeping the cottage for Libby's sake and going to London for Reah's. Now he had his answer.

He paused as he dialled the estate agent's number. He was remembering Libby standing on his desk to look for his famous view. He remembered the tall black boots, the backs of her knees clad in those leggings. He remembered standing with her outside watching Lee depart in his van, his hand probing between her buttocks, and her words: "You haven't attacked me in the shower yet."

Bill put down the portable as his legs seemed to cave in on him. How did it all go so wrong? He had preferred Reah over Libby hadn't he? No, he had just put her first. Libby had said she didn't want to go. He had said stay, hadn't he? And she had said "But your daughter's coming." What should he have done? Put Reah off?

Now Bill felt cold, but this was not the chill lock on his wounded heart that he knew so well. This was the sudden tremor of shock pricking his skin. What had he *done*? Of course what Libby had wanted was to be first in his affections. Was that why she had hit him when he'd joked about sharing the room with Reah? But Reah was his daughter for goodness sake! She had always been so loyal, he owed her something surely?

A new wave of emotional incoherence swept over Bill. To give Tamsin her due, she had run the relationship for them both. He did not have to decipher her; if anything, it was she who deciphered him. What on earth did he do now?

Suddenly Bill was sure. He had to speak to Libby. It didn't matter what it cost. He had to claw his way back to her. He had to tell her that he loved her. Why did he not tell her that yesterday? Bill went back to the cold dusty screen. He would write to her again. The only reason he hadn't so far today was that he dreaded the words he knew he would see when he went online: *No New Messages.*

It had to be done.

> *Dear Libby,*
>
> *A love like ours is rare, I believe. We did not come back into each other's lives for no reason. Please let us try and resolve this. If it were simply a matter of my giving up journalism I would.*

That statement rather shocked him. Well he would. There was nothing so great about this life. Nothing compared to what his life could be with Libby. Good God, he loved her, didn't he? He loved her so much.

> *I love you. Please contact me.*

He thought about saying that if she didn't, he'd sell the cottage because he couldn't bear to live there without her, but that sounded like a threat.

Bill noticed that there was no subject heading to his e-mail. He typed in the four letters that summed it all up. Then he pressed send.

Now there was washing to do and he ought to see if he had a bottle of wine to take to Marika's, assuming he was still going. And there was no food in the house for goodness sake! How did one find time to earn, eat, travel and have a personal life? Maybe we were supposed to get all that sex out of the way in our twenties. The telephone rang. Bill half hoped it was Siobhan so he could complain about all the money *Arts International* owed him.

"Mr Wheeler," said a voice. "We haven't met. I believe you may have a letter of mine."

"Really?" said Bill. He sat down at the desk and fished for a pencil. "And what might your name be?"

"I don't think it is necessary for me to give you my n-name," said the voice. A man. An American perhaps. There was a hesitation on that last syllable which distracted Bill. "N-not at this stage and n-not until we have an agreement for you to return the letter." The timbre and accent were curious. Then he realised his caller was not American but another of those Germans or Swiss whose command of a foreign language is so complete it takes a while to pinpoint what it is about the accent that doesn't sound entirely British.

"How do you know I have a letter of yours?"

"We have an acquaintance in common," said the voice.

"Ah," said Bill. Mr Katz no doubt.

"The Baroness de Teisier von M-m-meck," said the voice, making quite a meal of Heidi's name. "I am a friend of her husband too."

"Ahah," said Bill. "Good old Willy." So this was the mystery man who had been waiting for the Baron to bully that letter off Bill.

"I believe Baron von Meck told you I am willing to pay you for the safe return of this letter."

"Yes," said Bill. "But how do I know it's yours? I mean if you won't tell me who you are..."

"There are certain c-conditions," the voice continued, ignoring Bill's procrastination.

"Ah. And what are those?" Up until now Bill had been doodling idly. Now he turned to shorthand.

"You are not to keep a copy of the letter, n-nor to publish it nor write about its content in any newspaper, academic publication or book. If you are willing to agree to these conditions, I will pay you a sum of money–"

"How much?"

"We can discuss that."

"I'd like to know how much," said Bill. "I'd like to get an idea of how much you want it and I'd like to know why."

"Mr Wheeler, this letter isn't your property," said the voice. There was a pause while the man took a breath. "You are not in a position to dictate terms."

"I get the feeling it's not yours either," Bill retorted. "Otherwise you'd have resorted to the law by now. And don't try and steal it from me. Like you did before."

There was a longer pause, and then barely surprised surprise. "Mr Wheeler, to my knowledge no one has tried to steal that letter."

"Well someone broke in here," Bill insisted.

"Maybe you have property belonging to several people in your house," said the man. He remained calm and polite but he was no fool, this guy.

"I want to meet you," said Bill.

"Mr Katz is acting for me in this matter," said the voice.

"Nevertheless I want to meet you," said Bill.

"That is n-not possible."

"Think about it," said Bill, and he put the phone down. Quickly he dialled 1471 but was only told that he had been called today at 10.03. The caller had withheld their number. Mr Mystery Voice was probably phoning from abroad.

"Interesting," Bill said aloud to himself. He might get to the bottom of this after all. He must contact Vita. Bill paused. He had just remembered something, something rather awful. Didn't he give the letter to Libby in Torcello? Did she ever give it back? Bill tore open his notebook. The damn thing wasn't there!

Of course not.

"*Dear Libby,*" Bill typed. If he'd been looking for an excuse to write again, he could not have asked for anything better.

> *I have just received a phonecall from a man who purports to be the rightful owner of the Werther Freund letter. I'd like to meet this man and find out what the significance of this letter is. It's only now however that I realise that I gave it to you on Torcello. Is it possible we could meet for you to hand it back to me? Hopefully we could then discuss our other differences. I'm sure we can overcome them.*

He signed it "*with love*" and then pressed Send. The machine whirred and shashed. *No New Messages*, it reminded him.

Bill spent the rest of the day completing various bits of journalism, sending out invoices and writing a long letter, replete with peevish demands for money, which, given Louis' aversion to e-mail, he faxed in. From time to time he checked for e-mail but without worrying too much about the silence. Bill felt confident that Libby would reply to him about the Wagner letter. It wasn't in her nature to ignore the business of restoring archival treasures.

For a moment Bill was afraid that she might decide to act independently of him. After all Heidi knew how to contact Libby and this mystery man was her friend. He sat down with his coffee and thought about that one. Surely, though, if Heidi had gone to Libby – and Libby were minded to hand the letter over – Heidi's mystery friend need not have called. Besides, he trusted Libby didn't he?

Well he loved her, yes. Bill was fairly sure of that, but trustworthiness is not always the first thing we look for in a lover. It's a useful quality in building a relationship but it's not what makes us fall in love. Uncomfortable with that thought, Bill reminded himself that Mertens and Plod had known how to contact him. So had Katz. And this man was in touch with Katz. So, no, there was no saying that Libby was involved at all. This was a relief given that she had the letter in her possession. On the other hand, it was sad that what he took consolation from was not the fact that he trusted Libby, but that she was not involved.

Why couldn't he trust her? Was it that he could not trust where he also loved? Bill wished he hadn't had that thought.

He went out to check the morning post. It was just possible of course that Louis' long-promised cheque was already waiting for him outside. It was also possible that Lee would be accompanying himself on the banjo in a rousing chorus of *Cwm Rhondda*. Once again Bill remembered standing at the mail box with Libby. He could see the two of them now, his hand discreetly taking liberties with her buttocks.

"Bill, would you make me pregnant?"

But memory had relocated the conversation. Opening his mailbox, Bill realised that he was in fact replaying a conversation they had had in Venice.

"I've stopped taking the Pill. There didn't seem much point carrying on with it this month," she was saying. "What if I don't start again? Would you make me pregnant?"

He'd asked her why she was still taking the Pill if she and Gustav

Mahler hadn't had sex for a year. And what had she said?

"That's not the issue here." She'd turned away, sulkily hurt. "*OK, fine. I get the message.*"

Women of Libby's age, particularly those who were hoping for children, don't take the Pill unless they have to, thought Bill. It lowers fertility. Someone had told him that, possibly Tamsin. So why did Libby continue taking the Pill for a year? Maybe the last twelve months with Gustav hadn't been as chaste as she'd had him believe.

Bill really wished he would stop having these suspicions. The sad thing was that there were things that didn't add up about Libby. Why had she, in this very cottage, told him not to question her work? She'd had no qualms about objecting to his. And she'd been evasive when he'd asked her about how she financed her trips round Europe.

Bill checked the play in that loose gatepost which marked off his land from Tamsin's. She's 34 now. She's not a child. Who knows what she's done with her life? There may be secrets. It didn't mean that he couldn't trust her at the level that mattered, surely. After all, wasn't he planning to go and see Marika tonight? It hadn't occurred to Bill until this point to consider that Libby might think his protestations of love less than trustworthy if he sought out Marika. But Marika wasn't that kind of experience. Not that Libby would necessarily see it that way. All in all it was best she did not know. All in all it was best he did not go. Good grief, not if there were any chance that he and Libby might still have a future together.

The phone started to ring back in the cottage. Should he phone Marika, Bill thought, as he wandered back inside. Does *she* have feelings in all this? He remembered her sitting there silently rolling a cigarette after that unfortunate failure of his last time. No, he said to himself. She didn't have feelings. Their encounters were not about feelings.

The phonecall had in fact been a fax: a brief note typed and signed by Siobhan.

> *Dear Bill,*
>
> *I have passed your faxed letter to Louis. He has meetings all day. I am sure he will deal with it when he has time. You are not, however, the only contributor to Arts International.*

What was it with that woman? Still, Louis' antiquated use of the faxed letter did afford Bill the pleasure of rolling this particular communication into a tight little ball and lobbing it in the basket.

Bill went for a walk in the afternoon. Suddenly he felt absurdly optimistic. He didn't head towards the Pulpit where he'd met Marika that time after Munich, but strode off through the woods, through his own killing-fields, daring the images to haunt him on such a day. What was making him so positive? It had to be that third e-mail he had sent to Libby. He was sure that when she received it, she would answer and when she answered, they'd have to arrange to meet. And when they met, he would convince her that she must come and live at Holt's Cottage. So that was it, Bill decided. He was back to playing happy families with Libby Ziegler. Despite all his doubts, he seriously could not believe that they wouldn't meet. Unless she sent Hauke with the letter of course. Bill didn't like that thought. No. She wouldn't do that. He knew she wouldn't do that. How did he know? Because when you have laid someone open and vulnerable and they have looked into your eyes the way that Libby had looked into his, then you know them. You don't know everything. You don't know how they fund their work. You don't know why they continued to take the Pill when not having sex with Gustav Mahler, but you do know the inner person. He knew Libby. At that moment, at least, he trusted her.

Bill strode into the office and switched on his PC. She would have written. She had. "Ziegler Dot 409," he said to the screen. "Welcome back." "*Letter*," the heading read.

> *Dear Bill,*
>
> *Thank you for your three. I am sorry that I walked off with the famous letter. I am sorry for my behaviour generally. It is too soon for us to meet but I agree we should. There are things that need closure. If you need the letter urgently I could FedEx it.*

"No," said Bill. Sod that. He wanted her in front of him. She needed to feel how much he loved her.

> *Let me know what you want to do. I have looked again at the letter. I think we have both missed the obvious. Lusch. Not entirely inappropriate.*

The kitchen maid? thought Bill.

> *Look her up. You'll find her in all the biographies. Hauke and I are going to be here a while longer. Then I'm going back to Munich and possibly Helsinki. We could try and meet somewhere en route.*

Bill was worried by her tone. It might be she was aiming at dignity. It might be she was speaking from a position of sadness. He didn't like this term 'closure', though. It needn't necessarily mean endings, Bill knew that, but it did have unfortunate resonances.

Bill, I don't know whether we came into each other's lives for good reasons or ill but if you want to keep in touch until we can meet again you can always e-mail.
    Libby

He liked the way she used his name. She was clearly shaken, but she wasn't entirely gone. He just knew he'd get her back. Bill found his attention drawn back to the Lusch reference.

I have looked again at the letter. I think we have both missed the obvious. Lusch. Not entirely inappropriate.

Libby was being annoyingly cryptic. *Lusch.* If only he had that biography still. Bill dug out Grice's translation of the last section of Wagner's letter.

As for my wife, she refused this morning to embrace me. She knows my heart as well as I do. You will understand therefore why this matter of S—— has not touched me but I thank you, my friend, for concerning yourself with it on my behalf. Our dearest Lusch leaves to meet her father at the end of this month. This matter affects me deeply you may imagine.

Bill had never considered Wagner's last paragraph of particular interest before but when he read the words that followed the Lusch reference he suddenly saw Libby's point. Why on earth had he assumed that cry of anguish had no relevance to Lusch the kitchen maid! Excitedly Bill read on:

I am tolerably well in other respects and am resuming work on the Bühnenweihfestspiel which I hope to see finished this year. Forgive me my despair!
    Mit den besten Grüssen
    Ihr sehr ergebener
    Richard Wagner

Of course! Until now he had always assumed that Wagner was winding up the letter with a series of stray thoughts. Firstly Lusch is leaving. Secondly a repetition of his woes about the woman he loved from top to bottom – *"this matter affects me deeply you may imagine"* – and then references to his health and the resumption of work on *Parsifal,* plus more despair and a dash of humble-servant nonsense to finish off. But, but, but... looked at differently, that second sentence could of course refer back to Lusch. *"Our dearest Lusch leaves to meet her father at the end of this month. This matter affects me deeply you may imagine."* Why had he not seen it?

He had not seen it because he had not expected the name of Wagner's new Brünhilde to be slipped so late into the letter and with absolutely no fanfare. Now he thought about it, however, it was obvious. The Worthy Friend already knew who she was, so Wagner would feel free to launch in, with all his allusions to Brünhilde and Sieglinde, and only come to her actual name at the very end of the letter, if at all.

So whose wife was Lusch? Once again Bill cursed the loss of that biography. He could always try the web, but could already predict the mind-numbing results of typing in Wagner + Lusch: *Randi Wagner due to meet Robin Lusch in some American blah blah college tennis fixture... Recipients of Colorado State Governor's GSS Awards 1997 going, amongst others, to J.D. Wagner II and Julie Lusch, blah di blah...*

And of course some idiot who was using his personal website to tell the world that he had bought a *lusch* Cadillac once belonging to Robert Wagner and Natalie Wood.

No, life was too short to scour the worldwide web. Try international Vita. "*Wagner Letters,*" Bill typed.

> *Dear Vita,*
>
> *Please thank Lyndon for sending that copy of the new Wagner letter. I may have made some progress but need to check a reference. Does the name Lusch mean anything to any Wagnerians over there?*

Bill realised that he was running a risk. Vita might well decide this Wheeler guy was a liability. Investigative journalists are supposed to find things out for themselves, not keep asking the editor for help. However Vita hadn't commissioned him as yet. This was a bit of informal research he was doing to see if the story stood up. Besides, he wasn't an investigative journalist anymore, if he ever had been. He was doing this for Libby. Bill felt a test had been set for him. He clicked Reply.

> *Dear Libby,*
>
> *I'm very glad to hear from you and am following up the lead on Lusch. More important however is Us. When can we meet? This is very important.*
>
> *You are very important.*
>
> *We are very important. Will any of those flights be through London? I could meet you at Heathrow? Hope things are going well over there. I miss you.*
>
> *Bill*

It was short. He didn't feel the need to overwhelm her with words at the moment. He wanted her attention. He wanted her to know that he saw them moving forward. He wanted to hold her again. That would be the time for big speeches. Bill noticed the hour. If he didn't get off soon the shops in Chepstow would be closed and there'd be nothing to eat.

It was completely dark when Bill got back. The red light on his machine was flashing. "William." Louis was sounding weary. "Sorry for the delay. Some things have come up here. I tried ringing you on your mobile but I don't think it was switched on."

"Yes it was," said Bill.

"Perhaps it was all those valleys and coal-tips getting in the way. Anyway give me a bell as soon as you're up in town."

"What about my bloody cheque?" said Bill to the machine, but Louis was gone. Bill flung himself into his chair and punched the PC's power button. *Lusch* said an e-mail from New York. My kind of woman, thought Bill. Lucrative, prompt and erudite.

> Bill,
>
> *I enclose an extract from our fiche which contains the only use of Lusch that cross-references with Richard Wagner. I presume this is not the object of affection were you looking for. Woody Allen only lives across the park. We don't want another one.*

What on earth was Vita talking about? Prompt, erudite and completely cuckoo. Then he saw what she meant.

> *Daniela Senta von Bülow b.12 October 1860 Berlin Germany eldest da Hans von Bülow (qv) and Francesca Gaetana Cosima Liszt (qv) known within the family as 'Lusch' (see Richard Wagner 'Letters To His Family').*

Bill was stunned. *Our dearest Lusch leaves to meet her father at the end of this month,* he said to himself. Lusch was not the kitchen maid – never had been. She was Cosima's daughter by von Bülow, one of the children that Madame von Bülow took with her when she forsook Wagner's acolyte for the Meister himself. "*The fruit of entwined roots.*" That was what Wagner had written in the second letter. Bill dug out his notebook in which he'd pasted the copy Lyndon had sent him.

> *When I gaze upon her I feel like Siegmund gazing for the first time on his Sieglinde, his but yet another's.*

My God it made sense. The entwined roots would be Wagner and von Bülow, entwined around the same woman, Cosima. They were also

Cosima and von Bülow entwined around the same genius, Wilhelm Richard Wagner. Daniela and her sisters were the fruit. Two of these von Bülow girls were definitely Hans' children, while the third went to law to prove she was Wagner's natural daughter, even though Hans had claimed she was his because Cosima was still legally married to him at the time of her birth. Yes, these were indeed the fruit of tangled roots. Four girls with two fathers between them and two girls who grew up thinking of Wagner by Cosima's coy euphemism, 'Our Friend'.

But what else had they known?

"*I have tried everything,*" Wagner had written in that second letter. Had he indeed?

> *What more is left to me? I have known what it is to be Siegmund. In my youth I was brave enough to be Wehwalt, son of Wolf, hunted in the forest, an outcast and ill-fated one but no more. It is not just my own bravery that would be tested but hers. This I cannot do. Already I sense her own despair in this matter. What was can no longer be.*

What the hell had been going on? How old was she? Bill tried to remember when this letter was written. His estimate had been around 1880/1881 when Daniela was... Bill checked the fiche... coming up to her twenty-first birthday. Would that account for Daniela going from Wagner's household to her father's? Of course it might! At the age of 21 she was an adult, allowed at last to decide that enough was enough. Bill looked again at Wagner's words: "*What was can no longer be.*" What exactly *was* that which could no longer be?

> *It is not just my own bravery that would be tested but hers.*

There was something distasteful about all this. He sat back in his chair. Now he could understand Vita's pointed reference to Woody Allen. Daniela and the other one were adopted daughters living in Wagner's household, like Allen's Soon-Yi Previn. And Daniela had lived with the Meister from – again Bill had to check – from when she was about six. God he detested that man.

> *My worthy friend, I ask you to destroy this letter and with it all knowledge of the deeds of which I spoke to you.*

Bill looked at the clock. It wasn't as late as it suddenly felt. 8.30. He ought to ring Marika and say he wasn't going. Assuming he wasn't. Bill had a sudden recollection of Marika giving him a graphic account of the "old bastard" who had transferred his 'affections' to her after the death of her mother. There had seemed to be an assumption on the old hill-farmer's part that when death prevented one woman from satisfying his needs the next should assume her duties. Marika's mother had cooked for him and responded in docile fashion when the old boy had told her on a Friday night to go to his room. He expected Marika to do the same. When she hadn't got up from the table and obeyed his drunken command, the owner of Tredossor had bent her arm behind her and tried to force the girl upstairs. She'd struggled free of that grip, so he used his weight to force her back on to the kitchen table.

"I waited till he thought he was getting what he wanted and then I knee'd him hard," she'd told Bill. "Right in the balls." And to make doubly sure that the old man never got any ideas about trying it on again Marika had gone over to where he lay, sprawled, in front of the sink, and stamped on his genitals three or four times. "After that I had no problems."

Bill had winced thinking of problems the farmer himself might have had after that encounter. Bill had not stayed much longer that particular night. Now, however, when he thought of old men and young women, he could only think of Daniela von Bülow – "*Our dearest Lusch*" – and that dreadful old German egomaniac. Where was Cosima in all this? Wasn't her role to protect the children for God's sake? He had heard of mothers who didn't, women who kept their marriages going by sending their daughter into the marital bed as substitute. Very unpleasant.

Disquieted, he picked up his post. This morning Bill had skimmed through quickly to make sure that *Arts International* hadn't sent the long-promised cheque. The only post of any interest these days was hand-written or hand-typed. The individual missive has never been so highly valued, by dint of its very rarity. The potency of the individual communication over the mass-produced. Wagner confessing disturbing secrets to his *Werther Freund*. Bill and Libby falling in love. Libby getting shafted by Gustav Bloody Mahler... now *there* was a man who recognised the significance of personal communication.

The phone went before Bill had got round to opening even one of these unappetising envelopes.

"It's me," said the voice that used to be known as Tamsin.

"Hi," said Bill.

"Look, Reah's passport," she said.

"What about it?" said Bill.

"You said you were going to let me have it."

"Oh yes." Indeed he had.

"But you didn't send it back with her on Monday." Tamsin seemed more than necessarily bothered about all this.

"I'm sorry," said Bill. "It was tucked inside mine for safe keeping."

"Well can you make sure you dig it out at the weekend?" Tamsin asked him.

"What's the hurry?"

"I didn't say there was a hurry."

"No, I did," he replied. "I feel you're really bugging me about this. I've accepted you can keep it, but you forgot to ask for it on Monday and I forgot to give it you. That's all."

Tamsin took a breath. "I just feel that if this were anyone else asking you'd have remembered and done it by now."

"Well other people ask me things directly rather than getting solicitors to write letters for them," Bill told her. He was getting riled again. "That always slows the process down."

"Are you doing this to annoy me?"

"No, I'll give it you on Friday night, OK?"

"OK," said Tamsin.

"You're not planning to take her abroad, are you?"

"No..."

"I'm just wondering why this damn thing is so important."

"I'm not saying it is," she replied. "It's just... oh you wouldn't understand, Bill. A passport is... to my people it's something that was denied us. Jews were trapped, unable to escape from persecution because of passports—"

"I don't think anyone's persecuting Reah, or you," Bill pointed out.

Tamsin sighed. "I said you wouldn't understand."

They left the phonecall at that and Bill finished going through his post. It was already dark outside. Spring might be evident during daylight hours but evenings at this time of year seemed no more hopeful to Bill than all the winter months that had preceded them. He wondered about a glass of whisky. The fire wasn't made up so he might take it to bed with him. Bill wished he had a biography of Daniela von Bülow to study. It was at times like this that he regretted living so far from a decent library or a tame academic. He could imagine someone like Rory Llewellyn Goetz having the Bülow family at his fingertips. Bill went to the sideboard and poured himself a glass. Oh God, he knew the spirit could prove all too tempting on a dark and empty evening like this.

Dear Libby,

Bill was back at his computer and typing before he'd even realised the decision had been made. Whisky had short-circuited conscious process.

You were right about Daniela. From what I can see she is Our Dear Lusch but why was Wagner so exercised about her going to her father? Why was it a trial to him that she was in Venice and what was so awful about Berlin? The Bülow Studies section at Chepstow Public Library was sold off last year to fund the bilingual Gameboy project. Any thoughts? The days are getting brighter here. But the nights are no less lonely. How are things in Finland?

He sent the e-mail not expecting to have heard more from her. They were rebuilding, but slowly. Bill still had every hope that Libby would be back with him in due course. Back online and back in Holt's Cottage. He could cope with that evil little *No New Messages* icon at the bottom of his screen.

That night Bill was very aware of trees. He couldn't escape their presence. At first he thought he was dreaming but he awoke to hear rain spattering and storm winds blowing the branches wildly overhead. They seemed to roar at him. Hagen was still out there, prowling the savage night.

In the morning he stepped out to see if there were any damage. The world was damp but bright, clouds rolled at speed across the light blue sky. That was all. How could Nature rage so angrily and then greet the dawn so vibrantly? Bill looked to the distant treeline. Had he seen one figure or two that day? If it had been a couple, were they Mertens and Clements, spying on him, or just the purchasers of Tamsin's farmhouse out for a pre-completion ramble? He looked over to the farmhouse, to the home that Tamsin would soon be ceding. To get a better view he walked up the small slope to where his Jeep was parked. Bill rested against its bumper, not thinking, just indulging in the sadness of it all.

There were large puddles all the way back to Tamsin's farm. Bill thought about Reah, whose room there would soon lie empty, and about Daniela von Bülow. How old had she been when her parents split? Six? Yes, six when Cosima had gone to join Wagner in Switzerland. Six – the same age that Reah had been when they moved here. That's what he remembered. The adulterers had waited there with her children in an empty house by the lake for all the fuss to die down. And for Ludwig to recall Wagner from exile. To return and complete his three great enterprises: namely *The Ring*, the financial ruin of profligate Ludwig and of course the destruction of von Bülow's marriage. And at what stage did Wagner's attentions turn from mother to daughter?

He went inside and decided to see if Libby had written. Unlikely, but she did always begin her days early, and the Continent was one hour ahead.

Something disturbed Bill just as he was about to enter the office, a recognition of that which is alien. Though he could not have given the police a detailed description of his living room at Holt's Cottage, Bill knew straightaway that something about the room he had just passed through was different.

Behind the sofa stood an old table which divided the living area from the kitchen. It was a hall table really, too small to eat off but useful for piling up those things – like the post – that were to go out, and for dumping those things – once again mainly post – that had just come in. That table had been empty when he went out to look for storm damage. Bill knew that. He would never have been able to say *how* he knew, but thinking of the varnished and dusty surface behind him now he was convinced something had changed. Bill turned back.

A magazine of sorts. Not his, and definitely not there before. As he was drawing closer it became obvious. There on the cover the words "*Sotheby*" and "*1938*". It was Libby's missing catalogue. The one she had left behind with such anguish. The one that they had turned the place upside down to find on her last morning in Holt's Cottage. This was bizarre.

Shock was becoming a way of life for Bill. This time it was the shock of recognising something supernatural entering his world. Fears were one thing. Images of mass graves as he took his daily walk, these were macabre but they still occurred to him within a real world – the world of Lee The Post and Video Magic down in Chepstow. Even his dreams were only ever dreams, however much malevolence he attributed to the trees at night. But this was real. This was tangible. This shouldn't be here. Bill reached out to touch the catalogue.

Part of him wondered whether in fact he were in a dream now. Maybe his hands would pass through this faded, dog-eared mirage but no, his fingers took it, lifted the printed pages and held them for inspection. This had weight. It had texture. It had monochrome illustrations too.

Bill flicked through the catalogue. It was unremarkable, wholly unre-markable, exactly the kind of thing Bill would have expected to see. Except that he couldn't possibly have expected to see it, could he? That was the point. This thing was lost. It wasn't here. Had he found it last night perhaps and placed it on the table but forgotten doing so in some drunken stupor? No, he had only had two glasses. Had Libby returned to the Wye Valley without telling him and placed this here as a calling card? Preposterous. Alas.

OK, said Bill to himself. OK, so if this were some kind of poltergeist... was there any rationale as to why such a catalogue would turn up now?

Was its presence significant in some way? Was it telling him something about Libby? Bill was not the kind of man to have such thoughts, but a journalist has to respond to the inexplicable on the basis that there must be some kind of rationale behind it.

He sat down, switched on the computer and decided to e-mail Libby. She should know about this. Pondering exactly what to say, Bill was still wondering whether this news should be couched in terms humorous, matter of fact or astonished when a message from ziegler.409 was delivered with a bing. "*Lusch*," it read. Of course. The world was bizarrely serendipitous like that these days. Bill clicked to read.

> *Dear Bill,*
>
> *Daniela was Cosima's first daughter by von Bülow. The two visited Wagner on their honeymoon. He was a third presence in their marriage from the start. You have to understand the importance of Richard Wagner in many people's eyes at the time. He represented a way forward when people like Brahms could only hark back, and society seemed to have lost all spiritual values. Liszt, Cosima and von Bülow were devoted to him, though none was blind to his personal failings. They protected him from the press who sensed scandal wherever he went. Even some of Cosima's correspondence – heavily edited as it was – betrays the fact that she wasn't entirely enamoured of Wagner's ego at first. I think it took a while to love him. By the time Daniela was born the Bülow marriage was on the rocks. Correspondence that I have seen shows that Cosima threw herself first into desperate adoration of Karl Ritter. Only later did she become the high priestess of the Wagner cult.*

God bless Libby, Bill thought. Her e-mails were like Apollo descending at the end of a baroque opera, answering all questions and resolving all ills. Faced with the calm typeface of a Ziegler e-mail Bill found it easy to forget that phantom catalogue lurking in the room next door.

> *I only worked on the early Wagner correspondence but I do know that Lusch was christened Daniela Senta, Daniela after Cosima's brother, Daniel – Liszt's son (he'd died not long before) – and Senta after the heroine of The Flying Dutchman, whom von Bülow used to jokingly refer to as "Wagner's eldest daughter". It was a joke whose irony can't have been lost on him when Cosima left and took their daughters so that she could live with Wagner at Triebsching. What the domestic situation was chez Wagner by the time your letters were written, I really don't know. This is not my period but it sounds as if there were something a*

tad prophetic about the association of Daniela with Senta. The Dutchman's girlfriend was after all Richard's ideal woman. Weather here intolerable. Hauke invaluable. Helsinki dates imponderable. At the moment. L

Bill clicked Reply.

Dear Libby,

Wagner says "What was can no longer be". And that he already senses Daniela's own despair. What are we to presume has been going on? The Worthy Friend is asked to destroy that second letter so that no one would know "of the deeds of which I spoke to you". What on earth has been happening? I know what it sounds suspiciously like, but that's not necessarily the case is it? Daniela was in her late teens, early twenties when this letter was written. Can we assume there had been some kind of relationship between her and the old man? Is this pure scandalmongering on my part? Or do you see a reasonable justification for such questions?

Bill thought about Louis after he had written that last line. Louis, with his perfect cuffs. Oh Louis would relish Bill muddying his hands with scandal like this. He may as well acknowledge straightaway that he recognised the journalistic agenda here and that he knew this presented a new problem for the two of them.

Libby espoused the truth. So did he, but Bill earned some of his income from sensation in the arts world. Scandal could arise as much from truth as falsehood. Wagner and Cosima were long suspected to be lovers by Munich's tabloid press and the muckrakers were proved right in the end, even though the couple had managed to get young Ludwig to write a letter to the press, extolling their innocence. No, scandal wasn't always misguided and undeserved. What poisoned the world was the mentality of those who looked *only* for scandal.

"Any further with the imponderabilities of Finland?" he wrote, adding, as if it were an afterthought:

Your Sotheby's catalogue has turned up by the way. I've no idea how. Shall I send it or shall we exchange at Heathrow?

Bill felt pleased with this letter. It gave Libby more reasons to see him again and it also addressed the main point of contention between them with neither fear nor resentment. He had made light of the catalogue, but then what should he make of such an unnerving mystery? Libby could cope with his fears about the landscape and with the violence of their love-making. It was rather a lot to ask her to cope with a poltergeist too.

Bill was about to press Send when the telephone went. He answered it only to be greeted by silence at the other end. It was a silence that sounded familiar, particularly when Bill became aware of someone breathing.

"Hello," Bill repeated.

"Mr Wheeler," said the voice, taking another breath. "I believe you have a letter of mine."

"Is that Mr Katz?" Bill asked.

"We met in Israel," Martin Katz wheezed by way of an agreement.

This was a conversation that had been bound to happen one day. Bill was not prepared for it but he was certainly ready to fight back. "I understand that the letter is not actually yours," Bill pointed out.

"It was in my possession when we met," said Martin Katz. "The next morning I find it is no longer in my possession, but in yours."

"Did you send people to break in here and take it?" Bill asked, refusing to be cowed.

Katz paused. "No I did not," he wheezed. "So, do you agree you have the letter?"

"You left it with me," Bill replied, recognising that somewhere during the last few weeks he had crossed a line. Despite initial denials to various people, Bill Wheeler was now admitting possession. This transition had happened without his noticing how or when, just as a transition had occurred from fighting Tamsin over the London move to a position of accepting the inevitable.

"Ya, ya," said Katz, sounding distinctly German and unwilling to listen to Bill's excuses. "I am in a position to offer you a sum of money for the return of that letter."

"That's exactly what someone else said to me only yesterday."

"Yes, yes," said Katz sounding repugnantly superior. "That is my client, the person on whose behalf I am speaking."

"Really?" said Bill.

"This man was already dealing with me when I spoke to you in Israel," Katz continued before pausing to take in another lungful of air.

"Why did you go to such lengths to interest me in the letter?" Bill asked.

The discomfort in Katz's breathing increased. "You are a journalist, Mr Wheeler. You know the value of a good story."

"But a true story preferably," Bill replied. "As I recall, you told me that if you didn't log into your computer every few days, copies of the letter would be sent to three journalists of whom I was one. That was your 'safety net' as I recall. Was that a fabrication?"

"Mr Wheeler, I don't have time for this," said Katz with distinct irritation. "Are you willing to hand over that letter for a sum of money?"

"How much?" Bill asked.

"That can be discussed."

"Let's discuss it then."

"Am I to take it," Katz asked as if he were ticking the first concession before moving to any others. "Am I to take it that you *are* willing to hand over that letter?"

"Not necessarily," said Bill, digging in his heels. "I want to know who the rightful owner is to start off with, and I want to know how badly he wants it. That's why I want to know how much he's willing to pay. And I'd like to know how you came by that letter in the first place."

Katz wheezed and then said nothing. Behind his silence Bill could hear the distant infinitesimal line noise that accompanies an international call.

"The gentleman who wishes to purchase the letter," Katz began in a delivery so pedantically slow that Bill was able to jump in straight away.

"I thought you said he was the owner."

"Owner, purchaser what is the difference?" said Katz.

"I think you'll find there is quite a big difference if the police get involved," Bill replied.

"This man, he does not wish to be known to you," Katz continued.

"You tell him that that's the deal," Bill insisted. "As you say, I am a journalist. I want to find things out. If he's willing to talk to me then maybe we can do business."

"Not possible," said Katz, now distinctly out of breath. "I am appointed to acquire the letter."

"I think this man is remarkably trusting of you," said Bill. "Given your capacity for untruth, Mr Katz. But I'm afraid I certainly don't want another evening with you. We have an expression over here about preferring the organ-grinder to his monkey." Bill was starting to enjoy this exchange.

"You have cost me money," Katz snarled.

"I suppose I have," said Bill. "Tell your man I'm willing to *give* him the letter providing he'll talk to me. Persuade him to that, Mr Katz, and you can keep whatever money you were told to offer me."

There was another pause on the line. "You will hand the letter over?" Katz checked.

"In person, when I'm convinced that I'm dealing with the Organ Grinder. Don't get any ideas about having someone come along and pretend. I've spoken to Herr Grinder. I'm only giving this letter to the person with that voice."

"Where do you propose this meeting happens?" asked Katz.

"Heathrow," said Bill. "Ring me back."

He came off the phone feeling exhilarated and returned to his e-mail.

Any further with the imponderabilities of Finland? Your Sotheby's catalogue has turned up by the way. I've no idea how. Shall I send it or shall we exchange at Heathrow?

Bill prepared to type.

I have to be at Heathrow to meet Willy's friend and hand over the letter. Could you be there too? You can decide when but I'd like you to be there. I'm sure I'd find handing the letter over much easier if I actually had it!

He felt light-headed. The world was finally beginning to make sense. As long as he forgot that mysterious catalogue next door.

❖ THE DIVINE PLAN

IT WOULD BE AN ODD EXPERIENCE to be waiting at an airport, Bill reflected, as he drove into the short stay car-park. Usually when he pulled up at Heathrow it was to stick the car in long-stay and take a bus over to whichever terminal would whisk him away that day. This time he was a civilian, the meeter, not the met, one face amid those clumps of listless individuals behind the barrier, scanning to see if this time the doors would disgorge someone recognisable. Someone loved, even.

Bill found it hard to imagine Libby in one of the random clusters of trolley-pushers passing left and right. She was too specific. Too much of her own world to belong among the bland and neutral hues of an international arrivals hall.

Walking underground to Terminal 1 Bill fell to wondering how this was all going to go. He needed to get Libby to the cottage. If they made love there again all would be well. At the moment, short of kidnapping *La Bella Dottoressa*, he had no idea how it would happen.

Their e-mails had warmed up this last week. They'd even begun joking with each other again. Libby was finding Finland colder than Maine in February, something she had not imagined possible. Bill had teased her about the thinness of her adoptive Mediterranean blood. She had told him that Hauke was having to rub her feet. He had e-mailed back that he hoped that was all Hauke was rubbing. He'd wondered how Libby would respond to the possessive intent behind that jest but she had not taken up the reference. Bill had been in torment for a while. He did not really imagine Libby was taking solace in *Der Junge Hauke,* but having summoned up this jealous demon, Bill needed her reassurance that she was his and his alone. He had sat for a long time staring at his PC and at Libby's anodyne witterings about temperatures that would freeze the brain of an Inuit, let alone an urban Bostonian like herself. He so wanted to fasten his teeth on her nipple, to hear her gasp with momentary pain. How the hell did he put that in an e-mail? Especially if Gustav was still hacking into their correspondence.

Entering the arrivals hall, Bill failed to be possessed by the possibility of flight, what possessed him was the surge of desire that accompanied any remembrance of Libby's body. What was it about the very idea of her that could have him aching for those limbs? It wasn't just sex. Just sex was what Marika offered. Just sex was something he could cope without quite happily. Had coped without, in fact, since Torcello. Libby was so special.

These feelings had been stoked at the weekend by Libby's account of a sauna that she and Hauke had taken. Her Finnish hosts had insisted that this was the answer if Libby wished to feel warm and refreshed. Bill felt sure she had mentioned this in her e-mail to provoke him. Libby was aware that Bill had travelled in Finland, that he knew how men and women sat naked in saunas together over there. And where was Hauke while all this was going on? Nowhere on either page of the e-mail. Nowhere to be seen. Was he rubbing her steamy feet or beating her buttocks with birch sticks? Bill had clicked reply. *"Please state exact location of Hauke's penis in aforegoing e-mail,"* he typed. Thank God for humour. He deleted in a better frame of mind.

Libby would not be drawn on what would happen when they met up. Bill had told her that he'd arranged a meeting with this friend of Heidi, this employer of the dubious Martin Katz. He'd also written that he assumed she'd want to be there. Maybe they could have dinner afterwards. Libby had said dinner would be nice but she had a connecting flight back to Venice. Bill had told her that connecting flights can always be delayed. Wasn't this relationship more important than a flight?

He had printed out her reply.

> *Dear Bill,*
>
> *Yes it is, but whereas a connecting flight is possible, are we? You know that I want this to work out between us, but aren't we storing up more heartache if we know that it cannot work but continue to pursue that pain in the hope our forebodings are wrong? The heart is wise as well as impulsive. I know in my heart that I love you but I am not sure that we can live together and be happy. If I were, I would tear up my ticket to Venice now. Let us see what happens. I can make no promises.*
>
> *Libby*

She loved him. She admitted it. That was all the answer Bill needed at the moment. He had hoped that curiosity about Heidi's friend would keep Libby at the airport. Now he knew that he could rely on an impulse far more powerful. Bill did not know why she had run away on Torcello but he knew that he must never let her do that again. He had to hold on to her and gradually she would be his.

Things had fallen into place with dreamlike precision. On Sunday Katz had rung to say that his client was willing to meet Bill at Heathrow airport and when Bill suggested the following Thursday afternoon it turned out that there was indeed a flight from Lucerne which got in at 4pm, one hour and ten minutes after Libby was due to arrive from Helsinki. Bill would be able to pick up the letter, ply Libby with a heady draft of his amorous convictions and then the two of them would meet the man who claimed to own the letter that had brought them back together. They might even find out what all the fuss was about.

Katz, with wounded self-importance, had made it clear that his client had business in London that evening, so they would only be able to meet for fifteen minutes. That suited Bill fine. He and Libby would pass an interesting quarter of an hour getting to the bottom of this Wagner business and then it would be time either for her connecting flight or dinner in town. Bill prayed that Katz's man would be late. If he could rely on British Airways being delayed by half an hour, Libby would have to choose between finding out all about the letter or getting back to Venice. Bill knew he could persuade her. He had even checked on room availability at a Hilton in west London with overnight parking for the Jeep.

It had to happen. The gods were smiling on this endeavour, Bill felt. For him to be able to fit Katz's man and Libby together with such synchronicity was an endorsement of what he was setting out to achieve. They were even flying into the same terminal! Bill had set off that morning with a spring in his tyres. Sunshine was being poured on to the Wye Valley, causing a riot of colour to ripple round its steep wooded slopes. God was backing this day. The Almighty had even made it easy for Bill to book the VIP lounge so that this interview could be conducted discreetly. He had never been in the VIP lounge before.

Bill scouted round looking for a monitor to check on arrival times. BA flight from Lucerne was currently still on time. And as for Finnair from Helsinki... As for Bloody Finnair! Bill swore, as God switched off the sunshine. FINNAIR: DELAYED. Bill made his way to the information desk. "How delayed?" he asked in a tone that was trying hard not to attribute blame.

The poor woman did her best and discovered that the incoming plane had been late arriving in Helsinki. How late, she didn't know. Had it even set off for the UK yet? She didn't know that either. Bill sighed heavily. Normally this would be merely tedious but today it was potentially disastrous. He needed time alone with his own Very Important Person before being summoned to the lounge. He also needed that letter!

Bill was tempted to tell the woman what a nuisance this was for him, even how it endangered his reunion with Libby, but what was the point?

In the overall scheme of things, it was genuinely more important that Libby Ziegler landed on time in London than every Finnair headset and blanket were picked up and stowed away. But even if the woman were to telex Helsinki that Bill Wheeler's lovelife hung in the balance, it was hardly likely they would work faster to get that late arrival back in the air.

Bill went to have coffee and do some calculations. If Libby were three quarters of an hour delayed he'd be OK. An hour was cutting it tight. 70 minutes would mean Libby and Katz's friend arriving at the same time. That would be awful. He could only hope that BA 890 from Lucerne suddenly hit a snag. Strong headwinds causing it to miss its window. Maybe the flight controllers would then stack Flight 890 for the necessary half an hour, subjecting Katz's client to pointless aerial vistas of the M25 as he circled London. No. They always gave British Airways priority, Bill thought grumpily. It was carriers like Air Malta and bloody Finnair that had to wait forever in the gloom above Surrey.

His mobile rang. At first he thought this might be the *Dottoressa* with news of her delay, but it only took him a moment to recognise Home Farm's number on the screen. "Dad it's me," said Reah with the simple presumption of an only child.

"Dad, you know I'm coming to you this Friday..."

"Yes." Bill reflected on the fact that children never pause to ask whether they've rung you at an inconvenient time. No time is inconvenient for a parent in the mind of its offspring.

"Only mum's saying she wants me there for boring Shabbat *again*. You know, candles and all that, and I said I'm eating with you this Friday and she says I can go over after and she's sure you won't mind, but I will. There's all sorts of programmes I'll miss and she's only doing it to impress Ben."

"Who's Ben?" asked Bill. He'd already written down the name in his notebook.

"Oh, you know, this guy we went out to lunch with."

"No I don't," said Bill, forming a question mark against the name.

"Oh well, maybe I didn't tell you but he's really dull and very Jewish and Mum wants to impress him. He's coming down on Friday."

"Where from?" Bill asked.

"Dad!" said Reah, as if through gritted teeth. "That's not the point."

"What is the point?" Bill asked her as he underlined the name in his notebook several times.

"The point is, will you talk to Mum and tell her that I don't have to say the blessings tomorrow night?"

"I'll speak to her," said Bill. "But it doesn't take long and it is part of your heritage, love."

"Did I ask to have a heritage?!" Reah exploded. "Please Dad, I don't ask much of you but I don't want to do stupid Shabbat with Ben, not when there's so much on TV that I want to see."

Well, it was debatable that Reah never asked much of him but he promised he'd do his best. "Tell me, this Ben. Where does he live?"

"Like that really makes a difference, Dad."

"Just curious."

"London," said Reah.

"What does he do?"

"No idea," said Reah. "He's a friend of Grandpop's or some family connection. I dunno."

"How old is he?"

"112. Can I go now?"

It was a bit of a shock to think that Tamsin had a visitor in the farmhouse. A man with whom she and Reah had been out to lunch. A man and yet not a boyfriend. Bill assumed that Ben could not be a boyfriend. If he were, Reah would have said. After all, in Venice she'd told Tamsin that Libby was "Dad's girlfriend". And this Ben was 112, wasn't he? A friend of Old Man Walken. Or was that just Reah keen to get off the phone? Ben was probably a family friend come to help Tamsin with some aspect of the move. A family friend who had already been out to lunch with Tamsin and Reah... Forget it, Bill decided. He had two important meetings to think about, one of which was more important than any he'd ever had, or so it felt.

Bill looked at his notepad. Lots of slow circles round the word BEN. Really he'd be better employed working out what he wanted to ask the mystery man on Flight 890. Bill hadn't had a meeting with an anonymous contact since he worked in news. He'd once gone to meet a guy in Croydon who wouldn't give his name, a headcase who believed that dry- roasted peanuts were poisoning the planet. This was different though. Whatever else Mr Katz's client might be, he didn't sound like a headcase. From their one brief conversation it was obvious to Bill that this man wanted only one thing and it wasn't to save the Earth. In exchange for Bill's letter, the guy with the speech impediment was willing to answer some questions. The less a man wants to say to the press the more interesting he must be. It was a variant on Groucho's paradox, Bill surmised. A true journalist is only interested in talking to people who don't want to talk to him.

After ten minutes of caffeine Bill picked up his bag and went to have a look at the screens again. Lucerne was still expected on time. AY389 from Helsinki remained delayed.

"You must have *some* idea," Bill was insisting now. The woman typed a series of inexplicable commands on to the screen that lay between them. For all Bill could tell she was writing '*This man is really getting on my nerves*' over and over again.

"Ah, it left twenty minutes ago," she said with a smile, as if that solved everything.

"And the flight's two hours?" Bill checked.

"That's right."

"So one hour and forty minutes, if we're lucky," said Bill grimly. A delay of a good ninety minutes. Not bad considering the plane had been late in from LHR. Not good considering that BA890 from Lucerne was going to be down in thirty minutes, leaving Bill with no letter to produce for over twenty minutes. If he were lucky.

He was starting to feel uncomfortable. In the hermetically sealed atmosphere of the airport it doesn't take long for unwholesomeness to steal over the weary traveller. Bill felt as though his body were a breeding ground for germs. Time for a walk outside. Pick up some diesel fumes.

The contrast between real air and the stultifying atmosphere of Terminal 1 was invigorating. Bill paced, swinging his arms wondering what to do when he got the call to the VIP lounge. The plan had been that his visitor, who was travelling under the name of Dr Schmidt, would ring him on his mobile. If that failed he'd have Bill tannoyed. Finally, if that didn't work, Bill would make his way to the corporate hospitality desk and ask if there were any messages for him.

He did a few more calculations. Libby and Herr X were currently due to arrive at the same time. Allowing for the fact that her plane might well get stacked, Herr X might be out fifteen minutes ahead. He'd probably have an EU-valid passport and she wouldn't. That might add another five minutes or so to the delay. Plus the fact that Herr X might only have hand luggage and so not have to endure the cyclical tedium of the reclaim hall which Libby would, unless she'd checked her luggage through to Venice. And Bill seriously hoped she hadn't, for reasons that were getting lost under all this timetabling minutiae. Bill exhaled and swore. All in all he was likely to get the summons half an hour ahead of Libby's emergence into Arrivals. Therefore no letter. Somehow the life of Bill Wheeler was no longer matching the divine plan as well as it had this morning.

Ah well, Bill thought to himself, he'll just have to wait. It's not as if Bill were personally responsible for Finnair's late arrival into Helsinki. Hopefully Herr X would be willing to make small-talk ahead of the letter being handed over. "Bet he won't though," Bill muttered to himself. He could foresee a rather frosty time checking watches in the VIP suite.

By the time Bill had wandered back inside, AY389 had finally decided to go public. It was going to be touching-down one hour and forty-five minutes later than scheduled: thirty-five minutes after the good Doktor. "Bugger," Bill said to himself. He was getting bothered about the state of mind in which he'd meet Libby. That was actually what mattered after all. Maybe it was a good thing she wouldn't be touching down alongside the evil Doktor. The last thing Bill wanted was to snatch the letter and then treat her to a virtuoso display of journalistic interview techniques. She needed time to get to like him again.

Maybe if he got that interview out the way first it would be better. Libby knew to ring him on his mobile if he weren't there to meet her. There was nothing to worry about. Bill checked the battery level on his mobile. No, definitely nothing to worry about.

This time Bill did go shopping. Or at least browsing. Of all things he found a biography of Rossini in the bookstore, but nothing on Wagner. The biog had been a number-one best-seller in Pesaro and promised to be sensational. Bill did not believe it for one moment. Rossini lived a happy life and gave up music for celebrity retirement when he realised people no longer cared for his style. He was not dramatic and Wagnerian in outlook but then what Italian could ever take himself quite as seriously as Herr Richard? His clothes as seriously, yes, but not his art. Even Verdi, that angry and embittered old tyrant, achieved a certain self-deprecation with success. Wagner just took himself more and more seriously as the rest of the world joined in with his monumental act of self love. Really he wasn't being fair. Hadn't Wagner once threatened to push Cosima across the town square in a wheelbarrow when she was taking herself too seriously? He had been going to do it too. In Germany, that kind of thing is considered very funny.

The memory of that story about Cosima and Wagner made him smile. What had happened in between Wagner's horsing around and the *Werther Freund* letter in which Cosima refused to embrace him? What had happened to her laughter? What had happened to him and Tamsin for that matter? Bill could remember laughter in the town square too. It was difficult to get a clear image of Tamsin laughing nowadays, but he had known her in so many ways. She was so much more than the hurt, stressed and angry person he seemed to meet now. How had they come to this?

An image. The two of them taking a bottle of champagne on to the roof-garden of some office. His paper, one summer evening. There was a party and they'd both ended up standing in this ornamental pond drinking from champagne glasses. No. Not him and Tamsin? Yes. *Bill and Tamsin.* Her red dress. She had been complaining about the heat so they'd gone outside. It was one of those rare London summers that are not so much hot, as Mediterranean. The girl in the red dress was still hot even out on the roof.

"Take something off," he said. She'd laughed. She always did laugh when he was too obvious. "OK, go for a swim then," he'd said.

"In that pond?!"

It was like a challenge. So he picked her up in his arms and she hit him with her fists. Had he really walked into an ornamental pond with Tamsin Walken in his arms? Had he really, really stood there in the middle, water up to his calves and kissed her? And had she really kissed him back and insisted they had a drink? That's right. Her eyes, bright with the future. She had had a bottle in her hand. They had stood there, the water round their legs, and drunk from two glasses that appeared from nowhere. Did memory supply the glasses or did she?

"I love you," he might have said. No, "I love you," he *did* say.

"I love you," she said too.

Christ, the memory certainly chooses its time. Here he was, about to meet Libby with the intention of persuading her of his undying devotion, and suddenly his memory is making love to Tamsin on some roof-garden. A different woman, in a different century, in a red dress.

What had happened to him and Tamsin? What had happened to Wagner and Cosima? Was it just children? Had little Eva and Siegfried come between the Meister and the Eternal Female, the woman who would sacrifice anything for him? Had it been Reah who had pushed him and Tamsin apart? Little Reah who had intended to keep her silly parents together. Bill could remember Tamsin seizing Reah from him. In his mind they were at that same ornamental pool on the roof, that very same evening.

"You'll kill that child," said Tamsin. Now this was fantasy. Had she ever said those words? He wasn't sure. Had she seized Reah from him? Possibly, but not on the roof of his paper in London and certainly not in that same red dress.

Symbolism, Bill decided. A rare proof that at least part of him worked creatively. Tamsin the woman had loved his bravado on a hot and steamy London night. Tamsin the mother had less time for it, less time for *him*. So what had she wanted of him after Reah's birth? Reah Christabel had been the best thing for Bill Wheeler. The worst for Bill and Tamsin. Why was that? Suddenly they were no longer facing the same future. Maybe that was why Bill had become an arts journalist and met a 27-year-old

American who helped him wreck his marriage.

Why on earth was he having these thoughts? Why was his mind trying to sabotage the grand reconciliation with Libby? Did he still love Tamsin? Of course he still loved Tamsin. Bill was leaning, his head inclined forward, resting against the bookshelves. And she loved him. *Christ.* And Wagner probably still loved the woman he abandoned for Cosima. Minna. Minna Planer, actress. Loved the Meister until her death. A difficult woman but he kept taking her back after all. Loving isn't hard, Bill thought. Living in happiness and harmony, now there's the challenge. He thought of the *vaporetto* taking Libby away from him and of Tamsin walking away in her ridiculously tight skirt and ankle boots and of Cosima refusing to embrace her Richard. So what goes wrong, Herr Meister? With so much love in the world where do we screw up?

His mobile rang. *Guten Tag, Herr Doktor,* thought Bill to himself. He put the Rossini book back. Again it rang. Bill sighed and accepted the call. "Mr Wheeler," said a voice.

I have absolutely no interest in this conversation, thought Bill.

The VIP suite was nowhere near as opulent as some of the airline hospitality lounges Bill had passed through in his time, but it had the advantage of being on his side of passport control. It was well decorated but had an empty feel to it. Whereas business lounges reek of indulgence and fat men on expenses this suite of rooms had the serious aura of an arena for briefings. A hefty man with a key-card unlocked the door for Bill and told the room ahead that he had brought Mr Wheeler. He then held the door open and an immaculate young man proffered Bill a hanger for his coat and asked to put his shoulder bag through a scanner. The young man was formal but not unfriendly. He reminded Bill of the reception staff at Hotel Danieli.

"I'll tell Dr Schmidt you're here," he said when the formalities were complete.

Schmidt, thought Bill. Was this really a ruse, a little joke at the expense of the most basic hotel registration subterfuges or did Martin Katz's client really go by that name? Was there really a Schmidt of Interlaken as Mertens and Clements had claimed? Certainly the man who rose to meet Bill did not look like a joker. He was tall, balding and bony-faced. Bill noticed he was wearing an expensive Burberry overcoat. No one else was in the room.

As Schmidt advanced, Bill took in the plain decor and unremarkable carpeting of his surroundings. A single photograph of the Queen graced these walls. She was looking much younger and remarkably happy about something. The whole place had the air of a British High Commission. Nothing ostentatious, nothing to offend. There were two leather armchairs in front of Bill, and not much else. Until now he had had the idea that entering a VIP lounge would be rather like visiting Madame Tussaud's, full of statesmen, pop idols, actors and athletes. But here it was just Herr Doktor Schmidt, two chairs and Her Maj.

As they shook hands, Mr Katz's employer was already beckoning to the chairs. "Do you have the l-letter?" he stammered. Damn, there wasn't going to be much in the way of small talk.

"It's arriving in 40 minutes. The flight from Helsinki was delayed." Bill waited to see what reaction this information might elicit. Dr Schmidt inclined his head sideways for a moment as if he were registering this delay. Bill waited. There seemed to be no point going into profuse apologies.

"That is unfortunate," said Schmidt without a trace of a stammer this time. His voice was much quieter person-to-person than on the phone and it hadn't exactly been stentorian then.

"The plane should have been in an hour and a half ago," said Bill.

Schmidt sighed. "These things happen," he conceded, looking slowly round the room.

"The letter wasn't supposed to be in Helsinki," Bill added, kicking himself. Suddenly he was sounding amateurish.

"The important thing is that you hand it over," said Schmidt. "I understand that you are willing to do so."

"Yes," said Bill. "Providing that you'll explain its significance to you and Mr Katz."

Schmidt was silent for a moment. He seemed to be making an assessment of the situation, then he inclined his head sideways again. "Mr Katz came by the letter as one does. I believe he bought it. He then offered it, unseen, to me for a sum of money, knowing that I collect such things. It was an absurd sum of money that he was asking." For a moment Schmidt's guard had dropped. He was actually confiding something to Bill. "When I said n-no he attempted to publicise his acquisition of the letter in order to get a better price. He believed that if he could persuade j-j-journalists that its value was sensational I might be willing to pay him more." Schmidt had looked directly at Bill as he stammered over the word 'journalist', but Bill was the one who felt uncomfortable. That word spluttered, each superfluous 'j' a damning accusation. "I believe he may even have told you that his life was in d-danger."

"I didn't believe him," Bill replied. Schmidt inclined his head and smiled politely but he was hardly going to applaud Bill Wheeler for his perspicacity. The subject of Katz seemed to have stalled them. "Someone broke into my cottage and removed a Wagner biography," said Bill. "At the time I took this to be a signal. They were looking for the letter and stole that book as a warning," Schmidt looked up at Bill as if he were just a little mad. "You told me that you had nothing to do with that," Bill prompted. He meant it as a question.

Schmidt understood. "No, I had nothing to do with it, and neither had Mr Katz. Since his return from Israel he has not left Switzerland."

"Could he have arranged it from Switzerland?"

Schmidt's face suggested surprise and distaste in equal measure. He clearly could not imagine the point of this conversation but he stuck by his agreement to answer Bill's questions as best he could. "I'm afraid I do not know how easy it is to employ burglars in this country down a telephone line. I would imagine if it were possible it would be very expensive. This letter is not worth so much money."

"How much money is it worth?" Bill began to ask, but Schmidt leaned forward and interrupted him.

"Mr Wheeler, let me ask you something," he said. "Why do you assume that your burglars took this book as a 'calling card'? Wouldn't it make much more sense – isn't it more normal – to *leave* something as a calling card. After all the house-owner will notice an object which has unexpectedly materialised. He may not notice something that has disappeared. Not for days. If at all." Bill felt taken by surprise. The man was right. And he wasn't leaving it there. "Burgling a house is a dangerous activity. People get arrested. They fall. They get dogs set upon them. Would someone really take that risk just to remove a biography of Richard Wagner?"

"It felt like too much of a coincidence," Bill admitted.

"Not everything that happens is significant. Maybe it fell down the back of a sofa." Schmidt looked quizzically at Bill then lapsed back into silence.

"The couple who came to see me," said Bill. "Who are they?"

"Miss Mertens currently works in my Bristol office," said Schmidt. "When Mr Katz told me that he couldn't produce the letter and where he thought it might be, I asked her to contact you. She telephoned twice, I believe, without getting an answer and then kindly asked me whether I wanted her to visit you. I suggested she took Mr Clements along for protection. I'm very glad she did."

Bill imagined Miss Mertens relating how Bill had pulled a gun on her. Herr Doktor must be a brave man to arrange this meeting. "You don't think they were the..."

"*No*," said Schmidt firmly. "I do not employ people who steal." He glanced at his watch.

"Why do you want this letter?" said Bill, feeling hurried.

Schmidt thought for a moment. "I am a collector."

"Why did you say that you were the owner of the letter when we first spoke?"

"I inherited some letters from an archive," said Schmidt. "When I went through them I found that a certain number were missing. Since that time I have been trying to track down the missing letters."

"How could you tell some letters were missing?" Bill asked.

"I'm not w-willing to say." Dr Schmidt glanced at his watch again. Bill wondered what kind of engineer he was. If he employed staff in a Bristol office he must be fairly successful. He was very clear in his own mind about what he would and would not say and yet Bill felt he had detected a vulnerable streak. But maybe it was just the stammer.

"Had the archive been broken into?" Bill asked, probing. "Had the parcel been tampered with? Or did some packages fail to arrive?"

"I'm not willing to discuss that," said Schmidt, still watching the monitors.

"Are you willing to tell me how you came by the archive?" Bill asked. One question after another.

"As I said, I inherited it," said Schmidt looking back at him.

"Who did it belong to before you?"

"I'm not willing to discuss that."

"Were you given it? Did someone die and leave it to you?"

"I'm afraid I'm not willing to discuss that."

"OK," said Bill, trying not to let it show that he felt woefully under-prepared for this interview. "OK, just tell me this. Why is that letter so important?"

"It is one of the few that are missing and if I have it I am completing my collection."

"OK..." said Bill, wishing like hell that he had something to pull out of the bag, some piece of evidence which would oblige Schmidt to tell him something interesting. "OK. Tell me, did you buy that letter which came up for sale in New York recently."

"No."

"Why not?"

"The reserve price was r-ridiculous," said Schmidt with great diffi-culty. Bill was going to point out that this left Schmidt's collection incomplete but an instinct told him to wait, to let the man talk. "Besides, the *Boston Globe* published it in full on their website before it came up for auction." Schmidt waved a hand. The gesture suggested that this meant the letter was no longer of any worth. Bill found the gesture strange in a way that he could not define, but he saw Schmidt making to move. "I'm afraid I cannot wait for your flight from Helsinki, Mr Wheeler." Schmidt was consulting his watch again. "The time says I must go. I will give you the address of my hotel. Perhaps you would deliver the letter there. I will then arrange for a cheque to cover your expenses."

"We haven't discussed money," said Bill.

Schmidt stood up and handed an envelope to Bill. "This outlines the conditions under which you place yourself in return for the payment of £1,000. I would have asked you to read it before handing over the letter. Read it now. If you agree, bring the letter to my hotel and I will send you a cheque."

"Where are you staying?" Bill asked.

"The Langham Hilton."

This was all happening quicker than Bill wished. He had more questions to ask. He wanted a discussion. He needed Schmidt to sit down again. "Before we finish I'd like to ask you some questions about the person Wagner was writing to–"

"I'm sorry," said Schmidt, looking uncomfortable. "I am not willing to discuss the ar... the ar," Bill could tell that Schmidt was trying to say 'archive' but the word was defeating him. Before Bill could supply it, however, Schmidt had given up. "If you will excuse me." He was on his feet, paused awkwardly, hands in pockets as if he were trying to find something, prior to leaving the room.

Bill stood up too. There seemed to be little chance of getting Schmidt down again. "I don't really care about your money," he said. "I want to understand the significance of that letter."

Schmidt had found what he was looking for now, a piece of paper with what seemed like a telephone number written on it. "I have told you its significance as far as I'm concerned, Mr Wheeler." Was Schmidt looking at Bill over his shoulder. "I assure you anything else you may have heard is conjecture and f-fantasy." Schmidt opened the connecting door and Bill heard him ask the uniformed man to telephone for his driver.

"When I bring the letter round I would like to talk to you again," Bill told him.

"I'm afraid I shall be *out*," Schmidt replied. Bill couldn't see his face so he had no idea how offensive Schmidt intended that remark to sound. It may just have been a statement of fact.

Schmidt turned back to Bill. "Read that contract Mr Wheeler. If you are agreeable leave the letter at Langham Reception for me by ten o'clock tomorrow morning."

"Is that when you're leaving?" Bill asked. Colour flushed into Schmidt's cheeks. "D-do not think of door-stepping me, Mr Wheeler." There was distaste in that look. It was as if Schmidt never wanted to see a journalist called Bill Wheeler ever again.

Bill found himself stepping back, chastened and alarmed. "To whom should I address the envelope?" he asked.

Schmidt looked surprised. "My name is Schmidt. Georg Schmidt."

"Of Interlaken," said Bill.

"That is George but without an 'e'."

After he had gone Bill reflected that Schmidt had not presented a business card, which seemed unusual for a man in his position. Clearly he wanted to limit the extent of contact between them. Bill felt as if he were contagious and Schmidt had been advised to keep his distance. Not a good feeling.

He sat down and opened the contract. It turned out in fact to be a letter in which he, Bill Wheeler, undertook, in exchange for the sum of £1,000, to hand over in good condition a letter written by Richard Wagner that was currently in his possession. No mention was made of how that letter had come into his possession. Paragraph two stated that Bill would not make any reproduction of the letter, would surrender any copies already made, would not quote the letter in any publication, article or broadcast either in part or full. He then had to sign, date and even have the damn thing witnessed.

So that was it. In exchange for £1,000 the *Werther Freund* letter would cease to exist as far as Bill was concerned. He was disappointed by the sum; not that he didn't need £1,000, but Bill wanted the inducement to be big enough to make him feel there was real significance in that letter. A letter currently stacked in a queue of aeroplanes somewhere over Heathrow. He wanted a big story but Schmidt was paying him for his trouble, nothing more. Maybe this had been a wild-goose chase, after all.

"Then again," Bill said to himself as he turned the contract over idly in his hand. "Then again Schmidt is no fool. He knows that the more he offers me the bigger I'm going to think the story is and the less likely I am to part with it."

Some words of Schmidt's came back to Bill. "Mr Katz came by the letter as one does." What exactly did 'As one does' mean? At an antique store? On the blackmarket? Given away with a packet of Swiss nonbiological washing powder? And that other thing that had struck him as strange at the time: Schmidt no longer cared about the New York letter once it had been published.

"Because it leaves his archive incomplete," Bill said aloud to himself "So..." he wished his brain had not been numbed by two hours of air-conditioning and flight announcements. "So the reason Schmidt wants this letter is not to complete his archive. He doesn't care about complet-ing the archive." So what does he care about? Bill wondered. Even wealthy men like Georg Schmidt don't just give away £1,000 to cover a journal-ist's phone bill. What was in it for him?

Bill looked at his watch. He ought to go and see about progress on Libby's flight.

She looked smaller than he remembered. It had been less than two weeks but the Ziegler in Bill's memory must have grown a few inches. Or the real one had shrunk. For a moment the combination of slight build and long hair presented an impression of the teenage Libby, the girl whose father had left her in such a spectacular fashion. Her face was tired though, poor love. And not just from the flight. Every day in her thirties was taking its toll, Bill thought, wishing he could scoop her up and protect.

Libby's eyes found him in the crowd and they lit up. She seemed to grow, almost, as if her whole body regained energy from the recognition. Maybe that poor vulnerable child was Libby without admiration, Bill thought. He moved towards the barrier but it was a bad place to embrace. Her trolley, with its pile of Arctic gear, kept them resolutely apart.

"Welcome to the temperate zone," he said, as they walked in parallel to the end of the barrier.

"I'm sorry to be so late," she told him. "Goddam Finns."

"It was the plane from here arriving late in Helsinki," Bill explained.

"I need to find out about my connection."

God this conversation was going wrong. They had been walking and talking in parallel, making a mess of things.

"There's a plane first thing tomorrow," said Bill, improvising wildly as they came to the end of the cordoned off area and were finally unimpeded. "I've booked us into a hotel and I've got the car outside."

It wasn't what he had intended to say at all. They were going to talk. They were going to eat. He was going to persuade. She was going to be won round. Still it got them off the subject of Finnair delays.

Libby looked up at Bill and for a moment he thought she might upbraid him for his presumption. "Well I could do with a shower," she conceded.

On the drive into London it began to rain heavily. In between the rhythmic swishes of the wipers Bill told Libby about Schmidt and she told him about Helsinki. There was a picture that had come into German hands during World War II but had originally disappeared during the Finnish Civil War. Libby wouldn't name the artist, but it seemed he was a Modernist big-hitter.

Bill quickly grew confused.

"Don't forget the Finns were allied with Germany for part of World War Two," said Libby. "It was a defensive pact because Soviet Russia was threatening their eastern border. In fact, during the Winter War of 1940 the Finns were so successful holding back the Russians that Hitler was encouraged to think he could invade the USSR. Later when the Finns changed sides the Nazis took revenge. Rovaniemi was razed to the ground."

"That's where you've been?" said Bill. The street lamps of London were beginning to whizz past, making it easier to see through the water-swept windscreen.

"Uh-huh. Two inches inside the Arctic Circle. God it felt like it too."

"And this picture," said Bill. "You think you've found it?"

"Oh no, it's definitely found," said Libby.

"So what's the problem?"

"It was more a question of getting permission for the guy who wanted to buy it."

"I thought you were restoring it to its rightful owner," said Bill.

"Sometimes things get given back. Sometimes they're bought. The Finns are very high-minded about these things. The past is a mess, Bill, and they don't want their citizens to be seen to be purchasing looted artworks. It has to be seen as *restoration*."

"So what was your role in all this?"

"Persuasion," said Libby. "Persuasion and freezing my butt off."

"What if your guy hadn't got the best claim to this picture?"

"That's my job," said Libby. "To prove that he had."

"But he's paying you to do that?" Libby nodded.

"So you're not really making a *judgement*, you're acting as an advocate on his behalf."

"So?"

"What if someone else has got a better claim to that picture?"

"Nobody has," said Libby. "That's what I went out there to prove."

"But you prove what your client wants you to prove?"

Libby flashed him a look. "Where's all this going Bill?"

"I just thought you were more of an independent authority."

"Sometimes I am," said Libby. "What's the problem? The fact is this picture has now been catalogued. It exists again. That's great."

"Can people go and see it?" Bill asked.

"Yes, I should think so. If they write asking to visit. It's not a secret. Nothing's a secret in Finland." She turned in her seat to face him. "Bill, previously this was a *non*-picture. It was hidden away, people thought it had been destroyed. Now it exists. I think that's something to celebrate."

"Yes, it is," Bill agreed uncertainly.

"That's the thrill of this job. You see things that no one's seen. Hauke, for instance, he's been shown a book of photographs. I can't tell you any more but I had no idea they existed. No one even knew they'd been taken. They were going to be destroyed, too incriminating, but they've come our way."

"What photos?" Bill asked.

"Maybe one day I'll tell you. The thing is, in this business you have to be so discreet. If someone gets wind of the fact that you're out there blabbing, they might just decide it's easier to destroy what they've got. Like that Canaletto I told you about in Minsk."

"Why does everything you deal with have these problems attached?" he asked.

"Bill, if you think all works of art change hands openly you are naive." They were beginning to decelerate sibilantly through puddles of surface water. Libby noticed Chiswick House on their right. "Just think what happens if someone stole statuary from over there. Do you think the guy puts £200,000 worth of eighteenth-century shepherdesses in his own backyard? No. It gets handed on. In fact a lot of thefts are commissioned. If that stuff's ever going to see the light of day again the whole thing needs to be handled very carefully."

"So you don't just deal with stuff from the War?" Bill asked.

It seemed odd to be passing near where he and Tamsin used to live. Seven years on from those faxes, here she was in the Jeep with him, discussing how thefts from historic houses get fenced around the world.

"Oh stuff is always disappearing," said Libby, and their conversation seemed to come to a halt. In the neutral silence Bill heard Schmidt's curious words coming back to him and he asked her what he might have meant. Libby thought for a moment. "In German it's '*wie es halt so geht*'. I guess he's talking about the fact that once you're collecting and known to be collecting all sorts of people come your way. Sometimes they're crazies, sometimes they've got a serious proposition."

Bill didn't like the idea of Libby being mixed up with the likes of Katz.

Georg Schmidt was all right. Schmidt seemed to have integrity, even if he didn't seem to have much respect for Bill, but bloated vermin like Katz... Bill hated the thought that Libby might be in his sights.

"Have you come across this man Schmidt?" he asked. Libby had shown surprisingly little interest in whom the Baron's friend had turned out to be.

"Don't think so," she replied. "He wasn't around when I did that edition of the letters."

"Where d'you think he would have got his archive from?" Bill asked. They were passing darkly through Hammersmith now. Libby was watching the wipers as they scooped up water and hurled it to either side of the windscreen.

She seemed hypnotised. At first Bill thought she hadn't heard his question at all. Then she shifted back in her seat.

"There are so many ways. Maybe he bought it or found it in some family *schloss* in East Germany once the wall came down. A whole lot of stuff the Stasi had was just thrown into dumpsters. Maybe Schmidt used to work for the secret police and just appropriated it, *wie es halt so geht*."

"Why would the Stasi have Wagner's letters on file?"

Libby was tracing condensation patterns on the passenger window. "They had everything." She yawned. "You have no idea, Bill. Remember Wagner's family came from Leipzig and the whole of Saxony was in the DDR. Maybe the guy who kept his letters, this *Werther Freund*, was a Leipziger. The letters stayed in a box in some attic till the city was bombed during World War II. In the rubble someone rescued them, thought they'd got the family treasure-chest, forced it open with a crowbar late one night and found nothing of value. So he stands up, wipes his hands and is shot by a sniper. Two days later a Russian intelligence officer finds this bundle of papers and takes it back with him. Before he gets round to working on it he's eliminated by his own side as a spy. Stalin's thugs were profligate with human life. All the intelligence officer's stuff was bundled up to be gone through back at HQ. Sits in a shed for three months. The war ends. A conscript who can read is assigned to catalogue what there is, realises this is German and tosses it into a lorry-load of stuff to be sent to Berlin. Total chaos in Berlin. Someone sees a date in the bundle of letters and realises none of this is relevant to tracking down Nazis. As nothing is thrown away in the DDR, it gets piled in a bunker on Normannenstrasse. Forty years pass, not a letter is opened, not a page is read. Maybe the cupboard in which these letters sit is just never unlocked. The Wall comes down. Maybe this bundle gets thrown out when the Stasi are covering their tracks. Maybe no-one knows it's there, not until the *Polizei* go in and start sorting through what's been squirreled away. Someone takes a decision that this stuff is of no interest – no old scores to be settled with a pile of hand-written letters addressed to some *Werther Freund*. Send it to the *Preussisches Geheimes Staatsarchiv*, a museum, absolutely deluged with stuff. They bin it. Or maybe it never gets there. It goes straight from Normannenstrasse into the dumpster outside. Georg Schmidt notices it and decides to start his collection."

"He didn't look like the kind of man who goes round skips," said Bill.

"A lot of people have made a lot of money since the Wall came down," said Libby.

"Nearly there," said Bill, decelerating and turning his attention from Wagner. "I shall be glad to get out of all this."

"Me too," said Libby. "I'm beat."

He didn't like the sound of that.

Bill sat in the window of their hotel room. This place was anonymous. It had two huge double beds and an en-suite bathroom where Libby had gone to shower. There was a small table where one person might eat an overpriced club sandwich, and a pert little leather armchair which Bill was currently occupying.

Libby had wanted the curtains drawn but until she came out of the bathroom, Bill decided he'd enjoy the view. Not that he did. Out there, in every direction he looked, people were living their lives. They might be lost in the darkness, huddling together against the lashing rain, but Bill still couldn't help feeling that the majority of lives in west London were in far less of a mess than his.

He considered that bundle of letters mouldering for more than forty years in an unopened cupboard. It was just a story that Libby had woven, but it felt ghastly. Nightmarishly bleak.

What are you doing? Bill continued to stare down the dark unlit corridors of Normannenstrasse. Are you really wasting your time imagining what it would be like to be a bundle of papers that no one has read for more than forty years? A pile of letters doesn't feel what *we* feel. Assuming it feels anything at all. God would not give human consciousness to something as inert a stack of stationery! You're cracking up, Bill Wheeler.

The Almighty doesn't work in such a vindictive way. He gives to each of us just enough consciousness to make us happy. So why aren't we? Bill thought. Because he also gives us the potential to *wreck* that happiness. God doesn't makes us unhappy. He doesn't need to.

*

The rain fell still. Bill got up and drew the curtains. Libby had been awkward when he'd tried to kiss her on arrival in their room. "I really smell, Bill," she'd said, her hands raised to keep the distance between them. He'd taken it amiss of course, even as he'd tried to reassure her that she smelled wonderful to him. Libby needed space, Bill could tell that.

Tonight wasn't going to be easy. We have the potential, Bill thought, the potential to wreck.

He thought he'd offer Libby a soft drink. By the time he was within an arm's reach of the bathroom door Libby was emerging, a vision in white towelling robe and matching turban. She stepped back in surprise.

"Have you been there all the time?"

"I was just coming to ask if you wanted a drink."

Libby pondered. "Is there wine in the minibar?"

Bill was surprised.

"I feel like a glass of wine," she told him. "White. French. Preferably Loire." Bill laughed. "Chablis would be ideal."

The laughter had made him feel better. "For someone who doesn't, you certainly know what to drink." Bill went to look.

"Just because I don't own a car doesn't mean I don't know what I'd buy if I could," Libby told him.

"And what would that be?"

"Aston Martin." Libby clambered on to the bed. "Two door, leather upholstery. The car has not been made that looks as good with four doors."

"And what about nightclub," said Bill. "Do you know what kind of nightclub you'd frequent?"

"How do you know I don't go to nightclubs?" Libby asked, settling herself, a pillow behind her back.

"I can't imagine you bopping the night away. There's a Tourraine Sauvignon," he added.

"That's Loire. Isn't it?"

Suddenly Bill felt very fond of her. A moment of uncertainty for this overgrown schoolgirl who was also his mistress.

"Yes."

"And as for nightclubs..." Bill looked up at the bed. Libby was enjoying this conversation. "As for nightclubs, I can name you two in Munich that are much better than you'd think and several in Venice. I even know the only decent place in Boston that's not a student dive or gay bar."

"What have you got against gay bars?" Bill asked.

Libby shrugged. "Well, my Dad did leave me for another man. Though Carey's fine now I know him."

"Your father didn't leave you," Bill told her as he uncorked. "A father is always a father." Libby didn't reply. "Here."

She accepted her glass. "Thanks."

Bill started to pour one for himself and was going to propose a toast but Libby had something to say. "I was nearly sixteen. They'd pushed me ahead. I'd be in college in a year." Bill looked at her. He felt there was more. "Well he could have *waited*."

"What happened?" They both took a sip.

"Oh I went back to my grandparents. Everyone thought it was better I stayed with them till I went away and – hey – I never came back. Cheers."

With that Libby suddenly downed her glass. Bill reached for the bottle to refill her.

"Do you want to talk about it?" he asked.

"Just have." Libby wasn't looking at him now. Bill took another sip and was about to suggest they think about food when Libby resumed. "Still, got me to college didn't it? I was the youngest by nine months in my year at Wellesley."

"I bet your father was proud of you," said Bill, thinking of Reah.

"Oh yes, child prodigy," said Libby. "I didn't have much in the way of friends, given the kind of childhood it was, but I had the world at my fingertips, well, ocular receptors. They used to call it a photographic memory but it isn't. It's a facility that's all. I don't forget detail. In some ways it's an aberrant form of intelligence."

"I wish I was even remotely as aberrant," Bill told her.

"Doesn't mean I have great ideas," said Libby. "Just that I can substantiate them with data. Half the time I wish I could forget some of the things I know."

"You are amazing," said Bill, the wine helping him recall how amorous Libby made him feel. He slid a hand inside her robe and saw Libby fight her reaction down. "What?" he asked.

"Your hand's cold," she said, taking another gulp of her wine. "Here." She took his hand and moved it up until he cupped a breast. Bill moved to kiss Libby. Her glass was between them. She downed what remained in one go and then kissed him back. Bill tasted her wine flowing into his mouth. "Well then," she said, seizing hold of his belt.

Later that evening they skeetered through the rain and dove into the first restaurant on the Edgware Road, an Italian.

"Bloody hell," said Bill as water cascaded from their coats on to the inadequate matting of the lobby.

Libby nuzzled into his shoulder. "You're not still mad?" she asked. Bill said no, he understood, but the need to get away from that hotel had been his. Regardless of the weather he didn't want Room Service tonight. He'd needed out. "Now that I'm not taking anything, I'm just not so relaxed about penetration," Libby told him, not for the first time. "And that makes it difficult."

"It's fine," he said, but he still didn't understand. He had provided condoms but Libby seemed not to trust them anymore. "You have more chance of being eaten by a shark tonight than getting pregnant with a condom," he'd told her.

"Plenty of people get eaten by sharks," Libby argued.

"Not in West London they don't."

He had tried to make light of it. Bill knew he had to be kind. He had to abandon his expectations about their love-making in the hope that this, whatever *this* was, would pass. They had managed something in that hotel room but it had seemed crudely sexual and sadly separate. At the centre of his being, Bill had felt very alone when he climaxed and Libby had not lingered fondly like she normally did.

"*Food*," she had said, moving back to the bathroom.

Now Libby was looking at the wine list. She asked for a Petit Chablis.

"This isn't like you," said Bill when finally the bottle was being poured.

"It's a lot more like Chablis, though," said Libby, taking a swig. "Sauvignon's too subtle for my palate. I guess I've never educated my olfactories."

"Nice to know there's a bit of you that's still in need of education."

"Bill, you have *no* idea," said Libby with a heavy significance that was probably entirely random and the result of her rushed intake of wine. This new Libby was much more skittish than any he had seen before.

They talked about his meeting with Schmidt. "Do you think I should hand the letter over?" Bill asked.

"I don't know," she replied. "Depends if you need £1,000, otherwise I don't see what's in it for you. You sign up to some deal where you can't even keep a photocopy and still you don't get your questions answered."

"No, I don't really see what's in it for me," said Bill.

"He just thinks you're some jerk of a journalist on the make. He's basically giving you a bit more cash than you'd get if you wrote it up as a story." Bill didn't like her casual alliteration. "I mean come on," said Libby, her hand-gestures extravagant. "What are you actually in this for?"

"In *what* for?"

346

"In this whole letter-business for. I mean is it death and glory or a good story – or a fast puck? I mean *buck*." Bill was beginning to think Libby had had enough.

"I want to know the truth."

"Don't give him back the letter then," Libby said with telling simplicity. "Jeez! I feel hungry." She gazed around the restaurant in the vain hope of hastening on her main course.

"It's the wine," said Bill. "It stimulates gastric juices. Your stomach's raring to digest, and wants to know where all this food is that it's heard so much about."

"I've had too much," said Libby. "Two glasses on an empty stomach."

"Three."

"Can you order us some *water*?" Libby appealed to him extravagantly, as if it would be the greatest favour.

"Why are you drinking tonight?" Bill asked.

"No reason," she replied, then she reached out and took his hand. It was not the kind of gesture Bill associated with Libby. There was even an engaging clumsiness about it. "Bill do you think you can cope? Really?"

"With what?"

"*Without*," she said, her face full of compassion. "Without penetration, Bill." Her diction was clearer than he would have liked in a restaurant full of people. Bill wished she'd stop mentioning it, and assured her there was no problem, as long as this wasn't a long term phenomenon.

"Only I know how important penetration is to you," she insisted.

Now he was embarrassed. "Libby."

"What?"

"You're speaking too loud."

Libby looked across at the nearest table. "Sorry," she said, and she leaned forwards to whisper. "Only I wish I weren't doing-ing this to you."

"You're not doing anything," said Bill. Libby looked at him with exaggerated feeling. "Do you really think I'm some jerk of a journalist on the make?" he asked.

"No," she said. "I think you're a Wonderful Man." She looked so sad, no longer the wild child of their early days in London nor the teenager he'd taken her for at Heathrow but a woman older than she used to be. Someone who had not found happiness.

He wanted to change the subject. "Why do you think Schmidt wants all these letters?"

"Oh people are very strange," said Libby as the water arrived. "I know a man who bought up clothes that Maria Callas had never worn. She'd never taken them out of the box in fact. Never tried them on in the store. They'd been made up for her, delivered to her apartment and stacked away in a closet. Never opened. Seals still in place. Those clothes that Callas never saw were last viewed forty years ago by a seamstress in Paris. This guy has the complete collection. Nothing that she's actually worn, you understand. Just unopened boxes from the couture house. Once he was offered a dress she wore. To Onassis' birthday, I think. *Not interested.* But when he heard there was an unopened box in the London premises of this couturier he went berserk. *Unopened!*" she reminded Bill unnecessarily. "He got the next flight over, virtually camped on the doorstep until they let him buy it. Sent two telegrams saying on no account open it. He couldn't bear the thought of sharing that bit of Callas. Even with Callas! Collecting is not a rational activity, Bill. The strangest people do it – most of them men – and it's pointless trying to work out why. Look at *Citizen Kane* where they try to bolt on cod-Freudian analysis to explain why Kane filled Xanadu with all that stuff. Spoils the film. There is no Rosebud. There is no answer. People do because they do."

"What's he going to do with his collection though?"

"Ask him."

"He won't talk to me. Remember?"

"Gloat probably." Libby grinned at Bill over her glass. "The collector has something that no one else has. There are people who collect to make money but they're only acquiring stock – like your man Katz. The true collector wants it for himself and part of the joy of that is knowing that no one else will ever see what you have."

"Like your man in Helsinki," said Bill.

"Maybe."

"No one's ever going to see that painting are they?" Bill asked. He was suddenly sure.

Libby looked at him. She realised that Bill had scored a point here and didn't like it. "Why are you so antagonistic about my work?" she asked and suddenly she seemed sober again.

Bill hadn't meant to provoke an argument. His insight had surprised him as much as it had Libby. The waiter arrived.

"I'm sorry," said Bill.

"*Prosciutto,*" said the waiter.

Later, when they dashed back up Edgware Road and the rain was being hurled down upon them with positive malice, Bill and Libby had to take refuge in a shop doorway. Huddled together he told Libby that he loved her and that he would do everything he could to make sure they had a life together. He had wanted to say it over their meal but it had taken a while for the two of them to recover from that spat about her work.

Libby held on to Bill and shivered in the night air. "How can I live here, Bill? It's so goddam cold and wet."

"It isn't normally like this," said Bill. "This isn't real. This is Storm Force 80, care of Hollywood. Besides, I'll put central heating in the cottage." She didn't reply. "I love you Libby." The rain on Edgware Road took no notice of his protestations. Bill heard a few cars battling their way through the sea of surface-water but nothing from her. He noticed she was looking down, thinking. "What?" he asked.

"What about my work, Bill?" Libby asked the ground at his feet. Then she gazed up at him, full face. "Do I have to give that up to live with you?"

"No. Of course not." He held her tightly.

"And what about Reah?"

"What about her?"

"Do I have to go into hiding when she comes down to stay?"

Bill laughed. "Of course you don't have to... she's going to like you, given time." Libby snuggled into Bill's embrace and said something into his coat. "What's that?" Bill asked.

"I said I love you too, Bill Wheeler." Bill tried to kiss Libby but only got an ear.

Back in their room Bill and Libby had the unusual experience of undressing in front of each other. Up until now they had always tugged at each other's clothes.

"Which bed do you fancy?" Bill asked, trying to lighten the mood. "I could ask Room Service to bring up a few more if you like. I'm sure we could squeeze in another."

Libby came out of the bathroom and slipped out of her underwear. Her body never ceased to arouse him. She was already inside the bed on which they'd tried to make love a few hours ago. Bill joined her as quickly as he could.

"Could we have some more wine?" Libby asked as he settled himself alongside her. Bill was surprised. He was about to make some joke about her burgeoning addiction when the connection became obvious.

"*Why?*" He didn't want her to hide like this.

"I want to be intimate with you," Libby admitted "But I know my personality too well. This is awful I know, but I really can't manage penetration unless I have wine."

"You haven't needed it before," said Bill.

"I know," said Libby. "That was then, this is now. I hate it when this happens. Hell, I thought a drink would help."

"When what happens?" Bill asked. "I mean is this something emotional or sexual or medical? I don't understand."

"Will you put your arm round me?" said Libby, curling up against him. "I just get a sort of holy terror. This same thing happened with The Other Man. Not so soon, but after a while. We tried to pretend it wasn't happening but things never got any better. I don't want that to happen to us, Bill. If there still is an Us after tonight."

"But if I wear something..." said Bill.

"No, it's just penetration. I simply can't have a penis inside me."

Bill was so glad they weren't still in the restaurant. "Do you know why?"

"I've been trying to understand while I was away in Helsinki. I thought it was just with *him* but I think it's a commitment thing. When I go for someone as I did for him, as I did for you, I hold nothing back. Something throws me forward. Remember that knife in your cottage? I so much wanted you to put that inside me. I felt at that moment as though there was nothing you could ask of me that I wouldn't do."

"Have you ever done that?" Bill asked. "With the knife?"

"I tried it once before, I couldn't."

"You shouldn't," he said. "It's dangerous."

"I just wanted to completely subjugate myself to you," said Libby. "It was the same with him. Do you think I'm weird?"

"No," said Bill.

"One night at your cottage I woke up and you were asleep and I imagined you dying. You know Cosima threw herself on top of Wagner's coffin and didn't move, eat or sleep for three days? I know how she felt. I knew it then, Bill. What I actually thought though was I'd kill myself if you died. That's what reminded me of the knife. I'd eviscerate myself. It's the quickest method. It's certain."

"You even know the best kind of suicide." Bill squeezed her shoulder.

"The trouble is that when there are problems – like in Venice – my body panics. I'm just so far in I... I can't cool down, I freeze up. With The Other Man, I knew it was important for his work that we continue to make love so I tried. I really tried, but it got worse and worse. In the end I just couldn't have him come near me. I kept hoping something would happen, something would unlock me but it only got worse."

"Is that why you continued to take the Pill while you were with him?" Bill asked.

Libby nodded. "I kept hoping there'd be this breakthrough. I tried everything. That's when I discovered wine," she smiled ruefully. "But too much makes me feel sick. It had to be something French. I can't abide Qualitats anymore."

Bill laughed despite himself.

"The awful thing is I so wanted him inside me," Libby continued with a childlike lack of tact. "I so wanted it for him. It was very important for him, Bill. You don't understand, he's – well I don't want to go into what he does, you're bound to know of him – but really he was *such* a penetration person. You have no idea. It was as if when he wasn't inside me, all his creativity left him. I tried, I really did. He was working on this major work. Something so beautiful, so important, and I knew that if I did manage to put him off – I used to try and fake periods, I had so many. Can you imagine that? – you see, I knew if he knew I didn't want to he'd be so demoralised. He was. Bill. I could see his work suffering. Right in front of me. I tried. I tried *so* hard."

"You poor thing," said Bill, stroking her hair, partly out of compassion, partly because he was stunned and not really aware of what he was doing.

"So when I realised the same thing was happening again –"

"When did you realise?" Bill asked.

"As soon as I left Venice. I just knew that I'd lost it. Not love. I didn't stop loving you but, well to put it crudely Bill, I found I wasn't wet at the thought of you anymore. It's not you," Libby ploughed on relentlessly. "It's me and I don't know why. As soon as I feel things going wrong. Anyway, tonight when I got into bed I decided I had to tell you. We can deal with this together can't we?"

"Sure," said Bill.

Libby tucked herself closer to him. "I feel better already. What was so awful with The Other Man was that I kept inventing excuses. I couldn't bring myself to ask him to accept this. I think in the end I upset him more by not telling him the truth."

Bill had never imagined this.

"Do you still want to make love to me after this?" Libby was asking.

"Of course I do," said Bill, though he wondered how.

"Breasts are fine," she said, peeling back the sheet. "In fact they miss you."

"I miss them too," said Bill.

Later that night Bill lay and watched the silence of the ceiling. Libby slept curled in a ball, facing away from him. Occasional clanks and vibrations in distant elevator-shafts spoke of life continuing in the dark hotel night.

Life seemed to be a darkness to Bill, an unlit corridor down which we walk alone. Every so often there may be a pool of light to brighten our darkness. A moment of happiness. But then we pass on, slower each time, dragging the weight of regret behind us. He was so tired. And yet he did not sleep. When would he stop? When would he be able to take time out of time, to rest and find peace? A long way behind him was a marriage that wasn't so bad. Yet he had wrecked it, hadn't he? Why had he and Tamsin turned to hating? And now here was this woman, this beautiful stranger with whom even more things had gone wrong. Only with Reah had life ever run smoothly, and now even that happiness hung in the balance.

Bill thought of Schmidt in his hotel room. Not of Schmidt's surprise when he checked out in the morning to find that sexual dysfunction in the Hilton equalled no letter at the Langham. No, he was imagining the calm and ordered life of Herr Doktor S. The life of a man who writes down what he wants and leaves you to decide whether or not you'll provide. A man who names the price he is willing to pay. What a great way to live a life. No surprises. No emotions. No, Herr Doktor Georg had found a way to deal painlessly with existence. Only with inanimate objects could you ever get the complete set. They were out there. Locked in some cupboard down in the basement of Thingiestrasse.

Bill sat up suddenly and sought for his notebook. Hurriedly he clicked on the bedside lamp. There was something buzzing in his head and he was sure it was just about within reach. Libby didn't stir. Bill picked up his pen and lifted up his knees to provide a bookrest. He slipped the band from his note-book. That blasted contract of Schmidt's fell out and slithered away over the duvet and on to the floor.

"*Why does Schmidt want to buy my letter?*" Bill wrote.

   (1) So he can complete his collection?

Bill crossed this out and wrote by the side of it:

   No. He cannot be concerned to complete his collection else he would have bought the New York letter when that was offered to him.

   (2) So he can learn what is in it? Is the commodity Schmidt collects knowledge? Does he want to know what no one else knows? Is he like that guy in Finland who has the Picasso or Braque no one will ever view or the freak in Paris who knows that no one else has ever seen what's inside Callas' box??

It certainly made sense. And it would explain why Schmidt didn't want the New York letter once it had been published. It was no longer information to which only he could be privy.

> *BUT, he is still privy to special information because if he has the rest of the letters he knows things about that New York letter – and my letter – which others will never know, because he'll understand the context. He may know who S—— is, and all that led up to the emotional crisis over Lusch. If Schmidt wants control over the story he'd still want the New York letter so that the whole story is his and his alone.*

Bill was moving towards his idea. It was there, it was there. If he just kept on writing he'd have it.

> *Surely the idea that someone else owns a fragment of the story would be anathema to him. He'd want it all in his greedy little hands. So why does he want my letter then but not the New York letter?*

Bill thought about the contract which now lay in its envelope on the carpet below him.

> *Not because he wants the story to himself. No. He wants to suppress the story.*

Bill looked at those words. Then picked up his pen again:

> *That is why he'll pay for my part of the story but not the part which was published in New York. That letter is already in the public domain. What Schmidt is doing is using his money to keep as much of this story as is possible out of the public domain. So what is the story that Schmidt wants to suppress?*

Bill paused for a moment, then continued as the fever grew in him.

> *And why does he want to suppress it?*

He underlined the word 'why' several times. An instinct told him that if he could find the answer to one of those questions he would probably have the answer to both.

Maybe the Almighty's day plan had included Bill Wheeler after all.

❖ A COLD AND HOSTILE PLACE

LIBBY WOKE IN THE NIGHT to see Bill engrossed at a table near the window. She watched him, flicking slowly through his notebook. That notebook, the one in which he had betrayed her. Page after page. Silent and unobserved, she remembered how she used to watch her father, the same quizzical look on his face. Suddenly she felt such tenderness for Bill. His seriousness made him seem vulnerable. Always had. Now she noticed he didn't seem to be wearing anything. He must be cold, she thought.

"Come to bed," Libby said, stretching out a hand across the duvet. He glanced up and smiled, this man. His face, arrested in introspection, looked careworn. Not young and godlike as it did when they made love. She remembered when she had first met him, the father who was also her child.

"I think I'm on to something," he said, coming over, still holding his notebook. Surely he was cold? He must be. Libby made space in the bed. Bill sat down, talking all the while. She wrapped the duvet round his waist and felt the strength in his body.

"Listen to this." He was telling her that he was sure that any understanding of the letters' significance must lie not in Schmidt's desire to possess, but in his wish to conceal.

Libby was soon ahead of Bill. She knew where this was going before he finished. Her mind was quicker than his but she was impressed nevertheless. He had found the answer. She was used to the manifold and curious motives of people who traded in this netherworld, but Bill was working it out from first principles. And he had seen what she had not even thought to look for. How she wanted him at this moment.

"So it is like Katz said, there is something that's dynamite in that letter but I don't think it's the anti-Semitic doggerel," said Bill. He had his hands on her shoulders now. He had turned from his notebook and was gripping her quite tightly.

Libby felt a thrill; it was as if he wanted to force the answer out of her. She would never tire of men who blazed, men whose eyes were dangerous because an idea or an image had possessed them. Ideas were her passion and yet she could only ever weigh them. They could never set her on fire as they did these men.

"I'm going to fax Schmidt now," Bill was saying. "I'm going to write him a letter and make sure they put the damn thing under his door tonight!" He laughed. She laughed, both of them caught up in the moment. "He can have that blessed letter as long as he tells me why he wants no one to read it. That's all I want. He can keep his money. I know his intentions and I won't stand in his way. I just want to *know*."

He paused. There was something in Libby's eyes that made him kiss her at that moment. And then kiss her again. Soon he had forgotten completely that he had a fax to send. He so wanted her. And she him. Oh yes, she wanted him. Libby felt the desire swell in her to a point of desperation. Then they seemed thrown together by some compulsion that exceeded anything Bill had known before with Libby. Her eyes. They overwhelmed him. How could he ever live without her? That was his last thought before he plunged forward and surrendered to her utterly. Bill lost himself completely. An energy arose in him and flashed through him. He was aware of a brilliance. Of light that was everywhere, within him and without. And then he was spent. Utterly. He ceased to be and with him everything that had ever hurt him also ceased.

When Bill returned to existence he felt wonderful, as if everything in his body had been brought back into perfect alignment. Such inner harmony made it seem unlikely that he'd ever wish to move again. "I love you," he said to the ceiling. Those seemed the only words that existed, the only syllables that belonged in this new world order.

"We both climaxed," said Libby softly. She was cradling him in her arms and looked like a child, an angel of sudden tenderness. What had happened?

"I want to die," said Bill, laughing quietly. "*Now*." He could feel himself slipping into the most perfect sleep.

"Do you really love me?" Libby asked.

"Completely," he said. He did. At this moment it was impossible to love any other way. The world only consisted of one place, one emotion, one couple. Bill and Libby. They had no complex history. They simply were.

"I took one hell of a risk," said Libby. "I didn't think until it was too late." She was sounding almost dreamy too. He could have floated away on her voice. "I don't know why. I just went for it. I've never done that before. Ever."

Bill could feel a cold slow squeeze of shock on his otherwise warm and open heart. "Oh God, you mean..." he said, gazing into her eyes. Was anyone ever so beautiful? These eyes did not hold the future like Tamsin's. Their openness held only the present. No history. The eternal present of

Bill and Libby. She had given herself more to him than he had realised.

"I don't care," said Libby, gazing at the ceiling. She seemed almost mystic about all this. Not like her at all.

"Look, if you are..." said Bill

"It will be a wonderful child," she said, but she looked back to check with him.

"Yes," he said, trying to smile at the thought that he may have just made her pregnant. "I would like you to have my child," said Bill. More words over which he had no control. These words existed outside him; they wished to be said, and so he let them. He felt himself slipping back towards perfect peace.

"I've only just stopped taking it," said Libby. It's not really likely..."

Not yet, please, thought Bill.

"Bill?" she was speaking.

"Mm?"

"Would you really make me pregnant?" Her voice was so quiet now. He could hardly hear her.

"Whenever."

"And will you love me forever?"

"Anything."

"Always?"

But he was already asleep.

Inside herself Libby tried to settle. She had done it. She had given herself so completely it could destroy her. She wanted it to destroy her. Surely now that she had committed herself so far there was no going back? Yet she had to look at him again. She had to be sure of him, this man. She had taken such a risk.

Bill was sleeping. Libby wanted to sleep too but already the voices inside her were sinister with calculation. How long after ceasing to take oral contraception did a woman's body return to its normal fertility?

But I love him... And she had been taking it for several years now, hadn't she? And this was a safe time anyway, wasn't it?

Love him so... She couldn't remember.

Suddenly she knew the fear again, a small worm in the pit of her stomach. It had crystallised, cold and abrupt. The tiniest evil growing into the possibility of abandonment. No matter what you do it remains, a small cluster of cancerous doubts. It only takes one cell but they grow, these cells. After all, this was just a man who thought he loved her. He wasn't a god. She wanted to believe him but always she knew these men better than they knew themselves. She was shaking.

*

Bill awoke to hear Libby in the shower. He seemed to have slept forever. When he looked at his watch indeed he had. It was 10.15. Hell! *Schmidt.* Bill didn't want to get out of bed: he knew when he did that he'd never return to such peace. But he had to get up. He needed to find his mobile and switch it on. Georg Schmidt would have checked out but maybe he would call Bill en route to the airport.

Bill went into the bathroom. Libby was crouched down in the bath showering with the attachment, her hair held in a cheap complimentary cap. She glanced up at him.

"Hi," said Bill. Libby stood up and smiled back. It was a smile with a question mark at the end of it. "What do I say after last night?" asked Bill. "That was just..." he lifted his hands to indicate that words failed him, while his eyes followed the rivulets of water down Libby's body and saw them come to rest briefly on the swelling of her stomach. He hadn't noticed before but she was slightly rounded there, a mature curve on her otherwise schoolgirl figure. The idea of making Libby pregnant resonated within him. He might watch her grow with his child.

Libby held out a hand in the silence, and Bill stepped into the bathtub, seating himself on the edge. He placed his head against her abdomen and the water from her breasts ran down through his hair. "Will you marry me?" he asked. Libby squatted down to look at him.

"Why d'you ask me that?"

"Because then I'll know that whenever I wake up you'll be showering next-door. It's the sound I want to hear for the rest of my life."

He saw Libby looking down at him, intensely. Water ran noisily through that silence.

"How do I know you'll still mean it in three months' time? Three years' time?"

"I mean it now when you're wearing a shower cap," said Bill.

Libby smiled at him but she still seemed to be seeking something in his eyes. "I have such doubts."

"You were married before."

"My mind tells me that marriage is impossible."

"Schopenhauer," said Bill.

"Schopenhauer lived with a poodle," said Libby. Then she laughed "Oh God, I don't want to end my days with only a pooch for company, Bill!" Now they both laughed.

"Is that a Yes then?"

"It's an 'I don't know.'"

"Look," said Bill. "Last night. You said you'd had this problem before and it never went away with Him. Well, look what happened with us."

"I know," said Libby.

"That was the best sex since written records began. And before then everything was oral."

"I know," she said. "Something in me opened up. And I don't just mean that," she added, noticing where Bill was kissing her.

"Marry me then." Bill could see Libby looking at him. Damn, she wants certainty, thought Bill. There is no certainty. Only love.

"Will you ask me again?" Libby said. "On Torcello." He loved the idea. "We'll go to Venice today," she said. "Hauke can meet us at the airport and we'll get the *vaporetto* over tonight. There's a place to stay by the basilica."

"I don't want Hauke coming," said Bill. Libby laughed.

"He could give me away!" Then she was solemn again. "No one gives me away, Bill. If I do give myself away then it is of my own volition. Wholly and without question."

Bill's mobile began to ring in the next room.

"That'll be Schmidt," said Bill. "I never sent that fax!" He shrugged. They laughed. They laughed so easily.

"I don't suppose anyone has ever turned him down before," said Libby. He kissed her and then asked her to stand up again.

"I love you," he said, his mouth against the rounded warmth of her stomach.

Bill's phone had stopped ringing by the time he got to it in a swathe of towel. He lay on the bed and pressed Last Ten Calls Received. To his surprise that call had not been from Schmidt's mobile nor the Langham Hotel. It was from Bill's messaging service.

"Dad, it's me. I've rung you twice this morning and I've got to go to school now." Reah did not sound at all happy. This time Bill felt it was genuine. "Mum and I had this really big row last night. She accused me of turning my back on my culture and I said that half my culture wasn't Jewish and that you wanted me to spend all of this Friday night with you. And..." Reah seemed to be at a loss for words. "And you said you were going to ring her about tonight and she says you didn't and, like..."

Bill felt his stomach turn. This wasn't Reah manipulating Silly Daddy with her pouts and sulks. She really was upset.

"Like... I really don't ask things of you, well maybe I do ask things of you, but this was really important, Dad. You said you'd do it and. Oh... I've got to go for the bus now. Dad I don't even know where you are."

Bill lay back on the pillow. He felt awful. He switched the phone to dial and tried Holt's Farm. It rang but there was no answer. Libby came in wearing a towelling robe, her hair snaking down darkly over its dense white collar. "Hi," she said, stretching out alongside him and sliding her hand up his leg. "What's the matter?"

"It wasn't Schmidt. I've got problems at home."

"What kind of problems?" she asked, for problems were something they shared now.

Bill wondered how he was going to deal with this. He sat up and put his hands on her shoulders. "Libby. Can we leave Venice till Sunday?"

"Why?"

"Come down with me to the cottage today. We'll spend tonight and tomorrow there and then go straight off to Venice Sunday morning."

"Why?" Libby asked again, only this time she felt more confused and less compassionate. She could hear her own voice getting thinner and harder.

"I promised Reah–" Bill began but Libby was already getting up.

"Oh God, not again!"

"What d'you mean?" he asked.

"I must be crazy!" said Libby. To Bill's surprise she walked over to her case and began stuffing things in. "I must be *totally* crazy to be involved with you."

"It's just two days," said Bill. "Two days against a whole lifetime–"

"It's not two days, Bill," shouted Libby, wiping away the angry strands of hair from where they had slicked across her face. "It's a whole lifetime of always coming second to your daughter."

"But I promised her–"

"What? One night with me and then whatever happens, however much you and I want to spend the rest of our lives together, you're back down that goddam motorway, tail between your legs, just because Reah orders you back! Was that the plan, Bill?!"

"It isn't like that; besides, I'm taking you with me. She has to accept you now."

"I am an *afterthought*!" yelled Libby. Bill had never seen her like this before. "Up until now you weren't thinking of taking me down there at all. You hadn't decided now was the time Tamsin and Reah recognised our relationship. Oh no, you were all for going off to Venice until Reah pulled you back."

"She's my daughter," Bill insisted. "There are things I owe her. I represent a certain kind of stability in her life."

"She twists you round her finger, Bill!"

"She isn't like that!" He was on his feet. Libby had no right to criticise Reah.

"She knows you feel guilty and she uses that."

"Leave Reah out of this," he snapped.

"I wish we could! I wish you and I could have a chance for once. Seven years ago you sent me that dreadful, *dreadful* fax, telling me that we couldn't meet again because of Reah, and here we are, seven years later, back in London and back with bloody Reah! God, I hate London," said Libby, gathering up more clothes and heading to the bathroom. Why did I ever come back here!"

Bill moved to intercept her. "Libby stop this."

"No more, Bill."

"You have to understand," he grabbed her by the arm. "*Libby*, it's just now. She's at a vulnerable age. I know she can accept you. I want her to accept you. I want you to be an influence on her life. Let me just make the transition easier for her. Your father left you, you know what it's like."

"My father left me and I had to get on with my life. Maybe he taught me a useful lesson!" snapped Libby. "Maybe I learned something about standing on my own two feet."

"She's thirteen for godsake," said Bill.

"I was ten when my parents split up." Libby was glaring at him. "And fifteen when he walked out of my life completely. I didn't see him for eighteen months! You're not doing that. All you're saying is 'Sorry, baby, this weekend something's come up. I love you but for once you're going to have to come second.'"

"But..."

"And d'you know what?" Libby continued. "D'you know *what*? I wish he'd just walked out when I was ten and not come back like he did. I wish he'd kept his tears and his guilt to himself. D'you think it did me any good having those years – *years* – of trying to manage him?" Libby turned away as if she couldn't bear another word.

"You don't understand, love. With Reah–"

"Oh for Christ's sake why don't you fuck Reah and be done with it!"

The shock brought silence and momentary numbness, then something truly frightening. Before Bill knew what was happening someone was shouting and he could hear Libby cry out in terror. Something he'd done must've frightened her. He saw her hurl herself into the bathroom and lock the door. Bill ran to the door and hammered on it.

"Libby!" He shouted her name over and over. At one point he even kicked the door. Eventually he sank down next to it and rested his back against its highly polished surface. He placed his right hand on the door jamb. The wood had been lacquered to a point where its smoothness felt almost moist to the touch. "*Libby*," he said.

"Don't hit me Bill."

"I wouldn't hit you." What was she talking about?

"I can't take being hit."

"I wouldn't hit you," said Bill. He couldn't believe what she was saying. "*I saw it in your eyes.*"

Bill dropped Libby at Heathrow. They'd passed several trees blown down in last night's gale and a car that had been crushed by a billboard. Yet again the sky, after its nocturnal rage, was wonderfully, painfully blue.

"Please don't give up on us," Bill said to Libby. White clouds rolled by at speed and sunlight dazzled on the windscreen. "I love you," he said.

"Loving's the easy part," Libby replied.

"Do you love me?" he asked. She refused to answer. "But that's not enough? Is that it?" he asked.

"I love you Bill. I loved you seven years ago. I suffered then. I'm not going through that again."

"You can't just tear up last night," he said, but Libby had already opened the door. "Or this morning, Libby–" He reached for her hand.

The car behind was getting impatient. Libby had asked Bill just to drop her at the terminal rather than park and see her off. She didn't even know when her flight was. She just wanted to get beyond passport control as soon as possible.

"If I write to you will you write back? We need to arrange something about that Sotheby catalogue."

"Sure." She was getting out already.

"I wanted to give it to you at the cottage. I was going to surprise you–"

"Look Bill, you're leaving me and going down to your wife and daughter." Libby took a breath. "Will you just go please."

It was the worst drive he had ever undertaken. The M4 had always represented pain as far as Bill was concerned. He had driven Tamsin down it when she wanted to find them somewhere new to live, in the dreadful aftermath of that heady summer of faxes, phone-calls and unrequited love. He had also driven along it during the difficult time when they were sharing Holt's Farm together, after Tamsin had found that farewell fax to Libby. The evenings when they would end up screaming at each other and little Reah would try and stop them being silly and he would drive out long into the night.

Once he drove all the way to London and parked in the road where Libby had lived. He'd never been to her flat. She had never invited him there, but that night he'd parked in the road and looked for her ghost, torturing himself with the fantasy that she too might be visiting NW5 on a similarly bizarre nocturnal pilgrimage from wherever she had flown after he'd sent that fax of farewell.

And in the years that followed he had often driven down the M4 to board planes. Many planes. Planes that would take him away, take him anywhere, during the days when Tamsin and Reah lived at the farm and Bill could not endure the loneliness of Holt's Cottage without his daughter. That was when he'd first started working for Louis. "Is there anywhere you won't go Bill? Anyone would think you had an aversion to Britain."

And he'd driven down this blasted road when he'd left Reah with Tamsin in London after returning from Venice. It was only a matter of time now before this motorway would take on its cruellest aspect ever: the road that separated him from Reah for good.

And Libby? thought Bill. Was it true that he always put Reah first? He had found the possibility of happiness and peace with Libby. Why could he not give her the priority that she felt she deserved – that he knew she needed?

For that matter, why had he not been able to give it to Tamsin seven years ago, when *she* needed that priority? He had loved her too. He had found great happiness with Tamsin. But he had left her for Libby. Not in the literal sense, maybe, but Libby had certainly displaced Tamsin. She had come to represent the future to which Bill aspired. This was what Tamsin knew, and this was why she had been so angry.

God, love seemed so vulnerable and transitory. So easily damaged by things that go wrong. We really should not place so much store by it. How could it be there the night he and Tamsin had drunk champagne on the roof-garden, then gone? How could it be there this morning, when he and Libby made love as no two people had ever made love, but not now? Libby was right. Loving wasn't difficult. It was loving someone every day that proves beyond us.

His mobile phone rang. Immediately Bill hoped it might be Libby. It wasn't. "Look, this business with Reah coming over tonight." *Tamsin.*

"Ah yes."

"All I've asked is for her to stay for the blessing, but she says she's arranged to come over to you straight away."

"Right."

362

"Well has she?"

"What?"

"Has she arranged to come to you straight away? Only this was supposed to be my weekend with Reah and I've already agreed that she can have the Friday with you. I don't like the two of you making arrangements without talking to me." Tamsin had clearly had enough of Reah that morning and was spoiling for a fight.

"Nothing's been arranged," said Bill. "She asked me to ring you and discuss it and I forgot."

"Oh. So you haven't arranged for her to come over before the blessing."

"No."

There was a pause with the name of Ben hovering on the edges of it. "It's difficult to know what she objects to half the time," said Tamsin. "One minute she wants to go off to Israel to stay on a kibbutz. The next she won't even come to Synagogue." Bill didn't know what to say. "I mean she knows we always have the blessings for Shabbat when it's her Friday with me. What's so awful about having it this Friday?" He felt Tamsin turning to him. It was an odd experience, because still his instinct was to be there for her. "It's not that she objects to Ben," said Tamsin. *The name spoken.*

"No?" said Bill, trying not to sound sceptical.

"He's an old friend of the family," said Tamsin. Obviously the party line. Bill wondered how much Tamsin thought he knew. He may as well tell her.

"It is the first time he's come down to stay though, isn't it?"

"Yes it is," said Tamsin, trying not to sound thrown. "But he's an old friend of the family. She's known him for years."

Bill suddenly felt very sorry for his ex-wife. She was feeling uncertainty, not a state in which Tamsin Wheeler was ever comfortable. "Why don't you tell her that we've talked. That she's sleeping with me tonight but she has to stay for the blessing. I can record whatever programmes she's going to miss."

"What about tomorrow morning?" asked Tamsin.

"What about it?" said Bill.

"Synagogue."

"No," said Bill, that was too much. "You said you wanted her back Saturday evening."

"Oh," said Tamsin. She obviously wasn't happy.

"That was what we agreed," said Bill.

"It's just that we've let some observances slip," said Tamsin. What had got into her?

"She is my daughter as much as she is yours," Bill told her.

"But she shouldn't lose touch with her people." Bill wondered if this were Ben talking.

"Reah is from mixed blood, Tamsin."

"But I'm her mother," protested Tamsin. "To my people that means she's Jewish."

"And I'm her father," said Bill. "You do *not* try and write me out of the picture."

"I'm not trying to do that," said Tamsin, suddenly tearful. "It's just a fact that if the mother is Jewish–"

"It may be a fact for you. It may be a fact for your father and this Ben person but for me the fact is that Reah is only half Jewish."

"That's what she says," said Tamsin. "But it's not true!"

Now she was crying. Bill hated it when women talked bollocks and then cried. It left him feeling bestial for simply pointing out the obvious. "We have to try and work together," he said. "I'll support you over the blessings but no more. Reah has the advantages of being born into two cultures. You try and write me out–"

"I said I'm not doing that!" cried Tamsin. "That's what I keep telling her."

What had been going on at Holt's Farm? Bill wondered. "I've got to go now," he said. "There's roadworks or something. I need both hands.

"OK," said Tamsin.

"You'll send her over at what time?"

"6.30"

"Ask her to ring me with what she wants recorded."

Bloody hell.

When Bill turned off the Chepstow road to begin the climb up to Holt's Cottage he found a group of jolly men from Dŵr Cymru digging up the track. "What's the problem?" he asked.

"All that rain," said one fluorescent jacket. "Knocked out your main sewage pipe."

"I'm at Holt's Cottage," said Bill. "Can I get through?"

"Ah well. We've got the road up just afore you get to the top. Be down again this evening mind."

"OK." Bill was about to drive on when he was struck by the thought that there might be no water at the cottage.

"Oh no shortage of water!" laughed another fluorescent man.

"You'll be all right," said the supervisor. "We've had to turn it off below you. Mind, bit muddy up there you'll find."

"Bit!" laughed someone else.

"I'll risk it," said Bill, putting the Jeep into four wheel drive.

"There's a parking space just afore the trees," shouted the supervisor. "Just off to the left. We've got a genny up there. If you can pull in alongside till five."

"No problem," said Bill. He knew the pull-in they meant. Tamsin had left her car there once or twice when it was too icy to get all the way up to the farm.

He had enjoyed speaking to the water board men. By comparison with Libby, Tamsin and Reah they seemed so simple and straightforward. They seemed so compared with Bill, in fact. What they liked was a practical problem to tackle, a laugh with the boys and a pint at the end of the day. Maybe he didn't spend enough time with men, Bill thought as he negotiated the slope. Mind you, that's how they were with each other. Who knows what pain and convoluted resentments they carried daily to and from their marriages?

He managed to get as far as where the generator was parked and took everything he might need from the Jeep. Bill remained strangely cheered by the waterboys. As he checked his mailbox he felt his horizons expand beyond the internecine strife of lovers past and present. Here was a letter from Dŵr Cymru, somewhat overtaken by events no doubt, one or two letters and a cheque. From *Arts International.* An actual, tangible cheque! Bizarrely Bill concluded that it was his jovial encounter with the lads in fluorescent that had made this cheque possible. The log-jam that had been his life of late had burst. He'd needed to shift focus and their humour had provided that.

Once inside, however, his spirits sank. Bill couldn't help but remember his image of Libby, here in the cottage. Only yesterday morning he'd returned the Sotheby's catalogue to the hall table. He'd imagined recounting the tale and then Libby picking up the damn thing and furrowing her brow and the two of them laughing at the upmarket pretensions of modern-day poltergeists. What did he do with it now? He could always e-mail her. It was inevitable he would.

Entering the office, Bill felt the pangs of long empty nights ahead. Nights when he would check-in to find *No New Messages.* Nights when Reah was not with him and Libby never would be again. He tried not to think of that. The red light on his answer machine was flashing. Of course it was, but it would not be Libby. Life was not like that.

Indeed it wasn't. The voice was male. "Mr Wheeler, Georg Schmidt."

Bill sat down to hear what his would-be patron had to say. "Mr Wheeler, I assume that my t-terms are not acceptable to you. If you wish to discuss this matter further I am remaining in Britain and will be on my Handy until Saturday evening." There was a pause after which Schmidt added, "If you are not willing to come to an agreement with me I would appreciate knowing what you intend to d-d-do with that letter." Schmidt then gave Bill his mobile number.

Bill couldn't help but warm to the man. He must have been surprised when no letter materialised, but he was handling the situation. Tactically, it had probably been to Bill's advantage that Schmidt had heard nothing at all from Bill. A fax might have left him feeling his adversary was too eager to negotiate. The inadvertent silence emanating from Room 702 of the Kensington Hilton meant that Bill was now in a stronger position to negotiate. If he could be bothered.

Bill leafed through the post. Dŵr Cymru were indeed regretting what they had now done to Bill's sewage system and some press releases were trying to be enthusiastic about the appointment of another new idiot to run this and that. Then there was *Arts International*. From long experience, Bill could tell by touch whether or not an envelope contained money. There were, however, two here from *Arts International,* one of which contained the obligatory comp slip and a cheque, a cheque indeed for more money than Bill had been expecting. He counted the digits to be sure. No, it genuinely was £2,550. There was no breakdown given on the slip, so Bill couldn't surmise what he'd been paid for but even if you added together his various expenses plus the two pieces in the last edition it still shouldn't come to £2,550. "Thank you," said Bill. Maybe Siobhan was in love and wanted to spread a little extra happiness.

The second envelope contained a brief letter on headed paper signed by Louis with a PS scrawled at the bottom. "*Bill – ring me, L.*"

Dear Contributor,

As you may know Arts International has for some time now been competing in an overcrowded marketplace. Our belief that there is room for quality reportage across a number of performing media has proved difficult to reconcile with the title's diminishing returns and distribution difficulties.

Gonforth, the publishers of Arts International, have therefore decided that this magazine should cease publication forthwith. Conveying this news is very painful for me as many of you have become close friends over the years.

I am arranging for all outstanding fees and expenses to be paid

where possible and also kill fees for any articles that are waiting on the
stocks. These cheques should reach recipients within the next few days.

Bloody hell, said Bill. So that's why Siobhan had been so generous. He
was getting his marching orders. Those four pieces, including the tale of
Paolo Bardini, were never going to see the light of day.

Bill picked up the telephone and dialled. When he'd last talked to Louis,
the man had claimed he was spending money to stop anything of his
budget being handed back at the end of the financial year. Now it seemed,
far from having a surplus, *Arts International* was having its few remaining
resources squandered.

Both lines were busy. Of course. Bill hung up. It made little difference
when he spoke to Louis. He might understand more after they'd talked but
he'd wouldn't be able to change anything. That letter would have been
vetted by Louis' employers. It was official.

Bill sat back in his chair. In one sense, given that *Arts International*
underpaid him and did so always with great reluctance, several months in
arrears – and indeed frequently forgot to pay him at all – it made little
difference to his parlous financial situation. Bill did have other sources of
income. But the magazine had been his passport to stories all round the
world. Airlines gave him flights, hotels gave him discounted rates, opera
houses gave him seats and large-chested PR women gave him champagne,
all because he had a roving brief from Louis Montgomery to go wherever
he wanted and to follow his nose. He was a free agent because when it
came down to it Louis would always back him up and say yes, William R.
Wheeler was researching for *Arts International,* even if he had no intention
of running the story or even much idea what Bill was doing in Portugal,
Rimini or Helsinki. Louis had given Bill his wings to fly. Getting the likes
of Vita in New York to back him was going to be much more difficult. Even
if she grew to like his work, she wasn't going to let the *New York Times* be
used as Bill Wheeler's calling card.

Poor Louis, thought Bill. No, Louis would have some lucrative deal set
up already. He had friends everywhere and had known this was coming.
He would have been preparing to jump ship ages ago. Louis could look
after himself. Still, Bill was going to miss the bastard. Working for Louis
had even made it possible to live in the wilds and be with Reah. Bill could
not go back to newsroom life now. So it was that Bill sat with his whisky
and stared up at the sky above his office window. Since this day began Bill
had gone from the loneliness of a frigid bed to investigative triumph and
the best sex on four legs. He had then tumbled into the worst kind of strife

with Libby, seemingly lost her, argued with Tamsin on the phone and come home to find he was out of a job.

He switched on his PC and waited for it to whirr and fume into action. New Message, he told the machine. *"Dear Libby."* Bill wondered how he might head this one. *After London? Instead of Venice? Death in Chepstow?* He settled on *"Sotheby"* and returned to the message box.

> *I have the catalogue we spoke of here in front of me. Do you want me to post it? I'd rather bring it over. Libby – I am desperately sad about what has happened. I cannot believe that we will lose so much because of one thing that I did wrong. Please try to forgive me. As things happen, it seems there is a bigger storm brewing here between Tamsin and Reah than I realised. I really do need to be here this weekend but afterwards I'd so like to come to see you in Venice, to see if we can put things right. Surely that is possible? I know that I have always put Reah first but ours has always been a special bond. She needs me and I believe a father should answer that need. I realise ultimately I must wean her from dependency. At the moment with Tamsin's new-found fundamentalism raging, I recognise that it's necessary to be near to hand. We did a terrible thing by splitting up. I do owe Reah. But things will change. Soon she will have gone to London. Soon she won't want to spend so much time with me.*

Bill felt this looked as if he were advocating waiting a few years till the situation normalised. He deleted everything after *"I must wean her from dependency"* and continued.

> *Your own parents split up when you were young and I know this cost you dear, however I don't see why both things can't be possible, for a child to have their parents and the parents to have people they love. This weekend I intend to tell Reah that I wish to live with you, marry you even, if you will have me. Please, for all that we have meant to each other and do mean to each other, don't throw this away.*

He signed it *"with love"* and then pressed Send. There were some fresh e-mails in his Inbox but none was from Ziegler.409. Of course not. Bill clicked off, the phone went. It was Reah with a list of programmes she wanted him to record.

Soon after 5pm Bill heard a car go past, not an engine he recognised. Ben must be down from London for the weekend. That section of road between the lay-by and the farm must have been temporarily restored by the water-boys. Bill was tempted to go and move his Jeep closer but the thought of

Good Old Ben in Holt's Farm sapped his energy. He'd been going to prepare the fireplace for tonight but now he sat back wearily on the battered old settee where he and Libby had made love, where Reah had lain with a temperature and Miss Mertens had interrogated him and sipped her tea.

Bill didn't like the idea of Ben. Not because Ben was sitting down at what had once been his table or looking at what had once been his pictures or even putting an arm round someone who had once been his wife. No, it was the thought that Ben was witnessing moments in his daughter's life which Bill would never see. Was Reah cheerful or sulky at the moment? Bill would not know but Ben would. Was she doing one of her dubious paintings or slumped in front of the TV? Were the floorboards creaking up above because Reah was dancing too heavily in front of the bathroom mirror again? Was she back in love with Jethro or was he out of favour yet again for not making enough fuss of her? All these tiny, wonderful things Ben would know and yet hardly notice. They would be inconsequential to him. Tonight he was here to see Tamsin and the child was just a blur, a bundle of noise or maybe a sulky teenage figure at the other end of the table. Always peripheral. However much he liked her, however cute or amusing he thought her, this well-known friend of the family would never treasure the minutiae of Reah's existence the way that he, Bill, did. The slightest surly shrug of shoulder or toss of hair was to Bill yet another instance of the miracle of her existence.

He could have easily jumped on the phone and demanded that Reah come over straight away. He really could have done that. But she was Tamsin's daughter too. That was the hard thing. Difficult as Bill found it at times to imagine, Reah was also her mother's child. They probably sang Jewish songs together, went shopping, and discussed characters in TV soaps. He did not resent Tamsin having Reah when he did not. However much they argued, he knew that Tamsin valued their daughter as much as he did. It was Ben that Bill objected to.

After a few moments of plumbing the quiet coldness within him Bill rose and wandered upstairs. He thought he'd fetch a sweater but he also knew at the top of the stairs that he'd open the door of Reah's room and look in. He'd switch the fan heater on. Warm it up for her. It was a room that had less of her character than he would have liked. Her real room was in the farmhouse. He had the second league teddies here, the out-of-date pop posters and old bits of bookcasing from Chiswick.

The phone rang. Bill made it before the answer-machine could cut in. "Mr Wheeler," said Georg Schmidt. "You left me a message this afternoon." It was true, Bill had. He'd failed to get through to Schmidt or Louis on his return but at least in the case of the good Doktor he'd been able to leave some record of his attempt.

"Yes," said Bill. "I feel we have more talking to do."

"What is it you want?" Schmidt asked, as if Bill had never once outlined the nature of his interest in the letter.

"I believe there is a story you want to suppress, Dr Schmidt. If I hand over my letter you will have moved one step further towards completing that suppression."

"I see," said Schmidt.

"I want to know what the story is."

There was silence while Dr Schmidt considered this.

"If we assume for the moment that you are r-right," he answered at last. "That I do wish to s-suppress something, why should I tell you, a journalist, of all people, what that story is?"

Schmidt had a good mind, Bill thought. Fortunately he'd anticipated this. "Without the letter I have no evidence. If I hand it over, I am sacrificing my chance of ever proving my story. Whatever my story is. I think in recompense for that, you can at least tell me what it is I'm giving up. Don't forget I may piece it together one day and if I have to do that then I'll still have my one piece of proof. Tell me what this is all about and I will give that up."

There was a further silence while Schmidt thought about this. "How will I know you won't take c-copies?" he asked.

"That's a risk you always take. It's the risk you would have been taking yesterday if I'd signed that contract of yours."

"But even if you had k-kept a c-c-c," Schmidt's stammer held up the word for so long that he began the sentence again. "Even if you had kept a copy, you still would not have understood the significance of that photocopied letter, Mr Wheeler. If I agree to your terms, and assuming that there is significance in the letter you possess, then you will come to understand it."

"That's the idea," said Bill. "The most I'll have is a story with no evidence, assuming you trust me not to keep copies. Even if you can't trust me the most I'll have is a story and a photocopy. No original."

Schmidt was silent. After a while he said. "It isn't what you think it is. It isn't what Mr K-K-Katz thinks it is. He thinks that because I paid him a retainer to find me letters that there is big money is involved here."

"So what is involved here?" Bill asked, trying to reel him in.

"I shall think about this," said Schmidt. "You shall hear from me on Saturday. If you have genuine interest in that letter, Mr Wheeler, can I suggest you don't dispose of it any other way."

"I do have a genuine interest," said Bill.

"Yes..." said Schmidt, as if he were turning this very novel idea over in his mind. "But if this gets out into the public domain, there will be nothing left for us to say to each other. You do understand that?"

"I'll wait to hear from you," said Bill.

It was growing dark. Bill took out the famous letter from his notebook and married it with the translation in his filing-cabinet. He had looked at it so often he felt he was even beginning to understand what the individual words of German said. So, what was this terrible grief that Wagner was suffering? Why was it painful that Lusch was in Venice now and going to her father later? Bill picked up the print-out of that *Boston Globe* article.

> *She is the fruit of entwined roots. When I gaze upon her I feel like Siegmund gazing for the first time on his Sieglinde, his but yet another's. I have dared but now I may dare no more.*

What was it that Wagner dared and what did he mean, "*It is not just my own bravery that would be tested but hers.*"?

No man must know of what Wagner had done.

> *My worthy friend, I ask you to destroy this letter and with it all knowledge of the deeds of which I spoke to you.*

Bill thought of those terrible words that Libby had used. Her face red with anger in the hotel room. The next thing he'd known, she was recoiling as if he'd hit her. He hadn't hit her. He wouldn't do that. What had she seen in his face?

He switched on his PC to see if Ziegler.409 had replied. She must be in Venice by now. Did she rush to her internet connection as he had, or would she wait till tomorrow?

Bill noticed that one of the e-mails he had left unopened had the address llewellyng@kcl.ac.uk. Good old Rory had joined the twenty-first century, thought Bill.

> *Dear Mr Wheeler,*
>
> *I have tried telephoning you and left several messages. I believe there is another interpretation of the word we were discussing. If you are still working on this letter perhaps we should speak.*

Not interested, thought Bill. Whether the ABCGH was up and under, over and above or dangling upside down with its toes in the air didn't seem to matter anymore. He couldn't bring himself to reply, not yet. Maybe when he had the full story he might tidy up all the loose ends.

Bill went online and asked his machine if there were any more messages. Indeed he had two, but they seemed to take forever to download. As his screen filled with little graphics Bill fell to remembering one of Libby's e-mails from last week. "*I think we have both missed the obvious. Lusch. Not entirely inappropriate.*"

What did she mean "*Not entirely inappropriate*"? Libby and her blessed double negatives. He hadn't thought much of that remark at the time. What was she suggesting, then? That his relationship with Reah was in some way comparable with that of Wagner and Lusch? Wagner who had dared but would not dare any more. Bill felt annoyed with her. Libby's problem was she never had a proper relationship with her own father. Too distant and then too close. Inevitably she was suspicious.

Suddenly the little bar-diagram charting the turgid process of downloading, had filled up and disappeared. Both messages were from ziegler.409.

The first was still headed "*Sotheby*". Clearly Libby had simply clicked reply to his earlier message.

"*Bill,*" it began. Not exactly affectionate.

> *I too am sad about what has happened. More than sad but in ways that you wouldn't understand. You offer and withdraw without realising the cruelty of such prevarications. You talk of love and of marriage but these are not just words, Bill. They are commitments of which I do not believe you truly have the measure. When you first asked me to live with you at Holt's Cottage I believed that that was what you truly wanted. I no longer have that certainty. I spent my 'plane journey thinking a lot about what occurred between us and came to the conclusion that love and marriage – concepts which mean a lot to me as a woman – are to you just words to be used for the moment. I also realised that I have been foolish to think that you use these words with the same respect that I and many others accord them. I was unsure whether I was going to tell you this. For you the misappropriation and misapplication of words has probably been the habit of a lifetime. Nothing I say is going to change you now.*

Bill paused. It was an outrageous and unforgiving thing to say. By attacking the written word she knew she was striking him where it hurt most. There was more to come.

> *However when I arrived here and read what you wrote about Reah, I felt that it was finally incumbent on me to tell you these things. Maybe if you are aware of the damaging way in which you fool yourself on a*

*daily basis you may stop and think the next time you are extravagant
and irresponsible with the vocabulary of love and commitment.*

Something at the bottom of the screen was written in inverted commas.
In a mixture of fascination, confusion and outrage Bill scrolled on down.

*You write to me:"I know that I have always put Reah first but ours has
always been a special bond." This echoes what you wrote to me seven
years ago – I did keep a copy even though I tore that fax in two when
first I received it. These were the words you wrote me when deciding to
end our friendship: "For the sake of Reah we have to end this relationship. We cannot meet anymore. This saddens me greatly but she is my
child. I could not bear to do her harm. We have a special bond.*

Quite right, said Bill to himself.

*I kept two faxes from that period. The other you may not remember
sending, so many passed between us as we discussed our ideas and our
hopes across the skies of London. This second fax is undated but I
received it about a month before your last to me and it in part explains
why it was such a cruel shock to receive that disingenuous farewell
missive three and a half weeks later:*
    *"Life in this house has become a prison to me. The love that Tamsin
and I had for each other seems not to have survived the changes in our
lives. My interests have altered. I feel that there is so much that I want
to know and want to write. I want you to help me learn and grow."*

It was an odd experience for Bill to see his younger self suddenly
appear like this. He had no recollection of this faxed letter and yet he
recognised the voice. This younger man seemed very full of himself, very
impatient and very aware of his own needs. He was also making a direct
appeal to Libby, Bill now realised. The two of them may never have spoken
of their feelings for each other all those years ago but Bill Wheeler knew
that you didn't lightly tell a woman that you need her in your life. He
certainly knew that now, even if he didn't know it then.

    *"As for Reah she is a charming child but maddening. Over these last
few months I have come to the conclusion that I am not cut out to be
a parent. Tamsin wanted us to have children and I agreed, but now I
realise the mistake. Much as I love my own daughter I have to admit
she bores me."*

Bill felt as though he had been hit. He could not possibly have written
those words and yet they were already finding their echo within him. Even

now, even inside the shock from which he was now reeling. It was like being told in the prime of life that you have a terminal disease. Within the first seconds of disbelief, the truth of that prognosis surely begins to resonate. Even though those words and ideas were contrary to everything Bill would claim ever to have believed, they were his. His words. His ideas.

"*Can you see?*" Libby resumed.

> *Seven years ago I felt I had to leave London. Can you see that I could not fight for a man whose grasp on the truth was so tenuous? Tonight I feel that same sadness all over again. I can never give myself to a man who may one day forget he ever said he loved me. Goodbye Bill.*

He needed a glass of water.

Bill was still standing at the sink, gripping the tap, when Reah arrived with her enormous bag.

"Hi there, Daddy Boo."

He tried to speak. It was difficult. Bill moved to where she stood and enveloped her in his arms.

"Oof!" said Reah as Bill squeezed her tight.

"I love you Boo Boo," said Bill. "I love you so much."

"I love you too," said Reah. "Did you record my programmes?"

Bill felt a need to cook and prepare food. He wanted to be domestic. He asked about homework. He asked about dates for the new school. He even offered to do any washing she needed.

"Mum has got a washing machine Dad and, like, I only arrived here five minutes ago."

Reah put the headphones back on and returned to nodding her head in time to the music.

He wasn't trying to prove something to Libby or to himself. On the inside Bill knew he was a good father but he felt the need to make amends for ever having said that of Reah. She was six at the time. She had a voice like a chipmunk and a bossy, busy manner like some portly, shrunken pensioner forever trying to organise a Women's Institute meeting in the home of Bill and Tamsin Wheeler. Looking back Bill remembered her only with fondness but she had been a trial, instinctively arguing with Tamsin about who knew best, and forever squirming on to Bill's lap when he was trying to work.

He could see now that, with two parents poring obsessively over the fissures in their relationship, little Rachel Christabel Wheeler was being neglected long before a 27-year-old Bostonian academic answered a phonecall from Bill Wheeler one morning. He may have found Reah tire-some. Indeed it was true, he *had* been irritated by her but the reason Reah had seemed troublesome was that her parents had only one subject of conversation after seven and a half years of marriage. Every hour of the day was devoted to Bill and Tamsin, the possible cause of their difficulties and the seemingly impossible solution. When Libby had come along she had been welcome because she and the world she represented were new. If Reah had been tiresome and boring it was because Bill and Tamsin's introspection had made her so. With Libby Bill had found an escape, not from Reah but from the world that had made Reah troublesome. He felt so sorry. How could he have identified his daughter with the malaise when really she had been one of its symptoms?

So what was the malaise? He used to say that Tamsin lost interest in him when Reah was born. He had even created that image of her in his mind, Tamsin snatching the child away from him as she stepped out of the ornamental pond that hot summer night. But they were already drifting apart. And on this slow dull drift they both seized on new futures. Tamsin had her anxieties about Reah; Bill his opportunity to move into Arts jour-nalism. Both kept them busy and away from each other. Neither really knew what was happening till Libby. She was their angel of revelation.

Bill drained the pasta and started chopping vegetables on automatic pilot. He felt numb and sad. Curiously, his course of introspection must have coincided with Reah's because over supper she suddenly asked, "Dad was it really Libby who broke up you and Mum?"

"No," said Bill. Maybe the subject of Libby had been hanging in the ether. Bill had certainly spent the meal with snatches of her e-mails running through his head. "No, your mother and I broke things up. Libby just filled the gap when I was lonely. When she realised that it was affect-ing my marriage she backed off."

"Oh," said Reah, trying to think about this. Clearly it wasn't what Tamsin had been saying. It wasn't entirely true either. Suddenly Bill felt the weight of Libby's disapproval just as clearly as if Dr Ziegler were sitting opposite him at that very moment. Yes, he knew what he had said wasn't true, but he wanted Reah to think well of Libby. If that could ever be possible.

"Why did you split up then?" Presumably the arrival of Ben at Holt's Farm was provoking all these questions but they were remarkably in tune with his own current obsessions. After all Bill would never have split from the woman in the red dress who stood drinking champagne with him on the roof-garden that hot summer's night.

"I think that's the wrong question," Bill said pushing his plate away. "I think the real question is, How do people manage to stay together?"

"Because they love each other," Reah replied.

"Loving's the easy bit," said Bill. She looked quizzically at him. "You have to find a way of accepting the other person with all their faults. When you're first with someone it's very easy to be what they want you to be. Then they get to know who you are, I suppose."

"I really don't like the way Mum is with Ben," said Reah, who was on her own wavelength in this conversation.

"You didn't like the way I was with Libby."

"At least you weren't bending over backwards to please all the time and giggling."

"I'm glad I wasn't giggling," said Bill. They went and sat down in front of the TV. "I've got *Touch Of Evil*, that's Orson Welles again. Or I'd really like to show you *Immortal Story*."

"When we go to London we're going to be seeing even more of Ben," said Reah. "More Friday nights of that yukky wine and plaited bread." Once again Bill wondered how much Reah really objected and how much she grumbled habitually.

"You'll be having weekends with me as well," he told her.

"And you will come and live by us, won't you?" she asked.

"Well not very near," said Bill. "Do you know the prices of flats in St John's Wood?"

"I told Mum she should give your money back."

"And what did she say?" Bill asked, putting his arm around her shoulder.

"She said I didn't understand, that you had given her a lumpy sum."

"Lump sum."

"Instead of the maintenance most wives get. How much will you get for this cottage Dad? If you tell me I can look out for flats and things."

"Well I have to ask an estate agent to value it first."

"You were going to do that ages ago!" Reah protested.

"I've been so busy. I forgot. I'll do it tomorrow I promise."

"Love you Daddy Boo," said Reah getting up. "Can I play on the computer for a while?"

"What about Orson?" Bill asked.

"Twenty minutes?" said Reah.

It was true what Libby said. Maybe she couldn't exactly twist him round her finger but he never resented a single sacrifice for Reah. Now that was something he could not say either of his feelings for Tamsin or for

Libby. Lovers come and go, Bill thought to himself sadly as he got up to finish clearing the table, but our children are always our children.

No wonder we are never at peace when we're in love. We want the headiness to last forever but maybe it's heady precisely because we know it's doomed to fail. Love is transient. We are always waiting for the first crack of disappointment. Parenthood, on the other hand, is reassuringly permanent.

It started to rain again while Bill was washing up. The first he knew of it was a surge of wind in the trees outside and then a splatter of rain across the window pane above his head. Soon water was veritably flowing down the skylight. The storm was back and with it there came a chill into Holt's Cottage.

Bill went back to the fire to poke the logs into life but still he was cold. A few dark raindrops had already made it down the chimney. Bill noticed how they'd created splashes in the ash.

Then it happened. Not the storm. The something that was wrong. The something that was worse than any storm. He heard it in the rain. He felt it on the back of his neck. He sensed it as he stood up from the hearth, his back to the office door. Bill turned round, the poker still in his hand, wary. Reah in the doorway, her face as white as illness.

Bill didn't know at first what was happening but he let the poker drop slowly through his fingers. Normally, seeing her like that, he would have gone over to hug her and tell her it was OK, whatever it was. But it wasn't OK, was it?

"You're not selling this place are you?" said Reah. "She's moving in with you here."

Now Bill knew what it was he had heard in the rain. He hadn't closed that e-mail from Libby. It was still there on the screen when Reah went into his office.

"No, that's not true," Bill said slowly. "Libby is not moving here to be with me. I believe I'm never seeing Libby again."

"But you did ask her to," said Reah. "You did ask her to marry you. You were going to have a happy family here while stupid Reah went about stupidly thinking Daddy was coming up to London."

For a moment Bill thought about telling Reah that she shouldn't have been reading his e-mails but what was the point? They were way beyond decorum now. An instant, a moment within the storm, had changed everything.

He felt weak and needed to sit down. Reah, he noticed, was shivering. Or maybe she was trembling. How much had she read?

"Do you want to sit down?" said Bill, lowering himself on to the hearth.

"Stupid, that's how you treat me," said Reah. "Stupid and boring. Reah the mistake."

He had his answer.

"I didn't write that," said Bill. His voice was so quiet. He could do nothing to make it louder.

"What did you say?" Reah demanded. She seemed to have taken on the form of Tamsin and Jessica. Another angry woman in a doorway.

"I said I didn't write that. Libby wrote that."

"But she says you said that, that you wrote it to her in one of your lovey-dovey faxes."

He deserved such scorn.

"Well did you?"

"I don't know," said Bill. "It was a long time ago."

"I think I have a right to know, Dad. Did you write to Libby seven years ago and say 'I have to admit my mistake of a daughter bores me'?"

Bill did not know how to reply.

"Is Libby making that up?" Reah asked. "Is she lying when she writes that?"

Now this was a question he could answer. "I don't think Libby's the kind of person who lies, Boo."

There was a moment's silence before Reah hissed, "Don't you ever call me that again."

The next thing he knew, Reah had marched upstairs and slammed her bedroom door. Bill slowly covered his face with his hands. He felt as though the worst thing in the world had happened and yet those things on the screen were just words. Words he probably hadn't even meant a few minutes after writing them. My God, Libby was right, Bill thought. I claim to value words but maybe I only mean them for the moment they're occurring to me. I clearly don't mean them seven years later. He had to try and make Reah understand, but regret overwhelmed him. "I should never have written that down," he said aloud. Nothing should ever be written down. Ever, ever, ever.

Reah was coming downstairs tugging that great bag of hers.

"Where're you going?" Bill asked fatuously.

"Back to Mum's."

"But you're with me tonight."

"I don't have a father anymore!" shouted Reah. And, my God, she meant it too. Bill got up and ran to the door to stop her. Reah's face was horribly swollen with white and red blotches. Tears had made her eyes angry and she seemed to have bitten her lip.

Bill put his arm across the door to stop her. "Not like this. Not like this, Reah."

"Get out of my way," snarled Reah. "I'm a mistake and I want to get out!"

"I never meant you were a mistake," Bill tried to tell her. "I meant I felt I was wrong to think I'd be a good parent. That letter wasn't about you it was about me."

"Let me *out!*" Reah's lip was indeed bleeding.

"You can't go out there like this. It's raining."

"I don't care about the rain!" shouted Reah. "Dad let me go of me!"

"Reah, love," said Bill, trying to take her by the shoulders. She shook herself free of his embrace.

"Let me go or I'm ringing Mum to come and fetch me."

He was shocked by how much she meant it. "Sit down," said Bill, trying to sound as if he had an ounce of authority left. "I'll ring Tamsin."

Bill had arranged that Reah would wait in the car while he and Tamsin talked in the cottage. He watched as a figure in the passenger seat, presumably Ben, helped Reah manhandle her overnight bag on to the back seat of Tamsin's car.

"This is not a normal bust up," Bill said as he closed the door. Tamsin was taking off her coat. She was smartly dressed for dinner *à deux* but had put a thick and inappropriate cardigan over her outfit. Presumably she was not expecting Bill's cottage to be warm. Bill asked her to sit down. Tamsin moved slowly to one of the chairs. All the time her eyes were taking in the detail of Holt's Cottage. It was a very long time since she'd been inside.

"Oh, I brought you this from Israel," said Bill, handing over the necklace he'd picked up at Ben Gurion Airport. "Seems an age ago. I never got round to giving it to you."

"Thank you," said Tamsin, taking the tissue-wrapped parcel but not opening it.

Bill did not sit down. He began speaking while gripping the back of the settee. "Reah saw something tonight. Libby sent me an e-mail and quoted back at me words that I'd used to her seven years ago." He saw Tamsin flinch. Her body language was always so explicit. "It wasn't the fax over which... it wasn't the fax which you saw."

"I don't know whether I wish to discuss this," Tamsin said quietly. She looked away unhappily, as if trying to remember where the exit was.

"No, please. I wouldn't have mentioned this if it weren't really important. It's as difficult for me as it is for you."

Tamsin smoothed down her dress over her knees.

"What Reah saw was something Libby claims I wrote to her about finding it very hard to be a father. Well it was worse than that. I said that I found Reah boring at times."

As Tamsin did not reply, Bill added, "That's what Libby said I said."

"Can we leave Libby out of this?" Tamsin asked succinctly, holding on to her feelings as best she could. "I'm not interested in her or concerned about her. I'm only concerned about Reah."

It seemed a reasonable request. Tamsin clearly still blamed Libby for the break-up of their marriage. If they were going to be able to deal with this problem, it was probably best to eliminate such a major cause of contention.

"OK," said Bill. He was pacing up and down. "OK, the fact of the matter is that that was a very unfortunate thing for Reah to read. I don't know if I said it or not seven years ago but I couldn't say it was complete fabrication–"

"You did used to say that," said Tamsin. Bill felt his heart sink. Was she going to use this against him?

"You did find Reah a trial at that age. I think a lot of fathers do. At the time it was very difficult for me, Bill." Tamsin looked up at him. "I felt I had no support from you, but I have come to realise since that men are like that. Some men, anyway. My own father was always at work when I was young. I probably saw him for half an hour a day at the most. Even then I can remember feeling that I was a bit of a nuisance to him. All these women in the house. He used to retire to his study as soon as he could. You worked from home," she conceded. "I think you probably saw a lot more of your daughter than most fathers do."

She gave him the smallest flicker of a smile. Bill was amazed how reasonable Tamsin was being. Was this the woman who had conspired secretly to move away, refused to take his phone-calls and claimed he had raped her? Or was this the woman who had spoken such sense when Reah had rung her in distress from Venice? It was as if there were two ex-wives, and he never knew which he was going to get.

"But you were a fool to ever put it in writing," she added. No malice. Fact.

God he could feel such tension in the air.

"I know."

There was now a great deal lying unspoken between them, not just the fax that had so distressed Libby and Tamsin, but the rolls and rolls of faxes that had passed between Bill and Libby seven years ago and which Bill had burned in a pointless gesture to save his marriage. After the bonfire, in the garden outside Holt's Cottage, Tamsin had turned angrily on her heel.

"She's still got her copies though, hasn't she?"

Bill remembered Tamsin staring at the flames her hands deep in her windcheater, while Reah danced around thinking it was Bonfire Night come early. One rolled sheet had detached itself and floated off into the air. That was the only time Tamsin's attention had shifted. She'd watched the translucent printed page rise and fall until Bill caught it, screwed it tight and pushed it back into the flames.

Then when the blaze was over Tamsin had walked away. Her words hanging in the air. "She's still got her copies though, hasn't she? The Bitch." Indeed she had, and Bill could see that as far as Tamsin Wheeler was concerned havoc was still being wreaked by the grotesque folly he committed all those years ago.

"And she's wholly irresponsible sending you that," Tamsin was saying. "What was she trying to prove? She has no idea has she! No idea the damage–"

"She didn't intend it for Reah to see," Bill interrupted. "And she wasn't gloating. If you must know, I think she was saying that she'd never believed that I gave her up for Reah."

Tamsin stood, indeed fairly sprang out of her seat. "I'm sorry I can't talk about this any more." She put her hands up between them as if trying to push the idea away. "I don't want to hear another word about that woman."

Bill came towards her. "Please Tamsin, just wait. We've got side-tracked. I only want to talk about Reah. She's going to talk to you. She's very upset. Can you tell her what you said to me? About fathers often feeling like that with young kids, that it doesn't mean anything?"

Bill realised that by appealing so directly to Tamsin now he was making plain his own desperation. He had always taken pride in his relationship with Reah. How that pride had fallen now.

"Why did you have to put it all in writing, Bill?" Her words stopped him literally in his tracks. The old wounds were still there. "Why?"

"It was a long time ago," he replied, helpless.

"I must go," said Tamsin, shaking her head. "Reah's in the car with Ben."

"It's partly her weekend with me," said Bill. "*Please*." He saw Tamsin shudder but continue moving towards the door. "Look, if Reah won't come back tomorrow, I want to see you. We need to discuss this. You know the danger to my relationship with Reah at the moment. If you weren't going to London none of this would've happened."

There was a causality in that which made sense to Bill but he didn't really expect Tamsin to grasp how her plans to take Reah away had precipitated his recent affair with Libby. To her it must've seemed like another desperate appeal.

Tamsin had reached the door.

"She's my daughter too," Bill called out to her.

"If only you'd thought that seven years ago," she muttered.

The winds were vicious that night. They seemed to hurl themselves against the casement of Bill's cottage with specific malevolence. They even forced rain round some of the older panes. Bill sat in front of the fire with his bottle of whisky but didn't get drunk. He was too much in shock to feel the effects of the alcohol.

When he got up to climb the stairs his legs seemed perfectly steady although the storm did sound absurdly loud. He thought the booze had somehow affected his hearing until he got upstairs and found that the skylight in his room had been blown out. It was odd that he'd not heard the noise of wood splintering. Fortunately it had lodged diagonally, halfway in and halfway out and the rain had mostly continued to drain down the roof. What water had come in had soaked his bed. Bill swore, pulled the mattress and bedding clear and brought up some buckets from downstairs to catch the rain still dripping in.

The worst of the downpour had fortunately come to an end but the wind roared on ferociously above. Bill went back downstairs to find a hammer and some nails to secure what he could of the skylight. Now the alcohol began to bite. Barely up to the job, he left the tools where they lay on the floor, before trailing into Reah's room where he fell immediately asleep on her bed.

An hour later he woke, with an incipient headache and a dry throat. Bill went to the bathroom and decided to look in on the storm damage en route. His room was quiet now, which seemed eerie until Bill worked out that his meant that the storm had blown itself out. Or was simply regrouping its forces out at sea.

Nevertheless the view up through his smashed skylight was bizarrely serene. White constellations in the pitch black sky wheeled slowly and silently above him, immune and unaware. The suffering and torment of this petty world was nothing, Bill thought. Faced with infinity like that, storms are also nothing, indeed nothing on this earth matters. Apart from love, he thought. Suddenly Bill felt very alone. Without Tamsin, Libby and Reah the world indeed seemed a very cold and hostile place.

❖ BREAKING POINT

JUST BEFORE 9 O'CLOCK, Bill lifted the phone to Tamsin, but his line wasn't working. He then tried his mobile but found that her landline wasn't working either. The storm had presumably brought down cables. Bill rang the operator who put him through to Faults. Faults then tested both lines but all they could do was confirm that there was indeed something wrong. Pacing up and down with his coffee, Bill rang Tamsin on her mobile but got through to a messaging service. She'd presumably switched it off.

He couldn't take this.

Bill needed to get some wood to cover the damaged skylight. But before he drove down to Chepstow he had to know from Tamsin what was going on. He dressed and walked over to Holt's Farm.

There must've been a phenomenal amount of rain over the last few days. Several distinct ponds had formed in the field that separated him from her house. The natural drainage system of this upland area could not cope with what had been thrown at it. Goodness knows how things were further down in the valley.

The farmhouse itself looked unharmed but its stone and mortar were clearly drenched. Every trace of colour in the exterior walls seemed dense and vibrant. The world was truly saturated this morning. Bill had pulled on his boots, expecting mud. Even so he was amazed how much had accumulated round his feet by the time he got to Tamsin's front door. He used the scraper, knocked, then waited, remembering the last time he had stood here and Jessica had thrown that vase. Bill was not expecting a warm welcome this time, either, but that was the least of his concerns. He needed to make his peace with Reah.

The smell of coffee was escaping through the door. Bill had fond memories of the Walken aroma. Tamsin's parents' house, even her sister's house, smelled the same, a mixture of coffee, cleanliness and very good quality carpets. There was security in that smell. It spoke of the home well-maintained. Domestic virtues. Bill was sure his cottage smelled of woodsmoke and damp. He had not been aware of the Walken smell in their Chiswick house but then Tamsin had been keen to break from her parents' style when they set up home together. It amused him now to realise she had not only returned to her faith and her family but also to their aroma.

Tamsin glimpsed Bill through the central diamond pane and disappeared to unlock. She hadn't long been up, he thought. The door opened. Tamsin's hair was unbrushed but she was dressed for stepping outside: jeans, boots, cardigan and waxed jacket.

"I saw you coming," she said. "Reah's still asleep." Bill almost asked her where Ben was but he knew the answer already. A decree absolute doesn't mean we lose the ability to pick up on our ex-spouse's signals. Tamsin had clearly just come from the bed where she and Ben had, however discreetly, slept together. Bill had images of that bed. No longer did he see it as a place of depravity, his daughter standing traumatised in the doorway; it was now a place of comfort and fondness. He could see the richly plumped pillows and expensive camberwick throw, even feel the warmth of the duvet and welcoming depth of Tamsin's mattress. Bill had enjoyed losing himself in that mattress. He was jealous. Not because this Ben person had probably made love to Tamsin last night, but because Ben had shared in her warmth and softness, waking this morning to the tenderness of a marital duvet.

"Are you proposing to go for a walk?" Bill asked.

"I'd rather be away from the house," she replied.

They set off into the trees on a narrow path that ran parallel to the walk Bill often took after his morning's work. On the way they spoke inconsequentially about the storm. Bill noted that 'we' had been worried about the chimney pot. He didn't assume Tamsin meant she'd been discussing it with Reah. 'We' had also discussed the phone lines. It seemed Tamsin had brought her mobile but left the charger in London. She had always been pretty cavalier about mobiles but when it came to the landlines being down Tamsin grew uncomfortable. "Oh. Oh dear."

"Doesn't Ben have a mobile?" Bill asked, speaking the name at last.

"No..." Despite her concern, Tamsin almost laughed. Clearly anyone who knew Ben as well as she did would certainly know how extraordinarily out of character it would be for him to be seen with a mobile phone. Bill disliked her fondness and pride.

They hadn't gone very far but already mud was becoming a serious issue. Then suddenly the forest seemed to part before them and they stumbled into a small clearing with space to talk. Some pretty barbaric tree-surgery had been going on here. That or the winds. A tall conifer had broken off and blocked their path entirely. Tamsin gestured to suggest they might make use of it. Bill waited while she brushed the trunk with her knitted glove and then sat down, preparing to be the one who spoke. Up until now they'd not mentioned their daughter although her name hung painfully in the air.

"Reah hasn't said very much," said Tamsin. "I know she's found it a pressure coming to see you–"

"How can you say that?" Bill interrupted.

"She's talked about it in the past." Bill didn't believe her, not one word.

"I thought you said Reah wasn't saying very much."

"About what happened yesterday evening," Tamsin told him. "She's talked generally in the past but to be fair to her I think she feels it disloyal to say much to me at the moment. Disloyal to you. Certainly with Ben there."

"Does he have to be present?" Bill asked, feeling riled again. Tamsin did not seem to understand the question. "I mean this issue affects you, me and Reah," Bill continued. "It's got damn all to do with Ben – or anyone else who's staying with you." He could tell she didn't like the way he had marginalised her man.

"He isn't just 'staying with me'," Tamsin said. "And he is fond of her."

"Well Libby's fond of Reah," said Bill. "But that's got bugger all to do with anything." A mistake.

"I would say she has a great deal to do with this," Tamsin snapped back. "If she hadn't sent that stupid e-mail, none of this would have happened."

"OK," said Bill. "But can we just leave her out of this? Her and Ben."

"All right," conceded Tamsin, finding her composure again.

"I mean are you planning to marry him or something?" Bill asked, totally losing it. "I mean, if *I* may speak for Reah, she seems not to know what the hell is going on."

"That's nothing to do with you," Tamsin replied, remaining icy calm. She knew and he didn't, and that was how it was going to stay.

"But as Reah's father–"

"As Reah's father, I will tell you anything that affects her. At the moment nothing is fixed. He's asked me. I haven't decided."

Oh God.

Bill felt absolutely awful. He got up, not wishing to show anything in his face. He took a look around the clearing in which they sat. He should have known, he thought. All the signs were there.

"So... he's asked but you're trying it out. Seeing how it feels..." He disliked himself for resorting to jibes.

"I don't have to listen to this," said Tamsin, getting up.

"I'm sorry," said Bill. "It's a bit of a shock, that's all." He looked at her. Tamsin sat down again. "Is that why you're moving to London. To live with him?"

"No," said Tamsin. "I'm moving to London to be near my family because I need their support."

"With what?"

"With bringing up Reah–"

"I supported you in that," said Bill.

"Within the traditions of her family."

"Your family," said Bill after a pause.

"I'm not denying you contact, Bill."

"Oh no, but you're moving her to one of the most expensive parts of London."

"It's where my family live."

"And Ben?"

"I thought we were leaving Ben out of this?"

"I want to know. My relationship with Reah is being seriously threat-ened. I want to know what else you have planned." Bill was pacing now, as he had yesterday, although the mud made it difficult to do so with any dignity.

"If your relationship with Reah is under threat that is your own doing," said Tamsin. "Not mine. It wasn't me who sent that stupid fax."

"Shall we leave Libby out of this too?" said Bill, resorting to sarcasm now.

"I don't mean Libby," said Tamsin. "She's nothing to me. I mean you. You were the stupid one. Seven years ago. Why did you have to write it all down? Don't you see what this has done?"

Bill realised that they had suddenly stumbled into a much bigger clear-ing altogether. An arena for the unresolved enmity between Bill and Tamsin Wheeler. Seven years on they were still dealing with the conse-quences of that summer of faxes and late night phonecalls. Why had he felt the need to write so much down? His eyes felt hot. "Don't you think I don't regret it?" he said, turning away from her. Bill did not cry, but he knew he was close to it at that moment.

There was a silence. Tamsin stood up, this time out of compassion. "Do you ever think that if you two had gone off to a hotel the day you met and I'd never been any the wiser..." Bill nodded. "If you'd just gone to bed once or twice instead of sending faxes to each other every hour of the day. Do you think..."

"Of course," said Bill, pinching the bridge of his nose and looking at the view, which was no view, just trees blocking the light. No, he was OK now. He turned back. Tamsin was standing close to him. It was an awkward moment. They'd been through so much. His instinct was to embrace her. Bill took half a step back. She did too. It had been just like the moment when he was left face-to-face with Libby in Venice. So close you either kiss or retreat.

"*Why* didn't you just go to a hotel room?" Tamsin asked. She sounded absurdly regretful.

"We thought we were moral people," Bill replied.

"God," said Tamsin and now it was her turn to look away. "God, the Nazis thought they were moral people! It's not what you intend, it's the effect you have."

"Please," said Bill. "I'd rather not be compared to the Nazi party. I think the worst you can say is that I hastened on the end of our marriage. I didn't kill six million Jews."

"You nearly killed me," said Tamsin, sitting down, heavily.

"That's ridiculous. We were both responsible for the break up."

"Yes, well, that's modern day relationship-speak," said Tamsin. Clearly neither she nor Jessica held with such ideas.

"God, you're so unforgiving," Bill told her.

"I think I've been very forbearing," said Tamsin quietly, glaring up at him.

"Not the same thing," said Bill.

"No it isn't, but some people might say it's more than you deserve."

"Oh yes, I can just guess who," snapped Bill. Tamsin's bloody parents of course. Ben, no doubt, and certainly Jess.

"No I don't suppose you can," she replied angrily.

"Who then?" This was petty.

"Reah for instance."

After a moment's cold panic Bill said "I don't believe you."

"I know you think you have a special relationship, but she's said that to me several times," Tamsin replied, unable to keep a small note of triumph from her voice. "She knows you were responsible."

This was no longer his calm and considerate ex-wife. This was the demon of an angry, vengeful woman who had battled with the calm and reasonable ex-wife for possession of Tamsin's troubled heart.

Bill swung round and pointed an accusatory finger. "If she blames me, that is because you've been telling her lies."

"I have not told her lies." Tamsin flushed. "I do not tell lies."

"Oh yes, and what's this I hear from Jess about me 'raping' you? Last summer, was it?"

Tamsin looked at her feet. For a long time she said nothing. At first Bill thought she was embarrassed at being caught out, then he realised she was on the edge of tears herself. He took a step towards her, part of him was rent with compassion. The other half with anger. He didn't know whether to speak or not.

"That's how it felt," she said. "To use someone and then walk out like that. And you wonder why I want to leave this place." Now she stood up in a massive effort to control her feelings. "You wonder why I want to leave this place! I have been to *Hell* because of you," she said. There didn't seem anything more to discuss on that subject.

"I want to see Reah today," Bill told her. There was no point in apologising again. He had to hold on to what mattered. "I want you to tell her that I want to see her."

"I'll tell her," Tamsin replied. Her voice very quiet. "I ought to get back."

"Will you bring her over at 11?" Bill asked.

"I'll ring you," said Tamsin, starting to walk.

"You haven't got a phone," Bill pointed out.

"I'll try and get her to come over at 11."

"I'll see you then."

It seemed inappropriate to walk back with Tamsin so Bill struck off into the woods.

As soon as he got back in Bill went to check for messages. Then, remembering that the phoneline was down, he diverted his course to make some more coffee. Halfway through tightening the machinetta he remembered that Schmidt was supposed to ring him today. That was annoying. Bill had given him his mobile number in case the airport meeting went awry. With a bit of luck he wouldn't be put off by the landline's failure. Of course, now he thought about it, if he did go down to Chepstow he'd pass through stretches of the Wye Valley where reception was poor. It would be maddening to emerge from the valley into an area of reasonable reception only to find a message from Schmidt explaining that he had already returned to Germany.

Should he ring him pre-emptively? Bill went out and looked at the sky. There were some dark clouds mustering in the south west. He really couldn't afford to leave that skylight in its current state. Bill decided to forgo coffee and phonecalls, and went up to measure for wood.

As he approached the lay-by where he'd left the Jeep last night he could hear an engine revving wildly and recognised the stench of petrol fumes hanging in the air. Turning the corner he saw Lee's van spread-eagled across the road in a sea of mud.

"I thought the post was a bit late," said Bill.

Lee was in no mood for joshing. "I mean why d'you people have to live up here?" he moaned, red-faced through an open window. "It's only the bloody English who buy these places. The rest of us go for somewhere with central heating, parking space and a little conservatory round the back. Somewhere on the *flat*, right?"

"Let me give you a push," said Bill.

"Bloody English," Lee repeated, but his mood was lightening. Together they turned the van round. "I'm not coming up here again till they've done something to this road," he grumbled. "I'm tellin' 'em straight. Here, your post and the bloody farm's."

"Thanks," said Bill.

"I mean what you been doing up here? Last few days it's been like the bloody Somme."

"Water Board," said Bill. "Seems we've got drainage problems. All the rain."

"Too bloody right you got drainage problems," said Lee. "You're going to have to call into the sorting office next week. I tell you I'm not coming up here again till someone finds where the bloody road's gone."

Bill followed Lee down in his Jeep. The track was indeed hazardous. Fortunately 4-wheel drive made all the difference even if it did stink the engine out.

On his way back from buying timber Bill made an attempt to get all the way up to Holt's Cottage in his Jeep but some substantial rocks, washed down in the night, blocked the road. In trying to skirt the debris he found that the excavation dug by Dŵr Cymru yesterday had filled up with mud. Closer inspection showed that the temporary surface laid on Friday had sunk, creating a substantial pot-hole across most of the road. Bill pulled off once more in the generator space and carried his strips of two-by-two back to Holt's Cottage.

He was up on the roof when he saw three figures coming out of the farmhouse. Bill had been glorying in the view. It was good to see beyond the all-oppressive tree-line and the sight of sunshine on the distant fields was cheering. Now, though, he noticed a chill in the air, as he saw Reah and two adults emerging from the farm.

Bill slithered down into the bedroom, taking his hammer and mobile with him. When he came out of the front-door the first thing he noticed was that the incubus known as Ben had fallen back and was waiting in Tamsin's field. He seemed to be undertaking a detailed inspection of the ponds that had formed overnight, and which were now seeping across the track and coagulating. Bill got no indication of what kind of man he was, not even much idea of age. He was not particularly tall, that was all Bill could tell.

In any case, the Reah and Tamsin delegation was much more important. Bill watched as it made its way over. When Reah got to the gatepost she spoke to Tamsin, presumably to ask her to wait. Reah then approached the cottage on her own. For a moment Bill had that curious image of his daughter running towards him again, falling, the blood and mud streaking her hair. He wanted to run forward and catch her up in his arms. But that was the past of his nightmares. This Reah was real and did not need rescuing.

She was dressed up against the cold, in an oversized black quilted jacket that she had probably borrowed. Her mass of hair disappeared into the folds of the hood which lay crumpled round her neck. She too wore knitted gloves and in one of them she held a letter.

Bill stepped towards her. "Please Reah," he said. "Not in writing, please. You can't undo anything that's been written down."

"I wanted you to have this," said Reah. "Because we're going back to London." She held out the letter. "I've tried to explain how I feel, Dad."

"You must feel very hurt," he said.

"I don't want to talk about it."

"I love you, Reah," said Bill. She was still holding the letter out. "I love you more than I've ever loved anyone."

Reah shuddered but despite her best resolve she was being drawn in. "Why did you say I bored you then?"

"I didn't say that," Bill insisted. "Libby said I said that. Seven years ago. I don't know if I ever said it."

"You said Libby never lied."

"No, I said it wasn't *like* Libby to lie. She may have done on this occasion. I don't know." Bill felt himself bending the truth right up to breaking point, but he really couldn't care less. He wanted his daughter back. That was all that mattered. "The thing is, even if what Libby wrote *was* true, that was seven years ago. It isn't true now. You are my happiness," Bill told her.

"Don't say that, Dad."

"But it's true."

"Yeah, and you were going to live here with her and let me keep on thinking that you were coming up to London to be with us. That's true too, isn't it?"

"I didn't have any intention of staying here with Libby. I just wanted her to be with me. I'm lonely, Boo," He saw Reah shudder again when he used that name. "I'll be particularly lonely when you go up to London. I was thinking of Libby moving in with me, yes, but that would be wherever I was living. Until I sold this place it would be here. If I moved to London it would be in London." Yes, he was definitely reaching breaking point now. "Libby likes London." Bill reassured her. *There*. Now it had been done. He had lied to her. For the second time. In the cause of a greater truth? Bill wasn't sure.

"Well I don't like any of it," said Reah, suddenly a little child again. "You've got her and Mum's got Ben and it's not right. That's why I've told Mum I want to go back to Gramma and Grandpops."

Bill looked over at where Tamsin stood and where Ben waited. His eyes were no longer drawn to the submerged section of road but were watching this scene as it unfolded in the distance. "You were going to have this morning in my cottage, Reah."

"I don't want today here," she replied. "It's always so gloomy. I want Gramma and Grandpops. Mum!" Bill wished she hadn't brought Tamsin in at this point. "Mum, I've told Dad we're going to Gramma and Grandpops today."

"It's ridiculous to go up to London today," said Bill. "You'll only have to come down again tomorrow for school."

Tamsin walked forward slowly. She looked uncomfortable. "I've got permission for Reah to go and visit her new school. She could stay up in London a few days."

"I'm not happy with that," said Bill. He could feel Reah being taken from him, his daughter absorbed into another community and never coming back.

"It's only for a few days," said Tamsin, half-heartedly. Clearly the prospect of this journey wasn't exactly delighting her, either. No doubt Reah had been giving Tamsin hell this morning about her parents and their various lovers. "Ben says he doesn't mind driving–"

"Can we leave bloody Ben out of this?" snapped Bill. "Besides, you can't get out at the moment, the road's a mess. Lee couldn't get through with the post. I've got yours for you, here." Bill dug in his pocket. "I tried getting up in the Jeep this morning. I had to park below where they've been working. It's not safe."

Reah took the letters, Bill noticed. Tamsin's face was registering panic. He could remember her fear of being trapped from when they were married. She rarely travelled on the Underground and once rang him in a panic from the Special Unit where she was teaching because she thought she'd been locked in for the night.

"I want to go to Gramma and Grandpops," said Reah, digging her heels in. "They're the only family I've got now."

"That's silly darling–" Tamsin began.

"You said you'd take me," Reah growled.

"Look, it's not feasible," said Bill. "Why don't you spend some time with me today and some time with Tamsin, and we'll see how the road is tomorrow?"

He felt if he could just get Reah into the cottage for a few hours he'd win her back. He was Daddy Boo, she was Boo Boo Bear.

"No!" said Boo Boo, and she turned round and stalked back to the gatepost.

"This is your doing," Bill told Tamsin.

"It's not," Tamsin protested, pinioned between the enmity of two people. "I promise you, Bill. You've no idea what she's been like. She was so rude to Ben."

"I don't give a stuff about Ben!" Bill told her. In the distance he saw Ben look up. For a moment Bill wondered if the man might have heard his exclamation but, no, Ben was watching Reah who had turned round and was marching back towards Bill with that letter in her hand.

"I want you to read this," she said. "If you take me at all seriously–"

"OK," said Bill, hoping that showing that he took his daughter seriously might indeed help the situation. Bill took the letter. Reah walked away. Bill glared at Tamsin.

"It's not my fault," she told him and then followed behind Reah. Bill watched them go. He saw Reah brush past Ben, and Ben and Tamsin exchange a few words before following in Reah's wake. Ben put an arm round Tamsin. Bill didn't blame him for doing so, but he hated him too.

Bill wandered inside, sat down and opened Reah's letter. There had been too many letters, he thought. All those e-mails and faxes that he and Libby had sent each other. All the letters that Wagner had showered on his *Werther Freund*, each one costing Georg Schmidt £1,000. What were letters costing Bill?

"*Dear Dad*," read Reah's wonderful spidery handwriting. He had seen it evolve from early spidery scrawl to adolescent spidery scrawl. Presumably even as an adult Reah Wheeler would always scuttle across the page, her script plunging relentlessly down to towards the right hand margin, never quite managing to pull out in time.

This is the third time I have written to you. The first two were so angry I threw them away. Dad I am cross with you. You used to say when we first moved here that you needed to get away when you were

angry well that's how I feel too. I'm going to stay with Gramma and
Grandpops for a few days. They say I can stay as long as I want.
Sometimes I feel like they are the only family I've got.

The handwriting suddenly changed as if Reah had left the letter and
come back to it in a different mood. Her script no longer sloped so alarmingly. She had decelerated and pulled out of her tail-spin.

I also want to say that if you want to marry Libby then I won't want
to live with you at all. I don't care what you say I know that she broke
up your marriage to Mum and if that hadn't happened none of this
would have happened either. I want two parents who are married to
each other. Not to other people. I've told Mum this too.
 Your daughter (not that you ever wanted her)
 Reah Wheeler

Bill felt his heart go out to Reah. He hated that last little jibe but also
felt desperately sorry that she felt the need to make it. He knew he could
persuade Reah and win her back. After all, it was the truth that she was the
focus of his happiness. It wasn't difficult to persuade people of the truth,
assuming they wanted to believe it.

His mobile rang. Bill folded Reah's letter and left it on the hall table
while he picked up the phone. "Mr Wheeler? Georg Schmidt. Your other
number isn't working, I believe."

Bill sighed and tried to focus. "We've had bad storms here. The landline is down."

"So. What can I do for you, Mr Wheeler?" Schmidt was sounding inap-
propriately affable today. "You say you want a story that you will not
publish. I find this curious in a journalist."

"Maybe I'm not a very good journalist," said Bill.

"I have been thinking about this famous letter," said Schmidt in a jovial
turn of phrase that quite surprised Bill. "If I tell you the story, as you
request, how do I know that you will hand it over?"

"I have your contract here," said Bill. "Tell me where you are and I'll
fax it over signed."

"I thought your l-l-landline wasn't working," said Schmidt.

"Oh yes, I forgot," said Bill. His mind was still on Reah's letter. "Look,
Mr Schmidt. Is this story really going to set the world on fire? I get the
impression from you that it won't."

"That is true," said Schmidt. "It is a footnote in history."

"Well I have to take your word that the story you're going to give me is
the truth," said Bill. "I'm sure if you tell me it's not going to get my editors

excited you're right. But how will I know I'm getting the real story? You may have made something up to put me off the trail."

Schmidt started to protest.

"It's in your interest to keep it dull after all, isn't it?" said Bill.

Schmidt's stammer interposed itself for a moment. "Y-yes," he conceded finally.

"So what I'm saying is why don't we trust each other? Give me the address you want it mailed to. Tell me the story and I'll put it in the post first thing Monday."

"Why Monday?" Schmidt asked.

"Post offices close at lunchtime round here," Bill told him. "I live in the wilds."

This detail seemed to convince Georg Schmidt. "Very well. Do you have an envelope and pencil to hand?" He then dictated what sounded like the address of some factory or office in Lausanne. "So tell me, then. What is it you want to know?"

Bill had been transcribing in the office. Now he took his mobile and the Wagner file into the living room and settled himself with a notepad by the fireplace. "In this letter Wagner addresses someone he refers to as his *Werther Freund*. Do you know who this man or woman is?"

"Man," said Schmidt. "I see your command of German isn't all that it should be, Mr Wheeler. The female form would be '*meine werthe Freundin*'."

"OK," said Bill, refusing to be sidetracked. "Who is the *Werther Freund*?"

"I don't know," said Schmidt. "Originally these letters were offered to me through an intermediary. No explanation was proffered. I believed I had bought them all. Only afterwards was I told that some letters from the archive had been pilfered."

"OK so who offered you the letters?"

"A dealer approached me with the archive. Such men exist. You do not need to know the name."

"Why did that dealer come to you?"

"You do not need to know that either."

Bill was beginning to get annoyed by the way Schmidt blocked him. "I thought you were going to answer my questions," he said.

"About the letter, yes."

"Do you have any idea who the *Werther Freund* might be?"

"I have theories," said Schmidt.

"I'd like to hear them," said Bill. If Schmidt didn't come clean now he was ending this call. "Well?"

"Richard Wagner writes with great openness to this man," said Schmidt. "For the time in which he is writing he is altogether much more confessional than one might normally expect. For this reason I do not believe that his correspondent was a family member. Wagner's relations with the men in his family were for the most part formal. He was the oldest son. He was inclined to strut too. Personally I have wondered if the friend might not be Pusinelli, the family doctor whom we know Wagner did address as his *Werther Freund* on occasions. Within the letters that I have studied which are known to be written to Pusinelli, intimate details are revealed, but these are of a more medical than psycho-sexual nature. Richard Wagner did not discuss problems of his sex-life with Pusinelli. As far as we know. Nevertheless, in the archive I acquired he does touch obliquely on such issues."

Bill made a note of this point.

"In fact you might say that what I have is exclusively the 'hidden Wagner' archive. As if someone has assembled it to that purpose. Moreover it can be slotted into the existing correspondence with Anton Pusinelli. There is no question, for instance, of Wagner writing two contradictory letters on the same day. I have checked. But then I have not seen all the letters yet. It may be when I look at yours that my theory is blown apart, that when he writes to Pusinelli, 'I am well', he writes on the same day to the *Werther Freund*, 'I am ill'. This is why I wish to see your letter."

"There is no date on it," said Bill.

"Mostly the date is torn off. I can only assume the *Werther Freund* was trying to protect Wagner. And yet he is unable to destroy the letters. He may burn a few. I imagine there are gaps. Occasionally he even removes the signature, but that is as far as he goes. And this despite the fact that Wagner frequently begs that this correspondence be destroyed."

"Difficult," Bill admitted.

"We can assume that Cosima or Eva, or maybe even Glasenapp, destroyed the other side of the correspondence if Wagner himself did not. I have not come across any letters that might be construed as those of the *Werther Freund* writing in reply. Maybe Wagner was responsible. He always had an eye to posterity, though I doubt he could have anticipated our – what is the word – our '*prurience*'."

"Who's Glasenapp?" Bill asked.

"Wagner's 'in-house' biographer," Schmidt replied. "Richard Wagner's not really your subject is he, Mr Wheeler?"

"I'm not even sure I like the man," Bill replied.

"D-d-difficult," Schmidt agreed. He was in an altogether more easy-going mood today. "Some people are easier to love than like, easier to admire than live with, wouldn't you say?"

"So am I right in thinking 'Our Dearest Lusch' is Daniela von Bülow?" Bill asked without preamble. There was a pause. Bill felt that he had struck Schmidt below the belt, but he couldn't imagine why the name had such an effect. Vita had sent him that fiche about Lusch being Daniela's pet name. This was no secret.

"Ah," said Schmidt. "So she is mentioned. In your letter she is mentioned?"

"Very much so," said Bill.

"In what context?" asked Schmidt. He sounded weary, resigned even.

Bill was intrigued by the change in Schmidt's tone. "Oh," said Bill, searching for the memory. "Well, for instance, Wagner writes that he is distraught that she is currently in Venice. What's so wrong with Venice, just out of interest?"

"In 1882, when I believe your letter was written, Daniela accompanied her grandfather, the composer Liszt, to Venice," Schmidt explained. There was something very odd in his voice. "There they stayed with the Princess Hatzfeldt. The princess's daughter, Countess von Schleinitz, then took Daniela into her household in Berlin. This move was prior to the launching of Daniela into society."

The man was talking like a robot, reciting facts. He sounded wholly disengaged.

"I still don't see why that should bother him," Bill replied. Schmidt didn't answer so Bill continued. "Wagner also says that Lusch is going to meet her father. That seems really to upset him."

"Yes. I can understand. They had already met the previous year, through the agency of Liszt," answered Schmidt with what felt like needless pedantry.

"I don't think you're really answering my question," Bill replied, but Schmidt continued regardless.

"Cosima had tried to reintroduce Hans von Bülow to his elder daughter when she was nineteen, but von Bülow sensed that she was using their child to make reparation for the elopement and betrayal. And he had blown up at her. You may know he was a difficult man, Mr Wheeler. When they did meet finally, von Bülow was overjoyed with Daniela and wrote to Cosima that his estranged daughter was a dear creature who had captured his soul in an instant. He even went as far as to ask Cosima Wagner what his fatherly duties should be toward such a sweet soul. Do you know the letter?"

"No."

"I must translate then – given that you do not have German." Bill wished Schmidt would not keep pointing that out. "*Teach me, great generous, noble woman, what could be the fatherly duties towards this d-d-dear creature, I am in debt to you for an incomparable happiness.*"

"Generous man," said Bill. "Considering Cosima ran off with Wagner and took Daniela and Blandine with her."

"Von Bülow was a man of the noblest nature," said Schmidt, then he paused. The comment had been made without any irony. "Un-unfortunately his nobility manifests itself best in his letters. He was a difficult man to be with. He continued to raise money for Wagner's projects even when he had none of his own. And yet he could be spiteful to Cosima if ever they were in contact. Have I answered y-your questions now?"

"No," said Bill, "very much not so."

"What else can I tell you?"

"You say Daniela was going back to live with von Bülow, this is Cosima's plan?"

"Yes."

"So why was Wagner so upset about this? I have here some very, very unhappy stuff indeed, claiming she was Sieglinde to his Siegmund, Brünhilde to his Siegfried. At one point he actually says – this is my translation so it may not be wholly accurate, of course – '*What hope is there for me? She cannot love me as I her.*' He later says, '*This matter affects me deeply you may imagine.*'"

Schmidt sighed as if this were all so familiar. "Yes," he said. "Wagner was a big baby in many respects. He knew nothing of half measures. You should not read too much into that. No one could love Wagner as he them, with the possible exception of Cosima."

"But what about the letter that was published in America? He says there that he has dared but now he can dare no more. That it would be asking too much of her bravery. Are we to assume he is talking about Lusch here?"

Schmidt paused and then replied somewhat distantly. "I should imagine so. I dearly wish you did not have that letter, Mr Wheeler."

But Bill's mind was elsewhere. He scrabbled to where the printout from Vita lay on the settee. "Here," he said. "Listen: '*I have dared but now I may dare no more. It is not just my own bravery that would be tested but hers. No man must know what I have done. My worthy friend I ask you to destroy this letter and with it all knowledge of the deeds of which I spoke to you.*'"

Bill waited a moment. "What deeds, Mr Schmidt? Presumably if you have the rest of the correspondence you know."

Schmidt did not answer so Bill repeated the penultimate sentence: "'*No man must know what I have done.*' What had he done, Mr Schmidt?"

Schmidt breathed heavily. "This is the kind of salacious scandalmongering I wished to avoid."

"If there is a scandal there it's not of my making," protested Bill. "I'm just trying to understand."

"Are you r-r-really?" Schmidt's stammer was getting more pronounced. "S-so tell me then, Mr Wheeler, what does it sound like to you?"

Bill felt reluctant to say what was on his mind. "I thought you were answering my questions."

"So. You will trail your innuendoes through the supposedly upmarket broadsheets," said Schmidt. "But you won't put them up to be tested." A challenge. No doubt about it.

"OK," said Bill. "To me it reads as if Wagner became over-fond of Daniela and that Cosima couldn't take that."

"I see and is this the story you wish to publish?"

"I don't want to publish any story," said Bill. "I've told you that. I just want your version of the truth, which ought to be closer than mine. What was it that Wagner had dared? What asked too much of Daniela's bravery? What was it Wagner dared now not do? Why, for that matter, had Cosima refused to embrace him that morning, something that he attributes directly to this business of Lusch?"

"Well," said Schmidt. "Well, yes, I cannot entirely blame you. The American translation of that letter was quite melodramatic."

"So?" Bill asked.

"Wagner did grow over-fond of Daniela," Schmidt admitted. "He and Cosima never differentiated between their children and the children she had had with von Bülow. Indeed the true parentage of Isolde – the middle child – remained a mystery, with both Wagner and von Bülow claiming to be the natural father. Daniela and her sister Blandine were von Bülow's, but they lived most of their childhood with Richard Wagner. We do not know how close the relationship between Wagner and Daniela was but there can be a closeness that exists between father and daughter that is very special.

"When you look at Wotan the Allvater and Brünhilde you can see that Wagner considers the illegitimate daughter a much closer connection than that with the legitimate wife, Fricka, or mistress Erda. Erda, the mother of Brünhilde, even. Brünhilde it is who alone understands Wotan. She is, as you may know, the agent of his wishes, his *Walküre* or *Valkyrie*."

"I do go to the opera," Bill pointed out.

"I believe Daniela was Wagner's Valkyrie," said Schmidt. "That is my opinion. He uses Wotan's words that his wish alone brought her to life. '*Die mein Wunsch allein ihr schuf.*' She is his '*wunschmaid,*' his wish-maid, if you like. He was distraught about the idea of her going away."

Bill felt he could understand that alright.

"Going away to a man who hardly knew her," Schmidt continued, then the phone connection seemed to give out.

"I beg your pardon, I missed that."

"I said, she was going away to a man who had never seen her grow up. A m-m-man who had taught her nothing, never read her a bedtime story. Wagner was quite '*ein neuer Mann*' when it came to parenting, I should say."

"But what was it Wagner had chanced his arm at?" Bill asked. "He said he'd dared but now he'd dare no more. That it asked too much of her. Am I right in assuming the obvious?"

"Well if the woman Wagner writes of is Daniela," said Schmidt, "then we know that he wished to adopt Daniela, to give her his name and keep her with him, contrary to Cosima's wishes."

Bill felt a sudden cold sickness.

"There is no doubt in my mind that he loved Daniela deeply," said Schmidt. "But as a father. When he made moves to keep Daniela and Blandine from their natural father it was the desperate act of a man who truly felt they – Daniela in particular – were his. The Count von Schleinitz was the man who finally stood up to Wagner and told him that not even he could do this. Schleinitz was at court, the Prussian court in Berlin. He knew the limit to which special pleading could be made on behalf of a man like Richard Wagner. If it is Lusch of whom Wagner is writing, then I believe this may be what he means when he speaks of having dared but daring no more."

There was a pause during which Bill's mobile beeped to tell him that its battery was low.

"Mr Wheeler, do you have your answer now? Do you see why Wagner tells his friend that he must destroy these letters so that no man must ever know what he had attempted to do?"

"Yes," said Bill.

"Do you see that your letter, if published out of context, would simply give an identity to the young woman cited in that wretched American website. And if your letter gives her a name then, in the wrong hands, we could have a truly sordid and wholly false scandal on our hands?"

"Yes," said Bill.

"I am glad we talked," Schmidt continued. "The letters in my possession spoke of a great rift between Cosima and Richard that took time to heal and that its cause was someone whose love Wagner feared to lose. Cosima wrote and said that until now she had known that, while his heart erred, his soul had always remained with her. The implication is unfortunate. And yet her letters never identified the person of whom she spoke. I knew that one of Wagner's own letters was bound to. I had fears that yours might. This is a very important letter."

"Yes," said Bill.

"Now you will send it to me?"

The phone beeped again.

"My mobile needs recharging," said Bill. "Can I ring you back? Or will you ring me back in two hours when I've recharged?"

"Mr Wheeler we made a d-d-deal—"

"I need to know!" said Bill.

"What do you n-n-eed to know?"

"Why! Why all this bothers you so much!" But the line was already dead.

Bill spent the afternoon tormented by what Schmidt had told him. On the one hand he identified totally with Wagner, losing a daughter who is the dearest thing to one's heart. On the other, he hated Wagner the parasite, siphoning off von Bülow's children in that way. It was one thing to imagine the waste of Reah living out her childhood in the presence of this Ben, a man who could never care for her, never take delight in her as Bill did. But the idea of Ben taking that sort of interest, developing such feelings for his child, made Bill angry beyond measure.

He had just finished sealing the skylight when he noticed water-drops spatter angrily across it. Right on cue, the storm was beginning again.

Bill squatted by the fire wondering what he should do. Bizarrely he was drawn to his shotgun again. Ben was indeed a threat. It was his doing that Tamsin wanted to return to London, and that decision to return had cost Bill his daughter. He should never have agreed to her having all their capital. At least if he paid her monthly maintenance he would have some leverage now. Bill went to the door and took down his gun. He broke the barrel but wasn't sure whether he was checking there were no cartridges within or secretly hoping to find some. One way or another he had to stop Ben taking his daughter to London.

It was cold. Bill replaced the gun and sought out his battered waxed-jacket from where it hung on the door. He returned to the fireplace and sat hugging his knees, trying to keep warm. He had to get Reah from that house.

There was a knock on the door. Bill's heart leapt. It had to be Reah. He struggled to rise. Could it really be? He was stiff from crouching too long on the cold slabs. "Come in!"

The door opened but admitted Tamsin. Tamsin. No one else. "It's dark in here," she said.

"What do you want?" Bill asked, taking a step towards her.

Tamsin was closing her umbrella. Her coat was lightly sprinkled with rain. "I wondered if we could use your mobile."

"Why?"

"Reah's very keen to go to London. I thought if we could get a taxi to meet us at the bottom of the lane we could catch a train from Newport."

"No," said Bill. "My phone's run out anyway. I had a long call this afternoon. It's recharging." With a nod he indicated where his mobile was plugged in on the floor.

"Well, when it's recharged," said Tamsin.

"No." Bill moved so that he stood between Tamsin and the phone. "You're not taking Reah away."

Tamsin looked tired with him. "Please, Bill, I've tried reasoning with her. You don't know difficult she can be. She's all sweetness and light when she's with you. I get all the tantrums."

"I'm not letting you take her and that's an end to it," said Bill. He realised he was being very hardline, offensive even. "It's getting dark anyway, and the track down there is unsafe."

Tamsin looked unhappy. "Well you could take us down in your Jeep if you didn't want us to walk–"

"No!"

The bark shocked them both. Tamsin blinked. Clearly in her heart she still expected to be able to turn to Bill if practicalities proved difficult. But not this time, not when she was taking his child away from him. "It's only for a few days," said Tamsin miserably. She looked close to tears.

"Oh yes and what guarantee have I got that I'll ever see her again?" snarled Bill.

"What do you mean? That's ridiculous. I'll bring her back on Wednesday, I promise."

"I don't believe you."

"Please Bill. If you won't let me ring from here then I'm going to have to walk down the track and find somewhere to phone. I can't stay here. I feel..."

Trapped, thought Bill. "You'll find it pretty difficult to get down there in the dark on your own," he told her. "Do you have a torch?"

"No, Jessica brought the electric box back with her."

"That's unfortunate."

"Do you have one I could borrow?" Tamsin asked, her voice trailing away. Bill shook his head. "You're trying to keep me a prisoner!" she said and burst into tears.

"Don't be ridiculous." Her tears always moved him. This time they moved him a step closer to sanity. "Listen I'm not stopping you and Ben. I just don't want you taking Reah away."

"Even if you keep her here she won't come to the cottage, don't you see!" Tamsin was shouting now. "She's been complaining about it for ages. I don't think it's the cottage *per se*. It's as if she associates it with trying to cheer you up." Tamsin was trying to make him see reason but she had the opposite effect.

"If Reah doesn't want to come here, that's because you have poisoned her against me." His anger was seething.

"No!" cried Tamsin. "I haven't, I'm the one who's been telling her she needs to come."

"I don't believe you," said Bill. He got up, walked to the door and held it open. "I don't think we have anything more to say to each other."

Rain skeetered in. Suddenly Tamsin grabbed his arm, digging her nails angrily into the fabric of his coat. "What are you trying to do, Bill?! Is it so awful that I've got a life again? Is it? Is it?"

"You're being ridiculous," Bill told her, still holding the door.

"I don't want to stay here!" Tamsin gazed wildly round the cottage. "Bill, I can't bear being trapped!"

"You've brought this on yourself." He realised he was being unfair. He wanted to stop but suddenly Tamsin aimed a slap across Bill's face. He stepped back and caught her wrist in his hand.

"Why are you doing this to me?!" she cried.

Bill held Tamsin. "Bring Reah over."

"*She won't come!*"

The two of them stared at each other, their faces alarmingly close. It was a curious intimacy. One of her hands was dug into the sleeve of his coat, the other he held at the wrist. They stood at the open door pressed against each other. Neither knew what to do. Bill could have kissed her at that moment. The old arousal was still there. He moved slightly closer so that their bodies made more intimate contact. Tamsin gazed up at Bill.

"Please," she whispered. "Let me phone."

He desired her at that moment. It was grotesque but he did. Maybe it was just because of Ben being on the scene, but Bill wanted Tamsin now more than he could remember wanting her – ever. Would she? If he promised to let her phone? It felt diabolical. A black infamous bargain. What had he become?

Bill stepped back and Tamsin released her fingers from the sleeve of his coat. The moment passed. Both knew what had happened but they were strangers again now. Strangers, after all that they had shared, because essentially his people were still the oppressor in her eyes. Rapist. Captor. Bill realised that the currency of their relationship now was Tamsin's victimhood. However honourably he behaved towards her, he could never make amends. His kind never could. In rejoining her people she had gone over to the other side.

Tamsin had already taken a few steps back into the room. Now she walked purposefully to where Bill's phone was charging. This was the least he owed her.

"No!" shouted Bill and he leaped across the room. Tamsin had the phone in her hands. Bill tried to seize it from her.

"Give it to me!" Tamsin hissed. Bill tried to pry her fingers clear but the grip he encountered was superhuman. "Give it to me or you'll never see Reah again!"

It might have been the thing to say. It might have intimidated him sufficiently, but in her desperation Tamsin had misjudged. The next thing both of them knew she was spinning backwards, crashing into the sofa. The phone was somewhere in mid-air. Bill seized Tamsin and pulled her to the door. He was aware momentarily that she had no weight and when he threw her out through the open door she seemed briefly to fly. Then the world shifted again. Time spun back into reality. Bill found himself leaning against the door-jamb, his hand bleeding. Tamsin lay in the rain on the garden path, looking confused and ungainly. Bill was shocked. He went to help her but she scrambled away from him in the mud and spat that she would see him in Hell. Surely they were there already, thought Bill, in a moment of curious calm.

He closed the door and took his gun down from its hooks. His ex-wife had never seemed so alien to him, or so dangerous. Bill squatted down by the fireplace again and wrapped his arms round the gun.

Of course, it was obvious, he thought. Tamsin had been asking for Reah's passport. Tamsin had been away and wouldn't tell him where. Of course she was planning to take the child to Israel. All this London school business was just to put him off the scent. For all Bill knew, this Ben person held Israeli citizenship. He'd been helping Tamsin apply for residence. It was illegal to take Reah out of the country without his permission but would the Israelis care about that? Once Tamsin got her over there she'd be protected. Israel believed in rescuing any Jew who could make it to Israel, wasn't that so? Particularly from a rapist father. Well not his daughter.

Bill got up and picked up the mobile. It felt oddly wet in his hand. He checked it was not broken, switched it on and stuffed it in his pocket. He would wait for Tamsin and Ben to make their move. Bill squatted down by the hearth again. It was cold with the door still open. Really Bill knew he should wait in the doorway until he saw them, but he was cold enough already and the rain was splattering everywhere. He would close the door for a while and then take up his sentry-post, maybe when the rain had passed. They'd wait until then.

He closed the door but didn't bolt it. He had to be ready. Seeing the coffee machinetta half-assembled Bill remembered that he hadn't eaten today. That might be another reason why he was so cold, but he didn't feel like food.

Bill resumed his place by the hearth. His mind turned to thoughts of the weekend he should have had here with Reah. They were going to watch *A Touch Of Evil* together. Libby had wrecked that. At that moment Bill felt he hated both of them, Tamsin and Libby. The only certainty in all this was that he loved Reah and they had driven him and Reah apart. Tamsin and Libby, two women who had sought to destroy his relationship with his daughter. Why had he given them the ammunition? If he could have cried he would have.

Bill wasn't aware of sleeping but he knew that he passed into a state that seemed outside time. Grief, tiredness and hunger were doing strange things to him. The unlit cottage seemed only intermittently real. At one point he thought he saw the door open and Reah enter but he knew that to be the cruel prickings of hope which plague us long after we have lost all reason to hope.

The door was opening nevertheless. Bill knew himself to be invisible where he sat, and so he waited to see who or what would enter. Someone was in the room moving slowly, a figure he did not recognise. She did not shut the door, this figure. The dim light from the night sky outside illuminated her progress. The rain had stopped and Bill was awake. The intruder was dressed indistinctly in country garb, rendering her shapeless. How then did he know it was a woman? It was the way she moved, thought Bill. He watched, fascinated to see how someone behaved in his cottage when he was not there. This was a rare experience, mused Bill. This is how someone moves around my cottage when I am not here. He felt no alarm. No sense of outrage or even invasion, just curiosity.

The figure was moving towards Bill's stairs. Surely she must see me now, thought Bill. Were I not invisible she would see me now. He heard a creak as a foot pressed down on the loose bottom step. Bill had forgotten how that step groaned. It had made quite a noise the time he and Libby had made love on the stairs. The same noise as when Reah had marched out, dragging her overnight bag. No, this is not a dream, thought Bill. I have willed myself into a state of invisibility.

Another step creaked and then for no apparent reason the intruder recognised Bill's presence in the room. She was looking down directly into the fireplace.

"You weren't expecting me?" said Bill.

"Rain lifted," she said, stepping down. "Thought I'd bring your book back."

Marika.

"Do you often come in when I'm not here?" Bill asked. He didn't move.

"Didn't see the car," said Marika.

"You thought I was away."

"Aye."

Bill felt no need to prolong the conversation. He was happily beyond the kind of conventions that attend on welcoming a visitor. Even of chasing off a burglar.

Marika watched him for a while. "You 'bin hurt?" she asked. "Your hand's a mess."

Now that Bill thought about it, his hand was painful and sticky. He didn't want to move it to check. Movement was a distraction. Marika came closer. "Dammo, you covered in blood. This thing loaded?" she asked.

Bill shook his head. Marika crouched down beside him. He saw the light from the doorway highlighting the creases on her forehead, the folds around her eyes. He saw the brightness of her eyes. She had most unusual eyes, he thought. Tamsin's were hungry, Libby's – from when he chose to remembered them – were happy, but Marika's were like an animal's. Ever alert.

"D'you often come here?" Bill asked, as Marika took his wounded hand.

"Well, seeing as you don't ever invite me," she said. "An' seeing that you don't often lock the door."

"And d'you take things?" said Bill.

"*Borrow*," said Marika. She got up and walked to the kitchen area where she washed a dishcloth to bind round his hand. On her way back she saw the Sotheby's catalogue that Bill had left out to amuse Libby. "I bring 'm back," she said, nodding.

Marika pried Bill's hand away from the gun again. "You gonna need stitches in that 'un."

Bill winced with the pain. "*Why*?"

Marika looked up at him. Her eyes were intense and attentive, he thought. Not dull and bovine as he'd always imagined. Feral, but incapable of love. "Why what?"

"Why do you come here and take things?" That deep shaft of pain had broken through the silent composure of Bill's soul. He was feeling uncomfortably reconnected to the world and to curiosity again. Marika shrugged.

"Why?"

"No reason."

"*Why*?" She sat back, the job complete.

"Maybe 'cause you come to my place and never leave nothing of you behind." She was silent again. That was a significant statement, thought Bill. It suggested that for Marika, their couplings had been something more than animal. "An' like when you don't turn up sometimes I think, right I'm going over there. I come over last week. Saw you working away. It's all dark out there. You never saw me."

"No, I didn't," said Bill. He stretched his legs, aware that cramps were developing. "So tonight you decided to pay me a visit?"

Marika shrugged. "The buggers were quiet. Storm passing, I thought I'd get out. Maybe bring your book back if the car weren't here. Which it weren't."

"Parked down the lane," said Bill. "Flooding."

"Ah."

"What book?" he asked. Marika slipped it out of her pocket. Bill recognised the cover with its photo of Richard Wagner in profile. He laughed. Laughed at life's rich ironies. How many go past that we never discover? What a fool he'd been.

"You 'ent angry then?" asked Marika. Bill tried to rise.

"How could I be?" said Bill. She helped him get to his feet. "But I'm getting a bloody lock for that door."

"Got some other stuff if you want to come over," said Marika. Somehow she seemed much more innocent than he'd ever known her to be. It was as if without the cigarette and her customary carapace she was less a desiccated misanthrope, more the feral child on whom the old bastard had made his move. Marika had dug her boots into his genitals till the old man had shrieked, but she was probably damaged too. Bill now remembered how Marika had compared the farmer's cries to those of a stuck pig. Thank God he'd been fighting with Tamsin today and not his resourceful neighbour. Bill noticed that his jacket was covered in dark crimson too.

Marika put the book on the hall table as she had the Sotheby's catalogue. Now he thought about it, this had always been her calling card. She could have sneaked things back in without making their reappearance noticeable, but no, she'd wanted him to wonder who had placed the catalogue there. Reah's book would probably turn up on the kitchen table one day. How ridiculous that he'd considered the possibility of poltergeists. He'd turned that gun on Mertens and Plod.

"So I'll expect you sometime?" said Marika, standing at the doorway now.

"Aye," said Bill, involuntarily picking up her way of speaking. "One question," he added, "have I seen you sometimes on the edge of the Forestry Commission plantation, looking this way?"

"Maybe," said Marika. "I don't always come over."

"Thanks," said Bill.

Bill sat in the porch nursing his hand. He felt less inclined to stand guard now. It was gone ten o'clock. Surely Tamsin and Ben would not think of leaving this late. There were no trains to London at this time of night anyway.

He felt he needed a whisky. His hand was beginning to throb badly. He was worried too that the dressing Marika had applied was not as clean as it should be. What the hell had happened in that fight with Tamsin?

Limping to the sideboard, Bill found himself wondering about the scene in Holt's Farm. Tamsin distraught because she felt trapped, and Reah angry because she was not going to London as they'd promised her. No doubt Tamsin had told Ben that Bill had attacked her. Would Reah overhear? She would not want Tamsin denouncing him in front of Ben. He could imagine her denying that her Dad would do such a thing. He hoped so anyway. But Ben, what must Ben wonder about the family with whom he had become mixed up? They'd probably all given up now and gone to bed. So should he.

Bill fished the mobile out of his pocket with his good hand, wiped off some of the blood and dialled Tamsin. Maybe if he could speak to her on the phone they could settle this. He did not want to be at war with her. He just wanted his old life back. He wanted to see Reah's face every day. He didn't want to live on his own. If the truth be told, he would probably have settled for being married again. If only there were not so much anger between him and Tamsin.

God what a mess, thought Bill. He let the whisky find its way within him. For the spirit to rise up and spread peace. If it could anaesthetise his hand at the same time that would be even better.

But of course Tamsin's phone wasn't working. Bill lay back on the settee and thought of what his life had come to. He was no longer young. All he had for his years was a divorce, an itinerant career on the periphery of the arts, a cottage that had only once been a home – for those five brief days when Libby had stayed here – and a daughter estranged from him.

Like the *Allvater* his daughter, thought Bill. Maybe he too had made Reah in his own image. He hardly remembered his relationship with her before he separated from Tamsin, but since then they had watched films together late at night and gone for walks even later to look at the stars. Waking on a Saturday morning to make coffee and stand at the window in his office, knowing that, after a while, Reah would emerge, a mass of night-clothes and hair, wander downstairs, hug him and blearily plug herself into the TV: this had been happiness for Bill.

Maybe this was what Wagner had found with Lusch. Libby didn't understand. He wasn't in love with his daughter, but maybe it was as complete a relationship as he, Bill Wheeler, could manage.

And yet something niggled Bill and disturbed him in his weariness. Why had Cosima refused to embrace Richard? It didn't quite make sense, did it, if Schmidt was right that all Wagner had dared was to try and adopt Daniela? No doubt that was true. And Cosima might have thought it tactless and overbearing, but would she really refuse to embrace him because of that?

Why had Wagner written about that to his *Werther Freund?* He must have known he was storing up trouble. That's why he begged the friend to destroy the letters. So why does he write so much? Because sometimes it is the only way we can cope with the extremity of our feelings, thought Bill. Or convince ourselves of their validity, of course. Hadn't he twice conjured-up an affair with Libby out of the air with words alone? Why was it that he and Reah had such love yet had hardly ever written a word to each other? Some has to be created but some love just is.

Words, thought Bill. Words and women. He didn't think much more until he registered a noise, distant, worrying. But Bill felt too tired, too weary to even think about what it was. This had been an extraordinary day.

Two battles with Tamsin. Things unsaid from seven years ago. Then Reah rejecting him and Marika arriving in the dark, a ghostly visitation. That last was almost unreal. Were it not for the throbbing stained dishcloth round his hand Bill would not have believed any of it had happened.

Again that noise. And with it recognition. My God, it was the sound of a car's engine turning over. Now firing. Bill leapt up. They couldn't be so crazy as to try and drive out tonight. The circulation in one of his legs was playing up after all that squatting by the fire. Bill limped as best he could to the door using the gun as a crutch.

Damn it, as Bill opened the door he realised it was raining again now. Didn't Tamsin believe him for godsake? As soon as he was outside, Bill could see that a largish car was moving down from the farm. He rushed as best he could towards the gatepost. They'd have to slow down to pass through there. The car was already encountering difficulties in the hollow where Tamsin's track was now fully submerged. Bill reached the gatepost and dropped the gun out of sight. He didn't want to alarm the car's occupants. His presence had already been picked up in the undipped headlights. He saw the car – Ben's presumably – suddenly accelerate through the floodwater. Spray flew everywhere, caught in the white dazzle of the car's lurching headlamps.

"Stop!" shouted Bill as the car regained its momentum on the near-side of the hollow. Instinctively he fell back behind the gatepost. Rain was falling faster now. He saw the car's wipers switch to a faster setting and heard the driver accelerate. This was madness. And Reah was inside. The car, not twenty yards away, hit a pothole and lurched violently up out of it. Bill felt he heard a cry from inside. He had to make them stop; moving at that kind of speed on the mud that lay across the road further down could be catastrophic.

Had Reah not been in the car Bill might not have done what he did now. The speed and noise was certainly intimidating but his daughter was there. She was within, and whether this desperate escape plan were her idea or not she needed him. That meant he had no choice. Bill pulled the gun up with his good hand and advanced into the path of the speeding vehicle. Surely it would stop now?

It took him only a moment to realise that he was wrong. Very wrong. Whoever was driving was not in a mood to be intimidated. With a roar and a blaze of headlights the car seemed to come straight at him, leaping like a wild animal. Bill just had time to hurl himself into the wire-fencing to the left of the gatepost and bring his rifle butt across the windscreen as the recoil of the wire hurled him back and into the side of the passing car.

As he hit the front-door panel Bill was briefly aware of Tamsin in the front passenger seat looking straight ahead and Reah in the back screaming. The vehicle slewed to the right as if in a belated attempt to avoid Bill but as he hit the track Bill knew that the car's windscreen had been smashed. The driver presumably had no idea where he was going now. It must be pandemonium inside, thought Bill, as long microseconds of calm passed by him. Why doesn't he brake? Bill struggled to his feet as Ben's car with alarming and ridiculous thoroughness ploughed off to the right and straight into the gatepost, which it hit with an enormous bang that echoed round the skyline.

Bill staggered to his feet and ran towards it. Before he could see anything clearly he was aware of steam hissing from the roaring engine and the sounds of pain. Bill found his shotgun on the road and used it as a crutch again. But hitting the car had really done something to his leg this time. Reaching the back door he flung it open and Reah fell out into the mud. There was blood on her forehead and down her nose. He couldn't tell if she were conscious or not.

"Come on, Baby." Bill pulled her clear and on to the grass verge. He could hear Tamsin shouting, but for the moment he ignored her. "Come on, Baby!" he said, slapping Reah gently on the face. Suddenly, with a huge intake of breath she was back and looking at him with terror. "You OK?" Bill asked. Reah nodded; she still looked like a startled rabbit, but she was breathing. She was OK. There was rain on her forehead.

"Dad–" she started to say, but Bill was heading back to the car. He tried opening Tamsin's door but she'd jammed the safety-catch down. She was hysterical, so Bill reached through from Reah's open door and released it. Tamsin's screaming was growing more frenzied and Bill had a sickening feeling that her knee might be damaged. He knew he shouldn't move her, but the roar of the car's engine was worrying him. He didn't want the damn thing blowing up. Bill picked up Tamsin and lifted her bodily out.

"My leg!" she screamed.

"Bloody stupid thing to do," Bill told her. Rain was soaking both of them now. "My God, love, you could have both been killed!"

"Oh Bill!" she hung on to him. The sound of her voice pierced Bill to his core.

Then he remembered. He who had driven. The man who would have killed them all. Bill picked up his gun and ran round the front of the car. That loose old gatepost had sliced into the bonnet like a knife. Bill wanted the blood of whoever had been at the wheel. It was as simple as that. Through the open windscreen he saw a figure staggering out of the car.

Bill had no idea what he shouted but the man was sufficiently startled to make a run for the back of the car, pushing the driver's door wide open in the hope of blocking Bill's pursuit. Tamsin screamed. Bill battered through the open door, hardly noticing how it winded him, and collared the man, bringing him down in the mud. With the gun in his one good hand Bill's grip was weak. Ben struggled free and ran round to the passenger side of the car, Bill pursuing.

"You stupid bastard!" shouted Bill. The man turned round. For a moment Bill saw an intelligent face, a reasonable face, a man a little older than himself, someone who might have been a friend had things turned out differently, a well dressed man, spattered with blood and clearly terrified. Only for a moment. Bill brought the gun powerfully round into his adversary's ribs. The man fell. Bill heaved himself up along the side of the car to get a better aim. He stepped over Ben who was trying to get up on to his hands and knees. Bill kicked Ben in the thigh and stomach and saw him roll over in pain.

Tamsin shouted "Stop it Bill. Stop it! It's over, please."

It isn't over, thought Bill raising the rifle swiftly. It's never over. Ever.

Then at that moment he saw her, Reah running towards him, her hair streaked with mud, her face smeared with blood. Bill froze. It was as she'd always been, falling towards him. But she was not falling in death, her head thrown back. She was falling into his arms.

"Don't Dad! Don't!" she cried. Bill could not move. For what seemed like forever Reah fell towards him, and then she was there, holding him. "Don't," she said. "Don't. It's not worth it."

Bill let the gun slip from his fingers. He was aware of Ben edging away through the mud. He no longer cared. He held her. He held his daughter for the last time as rain beat down. Bill felt something convulse within him, a great sob that rose up and split his heart. He howled. The tears that had never come poured out of him. He stood in the rain and held on to Reah and wept.

❖ DEATH IN VENICE

TAMSIN AND REAH did move to London although Bill got the impression that Ben was not so welcome in St John's Wood as once he had been. Fortunately Reah could not remember the crash in much detail, but Bill noticed that she too blamed Ben for panic in the car, for hasty decisions and that near fatal acceleration. Blame, thought Bill, how easily it sours.

None of them was seriously hurt in the crash. Bill and Tamsin suffered most but this was as it should be. It had been their fight all along. Now it was over. Bill even helped Tamsin pack the last few books away after contracts were exchanged on Holt's Farm. Neither of them spoke of that dark Saturday night two months ago. They only talked of the future. Reah was supposed to be coming to Bill one weekend in three. The rest of the time she'd be in London, but Bill could take her out any time he wanted, should he be in town. That was the theory, but Reah had many reasons why she would not revisit the Wye.

Whether he was likely to follow his ex-wife and daughter to London was something else of which Bill and Tamsin didn't speak. After the crash, Reah had become more determined than ever to be with her grandparents. They represented security. Tamsin had been planning to buy a flat somewhere nearby for the two of them but in the short term she acquiesced to her daughter's desire to live with Gramma and Grandpops.

Bill truly believed he had lost Reah. She resorted to elaborate excuses not to come to the cottage and the first weekend, when Tamsin finally put her foot down and said Reah must go, she and Bill argued on the drive down from the M4 handover. Reah resented Bill's questions. She was uncomfortable with the formality of having to give Bill an account of her new school, her new friends, her new teachers. Like, a dad shouldn't need to ask you questions. A dad should just be there. And Bill wasn't.

As for Bill, he was already on the defensive about Holt's Cottage.

"But Dad I was never happy here," said Reah. They were parked outside now, inert in the Jeep, rank with incipient discord. "We came to the Wye when you and Mum were breaking up–"

"We didn't know we were breaking up," Bill insisted.

But they had been. It wasn't what either of them intended but all Bill and Tamsin had ever been able to do was slow down the process of disintegration. Their new beginnings had only ever been illusory. Was it really Libby Ziegler who had put an end to his marriage? Bill wondered, for this was what Tamsin and Reah believed.

Bill pondered such questions as spring turned to summer and Libby still failed to respond to his e-mails. It was a subject that he discussed with Louis when they met for their farewell lunch.

"I see your friend Bardini has gone spectacularly overbudget again," Louis announced as he finished ordering. "Do you think genius needs to overspend? Or do we just let it? Maybe we want it to. Now there's an article. What a shame there are no decent publications left."

But Bill was in no mood for gossip.

"Put that place on the market," Louis insisted when the conversation returned to the emptiness of Bill's life these days. "Come to London. How much longer are you going to endure that parochial purgatory?"

"I've lost three women you know." They had reached the brandies now. Bill was aware that he too easily tipped into self-pity and sentimentality these days. It had been a very long lunch and Louis no longer seemed to be teetotal. Indeed the editor's last week on the payroll at *Arts International* had turned out to be a veritable feast. Siobhan was holding what was left of the fort but Louis had skipped over the ramparts and was feting the peasantry handsomely. "Tamsin, Libby, Reah," said Bill, just in case Louis had missed his point.

"You haven't lost Reah," said Louis, fond but firm. "She's your daughter. She's a teenager, Bill. It was probably overdue. How many thirteen-year-old girls spend their weekends watching black-and-white movies with their fathers? Come to London. Get a room. You don't need anything more at the moment. As for Libby, Bill, if I may say so I think you're well out of that. Reah would never forgive you."

"Should I really be choosing my daughter over my lover?" Bill asked, focusing again on the bottom of his glass.

"Only if Libby really is the woman for you."

"*I don't know*," said Bill, with all the emphasis he could muster.

"Then you've done the right thing," Louis told him. "If you're not sure of something, don't sacrifice everything just to find out." Louis leaned forward. "Promise me two things."

"What?"

"After a while you'll stop drinking so much." Bill nodded. It was true he had succumbed. "Not straight away. Give it time. Cut back to only drinking with friends. Then give up your friends."

"What's the other thing?" Bill asked.

"Promise me when you get maudlin over Libby you won't listen to *Tristan and Isolde*."

"Too late," said Bill.

"Then you are lost," Louis told him. "Lost my boy, and you will go to Venice and make a fool of yourself."

"No I won't," said Bill.

But he did. After all, there was a story that interested Vita over there. Eventually. And there was a woman who interested Bill.

Where did it all go wrong? Bill wondered on the plane over, as he watched a family, whose noise he took for happiness, starting off on their holiday. He had never really asked himself this question before. Libby had seemed to be the answer, when in fact she had just been a reason not to ask the question. Not to ask it for years. Meeting her again in Venice, Munich and Chepstow had made Bill realise that it wasn't so simple. Libby's role in the final disintegration of Bill and Tamsin Wheeler had been that of catalyst and scapegoat. Their marriage, once so healthy it could cope with anything, had developed a malaise along the way. The pain from that malaise was so intense it obliterated their lives eventually and yet all that Bill and Tamsin did was argue about the analgesics.

So where *did* it go wrong? Bill asked that a lot. He even asked the trees as he went for his afternoon walk.

Somewhere along the way they had stumbled. They had seen different futures and gone in pursuit of them, not realising how far apart they were travelling. Maybe it too was overdue. Maybe at some level they both needed their marriage to fail.

Bill didn't see the graves and the slavering guard dogs on his afternoon walks any more. He didn't hear the screams in the dark unfeeling forest either. Some things pass, he thought, as he sat on that rock which commanded the Devil's view of Tintern. Here, where he'd lain, full of love for Libby, Bill began to feel the transience of grief, the thankful numbness that eventually erodes the sharpness of our pain. In time he knew he'd feel happy again.

Things did get better with Reah but they were never the same. Maybe she hadn't seen their time together in the same rosy light as he had.

Bill had imagined that once he had put his cottage on the market Reah would become fond and even sentimental about the Friday nights they used to spend together. Maybe the problem had been that all the time he procrastinated about selling, she was losing faith in him.

But it was not as Bill had hoped. Something ended that night in the rain. Reah Wheeler felt she had done a lot for her father. She even clung on to him until he had lowered the gun. Now it was time for her own life. The glorious hair was cut and styled, much to the sadness of everyone except Reah and her new friends.

Going to see the estate agent had been a very difficult thing for Bill to do. It meant letting go of a dream, a dream in which Bill and Libby lived peacefully in Holt's Cottage and Reah was still there at the farmhouse, free to come over whenever she chose. Bill had known this was never possible but that hadn't stopped him holding on to the hope. Venice changed all that. He put his cottage on the market as soon as he returned. It had been the final blow, the final letting go.

The night before he travelled, Bill had had an unexpected call. Most calls were unexpected to Bill. He was a journalist, people did not ring him back.

"Mr Wheeler, Goetz here. You know I'm still troubled by that '*neben*'"

Bill apologised for never having got back to Rory Llewellyn but a lot had happened recently.

"Are you still proposing to publish something about that letter?" Goetz asked.

"No," said Bill.

"Ah." The man sounded relieved and disappointed in equal measure. "Well I wouldn't want my imprecision to have landed you in any hot water, Mr Wheeler."

Bill smiled. The sun was setting slowly outside his window. The world seemed bright and beautiful this evening, especially with the prospect of St Mark's by tomorrow lunchtime.

"So did it prove a forgery?" Goetz asked.

"No. Not a forgery."

The academic in Goetz was clearly thrown. "But you had some doubts?" he asked.

"No," said Bill. "I think it was authentic. But not for publication."

"Ah," said Goetz for a second time. "May I ask why?"

It was a good question but the answer was too personal. Bill could not expect a man whose cause was the dissemination of knowledge to have much sympathy with the suppression of it. A few months ago Bill himself would not have had much sympathy with that idea either, but two days after the crash he had been visited by Georg Schmidt and they'd had a long talk. Schmidt had been concerned that he'd heard nothing further from his Chepstow source since that fateful weekend.

"I'm afraid there was a car crash here," said Bill; his arm was still in a sling at this stage. Gesturing to it as he stood in the doorway lent graphic, almost comic, credibility to such a story. "Nothing major," he said in answer to Schmidt's expression of polite concern. "But I only got back from the hospital last night."

Schmidt was out of breath, having had to walk up the lane with his briefcase. His car was parked in the valley below. It was to be over a week before the road up to Holt's Cottage was passable again and Lee could resume his round.

"So I'm glad you've come," said Bill, stepping back to admit Schmidt. "I was wondering what to do about the letter."

"I thought we had agreed that you would hand it over as long as I explained its significance, Mr Wheeler." They were now sitting in Bill's living room, Schmidt's Burberry looking even more incongruous in these surroundings.

"I'd still like to know why that letter means so much to you," said Bill.

"I believe I explained that."

"But why do you want to suppress its contents?"

"I didn't say I wished to s-s-suppress it," said Schmidt, stammering and glancing round the room. He clutched the briefcase that lay on his knees.

"I'm assuming that you may well burn it though," said Bill. "And as I don't believe in burning books I'd like to know why you do."

Georg Schmidt did not reply. Maybe he detected a taunt.

"Oh, you can have the letter," said Bill, determined to make up for sounding snide. "I'm not going to be difficult." He extracted it from his notebook. "It's been a bit like the Rhinegold for me – nothing but trouble." Bill passed the two pages over, small and crinkly within the plastic bag that a man called Katz had purchased for them the afternoon he set out for Herbert Samuel Esplanade in order to meet a journalist called Bill Wheeler.

Schmidt opened the package, detaching the Israeli sticky-tape that had grown dull with frequent use. Bill waited as Schmidt read. He had plenty of time. The doctor had told him to convalesce. He wouldn't be working for a while.

Eventually Schmidt finished reading. He sighed, looked with some concern at what lay before him and then refolded the letter, placing it back in its bag. "Thank you," he said, tucking the letter in his coat pocket. "I think we do indeed have our *Wunschmaid*." Then he took out a cheque-book and began to write.

"There's something that doesn't quite make sense to me," said Bill as

Schmidt filled in the amount. "I don't really understand why Cosima would have refused to embrace Wagner over the matter of adoption."

Schmidt signed the cheque slowly. "No?" he said.

"I mean, that's the kind of thing that they might disagree about, but would she really spurn him in that way?"

Schmidt returned the pen to his breast pocket. "Who can say? She wished to make reparations to von Bülow. For Wagner to take from the girls their von Bülow name would be a further insult to the poor man."

"It still doesn't make you a stranger to someone's bed."

Schmidt put the chequebook back inside his case and thought for a moment. Then he re-opened his briefcase and put his glasses on again. "The past is never clear," he said, checking through his papers. "But there is something here that may interest you." After leafing through some plastic sheets Schmidt withdrew a folded sheet of paper. "It is a fragment only. I have been unable to find the rest and now imagine that this page alone survived the incineration of 1930." He passed it to Bill. "I think you should have this. Keep it."

It was a photocopied sheet that had been folded once in the middle. When Bill opened it fully he saw one page from a letter written in German. A different hand from Wagner's but a hand from an age before our own.

"What is it?"

"Cosima to Richard."

"I don't read German," said Bill, trying not to apologise.

"I'm sorry," said Schmidt. "I forget."

"*Du warst mein grösster Freund und weisester Lehrer*," Bill picked out the phrases with his finger and spoke them haltingly.

"'*You have been the greatest friend and wisest teacher*,'" Schmidt translated. Then to Bill's surprise he continued from memory. "'*Once I believed you were a man without a flaw.*' I think she says, '*Mann ohne Makel*'?"

"Yes," said Bill.

"'*When, in time, I knew your flaws I did not know whether I would ever be able to love you as much again.*' *Es war meine Jugend und Unwissenheit.* '*That was my youth and ignorance.*'"

"What is she talking about?"

"Something happened," said Schmidt. "Exactly what we do not know. When I first read through my archive I believed it to be another of Wagner's affairs. Cosima writes to him that she always knew his heart would 'quicken' but that even when it did she had been sure that his soul remained with her. This is what many women like to tell themselves, no?"

He had strayed from the point. Realising this, Schmidt cleared his throat before continuing. "'*But this, this was harder to bear than I thought possible.*'" That is what she says, I think you'll find."

"What is *this?*" asked Bill.

"It has been my quest to discover," said Schmidt. "The letter that you have given me contains the first evidence that Daniela was involved. It is the only letter that gives a name. Although I had myself suspected Our Dearest Lusch."

"But," said Bill, "but you said that the thing that Wagner dared was to try and adopt the girls."

Schmidt made a gesture with his hand. He was conceding something or maybe he was admitting – or feigning – ignorance. "We do not know. Who can say? Adoption is what I would prefer to think."

"Why are you only telling me this now?" Bill asked. He suspected Schmidt of punting that adoption story just to get the letter back. He suddenly felt tricked, defeated, even though it was a battle he no longer wished to fight.

"Because," said Schmidt, in all innocence. "Because, you are only asking me now. Besides, the past is unknowable Mr Wheeler. We can only ever guess." Bill sat there in his annoyance, the photocopied letter still in his hands. "Who knows exactly what happened? Myself I believe the letters will never tell us the full story. They were not intended to."

"Here," said Bill, handing over the photocopy.

"May I read you the rest?" Bill realised that to Schmidt he must be exhibiting the demeanour of a sulky child.

"Of course."

Schmidt adjusted his glasses. "'*Jetzt weiss ich, dass ich Dich mehr liebe als je zuvor.*' 'Now I know I love you more than ever.' '*Ein Herz, das nicht lieben kann, kann auch nicht verzeihen.*'"

"*Ein Herz,*" said Bill. "A heart that cannot something-something love?"

"Forgive. *Verzeihen,* yes. That for me is the story, Mr Wheeler. A heart that cannot forgive cannot love. We may never know exactly what Wagner did but we do know that Cosima forgave."

"Quite a woman," said Bill.

"So why did he want the story kept quiet?" Libby asked. They were sitting in a small square near the Chiesa San Zaccharia. Nothing Bill had said so far seemed to have impressed her.

"I did ask him," said Bill. He had been saving this story up, assuming she'd enjoy it. "I told him I'd had a theory at one point that he might be a descendent of Daniela. That he didn't want the taint of abuse, illegitimacy or incest to affect his line."

Schmidt had been amused at the idea. "Daniela had no children," he said as they walked to the lane. "She married a Mr Heinrich Thode, they divorced and she spent her later years looking after Cosima in Bayreuth."

"Ah," said Bill. "Well I'm a journalist. You can't blame me for plumping for the obvious."

"I think you are an honest man, Mr Wheeler," said Schmidt. It sounded like a question.

"I used to think so too," said Bill. "Maybe I was naive."

Georg Schmidt took that for a joke. "I apologise if I was curt with you when first we spoke. I believed you were seeking sensation."

"Not any more," said Bill. "There's been too much of that recently."

"You are not entirely wrong," said Schmidt. "About my, shall we say, my c-c-connection to this letter."

This was the story that Bill had been keen to tell Libby. "Our friend's name genuinely is Schmidt but he isn't some great grandson of Lusch, as I suspected. Or anything like that. He is related, but very very distantly. On the von Bülow side."

Libby sipped her water appreciatively. It was summer in Venice, noisy, garish, and popular for all the wrong reasons. They had had some difficulty finding a cafe that was quiet enough.

Bill was surprised that she had not been more pleased. "His great grandfather was Hans' brother. Or cousin. I think that's what it was. The line is indirect."

Libby was wearing sunglasses so he couldn't tell what she made of his little scoop. "So what's the motivation?" she asked. They were keeping it friendly. Interested and polite. Treading water.

Despite Bill's encroaching sense of disappointment, he described his conversation with Schmidt as they had walked down to the valley floor. It had turned out most unlike anything he'd expected.

"I am a business man," said Schmidt. "I have an interest in the arts but myself I am not artistic. I am a great lover of Wagner's music and I take a pride in my relation with Hans von Bülow, even if I am of mongrel stock and the connection is not direct. He was a difficult man to be married to, I am sure, but when it came to the arts von Bülow was a man of infinite generosity and nobility."

Bill had read about Cosima's taciturn first husband but he didn't feel this was the time to quibble, not when Georg Schmidt was finally coming clean.

"You know that he continued to support Richard Wagner by conducting concerts for him – and this long after Wagner had taken his wife and children away. Even when he had little money himself?"

"Yes, you told me."

"And this because he believed in serving a higher ideal. An ideal that was more important than the way Wagner and Cosima behaved towards him. An ideal that was more important than Wagner."

Bill nodded.

"As I say," Schmidt continued, "I am a business man, but Wagner's music has always m-m-moved me. I can still remember the first evening I heard *Tannhäuser*. It is music that speaks not of this life with all its brokering of deals, qualified love and conditional support. It speaks of the absolute to which we all aspire. I'm sure if Wagner were here today he would probably despise a man such as me but, like von Bülow, I prefer to differentiate the music from the man."

"Is that why you began collecting the letters?"

"No. I inherited them. A relative died, a distant relative. He left me a lot of material relating to Richard Wagner."

"A von Bülow relative?"

"Distantly, yes."

"Did he know who the letters had been addressed to? Did he know the identity of the *Werther Freund?*"

"No. You must remember these were not the only letters. There was much material. You must know that Cosima Wagner made plans that all journals and letters of a personal nature were to be destroyed after her death. When I told you that maybe Wagner destroyed the letters he had received from his friend, I was not entirely honest," said Schmidt. "It is possible he may have destroyed them but more likely that Cosima ordered their destruction, if she did not destroy them herself. But the letters Wagner sent *to* his friend were not destroyed. Obviously. They survived because – and this is my opinion – because Cosima had been told the *Werther Freund* had already done so. Maybe that is what he told Wagner too. Repeatedly Richard begs that these letters are destroyed and yet he cannot stop writing more. Now why is that? Tell me, you are a writer, Mr Wheeler."

"I do it for the money," said Bill, but that wasn't the only answer. He too knew something about the compulsion to write? Sometimes an experience wasn't understood – or even complete – until written down.

Sometimes the act of writing *was* the experience. Bill thought of that e-mail he had never intended to send to Libby. They were still experiencing its consequences, even now.

"But are you saying Wagner was writing to a relative of yours, a von Bülow, about his love for Hans' daughter?"

"No," said Schmidt. "No I don't think so. That would be highly unlikely. I do not know how these letters came into the hands of my family. I have asked myself, though, given that these letters refer to someone whom Wagner greatly loved and that the recipient was unwilling or unable to return them to Richard Wagner, who would he pass them on to?"

"The object of the affection, I assume," said Bill. "That would be the obvious thing to do, but why couldn't they be returned to Wagner?"

"He was dead in Venice within less than a year," Schmidt replied. "Let us assume the friend was Pusinelli, the family doctor. Let us say that this man felt unable to destroy what Wagner had written. He will feel he must bequeath these highly personal letters to someone and that that someone should be someone better able to judge what should happen to them..."

"Daniela," said Bill.

"Exactly my thought. I feel I can see Pusinelli's indecision in the way he tries to obscure the signature and tear off the date. But do you see now why I needed to know if a name was mentioned in your letter? I had wondered if, as Blandine and Daniela were of von Bülow stock, they might have been involved in spiriting away some of this material for safe keeping to a relative of mine who wasn't caught up in the craziness of Bayreuth after Richard Wagner's death. On the other hand, my relatives lived in the East. The family connection may be an irrelevant coincidence. However, now you have a letter citing Daniela's pet name, I think this confirms my theory. I believe they went to her and that she was the person who passed them for safe-keeping into the possession of my family. She would have known that Cosima was destroying everything. For whatever reason Daniela did not want her relationship with Richard Wagner destroyed as well, not all the traces. She was his *Wunschmaid* after all."

That word again. Bill had asked Schmidt what he meant by it, but this was one discovery he didn't share with Libby. In fact, when they sat together in Venice, he talked more about Schmidt than Wagner. "Originally Schmidt had intended to make use of the material himself," Bill explained. "He'd set himself the task of reading and dating it all. It had taken him the whole of one summer. Doesn't it seem ironic that when you were working on the Wagner letters there was a whole private archive no one knew about?"

"It figures," said Libby, putting down her glass. "Scholarship is always circumscribed by what's available. In the end that's why I lost patience with it." She seemed downcast.

"Why you preferred to get out there and extend what's available?" asked Bill, still hoping that generous words would help him patch over their former quarrel about her work. Libby didn't seem to notice the gesture. "So anyway," he said. "Once he got reading, he realised that there was much about the Wagner marriage that no one knew. That it wasn't so ideal."

"I could have told him that."

She was not making this easy. Sadly, Bill realised that he had enjoyed his conversation with Georg Schmidt a lot more than he was enjoying today with Libby in San Zaccharia. There was a weariness and cynicism about her now. Schmidt, on the other hand, had spoken with something approaching reverence about his subject:

"The more I read about these two people the more they came alive to me. Richard and Cosima as I came to think of them. The more, too, I began to realise that I was not equal to the task of telling this story, the true story of their marriage – not the ideal marriage that they presented to the world but the marriage as it appeared in my archive. Do you perhaps know the German phrase *Bürgerliche Wohlänstandigkeit*?"

"Indeed I do," said Bill.

Schmidt hesitated. "Your German is obviously improving, Mr Wheeler. "Well, I felt that fate had placed on me the responsibility. Pusinelli had not dared to publish these letters. Nor to destroy them. Neither had Daniela – if indeed I am right that they had been passed to her. Now it was my turn to decide what to do. I contacted this man, a distinguished author. I did not know him but I knew of his work. I asked him whether he would wish to read this archive. Of course he expressed great interest.

"Then I read through again what fortune had placed in my lap and I realised that another person might not read these letters and journals as had I. Viewed with a colder eye, what we seemed to have here was the making of scandal. Richard was a man who fell in love many times in his life. He seemed to need to be in love. When I reread Cosima's letters to him, letters in which she took him to task for his flower girls and *Parisiennes*, when I read his to his worthy friend, letters in which he accused Cosima of loving Liszt more than she ever loved him, of making him a stranger in her bed after the birth of Siegfried, I began to see why Cosima ordered the destruction of so many letters.

"Their existence, their continuance, reduced this marriage – the foundation of Wagner's great achievement – to a squabble between two emotionally inadequate people. Indeed it was more than a matter of their 'continuance'. Letters have a permanence. That permanence outlasts the memories of love and laughter. The word, Mr Wheeler, spoken in truth, recorded in good faith but re-read in distortion. These words, it seemed to me they were both true and yet not true. Not in terms of what is genuinely worth saying. That is my opinion. Can you understand why the idea of handing over this archive began to horrify me?"

Bill nodded. He could understand. Wasn't he thinking of asking Libby Ziegler for that fax back, the one in which he had so foolishly committed his passing thoughts about Reah to paper seven years ago? It was one of the reasons why, in the end, he went to Venice to see Libby. It was one of the reasons she was sitting opposite him now.

"So Georg Schmidt bought into the perfect marriage?" said Libby.

"I think he felt that we weren't ready for any more revelations about Wagner's private life," said Bill. "And he's right. Look at all that stuff about Lusch. Can you imagine what people would make of lines like, '*I have dared, but now I may dare no more. No man must know what I have done. It is not just my own bravery that would be tested but hers*'?"

"So he is destroying the archive?"

"He says he's keeping it, hanging on to it until we reach 'a more tolerant age.'"

"Oh come on Bill," Libby was not impressed. "He's suppressing the truth."

"Do you really think that anyone in the arts at the moment is interested in truth?" Bill asked. Now there was a subject his beloved might have enjoyed discussing with Georg Schmidt.

"I cannot destroy these letters!" the man had said with a burst of laughter. "And yet I cannot hand them over either. I can only keep them for a time when they might be read with a more generous spirit. Perhaps this is what Pusinelli thought too. For the moment Richard Wagner is *persona non grata* for his anti-semitism. I do not wish to further alienate people by revealing the complexities of his private life."

"When did you discover there were missing letters?" Bill had asked.

"An envelope was sent to me two years ago. Inside was one of those that you call the '*Werther Freund*' letters. I had no idea how some had been separated off from the archive or indeed how the sender knew that I would be interested. But remember that in the DDR people kept files on everybody and not just on those in the DDR. I have lived nearly all my life in Switzerland and yet I'm sure they had a file on me too. The person who sent me that first letter said that there were some twenty more and he named a price. That first letter was enough to make me pay for the rest. It alluded to a great but forbidden love. In Richard's own handwriting I saw him confess '*Ich habe gewagt*'. You recognise the phase? 'I have dared.' '*Was womöglich kein anderer Ehrenmann wagen würde*'. From this source I bought nine letters in all and then the contact dried up.

Then Mr Katz approached me. I do not know if he were the person who had sold me the first ten letters, but he knew that I was buying and he offered to act as an intermediary for me. I was grateful. This is not my world. I am an innocent in such matters. Fortunately I have friends like Heidi and Willy. And I had Mr Katz, to whom I gave a desk and a telephone. He produced two letters which I bought. For the third he asked much more money. When I refused, that was when he turned to you."

Bill nodded. He understood his role now. Katz's cupidity needed the cupidity of others in order to function. The equation required a greedy, vainglorious journalist in order to be completed.

"So this guy is just a regular Wagnerphile protecting his hero," said Libby. She seemed disappointed. Bill was disappointed too. He had saved the story for her. With Goetz he'd remained circumspect, simply said that he'd felt the source unreliable. But Libby had had most of what Bill knew, almost all of it, in fact. And somehow, because this curious tale had brought them together, Bill had felt it would resonate between them, yet today nothing did.

"So how have you been?" asked Bill.

"OK," said Libby. The eyes behind her glasses did not concur.

"I've wanted to say so much," said Bill. "I've missed you." His words fell flat and lay on the table between them. "It was a difficult time," he continued. "Things got said that shouldn't have been said."

"Things got read too," said Libby.

"Yes."

After Schmidt had left that morning Bill had gone to the PC for the first time in several days. He wanted to tell Libby something about their curious meeting. He had absolutely no wish to get on with his work, but he had an overwhelming desire to share. When he switched on, Bill saw that there had been a second ziegler.409 which he hadn't opened that awful Friday night. It had arrived in tandem with her fateful account of his fax from seven years ago, the night when everything had gone so horribly wrong. The subject heading was "*PS*".

Bill – I can't unsend what I've just quoted. Suggest you delete. As we know, sometimes the wrong people get to read these things. Libby

He had been touched by Libby's concern. In the silent weeks that followed, it had been one of the things that kept him writing to her. Eventually Libby had written back. She'd been in Finland again. There was a lot of interesting work up there. Bill noted that she did not reply to his suggestion that they try again, nor his later suggestion that they meet up. Only when Bill e-mailed her with details of when he would be in Venice visiting La Fenice did Libby respond. Yes, finally she would meet.

They'd met in St Mark's again but walked down as far as this small cafe on the edge of San Zaccharia to find somewhere quiet enough.

Bill was saddened at the lack of energy between them. This was never how it had been. He thanked her for that warning e-mail.

"Don't tell me Reah saw it."

"Yes, I'm afraid she did."

Libby flinched. It was the first time he'd seen a response escape her sunglasses. "I wished as soon as I'd sent it that I hadn't. Was she very upset?"

"Yes."

"I hope you told her I was a lying bitch."

"Why should I lie to her?" he asked.

"Bill, it's not the kind of thing a girl wants to know her father has said about her." Libby spoke as if she suspected he had some faculty missing.

Another time he might have made some kind of speech to Libby about the fact that no good was ever served by suppressing the truth. Now he wasn't so sure. "She's getting over it," he assured her.

Libby opened her paperback and passed something over to Bill. It was a folded piece of fax paper, grey with time. He took it without looking. "I guess this is what you came for."

"No," said Bill. "I came here to find you."

"Aren't you going to destroy it?"

The fax paper felt chalky and prematurely old where it lay on the table under Bill's hand. So there it was, a direct link with those heady months when his life had changed direction. For good or bad, he still didn't know. The past was in that fax, tangible and potent. It was like seeing Wagner's first letter to his *Werther Freund* all over again. Did she really expect him to destroy it just like that?

"What about the other fax?" he asked. "The one where I think I almost said I was in love with you. Said it as far as I dared in those days. Have you destroyed that?"

Libby looked away. "I'm not ready to answer that."

Bill inclined his head, trying to enter her line of vision. "Libby..."

"Oh hell, Bill, forget about me. I know my fate. You can't do anything to alter it." She was looking up now.

"I can be part of it though," said Bill. What was he saying? Hadn't Louis told him that Reah would never accept Libby? Hadn't he decided it was all folly? And yet this was how he felt each and every time he was with her.

"No," she said. "You don't want that. You want some nice English woman to come and share your cottage."

"You're nice," said Bill.

"I'm impossible," said Libby. "And I go for impossible relationships. And each time I really think this is the one. And each time something goes wrong."

"OK, it's gone wrong with us," said Bill. "We've got that out of the way. Now we can start rebuilding."

He had come to Venice wondering if he could forgive her, and had found his answer as soon as he'd set eyes on her. We cannot love someone and yet also hold resentment. It seemed so easy now. He loved. He forgave. They would make it work.

Libby looked past him at the old church. It seemed as if she could be tempted. Bill waited, so much wanting her to open her heart again. A bunch of children burst into the quiet grey piazza. The pony-tailed patron came out and watched them for a while, wiped his hands on a grubby white T-shirt, and went back inside.

"Too late," Libby said, meeting his eye. "Too much has gone wrong, Bill. Hauke and I are going to Finland. I've given up the apartment here."

"Why with Hauke?" Bill asked.

"Hauke knows the market. He's not my lover, Bill. Never was."

"Well then," said Bill.

"Well what?"

"Don't keep running away," Bill urged her. He'd taken her hand. Warm. Familiar. It felt so good to connect again. She didn't withdraw. She didn't respond at all. The fax fluttered in an imperceptible breeze which swept across the table. Libby looked down at Bill's large and capable hand as it rested over hers, but suddenly the fax left their table and hovered over on to paving stones outside the *osteria*. Bill relinquished Libby and went to retrieve it.

When he came back Libby had already risen. It was time to go.

"Don't get involved with someone unsuitable in Finland," said Bill, as they parted. "You've already found someone unsuitable here."

Driving back from Heathrow in the early evening, Bill Wheeler spent two hours facing a setting sun. His eyes grew tired. Inevitably, he replayed the conversation with Libby. Several times in fact. Bill felt he knew it off by heart now. He certainly had a better record of it in his mind than he had of the interview he'd just concluded at Palafenice, of which Bill could remember not one word. Yes, he was going to get out of freelance journalism. Not for the first time in recent years Bill wondered about going back to London and working in a newspaper office. Libby had said don't. Libby had said he was worth so much more. But then so was she.

"You know so much," he'd told her at the *vaporetto*.

"I know diddly-squat," she'd replied, smiling but shaking her head.

Maybe we have to settle for what the world wants of us, Bill thought as he approached the Severn Bridge. Not what we want. Nor even what we can do best. He had checked his finances. They were not good, but he had enough money to live on this summer. He needed time out to think about what he really wanted.

Libby.

Perhaps.

But there was no point in making his plans around her. Libby seemed to have given up hope. Maybe it was too late. Had life's cruel ironies repeated once too often for her? Whatever, she was not coming to Holt's Cottage. Not ever. Bill knew this and felt the loss of something very special. He would put it up for sale on Monday.

Once Bill had decided what to do there was relief. He had made the last in a long line of concessions. It would be good to fight no more.

Crossing the suspension bridge, Bill was struck by the magnificence of its twin white towers and how they sang in the setting sun. He swung the Jeep up past Chepstow and headed home. There was an area above one of the Wye's broadest meander-loops where cars could pull off the road should visitors want to gaze down 120 feet to mudbanks and a very sluggish river. Here Bill stopped. He had one last thing to do. This was the spot where several months ago he nearly threw away a cassette of Wagner's music. Then his scruples had prevented him. Now Bill had an act of destruction to complete. He looked at the package in his hands.

"What Wagner did was not important," Schmidt told him as they parted. "Indiscretions and betrayals, they are the common stuff of life. Are we surprised when mankind is cruel? What is remarkable is love. And forgiveness of course. *Lieben heisst verzeihen.* Keep that photocopy," he said, as he folded his long body into the hire car. "It is the one letter that makes sense of it all, even without the facts."

Bill had stepped back so Schmidt could close the door. It was time his loquacious new friend went, but then Schmidt wound down the window. "Mr Wheeler. I'm sorry if I showed myself suspicious of you when we met. I did not believe that a journalist would be interested in anything but scandal."

"Maybe I'm not a very good journalist," Bill reminded him.

"Let the past rest," said Schmidt. "Do you think me strange?"

"No," said Bill. Long-winded perhaps. Sentimental even. A most unbusinesslike business man.

"And read Cosima's last paragraph," said Schmidt as he engaged the engine.

"I don't speak German!" Bill shouted but the man was already reversing. Of course he could always ask Libby, Bill thought. That was before the long months when she did not reply. So in the end he asked Tony Scribbleman. Bill was loath to involve himself again in Goetz's endless stream of clarifications and pedantries.

What came back to Bill via e-mail made him smile one glorious early summer morning.

> *We have spoken so often of what happened and yet you do not understand. I thought I could forgive you everything, such was my Love. I forgave your heart, I forgave your soul. I could forgive your pledging both to another, for these were private things still. But that you wrote, those things I could not forgive. To truly love, a woman needs to know her love is a private thing. To open her heart fully is possible only in the silence of true intimacy.*

Bill wondered how Cosima had discovered what Wagner was writing to his *Werther Freund.* He didn't want to imagine the scene.

> *These words you wrote took that privacy from me, my husband. I could not love while the world looked in upon us through those words. But now you tell me that our friend has destroyed what you wrote, and that you too have destroyed every word, my heart can, within its silent devotion, open to you again, for to love is to forgive.*

Bill thought about Tamsin. He thought too about the copies of e-mails he and Libby had exchanged and the cruel revenge of that bitter Other

Man in Munich. How nothing had quite gone right thereafter. Maybe Cosima had a point.

Now he took out a box of matches and struck one. The first sheet of paper ignited with sudden beauty as if a vibrantly-coloured bud had just bloomed. Bill lit the second. These were his photocopies. Whatever terrible or foolish things Richard Wagner had once done he had done them no more now. Bill torched the translations too. Schmidt could keep the archive until this world was ready. Part of Bill still hoped the archive wasn't destroyed already. But it had better be well hidden. Finally he incinerated that single page photocopied from Cosima's letter to Wagner. It was not for Bill to leave clues.

And now there was only one sheet of paper left. That chalky grey fax that Libby had given him. A folded rectangle of paper, once torn in two, then reassembled and run through the machine again to produce this fading copy of one moment in Bill's life. One moment, one single phrase, hiding there like a dormant bacillus, growing more malignant with the years. Bill opened it and started for the first time to read. Yes, he knew those words. Despite the years that separated the Bill Wheeler who read now from the Bill Wheeler who once wrote them, he recognised immediately how close he had come in those early days to telling young Libby Ziegler that his soul too had been captured. Even now an absurd sentiment made him want to hold on to these words. But they were a moment in time that had been preserved too long already. What mattered was the present. Now is all we have and all we are. The written word is only ever a record of how we once were. This document blew the past out of all proportion. Out of context and out of control. What if Tamsin were to see this now? Words that he had written while married to her. No, these words should not hurt anyone anymore. Nor those other words. Those that he knew were there, two thirds of the way down this page. Words that his daughter must never see. Words he did not wish to see again either. Bill struck another match. The past blazed for a moment then was no more. Bill had deleted it.

As he climbed back into the Jeep, Bill remembered the last words Schmidt had said to him. The man had turned his car round in a cautious circle and then stopped alongside Bill to check directions. Bill meanwhile was already thinking of e-mailing Libby with questions about Cosima's letter.

"You know, I don't suppose he'd give a damn, our friend," said Schmidt, his mind more on Wagner than the route back to Heathrow.

"Sometimes we have to protect people from themselves," Bill replied. "Tell me though. *Wunschmaid*..."

"Ah," said Schmidt.

"Why?"

"German is a complex language, Mr Wheeler. *Wunschmaid* has many meanings. She may be a maid who understands one's wishes, the maiden of one's desires, or the perfect female. You might say the 'dream lover'".

Yes, Bill had feared as much. He wanted to go back inside now and get on with his life, maybe send an e-mail, but he wouldn't bring up that particular compound with Libby. This might need talking over.

"You know what I think? I think Wagner was lonely," said Schmidt. "Despite all his acclaim. It is all too easy. It is all too easy to use the child as an extension of oneself, particularly if one is unhappy. He was just a man after all. Who knows? Are we right to forgive a man anything for his music? That is what the Wagnerites would say. Myself I try not to judge. Among my people it's a common failing."

Bill understood.

"I cannot condone what he wrote about us in *Das Judentum* – and who knows what he put Cosima through – but let God judge the man, that is what I say. Let God judge the man and let us have the music."

That was two months ago. This was now.

Bill started the Jeep. He needed to go home.

Lieben heisst verzeihen, Verzeihen heisst lieben.

Acknowledgements

FIRST AND FOREMOST my thanks must go to Kate Tadman, then to Carolyn Watts, Mark E. Smith, Ashutosh Khandekar, Tamar Hodes, Jeremy Loeb, David Vaughan Birch, Anthony Whitworth, Siân Williams and Will Atkins.